THEIR RADIANT FUTURE ...

Abigail Tempest—Arriving in Sydney with her sister Lucy, she found herself an heiress. On every side men offered love and "guidance," but whom among them could she trust?

Jenny Broome—Alone, she struggled to raise her children in an alien land. Her spirited faith and indomitable courage would be tested yet again as her new homeland was shaken by the lust for power and naked greed.

Andrew Hawley—Governor *Bounty* Bligh's trusted aide, he stood at the very center of the storm with the military against him and the colony's richest landowner his most bitter foe.

Justin Broome—With his father's seafaring blood in his veins, he longed for adventure. But love and loyalty bound him more strongly than any convict's chains.

... HELD RANSOM BY DRUNKARDS, MURDERERS, AND THIEVES!

THE TRAITORS

Also by William Stuart Long

THE
TRAITORS

WILLIAM STUART LONG

A DELL BOOK

*To my daughters, Jill,
Jenny, Vary, and Val.*

Published by
Dell Publishing Co., Inc.
1 Dag Hammarskjold Plaza
New York, New York 10017

Produced by Book Creations, Inc.
Lyle Kenyon Engel, Executive Producer

Dell ® TM 681510, Dell Publishing Co., Inc.

ISBN: 0-440-18131-3

Printed in Canada

First printing—May 1981

THE
TRIATORS

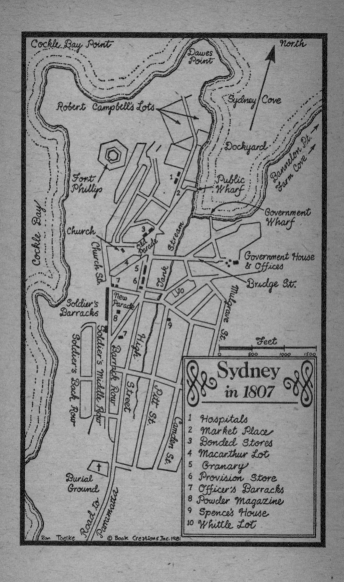

Cockle Bay Point

North

Dawes Point

Robert Campbell's Lots

Sydney Cove

Dockyard

Fort Phillip

Public Wharf

Bennelon Pt.
Farm Cove

Cockle Bay

Church

Government Wharf

Church St.

Old Parade

Tank Stream

3

1
2

5
7 6

Government House & Offices

Bridge St.

10

McGrave St.

Soldier's Barracks

New Parade

8
7

9

Feet

500   1000   1500

Soldier's Back Row

Soldier's Middle Row

Barrack Row

High Street

Pitt St.

Camden St.

Sydney
in 1807

1 Hospitals
2 Market Place
3 Bonded Stores
4 Macarthur Lot
5 Granary
6 Provision Store
7 Officer's Barracks
8 Powder Magazine
9 Spence's House
10 Whittle Lot

Burial Ground

Road to Parramatta

Ron Toelke   © Book Creations Inc. 1981

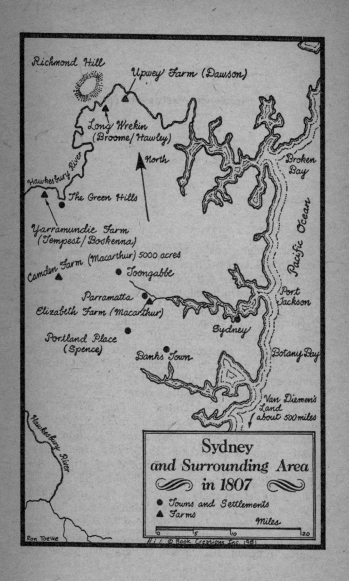

Richmond Hill

Upwey Farm (Dawson)

Long Wrekin
(Broome / Hawley)

North

Broken
Bay

Hawkesbury River

The Green Hills

Yarramundie Farm
(Tempest / Boskenna)

Pacific Ocean

Camden Farm (Macarthur) 5000 acres

Camden Farm

Toongabbe

Parramatta

Port
Jackson

Elizabeth Farm (Macarthur)

Portland Place
(Spence)

Sydney

Banks Town

Botany Bay

Hawkesbury River

Van Diemen's
Land
about 500 miles

Sydney
and Surrounding Area
in 1807

● Towns and Settlements
▲ Farms

miles

0   5   10   20

Ron Toelke

© Book Creations Inc. 1981

Acknowledgments and Notes

I acknowledge, most gratefully, the guidance received from Lyle Kenyon Engel in the writing of this book, as well as the help and cooperation of the staff at Book Creations, Incorporated, of Canaan, New York: Marla Ray Engel, Rebecca Rubin, Marjorie Weber, Charlene DeJarnette, and, in particular, Philip Rich, whose patience was seemingly inexhaustible.

Also deeply appreciated has been the background research so efficiently undertaken by Vera Koenigswarter and May Scullion in Sydney.

The main books consulted were:

The Life of Vice-Admiral William Bligh: George Mackaness, Angus & Robertson, 1931; *Bligh:* Gavin Kennedy, Duckworth, 1978; *Rum Rebellion:* H. V. Evatt, Angus & Robertson, 1938; *The Macarthurs of Camden:* S. M. Onslow, reprinted by Rigby, 1973 (1914 edition); *Mutiny of the Bounty:* Sir John Barrow, Oxford University Press, 1831 (reprinted 1914); *A Book of the Bounty:* George Mackaness, J. M. Dent, 1938; *Description of the Colony of New South Wales:* W. C. Wentworth, Whittaker, 1819; *The Convict Ships:* Charles Bateson, Brown Son & Ferguson, 1959; *Cap-*

tain William Bligh: P. Weate and C. Graham, Hamlyn, 1972; *History of Tasmania:* J. West, Dowling, Launceston, 1852; *A Picturesque Atlas of Australia:* A. Garran, Melbourne, 1886 (kindly lent by Anthony Morris).

These titles were obtained mainly from Conrad Bailey, Antiquarian Bookseller, Sandringham, Victoria. Others relating to the history of Newcastle and Hunter River, New South Wales, were most generously lent by Ian Cottam, and extracts from the *Historical Records of Australia* were photocopied for me by Stanley S. Wilson.

My gratitude for her efficient help in speeding typescript across the Atlantic goes to my local postmistress, Jean Barnard; and I owe an immense debt of gratitude both to my spouse and to Ada Broadley, who, in the domestic field, made my work on this book easier than it might have been.

Truth, it is said, is sometimes stranger than fiction. Because this book is written as a novel, a number of fictional characters have been created and superimposed on the narrative. Their adventures and misadventures are based on fact and, at times, will seem to the reader more credible than those of the real life characters, with whom their stories are interwoven. Nevertheless—however incredible they may appear—I have not exaggerated or embroidered the actions of Governor Bligh, his daughter Mary Putland, John Macarthur, George Johnstone, or their contemporaries in retelling the story of Australia's Rum Rebellion. They behaved in the manner described, although, of course, their dialogue—necessary in a novel—had to be imagined.

In the light of hindsight, opinions differ as to the merits or flaws of Bligh and Macarthur. Each has his admirers and his critics, just as each, being human, has his vices and his virtues . . . but it is a fact, which I acknowledge, that John Macarthur played a very prominent and valuable part in rendering the colony prosperous by establishing its wool industry. He also, as this book will illustrate, came perilously near to destroying it, in order to retain the trading monopolies by means of which he and the officers of the New South Wales Corps made their personal fortunes.

Very extensive reading has convinced me that, judged by the standards of their day and age, William Bligh was the more honorable man, John Macarthur the cause of his downfall . . . almost single-handed.

It is interesting to note that, of the governors and acting governors who followed the upright and farsighted Admiral Phillip, Colonel Paterson—in a single year—disposed of more land, 68,101 acres, than any who went before him. The rebel administration between Bligh's arrest and Governor Macquarie's arrival granted a total of 82,086 acres in, one can only suppose, an endeavor to reward those who gave their support or whose loyalty had to be bought. John Macarthur, however, received a grant of only three acres in the town of Sydney, two of which he exchanged, quite legally, for a similar acreage in Parramatta. Nevertheless, he was the colony's largest and wealthiest landowner, with a holding of 8,533 acres in all, against Governor Bligh's comparatively modest 1,345. (See *Historical Records of Australia* and Mackaness.)

Finally, I should mention that I spent eight years in Australia and traveled throughout the country, from Sydney to Perth, across the Nullabor Plain, and to Broome, Wyndham, Derby, Melbourne, Brisbane, and Adelaide, with a spell in the Islands and the Dutch East Indies, having served in the forces during World War II, mainly in Burma.

PROLOGUE

Abigail Tempest watched in unhappy silence as her father set spurs to his horse and cantered off down the long, weed-grown drive. She waited until he was out of sight and then said, her forehead still pressed against the glass of the window, "Papa has gone, Rick. I was so hoping that he would change his mind . . . because he promised, you know. He gave me his word."

Her brother, Richard, came to stand behind her. He was in naval uniform, wearing the white patches of a midshipman earned after two years at sea as a lowly volunteer. He eyed her bent fair head a trifle skeptically. He was seventeen, only a year older than Abigail, but already he was more than a head taller than she was and, in his considered opinion, vastly her senior now in worldly experience.

At pains not to sound condescending he said, "You don't understand, Abby. Papa could not refuse an invitation from Lord Ashton. He's a rear admiral and Papa's patron and besides, he—"

"A *retired* rear admiral," Abigail pointed out. "And poor Papa doesn't need a patron to advance him in the naval service now, does he?"

"No," her brother conceded, "but I do. It is thanks to His Lordship's influence that I have been appointed to the *Seahorse*. She is a forty-two-gun frigate, you know."

"With the country at war, you would have had no trouble finding a berth," Abigail assured him.

She turned from the window to face him, and Richard was shocked when he glimpsed the pain in her eyes. She was such a pretty girl, he thought, with her slim, lissome body and shining, corn-colored hair . . . pretty and talented, possessed of a charming singing voice and no little skill at the piano. On the threshold of womanhood, she should have been carefree and happy, with a host of admiring young beaux vying for her favors, but instead . . . He sighed, reaching for her hand as she went on bitterly, "They will play after dinner, Rick— they always do. And for high stakes, which Papa cannot afford."

"He might win," Rick offered, but without conviction.

For answer Abigail gestured to the sparsely furnished room behind them. "Can't you see . . . are you blind? The pictures have gone, all Grandpapa's books and Mamma's cherished china—even the cabinet she loved so much, the one Thomas Sheraton made. I know you've been away for two years, Rick, but surely you've noticed how different things are now."

"I did notice that there were only three horses in the stable," Richard admitted, "and no carriage. But—"

"They were all sold," Abigail told him. "The bailiffs came, three weeks ago, to take Mamma's cabinet and the piano away. They would have taken poor little Lucy's silver christening cup if I hadn't forbidden it. They were sent by the court on Mr. Madron's behalf— he applied for a court order."

"Madron? You mean the feed merchant, *that* Madron?"

"I mean his son, Reuben. Old Tobias Madron has retired. Reuben claimed that Papa had not paid his account for horse and cattle fodder for twelve months." Abigail spread her hands in a despairing gesture, and Richard's heart sank as she continued the unhappy litany. "At least Reuben Madron does not need to worry anymore about being paid, for there are no cattle to feed now. Papa sold the last two farms at the beginning of the month, and the three horses we have left have to live on hay."

"But . . . Papa's not in debt *now*, is he? Surely if he's sold the farms, he must have paid off whatever he owed?"

Abigail's lower lip trembled, and, hanging on her answer, Richard saw her shake her head. "He still owes money for gaming debts. I don't know how much, he will not tell me. Rick, dear, you have not heard the worst of it yet."

"Have I not? Then tell me, for pity's sake!"

She hesitated, eyeing him uncertainly. "Papa said nothing to you? He gave you no hint of his—his plans for the future?"

"No," her brother denied. "Dammit, Abby, I only arrived here yesterday afternoon. He's hardly spoken to me of anything—except my voyage. He wanted to hear about that, and I told him, naturally. There wasn't time for much else, and I was dropping with sleep. But . . . well, he talked to me of Mamma, of course. He told me how bravely she had borne her last illness and how much he misses her. And he does, Abby, truly . . . he was in tears when he spoke of her."

"I know that," Abigail responded, her voice flat. She turned away from him and walked over to one of the wing chairs drawn up in front of the spluttering log fire. The fire gave off little heat, and she poked at it resentfully before adding another log. Over her shoulder she added, "We all miss her, Rick. It . . . Oh, it might have been different if Mamma had lived, *so* different! Papa listened to her. He took her advice, but he will not listen to me. He says I am a child."

"And are you not?" Richard quipped, thinking to make a joke of it in the hope of bringing a smile back to her lips. The joke fell flat. Abigail shook her head. The fire woke at last to a semblance of life and she seated herself in the wing chair, holding out both hands to the blaze she had created.

"No," she asserted. "I am not a child anymore. In the—in the situation in which I find myself, I cannot afford to be. Papa is not himself, Rick. That terrible head wound he suffered at Copenhagen has affected him very badly, and it is getting worse. Whilst Mamma was alive, and during her illness, he kept himself in check, for her sake. Oh, he was drinking then, quite heavily, and gaming with his friends, but not to—not to excess. He was hoping, I think, when the war with France was resumed, that Their Lordships of the Admiralty would have need of his services. He wrote, he waited on the First Lord, but they would not give him another ship."

"He's not fit to serve at sea," Richard put in when she paused. He came to sit opposite her. "Go on, Abby. You mentioned his plans for the future, but you haven't told me what they are."

"I'm coming to that," Abigail promised, "but I want you to understand, to realize how Papa has changed. He . . . the last time he went to the Admiralty was when Mamma was still alive. He stayed in London for almost a week and someone, a friend he met there, introduced him to a gaming club. It's called White's, I believe, and the Prince of Wales goes there, with a lot of very wealthy noblemen, so the stakes are high. He . . . Rick, Papa *won*—he won a great deal of money. I remember, when he came home, he bought a new hunter for himself, and a dogcart and a beautiful little pony for Mamma. He said she could go for drives in it, when she—when she got better. Only—" She broke off, a catch in her voice.

Only poor Mamma had not got better, Richard thought. And probably his father had never won so substantial a sum again. He had gone on playing, but he had become a loser. The evidence of this was, as Abby had indicated, all about them. He glanced up at the walls where the pictures had hung, family portraits, for the most part, and mainly of his mother's family. There were lighter squares on the wallpaper in the spaces which the pictures had occupied, smudged stains in the corner in which the Sheraton china cabinet had stood. He had not noticed these signs when he had first entered the room—he had been too pleased and excited by his homecoming, too eager to detail his own adventures to observe the change in his father.

Looking back, however, he realized that there had been a significant change. The maudlin tears, the amount of brandy his father had consumed as they talked, his explosive burst of ill temper when one of the slovenly servants had interrupted them . . . these had all been indications which he had observed and chosen to ignore, together with the fact that the servants *were* slovenly and that there were now very few of them.

Most significant of all, he supposed, had been the manner in which his father had taken leave of them, only a short while ago. The boy frowned, remembering. Normally the most courteous of men, Edmund Tempest had rebuked Abby when she had sought to persuade him not to accept the admiral's invitation, and he had barely acknowledged his own son's presence. And when thirteen-year-old Lucy had come running down the steps from the front door to wave to him, their father had ordered her brusquely back to the house, seemingly indifferent to the tears his harsh words had provoked.

Abigail was crying now . . . silently, trying to hide her face from her brother. His own throat tight, Richard went to kneel at her feet, taking her thin little hands in his. "You had better tell me the rest, Abby," he urged. "I shall have to know, shall I not—even if Papa has not seen fit to confide in me? What plans has he made?"

She made a brave attempt to speak calmly. "He intends to go out to Botany Bay to settle, taking Lucy and me with him. To—to start a new life," he says. You are provided for. So he will sell this house lock, stock, and barrel—all we have left—in order to raise the capital he will require and to pay the cost of our—our passages."

Richard stared at her in stunned disbelief.

"*Botany Bay?* But that is a penal colony! And it's half the world away! It's . . . For God's sake, Abby, whatever put such an idea into his head? Has he . . . has Papa taken leave of his senses?"

"There are times when I truly fear he has," Abigail confessed. She lifted her tear-wet face to his. "He has changed so *much,* Rick! But . . . as to what put the idea into his head, he met an officer who is on sick leave from the colony. A Major Joseph Foveaux of the New South Wales Corps—he is staying as a guest of the Fawcetts at Lynton Manor. And," she added wryly, "I fancy *he* will also be dining at Lord Ashton's this evening—they say he is a very good card player. Certainly Papa has spent a great deal of time in his company since his arrival here, talking to him of conditions in the colony."

"But it is still a penal colony," Richard objected. "What sort of new life would that offer?"

"A very good one, if Major Foveaux is to be believed," Abigail answered. "He appears to have made a fortune there—on the mainland first of all, where he owned two thousand acres of land, and then in command of an island over nine hundred miles away—a place he calls Norfolk Island. He told Papa that the worst and most recalcitrant of the convicts are sent to the island—those who rebel or try to escape from the principal settlement at Sydney."

"And Papa plans to go *there*?"

"No, not to Norfolk Island—to Sydney. It seems that all who go out there as free settlers are allocated as much land as they want at a purely nominal price, with convict laborers to cultivate it in return only for their keep. Major Foveaux has assured Papa that he cannot fail to show a most handsome profit if he brings out livestock of good quality for breeding, and joins one of the trading syndicates which the Corps officers have organized. Jethro Crowan, the shepherd Papa engaged at Michaelmas, is to come with us as foreman and to care for the livestock on the voyage."

Richard was silent, endeavoring to assess and evaluate the prospects his sister had outlined. For his father, perhaps, they were hopeful, even—in his present circumstances—desirable, but for Abby and for the delicate little Lucy . . . He got up abruptly and started to pace the floor, a prey to deep misgiving.

"Do you want to go, Abby?" he asked at last, returning to face her.

"Oh, Rick, of course I don't!" Abigail answered miserably. "This is my home—I've never lived anywhere else and neither has Lucy. I dread the very thought of leaving England! And besides that, New South Wales is a terrible place, from what I have heard of it. They say there are black savages there, as well as the lowest kind of convict felons, and it *must* be true since Major Foveaux does not deny it." She shivered. "And, Rick, that monster Captain Bligh of the *Bounty* is governor . . . imagine it!"

"Papa admires Captain Bligh, Abby," Richard felt compelled to point out. "He has always said that his conduct at Copenhagen was little short of heroic. And even Lord Nelson singled him out for approbation. He—"

Abigail sighed. "I've not said I will *not* go, Rick . . . only that I do not *want* to. If it will help poor Papa, if it will provide a new life for him and enable him to pay off his debts, then I cannot think of myself. If he goes, Lucy and I must go with him. In any event," she added resignedly, "we shall have no choice, shall we?"

That was true, Richard thought. If his father had really made up his mind to sell up and leave England, the two girls could hardly stay without a roof over their heads or anyone to support them. He, alas, could not afford to maintain them on a midshipman's meager pay. He could barely support himself, even when he was at sea. And the country was at war, the navy in the thick of it. He might be killed or severely wounded, as his father had been. Like his father, he might be invalided out of the service, cast ashore without hope of further employment, to exist as best he might on the pittance Their Lordships deemed sufficient compensation for their junior officers.

His father had had this house and a well-endowed estate, which he had inherited, as well as a first lieutenant's wound pension. But he himself would have nothing once the house was sold . . . and it might be years before he obtained his lieutenant's commission.

Abigail said gently, as if she had read his thoughts, "We are not your responsibility, Rick. You have your career, and I thank God that you have." She managed a wan little smile. "Dear Rick, it is *so* good to see you again! And a great relief to have someone in whom I can confide—someone who can understand my anxieties concerning Papa. I could not talk to Lucy as I have to you. She is so sensitive, and she worships Papa. She—"

"You used to worship him, too, Abby," her brother reminded her.

"Yes," she agreed, without warmth. "I did."

Her use of the past tense was indication enough of her feelings, and Richard sighed, bitterly conscious of his own helplessness in a situation that affected them all so poignantly. "I wish I could do more to aid you, I . . . When does Papa plan to leave? Or has he not yet decided?"

"Oh, he has decided. He told me a week ago that he has booked passage for all three of us and Jethro on board a ship called the *Mysore*. He said she is an Indiaman of four hundred tons burden and that her master, Captain Duncan, has assured him that she will make a fast passage. But"——Abigail shrugged despondently——"it will still take us about six months to reach Sydney, will it not?"

Richard nodded. "I believe so. Some ships do it in less." The *Mysore* was probably a convict transport, carrying a few fare-paying passengers in upper-deck cabins. Most of the ships plying between England and New South Wales were hired by the government to transport convicted felons to the colony, he knew, but, anxious not to upset his sister, he refrained from saying so. Time enough for her to find that out when she went on board, poor girl. . . . At least such transports were now required to carry a surgeon, to ensure that the convicts were properly fed and cared for, and the conditions in which they traveled had been improved.

"When is the *Mysore* due to sail, Abby? And do you know from which port?"

"In three or four weeks' time, I think," she told him. "And she is at Plymouth—she had just docked there when Papa called on her master. At least that will mean a short journey—the Bodmin coach stops at Half Way House now."

"Good," Richard approved. "I may be able to see you off. The *Seahorse* is refitting at Devonport, and I'm told she will be joining Lord Collingwood's flag in the Mediterranean when she's completed." He talked of his ship more to gain time and to introduce a change of subject than because he expected Abigail to share his enthusiasm, but she made a selfless attempt to do so, and only when the subject was exhausted did she return to that of their father.

"Rick," she said, with a catch in her voice, "I don't believe that, in his heart, Papa wants to leave England or to sell this house. He was brought up here, just as we were, and I know he loves the place as much as we do. It will be so different in New South Wales for him and for us. I . . ." She hesitated, again eyeing him uncertainly and clearly wondering whether or not to confide in him further.

Richard reddened. "You can trust me, Abby," he assured her. "I'll not repeat anything you do not want me to—least of all to Papa."

She accepted his assurance and went on almost eagerly, as if it were a relief to unburden herself, "As I told you, Papa has been talking to this Major Foveaux, who is all enthusiasm for the prospects Sydney offers. But I . . . that is, I sought another opinion—a woman's, Rick—and as I feared, it was much less favorable than Major Foveaux's. That was how I found out about the black savages—they call them Indians, and it seems they rob and murder at will in the isolated settlements, which have no troops to guard them."

Richard stared at her incredulously. "A *woman* told you that? But where in the whole wide world did you contrive to find a woman who knew anything about Sydney, pray?"

Abigail smiled, savoring her small triumph. "Oh, quite near at hand, as it chanced . . . in Fowey village. A Mary Bryant, who is a widow and something of a local celebrity. I had heard her talked about, so I went to see her, and—"

"But Fowey's fifteen miles from here!" her brother

interrupted. "How did you manage to get there and back without Papa knowing?"

"I drove the governess-cart, with the old pony, Pegasus. He's slow but reliable. Papa thought I was going to St. Austell to visit the Tremaynes, as I often do, so he raised no objection. It was after eleven when I got back, but Papa was out, so it didn't matter." Abigail shrugged off her deception as of no account, but her smile faded as she added, "In a way I am sorry I went. The picture Mrs. Bryant painted of the colony was—oh, it was horrible, Rick! I've had nightmares about it ever since. She said that Sydney Town was a veritable den of iniquity and the convicts cruelly maltreated and made to work in chains. They—"

"Was this Mrs. Bryant a convict?" Richard asked suspiciously.

"Yes, she was, but she is a most respectable woman, truly, Rick, and she received the King's pardon. She told me that she was one of a small party, organized by her husband, which escaped in an open boat—a sailing cutter, I think she said—to Timor, in the Dutch East Indies. Poor woman . . . she lost both her babies, as well as her husband, on the voyage home."

Memory stirred and Richard slapped his thigh, suddenly excited. "Why, Abby, she was a heroine! I heard the story—our first lieutenant was talking about it not very long ago, when he was instructing some of us in navigation. He said it was an epic . . . a feat of navigation that even put Captain Bligh's passage from Tofua into the shade, because it was longer and the Bryant party had only a compass to aid them. Their navigator was a man named Broome—or some name like that— and he's serving in the navy now, as a master's mate. But—" He broke off, sensing Abigail's lack of response, and then added, thinking once again to offer her consolation, "it was a long time ago—fourteen or fifteen years at least. They escaped when Admiral Phillip was governor. Conditions will have changed, they'll have improved, I'm quite sure. After all, from what I've heard, free settlers are going out to Sydney now in increasing numbers. And I doubt if a taut hand like Captain Bligh will permit the town to remain—what did your Mrs. Bryant call it? A den of iniquity—for long."

Abigail's brows met in a thoughtful pucker. "Perhaps you are right, Rick," she allowed, "but there is someone else I can ask—Mrs. Bryant told me of her. A Mrs. Pendeen, who is the wife of the vicar of St. Columbia's in Bodmin. She was Bishop Marchant's daughter, and she returned more recently from Sydney, I believe. She—"

"At least she wasn't a convict," Richard put in, relieved. He held out both hands to her, and Abigail took them, rising from her chair to stand facing him. Mary Bryant had hinted that the bishop's daughter had, like herself, been granted a royal pardon, Abigail recalled . . . but she had doubted this, supposing the woman to have been confused. In the light of Rick's observation her doubts returned. Old Bishop Marchant had died a long time ago, during her own early childhood, but he was still talked of as a much-loved and widely respected—even saintly—man. It was absurd to imagine that his daughter, who was now the wife of a Church of England vicar, could possibly have been transported to New South Wales as a convicted felon.

She shook her head and answered, with certainty, "No—no, of course not. That is why I want to see her. Will you come with me, Rick? You could make some excuse to Papa, and he wouldn't question it if we went together."

"In the governess-cart, with old Pegasus between the shafts?" Richard questioned. "It would take us all day to get there!"

"We can go with the carrier's van from St. Austell if

we leave early," Abigail insisted. "Oh, please, Rick—do say you will."

He smiled down at her. "I'll come," he promised, "if it matters so much to you, Abby dear." It was borne on him, as he spoke, that if his entire family went to New South Wales, he might never see them again. A lump rose in his throat, and as his glance went to the shabbily furnished room, with its pictureless walls and the denuded bookshelves, he found himself, for the first time in his life, bitterly critical of his father. Like Abby and little Lucy, he had worshipped and looked up to both his parents, but now . . . His fingers tightened about his sister's thin, work-roughened hands.

"Perhaps," he suggested, "perhaps Papa will have a big win at the tables tonight and then all our fears will be groundless."

"That is what I pray for," Abigail confessed. She avoided his gaze, two bright spots of color rising to burn in her cheeks. "One should not ask Almighty God for such—such mundane things, I know, but it is what I ask Him, every night, Rick. I pray that Papa may win enough to enable us to stay here and"—she looked up at him then, her lower lip tremulous—"I prayed for your safe return. He has granted *that* prayer, but I fear He will never grant the other one."

"In His wisdom and mercy, He might," Richard said, but without conviction. He tucked his sister's hand beneath his arm. "It's time we dined, is it not? Let's go and find Lucy and enjoy a meal together . . . poor little scrap, we've been neglecting her, and she'll take it amiss. We'll put the clock back, shall we, and pretend, just for this evening, that nothing has changed?"

Play at the loo table had started at a little before midnight following a late and somewhat protracted dinner at Pengallon House, and after fewer than a dozen hands it had been agreed, at Major Foveaux's suggestion, that the pool should be unlimited.

Now, with the first glimmer of light seeping in through an uncurtained window at the far end of the musicians' gallery and the candles in the room below spluttering to extinction, a fortune was at stake. Each of the red counters in the pool represented a bid of three hundred guineas, the whites a hundred, and bidding had, from the outset, been high.

Conscious of his obligations as host to the party, Lord Ashton was worried, although less on his own account than that of his guests. He had retired from the Royal Navy as a very rich man, with the rank of rear admiral and, after a two-year command in the Caribbean, an enviable share of his squadron's prize money accredited to him. But . . . He frowned, looking across the table at Edmund Tempest's downcast head.

The poor devil had elected to play the widow in the previous deal and failed to win a single trick, and his hand was shaking as he paid his forfeit from the dwindling pile of red counters in front of him.

"Foveaux," he began sourly. "Damme, you—"

Fearing an outburst, Lord Ashton waved to a footman to replenish the candles in the chandelier. As the man hastened to obey him, he himself turned up the wick of the oil lamp at his elbow and moved it with careful deliberation to the center of the table, so that its light shone on the accumulation of counters there and on the two packs of cards the players had been using.

"We'll have fresh cards and another decanter," he instructed his majordomo, and when these were brought, he added, his tone intentionally jocular, "A plague on you, Major! You've the luck of the very devil, have you not? Who'd have imagined that you would come up with two flushes in a row, eh?"

"Who indeed, sir?" Major Joseph Foveaux met his

host's quip with a smile that bordered on complacency, but his dark eyes were wary. He was a handsome man in his early forties, running a little to seed, and was, the old admiral knew, on leave from the penal colony in New Holland, of which his regiment—the New South Wales Corps—formed the military garrison. He had lately acted as lieutenant governor of some outlying settlement, Arnold Fawcett had said . . . and it had been an appointment that had paid him generously, judging by the stakes he played for and the style he affected, although the Corps to which he belonged had a less than distinguished reputation. It was an infernal pity that poor Edmund Tempest had allowed himself to get mixed up with Foveaux, in the circumstances, but . . . Lord Ashton gave vent to an audible sigh.

Major Foveaux went on, quite pleasantly, as he made change with white counters to enable the pool to be divided, "You know what they say concerning one's luck at cards, Admiral. Mine, alas, seems at present to be confined to the gaming table, and I fancy they were glad to see the back of me at Boodles's! His Royal Highness certainly was. But if one's on a winning streak, one must see it through . . . and count one's lack of success with the fair sex as a small price to pay. My own wife's displeased with me, and Edmund's lovely daughter won't give me the time of day, damme!" He snapped the seal on one of the new packs and, still smiling, thrust it in Tempest's direction. "Be good enough to shuffle the cards, Edmund. It's Judge Grassington's deal, I believe."

Edmund Tempest did as he had been asked with sullen clumsiness and reached for his glass without speaking. The pack lay waiting for Lord Ashton's cut, but he delayed restarting the next hand, resenting Foveaux's ill-mannered eagerness to continue a game in which only he was a major winner. Such behavior smacked of an ungentlemanly lack of sensitivity, but

then, the admiral reminded himself, Joseph Foveaux
was noticeably lacking in the finer feelings that came
with breeding.

Rumor had it that he was a by-blow of the Earl of
Ossory and that his mother had been employed in the
Ossory kitchens . . . a damned Frenchwoman, if the
rumor were to be relied upon, and it probably was. Lord
Ashton repeated his sigh and cut the cards. He had not
taken to the fellow from the start of their brief acquaintance, he reflected, but since he was a guest of the
Fawcetts, it was impossible to avoid meeting him
socially, at the houses of friends or in the hunting
field—Arnold Fawcett took him everywhere and
Tempest, too.

This was the third or fourth occasion on which they
had encountered each other at the loo table, and the
last two occasions had proved costly enough, in all
conscience. Tonight, though, his luck was almost beyond belief. Lord Ashton made a swift mental calcula-
tion. The last two hands alone had netted Ossory's
damned scallywag of a son a cool two thousand
guineas, the losers himself, Fawcett, and Edmund
Tempest, who—poor feckless devil—was the least able
to afford such a loss, though of course it was his own
fault.

"Judge Grassington," Foveaux persisted, "the cards
are yours, sir."

"Why, 'pon my soul, are they?" Old Judge Grassington, who had been nodding, roused himself to peer uncertainly at Foveaux over the top of his thick-lensed
glasses. In addition to being shortsighted, the judge
was deaf, and for the past hour he had taken little part
in the play save when it fell to him to deal.

He had not lost, however, Lord Ashton observed
without surprise. Grassington might be over seventy
and inclined, as the night wore on, to lapse into a doze
—a habit acquired during his years on the bench—yet

for all that his passing had been shrewdly calculated, and when he did elect to stand, he invariably took sufficient tricks to ensure him a share of the pool. But now it was evident that he, too, was out of patience with the overly lucky visitor from New South Wales. He tugged a heavy gold timepiece from the pocket of his brocade waistcoat and clicked his tongue in well-simulated astonishment, as if only just aware of the lateness of the hour.

"Have to go, Gilbert, me dear feller," he announced without apology. "Cash me out, Major, if you please." He rose ponderously to his feet, a restraining hand on Admiral Ashton's shoulder as his host also rose, prepared to escort him to the door. "No need for you to disturb yourself . . . carry on with the game. Your man can call me carriage and see me on me way. Don't want to break up the party, you understand, but I'm not as spry as I used to be. Can't keep awake, and that's the truth, damme!"

Lord Ashton, with a rueful glance at his own depleted stake, was about to use the judge's departure as an excuse to end the game when Foveaux, anticipating his intention, slid the pack across the table and said smoothly, "Then I fancy it's your deal, Edmund, is it not?"

Edmund Tempest reluctantly raised bloodshot eyes to meet those of Foveaux, his pulse visibly beating at the center of his hideously scarred left temple. He had sustained the ugly head wound six years before at the Battle of Copenhagen when serving as first lieutenant of poor Robert Mosse's seventy-four, H.M.S. *Monarch,* the admiral recalled. Indeed, as his patron, he had obtained Tempest's appointment for him, hoping to afford him the chance to make post rank.

He had been able enough, as a young officer—promising even—but since then the wretched fellow had steadily let himself go to the dogs. He had been deuced unfortunate, of course. First he had been invalided by his wound. Then his wife had died not long after his return to his native Cornwall, leaving him with a son and two young daughters. The boy was all right, he was in the navy, but both girls were little innocents of less than marriageable age—pretty as pictures, the pair of them, they did not deserve to be in the straits to which their father had reduced them.

A footman, unbidden, refilled his glass, and Lord Ashton sipped at it, scowling, as Tempest picked up the cards. After a moment's hesitation his cheeks turned brick red. The fool had started to gamble heavily of late, with a lack of success that was becoming notorious. The small estate he had inherited was now, if local gossip had not exaggerated, partially in the bailiff's hands, with farms sold off and the manor house denuded of furniture and pictures. Yet Edmund Tempest went on playing, presumably in the hope of a miracle which would enable him to recoup his losses.

Recently, he had talked of going out to New South Wales—an idea, no doubt, that Foveaux had put into his head—and watching him now, the old admiral found himself wishing that the wretched fellow would summon up all his resolution and go, since it might be the saving of him.

It had been a grave mistake to permit him to take a hand at the loo table tonight, but Tempest had been with the Fawcetts when the invitation had been issued, casually, at Judge Grassington's garden party the previous week, and had taken it to include himself. Short of insulting him publicly, there had been no way in which his participation could be avoided and, even with the best of motives, one could not insult an old friend and one-time protégé. But for all that . . . Lord Ashton opened his mouth to utter a warning, only to close it again when Judge Grassington forestalled him.

"Edmund, me dear boy," the old man said quietly. "I

promised you a lift, did I not? Almost forgot but there's a sea mist set in, His Lordship's man tells me. Not a night to ride across the moor in evening dress, and since I gave your little Abigail me word that I'd see you safely home, I fancy we'll both be in her bad books if I don't, eh?"

Tempest did not raise his head. "Abigail has no call to concern herself with my safety, the impudent chit!" he retorted, his tone peevish. Then, belatedly recalling that the old judge had been his wife's uncle, he managed a surly apology. "I cannot possibly leave the game now, sir. Plague take it, my luck *must* change!" He started to deal, and Judge Grassington shrugged resignedly. He moved toward the door, and Lord Ashton, with a curt "Excuse me, gentlemen," to the players went with him.

In the long, stone-flagged hall, out of earshot of the players, the white-haired judge said explosively, "Damme, I did me best, Gilbert! But I can't drag the demmed idiot out by the scruff of his neck, can I?"

"No, unhappily," Lord Ashton concurred. "And I can't throw him out. I've known Edmund all his life—took him with me into his first ship when he was ten years old."

The judge accepted his hat and cane from a hovering footman and let the man drape his cloak about his shoulders. "It's those poor little gels of his I'm sorry for," he asserted. "Abby's got plenty of spirit, but . . . d'you suppose he really intends to take 'em off to—what's the name of the demmed place? Botany Bay, New South Wales, or whatever it calls itself?"

"It might be the best thing he could do, Henry."

"You think so? A plaguey penal colony, for God's sake? When I think of the rogues I've had to send out there, I . . . demmit, Gilbert, I question Edmund Tempest's sanity, before heaven I do!" The old judge's rheumy eyes were bright with anger as he added, low-

ering his voice a little, "That feller Foveaux's no adver-
tisement for the place, is he? Arrogant, ill-mannered
upstart and too demmed good at cards into the bargain.
He took two hundred guineas off me before I'd taken
his measure. Feller's a bluffer, of course—bids on
nothing if he thinks he'll get away with it. Well . . ."
He extended a bony hand. "Thanks for your hospitality, Gilbert. Though if I said I'd enjoyed meself, I'd
be a demmed liar, I'm afraid."

Lord Ashton escorted him to his waiting carriage
and stood watching it drive away, his heavy dark
brows knit in a thoughtful frown. The new day was
already well advanced, he observed, a gray bank of
clouds to the eastward tinged with pink and the sea
mist swirling in across the open moorland without a
breath of wind to disperse it. There would be rain before long, he thought, conscious of a twinge in his
gouty right foot . . . the blasted thing always made its
presence painfully known when there was rain in the
offing. He started to pace the graveled drive, still deep
in thought, and then, his mind made up, he strode
purposefully back to the house.

To the devil with the obligations of hospitality. If
the only way to save Edmund Tempest from himself
required him to dismiss his guests in summary fashion,
then by God he would do it! Both Arnold Fawcett and
his brother Arthur had lost a fair sum between them—
they would not mind, and if Foveaux objected, then
to the devil with him, too. The infernal bastard could
have no cause for complaint on the score of his win-
nings, which had been substantial by any standards . . .
even by Boodles's and, damn it, the Prince of Wales's.

Besides, the admiral told himself wryly, like old
Henry Grassington, he pitied Tempest's two girls.

"Serve hot chocolate at once, Scorrier," he ordered
his majordomo, "and warn 'em in the stables. We'll call
it a night."

But when he returned to the withdrawing room, it was to find a remarkable change in the atmosphere. Foveaux was scowling and biting his lower lip; the two Fawcett brothers sat with their mouths almost identically agape, and Sir Christopher Tremayne, normally the most phlegmatic of men, who talked very little when he was playing cards, was offering effusive congratulations to Edmund Tempest. And Tempest, the admiral saw to his astonishment, had—judging by the pile of red counters in front of him—more than recouped his earlier losses. He was dealing, and, one after another, every player passed, except Foveaux, who said illtemperedly, "I'll take the widow and a plague on it! Your luck can't hold much longer, Edmund."

"Can it not?" Tempest retorted. "Well, we'll see."

His voice was slurred; the scar on his temple pulsating and inflamed. He had evidently been drinking more heavily than any of the others and his hand was shaking uncontrollably as he extended it to take Foveaux's original cards. The rules of the game called for the discards to be placed at the bottom of the pack by the dealer, but Edmund Tempest's attempt to do so was so maladroit that two spilled onto the floor. One, Lord Ashton noticed, was a heart, the eight or the nine, he could not be sure which, as, with a smothered exclamation, Tempest bent to pick them up and Foveaux said rudely, "Clumsy oaf!"

"For the Lord's sake, I . . ." Tempest faced him, red of face and angry, but to Lord Ashton's relief, he controlled himself and gestured to his stake in the pool. "I'm ready to double that, if you wish, as my forfeit."

"Then be so good as to do so."

Three more red counters joined the three in the pool; Foveaux matched them, his expression oddly tense. "Make your lead," Tempest invited.

A footman, with the majordomo at his heels, brought

in the chocolate the admiral had ordered, but he waved them both away impatiently, his gaze riveted to the table.

Foveaux led the queen of clubs and Tempest took it with the ace; his own lead of the king of hearts found his opponent with a void. He took the trick and his fingers closed about the top card of the pack.

"Hearts are trumps, Joseph," he stated thickly, and laid down his hand. "You are looed."

"Hold hard!" Joseph Foveaux snapped. "That card you just turned up, the nine of hearts, was in the hand I discarded. It was one you contrived to drop on the floor. For God's sake—" He appealed to the table at large. "Did none of you see it? You must have done!"

Silent headshakes were his answer; Lord Ashton hesitated, torn between his own strong sense of justice and his dislike of the upstart Foveaux. To speak now would be to bring about Edmund Tempest's ruin, he was unhappily aware. He had only glimpsed the fallen card, he could not be sure. Foveaux's next words decided him to join the others in their silence.

"Damn your eyes, Tempest!" the New South Wales Corps officer accused, his expression ugly. "You tried to cheat me!"

Before Tempest could speak, the admiral intervened. "My house is not to be made the scene of an unseemly quarrel," he warned them coldly. "Major Foveaux, I will thank you to take your leave forthwith, sir. Divide the pool between you and let's hear no more of these unpleasant accusations, if you please. The game is over."

"As you wish, sir," Foveaux acknowledged, his mouth a tight, hard line. He picked up his stake from the pool, cashed himself in, and added in a low, furious voice, "You've not heard the end of this, Tempest, by heaven you haven't!"

"My seconds will wait on you," Edmund Tempest began. "You—" But once again the admiral cut him short. The Fawcetts departed with their guest; Sir Christopher Tremayne wrung his host's hand with unusual warmth and followed them, and Tempest was making for the hall when Lord Ashton called him back.

"He was right, was he not, Edmund?" the admiral questioned sternly. When the younger man attempted to bluster, he added in a tone that brooked no argument, "I saw the card you dropped."

"It was only that one hand, sir, I swear it. My luck changed after you left the room. . . . I was winning, I had a phenomenal run of the cards. Believe me, I—"

"You will not be welcome in my house again, Edmund. Nor, I dare swear, in any house in this neighborhood. Foveaux will talk, so will Arnold Fawcett."

"But, sir . . . if Your Lordship would listen." Tempest's hectic color had faded; he was white and shaken, the admiral saw, guilt and shame written all over him. "I beg you, sir . . . I'm telling you the truth. I saw the card fall, and I was tempted, but I—"

"Spare me your excuses," Lord Ashton bade him. He drew himself up to his full, impressive height, making no effort to hide the disgust he felt. "You've made plans to go out to New South Wales, have you not? You've booked passage out there, for yourself and the girls?"

Taken aback, Tempest nodded. "Yes, in the Indiaman *Mysore*, sailing from Plymouth, but—"

"Then the best advice I can offer is that you take them up, now, at once. Go on board as soon as you can and don't show your face in these parts again if you can help it. I'll take care of your boy. And for God's sake, man"—the admiral's voice softened, became almost pleading—"make something of your life when you get to Botany Bay, so that those two little girls of yours don't have cause to feel ashamed of their father."

"I . . . I'll do as you say, sir," Edmund Tempest promised. "But there's my house. I have to sell it, and—"

"I'll have my lawyers deal with the sale. If you leave before the legal details are completed, I'll have a draft for the proceeds sent out to you." The admiral turned his back, feeling tears well into his eyes. The pity of it, he thought . . . Edmund had been a credit to the service as a young officer and, in the early days, like a son to him. But now . . . "Get out of my sight," he ordered harshly.

When he had his emotions under control again and turned round, Edmund Tempest had gone.

CHAPTER I

It was still an hour before sunrise, on the morning of July 28, 1807, but already Captain William Bligh, Royal Navy—governor and captain general of the penal colony of New South Wales—was at his desk. Mail from England, which had been delivered the previous evening by the master of the convict transport *Duke of Portland*, lay neatly stacked on his desk to await his attention, but the governor gave only a cursory glance at seals and handwriting, in order to identify the senders.

There was an official dispatch from the colonial secretary, William Windham, and, among a pile of private correspondence, a bulky missive from Sir Joseph Banks, and a slimmer package, with his wife's carefully executed copperplate on the outside, which he slipped into the pocket of his uniform tailcoat, to read later at his leisure.

Most of the news would be old, he knew, and Windham's instructions probably out of date, for the *Duke of Portland*—although she had sailed direct from Falmouth—had made a slow passage. But her master, John Spence, had brought out his entire consignment of one hundred and eighty-nine female convicts alive and in good health, and this, God knew, redounded greatly to his credit. Virtually every transport lost upwards of a score of her unwilling passengers during the long voyage to the place they still called Botany Bay . . . and some lost many more, from sickness or judicial execution.

Masters of the ships that came from Ireland frequently had to hang rebels transported for sedition when their continued defiance of authority led them to attempt mutiny, and only the previous year the *William Pitt* had landed a sickly band of unhappy wretches suffering from cholera, the arrival of whom had caused consternation throughout the colony.

The governor frowned at the memory but reminded himself that conditions had improved in the year he had been governor. Given a humane ship's master like Spence, who was assisted by a competent surgeon—both of whom were paid a bonus for every healthy felon they set ashore—then further improvements in the quantity of healthy convicts arriving might confidently be expected.

The home government, alas, still chose the people for transportation without regard for their suitability as future settlers or even for their usefulness as laborers. Indeed, the sole objective appeared to be that of emptying England's jails of thieves and prostitutes and Ireland's of her rebels. His predecessors, like himself, had pleaded in vain for some care in selection to be exercised, but successive colonial secretaries had turned a deaf ear to such pleas.

They had simply ignored them, as they had ignored even more urgent requests for more reliable troops to be sent out to replace the corrupt and dissolute New South Wales Corps as the colony's garrison. Pressed for a reason, the war with France was invariably offered to justify refusal . . . as, no doubt, it did. Perhaps the

Mysore—whose arrival off the Heads had been signaled yesterday evening—would prove to have on board the free settlers Captain Spence had predicted, as well as the usual scurvy sweepings of Newgate and the provincial prisons.

Aware that he could not count on this, William Bligh expelled his breath in a long-drawn sigh of frustration. Thrusting Secretary Windham's weighty dispatches aside, he reached for the latest muster list his own secretary had prepared for him, dark brows furrowed as he studied it.

The population had grown to 7,562 in New South Wales proper, he saw. Of this number over a thousand were free settlers and emancipist landowners, growing the crops and raising the stock which would render them self-supporting, provided that no disastrous drought—or sudden flooding of the Hawkesbury River —occurred to thwart their efforts and destroy, in a few short days, the toil and enterprise of years.

They were the lifeblood of the colony; recognizing them as such, he had done all in his power to protect and encourage them, in the teeth of bitter opposition from the military hierarchy and certain civil officials who were bent on enriching themselves at the settlers' expense.

The New South Wales Corps represented the most intractable obstacle to the future well-being and prosperity of the colony he had been appointed to govern. Since Governor Phillip's departure fifteen years before, it had earned itself the inglorious title of "Rum Corps" . . . and deservedly, Bligh reflected sourly.

His two immediate predecessors, John Hunter and Philip King—both naval post captains, like himself— had been driven from office by the machinations of the officers of the military garrison and by the dubious activities of one in particular, Captain John Macarthur, now retired from the regiment and the colony's richest

landowner. All had obtained large land grants, with
free convict labor to work them, and all had engaged
extensively in trade—a trade based mainly on the import and barter of rum. The common soldiers, as well
as the convicts and the free and emancipist settlers, had
been compelled to use rum as their currency. Wages
were paid in rum, purchases made in it, and Macarthur
and his brother officers had made personal fortunes
from their monopoly of the colony's liquor imports.

Bligh had been sent out with instructions from the
Colonial Office to put a stop to the monopoly and replace the barter system with that based on a stable
currency, but . . . Impatiently, the governor broke the
seals on William Windham's dispatch, swearing under
his breath as he glanced through the first of its closely
written pages. Windham's demands were much as Lord
Hobart's had been, his mind registered, if couched in
more forthright terms than those normally employed
by the previous colonial secretary. But it was one thing
for a cabinet minister in far-off London to issue instructions to His Majesty's representative in New South
Wales, and quite another for that unfortunate representative to implement them.

In heaven's name, it would take time! Sydney had
been in a state of virtual anarchy when he had arrived,
and poor King a broken and embittered man, full of
complaints concerning the iniquities of the military
garrison, but without any advice to offer as to how the
situation might be improved or the Rum Corps brought
to order. And there *was* no way, short of removing
them. Plague take the whole unsoldierly, disloyal
bunch . . . they were a disgrace to the uniform they
wore!

Gripped by his own futile anger, Captain Bligh rose
and went to stand by the open window. The calm, now
familiar beauty of the cove and the great harbor beyond, lit by the first pale-golden rays of the sun, seemed

somehow to mock him, as if, by its sheer expanse and grandeur, it were emphasizing his own helplessness.

He had been given authority without power, he thought bitterly, and yet, God knew, he had done all any man could to carry out the task entrusted to him.

He had made progress in the reestablishment of a stable currency based on sterling and, with the support and approval of the majority of the settlers, had pegged the prices of essential foodstuffs, prohibited all liquor imports, save under government license, revoked half a hundred grogshop permits, and appointed civilians of good repute to the magistracy, the land commission, and the constabulary. At every step the rum traffickers had opposed him. John Macarthur, with his five thousand acres of prime grazing land, his imported sheep, and the ninety-strong labor force he employed on his two farms, had proved a formidable opponent.

Macarthur was without scruples, devious and clever. He broke the law without compunction himself, whilst invoking it against others to serve his own ends, and the acting commandant of the Corps, Major Johnstone, was completely under his influence.

But . . . The governor's hands clenched into fists at his sides. Macarthur was not infallible; no man was, and sooner or later he would make a mistake. When that happened, it would be time to take action, and, as God was his witness, he would not flinch from the challenge. He unclenched his fist as he heard a knock on the door.

William Bligh let his anger drain out of him; then, composing his features, he resumed his seat at the desk before bidding the caller to enter.

"Good morning, sir." Edmund Griffin, his secretary, advanced with his customary diffidence to face him across the paper-strewn desk. Griffin was a loyal, hardworking young man, whose gratitude for his recent advancement to the post of secretary to the colony had manifested itself in innumerable small ways, and Governor Bligh greeted him with a smile.

"Well?" he invited. "What is it, Edmund?"

"My apologies for disturbing Your Excellency," the secretary offered, "but Mr. Atkins is here and—"

"At this hour?" the governor exclaimed.

"He says the matter is of some urgency, sir. The lawyer, Mr. Crossley, sir, is with him."

"Well, damme!" Bligh was surprised. Judge Advocate Atkins was not, by habit, an early riser, but the fact that he had Crossley with him might account for his unexpected arrival. George Crossley was a one-time King's Bench attorney, deported for perjury and pardoned soon after his appearance in Sydney by Governor King, to whom he had made himself useful as legal adviser. He was a shrewd, intelligent fellow, well versed in the finer points of the law, and Atkins —who was not—had lately commandeered his services, in the hope of combating some of Macarthur's more outrageous legal ploys.

William Bligh frowned, his lips pursed to form a mute question, and Secretary Griffin shrugged his well-tailored shoulders, clearly understanding the import of the question but reluctant to answer it in so many words.

"Mr. Atkins told me that they have talked through the night, sir," he finally conceded. "Both have— er—the appearance of having done so. Perhaps I should order coffee for them if Your Excellency deems it advisable. That is—"

"Yes, do that, Edmund," the governor decided. "But I will take tea, as usual. See to it as soon as you've shown them in, if you please . . . and warn Mrs. Putland that I may be delayed."

"Very good, sir."

"Has anyone gone out to meet the *Mysore*?" Bligh

asked, belatedly recalling the transport's presence off South Head.

"Captain Hawley has, sir," Griffin assured him. He cast a mildly reproachful glance at the scattered contents of the governor's mailbag, but, after drawing two chairs up to the desk in readiness for the visitors, went obediently about his errand, announcing both men with the formality on which Bligh always insisted.

They came in, the lumbering, ungainly figure of the judge advocate preceding that of the slim, soberly dressed emancipist, whose bow, as he greeted the governor, verged on the obsequious. Bligh waved them to their chairs, his greeting brusque. Atkins's eyes were red rimmed, he observed, his long face flushed beneath its coating of dark stubble, his clothing crumpled—unmistakable signs of a night's heavy drinking—although his companion, by contrast, appeared well groomed and alert, his cheeks freshly shaven.

But, the governor reflected resignedly, as his servant carried in a tray of coffee and set it at his elbow, Richard Atkins was seldom completely sober these days—a state of affairs for which he himself was not solely to blame.

He had come out originally as registrar to the colony's Court of Admiralty, but not long after his arrival the home government had appointed him judge advocate, despite the fact that he had neither legal training nor experience. To his credit he had served in that capacity since the departure of his predecessor in the office, Colonel Collins, giving unstinted loyalty to both the previous governors, Hunter and King, as well as to himself. To the best of his ability, Atkins had supported every government reform brought in to curb the iniquitous rum traffic and the Corps' trading monopoly, and inevitably his efforts had incurred their displeasure.

Watching him now, as he slopped coffee into his cup with a far from steady hand, William Bligh was conscious of both pity and exasperation. It had been, he knew, Atkins's long-standing feud with John Macarthur that had finally broken his spirit and driven him to the bottle for solace. Their differences dated back to the time when both had been stationed in Parramatta and had quarreled openly, and Macarthur, with more than his usual vindictiveness, had sought ever since to blacken Atkins's character and bring about his removal from the office he held.

The poor devil had lost heart during the last years of Philip King's governorship, when all his efforts were defeated and his integrity was called, again and again, into question by Macarthur and his supporters, but . . . The governor glanced across at Atkins's companion, his eyes narrowed and speculative. Since the advent of Crossley, Richard Atkins had found fresh courage to continue the fight. Crossley was undoubtedly a rogue, but he was a first-rate lawyer, astute and possessing few scruples . . . just the man, in fact, to carry the fight into Macarthur's corner with some hope of success.

His own tray, with its silver teapot, was brought in and Bligh poured himself a cup, replying absently to Atkins's mumbled platitudes, while continuing to study the face of the man who had inspired that hope.

In appearance Crossley was far from impressive. He was small and dapper, his dark eyes too closely set to counteract the unpleasing effect of a large and somewhat bulbous nose and a wide, thin-lipped mouth. His age was difficult to assess; initially the governor had supposed him to be past middle age, but his papers had revealed that he had been only thirty-three when his fellow King's Benchers had disbarred him for malpractice and perjury.

Not by any stretch of the imagination an ideal ally

in his struggle to rid the colony of its corruption, Bligh reflected cynically. But then neither was Atkins . . . and he had no alternative, as he had already learned to his cost.

Crossley met his searching scrutiny with a nervous smile and touched Atkins on the arm, as if to remind him of the purpose of their early morning call. The judge advocate set down the cup, spilling what remained of its contents into the saucer, and announced, with owlish solemnity, "We are of the opinion, sir, that Mr. Macarthur and Captain Abbott have transgressed against the order, promulgated by Governor King, which prohibits the import into the colony of— ah—liquor stills, sir."

"Apparatus intended for the illicit distillation of spirits, Your Excellency," Lawyer Crossley put in. He quoted the order and the date of its promulgation and added, with a hint of smugness, "The order is still in force and the penalty for contravening it is quite specific, sir. It calls for the seizure and confiscation of the apparatus and—"

"Devil take it!" the governor interrupted impatiently. "I *know* the infernal stills were landed! The ship's master informed me, quite properly, that he had them on board. I directed Dr. Harris, as port naval officer, to take them into the government store as confiscated goods, pending an explanation from those to whom they were consigned, and I received an explanation, from Abbott. He claimed he had no knowledge of them, had not ordered them, and he agreed that they should be sent back to the makers. Captain Spence will take 'em, in the *Duke of Portland,* on my instructions." He spread his hands in a resigned gesture. "I don't doubt that Abbott or Macarthur or both of them *did* order the blasted things, hoping to slip them in unnoticed . . . but how the devil can I prove it, eh? Tell me that!"

"Your Excellency," Crossley offered smoothly. "There has been a—ah—a fresh development, which puts a different complexion on the matter, as Mr. Atkins will tell you." He turned expectantly to the judge advocate, who nodded, and proceeded to explain.

"That's so, sir, indeed it is. Surgeon Harris has permitted Mr. Macarthur to remove the two copper boilers, which form part of the distilling apparatus, from the store to his property at Parramatta."

The governor swore. "Has he, by God!"

"Yes, sir, he has. On the grounds, as I understand it, that Macarthur told him that the boilers were packed with medicinal requirements for his livestock, which he *had* ordered from England."

"And Harris believed that cock-and-bull yarn?"

"He purports to, yes. It's my belief . . . that is, sir—" Atkins exchanged a meaningful glance with his companion. "Crossley recently stumbled on the—ah—the fact that one of Macarthur's Crown leases has been made over to John Harris and—"

He hesitated, as if reluctant to put his conclusions into words, but Crossley, with no such scruples, did so for him. "It is my opinion, sir, that Dr. Harris has been persuaded to change his coat. I do not think that Your Excellency can continue to count on his support in any matter in which, sir, Mr. Macarthur chances to be involved."

It was as clear an accusation as could be expected of a lawyer, the governor thought . . . yet Harris had been Philip King's man, supporting him through thick and thin on the magistrates' bench and recommended warmly for his loyalty. Indeed, his appointment as naval officer had been made on King's recommendation. He himself had never liked the one-time naval surgeon's assistant, considering him spiteful and less than a gentleman, but . . . He met Crossley's eye across the desk. There was no uncertainty in the lawyer's shrewd gaze.

"Not to put too fine a point on it, sir," Crossley said. "Mr. Macarthur is not above suborning those who have, in the past, gone against him."

That was true, as he also knew to his cost, Bligh reminded himself. There had been a number of other waverers who had accepted favors from the wealthy Macarthur and thereafter ceased to stand in his way. Soon after his own arrival in the colony, a covert approach had been made by one of the Blaxland brothers—both members of the Macarthur faction—when the offer of a lucrative partnership in a brewery had been dangled in front of him, in order, or so he had supposed at the time, to test his integrity.

The governor reached for pen and paper, his mind made up. He wrote quickly, the quill catching on the paper in his haste; then, after reading through what he had written, he passed the note to Crossley.

"This should settle it, don't you agree? It's a written order to Harris to repossess himself of the boilers and hand them over, with the rest of the damned apparatus, to Captain Spence of the *Duke of Portland*."

"Admirably put, sir," the lawyer approved. He passed the order to the judge advocate and asked quietly, as Atkins, in his turn, was reading it, "And should Dr. Harris fail to carry out your instructions, what then, sir?"

"Then, Mr. Crossley," Bligh thundered, "the infernal fellow will be dismissed from his appointment as port naval officer forthwith! If we are ever to stem the flow of illicit imports into this colony, it is essential that the holder of the office should be an honest and reliable man. And, by heaven, one who cannot be bribed by the scoundrels who seek to contravene our laws!" He paused, frowning. Harris would have to be given the benefit of such doubt as there was—he

was entitled to that—but . . . "If you are right about
Surgeon Harris, Mr. Crossley, he—devil take the fellow! He'll have to go."

"Your Excellency can be assured that I *am* right,"
Crossley asserted firmly. "If those two boilers are not
already at Mr. Macarthur's Parramatta farm, then
they are on their way there. And Mr. Macarthur will
claim that he had Dr. Harris's permission to move
them."

"But not mine, damn his eyes!" Bligh snapped. Undoubtedly Harris had exceeded his authority, but had
he done more than that? *Had* he let Macarthur suborn
him? And, if he had, where was the honest man to
replace him, the man who could not be bribed? He
thought suddenly of Robert Campbell and felt his
tension relax. Campbell and his nephew—also Robert
—were free settlers, both of them possessed of capital
and enterprise, their record for fair and honest dealing unsullied . . . even in this corrupt place. And
Campbell was a civilian, with his own shipyard and
wharf on the west side of the cove. He would be the
best possible replacement for Harris.

Relieved at having reached so satisfactory a conclusion, William Bligh turned again to Crossley.

"My note, if you please."

"Certainly, sir." The lawyer took the note from Atkins's uncertain hand and offered, with an eagerness he
made no attempt to conceal, "Shall I deliver this to
Dr. Harris, sir? It would be no trouble."

Bligh hesitated and then shook his head. "No. Griffin had better do that . . . or perhaps Gore, as provost marshal. That would make it official, would it not?
I don't want Harris to claim he hasn't received it."

He rose, intending to signify that the interview was
at an end, but Richard Atkins, who had lapsed into
a gloomy silence, roused himself from his apathy and
observed portentously, "Willie Gore will have to tread

carefully, Governor. He'll have to tread very carefully indeed."

"Gore? Good God Almighty!" The governor stared at him in shocked dismay. Apart from Andrew Hawley, his Royal Marine aide, William Gore was the best officer he had. Courageous, efficient, and transparently honest, he had carried out his duties in exemplary fashion and with a determined impartiality that merited respect. The office of provost marshal was a thankless one, underpaid and, at times, extremely onerous, since it involved command of the jail and the colony's constables, in addition to the heavy burden of court work. Bligh's lips tightened. "What exactly do you mean, Mr. Atkins?" he demanded bluntly. "You are not trying to tell me, surely, that *Gore's* been persuaded to turn his coat?"

"No, certainly not," the judge advocate assured him. "Quite the reverse. Gore is a most conscientious officer, with a high regard for his duty and the responsibilities he bears. Not that they haven't tried to win him over—they have, and they have failed." Warming to his theme, Atkins waved Lawyer Crossley to silence when he attempted to interpose a word of caution. "All right, George, I know what I'm saying . . . leave this to me. His Excellency must be informed of what's afoot."

"Pray continue," Bligh bade him, losing patience.

Atkins did so. "No doubt you will recall, sir, that a few weeks ago Gore recommended the removal of a scoundrel named Mackay from his post as head jailer here, on the grounds of his profligacy and the ill treatment of prisoners?"

The governor frowned. "Yes, I do indeed. Mackay's an unmitigated scoundrel, a time-expired convict who should never have been given the post. *I* ordered his removal."

Atkins permitted himself a thin smile. "As a con-

sequence, sir, there is a move afoot to discredit poor
Gore. Mackay's mistress has been induced to bring
a charge of theft against Mr. Gore, claiming that he
robbed her of some trinket, of sentimental value only.
The charge won't hold water, sir, as Mr. Crossley
agrees, but I'm bound to investigate it, of course. I
mention it simply to—well, to tender a warning, because now there's been a second charge. Simeon Lord's
partner, James Underwood, has accused Gore of issuing a forged note of hand."

Bligh swore. "Well, for God's sake—*that* charge
won't hold water! Surely you're not even thinking of
permitting them to bring it, are you?"

"It has been filed," the judge advocate answered reluctantly. "I have to take statements, but—"

Crossley put in smoothly. "Both charges are outrageous, sir, but in my view they should not be—ah
—suppressed. It will be in Mr. Gore's best interests
if they are brought and disproved." He talked on, and
finally the governor allowed himself to be convinced.
If the knives were out for an honest, upright officer
like William Gore, then those who were seeking to
use them must be forced into the open and publicly
exposed for the rogues and perjurers they were.

"Are you certain that Gore can clear himself?" he
asked, and both men asserted that they were.

"Provided," Crossley added cautiously, "that the
bench are not all of the—ah—of the military faction.
It is within Your Excellency's power to ensure that
they are not . . . in the interests of justice."

The governor frowned but offered no comment, and,
to his relief, the two law officers took their leave a
few minutes later. It was his custom to break his fast
in the company of his daughter, Mary Putland, but
. . . He consulted his pocket watch. Their visit had
delayed him for almost an hour; Mary would have
given him up by this time and taken the meal with

her husband, Charles. The poor fellow was still confined to his bed after the last severe attack of the lung affliction that was draining him of strength.

The secretary, Edmund Griffin, came in response to his summons. Bligh gave him the note he had addressed to Surgeon Harris and, after instructing him to deliver it in person and obtain a signed receipt for it, ordered fresh tea to be served to him at his desk.

"There are letters I must read, Edmund. Be so good as to make my apologies to my daughter. Tell her that we will take luncheon together before I set out for Parramatta. I ordered an early luncheon, did I not?"

"You did, sir—it will be served at midday. I'll see that Mrs. Putland is informed." Griffin hesitated, looking uncertainly at the note he had been given. "Do you wish me to deliver this to Dr. Harris immediately?"

"I do," Bligh returned emphatically. "Read it for yourself, Edmund—and having done so, mark Harris's manner well when he digests its contents! There's been a suggestion that he's changed his allegiance, and I'm anxious to be sure which way the wind is blowing." In a few brief and bitter words he repeated Crossley's warning and the conclusions he had drawn from it and, hearing the secretary's sharp intake of breath, knew that his loyal subordinate was shocked . . . if not, perhaps, surprised.

Left alone, the replenished teapot at his elbow, the governor dealt first with the colonial secretary's dispatch and then took his wife's letter from his pocket, conscious of a pang as he glimpsed its opening words.

He missed his Betsy sorely. Heaven knew, in twenty-five years of marriage he had been able to spend all too little time with her. Even during the five years when the navy had put him on half pay, he had been at sea, commanding a merchant ship engaged in the West Indian sugar trade, until Their Lordships had recalled him to command the *Bounty,* and embark on the ill-fated expedition to Otaheite which had ended in mutiny. His dark brows came together in a resentful scowl. A plague on it, he thought, as the painful memories came flooding back—the *Bounty* and Fletcher Christian's betrayal would always haunt him, in spite of the findings of the court-martial and the fact that he had been exonerated from all blame.

But Betsy, bless her kind and generous heart, had stood by him, comforting, encouraging . . . never losing faith in him, ready always to give him her loyal support. A lump rose in William Bligh's throat, as he read the first page of her letter. It was a source of constant regret to him that her frail health had precluded her from accompanying him to Sydney, for, God help him, he was in need of Betsy's companionship now. His daughter Mary did her best, but poor Charles Putland's illness and his needs had, of necessity, to take precedence over any other claims on her time, even his own, and . . . The concluding lines of the first page of his wife's letter caused him to draw in his breath sharply:

"The malice and cruelty of the people who were engaged in this business of rum trading exceeds everything I ever thought men capable of," Betsy had written.

"Kent went down to Portsmouth in the same chaise as King, and at Hunter's lodgings with Short planned how the trade might be continued. . . ."

Philip King, his immediate predecessor, Bligh thought, shocked to the depths of his being. . . . John Hunter, also a former governor, and his nephew, that fine officer, William Kent, who had come here with him in command of the *Supply*—were they allied against him now? Surely that could not be true, when both King and Hunter had tried as hard as he was trying to stamp out the iniquitous rum traffic? Lieutenant Short's enmity was to be expected—he had sent the fellow home for court-martial on charges of insubordination, for his disgraceful conduct when in command of his own escorting frigate a year ago—but it did not seem within the bounds of possibility that King and Hunter should seek now to undermine his authority. Of all men living, the two former governors had learned, from painful experience, what he had learned in the past year. . . . Devil take it, had they not suffered from treachery and betrayal? Did they not know from whom it stemmed?

Bligh mopped his brow, feeling beads of sweat break out on it as he reread the damning accusation Betsy had made and then turned the page.

"I wish that the troops could be changed," she had added. *"Foveaux is very ill-disposed to you and I hope you will send him back to Norfolk Island when he returns to the colony. Mr. Marsden thinks that you will have a great deal to encounter if you oppose the barter of spirits, by which everybody about you have made their fortunes."*

The Reverend Samuel Marsden—the colony's chaplain, who had gone home on leave with King—had not exaggerated, the governor reflected. No, dear God, he had not! Foveaux, recently promoted lieutenant colonel in the Corps, had always been a close friend and business associate of John Macarthur's; like Short's, his opposition was predictable, but since he was junior in rank to Colonel Paterson, Betsy's suggestion was a sound one. Foveaux could be sent back to govern Norfolk Island . . . at all events, until the Norfolk Island convicts were removed to the new settlements in Van Diemen's Land.

And Samuel Marsden, rough diamond though he was, had an exemplary record of loyalty. On *his* return to the church and the magistrates' bench, he could be relied on to oppose the rum traffickers of the Corps to the limit of his considerable ability. But . . . Bligh folded his wife's letter and thrust it back into his pocket.

There was still the vexed question of Governor King's apparent defection, if Betsy's conclusions concerning him were based on more than gossip and conjecture.

Wearily, he rose and crossed to Edmund Griffin's filing cabinet. An impatient search was finally rewarded by the finding of a list of government land grants made by King during the last six months when he had held office. Returning to his desk, William Bligh went carefully through the list. His own name, he saw, had been written at the foot of the fourth page as having, quite properly, been allocated agricultural land to the south of the Parramatta road and now known—by the name he had given it—as Camperdown. The preceding pages, however, covered grants of Crown building land within the boundaries of Sydney itself, and all were fourteen-year renewals of leaseholds, which had been granted initially for a limited period of five years.

Under Arthur Phillip's governorship, all building land within the boundaries he had drawn had been declared Crown property in perpetuity, but King had permitted the five-year lease to certain civil and military officials to be extended, and he had made a large grant to the church, which comprised the original military parade ground to the east of the Tank Stream.

Governor Bligh spread out the surveyor's map attached to the documents, on which the holdings were identified by numbers. He frowned as he ran his eye down the list, noting the names of those to whom his predecessor had granted the fourteen-year leases in January 1806—six months prior to his own arrival in the colony.

Among them he saw, with growing indignation, several names which had become all too familiar to him of late . . . those of John Macarthur, Surgeons Jamieson and Harris, Colonel Paterson, Major Johnstone, Captains Kemp and Prentice of the Corps, and the sergeant major, Thomas Whittle. The civilian leaseholders included Simeon Lord, James Underwood, Garnham Blaxcell, and . . . Unable to restrain himself, the governor swore aloud. A plague on it! Daniel Mackay, the infernal rogue whose dismissal from the post of jailer Gore had sought—even Mackay had been granted a building lease between the hospital and the public wharf, facing on to the High Street!

And Macarthur's lease, numbered 77 on the survey map, was on the church reserve . . . God in heaven, what could have possessed Philip King to authorize these grants, and to these men? Had he, aware that he was about to be superseded, attempted to curry favor with his enemies, with the monopolists and the rum traffickers who had brought about his dismissal and whom he had described as the secret assassins of his reputation? Had this been his way of buying peace during the last months of his governorship, or was it yet another example of the monstrous corruption that existed here?

William Bligh got to his feet and started restlessly to pace the room, beset by doubts and recalling, with bitterness, the accusations his wife had made. He had not wanted to believe them, had endeavored to dismiss them . . . but the list of Crown leaseholders offered proof he could not refute. Proof, at least, that King had weakened, if he had not been suborned. And if he had . . . It was almost with relief that Bligh heard a knock on the door, and, guessing from its softness that the knock heralded his daughter, he hurried across the room to admit her.

Mary Putland was small of stature and an exceptionally pretty girl, whose narrow, fine-boned face and deep blue eyes were the echo of her mother's. She had inherited his temper, though, William Bligh reflected ruefully as, bending to kiss her, he found himself held at arms length and greeted with an angry demand for his full and instant attention.

"Edmund Griffin insisted that I must not disturb you, Papa," she went on accusingly, "but the matter is urgent. Surely you can spare me a scant five minutes from the affairs of this—this brigand state?"

"Of course, my dear child," her father assured her. "You know that I always have time for you." He attempted to lead her to a chair, but she shook her head with barely restrained impatience.

"It's Charles, Papa. . . . Poor darling, he has had another hemorrhage. A really severe one, and it happened so suddenly I . . ." Tears filled the blue eyes, marring their brightness. "Papa, I have sent for Dr. Redfern."

She made this announcement defiantly, aware that it would displease him, but Bligh controlled himself. The poor child was seriously worried, and not without cause. Her husband's hemorrhages had become more frequent of late and infinitely more alarming, and it behooved him to show her sympathy and understanding, although he could not—either officially or personally—approve her choice of a physician. William Redfern had been assistant surgeon of the line-of-battle ship *Standard* at the time of the Nore mutiny and, at his court-martial, had been found guilty of all save two of the charges brought against him. Indeed, he had been fortunate that the court had recommended him to mercy, and transported him, instead of hanging him.

Mary said, before he could speak, "They say that young Dr. Redfern is by far the best in the colony. Dr. Jamieson has not helped poor Charles, you know he has not. He gives him opiates and wrings his hands, and Charles is suffering so. I cannot just stand by and do nothing, Papa."

"No. I understand you cannot, my dear." Moved by her distress, Bligh put an arm about her slim shoulders and held her to him. "Send for whom you wish. I shall raise no objection."

She turned and, raising herself on tiptoe, kissed his cheek. "Oh, thank you, Papa . . . and bless you! I— I'll go back to Charles now and do what I can for him until Dr. Redfern arrives. But I felt—that is, I felt I owed it to you to tell you." Her gaze fell on the dispatch box and the scattered papers on the desk. "Mail . . . was there a letter from Mamma?"

Her father hesitated and then inclined his head.

"Yes, there was. But," he added evasively, "apart from her affectionate good wishes to you and Charles, there was not a great deal to interest you in it."

Mary did not question him further. She kissed him again and then hastened back to her husband's sick-room, leaving the governor to peruse the rest of his official and private mail. He had barely started to read the lengthy epistle from Sir Joseph Banks when his secretary returned, looking angry and ruffled.

"Well?" Bligh asked, anticipating the reply he would receive. "Have you come to tell me that Dr. Harris intends to defy me?"

Edmund Griffin nodded, tight of lip. "He insists that he acted quite properly within the bounds of his authority as port naval officer, and he declines to go back on his word. He wishes me to inform Your Excellency that he does not feel obliged to take any steps to recover what he deems to be Mr. Macarthur's legitimate property, and he refused to sign a receipt for your order, sir."

"Did he, by God!" Governor Bligh drew pen and paper toward him. "I fancy he'll have to take notice of *this* order, damn his insolence! And you can give it to him at once. . . . It's his dismissal. I shall appoint Mr. Campbell as port officer in his stead; and his first official duty shall be the recovery of those infernal stills! They're going back to England in the *Duke of Portland,* boilers and all, and I shall tell Mr. Campbell so. You had better ask him to call on me, if it's convenient, before I leave for Parramatta. Oh . . . and I take it you arranged for my escort?"

"Yes, sir, they're here. Six troopers of the Loyal Association, and they are all mounted." The secretary permitted himself a gratified smile. "They make as smart and well turned out an escort as I've seen, for all they are volunteers."

"Good," the governor approved. "Be so good as to see they are given refreshment. Is Captain Hawley with them?"

Edmund Griffin shook his head. "No, sir, he went out to meet the ship that's just arrived off the Heads, if you remember. But I think I saw his cutter returning—I hadn't a glass, but it looked like young Broome's boat. He should be back within the hour, sir."

"Good," the governor repeated. "My compliments to Captain Hawley, and when he does get back, invite him to take luncheon with me, if you please. My daughter will not be joining us. She's waiting for Dr. Redfern to call." Glimpsing the surprised look on the secretary's face, he supplied crisply, "With my consent, Edmund."

"Sir," Griffin acknowledged, and withdrew.

Left alone, Governor Bligh was in a more optimistic mood when he once again gave his attention to the half-read letter from Sir Joseph Banks, pleased and relieved to read that the colonial secretary, William Windham, had expressed approval of the measures he had taken to end the barter of spirits throughout the colony.

"I can assure you," his patron had written, *"that you have the full support of His Majesty's Government, following a debate in the House and a statement by the Right Hon. Gentleman. In this, Mr. Windham as-*

serted that the import of spirits into the colony must be strictly controlled in order to prevent the illicit trading activities, by means of which certain individuals have enriched themselves . . . to the detriment of the farming interests and great injury to the morals of the colony.

"I urge you therefore to continue in your endeavors, no matter by whom you may be opposed. . . ."

William Bligh was thoughtful, as he folded the letter and reached for the list of Crown leaseholders he had taken earlier from the official files. Would His Majesty's Government support him if he were to invoke Governor Phillip's order of 1792 and declare Philip King's grants null and void because of the suspicion of corruption they aroused? He would consult Crossley, he decided, and instruct him to search the records for any evidence of Phillip's order having been rescinded. If he found none, then . . .

"Your luncheon is served, sir," his servant announced from the doorway, and the governor rose, suppressing a sigh. Scarcely half the day had passed, but he felt unbearably tired, and, not for the first time since his arrival in New South Wales, he found himself wishing that he were still in command of one of His Majesty's ships at sea. On his quarterdeck, even in action, he had not felt so vulnerable or so hard pressed by enemies as he did here and now.

"Captain Hawley is here, sir," his secretary told him, and the governor's expression relaxed. The tall marine officer was waiting for him in the dining room. A good man, Hawley, he reflected, and one on whose loyalty he knew he could depend. Had he not proved it at the Nore mutiny, when his whole ship's company had joined the disaffected rogues led by the renegade Parker and, for a time, his own life—and those of his officers—had been in jeopardy? Andrew Hawley had been only a sergeant then, and the self-styled delegates had threatened to hang him from the *Director*'s yardarm if he would not join them, but he had stood firm and done his duty with resolute courage. His rise to his present rank had been achieved on merit, without patronage or influence and . . . The governor greeted him warmly as he waved the newcomer to a seat at the table.

Hawley had displayed similar resolution in his refusal to exchange into the New South Wales Corps, a course which, he was aware, both Major Johnstone and Captain Abbott had repeatedly urged him to consider whilst, no doubt, laying stress on the financial advantages likely to result from such a move.

Soup having been served and the usual pleasantries exchanged, Bligh asked, "Well, what of the *Mysore*, Hawley? Has she brought us the free settlers Captain Spence led us to expect?"

"She's brought half a score, sir, and a hundred and twenty convicts from the West Country assizes—eighteen of them female," the marine officer answered. He went into careful detail concerning the convicts, emphasizing the fact that all were in good health and that—instead of the usual thieves and vagabonds from city back streets—the majority were fishermen, agricultural laborers, or tin miners, and that one man, whose family had accompanied him, was a thatcher. "They are country folk, sir . . . a rare cargo, and the master speaks well of their conduct during the passage."

"Excellent, excellent!" the governor exclaimed. "Can this be indicative of a change of policy on the part of His Majesty's Government, do you suppose? Will they now send us the skilled artisans and husbandmen we need so sorely?"

"I fear, sir," Andrew Hawley demurred, "that it is pure chance. The *Mysore* lay for six weeks at Plymouth and for a further two at Falmouth. The assize justices took advantage of her presence to order transportation for most of those arraigned before them."

William Bligh swort softly. "I don't doubt you're right, Captain Hawley." He helped himself sparingly from the dish his servant offered, without appetite and scarcely aware of what it was. It was always the same, he thought with bitterness; the authorities at home, be they politicians or His Majesty's judges, were guided by expediency. Those in Launceston would be congratulating themselves on the saving they had made, by keeping their jails empty. "We must be thankful for occasional examples of parsimony which work to our advantage," he said resignedly. "But . . . what of the settlers? Are they of the same caliber as the felons?"

To his surprise he observed an embarrassed flood of color rise to suffuse the scarred face of the marine officer. "There is a Missionary Society chaplain, the Reverend Caleb Boskenna, and his wife, sir, a master carpenter with a wife and child, a tailor with a wife and son, and a single shepherd. They will present no problems but—" He hesitated and Bligh prompted sharply, "Well? Are you implying that the others may?"

Andrew Hawley nodded, his blue eyes troubled.

"There are two young sisters, sir, who were orphaned during the passage. Their father died—by his own hand, I gather—after the ship left the Cape. He was a naval officer, invalided after sustaining a severe wound at Copenhagen and . . . well, as far as I could make out from the master, Captain Duncan, sir, he was not sorry to be rid of a somewhat troublesome passenger. But . . . the unfortunate gentleman purchased a considerable quantity of stock at Capetown, sheep, mainly, and some well-bred horses, Duncan said, intending to apply for a land grant and farm here."

"We can buy all the stock for the government farms," the governor put in. "That will present no problem. But what of the two young orphans? Did you speak to them?"

"I did, sir. The elder of the two young ladies, who is seventeen, sir, told me that it is her firm intention to retain her father's stock and carry out his wishes. She is . . ." Andrew Hawley smiled. "Miss Abigail Tempest is a most courageous and determined young lady, and I understand that she—"

"Tempest?" Bligh interrupted. "Good God . . . and her father was wounded at Copenhagen, you say! Was his name Edmund Tempest—Edmund Ashton Tempest?"

"I believe so, yes, sir. Did you know him?"

"I did indeed. He was first lieutenant of the *Monarch*—took command after Captain Mosse was killed and handled her most gallantly. I relieved him, after he was wounded, and brought the ship home. I did not expect to bring poor Tempest home—he was very severely wounded in the head, I recall. But now the poor fellow is dead . . . and by his own hand, God rest his soul! I am appalled, I—" The governor was deeply moved. "I shall do all I can for his children, although I fear they'll have to be sent home. In the meantime you did not bring them ashore with you?"

Andrew Hawley shook his head. "I thought it best to arrange accommodation for them first, sir. They're being well cared for. The missionary chaplain—the Reverend Boskenna—and his wife have assumed responsibility for them and the ship's surgeon assured me that he—"

"They must stay here, at Government House," Captain Bligh decided. "But damme, I have to go to Parramatta for the muster! When d'you think the *Mysore* will enter the cove?"

"Late this evening, sir, I should judge."

The governor rose, pushing his untouched plate aside. "There's no time for me to go out to her—I must be in Parramatta before dark. You'll have to look after those poor children, Hawley. Bring them ashore as soon as their ship drops anchor—I'll warn my daughter to expect them."

"I was to command your escort, sir," Hawley reminded him.

"That's of no matter. I can command 'em myself, can I not? Well"—as his secretary made his appearance from the anteroom—"what is it, Edmund? I must be on my way."

"Your Excellency wanted to see Mr. Campbell—" Griffin began, and Bligh swore softly.

"The deuce—so I did. Well, there'll be time for that, I suppose, if he's here. I take it you delivered my —ah—note to Dr. Harris?"

"I did, sir." The younger man permitted himself a wry smile. "It was not well received, sir."

"Good!" the governor exclaimed. "We've put the cat among the pigeons, I fancy . . . or perhaps 'stirred up the hornets' nest' would be a more apt metaphor." He shrugged with feigned indifference. "Well, a plague on them!" He laid a hand briefly on Andrew Hawley's broad, scarlet-clad shoulder and strode off to the anteroom, with Griffin at his heels.

CHAPTER II

The sun was sinking in a blaze of glory behind the wooded slopes on which the town was built when, at last, the *Mysore* came to anchor in Sydney Cove. Her female passengers, both convict and free, had been on deck for most of the day, exclaiming in wonder at the magnificent vista of Port Jackson Harbor spread out before them, as the ship weathered the two rocky headlands standing, like sentinels, at its entrance and worked her way to the anchorage under easy sail.

Dusky-skinned natives in flimsy bark canoes caused much excited comment when they had first been seen, but now the concerted attention of all on board was focused on the town that was to be their home—in the case of the convicts, almost certainly for the rest of their lives.

"There bain't a great deal of it, seemingly," the stout midwife, Kate Lamerton, observed, after a lengthy inspection of the rows of white-painted wooden houses, interspersed with a few larger buildings, constructed of brick or stone. "But it do look tidy enough, I s'pose, an' dem windmills is a pretty sight. Oh, ah . . . an' there's a clock tower, too—or be it a church?

Miss Abigail, dear, your eyes'm keener than mine. Can you make it out?"

Abigail shook her head, conscious of a feeling of bitter disappointment. Had they come so far, almost halfway round the world, only to this? The town might look what Kate called tidy but it also looked primitive, as if expediency had brought it into being and little had since been done to rid its scattered clusters of ramshackle dwelling places of their air of shoddy impermanence.

Government House, which one of the mates had pointed out to her, was the only two-story building she could see . . . although two others, as yet lacking their roof shingles, had men working on them and both appeared more extensive than the governor's residence. There were some larger houses on the gently rising slope to the rear of Government House and a huge building, half hidden behind a high log fence, which enclosed a square compound or exercise yard that appeared, at first glance, to be empty.

"That there's the jail," Kate said wryly, following the direction of Abigail's gaze. "Ready for the likes o' us, I reckon, when they takes us ashore. It bain't a prospect I relish, I tell 'ee true, m'dear. Plymouth jail were bad enough!"

Abigail squeezed her plump, work-roughened hand in wordless sympathy. Kate Lamerton was a convict, transported for seven years. She never spoke of the past and had maintained a stubborn silence as to the nature of the crime of which she had been adjudged guilty. A practical and eminently sensible woman, she had accepted her fate with dignity and had won the approval of the ship's master and the gratitude of the surgeon for her willingness to apply her nursing skills for the benefit of any who might require them.

And there had been many, Abigail reflected . . . her delicate little sister, Lucy, among them. Lucy had been afflicted with a severe fever on the passage between Rio de Janeiro and the Cape and only Kate's devotion had saved her. And then . . . She drew in her breath sharply, still unable to think of it with equanimity. Following their father's inexplicable decision to take his own life, the midwife had been a tower of strength to both of them, she and the young assistant surgeon, Titus Penhaligon. Between them they had done infinitely more and shown a greater degree of compassion than the man their father had appointed as their guardian.

Abigail shivered in the warm dusk. Why, she asked herself bitterly, had her father chosen the Reverend Caleb Boskenna and his acid-tongued wife to take charge of Lucy and herself? That he had, there could be no doubt; his dying wishes had been clearly set out in the letter he had left—a letter seemingly written only a few hours before he had put a pistol to his head, to end an existence he had found unbearable.

Titus Penhaligon had sought to spare her from all knowledge of the letter's contents, but Martha Boskenna had shown it to her, insisting that she must read it lest, Abigail could only presume, she were to question the provisions her father had made for his livestock, his money, and the furniture he had brought from England to be entrusted to Mr. Boskenna's care, in addition to his daughters.

There had been much in the letter that she regretted having read; disillusion had followed the shock and heartbreak of Edmund Tempest's death. Abigail bit her lip fiercely, feeling it tremble. Unlike Lucy, she had not been blind to her father's faults, but the letter, much of it couched in maudlin terms, had stripped the man who had written it of all pretense. It was as if he had revealed himself naked before her. . . .

Beside her, Kate Lamerton exclaimed, "Look, Miss

Abigail—there's another boat a-comin' out to us, I do believe! An' it's full o' redcoats."

The boat, Abigail saw, was putting out from a wharf on the west side of the cove, with four men at the oars and a cluster of scarlet coats in the stern sheets. It was the second boat to put out to them since the *Mysore* had dropped anchor; the first brought the tall marine captain who had greeted them off the Heads, and he was below, closeted with the Boskennas in their cabin. She had been mildly puzzled by his reappearance, but apart from a polite acknowledgment of her presence on deck, the officer had not spoken to her, although she had sensed that his business with the Reverend Caleb Boskenna probably concerned Lucy and herself.

She had spoken out, perhaps a trifle too freely, Abigail recalled, when he had questioned her earlier as to her intentions. Indeed, she had told him very firmly that she planned to take up the land grant which the Colonial Office in London promised her father, but then Mr. Boskenna had intervened, drawing the marine captain aside in order, she supposed, to establish his credentials as her guardian.

When they had joined the ship at Plymouth, the Boskennas had informed all who cared to listen that they were on their way to New Zealand, under the auspices of the Missionary Society, to seek for Christian converts amongst its savage inhabitants. For this reason it was odd, Abigail thought resentfully, that the Reverend Boskenna should, with so little reluctance, have agreed to act as guardian to Lucy and herself. To do so would mean that his journey to New Zealand must be indefinitely postponed—yet he appeared to have no qualms of conscience on this account. Rather the reverse, in fact; both he and his wife seemed pleased by their change of destination,

and they had pointedly ignored the diffident suggestions she had made, dismissing with adult scorn her
attempts to convince them that she was capable of
caring for her sister without their help.

"You are children," the missionary had reminded
her, "and Sydney is a penal colony. It would be the
height of irresponsibility were we to abandon you
there, Abigail. Mrs. Boskenna and I would never do
that. I am determined to carry out your father's wishes.
The God I serve is compassionate and wise, and I
have thrown myself on His mercy in the certainty that
He will understand and countenance my decision. So
there is no more to be said, my child."

In spite of this she had tried to argue, for Lucy's
sake, as well as her own. Lucy was frankly scared out
of her wits by the prospect of having to submit to the
Boskennas' guardianship, working herself into parox-
ysms of grief and fear whenever the subject was mentioned.

"I'd rather go back to England, Abby," she had
wept. "Truly I would—even if we had to beg for our
bread when we got there! And I don't care if Mr.
Boskenna is a minister of the church—he's an evil,
wicked man and I hate him! Please, Abby, make them
go away—to New Zealand or wherever they are supposed to be going. We don't need them . . . Kate can
look after us. She wants to, and Jethro, too. We should
be perfectly safe and happy with them."

But Kate had been dismissed as scornfully as all
her other suggestions. She was a convicted felon, Mr.
Boskenna had asserted, and Jethro Crowan, the shepherd who had accompanied them from Tywardreath,
an unlettered oaf, who could not be trusted to undertake so heavy a responsibility.

Abigail glanced uneasily at Kate and from her round,
honest face to the approaching boat, seeing both
through a mist of tears. If only her brother, Rick, had

been with them, she thought wretchedly, saddened by her own powerlessness. True, he was barely a year older than she but . . . he was a man. No one—not even the governor or the marine captain he had sent to represent him—would have questioned Rick's ability to assume responsibility for his sisters' care. But because she was seventeen and female and because Kate Lamerton was a convict, the alternative to acceptance of the Boskennas' guardianship could only be a return to England and penury . . . to beg their bread, as Lucy had put it. And that was unthinkable.

"They'm officers, Miss Abigail," Kate said, pointing to the boat. "Swords an' gold braid an' all. What d'you reckon they're comin' for?"

Abigail brushed the tears from her eyes with her knuckles, the gesture a childish one of which she was instantly ashamed. "I don't know," she admitted, and then, recalling the occasions when the *Mysore* had had to pass quarantine inspection at Rio and the Cape, she shrugged. "Perhaps they are the port health authorities."

"Well, we'm healthy enough," Kate claimed, beaming. "Earned a nice fat bonus for the cap'n and young Surgeon Penhaligon, I fancy. No scurvy an' not a sign o' jail fever—them officers won't have much to complain of, even if they try."

Abigail managed an answering smile. Captain Dun-can was a humane and kindly man; he had treated his convict passengers well, rewarding those of good behavior by removing their fetters and permitting them regular access to the deck in all but the worst weather. The male convicts' exercise deck was forward; that of the women where she was now standing, on the poop, where they had mixed freely with the settlers and their families. Glancing over her shoulder, she saw that most of them were still there watching, as eagerly as Kate, for the port officials' boat to come alongside.

Meeting Abigail's gaze, Chrissie Trevemper, the wife of master carpenter Robert Trevemper, lifted her small son high above her head and called out shrilly, "There be plenty o' work for my Rob to do by the looks o' them little wooden 'ouses on shore, Miss Abigail! Not much o' a town, be it now?"

"No, not much," Abigail conceded, voicing her own disappointment. She wondered, as the officers' boat drew nearer, whether, after they had made their inspection, permission would be given for the *Mysore*'s passengers to go ashore . . . and then, with a sudden pang, whether Kate Lamerton would be housed in the jail with the other convicts. She had asked Mr. Boskenna to make application for her as an assigned servant, but he had been evasive, saying that he must first arrange their own accommodation, and adding, repressively, that Kate was a convicted felon, and it must be left to the authorities to decide where and to whom she was to be assigned.

"We are new arrivals, Abigail," he had told her, "and I repeat, this is a penal colony. It would be unwise, in my view, to form anything resembling a friendship with a woman of Lamerton's class. You would do well to forget her once we land—for your own sake, if not for hers."

She would *not* forget Kate, Abigail thought rebelliously, whatever her new guardian said . . . both she and Lucy owed the good soul too much to forget her. But perhaps the marine officer—what was his name? Hawley, Captain Hawley . . . perhaps he would be able to arrange matters if she asked him. He had seemed concerned and anxious to be of assistance, but he had been a very long time below with the Boskennas, giving her no opportunity to speak to him. She moved to the taffrail and found herself looking down into the officers' boat as it rounded the *Mysore*'s stern and made for her larboard side.

There were five officers in the boat, four of them young. The fifth, clearly the senior, wore his iron-gray hair close cropped and his face, as she glimpsed it, filled the watching girl with an odd sense of foreboding. It was a dark, heavily jowled face, set in sullen lines, and its owner's cheeks were flushed, reminding Abigail of her father's after a night's hectic drinking. Instinctively, she stepped back from the taffrail, aware that the officer had glanced up and was watching her with frowning intensity.

Kate said, grasping her arm, "Maybe you'd best to go below, Miss Abigail, 'cause I don't reckon they'm port health officers by the looks of 'em."

Abigail was about to act on this sage advice when she saw Titus Penhaligon emerge from the midships hatchway and stride purposefully toward the entry port, as the bowman of the officers' boat deftly hooked his boathook onto the larboard chains. The assistant surgeon wore a white coat over his uniform and he was hatless, his dark hair ruffled as the breeze caught it. He was a quiet, sensitive young man, diffident and self-effacing in feminine company but at his best with the sick, Abigail knew. On his own admission he had been lacking in professional experience when, on impulse, he had accepted the post of ship's surgeon a few days before the *Mysore* was due to leave Plymouth, after the appointed incumbent of the post had suffered a stroke. But he had borne his responsibilities well and with growing confidence, and now it was his intention to seek employment in the colony as a physician, since the *Mysore* would have no further need of his services once her passengers were put ashore.

Abigail watched him greet the military officers as each, in turn, swung himself through the entry port, and she hesitated, still uncertain whether or not they were representatives of the port health authority, as she had initially supposed. Then she saw the red-faced captain thrust past Titus without apology and, with two of his companions at his heels, make for the after part of the deck, where she and Kate were standing with the other women. His gait was unsteady, his speech slurred, and when he halted in front of her, she caught the whiff of spirits on his breath.

"Turn round, wench," he ordered brusquely.

Abigail stared at him in bewilderment, making no attempt to obey him, and he growled impatiently, "Damme, you heard what I said, did you not? Turn round—walk away, so that I can get a look at you."

"They're not fettered, any of them," one of the younger officers observed. "Seems they've been treated overindulgently by the ship's master, don't it? But this one's a little beauty and no mistake. If you decide not to take her, Tony, I fancy I might, because the creature I have has turned into a veritable harridan, devil take her!"

"I want to see how this wench moves," his senior drawled, "before I make up my mind about her." He hiccoughed loudly and poked at Abigail with the cane he carried, his pale eyes narrowed and speculative as he studied her. When Kate stepped forward protectively and started to voice an indignant protest, the cane descended across her shoulders, shocking her into silence. "I'll have the lot of you put back into fetters if you don't show me proper respect," the officer warned. "Let's see your legs, my girl . . . lift your skirt and walk across the deck!"

Realizing belatedly that she had been mistaken for a convict, Abigail stared at him, resentful and humiliated, as shocked as poor Kate had been by the blow from his cane. But as she sought vainly for words, her cheeks suffused with shamed color, a hand reached out to grasp hers, and she turned thankfully to see that Titus Penhaligon had come to range himself beside her.

"The master's gone ashore, but I've sent word to Captain Hawley," he told her in a whisper, and then, raising his voice, he addressed himself to her tormentor. "Is this the manner in which you are accustomed to receive new arrivals in the port of Sydney, sir? I had supposed that an officer wearing the King's uniform would know how to conduct himself in the presence of a lady and, furthermore, that he would instantly recognize her as such, in whatever circumstances he might chance to encounter her. But you, sir, have failed to do so, which leads me to the conclusion that, despite the uniform you wear, you are no gentleman!"

It was a brave, even reckless speech, and it took Abigail by surprise, for she had never, during the six months' voyage, heard the *Mysore*'s young surgeon speak in such terms to anyone, not even to a recalcitrant convict. But Titus Penhaligon's stinging sarcasm was wasted on the angry captain . . . as well might a small dog endeavor to halt the onrush of an enraged bull, she thought, wishing now that he had not come rushing to her defense.

"It's the manner in which we receive convicted felons," the officer snapped. "And whores, whether or not they were once ladies. And this"—the cane, viciously wielded, cut a livid weal along the surgeon's cheek—"is how we treat the poxy sawbones who accompany them if they choose to be insolent!" He ignored the low-voiced warning of the younger of the two officers who had accompanied him to the poop deck, irately shaking off his restraining hand with a curt "Be damned to you, O'Shea! I'll thank you to mind your own business."

Titus clutched his bruised and swelling face, but when Abigail made to apply her handkerchief to it, he besought her to go below. "Go and take Mrs. Lamerton with you, Miss Abigail. It will only make matters worse if you stay."

Reluctantly she started to obey him, but the red-faced captain had not done. Crossing to the larboard side of the deck, he bawled an order for his sergeant to come on board. "I'm putting you under arrest, Sawbones," he flung over his shoulder at Titus. "You'll be charged with insulting behavior. As for the wench, I . . ." He saw Abigail then, at the hatchway with Kate, and roared at her to stay where she was.

The younger officer, whom he had addressed as O'Shea, moved swiftly to her side. "Get out of his sight, my dear, and quickly! I'm afraid he's—ah—not quite himself, if you take my meaning. I'll try to talk him out of it, but it will be easier if you're not here to —ah—enflame him. You—" He was interrupted, to Abigail's intense relief, by Captain Hawley.

The marine captain took in the situation at a glance. Abigail saw him cross to interpose his tall, imposing person between herself and her would-be pursuer, a hand raised to bring him to a halt.

"Out of my way, Hawley, dammit!" the older man demanded. "I want to teach that little wench a lesson before she makes off!"

"I fear, sir, you have made a grave error," Captain Hawley stated, with crisp authority. "The young lady you have mistakenly accosted is the daughter of a naval officer, on whose behalf His Excellency the governor is personally concerned. Indeed, I am here at his behest to invite Miss Abigail Tempest and her sister to take up residence at Government House. Their father, sir, regrettably, died during the passage and His Excellency intends to assume responsibility for their well-being. He—"

"A pox on His Excellency!" the New South Wales Corps captain exclaimed. But he was visibly taken aback and added irritably, "Why did not the infernal girl tell me who she was? How was I to know, damme?

Devil take you, Hawley, you should have kept her below, not permitted her to walk the deck with a mob of convict whores!"

He continued to argue in the same vein, and Kate whispered anxiously, "We'd best go, Miss Abigail, an' keep out of harm's way."

Abigail nodded, still shocked and as anxious as her convict companion to make her escape from the unpleasant scene, but at the foot of the hatchway the Reverend Caleb Boskenna barred their way, his wife hovering at his elbow.

"What"—he inquired of Kate with icy condescension —"what is going on up there, woman? The second mate came bursting into my cabin with some wild and no doubt distorted tale of an altercation between my ward and some military officers . . . that surely cannot be true! No!" He glared at Abigail as she attempted to answer him. "Be silent, if you please. I wish to hear what has occurred from Lamerton."

Kate told him, sparing no detail in her agitation, and Martha Boskenna's thin lips tightened in disapproval.

"I have told Abigail until I am tired that she should not mix so freely with the convict women," she asserted. "If there has been trouble, she has brought it upon herself. All the same, I think you should point out to the officers, Mr. Boskenna, that their behavior is not to be tolerated. This may be a penal colony but it is, surely, a Christian community? And if, as Lamerton says, the officer in question was inebriated when he came on board, then—"

"Quite so, my dear," her husband agreed. He drew himself up to his full height, his dark, bearded face alight with the religious fervor he habitually brought to his sermons, as he continued in loud, carrying tones, "God has indeed guided us to this sinful place, for it would seem to be sorely in need of spiritual guidance . . . if the conduct of these King's officers has been as Lamerton described it."

"It was, sir, truly, just as I were telling it—" Kate began, but Mr. Boskenna cut her short.

"I have every intention of getting to the bottom of the affair," he said firmly. "And, if it is merited, of administering a rebuke, as a matter of Christian principle. But I consider it inadvisable to permit either of the girls to accompany Captain Hawley ashore, as he is insisting . . . not, that is to say, until I have seen and talked to the governor in person and explained my position as their guardian. With a man like Captain Bligh in command, who knows what moral codes prevail, even at Government House?" Again he waved Abigail to silence with an imperiously raised hand. "You will kindly go to your cabin, miss, and remain there with your sister until I send for you. No, no, not you—" as Kate's fingers protectively closed about Abigail's arm. "Return to the convicts' quarters. No doubt you will be taken ashore sometime tomorrow morning and lodged in the jail where you belong."

He left them and Abigail felt Kate's fingers trembling and, sensing that she was about to rebel, whispered softly, "Better do as Mr. Boskenna says, Kate. But I'll see you before they take you ashore, I promise."

"If you say so, Miss Abigail." Kate went reluctantly, and Mrs. Boskenna gave Abigail a push, propelling her, none too gently, along the dimly lit passageway that led to the after passenger cabins.

"You are to stay in your cabin, as the reverend told you," was her parting injunction. "And tomorrow you will not go on deck unless I am with you . . . is that clear?"

Abigail's cheeks flooded with indignant color but

she restrained herself, deeming it wiser to make no reply. She felt drained of emotion, unable to think clearly, and the dark, cramped little cabin that had been her home for over six months now seemed less of a prison than a refuge.

Lucy was asleep in the lower bunk, her thin little face almost devoid of its once healthy, apple-cheeked color. With her dark hair and long, curling lashes she bore so close a resemblance to their dead mother that Abigail was conscious of a tightening of the throat as she looked down at her. To what, she asked herself wretchedly, to what manner of place had their father's whim brought them? If the officers who had boarded the ship just now were an example of Sydney society, what future could there be here for Lucy and herself? Or, come to that, for poor young Surgeon Penhaligon, who had almost certainly made a very dangerous enemy when he had come rushing to her defense. She bit back a sigh and started slowly to undress, her conscience pricking her on his account.

From the deck above came the sound of shouted orders. Abigail tensed, straining her ears. She heard the boat called and the thud of booted feet on the deck planking above her head and, anxious to ascertain whether or not Titus Penhaligon had been put under arrest as the arrogant captain had threatened, climbed onto the trunk she and Lucy had placed beneath the cabin's single porthole and peered out.

To her intense relief she saw that the boat contained only the red-coated officers and their crew—there were no women on board and no Titus. Evidently tempers had cooled or . . . Her lips twisted into a smile. Or the Reverend Caleb Boskenna's moral strictures had caused the military to see the error of their ways. Certainly his crusading zeal and the threat of hellfire— which all his sermons had contained—had won him a number of converts during the *Mysore*'s long voyage, particularly among the seamen, whose dangerous calling imbued them with a morbid fear of death.

But her father, Abigail recalled, had listened to only one of Mr. Boskenna's sermons. Afterwards, in a moment of tipsy merriment, he had nicknamed the missionary "The Reverend Brimstone," and some of the less respectful convicts, hearing of it, had henceforth gleefully referred to him thus behind his back.

A hail from the deck and the rhythmic splash of oars sent her once again to the porthole. The light was fading rapidly, but she was just able to make out the tall figure of Captain Hawley in the stern sheets of a second boat, which was pulling toward the shore.

So the governor's aide, too, had listened to Mr. Boskenna, she thought uneasily. Despite his insistence and the governor's invitation, she and Lucy were to remain on board the *Mysore* in the continued care of the guardian their father had appointed. Abigail plucked blindly at the row of buttons fastening the front of her dress, her eyes filled with tears. Why *had* her father chosen such a man to act as their guardian, she asked herself. . . . Why, when he had held the missionary up to ridicule with his bestowal of the satirical nickname and, in her hearing, had branded him a hypocrite?

Indeed the two had spent very little time together during the passage from England. They had had little in common; socially they were poles apart, and Mrs. Boskenna had made no secret of her disapproval of the nightly drinking sessions in which Edmund Tempest and the easygoing master, Captain Duncan, had indulged.

And yet, when death had faced him, her father's choice had fallen on the Reverend Boskenna. He had entrusted his daughters' future to a man he had openly despised because, she could only suppose, he was—

with all his faults—an ordained minister of God. There
could be no other reason and—the tears of frustration streamed now, unchecked, down Abigail's cheeks
—seemingly no escape unless . . . Suddenly remembering, she reached for the whale-oil lantern hanging from
the bulkhead and, careful to shade it from Lucy's
sleeping face, turned up the wick.

The letter, she thought—the letter Mrs. Pendeen
had given her, when she and Rick had journeyed to
Bodmin to seek her out. It was in the trunk somewhere,
concealed from prying eyes amongst the clothing she
had packed inside it. She dragged the heavy trunk,
with difficulty, from beneath the porthole and, finding
the key in her reticule, unlocked and opened it, the
memory of that visit to the quiet, austere vicarage of
St. Columbia's, a little more than six months earlier,
flooding back into her mind.

At first the vicar's wife had been reluctant to talk
to them, even seeming suspicious. Initially she denied
that she knew anything about the penal colony of New
South Wales or that she had ever left England, but
Rick's charm had won her trust, his evident anxiety
on his sisters' behalf had dispelled her doubts. She had
eventually admitted the truth and talked sadly of the
bitter years of exile she had endured, as one of the
convicted felons Governor Phillip had taken out to
the New World.

A slim, still-beautiful woman, Amelia Pendeen had
seemed to both Rick and herself the picture of respectability, Abigail remembered, and they had listened,
in stunned amazement, to the story she had confided
to them. "Only my husband and my mother know the
truth," she had said, when pledging them to secrecy.
"Here, in my dear husband's parish, they would not
understand, I am afraid, so I have learned to keep a
guard on my tongue. I have never spoken of my ex-
periences save to those two and now, of course, to

you. But I should like to help you, Abigail, if I can, provided that you will respect my confidence and will give me your promise not to betray it."

She had promised readily and gratefully and so had Rick; the two of them had even kept the reason for their journey to Bodmin a secret from both Lucy and their father. Abigail's hands were trembling, as she sought impatiently among the folded dresses and petticoats in the trunk for the letter she had hidden there.

Mrs. Pendeen had seated herself at her husband's writing desk, she recalled, and, her quill moving swiftly across the paper, she had written the letter, covering one and then two sheets with beautiful copperplate script.

"This is a letter to the bravest and finest young girl I ever knew," she had said. "And she was about your age when I knew her, Abigail. Now, of course, she will be a woman in—oh, in her thirties, I suppose, and married, no doubt, with several children of her own. Her maiden name was Taggart, Jenny Taggart."

She had paused to add a few more words at the foot of the page and her lovely face had clouded over as she went on, "Jenny has little reason to love me and yet I think she did love me, in spite of the injury I did her. Find her, if you can, when you reach Sydney, and give her my letter. She will help you, I feel sure, and she is one you can trust with—oh, with your life, if need be."

Her tone had been wry when she had added a warning that Abigail should make her inquiries discreetly on arrival in the colony. "There is a great, unbridgeable gulf between those who were transported as convicted felons and those who, like yourself, go out there as free settlers. And you are an officer's daughter, Abigail, so it behooves you to be doubly discreet. Jenny Taggart is an emancipist, and when I left, she had her own small farm near Parramatta. Even so, my dear, the convict stigma remains, and you could well be subjected to unkind criticism if it became known that you were endeavoring to establish contact with her. Do not fail, on that account, but make your approach to her without drawing attention to yourself. And be wise. Tell no one of my letter—not even your father, since it is conceivable that he might require you to destroy it."

With half the trunk's contents strewn over the floor of the cabin, the letter came at last to light, and Abigail expelled her breath in a long-drawn sigh of satisfaction. She would make her inquiries discreetly, as Amelia Pendeen had advised but, she decided, make them she would, and at the first opportunity—through Kate, perhaps, if that kindly soul were willing. And probably Parramatta would be the best place from which to begin the search. A loud, insistent knock on the door of the cabin interrupted her thoughts.

Abigail thrust the precious letter into the bosom of her dress, and, hastily buttoning it up again, she went to the door.

"Yes?" she called out cautiously. "Who is it?"

"Mrs. Boskenna. Let me in at once, Abigail." The reply was impatient, but Abigail took her time, replacing the contents of her trunk and closing its lid before she unbolted the door.

"You weren't in bed," the missionary's wife accused.

"No. No, I was reading," Abigail answered untruthfully, "but Lucy is asleep and—"

Martha Boskenna clicked her tongue, but for all her impatience, she had the grace to lower her voice. "I came to tell you that you are to stay on board until after the convicts have disembarked tomorrow morning. Mr. Boskenna has arranged with Captain Hawley that we shall all go to Parramatta, where the governor is in temporary residence. The chaplain's house is unoccupied, and we shall stay there for the

time being. The house is furnished and ready for occupation, I understand."

"Parramatta?" Abigail could scarcely contain her
excitement. "Is it . . . is it far away?"

"Only about sixteen miles. We shall go by boat and
our personal baggage will come with us. The heavy
baggage in the hold and, of course, your late father's
livestock cannot be unloaded until the ship is warped
into the public wharf, which will not be till much
later in the day. But his shepherd will be left in
charge, so you need not concern yourself, or . . ."
Mrs. Boskenna's sharp eyes lit on the trunk, with its
open hasps, still lying in the center of the cabin floor.
"Oh, so you were packing, were you, in anticipation?"
She crossed the narrow floor and opened the lid, frowning as she noticed the disordered contents. "Tst-tst!
And a very poor job you have made of it, my girl!
See that all these garments are refolded before you
retire and the trunk locked. You'll not have Kate
Lamerton to act as lady's maid any longer, so the
sooner you learn to look after yourself the better."

"Very well," Abigail acknowledged, with restraint.
"Good night, Mrs. Boskenna."

Lucy stirred, as Martha Boskenna let the door slam
shut behind her, and then sat up, suddenly wide awake.

"Abby, was that horrible woman here?" she whispered fearfully. "In here, in our cabin?"

"Yes," Abigail confirmed. "But she's gone now."

"What did she want?"

"Only to tell me that we are to go ashore in the
morning."

"With *them* or to the governor's?"

"With them, I'm afraid," Abigail admitted reluctantly. "But we're to see the governor, who is at a
place called Parramatta, sixteen miles from here. We
shall be going by boat. It'll be exciting, Lucy—you'll
enjoy it, I feel sure."

"I shan't if we have to go there with them," Lucy retorted sulkily. "They're hateful, both of them."

Abigail went to perch herself on the edge of her sister's bunk. "Lie down and go to sleep again," she urged gently. "At least we shall be going ashore. And I . . . I have a plan, I—well, I can't tell you about it yet, but there is someone I'm hoping to see in Parramatta. Someone who may help us."

Lucy eyed her uncertainly for a moment and then obediently settled back on her pillows. Abigail waited until the child's even breathing told her that she was asleep, and then, her fingers clumsy in their haste, she took Amelia Pendeen's letter from its hiding place.

If Jenny Taggart were still in Parramatta, it would not be difficult to find her, she told herself exultantly. And even if she had moved or changed her name on marriage, there would surely be someone in the settlement who remembered her, someone who would know where she could be found. It must auger well that the Reverend Caleb Boskenna had chosen Parramatta as their destination. Abigail was smiling when she reached up to place the precious letter beneath the pillow of her own berth.

CHAPTER III

A chill breeze ruffled the surface of the Hawkesbury River and stirred to whispering life the feathery tops of the eucalyptus trees growing along its banks.

Gesturing to the glowing red ball of the setting sun with his fish gig, the native boy, Nanbaree, warned in a quaint mixture of acquired English and the words of his own tongue, "Soon-time *moorundi* . . . maybe *kurana. Berrabri,* Jen-nee!"

Jenny Broome felt the strength of the wind as it swept across the darkening expanse of water and shivered as she, too, glanced skyward.

"I go *kyewong,* Nanbaree," she answered, and set her horse's head in the direction of the distant cluster of farm buildings, half hidden behind the screen of ironbarks and the towering blue gum trees which ringed the high ground on which they stood. Smoke was rising from the chimney of Nancy Jardine's cottage, just below the trees—an indication of the lateness of the hour, since it meant that her foreman's wife had started to prepare the evening meal—and Jenny clicked her tongue impatiently as her horse snatched at a tussock of grass, reluctant to abandon the lush grazing at the river's edge.

She had stayed out for longer than she had intended, in order to bid welcome to Nanbaree and bring him the sack of maize for which he had asked. The Bediagal boy had returned from a walkabout of almost two months' duration, with a new wife and the expressed desire to resume the employment he had abandoned so casually the previous June, but Jenny had taken him back willingly enough. Despite his periodic absences the young aborigine was a hard and skillful worker with both sheep and cattle, and his presence on the farm, with that of his brother, Kupali, had served to deter other members of their tribe from stealing crops and setting fire to the bush as, in this locality, they all too frequently did.

She could afford no more losses from any cause, Jenny was unhappily aware, if she was to continue to farm the land she had called Long Wrekin, after her father's small holding in Yorkshire. The disastrous Hawkesbury flood, which had struck with virtually no warning eighteen months earlier, had taken a heavy toll of those who had settled on its banks.

Many of her neighbors had lost everything—their homes, their farm buildings, their stored crops, their livestock—and some, like her husband, Johnny, had lost their lives in the chaos the flood had left in its wake. And Johnny . . . She kicked her horse into a canter, conscious of the familiar ache in her heart, as the memory of that terrible night returned to haunt her —the night she lost him.

Johnny and her elder son, Justin, with the aid of some convict seamen, had spent the night and all the previous day helping to rescue stranded settlers from their isolated holdings. They had come back to the Long Wrekin homestead at last, unscathed but ex-

hausted, after rowing an oared boat through the flood-
waters for hour after hour, and she had met them with
the news that her younger son, William, was missing.
Being the man he was, Johnny had gone out again
without hesitation—again with Justin and the seamen
—to search for the little boy. They had not even
paused to break their fast.

Soon after dawn, when she had been beside herself
with anxiety, the boat had returned, with Johnny's
limp, drowned body lying across the thwarts—and poor
old Watt's next to his. Justin had sobbed out the heart-
rending story of how his father had died. He and old
Watt Sparrow, both of them swallowed up by the ra-
paciously spreading river, which had risen ninety feet
above its normal level, engulfing all that lay in its
path.

Now any threat of rain in the mountain ranges to
the west was enough to fill her with a sickening fear
that it might all happen again. Jenny's brow was
beaded with perspiration, despite the chill of the wind.
Nanbaree had said "Maybe *kurana*" . . . and *kurana*
was the aborigine word for rain. She glanced apprehensively over her shoulder at the scudding gray
clouds. They were no longer touched by the glow of
the sunset, but they were blowing out to sea, and the
sky over the tree-girt slopes of Mount Richmond to
the west was clear, the peaks beyond innocent of mist.

Her fears dispelled, Jenny breathed a sigh of thank-
fulness and let her thoughts drift back to the after-
math of the flood.

Somehow she had found the will and the strength
to go on living, for all she had come close to despair,
Johnny's death a cruel and crushing blow to the
dreams she had cherished and the future they had
planned together. But there had been the children
to care for—William and little Rachel depended on
her, even if Justin did not. And there was work to be

done, as there had always been ever since she had
come to this alien, inhospitable land nineteen years
before, as a girl of barely sixteen, in convict's fetters,
bitter and bewildered but grimly determined to build
her life anew.

She caught her breath on a sigh. The governor—
the naval captain they still called *Bounty* Bligh—had
done all in his power to alleviate the distress caused
by the flood. He had replaced lost breeding stock from
the government herds, supplied bricks, timber, and
convict labor to restore damaged buildings, and had
allocated an entire ship's cargo of seed corn to the
Hawkesbury settlers, free of charge. She had toiled like
the rest to repair the devastation, but like the rest,
Jenny reflected, she was finding it increasingly difficult to make ends meet, for the prosperity of the
earlier years had gone, it seemed, with the receding
waters of the river.

Wheat yields were poor, rust had infected the growing crops, the vines she had so carefully tended shriv-
eled and died, the sheep suffered from foot rot, and
the ewes lost their lambs for no reason that anyone
could understand. Prices for all agricultural produce,
livestock, and labor were fixed, to enable the barter
system to be abolished and a stable currency introduced. Coin was now in circulation and settlers' promissory notes were officially approved for all purchases,
which was what they had wanted. She herself had
signed the petition with over 230 of the Hawkesbury
settlers, and Governor Bligh had taken swift and decisive action to redress the balance in their favor and
to curb the excessive profiteering the military had indulged in up to now.

It was no longer necessary to buy rum—at four or
five times its import cost—from officers of the Corps
or their agents, in order to pay wages, but money had
still to be earned and promissory notes honored. La-

borers, even if they were only seasonal, had to be paid and fed. With the price of wheat held at ten shillings a bushel, mutton at two shillings, and pork one and eleven pence a pound, a failed harvest and lost livestock could spell ruin, as she was only too well aware. Jenny looked about her and her brows met in a worried pucker, as she mentally totted up the promissory notes she had not yet been able to redeem.

True, she had sold her last harvest, but transport costs were high. At a shilling a bushel for delivery by boat to Sydney, the profit from thirty acres of good wheat barely covered the cost of the labor required to grow and harvest it.

When Johnny had been alive and in command of the *Phillip* sloop, there had been no such problem. The Hawkesbury settlers' produce had been taken to the government store free of charge, not only by the *Phillip* but also by other government-owned vessels. Unfortunately, Simeon Lord, the wealthy emancipist ship-builder, owned most of the river and coastal trading craft. . . .

Her horse shied suddenly, almost unseating her.

"Steady, boy," Jenny admonished the young animal. "There's nothing to fear." Out of the corner of her eye she glimpsed a movement among the trees to her right and heard—or imagined she heard—a man's voice raised in anger. But it was swiftly stilled, the clump of ironbarks too far away and too deeply in shadow for her to be able to identify the owner of the voice or even to be certain that she had heard it.

There were always escapees in this part of the Hawkesbury Valley—runaway convicts heading for the river and what they imagined was freedom on its far bank—and they would steal anything on which they could lay hands, given the chance of doing so unobserved. Usually, however, they gave the larger homesteads a wide berth, aware that most of the occupants were armed, and preferring to descend on isolated small-holdings, where only a man and his wife might be expected to oppose them.

They could not know, of course, that although she still had Johnny's musket hanging above the living-room fireplace, she had never learned how to use it and could not even be sure that, should the occasion arise, she could contrive to load and prime the weapon —still less discharge it at an intruder.

A second careful scrutiny of the ironbarks revealed nothing calculated to alarm her, and Jenny's tension relaxed. Andrew Hawley had offered to teach her how to use a musket, the last time he had come upriver with the governor, but she had evaded the offer . . . as she had also evaded the subject of marriage, which she knew was on Andrew's mind. Marriage to Andrew would solve all her financial difficulties, but it was too soon, she thought, her throat suddenly tight . . . too soon, with Johnny's memory too deeply enshrined in her heart and mind, and his children there to add to her aching sense of loss.

She soothed her horse, her fingers gently caressing his cropped mane, and continued on her way at a brisk canter, forcing herself not to dwell on memories of the past. Reaching the first of the sheep paddocks, she saw that the new convict laborer, a man named Martin, who had recently been assigned to her, was walking back toward the farm buildings. He had been sent by Tom Jardine to repair the fence but, to her critical eye, had made a poor job of it. He saw her coming and halted, watching her open the gate but making no move to come to her assistance, and when she called him over to explain why there was no padlock on the gate, he came reluctantly.

" 'Twere busted, the padlock," he asserted.

"*I* managed to lock it," Jenny pointed out unanswerably, and when he was silent, eyeing her with sul-

len hostility, she gestured to a sagging gap in the
wooden sheep fence. "Why did you not mend that?"

"Didn't have time, missus, that's why."

"You had all day."

"Well, 'tweren't long enough. Not wi' tools like
these 'ere an' hard wood." Martin held out the ax he
had been using and spat his contempt for its blunted
blade. "An' them nails ain't up ter much, neither."

There was a strong odor of liquor on his breath,
and, catching a whiff of it as she bent from her saddle
to inspect the nails, Jenny recoiled.

Samuel Martin was typical of the worst type of convict sent out here, she thought bitterly: unwilling to
put his back into whatever work he was given, surly
and truculent, yet expecting to be housed and fed,
supplied with clothing and tobacco, whilst giving nothing in return . . . least of all civility. She had applied
for one of the Cornish agricultural laborers who had
arrived a fortnight ago in the transport *Mysore,* having
heard excellent reports of them; but the Corps officers
had been quick to forestall all other claims, and instead she had been compelled to accept this man,
much against her better judgment.

He had stated that he was a carpenter, with experience on the land, but Jenny could see that was a false-
hood. Her gaze went again to the patched-up fencing.
Martin's carelessness might well have lost the breeding
ewes which normally occupied this and the paddock
beyond, for the Bediagal regarded strays as legitimate
plunder. When she told him so in a carefully controlled voice, the convict stared back at her with angry, defiant eyes.

"Ain't 'ardly my fault if you've let your fences rot,
is it, missus?" he retorted. "You need 'arf a score o'
men ter work this acreage—not jus' me an' Jardine
and them two scurvy blackfellers you set so much
store by! An' as fer that overgrown kid o' yours, al-

ways runnin' around wiv' 'is dog an' givin' orders
. . ." He swore insolently. "Hell's teeth, it's bad enough
'avin' ter take orders from a woman at my time o'
life, but at least you seem ter know what you're about
—the kid don't. Ferever on about danged sheep, 'e
is . . . an' dingoes."

Jenny reddened, hurt and annoyed by this unjusti-
fied criticism of her son William. True, the boy was
only seven, but he was a born shepherd, and when
released from school, he did the work of a man with
Nanbaree and Kupali, displaying a skill and knowledge
far beyond his years.

"Willie's cut out to be a farmer," Johnny had said,
not without a certain rueful pride in his younger off-
spring. "He'll make that dream of yours come true,
Jenny, my love, when Justin's at sea with me. He'll
be your husbandman in those fertile plains you're always talking about. . . ."

Jenny recalled Governor Phillip's promise, made all
those years ago, when the Union flag had first been
hoisted in Sydney Cove, *"Here are fertile plains, needing only the labors of the husbandmen to produce in
abundance the richest and fairest fruits,"* the colony's
first governor had assured his convict listeners. *"Here
are interminable pastures, the future home of flocks
and herds innumerable. . . ."*

Few had believed him then; they had all still been
in fetters, concerned only for their survival in what
had seemed a barren wasteland, incapable of sustaining either human or animal life, and peopled by hostile Indians, ever ready to dispute its possession with
any who ventured within range of their spears. But
she had believed, she had dreamed that one day the
prophecy would be fulfilled and Governor Phillip's
brave vision become reality. Jenny drew a quick, uneven breath. She had her freedom and she had her
land, and for all the burden of debt which might

threaten both, it was not for men of the caliber of
Samuel Martin to decry what the years of work had
achieved for her family and herself.

She met his gaze coldly and said, without compunction, "I'll have you sent back to Parramatta, Martin.
You can leave on the next boat."

"Leave?" The convict was taken by surprise, and
for a moment his expression was ugly, as he fingered
the ax in his hand. Then he recovered himself and
shook his head. "I didn't say as I wanted ter leave,
missus. 'Tis just that I—"

Jenny cut him short and returned, with finality,
"Your work is not good enough. I can't afford to pay
wages to idlers—and besides, you've been drinking
when you were supposed to be at work."

"I only took a drop, jus' ter slake me thirst," he
defended. "If you send me back ter Parramatta, they'll
put me on the road gang."

"You should have thought of that before. Where
did you get the liquor?"

Martin hesitated. Seeking some way of evading the
question but finding none, he mumbled sullenly, "It
were some I 'ad left over from a job I done at Cap'n
Macarthur's farm in Parramatta."

So Captain Macarthur was still paying for his casual
labor in rum, Jenny thought, but she let it pass; probably Samuel Martin worked better when promised his
reward in liquor—his kind usually did. She was about
to ride on but the convict caught at her rein.

"Gimme another chance, missus," he whined. "Look,
I'll fix that fence 'fore I knock off an' fix it good, even
if it takes me 'arf the night. Don't send me back, fer
pity's sake. The superintendent o' the road gang's a
swine, an' 'e's got it in fer me. 'E'll just about kill
me, if you send me back."

"All right," Jenny conceded, with some misgivings.

"But your work will have to improve if I'm to keep you on. One more chance is all I can give you."

"That's all I'll need," he assured her, and, picking up his tool bag, went shambling off to the gap in the fence. The sound of his hammer, briskly applied, followed her as she cantered on into the swiftly gathering darkness.

William and her six-year-old daughter, Rachel, greeted her in a state of some excitement when she reached the farmhouse.

"Callers, Mam," William announced, grasping his sister firmly by the arm in order to restrain her. "*I'll* tell her, Shelly, I'm the eldest . . . so just you hold your tongue."

"But I talked to them," Rachel objected, "while you went out looking for Mam. And you never found her, did you? Mam, there were two of them . . . new folk. A man, a reverend, and a girl about Justin's age."

Jenny managed at last to silence both children. Callers, on their remote holding, were a rarity, and she could understand their eagerness to tell her of them. "You said 'was,'" she reminded her son. "Does that mean they've gone?"

The boy nodded his small, carrot-colored head. "It was getting dark, they couldn't wait any longer, and I didn't know where you were. But they're coming back in the morning. The reverend said they were staying overnight at Mr. Dawson's. He's going to hold a service in their big barn on Sunday and——"

"I didn't like him, Mam," Rachel said, with a little grimace. "I didn't like him one bit. Oh, I know he's a reverend and has to be respected, but he . . . he wasn't nice to the young lady who came with him. She was pretty and sweet, but I think she was scared of him."

"She was," William asserted with conviction. "He kept saying, 'Leave this to me, Abigail,' whenever she tried to talk to us. And Nancy made them tea and dampers, but he hardly said thank you to her."

"What was his name?" Jenny asked, regarding their two excited faces with furrowed brows. "Did he tell you? Did he give any reason for his call?"

Timothy Dawson—now one of the largest and most prosperous landowners in the Hawkesbury district—had offered to buy her farm, she recalled, when she had spoken to him of her present financial problems. His had been a generous offer, which had included the promise that if he became the owner of Long Wrekin, he would continue to employ Tom and Nancy Jardine on the property, but . . . Her frown lifted. Surely Tim Dawson would never have confided these tentative plans to a stranger? He was an old friend, completely to be trusted, although his wife, Henrietta, had no love for her, regarding her—Jenny sighed, recognizing the absurdity of it—regarding her, wholly without justification, as a rival for her husband's affections. "Mam," Rachel began, "I—"

"Oh, be quiet, Shelly!" William exclaimed, losing patience. "I'm thinking. His name was Boss-something, Mam. The Reverend Caleb Boss-whatever it is."

Rachel gave him a push. "Boskenna, stupid!" she interrupted triumphantly. "You may be a year older than me, but you don't know everything, so there! And the young lady's name was Miss Abigail Tempest."

"Don't bicker, children," Jenny reproved them, and, remembering the convict Martin's strictures, she added sharply, "You're not to bully your sister, Willie."

"Oh, all right," William conceded. He added, with a shamefaced grin, "Mr. Boskenna didn't say why they had come—just that they wanted to see you.

But he was nosey—he asked me all kinds of questions about the farm."

"Questions? What kind of questions?"

"Oh"—he shrugged—"how much stock we have, what crops we grow, how bad the flooding was. . . . But I didn't tell him much. I said he'd have to ask you."

Rachel was dancing about the shadowed living room, scarcely able to contain herself, and Jenny turned to her, puzzled. "What's the matter with you, child?"

The little girl eyed her reproachfully. "You let Willie talk all the time, Mam. But *I* know why Miss Abigail came. She brought a letter for you."

"A letter for me? You're romancing, you bad girl! I don't know her . . . why should she write me a letter?"

"It's addressed to you," Rachel answered. She went on, savoring her triumph to the full, as William stared at her open-mouthed. "She gave it to me when Mr. Boskenna was talking to Willie and said I was to hide it and give it to you when you came back. That's how I knew she was scared of him, you see. She didn't want him to know about the letter."

"I see," Jenny acknowledged with restraint, aware that Rachel, in her efforts to hold her own with her brother, was prone to occasional flights of fancy. "And where is the letter, pray?"

"Where I hid it," the child said. She skipped over to the fireplace and, standing on tiptoe, took down the tea caddy from its place on the shelf which, when they had first come to Long Wrekin, old Watt Sparrow had fashioned to hold cooking pots and jars of herbs. She thrust the letter into her mother's hand. "It *is* for you, isn't it, Mam?"

And it was. Jenny saw the name Taggart, in a hand that was familiar, stroked out and replaced by her

married name of Broome, written in a round, childish
script she had never seen before.

She studied it incredulously and then broke the seal,
carrying the two flimsy sheets of paper over to the
lamp on the table to enable her to read the signature.
And it was there. . . . Melia had written to her,
after all these years. Only now she, too, was married;
the signature was "Melia" and, written beneath it
"Amelia Pendeen" and the address "St. Columbia's
Rectory, Bodmin, Cornwall." She had a swift mental
picture of Melia, a beautiful, gently born girl who
had been her closest—and often her only—trusted
friend when Governor Phillip's first fleet had brought
them into exile.

Feeling tears pricking at her eyelids, Jenny refolded
the letter and thrust it into the pocket of her dress.

"Aren't you going to read it?" William asked, disappointed.

"I'll read it when you're in bed," Jenny told him.
She smiled at Rachel who, equally disappointed,
seemed disposed to argue. "Thank you, Rachel love.
But now it's suppertime, isn't it? Lay the table, will
you, like a good girl, while I dish up?"

She served the stew Nancy Jardine had prepared,
and the children ate hungrily, their chatter momentarily stilled. Both were reluctant to retire for the night,
their curiosity concerning the letter undimmed, but finally Jenny contrived to pack them off to the small
loft bedroom they shared with the assurance that Abigail Tempest had delivered the letter for a friend she
had known in her girlhood . . . long before either had
been born.

In the silence that followed their departure, she
drew up a chair to the fire and settled down to read
what Melia had written.

The letter began,

It is sixteen years since I bade a thankful fare-well to Sydney, and I had thought never to be reminded of it again . . . although I have often thought of you, my dearest Jenny, and always with admiration and abiding affection, whatever you, alas, must think of me, for I betrayed our friendship and used you very ill.

But now, quite unexpectedly, I have received a request for what help I can give them from two young people, one of whom, little Abigail Tempest, is about to take passage to Sydney with her father and younger sister.

Abigail called on me with her brother, a mid-shipman in the Royal Navy, having heard of me through Mary Bryant—whose name you will know and who is now living nearby in Fowey, having been granted, as I was, a royal pardon. The two children were discreet; they confided to me that their father, invalided from the navy, is heavily in debt and that his intention is to build a new life in the colony as a free settler. As it happens, I have heard of Mr. Tempest and what I have heard leads me to fear that, due to his intemperate habits, it will not be easy for his two young daughters when they reach their des-tination.

For this reason, I am writing this letter to introduce Abigail to you and to beg that you will befriend her, should she be in need of a friend. I have told her about you—at least, I have told her as much as I can with a gulf of sixteen years now between us—and I have said—and with truth, dear Jenny—that you are the staunchest friend anyone could wish for, and that she may repose complete trust in you.

My own circumstances are happier than I de-serve. I have a good and saintly husband, who is vicar at my father's old church in Bodmin, and we have been blessed with four children . . . three beloved sons and a little daughter whom I adore.

My mother, widowed for the second time, lives near us and we are fully reconciled.

I wonder about you and Ned Munday and dare to hope that you, too, may have found happiness in marriage, with children to delight your heart. Though as to Ned . . . perhaps I should express no feelings, save the fleeting thought that the freedom that was ever solely his goal may finally have been his and you, God willing, the better for it.

Above all I hope that you may find it in your heart to forgive me the injury I did you and that you will permit me still to sign myself as . . . Your sincere and loving friend, Melia.

Jenny caught her breath on a long-drawn sigh as the old, half-forgotten memories came flooding back. Ned, she thought, foolish ne'er-do-well Ned, whom she might have married, had he not chosen to run off with Melia in his vain quest for freedom. Ned, who had died at the redcoat soldiers' hands when on his way to fetch the midwife for Justin's birth. . . . Was it possible that Melia still had this—her only breach of loyalty in all the years—still on her conscience? Surely she must know that all they had shared together, all they had suffered and endured on the long voyage and in the new, untamed land of their exile had forged a bond between them that neither time nor distance could ever break. . . . Jenny sighed again and, turning the letter over, started to reread it.

The callers returned early the following afternoon, mounted on two of Timothy Dawson's saddle horses.

Jenny received them hospitably, as was the settlers' custom, but as they ate the meal she and Nancy Jardine had prepared in readiness for their arrival, she found herself taking an instinctive dislike to the Reverend Caleb Boskenna.

As William had told her, he was a big, heavily built man with a black beard, and a pair of dark eyes set in a swarthy-complexioned face, which gleamed with an oddly fanatical light as he talked. And it was he who talked to the exclusion of the slim, pretty young girl who had accompanied him and whom he subdued with a gesture whenever she attempted to interpose a word . . . even of thanks.

"You will kindly leave this to me, miss," he admonished her, and Abigail Tempest, flushed and clearly ill at ease, did as he bade her. His talk was initially of his Christian mission; he quoted Bible texts with fluency, his napkin tucked into the knot of his long black cravat, as he attacked his food with lively appetite, only interrupting the flow of impassioned words to ask for his plate to be replenished.

As a minister of God, he said, he considered the colony of New South Wales in imminent danger of damnation. Sydney had shocked him; and Parramatta and Toongabbie appeared to be no better.

"All are veritable sinks of iniquity, peopled by whores and drunkards," he declared fiercely. "A corrupt convict society amongst whom, it would seem, little attempt is made by those in authority to preserve law and order . . . or even common decency! The female Factory at Parramatta is a school for harlots, who toil not, neither do they spin. My dear wife was appalled by the inmates' behavior when she went there, scarcely able to believe the evidence of her own eyes, as I was," he added feelingly, "when I found that priests of the rebel Catholic faith are permitted to preach to Irish seditionists and incite them to further rebellion."

Jenny knew well enough that conditions in the Factory were wretched. The ramshackle jail housed the worst of the colony's convict population. They were set to weaving and performing other useful tasks of manufacture, in the hope that such work would effect an improvement in their characters—a hope that was largely ill founded.

Growing weary of Caleb Boskenna's harangue and needing no lecture on the evils of the Factory, Jenny attempted to interrupt, but the reverend gentleman shook his head sternly and went on in ringing tones, "Truly it was the hand of God that brought me here, and although mine may be but one voice crying in the wilderness, I can only hope and pray that my words will be heard by those few who are not yet incorrigibly steeped in their own wickedness and evildoing!"

Sensing that both William and Rachel were listening in some bewilderment to the visitor's rhetorical outburst, Jenny sent them from the room. They went, for once, without protest, and Abigail looked after them longingly; but when Jenny suggested that the girl might care to go with them, the Reverend Boskenna denied it.

"No, she must stay. It is on Abigail's behalf that I have come here," he asserted coldly. "You are not perhaps aware, Mrs. Broome, that their late father appointed me as guardian to Abigail and her sister. Mr. Tempest had intended to settle here, and to this end he purchased livestock in Capetown, having received the promise of a substantial land grant from the colonial secretary prior to his departure. I have been in consultation with the government surveyor concerning the grant and—"

Jenny, after a quick glance at Abigail's pale, unhappy face, contrived at last to interrupt him.

"You spoke of their late father, Mr. Boskenna. I am sorry, I—do you mean to say that Mr. Tempest died on the passage out here?" Recalling what Melia's letter had revealed, she put out a hand to the silent girl, but before she could express any words of sympathy, Caleb Boskenna said brusquely, "By his own hand, alas. Mr. Tempest shot himself, Mrs. Broome. Leaving"—the dark eyes, Jenny saw, held an oddly malignant gleam—"leaving to my dear wife and myself the grave responsibility for the two orphans he so callously abandoned."

Abigail's fingers closed convulsively about hers as if seeking reassurance, and Jenny's heart went out to her. Melia, she thought, Melia had begged her to befriend Abigail Tempest if . . . what had she written? *If she should be in need of a friend.* And it seemed the poor child was sorely in need; that was why she had come, why she had given the letter to Rachel and asked her to hide it. She was seeking a chance to escape from this bigoted, insensitive, self-styled man of God who, in her presence, could speak so cruelly of the circumstances of her father's death and, in the same breath, complain of the responsibility her guardianship would entail.

Suddenly angry, Jenny saw the girl's lips form the words "Not now," and she hesitated. It might be more prudent to wait until they could be alone, but they might not be left alone.

Choosing her words carefully, she offered, "Mr. Boskenna, if the responsibility is too grave for you and your wife to undertake, I can give Abigail and her sister a home here with my own children, for as long as they may wish to stay. I should be more than glad to do so, I . . . was this the reason you came here, perhaps? To ask that I should? Did Mr. Dawson suggest it?"

"Indeed it was not!" The Reverend Caleb Boskenna

was on his feet, his sallow face suffused with indignant color. "You have misunderstood me—I am not one to shirk responsibility, far from it. I know my Christian duty better than most, Mrs. Broome. I also know that you are an emancipated convict. Mrs. Dawson informed me that you were. As such . . ." He had the grace to leave the sentence uncompleted, but its implication was plain.

Jenny reddened in her turn, but, meeting Abigail's pleading gaze, she offered no reply to the slight, and Mr. Boskenna went on, "I came here because I was told that you had run into debt and might therefore be willing to sell your land and buildings if a suitable offer were made."

And that, too, he must have learned from Henrietta Dawson, Jenny thought. Henrietta had never wanted Tim to buy Long Wrekin—fearing, perhaps, that he might leave her there to manage it on his behalf. She waited, afraid to speak lest she lose her temper and say more than might be wise, and Caleb Boskenna, adopting a more placatory tone, assured her that the offer he was prepared to make on behalf of his two wards would be a generous one.

"A desirable acreage is available in this area," he added, "but it is virgin land, with no buildings, and I shall require to house the late Mr. Tempest's livestock and ensure that we ourselves have a roof over our heads whilst the necessary work is done on the new grant. And I am told that it takes time, with convict labor in short supply."

"I don't think—" Jenny began, but he cut her short, resuming his seat and summoning up a wintry smile as he studied her thoughtfully across the table.

"Mrs. Broome, it stands to reason that considerable capital outlay is essential for any agricultural development if it is to be effective and permanent. Those who, like yourself, came out here as convicts clearly do not possess the funds or even the expert knowledge to use the land you were granted to the best advantage." Mr. Boskenna's tone was patronizing, and Jenny's color deepened under his critical scrutiny.

"My land is as productive as any in this area, sir, but—"

"But you have run up debts?" he suggested shrewdly.

"We lost livestock and grain in the flood, and with all prices pegged it has been difficult to recoup those losses."

"Mr. Dawson has recouped his, has he not?"

"He has more land than I have," Jenny insisted, "and he is in partnership with his father-in-law, Mr. Jasper Spence. Between them they own five times as much, and they employ more labor."

"Well . . . and is that not proof of my argument, Mrs. Broome? Out of your own mouth, you are confounded!" The bearded face was wreathed in smiles now, as if its owner scented victory. "Land grants are wasted on those without adequate means to develop them. What this colony needs if it is to become self-supporting and prosperous are free settlers with money. Governor Phillip fell into a grave error when he permitted pardoned felons to take up grants. Emancipists should be employed to work on the land but not to own it, in my considered opinion."

Thinking of her own long years of toil, Jenny could only stare at him in rebellious silence. Abigail said, her eyes downcast, "Mr. Boskenna, if Mrs. Broome does not want to sell her land and this pretty house, I don't think that you should seek to—to coerce her. She has been here a long time, much longer than we have, and as new arrivals surely we—"

"I did not invite your opinion," the Reverend Boskenna reproved her, an edge to his voice. "What I am doing is in your best interests, whether or not you give me credit for serving them." He rose, this time with dignified finality, and waved to the girl to follow suit. "We will take our leave, Mrs. Broome," he told Jenny, "and leave you to think over your—ah —your present somewhat precarious situation. If, having done so, you decide to take advantage of my offer, pray send word to me and I will go into the question of valuation. I will keep the offer open until Monday morning when, after holding divine service in this district, I shall be returning to Parramatta. And now perhaps you will be good enough to send for our horses?"

He offered no thanks for the meal and, thrusting Abigail before him, gave her no chance to do so either. Again meeting the girl's unhappy, pleading gaze, Jenny controlled her simmering resentment and dispatched William to saddle the horses. Aided by Kupali, with whom he had been watering stock, the boy led out the saddled animals, and Jenny was hard put to it to maintain her stoical silence when she saw the Reverend Caleb Boskenna thrust the aborigine aside and himself lift Abigail into the saddle.

His parting observation, as he mounted his own animal, was without doubt, she decided, intended to wound and humiliate her. "If you employ savages like that one to work your land, it is small wonder that you have incurred debts, Mrs. Broome." He touched the brim of his hat with a single disdainful finger and added brusquely, "I shall await word from you. Ride on, Abigail!"

"You will wait in vain, Mr. Boskenna," Jenny called after him, losing her precarious hold on her temper at last. "My land is not for sale!"

Caleb Boskenna gave no indication that he had heard her, but she sensed from Abigail's bent head and shaking shoulders that the girl was crying her heart out as she rode away beside him.

It was Tom Jardine who, all unwittingly, reduced Jenny herself to tears. The stocky, gray-haired foreman came from the brood mares' enclosure and said flatly, "Martin's run, Mrs. Broome—and the roan mare you call Ladybird ain't in the paddock. I reckon he's taken her."

Jenny looked at him with misted eyes. Samuel Martin was no loss, but the mare was in foal. "When," she managed, in a choked voice, "when do you think he ran, Tom?"

"Last night, probably." The foreman hesitated. "I can't say for sure, but I thought I saw him talking to a couple of men over beyond the far sheep paddock yesterday afternoon. They was too far away for me to see who they was, and Martin went back to his fencing so I left him be. Pity, plague take the little runt! Mind, he come in for his supper an' never dropped so much as a hint that he was thinking of lighting out." He shook his head regretfully. "I'm sorry, Mrs. Broome. I should'a kept a closer eye on him."

So that was why her horse had shied and nearly put her down the previous evening, Jenny thought. The men—almost certainly escapers—had been hiding in the clump of ironbarks when she rode past. It must have been from them that Martin had obtained his rum, not from Captain Macarthur, as he had claimed . . . and probably they had put the idea of escaping into the man's head. The temptation, coupled with her threat to send him back to the Parramatta road gang, had been enough.

"It's not your fault, Tom," she said. "I'm as much to blame as you are—I gave him the rough edge of my tongue yesterday and told him I'd send him back if his work didn't improve. But I wish he hadn't taken the mare."

"Aye," Tom agreed. He frowned and gestured after

the small cloud of dust which marked the passing of
Abigail Tempest and her guardian, now almost out of
sight beyond the screen of trees. "What did yon devil-
dodger want, if it ain't a presumptuous question, Mrs.
Broome? The wife seemed to think as he was trying
to buy this place off you, from what he said in her
hearing. But you won't"—there was an anxious note
in his voice—"surely you wouldn't sell out to him,
would you?"

"No!" Jenny answered, with grim resolution. "No,
Tom. Whatever it costs me, I will not sell out to
him, I give you my word."

Tom's frown faded. "I'm right glad to hear you say
that, Mrs. Broome. An' you can count on Nancy an'
me—you know that, don't you?"

"Yes, Tom, I know. I always have, haven't I? I've
always counted on both of you," Jenny assured him.

"Aye . . . and just you go on, see? We won't let
you down." The foreman sighed. "Times are hard but
. . . well, no use crying over spilt milk, is it? Reckon
I'd best take Kupali with me and see if we can't find
the mare's tracks. C'n we take your young horse an'
the old gray gelding? We'll cover more ground if we're
mounted." Receiving Jenny's ready assent, he observed
dryly, "The devil-dodger said as he was goin' to
hold a service at Dawson's Sunday—said the governor'd be attending an' all the folks from around here
as well. He told me it was my Christian duty to be
there, an' I was thinkin' . . . will you be going, Mrs.
Broome? You an' the young 'uns?"

Jenny stiffened. The Reverend Caleb Boskenna had
not made this suggestion to her, but if he were con-
ducting the service, there might be an opportunity to
speak to Abigail alone and renew her offer of hospitality.

She smiled, her spirits lifting. "Yes, Tom, we'll all
go. We can harness two of the workhorses to the dray

and go in style. I think that would be a very good idea, don't you?"

Tom's broad grin echoed her smile. "Aye," he said. "That I do."

CHAPTER IV

The six men were waiting at the agreed rendezvous when Samuel Martin jerked his sweating mount to a standstill at the entrance to the narrow, tree-shaded valley which had given them concealment. The valley floor was littered with rocks, and the exhausted mare stumbled and sank to her knees the moment he released her. Martin cursed her ill-temperedly as, with heaving sides, she struggled to regain her feet.

"Are you not the eejut, then?" one of the escapers exclaimed mockingly. "The craytor's in foal, so she is! 'Tis a wonder she was able to carry you here."

"Hell's teeth, it were dark when I picked her," Martin defended. He aimed a kick at the mare, resenting the big Irishman's mockery. "And I've had the devil's own job findin' you. Couldn't see me hand in front o' me face when I set out, and—"

He was curtly interrupted. "Never mind about that," the authoritative voice of the escapers' leader bade him. "Did you bring what we asked you to?"

"The muskets, you mean? Oh, aye—two of 'em." He caught the mare's rein and, pulling her to his side, started to untie the two weapons he had rolled in strips of sacking and roped across her withers. "Like stealin' candy from a baby," he added boastfully. "The bitch I was assigned to kept this 'un hanging over the fireplace. I lifted it two days since an' she never noticed it had gone!"

"It's rusty," the leader observed, after subjecting the musket to a critical inspection.

"She never used it," Martin said. He spat in the dry dust at his feet. "But t'other 'un's better. . . . It was the soddin' foreman's, and he kept it well oiled. An' here's the shot—buckshot, it is. Ought ter do the trick, eh?"

"What about powder?"

"I brought Jardine's primin' box an' 'arf a score o' cartridges." The convict emptied his pockets. "Goin' ter get a right shock when he wants to go off on a 'roo hunt, ain't he? Hey, you got anything ter slake me thirst? Ridden a perishin' long way, I have, an' I need a drink."

"There's water," the leader told him, "over there among the rocks." He gestured behind him, the gesture explicit, offering Martin no choice. "That's all we've had—you took the last of our rum yesterday, and we can't light a fire in case it's seen. And I don't doubt you'll be followed, when the Long Wrekin folk find out what you've made off with. . . . That mare will be missed, even if the muskets aren't." He stroked the mare's white-flecked neck with gentle fingers, pity in his eyes. "Fetch her some water, Christie," he bade the big Irishman whose mockery had so irritated Martin. "The poor creature needs it more than her rider, and that's a fact."

Christie went off willingly enough, but Martin held his ground. "You promised," he began aggressively. "You promised that if I—"

"I know what I promised," the leader retorted. He was a dark-haired, good-looking man, with an air of breeding about him that was evident despite his torn and filthy clothes and his emaciated state. As he moved to enable Christie to lead the mare into the shade of the trees, his ragged shirt parted to reveal that back and shoulders were hideously crisscrossed by the puckered scars of at least half a dozen floggings. Martin shivered at the sight. Joseph Fitzgerald, one of the other men had told him, had been a leading participant in the Castle Hill rebellion, when he and his Irish compatriots had armed themselves with pitchforks and met the soldiers of the New South Wales Corps in short-lived, unequal contest.

For his part in the ill-fated uprising, Fitzgerald— a one-time barrister from Cork—had been sentenced to two years' hard labor at the Coal River settlement. The poor sod had worked with the lime-burning gangs, the man known as Christie with him, and Martin's informant had added bitterly, "That's why their backs are scarred. 'Tis the unslaked lime, mixed with seawater, does it. When they'd taken their lashes, they were sent to load the barges moored offshore, wading waist-deep with the blasted lime carried in leaking baskets on their shoulders. . . . I was luckier. I only had to mine coal on Fiddlesticks Hill."

Samuel Martin shivered again. By comparison, he reflected wryly, the Parramatta road gang had not been too bad, but for all that, he had no desire to return to it. He persisted obstinately, "Mr. Fitzgerald, do you have a boat?"

Fitzgerald gave him a thin smile. "We have a boat in mind and the—er—the means to take possession of it." He tapped the musket he was holding, his smile widening. "Why do you ask? Do you doubt us?"

"No, but I . . ." For some reason he was afraid of this tall, well-spoken man with his scars and his cold gray eyes. He had given his word that his party had their escape well planned, with a seagoing cutter and an experienced navigator to keep them on course for the Dutch Islands. He had promised, in exchange for the muskets and ammunition, to permit Martin to join them. It had been done before; he had heard the tales of successful escapes, Martin reminded himself. Yet for all that . . . He licked his dry, dust-caked lips and ventured uncertainly, "Why are you waiting here, all this way from the river, Mr. Fitzgerald? I got you them bloody muskets, didn't I? Well, why not let's go an' take the boat, 'stead o' hanging about here, askin' for trouble. Like you said yourself, I might be followed."

"We are safe enough here for the moment, my friend," the one-time lawyer assured him. "But there is something we have planned to do before we put to sea and make our escape . . . a matter that will take another twenty-four hours or so. And we are short of one of our number—the seaman I mentioned to you yesterday."

"Him that's to navigate for us?"

"That's right. His name is Thomas McCann. The unfortunate fellow was involved in the naval mutiny at the Nore and was sentenced to deportation for life."

Another sodding seditionist, Martin thought nervously. If they weren't scurvy Irish rebels, they were mutinous English seamen. . . . God in heaven, what mess had he contrived to land himself in?

As if reading his thoughts, Fitzgerald said, "You do not have to stay with us, Samuel, if you have any doubts. As soon as McCann joins us, we shall move on and you can go back to your employment."

The color drained from Samuel Martin's thin, unshaven face. "I can't go back—Gawd's truth, I took Mrs. Broome's mare! She'd never forgive me for that, let alone the muskets."

"Then stay and do as you're told," the tall Irishman snapped. Christie finished watering the mare. Leaving

the animal to recover in the shade of the tree to which
he had tethered her, he returned, beaming.

"I truly think the craytor's on the mend, Joe. No
t'anks to t'at eejut there, though . . . for didn't he
ride her near to death? Can we lave her loose when
we move on, d'you suppose, an' hope she'll find her
own way home?"

Fitzgerald nodded absently, his thoughts clearly on
other matters of more immediate concern, and Martin, glad to evade any further reproaches concerning
his treatment of the mare, made his way to the thin
trickle of water welling up among the rocks to the
rear of where he had been standing.

Three of the others were there, filling a variety of
makeshift water containers from the little stream. It
was a slow and tedious task, for the water flowed
slowly, and it was not until he reminded them he had
ridden all night and was parched that, grudgingly, they
made way for him. All three were Irish; one, a hulk-
ing fellow from the peat bogs of Kerry, whose name
was O'Mara, had been with him on the road gang and
had first whispered to him of the escape plan. Sipping
the few drops of water he had been able to collect in
his cupped hands, Martin scowled at O'Mara, who
grinned back without rancor.

"Was it you who told Mr. Fitzgerald that I was
working on the woman Broome's farm?" he demanded.

"Indade it was," O'Mara admitted. "An' why would
you be askin', then? Are you not pleased I did? You're
with us now, are you not?"

Before Martin could decide on his answer, a shout
from a man he had not previously noticed, posted as
lookout on a grassy hillock to his right, set them all
talking excitedly.

"Ah, now, he's come!"

"He'll have word, surely, and we'll know!"

"God bless Ireland! Faith, 'twill be loike auld times, so it will!"

The water containers forgotten, the three rejoined their leader at a run. Martin finished his scanty, unrefreshing drink and followed them, curiosity overriding caution.

The new arrival—the mutineer from the Nore, he supposed—was a small, balding man, with a wizened, ratlike face and a pronounced limp, and as soon as he opened his mouth, it was evident that he, too, was an Irishman. He was armed with an ancient, long-barreled horse pistol, which he brandished above his head with little regard for his companions' safety as he shouted exultantly, "The *Bounty* bastard's on his way, boys! An' he'll be drivin' to the service in his horse-drawn carriage, so he will, leavin' at first light tomorrow. All we'll need to do is wait for him, and I've found just the place where there'll not be the smallest chance o' his escort seein' us! Are ye ready to leave, then? 'Twill take us most o' the night to get there."

"Hold hard, Tom lad," Fitzgerald cautioned. "I'll have to know a lot more before I—"

The one-time seaman waved his pistol in derision. "Is your heart failin' you, then? Sure, 'tis goin' to be as easy as fallin' off a log, you have my word on't. Holy Mother of God, Mr. Fitzgerald, amn't I the one who's waited near ten years for such a chance?" The light of madness blazed in his pale eyes and Martin recoiled, shocked and frightened out of his wits as it slowly dawned on him that, far from merely making a bid for escape from the colony, these men intended to set an ambush for the governor. Aye, and . . . to kill him, if they could, he told himself dazedly. He felt Christie's arm descend on his shoulder as the others joined in the noisy argument McCann's accusation had provoked.

"Ah, now, and wasn't Joe Fitzgerald tellin' me to keep me eye on ye, Martin," the big man said softly. "Not taken the notion to run out on us, have ye?"

Martin's headshake was unconvincing and the Irishman tightened his grasp. "You'd be a prize eejut if you do," he warned, still not raising his voice. "We have been plannin' this for a long, long time, an' we'll have no chicken-hearted English bastard givin' us away to the redcoats—make no mistake on *that* score, me boy!"

"I wouldn't, in God's name!"

"Would ye not? Well, 'tis better to be sure than sorry, so it is. I'll not be lettin' ye out o' me sight until I *am* sure."

"You're . . ." Martin burst out indignantly. He had been about to say "mad" but he thought better of it, choking back the word. He remembered McCann's reputation and recalled, much too late, the stories he had heard about the man when he had been working in the Sheerness dockyard.

At the Nore mutiny McCann had been one of the delegates from H.M.S. *Sandwich,* and even the mutineers' self-styled president, Richard Parker—whom they had hanged from the depot ship's yardarm—had found McCann too hot to handle and had endeavored to have him confined in hospital, lest he initiate some act of violence that might imperil the seamen's cause.

It was said that only some confusion over his name had saved the hotheaded Irishman from sharing the fleet president's fate, and here he was, God roast him, in the forefront of a crazy plan to assassinate the colony's governor! Samuel Martin swallowed hard, feeling as parched now as he had felt before drinking from the spring. Fool that he was, not to have stayed at his work on the Broome woman's farm . . . he should never have let these hate-filled Irish rebels talk him into stealing the plaguey muskets for them. But maybe if he could contrive to return the mare—he could not hope to regain possession of the muskets, he knew—maybe Mrs. Broome would take him back and say nothing. The mare was tethered beneath the tree, not a dozen yards from him and . . . Christie whispered, mouth to his ear, with deadly menace, "Watch your step, boy . . . watch your step!"

"I didn't move," Martin protested, quite truthfully.

"Sure an' I know you did not. But ye were thinkin' o't, were ye not, now?"

Martin glared back at him in surly silence. McCann was winning the argument, he realized; the other men were siding with him, overruling Fitzgerald's caution.

"Very well, then," he heard the leader say, with evident reluctance. "We'll do it your way, Tom, and on your head be it if the spot turns out to be ill chosen."

"It is not," McCann said. "I'll take me oath on't. *Bounty* Bligh will never know what's hit him . . . an' more's the pity, for 'twould gladden my heart if he did, the bloody swine!"

They began to prepare for departure, and Martin, his whole body clammy with sweat, came close to despair as he waited, praying for Christie to relax his vigilance. His moment came when the big man, out of pity for the mare, drew Fitzgerald's attention to the animal's predicament.

"Did you not say we could let that poor craytor go free, Joe? She'll die if we lave her tied up here, and t'e foal wid her."

"It will add to our risk," Fitzgerald pointed out.

"Not ours, Joe . . . only his." He gestured to Martin contemptuously. "Tell him to loose her!"

"All right," the leader agreed. "Untie the mare, Martin."

Martin moved to obey him. It was his only chance, he told himself . . . to grab the mare and leap onto her back. Even if Mrs. Broome carried out her threat and returned him to the road gang, that would be better than the consequences he might expect if he joined these madmen in an attempt on the life of the governor. Bligh was too well guarded. They would never get away with it, and the boat they had planned to steal, the escape by sea, would never materialize. They would be topped, the lot of them, and good riddance.

And they probably would not try to stop him, for had not Joseph Fitzgerald told him he could go, if he had a mind to, after McCann had joined them?

Martin untied the mare's rein, and, keeping her distended body between himself and the rest of them, he slithered awkwardly onto her back. With voice and heels, cursing her under his breath, he set her head toward home and urged her on.

"Gallop, yer bitch!" he swore at her. "Get along with yer, for Christ's sake!" His clenched fist struck her between the ears. "Gerrup, will yer!"

They had covered only twenty yards when Christie raised to his shoulder the stolen musket he had been carrying. He took careful aim, and the charge of buckshot struck Martin in the back. With a high-pitched scream of agony he came crashing to the ground as the mare galloped on, reins flying and terror driving her faster than her erstwhile rider had done, for all his frantic urging.

With Fitzgerald a pace or two behind him, Christie strode over to where Martin lay, motionless now, his eyes wide and sightless, his mouth still painfully twisted.

"The eejut," the big man observed dispassionately. "I had him figured, Joe . . . I guessed he'd try to run, so I did. But he'd no call to treat a poor dumb animal so, had he now?"

"Is he dead?" Joseph Fitzgerald asked.

"As a doornail." Christie turned the convict's body over with his foot, revealing the hideous wound the buckshot had made. "That was a powerful charge, was it not?"

"We'll need one just like it for Governor Bligh," Fitzgerald told him. A grim little smile hovered briefly on his lips and then faded. "Because a couple of shots will be all we'll get, whatever Tom McCann claims. And you're to be the one that fires the first shot, Christie."

"Why, sure, 'twill be a pleasure," Christie acknowledged. He started to sing, in a rich, exultant baritone, "But we trust in God above us and we dearly love the green! Oh, to die it is far better than be cursed as we have been . . . for that will be the way of it, will it not, Joe?"

Fitzgerald did not deny it. "We'll stand together, true together," he answered quietly. "And they'll have cause to remember us, God willing."

Christie was whistling cheerfully as they walked back, side by side, to where the others were waiting for them.

The coach and its four laboring horses rumbled slowly along the rough, uneven road, raising a choking cloud of dust in its wake. Ahead of it rode four mounted troopers, holding their horses back to keep pace with the carriage; those in the rear, also four in number, dropped behind after a mile or two, in order to escape from the dust.

Governor Bligh, in full dress uniform, sat under a canvas awning and cursed the sun beating down on them.

"As God's my witness," he remarked sourly to Provost Marshal Gore, who was seated opposite him, "only a man truly resolved to do his duty would endure this discomfort in order to be present at a church service conducted by that infernal fellow Boskenna! And in the open, what's more!"

"I fancy, sir," his secretary put in, thinking to offer consolation, "that Mr. Dawson has placed a large barn at the reverend gentleman's disposal."

"But he'll still rant and rave for an hour," the governor retorted. "Threatening us with the torments of hell, as if those we already have to suffer aren't enough. I made a grave mistake when I permitted Boskenna to stay here. . . . I should have put a ship at his disposal as soon as he set foot ashore in Sydney and packed him off to New Zealand. At least there the inhabitants would be unable to comprehend his blasted sermons!"

Gore and Griffin exchanged glances, but neither ventured to dispute William Bligh's admission of his mistake, and he went on, "And the fellow won't relinquish his—damme, his Christian responsibility, as he insists on calling it, for those two unfortunate young girls. *I've* offered to take responsibility for them and I'd do it, gladly. Their father was a brother officer and a friend of mine, so who has a better right? Their presence in Government House would ease my poor daughter's burden, and she would welcome it, I know, with poor Putland sinking fast. But plague take him, Boskenna won't hear of it. He flourishes the letter the unfortunate Edmund Tempest is supposed to have written before putting a pistol to his head, and if I attempt to dispute it or question Tempest's state of mind, he quotes the will of God to me! I may be misjudging the fellow, but I suspect his real intention is to get his rapacious hands on their land grant! He'll have to be watched, though I doubt if I can legally intervene."

His subordinates again exchanged wary glances and Griffin offered diffidently, "It is a pity Mr. Fulton is an Irishman and—er—an emancipist, sir. It gives Boskenna something of an advantage."

"Indeed it does, Edmund," Bligh agreed glumly.

They were speaking of Henry Fulton, a Protestant clergyman from Northern Ireland. He had been deported for having supported the rebel Catholics, but he was of such good repute that he had been appointed acting chaplain while the Reverend Samuel Marsden was in England on leave. Fulton was a good man, but his unfortunate background as an Irish seditionist offered little hope of his being brought to bear against Boskenna in the matter of the Tempest girls.

Giving vent now to a deep sigh, Bligh gestured toward the cultivated land on either side of the road. "There is so much that promises well in this colony, and there are good, loyal, hardworking folk here. It is a constant source of frustration to me that all their efforts—and most of my own, too—should be brought to nothing by the avarice of a few."

Both Gore and Griffin knew to whom his last observation referred, and the provost marshal commented, with some bitterness, "Despite all the unpleasantness Underwood and that drunken rogue Mackay caused me, Major Johnstone had to eat his words and order my acquittal. They will think twice, sir, before they indulge in that sort of litigation again."

"They will not, the devil take them!" the governor exploded. "Oh, you may have been acquitted, William, my boy, but now Atkins tells me they are after the Campbells. John Macarthur intends to institute proceedings against the younger Campbell for illegal seizure of those infernal stills he and Abbott imported. Robert Campbell senior who, as you know, I appointed as port naval officer in place of Harris, foolishly sent his nephew to recover the stills, instead of going himself . . . so technically he had no authority to take possession of them."

William Gore stared at him aghast. "But, sir, surely Mr. Atkins won't admit so—so frivolous a complaint?"

"The damned fool already has," Bligh told him. The carriage lurched into a series of potholes and he cursed irritably as he was almost precipitated from his seat. He added, with mock resignation, "Well, at least one good thing has come of it . . . Macarthur has decided to ostracize me. His wife— who is a charming woman, I am the first to concede —called on me when I was in residence at Parramatta. But when I returned her call, Macarthur sent his servant to inform me that he was out. In effect, I suppose that amounts to a declaration of open warfare between us." He shrugged his epaulet-trimmed shoulders. "By God, though, he'll live to regret it! I'll see the arrogant swine broken and exiled from this colony if it's the last thing I do. He's a damned blackguard and a seditionist, and Johnstone is as bad. Between them they—"

He was rudely interrupted. A musket cracked, the sound coming from a thickly growing clump of trees close to the road verge, and a charge of buckshot spattered into the dust a few feet short of the carriage, one or two actually striking the woodwork of the door.

"What the devil's that?" Bligh exclaimed wrathfully. A second shot and a single musket ball which embedded itself in the upholstery of the carriage gave him answer. Never a man to show fear in the face of danger, the governor was on his feet and out into the road, thrusting aside his secretary, who attempted to shield him. "Pull up, you damned fool!" he bawled at the coachman. As the carriage lurched to a standstill, he reached for the loaded blunderbuss that hung, ready to hand, from the box, and, using the vehicle as cover, raised the weapon to his shoulder. Gore and Griffin, moving more slowly, joined him there, both with pistols.

His escorts, in obedience to his shouted order, divided. They had been well trained and knew what was expected of them. Two dismounted and took post behind the carriage horses; two circled to the right, and the sergeant and the three men riding in the rear drew their sabers and galloped off in an attempt to take the attackers from behind.

Musket shots were exchanged between the governor's party and the men who had set the ambush, and Bligh himself, after thundering a demand that they surrender and receiving no reply, fired his fearsome weapon into the trees. A scream indicated that one of them had been wounded, but for the next few minutes pandemonium reigned. Buckshot and musket balls hummed through the air like a swarm of angry bees; one of the carriage horses went down, the coachman was hit as he endeavored to cut the dying animal's traces, and then, as suddenly as it had begun, it was over.

The sergeant came limping back, holding his shattered right arm, to gasp out the humiliating admission that he and his three troopers had themselves ridden into a trap.

"They took our horses, sir," the man said bitterly. "Up in the rocks, they was, an' they jumped us. They've made off ridin' our mounts." He winced with pain. "We won't catch the bastards now. Escapers they was, sir, armed with two or three muskets and some pistols. One o' my lads was hit an' two o' theirs, I think."

"Did you recognize any of them?" Gore demanded.

"Aye, sir—one." The sergeant gritted his teeth as Griffin attempted to staunch the bleeding from his wounded arm. "Have a care, sir, please—I reckon the bone's broken."

"Which one did you recognize?" Bligh asked thickly.

"Feller named McCann, sir, usta be a seaman. Irish and a bit o' a hot head. I . . . I'm sorry, sir, I—"

The unfortunate sergeant's legs buckled under him, and he collapsed at the governor's feet.

"We'll get the poor devil to a doctor," Bligh decided. "Lift him into the carriage, Edmund. We'll make for Toongabbie. The troops from there can start a search for the culprits." He swore softly, remembering Seaman McCann. The Irish delegate from the *Sandwich,* he recalled—the one who had come aboard his ship, the *Director,* and endeavored to incite *his* men to throw him over the side, when the Nore mutiny was at its height. He had good reason to remember Thomas McCann. "I shall offer a reward for their apprehension," he added, suddenly coldly angry. "God damn their infernal impudence! And, William"—as Gore returned, after assisting Edmund Griffin to carry the wounded sergeant to his carriage—"see to it that notice is published that anyone harboring these villains will be charged with them and with the same crimes!"

CHAPTER V

The roan mare, Ladybird, stumbled back to Long Wrekin, more dead than alive, just before sunset on Sunday evening. Jenny found her when, on their return from the public church service held in the Dawsons' barn, she went with William to water the other brood mares in the home paddock.

The poor creature stood with lowered head and heaving flanks by the gate, seemingly at her last gasp, and Tom Jardine, who had been rubbing down the dray horses in the yard, came running in response to William's piping summons.

"Away and bid Nancy heat some thin gruel for her," he bade the boy. "She's in a bad way, Mrs. Broome," he observed, after subjecting the mare to a frowning inspection. "But she's not dropped her foal. No thanks to that blackguard Martin, though . . . he's used her cruelly."

"As someone seemingly used him," Jenny said. She gestured, tight of lip, to the ominous dark stains on the rolled sacking the runaway convict had used as a saddle. "Look at that, Tom!"

Tom moved closer. "Aye," he confirmed grimly.

"It's blood, right enough. I reckon the rogue must've run into a patrol o' redcoats an' they fired at him. Unless he . . ." The foreman broke off, his frown deepening, and as Jenny met his gaze she knew that he was thinking along the same lines as herself . . . and drawing the same conclusion. News of the attempt to ambush the governor had reached the waiting congregation before the Reverend Boskenna had begun divine service, when a trooper of the governor's escort had ridden posthaste from the scene to offer apologies for Captain Bligh's enforced absence.

The soldier had made the most of his dramatic account, and as his story was repeated, it lost nothing in the telling. . . . Jenny shivered in the warm dusk. There had been talk of buckshot and of escapers armed with muskets, but surely that did not mean that Samuel Martin had been involved. She glanced again at Tom Jardine. "Martin had no reason—" she began.

"He stole your musket, Mrs. Broome, as well as mine. And they had two or three muskets, the sojer said—an' buckshot. Escapin' convicts don't find it too easy ter get their hands on arms, less'n they steal 'em from settlers, like Martin did."

The reasoning was irrefutable and Jenny sighed, her hands shaking a little as she caressed poor Ladybird's sweat-damp neck. "We'd better put the mare into the feed store under cover, Tom," she suggested.

"Aye," he agreed, and fell into step beside her. "I'll take care o' her, don't you worry. And when my Nancy fetches me some warm gruel, that'll put fresh heart in her. We haven't lost her yet, Mrs. Broome."

But they might have lost more than a mare and foal, Jenny thought uneasily. Settlers who permitted their assigned convict laborers to escape invariably met with official reluctance to replace the escapers, and those who were careless enough to let their weapons fall into the wrong hands could find themselves in

serious trouble. As she helped Tom to bed the exhausted mare down in the feed store at the rear of
the farmhouse, she said, "The soldier said that the men
who attacked the governor included one who had been
a seaman in the Royal Navy—he was seen and identified."

Tom nodded. William brought the gruel he had
asked for, and Ladybird drank thirstily, requiring little
coaxing. "It's bin a long day for you, Mrs. Broome,"
the foreman said, with gruff sympathy, as if he had
guessed the trend of Jenny's thoughts. "I'll stay with
the mare awhile. You go back to the house for your
meal. I'll call you if I need any help. Young Willie
can finish waterin', can't you, lad?"

" 'Course I can," William returned stoutly. He whistled up the dog that was his constant companion and
set off cheerfully for the paddock. Tom hung up the
mare's bridle and, reaching for a handful of straw,
started to rub her down, his big hands skilled and
gentle.

"Off you go, missus," he urged.

"All right," Jenny conceded. It *had* been a long
day, she reflected, as she walked slowly back to the
farmhouse . . . a long and anxious day and she was
tired. The attempt on the governor's life had come as
a shock to everyone, and with the stolen muskets on
her conscience, she had been more shocked than most,
convinced that even if he had not actually borne a part
in the attack, Samuel Martin had made it possible by
providing the weapons the would-be assassins had used.

But she had said nothing, not even to Tim Dawson,
excusing the omission by telling herself that she could
not be sure. Now, however, the mare's return and the
bloodstained sacking dispelled the last of her doubts—
for had not the soldier told them that at least one of
the assailants had been wounded? The wounded man
had to be Martin, yet, as she had told Tom Jardine,

he had no reason to want Governor Bligh dead . . . no reason, that was to say, of which she was aware. Unless, like the man identified as Thomas McCann, Martin had also been a seaman . . . one of those who had taken part in the fleet mutiny at the Nore and been sentenced to transportation in consequence. Andrew Hawley had talked of the Nore mutiny. He had been there serving in the same ship as the governor, but . . . Jenny bit back a sigh.

Apart from the shock of the soldier's news, she had been shaken also by the Reverend Caleb Boskenna's lengthy sermon, finding fresh reason in his harsh rhetoric to mistrust him on Abigail Tempest's account, for he had lectured his increasingly sullen congregation on the evils of female wantonness and the divine retribution which those who indulged in such weakness of the flesh might anticipate. Purity of body and spirit— added to hard work on the land—was, he extolled, the way to salvation from the fires of hell. Abigail had been present, sitting with downcast eyes and a white, unhappy face in the forefront of the congregation, but she had been with Henrietta Dawson, and Timothy's wife had bustled her away when the service ended, making it impossible for Jenny to approach her. She had even written a note, Jenny reminded herself, hoping for an opportunity to press it into Abigail's hand, but the note was still in her pocket.

She opened the door of the house and was touched to see that little Rachel had set the table and made tea and then, evidently weary of waiting for her mother to reappear, had curled up in Watt Sparrow's old rocking chair and gone to sleep. Well, it would not take very long to serve up the meal, and then both children —who had been up before dawn—could go to bed and sleep off their weariness. As indeed so could she, since most of the chores had been attended to before they had set out for the Dawsons' property, and Tom

Jardine could be relied upon to do what could be done for the mare. If the poor animal started to foal prematurely, he would send for her.

The meal was ready when William came in; his noisy arrival wakened Rachel, and she stumbled sleepily to the table to gulp down her food. To Jenny's relief both children departed to bed without protest, and she was cleaning away, intending to follow their example as soon as the pots were washed, when Tom Jardine came to the door.

A glance at his face was enough and Jenny said flatly, "Is the poor little mare dead?"

Tom nodded. "Aye, ten minutes since. I'm sorry, Mrs. Broome, I did my best, but she'd no fight left in her."

The blow was not unexpected, but it was a harsh one nonetheless, and Jenny thanked him with tears in her eyes. "You did all anyone could, Tom. Off you go and get your supper. Nancy must be despairing of you."

"If I ever get my hands on that damned rogue Martin," the foreman vowed, "I'll break his scurvy neck." He hesitated, eyeing Jenny uncertainly, "Will you be reportin' him as an escaper, Mrs. Broome?"

"I shall have to, shall I not?"

"Aye, I'm afraid so. An' the muskets?"

Jenny stifled a sigh. "Those, too, Tom. It's the law."

"Then you could be in trouble?"

She did not attempt to deny it. "I suppose I could. Tom, was Martin ever a seaman, do you know?"

Tom Jardine shrugged his broad, muscular shoulders. "He told me he worked in the Sheerness shipyard —as a carpenter, he said, but he wasn't skilled, was he? Them fences he mended down in the far sheep paddock, why they was cobbled an' no mistake. Well, you seen 'em, didn't you? An' like I told you, Mrs. Broome, I spotted him jawin' to a couple o' men down there the day before he lit out. I reckon that must'a bin when he made up his mind ter make off with our muskets an' join 'em."

He was probably right, Jenny thought, as Tom Jardine bade her good night and strode off into the darkness toward his own cabin on the far side of the farm buildings. It was a fine, clear night, the moon not yet risen, and she lingered for a few minutes by the door of the farmhouse, letting the cool southerly breeze take its refreshing will of her tired and aching body. An unsprung dray was not, she reflected, the most comfortable vehicle in which to travel close on sixteen miles in a single day . . . particularly if it were drawn by a single pair of workhorses more accustomed to pulling a plow.

But at least William and Rachel had enjoyed the outing, and she had been glad of the opportunity— both for them and for herself—to attend divine service, even if it was presided over by Reverend Caleb Boskenna.

"Don't make a sound, now, and you'll suffer no hurt," a voice whispered in her ear. The accent was unmistakably Irish. A big, calloused hand was clapped over her mouth, its fellow grasping her firmly about the waist, as if to emphasize the warning. Startled and afraid, Jenny struggled for a moment and then, realizing that her captor was too strong for her, she stood still, her heart sinking. The man's hand moved from her mouth. "Bide aisy and no calling out, d'ye understand. Are ye alone? Who else is in the house?"

"Only my children," Jenny managed. "And they . . . they are asleep."

"Where? Where are dey sleepin'?"

"In the attic. They won't hear anything."

"Ah, dat's fine, then." He sounded relieved, and, still retaining his grasp of her waist, he turned and emitted a low whistle, in response to which two others emerged from the shadows to the rear of the farm-house.

"Is she alone?" one of them demanded.

"She is. The man's away to his own place. I seen him go. There's just herself and her childer—she says they're sleepin'."

"I'll take a look," the other man said. His voice was educated, devoid of accent, and as he pushed open the door of the house and the lamplight fell on him, Jenny saw that he was a tall, dark-haired man, garbed like a scarecrow, with a pistol in his right hand.

His search was brief; he reappeared in the open doorway, the pistol now thrust into his belt, as he waved to someone beyond Jenny's line of vision.

"All right," he said, addressing her captor, "Bring the woman inside, Christie . . . and watch her, mind. I'll go and help the other boys with Michael."

He vanished into the darkness, his companion, who was armed with a musket, taking up a position a few yards from the door, his weapon at the ready.

"Fetch me out somethin' to drink, Christie," the self-appointed sentry urged, as Jenny and the big Irish-man passed him. "Lord God, I've the devil's own thirst!"

"Have patience," the man called Christie reproved him. "We've poor Michael to settle first." A hand on Jenny's arm, he thrust her before him into the house and said, smiling at her, his tone quite friendly now, "There's a sorely wounded man wid' us, Mistress Broome. Have ye a bed or a couch we can lay him on?"

"There's my own," Jenny answered. Since Johnny's death she had slept in an alcove off the kitchen, as much for convenience—since she habitually rose before dawn—as for warmth in winter. She indicated the bed and Christie beamed his satisfaction.

"Ah, that will be grand for the poor fellow, ma'am.

And some food, now, for de rest av us, if you'll be so kind. A pot av tay, maybe, an' bread an' cheese. We're not wantin' to rob ye, but none of us has eaten for two days past, and we're famished, so we are."

Jenny eyed him coldly, refusing to respond to his smile. These, she strongly suspected, were the men who had lain in ambush, waiting to fire on the governor and his escort. They were no ordinary escapers, for whom she might well have felt sympathy. They were dangerous men, seditionists, seeking to bring anarchy to the colony, and they knew her name, Christie had addressed her as Mrs. Broome. Which must mean . . . She drew in her breath sharply. "Did Samuel Martin guide you here?" she asked, an edge to her voice. "Did *he* tell you that I'd be willing to hide you and feed you?"

There was an odd look in the big Irishman's blue eyes, as if her question had confused him, but after a momentary hesitation, he shook his head.

"No, he did not."

"But he stole two muskets from here—muskets and ammunition. Were they not for you?"

He evaded her question, countering it with one of his own. "We have four horses, ma'am—have you anywhere we can put them where they'll not be readily seen?"

"There's a paddock," Jenny told him, and reluctantly gave directions which Christie, after thanking her with punctilious courtesy, passed on to the man outside. He called back a low-voiced comment, and Christie spread his big hands in an apologetic gesture.

"Now amn't I the forgetful eejut! They've saddles, so they have—military saddles, the which we'll need to conceal very well in case ony sojers come lookin' for dem. Have you a building with hay or straw in it, maybe, close to this house?"

There was the forage store, Jenny thought, where

Ladybird had gasped her poor young life away. She answered, with a resentment she made no attempt to hide, "Yes, there's a feed store across the yard, but there's a dead mare lying in the straw . . . the one Samuel Martin stole from me and rode to death."

The effect of her bitter words surprised her. Christie's blue eyes held genuine distress, and he swore under his breath. "Ah, now, I'm truly sorry to hear dat, Mrs. Broome, for she was a fine animal, so she was . . . an' you'll have lost the foal wid' her, will you not?"

"Yes," Jenny confirmed. "It wasn't due for several weeks." She heard the sound of subdued voices and the soft pad of horses' hooves, coming from outside. Christie went to the door, evidently to pass on the information she had given him concerning the feed store, and then, returning to her side, he went on as if there had been no interruption or, indeed, any attempt on his part to conceal the truth, "Martin rode the poor craytor to her death right enough, ma'am— and to his own. He'll not trouble you now, for he's lyin' out in the woods with a charge o' buckshot in his vitals. But I'd be the last to say 'God rest his soul' . . . and may I be forgiven for dat!" He crossed himself, a wry smile curving his lips. "But Martin was—" A stir by the open door caused him to break off. "Dey're bringin' the boy Michael Finnegan in now, ma'am. You'll help him, will you not?"

Jenny stood, silent and undecided what to do. But when two of the men carried in the limp, bloodstained body of a fair-haired youth of perhaps eighteen, she went to her bed and stripped back the patchwork quilt to enable them to lay him on it. She was a mother, after all, and the lad was so young.

"He has a musket ball in the chest," the dark-haired man with the educated voice told her flatly, "and I fear there's precious little anyone can do for him. But if you have some liquor in the house, Mrs. Broome, I'd be grateful if you would let me have it for the lad. It might ease his pain."

"There is a keg of rum in the larder," Jenny said. "Help yourself." She poked up the fire and set a pan of water to boil. "You'll find bread and cheese in the larder, too," she added as the dark-haired man crossed the room to inspect the contents of her larder. "And a fresh, cured ham. Take what you want, if you are hungry."

He thanked her with a polite little bow that contrasted oddly with his ragged, scarecrow garb and said, addressing Christie, "Give Luke a hand with the horses, Chris, will you? And get the saddlery well hidden."

"I'll do that, Joe," Christie assured him. He added, unprompted, "The mare came back, Mrs. Broome says . . . and the poor craytor's dead."

"I am sorry," the dark-haired man asserted, but his voice was hard and unfeeling, and it took on a harsher note as he went on, turning to look searchingly at Jenny as Christie left her side. "In any struggle there are casualties, but you and your children will be safe from us so long as you give us what we ask. I regret that we must trespass on you, Mrs. Broome, even for a few hours, but all our lives are at risk. You see, we—"

Jenny cut him short. "I know what you tried to do —I was at the church service which the governor was to have attended this morning. One of his escort brought the news of your attack on him. It was announced to the assembled congregation that His Excellency was unhurt."

"And you are glad of that? You sound as if you were."

His tone was accusing, and Jenny faced him, stung

to anger. "Yes, I thank God for it as the Hawkesbury settlers did this morning, Mr.? . . . I don't know your name."

"Fitzgerald," he supplied. "Joseph Fitzgerald, late of Naas, in the county of Kildare, and once an attorney in Cork and, I had the presumption to believe, a civilized gentleman. You'd hardly credit that now, would you?"

"What is a 'civilized gentleman' doing in the role of assassin?" Jenny challenged, too angry to be any longer conscious of fear. "And what did you hope to achieve by murdering Governor Bligh? He is the best governor we have had here since Captain Phillip left."

"He is a tyrant and the representative of a tyrant King!" Joseph Fitzgerald declared, with bitter conviction. "We failed yesterday, but we shall try again, have no illusions on that score. We are sworn to kill him, for it needs his death to rouse our people throughout the colony to throw off the English yoke and battle for their freedom once again."

"You will only invite savage reprisals," Jenny countered.

"And what if we do?" Fitzgerald demanded. "We'll meet them. Glory be to God, woman, have you not suffered injustice—have you not longed to be free and to return to your homeland?"

Had she not, Jenny thought, her anger fading . . . had she not indeed? Yet it was all a long time ago, the injustice of her conviction all but forgotten, and her homeland so distant a memory that she had no thought now of returning there, no sense even of loss.

"I have made my life here," she told the Irishman quietly. "And I have earned my freedom to live it here, Mr. Fitzgerald . . . after almost twenty years. But you are endangering my freedom by your presence, as you must know, for the soldiers will search until they find you. I cannot force you to leave—you are armed, and I am not. All the same, I hope you will stay no longer than you must."

"We will leave at first light," Joseph Fitzgerald promised, "provided that poor boy over there becomes no worse. Or if . . ." He hesitated, again subjecting her to a frowning scrutiny. "You are English, of course, and you came out here, I imagine, as an ordinary felon, but now you are a settler and you own land. I should not have expected you to understand the feelings of those who are bred as I am. You think of us as rebels, do you not? Even as traitors, perhaps."

"Yes," Jenny conceded. "That is how we think of you, Mr. Fitzgerald. Your attempt to kill the governor made you traitors in my eyes."

He shrugged. "We regard ourselves as patriots, fighting to free our country from centuries of alien occupation and oppression, Mrs. Broome. That any of us are here at all is the greatest injustice ever perpetrated by the tyrants who hold Ireland in thrall. And we're ready to die for the Cause, if that is all that is left to us. That scarcely makes us traitors, does it?"

Reminded suddenly of her friend Frances O'Riordan, who had so assiduously supported that same cause but who was now married to a wealthy landowner, Jasper Spence, Jenny said nothing as Fitzgerald carried the keg of rum over to the table. "You did say that I might have this for the boy?" Receiving her nod of acquiescence, he filled a beaker and made to cross over to the bed on which the wounded man lay, but Jenny stopped him, a hand on his fetter-scarred wrist.

She said, conscious of pity, "Let me cleanse his wound first and make sure that the bleeding has stopped."

"And this?" He held up the beaker.

"Drink it yourself," Jenny invited, with a faint

smile. "And share it with the others when you eat. I have another keg put by."

They were fugitives, she thought—dangerous fugitives, so far as she was concerned—but fugitives nonetheless, with every man's hand against them . . . the settlers' as well as the troops'. Had her beloved Johnny Broome not been a fugitive when she first set eyes on him? And on Frances, too, fleeing from the enforced company of whores and cutpurses, with the memory of her brother's hanging driving her despairingly into the bush. She poured water from the boiling kettle into a bowl, fetched some scraps of old linen from her sewing box, and went to attend as best she could to the wounded boy.

He was barely conscious, but he managed to smile his gratitude as she bathed and cleaned the ugly wound. But, as Joseph Fitzgerald had said, there was little to be done for him—the ball was deeply embedded in his bony chest, and each time he coughed, he spewed up blood from his lungs. Jenny propped him up on the pillows to give him ease, and when Joseph Fitzgerald brought the refilled beaker in response to her request for it, his expression told her that he knew there could be little hope.

"I wish we'd a priest for him," he said, all the harshness gone from his voice as he stood by the bedside, watching her hold the beaker to the boy's bloodless lips. "But since we have not, my prayers will have to suffice."

"And mine," Jenny reminded him. "For all they are English, Mr. Fitzgerald."

He bowed his head. "Michael will be thankful for them. I—" Christie's return, with three other men crowding in after him, caused him to break off with a smothered exclamation. "Did you deal with the horses and the saddlery, Christie?"

"We did," the big man answered, "but that rogue

McCann has made off wid' one o' them. He told
Luke he means to give himself up an' turn King's evidence against us and—"

"For God's sake, did you not try to stop him?"

"We tried, Joe," Christie retorted ruefully, "but the
swine had his pistol and he laid Luke out cold. And
you said we must not fire, lest we rouse Mrs. Broome's
laborers. The foreman's house is too close for comfort, an' I seen a blackfeller skulkin' around . . . we
had to let McCann go, we'd no option."

Fitzgerald cursed. "Perdition take the cowardly
devil—he'll lead the redcoats to us, nothing's more
certain! We'll not be safe here after daybreak, boys."
He glanced across at Jenny. "Have you a boat on
the river, Mrs. Broome?"

"Yes." Jenny lowered the wounded boy's head gently onto the pillow, and with the half-empty beaker in
her hand, she turned to face him. "I have a small
oared boat, Mr. Fitzgerald. But that boy—the boy
you call Michael—cannot be moved. It would kill
him."

"Sure and the poor soul's goin' to die anyway,"
one of the others began, an edge of panic to his voice.
"We'll have to leave him behind, Joe."

"Ah, hold your tongue, Liam!" Fitzgerald bade him,
"and let me think, will you? We've a few hours yet—
the soldiers will not move whilst it's dark, even if
McCann finds them. And Bligh's gone back to Toongabbie—that was what they said, was it not?"

For the first time since he had entered her house,
Joseph Fitzgerald seemed at a loss, Jenny realized.
He and the others talked in low voices, evidently arguing among themselves. She caught the name Michael
once or twice but little else and decided that the time
had come when she must assert herself.

"I will give you a meal," she told them, "and what
provisions I can spare, and I will tell you how to

find the boat. But you must leave as soon as you have eaten, because if the soldiers find you here they will charge me with harboring you. You know that and you cannot expect me to do more."

"An English emancipist bitch harborin' Irish Defenders," the man called Liam sneered. "Sure not even the plaguey Rum Corps would believe t'at, missus! Why dey'll likely pay you a bounty for—"

"Keep a still tongue in your head!" Fitzgerald ordered wrathfully. To Jenny he said, "Thank you, Mrs. Broome." He made no further mention of Michael, but as Jenny busied herself preparing their food, she saw him take a second beaker of rum to the bed in the alcove and kneel, his arm round the wounded boy's shoulders, as he aided him to drink.

The others ate hungrily, helping themselves to the rum with so little restraint that the keg was soon empty. She did not offer them more until Joseph Fitzgerald left the alcove and stumbled across to join them at the table, his thin face deathly pale. He met Jenny's gaze with blank, unseeing eyes and said in a choked voice, "Michael Finnegan's at peace now, God rest him. He'll be no further trouble to you—we'll bury him before we go. But if you have some more of that rum, perhaps you'd be good enough to let us have it."

The men crossed themselves. Christie got to his feet and followed Jenny to the larder, taking the second keg from her with a whispered "I'll give it to dem, ma'am. And whilst they're drinkin' the stuff, maybe you'll show me where you'd like the boy buried and I'll start diggin' his grave."

Jenny did as he had asked, sick with pity; but already the sky was lightening, she saw, as, having provided him with pick and shovel, she led him out to where the two wooden crosses marked the last resting place of old Watt Sparrow and her husband, Johnny. Christie peered at the inscriptions on them,

unable to decipher them in the dim light, but he asked
no questions. Bracing himself, he started to dig with
strong, rhythmic strokes of his powerful arms.

"Don't wait, ma'am," he said, pausing at last to
draw breath and exchange his pick for the spade.
"Michael Finnegan is not de first to give his life in
Ireland's cause, and he'll not be the last."

"It is a lost cause," Jenny said, the words wrung
from her. The dead boy had been only a year or so
older than her own son Justin, she reflected sadly, yet
here was Christie, seemingly also seeking martyrdom.
"Did not Castle Hill teach you that?" she asked him.
"Because you were there, were you not?"

He paused in his self-imposed task, shifting the
spade from one hand to another, and she sensed that
he was smiling at her in the dim light.

"Sure, I was there. An' I seen them hang five of
our boys. They reprieved Brian McCormack and
Johnny Burke, along wid' Joe Fitzgerald an' meself.
We all took five hundred lashes, ma'am, an' two years
workin' the lime kilns at Coal River. It killed the
other two, Brian an' Johnny, so it did. But Joe an'
me, we're alive, Mrs. Broome, an' we took the oath
like they did—the Defenders' oath. Dat can't be
broken, savin' only by death. We're pledged to go on
fightin'."

"And running, Christie?" Jenny challenged.

"Sure, if we must. But we'll make dem pay for it
. . . *Bounty* Bligh an' the blackguards o' redcoat officers." Christie resumed his digging. Over his shoulder
he added, his tone oddly flat, "We lost our chance
o' escapin' by sea, Mrs. Broome, when that plaguey
feller McCann made off to try an' save his own skin,
for wasn't he to navigate for us . . . de only one
dat could?"

Once again and almost against her will, Jenny was

conscious of a pity that transcended all other emotions. She said, with genuine concern, "I'm sorry, Christie."

"Ah, well." The big Irishman went on hacking at the loosened soil, shifting it in great spadefuls and gradually digging deeper, the sweat from his exertions pouring off him. " 'Tis the will of God, so it is. Would you see that the boy Michael has a cross to mark where he lies, Mrs. Broome, if I've not time to attend to it meself?"

"Yes, I'll see to it," Jenny promised.

He thanked her gravely. " 'Twill be ready by de time dey bring his body out. Would you tell Joe for me, if you please?"

Jenny nodded, tight lipped, and made her way back to the house. The men had been drinking heavily, she realized, the second keg of rum now empty and all the food gone. Even Joseph Fitzgerald appeared to have taken his full share of the liquor; his thin face was flushed and his voice thick and slurred, but he answered her civilly enough when she delivered Christie's message.

"We'll come at once, Mrs. Broome. Seamus"—he turned to the dark-faced man at his side—"we've to put poor Michael under now and then make for the river. Help me to carry him out, will you? And, Liam —take one of the muskets and keep a lookout. You—"

"Ah, what's your hurry, Mr. Fitzgerald?" the man he had addressed as Liam objected. "De woman's here and God knows it's been a powerful long time since I've taken my pleasure wid a woman. All dose months hackin' coal out o' flamin' Fiddlesticks Hill, 'twas all I thought about, an' now . . ." He came shambling unsteadily toward Jenny, his toothless gums bared in a leering smile. "She's a widow-woman, Martin said, an' glory be to God, amn't I de answer to

her prayers? Why . . ." This time it was the dark-faced
man who hit him, and as he fell to his knees, Fitzgerald
jerked his head in the direction of the door.

"Forgive him, Mrs. Broome," he begged unhappily.
"It is the liquor talking. Liam is a decent man at
heart, believe me, but when men are treated like brutes,
they become brutes, God help them! Send him on his
way, Seamus. Luke can help me with the boy."

Shaken, Jenny stood in silence as they lifted Michael
Finnegan's body from her bed and carried it out into
the gray half-light of newly dawning day. But they
had delayed too long and had moved only a few yards
from the door when a fusillade of shots rang out and
Liam came running back, a smoking musket in his
hands and his voice high-pitched and edged with panic
as he yelled, "Redcoats! They've taken Christie! Run
for it, boys!"

The warning was in vain. Trapped by the burden
they were carrying, Fitzgerald and the man he had
called Luke were surrounded; Seamus ran, only to be
pursued by a mounted trooper, who laid into him
with the flat of his sabre and knocked him down as
he sought to clamber over the paddock fence.

Liam, seeing that resistance was useless, dropped his
musket and raised his arms, but despite the gesture of
surrender he, too, was sent sprawling by a soldier's
musket butt. The officer in command of the search
party, a stout, gray-haired lieutenant, turned over the
body of Michael Finnegan with the toe of his boot
and, satisfied that he was dead, remounted his horse,
bawling to his sergeant to assemble the prisoners for
his inspection.

This was done, Christie—bleeding from a wound in
the head and scarcely able to stand—being jerked
roughly into line with the others.

"Five," the officer announced. "And one dead.
Where's McCann?"

A small, bald man with a pale face limped forward under the guard of one of the soldiers. "You want me, sir?" he inquired obsequiously.

"I'd as soon do without you," the lieutenant snapped, "But are these the men who ambushed the governor? Are they all here? Identify them by name!"

Avoiding the prisoners' concerted gaze, McCann mumbled a few words, his sallow cheeks pale as he sought the courage to utter the names. Jenny, listening, saw Tom Jardine coming toward the group, with boots and breeches beneath his nightshirt. She roused herself in order to sign to him to keep away. But Tom ignored the signal and one of the soldiers grabbed him and lined him up with the Irishmen.

"Joseph Fitzgerald," the bald man said. "Christian O'Hagan, Liam O'Rourke, Luke Brady, an' Seamus O'Mara." He ventured a nervous glance at Tom Jardine and added, "I never set eyes on de other feller, sorr."

"Let him go," the officer ordered, to Jenny's relief. "Those are the blackguards we're after. And that carrion?" He pointed to the body at Joseph Fitzgerald's feet. "What's his name?"

"Michael Finnegan, sorr."

"Right—see that he's buried, Sergeant. The rest we'll bring in. And the woman." The officer turned in his saddle to look at Jenny. "What's your name, woman?"

Jenny told him. Behind her the soft pad of bare feet brought her heart to her mouth as William, roused from sleep by the shooting, came stumbling drowsily to thrust his small hand into hers. "Mam, what is it?" he whispered fearfully. "What do the soldiers want? They were firing their guns, and I thought . . ." Glimpsing the still body of Michael Finnegan he broke off with a sharp intake of breath. "Oh, Mam, he's dead, isn't he? Did the soldiers shoot him?"

"Hush," Jenny cautioned. She endeavored to explain to the officer, praying that Joseph Fitzgerald would speak up on her behalf, but he remained silent, and the officer brushed her excuses aside. "The charge is that of harboring fugitives from justice," he said brusquely. "Fugitive assassins, Mrs. Broome! You'll have your chance to answer the charge in court. Put her under arrest, Sergeant."

"But my children, sir," Jenny began. "I have a little girl, as well as the boy here and I—"

He did not permit her to finish. "You, there," he shouted, gesturing to Tom. "Look after the children. You labor here, don't you?"

"Aye, sir, but Mrs. Broome had nothing to do with the attack on the governor." Tom ranged himself in front of Jenny, his honest face red with outrage. "I can prove it, sir—I drove her an' the childer to the church service over at Mr. Dawson's. If armed men come raidin' the homes o' innocent folk, what are they to do? Why—"

"Shut your mouth," the lieutenant bade him. "You can give evidence in court when the charges are brought. My orders are quite clear—anyone found harboring the assassins is to be arrested with them. We'll need horses to bring them in. Corporal, take a couple of men and go and round up those animals in the paddock. I think you'll find the ones they stole from the governor's escort among 'em . . . and their saddlery, too."

Jenny listened despairingly, William still clinging to her hand. If they found the horses and the hidden saddlery, the charge of theft might well be added to that of harboring the fugitives and that would mean . . . She turned her gaze on Joseph Fitzgerald, but as before, he remained obstinately silent. And Christie had slumped to the ground, holding his bruised and bleeding face in his hands, seemingly unaware of what was happening.

Gently, she freed William's hand from hers.

"You must go to Rachel," she told him.

"But she's still asleep, Mam," William protested. Two soldiers thrust past him, and he stared at them resentfully as they went into the kitchen. "I want to stay with you."

"I have to go with the soldiers," Jenny said. "But it won't be for long, Willie . . . a few days, that's all." She summoned a wan little smile, anxious to convince him and trying to believe it herself. The soldiers, she saw thankfully, had confined their search to the kitchen . . . Rachel, at least, was undisturbed. "Tom," she managed, "you and Nancy will take care of them, won't you?"

"We'll take care o' everything, Mrs. Broome," Tom assured her. He added bitterly, "However long it is, you'll have no cause to fret about the childer. We—"

The sergeant's red-coated arm came between them. "You're under arrest, ma'am," he said with wooden formality. "Come along with me, please."

With William's muffled sobs ringing in her ears, Jenny let him lead her to where the stolen horses of the governor's escort were standing.

"We found the saddles, sir," one of the soldiers announced. "They was hidden under some straw in the barn there. An' a dead 'orse wiv' 'em."

The officer asked coldly, "And how do you explain that, Mrs. Broome, eh? Not to mention a freshly dug grave beside that of your late husband, if I'm not mistaken. And the remains of a meal and two empty rum kegs my men found on your kitchen table!" He shrugged and motioned her to mount. "Giving aid and comfort to the would-be assassins of His Excellency Governor Bligh . . . what view, I wonder, will the military court take of your conduct? Or are you, perhaps, expecting its members to applaud you?"

Jenny made no response to the sneering questions; but her heart came close to breaking when the caval- cade started to move off and she saw Rachel come running to the door to wave her a tearful farewell.

CHAPTER VI

News of the arrest of the men who had attacked the governor reached Upwey, the Dawsons' farm, when the family were still sitting over a late breakfast.

Abigail, who had been helping to feed the fractious three-year-old Alexander, looked up in wide-eyed alarm when the master of the house came storming in, grim faced and angry, to make the announcement.

"Davie Leake says the blasted soldiers have taken Jenny—accusing her of harboring the Irishmen, if you please!" Timothy Dawson's rage was apparent in his face.

"Well, perhaps she did," his wife, Henrietta, put in spitefully. "You know what these emancipists are like, Tim . . . however long they've been free, their sympathies are always with their own kind, and—"

Timothy cut her short. "If it had been your stepmother—that patriotic Irishwoman, Frances Spence—I'd have believed that, but Jenny has no sympathy for Irish rebels and well you know it, Etta!" He shrugged his broad shoulders and went to help himself from the table, piling food onto his plate impatiently and wolfing it down, ignoring Henrietta's reproachful glances.

"Your manners leave much to be desired," she could not forebear to point out. "What will Abigail think of you, for mercy's sake?"

Abigail thrust a laden spoonful of oatmeal porridge into Alexander's small, pouting mouth and was rewarded by a howl of outrage.

"Give him to me," his mother said, holding out her arms. "He's had enough. There, darling, hush now . . . Mamma won't make you eat any more."

Catching Timothy's eye, Abigail ventured uncertainly, "Mr. Dawson, did you say that Jenny Broome—Mrs. Broome of Long Wrekin—had been taken by the soldiers?"

"That's right," he confirmed, still angry. "A damned oaf named Brabyn was in charge of the search party —used to be a ranker in His Majesty's Foot Guards, until they made him an officer and *a gentleman* in the Rum Corps." He gulped down a beaker of home-brewed cider and made no attempt to stifle the belch which resulted from his haste. "I'm going over there as soon as I've eaten and taking a couple of men with me to help Tom Jardine." His words, although he had addressed them to Abigail, were clearly intended for his wife, and Henrietta—who had neither forgotten nor forgiven his love affair with Jenny Broome—reacted predictably.

"I suppose," she suggested acidly, "you will want to bring the Broome children back with you as well?"

"The thought had occurred to me," Timothy admitted.

"I will not have them in this house, Timothy, let that be understood. They are convict brats and—"

"But I *like* them, Mamma," seven-year-old Julia protested. "Especially William. Couldn't you let them come here? Please, Mamma—Dodie likes them, too, don't you, Dodie?"

"Yes," her younger sister echoed dutifully, looking up from the bread she was buttering. "Yes, I do."

"No," Henrietta said, her tone one to brook no argument. "They are not to come here. William is too rough for Alex—you know he is."

"Alex is a milksop," Julia accused.

"You have Abigail for company. What more do you want?"

Julia flushed. "But she's practically grown up, Mamma. Rachel is the same age as me."

Abigail decided that it was prudent to intervene. "I could go with Mr. Dawson," she offered. "I know the house, and I have met Mrs. Broome's children. *I* could look after them, Mrs. Dawson."

It was her chance, she thought, hugging the knowledge to her. Mr. Boskenna had gone alone to inspect a property two days' ride away, and his hateful wife was in Parramatta, keeping poor little Lucy with her. Mrs. Broome had said that she might stay at Long Wrekin, and when the soldiers released her, then . . .

"Certainly not," Henrietta Dawson said, dashing her hopes. "Your guardian entrusted you to my care, and I am quite sure he would not approve were I to permit you to leave this house, Abigail. *I* need you here. In any event the Broome children have their convict foreman's wife to look after them. She is perfectly capable of doing so and, indeed, the children are left in her care for most of the time when Mrs. Broome is working in the fields or breaking in horses."

"That is so, Abigail," Timothy confirmed, to Abigail's chagrin. "But Jenny Broome is one of the most skilled agriculturists in this colony and, I might add, a better horse breeder than I am." He smiled, but his blue eyes held an oddly hostile glint as he looked across the table at his wife. "Mrs. Dawson is, alas,

one of those who refuse to give our emancipist settlers any credit at all for what they have contributed
to our prosperity, despite my efforts to convince her
otherwise. Isn't that so, my dear?"

"I simply do not trust them," Henrietta answered
tartly. "Julia—Dorothea, be off with you now and
wash your hands, both of you! And then perhaps, if
Abigail will be so kind, you could continue with the
lessons she's been giving you. It's high time you
learned to read, Julia."

Abigail smothered a sigh, as her two reluctant pupils got up from the table, both small faces set in
sullen lines as they made for the door. It had been
the Reverend Boskenna's idea that she should teach
them; he had volunteered her services to Mrs. Dawson without consulting her, and, with no experience
in the role for which he had cast her, she had made
regrettably poor progress. Both little girls were pretty
and well mannered, but they were spoiled, and Julia
in particular was self-willed and inclined to rebel,
even against the mild discipline she had endeavored
to impose on them. And as for their baby brother
. . . Abigail repeated her sigh, but said politely, "Yes,
of course, Mrs. Dawson. I'll do my best."

To her relief, however, Mrs. Dawson rose and, with
her son in her arms, she, too, made for the door,
pausing when she reached it to remind her guest not
to linger. "The children get very restless if they're kept
waiting, Abigail, dear . . . so don't be too long, will
you?"

"Their mother is inclined to indulge them, Abigail," Timothy Dawson observed unexpectedly, as the
door finally closed, leaving them alone together. He
refilled his beaker and sipped at it moodily. "You are
anxious concerning Mrs. Broome, aren't you?"

"Yes," Abigail admitted. "I only met her once, but
I . . . I liked her very much, Mr. Dawson." She hesi-

tated, somewhat in awe of him, and then added, reddening a little as she made the confession, "I had a —a letter of introduction to her from a friend in England. I did not mention it to Mr. Boskenna because he—well, he and Mrs. Boskenna have the same attitude to emancipists and convicts as your wife has, and Mrs. Broome's friend warned me to—to be discreet."

"But you are telling me?" His smile was reassuring. "Oh, have no fear, I won't mention it to a soul, not even to my wife. But . . . why did you tell me, Abigail?"

"Because I felt sorry for Mrs. Broome, and when I heard she had been arrested, I . . . well, I wanted to help, if I could. And you made it evident that *you* were going to help her, even if Mrs. Dawson did not want you to. So I thought . . ." Abigail broke off, fearing that she had said too much.

Timothy Dawson's next words dispelled her fears. "I owe my life to Jenny Broome," he told her quietly. "And very largely my present prosperity. Emancipist or not, she is one of the finest, bravest women I have ever known, and I shall help her, whatever it may cost, you may be sure of that."

"Is she in serious trouble?" Abigail asked. "The charge against her . . . that is serious, is it not?"

"Serious enough," he conceded. "But Jenny should have little difficulty in disproving it. The officer who arrested her is an ignorant oaf, as I said—he should never have taken her in. I shall go to Long Wrekin Farm this morning and find out precisely what happened from the foreman, Tom Jardine. If Jenny is brought to trial, I shall go to Sydney and ask to be called as a character witness, but I don't imagine it will come to that. She has an exemplary record—they will probably release her as soon as the judge advocate has taken a statement from her."

"Will they?" Abigail's relief was in her eyes, and he patted her hand across the table.

"I should expect them to. After all, if armed and desperate men were to raid this house when only Henrietta and the children were here, the redcoats could scarcely arrest her if she yielded to their demands and gave them food and shelter. It's always happening—there are always escapers in this area, Abigail, who hold the settlers at gunpoint." Timothy set down his empty beaker, crammed the last of his meal into his mouth, and got to his feet. "Well, I'll be on my way. And don't worry—I'll take you over to see Jenny Broome myself when she returns."

"Oh, *would* you?" Abigail cried eagerly. "Thank you very much, Mr. Dawson. Then I shall be able to talk to her and tell her about the friend who gave me the letter of introduction to her. I met her, you see, I met Mrs. Pendeen, and she told me about the early days here. I was longing to tell Mrs. Broome about it, but I—"

"But you were at Mrs. Broome's home with the Reverend Caleb Boskenna?" Timothy finished for her. "And he prevented your talking to Mrs. Broome?"

"Yes." Abigail lowered her gaze, feeling oddly ashamed of her own cowardice and lack of enterprise. But Mr. Boskenna had never left her alone, never given her the chance to talk freely. Even here, in his presence, she could seldom talk freely, but now he was not here and . . . She looked up, to meet Timothy Dawson's searching gaze.

"You do not greatly care for Mr. Boskenna, do you, Abigail?" he suggested gently.

She shook her head and, recalling Lucy's words against the reverend during their sad passage, said bitterly, "No, I—I hate him."

"And he a man of God!" Timothy exclaimed, but

his tone was cynical. "Tell me—*is* he your legal guardian?"

"Yes, he is, Mr. Dawson. My father left a letter appointing him. He has full authority over my sister, Lucy, and myself, until we are twenty-one or married. The governor confirmed his authority, and . . ." Recalling their interview with the governor, she came suddenly close to tears.

Captain Bligh had given them all lunch at Rose Hill, the government residence in Parramatta, and his reception had been warm where Lucy and herself were concerned. Indeed, he had offered initially to accept responsibility for them both and had spoken kindly of their father, with whom he had expressed himself proud to have served at the battle of Copenhagen.

"Edmund Tempest was a brave man and a fine seaman," he had told them. "And he would undoubtedly have reached post rank had it not been for the severe wound he sustained during the battle. Everything that is in my power to do for his daughters, I will most gladly do."

But his words had been addressed to the Reverend Boskenna, and the missionary chaplain had brushed aside all offers or suggestions the governor had made, insisting that it was his *legal* right—as well as his Christian duty—to undertake responsibility for "the two poor orphans" Mr. Tempest had entrusted to him. Abigail's teeth closed fiercely about her lower lip as she remembered. Even when the governor had plainly shown his displeasure, Mr. Boskenna had not allowed himself to be intimidated or weakened in his resolve.

"The all-knowing God whom I serve has chosen me to undertake this task, Your Excellency," he had declared. "And trusting in His guidance, for which I nightly pray, I shall undertake it to the best of my ability."

"Well?" Timothy Dawson prompted, moving toward the door. "What is to be done, then?"

"I fear there is nothing, Mr. Dawson," she answered flatly. "Lucy and I are entitled to a grant of two thousand acres of land, which my father had arranged through the Colonial Office in London before we sailed. The governor promised that he would speed up the survey of the land and also that he would see to it that labor is made available to erect a dwelling house for us, and the necessary farm buildings, should Mr. Boskenna's choice fall on virgin land. But it has been left to him to choose the land and to claim it on our behalf. Lucy and I are . . . we are considered too young to decide for ourselves. And, of course, we are females." Abigail could not hide her bitterness and she added wretchedly, "If only our brother, Rick, could have come with us! But he is serving in the navy."

The only good that had resulted from their luncheon with Governor Bligh had been his announcement that Titus Penhaligon had been accepted for the government medical service, she reflected. At least Titus was a friend and he was staying in the colony. . . . But she had been able to do little for poor Kate Lamerton, who was housed in the female jail in Parramatta, a hateful place they called the Factory. All her pleas to be permitted to visit the midwife there had been sternly refused, and indeed Mr. Boskenna, she suspected, had only brought her with him when he made his inspection of the land in order to insure that she did not do so, in defiance of his instructions.

Lucy, poor child, would be too much in awe of Mrs. Boskenna even to think of it.

Timothy Dawson laid his two big, work-hardened hands on her shoulders. "Boskenna told me his intentions," he said, smiling down at her. "But he'll choose land in the Hawkesbury area, Abigail, and you know where I live. If you ever need a friend, come

back here—or go to Jenny Broome. The Reverend
Caleb Boskenna may be your legal guardian, but that
does not give him the right to act as your jailer.
And the land will be yours and your sister's, remember!" He opened the door for her, still smiling. "We'll
talk again, Abigail, but now—off you go and try to
plant some seeds of learning in my daughters' unwilling
heads! We will keep you here for as long as we can
—Lucy, too, if it can be arranged."

Abigail thanked him, and it was with a new lightness
in her step that she went in search of her pupils.

Major George Johnstone was enjoying a glass of
wine with half a dozen of his officers, prior to a mess
dinner, when Captain Macarthur was announced. It
was not a guest night, and when the new arrival entered
the anteroom with his son Edward at his heels, the
commandant eyed him with some surprise.

"John, my dear fellow!" He held out his hand.
"You are most welcome—and Edward, too. But to
what do we owe this honor of your presence, if I may
ask?" He signed to a mess servant and the man
hurried across with his tray. "We have a good claret,
brought in by the *Mysore,* or Cape brandy if you
prefer it. Be so good as to help yourself."

John Macarthur shook his head impatiently. Johnstone, he thought, had already sampled enough of
the *Mysore* claret to leave him befuddled, and it was
important that his mind should be clear—a mistake
or a misinterpretation of the suggestion he had come
to make would be, to say the least, embarrassing.

"I'm dining with Charley Grimes, George," he returned crisply, "and my dear Elizabeth awaits me
there, so I can't stay, but . . ." Looking about him,
he saw that the other officers had moved out of earshot, and he laid a hand on his son's arm. "Go and
join them, Ned—Johnny Brabyn might have something

useful to say concerning your prospects of obtaining an ensigncy in his old regiment when you return to England."

The boy nodded in understanding and obediently walked over to join the little knot of officers by the bar. He was a good boy, John Macarthur reflected proudly, distracted for a moment as he watched Edward go up at once to Lieutenant Brabyn, an engaging smile on his lips. He had his mother's looks and her ready charm, and by heaven, his manners spoke most eloquently of the English public school education he had enjoyed. The school had been costly enough, in all conscience, but it had been money well spent— and money he could afford now. Edward was preparing for a military career; his younger brother John, now at school, would in all likelihood read for the bar. Their two younger brothers, James and William, would in due course be given the same educational advantages. The girls would perforce have to stay here, but between their mother and the excellent governess, Miss Lucas, who had come out with him in the *Argo*, they would suffer no deprivation. And when the time came for them to marry . . . Macarthur frowned, realizing that Johnstone had said something he had not heard.

"Yes, what is it?" he demanded testily.

Major Johnstone turned bloodshot blue eyes on him, taken aback by his tone. "I only inquired," he answered mildly, "whether you had it in mind to apply to Watkin Tench to interest himself in young Edward's concerns—they've made him a general now, and Francis Grose, too, of course. Or there is my own patron, His Grace of Northumberland. I could give Edward a letter to His Grace when he leaves here."

"I'd take it most kindly if you would, George," Macarthur acknowledged, contriving a smile. "But he's not leaving yet—I need him at Camden, to assist

my nephew Hannibal with the Merino flock. No . . ."
His smile faded, as he subjected Johnstone to a critical
scrutiny. The Corps commandant clearly was not quite
sober and the matter he wanted to raise was a delicate
one, but there was no time to spare. The damned
trial opened in the morning and was expected to be
concluded by midday. He could not wait until George
Johnstone had recovered from his night's drinking.
And such an opportunity to humiliate the governor
might not present itself again or, at all events, not
for a long time.

He took Johnstone's arm and led him still farther
away from the other occupants of the anteroom.

"I wanted a confidential word with you," he said,
lowering his voice, "before attending Grimes's dinner
party. It concerns the trial tomorrow in the criminal
court."

"Oh?" Major Johnstone stared at him in some perplexity. "D'you mean the trial of those infernal Irish
rebels who tried to shoot the governor?"

John Macarthur inclined his dark head, his eyes
bright with malice. "That's what I mean. You are
presiding, are you not?"

"Yes, I am. But it's an open-and-shut case, John.
The seaman—unpleasant feller named McCann—has
turned King's evidence. He's identified the lot of them,
and his testimony alone will convict them . . . even
that damned fool Atkins thinks so! The woman—what's
her name—Broome may get off." Johnstone reached
for his glass, which the mess servant had refilled,
and sighed, making an effort to concentrate.

"Why?" Macarthur flung at him, tight lipped.

"Oh, she has an exemplary record. Widow of a
naval warrant officer with war service, who was
drowned saving lives during the Hawkesbury flood
last year. And our mutual—ah—friend, Captain Hawley, is interesting himself on her behalf. Dawson, too."

The commandant drained his glass and shrugged. "There's a lot of feeling among the settlers against Johnny Brabyn for bringing her in in the first place. But Bligh's orders were clear, John. *He* insisted that anyone found harboring the villains was to be charged with 'em—and with the same crime! Nothing I can do about it, is there?"

"On the contrary, my dear George, I believe there is." Macarthur was smiling again now but his eyes were cold. George Johnstone was listening, he told himself, he was taking it in, even if some perplexity remained. "There's something *most* effective you can do."

"What d'you mean, for God's sake?" Johnstone exploded. "Hang the woman, too? I doubt if even *Bounty* Bligh would stand for that, John. The men will hang, of course—they haven't a cat in hell's chance and—"

"Why hang them?" Macarthur put in smoothly.

"Because it's the law. And because—"

"The findings clearly must be according to the law," Macarthur admitted, continuing to smile, "but is not the *sentence* the prerogative of the court, to be decided upon by its members? And who are its members, George? You, as president; Fenn Kemp and Tom Laycock, I understand, and Jamieson—"

"No." Johnstone shook his head. "Bligh has dismissed Dr. Jamieson from the magistracy since the Gore case . . . had you forgotten? He signed a certificate to the effect that Mackay's woman was in childbed when, in actual fact, she was merely reluctant to give false evidence against Gore and—"

"Yes, yes, never mind all that now," Macarthur put in impatiently. A roar of laughter from the group of officers round the bar caused him to look apprehensively over his shoulder. "Damme, I hope those irresponsible fools aren't making Ned drunk!" But his glance at his son was reassuring; the boy had not joined in the ribald laughter, and he had no glass in his hand. It had been Brabyn who had provoked the merriment. He turned back to George Johnstone. "Who are the others sitting with you, George?"

"Moore, Lamson, and Minchin are nominated, John. And Brabyn's being called as a witness."

"Excellent," Macarthur approved. "Then I would suggest that you make the sentences fit the crime."

"What d'you mean, John? I confess I don't follow you."

"My dear fellow, it is extremely simple. These Irishmen endeavored unsuccessfully to rid us of the tyrant Bligh, did they not? A laudable endeavor which I, for one, would have been tempted to reward had it succeeded."

The Corps commandant was eyeing him with something approaching dismay, and John Macarthur gave vent to an amused laugh. "Is their failure in so admirable a cause to be punished with the full severity of the law, for heaven's sake? Oh, they'll have to be found guilty, I concede, but . . . must they hang for it? Surely six months' banishment to Coal River or the Derwent would suffice?"

Comprehension began slowly to dawn and a moment later Major Johnstone's expression relaxed.

"God's truth, John, that is a brilliant notion! Damme, I wish I'd thought of it myself! We show our contempt for the *Bounty* bastard by imposing derisory sentences on the men who tried to assassinate him . . . oh, that is capital, indeed it is!"

"And it is perfectly legal," Macarthur asserted. "Even Atkins and that swine Crossley will not be able to question it." Satisfied that the purpose of his visit had been achieved, he took out his gold hunter and affected to consult it. "Time marches on, my dear George, and my dear wife will have reason for com-

plaint if I keep her waiting any longer. Ned"—he
raised his voice—"we're going now."

The boy came instantly, a mute question in his
eyes. John Macarthur gave him an affectionate smile
and took his arm. "*Au revoir*, George—gentlemen.
Corporal Marlborough"—he addressed the mess servant by name—"kindly summon my carriage."

The man set down his tray of drinks and obeyed
with alacrity. Macarthur said, as he was about to step
into the smart equipage, "You can tell Sergeant Sutherland that there will be a few gallons of Jamaica rum
put aside in the St. Patrick tavern, Marlborough. To
you and your comrades, my lad, the price will be half
a sovereign the gallon, with my compliments."

"Thank you very much, Captain Macarthur, sir."
the mess corporal acknowledged. He drew himself
smartly to attention and stood, grinning widely, as the
coachman whipped up his horses and the carriage
bowled away.

For Jenny it was a heartbreaking experience to find
herself once more being treated as a malefactor. The
men had been heavily chained for the journey down the
harbor from Parramatta to Sydney; Lieutenant Brabyn
had spared her that humiliation, but, once delivered
into the custody of Head Jailer Reilly, she had been
permitted no distinction. Fortunately—since the last
batch of female prisoners had been transferred to the
Factory at Parramatta a few days earlier—the part
of the jail allocated for the women's accommodation
was not crowded, and Jenny was given a cell to herself. But the hateful fetters were hammered onto her
wrists and ankles; there was no light in her cell, and
the prison fare—bread and water at night and morning
and gruel at midday—was stale and unappetizing
and swiftly turned her stomach.

Apart from an official visit from the judge advocate's

clerk, to obtain her statement, she saw no one from outside until, on the afternoon of the day before the trial was to be held, Andrew Hawley made his appearance. He was ushered in obsequiously by Jailer Reilly, who scurried off unbidden to bring a stool and candles. Jenny sensed Andrew's anger and frustration although, until the man left them alone together, he held himself under iron control: tall and handsome in his uniform, despite the scar on his cheek and the graying hair at his temples. When they were alone, he dropped to his knees beside her, and, taking both her hands in his, he burst out wrathfully, "In heaven's name, Jenny, what do these trumped-up apologies for King's officers imagine they're doing, putting you in here like a common felon?"

"I'm charged with harboring the men who tried to ambush the governor," Jenny answered, a catch in her voice.

"My dearest love, I know that—damme, I know what they've charged you with! Reilly told me—and he told me they'd refused to grant you bail." Andrew controlled himself and added apologetically, "But I only found out about it today—I was at Coal River, taking the muster there, and I did not get back here until noon. Since then I've been trying to have you released, but to no avail. Surely Justin—"

"Justin is at sea," Jenny put in regretfully. She, too, had pinned some of her hopes on her elder son, but his sloop *Flinders* was engaged in the transfer of convicts from Norfolk Island to Van Diemen's Land and had not yet returned. She went on, answering Andrew's unspoken question, "There is no danger of my being convicted, so long as the Irishmen's leader tells the truth in court. And I believe he will. He's a seditionist, of course, and a member of the Defenders, but I don't think he is a bad man at heart or an untruthful one. When the soldiers came and found them in my house, he refused to admit anything; but they were armed, and they forced their way in. With the children there, I could not prevent them helping themselves to food. And one of them was mortally wounded—he died in the house, Andrew, and—"

Andrew's fingers tightened urgently about hers. "Tell me the whole story in detail, Jenny. I'm to see Governor Bligh in an hour's time in the hope of getting him to order that you be given bail, and if I know the facts, I can make out a better case."

Jenny told him, omitting nothing from her stark recital. "I had some sympathy for them," she confessed. "The poor boy who died was very brave . . . and only a year or two older than Justin. The leader, Joseph Fitzgerald, is an educated man—he said he used to be an attorney in Cork. He and another man, whom they called Christie, were in the Castle Hill rebellion, and they have endured savage punishment for that. Five hundred lashes, Andrew, and two years working in the lime pits at Coal River."

"That is bad enough," Andrew observed grimly. "I saw them when I was there, but even so, the damned fools tried to murder the governor and for that they will certainly hang . . . and rightly so, Jenny, my dear. The governor is the King's representative—even the Castle Hill rebels did not attempt to take Governor King's life, did they? They only took up arms against the Corps."

"They do not acknowledge our King," Jenny defended, but her voice held little conviction. Even so, the Irishmen's action had been anarchy. "I think they believe in their cause and that all of them are ready to die for it."

"That still makes them attempted assassins." Andrew got to his feet and started to pace up and down the narrow cell. "And one's turned King's evidence,

Reilly told me. It was he who led the troopers to Long Wrekin."

"Yes. A convict named McCann, Thomas McCann. He used to be a seaman, I believe."

Andrew halted his restless pacing to stare at her in angry surprise. "God's truth, *Mad* McCann! He was one of the Nore mutineers, Jenny, and the rogue was lucky not to be strung up for his part in that! And he is a rogue if ever I knew one . . . and not the kind to suffer martyrdom for any cause save his own. But I . . ." He came back to her side, his blue eyes deeply concerned, and once again he knelt in the soiled straw that covered the floor of the cell. "I'm going to see the governor to plead for your release, lass. You shouldn't ever come to trial, and by heaven, you'll not if I have owt to do with it!"

Jenny thanked him, feeling her control start to slip. There had been other offers of help and support—a note from Tim Dawson, promising to attend the trial and be called as a character witness, a similar offer from the building superintendent, Tom Macrae. Frances Spence and her husband were at sea, not yet returned from a trading voyage to Calcutta; so they, like Justin, were not even aware of what was happening; but Rob Webb had offered, and Justin's mentor, old Tom Moore the shipwright . . . She forced herself to speak calmly.

"It's good of you, Andrew, and I'm grateful, truly I am. But it's too late, the trial is tomorrow. And they will not convict me—they cannot if—"

"They could not if you were my wife, Jenny," Andrew said. "No, wait before you say yea or nay . . . dear lass, you know it's what I've wanted ever since I found you again. When Justin brought me to your home at Long Wrekin last Christmas, I wanted to ask you then, God knows I did! But I knew Johnny

Broome, I knew the man you'd lost, and I'd an idea of what losing him meant to you. I . . ." His scarred face was brick red, and he avoided her gaze. "Jenny, I was anxious not to intrude on your grief. I was content to wait, to bide my time, like, until you'd had the chance to get over it. And I'll still wait if you want me to. But let me tell the governor that we're to be wed, will you, love? I'm on his staff and an officer in the Royal Corps of Marines, not a poor acting corporal, like I was when I first asked you to wed me, years ago. I'm in a position to protect you now, and, as God's my witness, Jenny lass, I want to protect you just as much as I want you for my wife."

Deeply moved, Jenny could not restrain her tears. Old emotions flooded over her, with the memories that flashed into her mind of the love she had once felt for him, and the heartbreak she had endured when Governor Phillip had parted them. It had been a long time, she thought, half a lifetime, in fact, since Andrew had first courted her on the deck of the transport *Charlotte*. And it was longer still since she had crossed London Bridge—going south, away from Billingsgate, in error—riding on his shoulders, an innocent child from the country, who had laughed with delight when he had promised to wed her when she was a woman grown. Yet he had kept faith with her, through all the long years of their separation; he had written her letters, and he had followed her here. And . . . had he not been a man Johnny was proud to call his friend? She put out a hand to touch his bent head, and Andrew grasped it in both his own and carried it to his lips.

"Think on it, lass," he begged her.

"I . . . oh, Andrew, I will, I give you my word," she assured him. "But I would not wed you just for—for protection or because I'm in trouble. And there are the children, too."

Justin, she knew, would give wholehearted approval to the match; he thought the world of Andrew Hawley and was on warm friendly terms with him. But William—admittedly jealous of his elder brother and inclined to hold an opposite opinion to anything Justin might advocate—William had taken a sullen dislike to her new suitor and had influenced Rachel against him. There was another reason, of course. . . . Jenny blinked away her tears. William and Rachel did not want to leave Long Wrekin and, come to that, neither did she. For all the drain on her slender financial resources and the backbreaking work her farm entailed, she loved the place.

She could not relinquish her homestead, the fulfillment of her dream; it had been her reason for living, the very root of her existence and the means of her transition from convicted felon to free and independent settler, on land that was her own, land her sons would inherit. As if he had read her thoughts, Andrew got to his feet and drew her up beside him, his hands resting lightly on her shoulders.

"I'm of farming stock, the same as you are, Jenny," he reminded her. "And if you'll wed me, lass, I'll resign my commission and take to farming alongside you. As for the children, why, if circumstances had been different, we should have married twenty years ago and they would have been mine, not Johnny Broome's. As things stand, I'd be the best father I could to all three of them, you need have no fear on that score."

And she need not, Jenny thought. Andrew Hawley was a man and would be a husband she could trust and, in the fullness of time, come to love . . . as in her still-remembered childhood she had loved him. And Johnny would not begrudge her this second chance of happiness. There could, surely, be no betrayal of Johnny's memory if she were to accept Andrew's proposal now and entrust to him Long Wrekin's future, together with her own? If this were what he wanted, then could not her old love be revived, born again, as passionate and eager as it had been on board the *Charlotte*? Surely it could. . . . Her heart quickened its beat as he took her into his embrace and she felt the stirrings of desire.

"Well, Jenny love?" he held her close to him, his lips in her hair. "What is it to be? Will you wed me or no?"

"I will wed you, Andrew," Jenny promised. "When the court frees me, I . . . I'll be honored to wed you."

"Then I shall tell the governor," Andrew said. He kissed her, with lingering tenderness. "I'll quit his service, and we will make Long Wrekin as fine a holding as any in the colony. It shall equal Dawson's and maybe even rival Macarthur's one of these days. Ah, Jenny, my dearest love, you've made me the happiest man on earth, and God bless you for it!" He lifted each of her manacled hands in turn. "And I'll have these infernal things off you, lass, whatever that rogue Reilly says."

He left her, shouting for Jailer Reilly to unlock the cell door, and when, five minutes later, the jailer returned to remove her fetters, Jenny felt her hopes revive.

CHAPTER VII

Mary Putland bent to kiss her husband's thin cheek,
observing with distress how hot and flushed it was.
She contrived an encouraging smile, however, before
tucking his bedclothes about him and following young
Surgeon Penhaligon from the sickroom.

"I will not be long, Charles, dear," she promised.
"Try to sleep if you can. I'll be within call."

Titus Penhaligon closed the door softly behind him.
He was a pleasant, courteous young man, Mary reflected, and was acting temporarily as Dr. Redfern's
assistant until he should be given a permanent posting. Dr. Redfern—himself unable to suggest what more
could be done for her poor husband—had sent the
new arrival to examine his patient. Clearly, he had
done so in the hope that, being more recently out of
medical school, Dr. Penhaligon might be able to offer some alternative to the constant purging and bleeding which, it seemed, was the prescribed treatment for
poor Charles's disease.

One of the attentive Government House servants
had set a tray of tea in her sitting room, and Mary
motioned the young surgeon to a chair. Seating her-

self behind the teapot, she poured out for both of them and then asked, unable to hide her anxiety, "Dr. Penhaligon, what is your opinion—your considered opinion—of Mr. Putland's condition?"

It was a concerned, straightforward question, and, sensing that the governor's daughter would expect him to answer it truthfully, Titus Penhaligon did not attempt to evade the issue.

"Your husband is very gravely ill, Mrs. Putland." He saw her eyes close for an instant, as if she were recoiling from a blow; then she opened them again to subject him to an earnest scrutiny, her blue eyes very bright. "*Can* anything more be done for him, Doctor?"

Her pain was a living entity, reaching out to enfold them both, and reluctantly Titus Penhaligon shook his head. "I would counsel you to permit him to be bled no more, ma'am. He is too weak to stand it. And in my view, opiates will ease him more than purges."

"Yes," she agreed, clearly relieved by this advice, for all the defeat it implied. "He scarcely eats enough to keep a sparrow alive, you know."

"Then give him wine—red wine, and brandy whenever you can persuade him to take it. Fruit, of course . . . and sometimes a glass of raw meat juice." He outlined a diet and again Mary Putland looked relieved. She also looked exhausted, Titus's professional eye told him, exhausted to the point of collapse, and he asked diffidently, "Do you nurse Mr. Putland yourself, ma'am?"

"Oh, yes. It is what he wants and the least I can do. I am his wife." She smiled faintly. "I have help when I need it from His Excellency's female servants. They are convicts, of course, but of the better type."

"Would you consider employing an experienced and most reliable nurse?" Titus questioned. "Also a convict, but a woman of excellent morals, Mrs. Putland, whom I could recommend to you without reservation." He saw her swift frown and added quickly, "You owe it to yourself and to His Excellency your father to take some respite from the cares of the sickroom. It will help no one, least of all poor Mr. Putland, if you, too, become ill from overexertion."

"No," Mary conceded. It had long weighed on her conscience that, with so much of her time taken up by her sickroom duties, she was able to spend very little with her father. And he needed her, needed her company and her support more now, perhaps, than ever before, for the attempt on his life by the Irish seditionists had shocked him greatly. She held out her hand for the young surgeon's empty cup, but he shook his head.

"I thank you but no, ma'am."

Mary refilled her own cup, scarcely aware of what she was doing. "This nurse," she pursued. "Tell me about her, if you please, Doctor."

"Her name is Kate Lamerton," he answered readily. "Sentenced to seven years for theft, and a midwife as well as a sick nurse. She comes from Falmouth, as I do myself. Her age is between thirty-five and forty, I should judge. She came out here on board the *Mysore,* and I confess, Mrs. Putland, that the healthy state in which we landed the convicts we carried was as much to Kate Lamerton's credit as to mine. More, perhaps . . . I was fresh from walking the wards, but she has had a lifetime's experience of caring for the sick."

"But she was guilty of a felony, Doctor, was she not?"

Titus Penhaligon shrugged. "The court found her guilty, ma'am," he admitted, and hesitated, reddening a little. "Miss Abigail Tempest, one of the two young ladies orphaned by their father's death during the voyage, also has reason to be grateful to her and would,

I feel sure, endorse my recommendation. You have made her acquaintance, I believe?"

Mary Putland was silent for a moment, sipping her tea. The two poor girls, whose father had shot himself, she recalled. The news had upset her own father a good deal, for the late Mr. Tempest had been a naval officer, who had served with him at Copenhagen. She shook her head. "No, Dr. Penhaligon, but I have heard about both girls from Captain Bligh. The only other—" Her mouth tightened. "The only other *person* from your ship whom I have met is the Reverend Boskenna. He called here, soon after the *Mysore* docked, for the purpose, or so I understood it, of informing my father that he had been appointed guardian to the two Tempest girls."

Her voice was flat, but she did not disguise the fact that the overbearing Caleb Boskenna had not impressed her favorably. "My father was in Parramatta, on government business, so that *I* received him, Dr. Penhaligon. I should have liked to make Miss Tempest's acquaintance . . . indeed, I blame myself because I have not done so, but Mr. Boskenna did not bring her with him when he called. And with my poor husband's illness, I . . ." Mary's voice shook, but she controlled herself quickly. "This nurse, Kate Lamerton, would be of great assistance to me. Where is she now—in Sydney?"

"No, ma'am," Titus apologized. "She was sent to what I understand is a factory where women convicts are employed in weaving and the like. It is at Parramatta, I believe."

"*That* terrible place!" Mary Putland exclaimed, and the young surgeon looked at her in surprise, puzzled by her vehemence. But again she controlled herself and went on quietly, "I will arrange for her to be sent here, so that I may interview her. If I do not think she will suit me, I will see to it that she is given more congenial employment than the Factory can provide—at the hospital or Mrs. King's orphanage. A skilled nurse is wasted in the weaving shop, and besides, it is a place intended for the more recalcitrant convicts or those of doubtful virtue. I am astonished that the poor woman was ever transferred there if she is the paragon you evidently believe her to be."

"It was on the orders of one of the garrison officers," Titus supplied. He hesitated, wondering whether he dare say more, and his honest indignation finally overcame his doubts. Mrs. Putland was sympathetic, and poor Kate had been treated abominably. He drew in his breath sharply. "Captain Kemp, ma'am, who deemed that she had been insolent to him. He and some of his brother officers came aboard the *Mysore* shortly after she dropped anchor in the cove and—er—an altercation ensued. During the course of this, the—er—the officer in question, Captain Kemp, put me under arrest and—"

"That unpleasant man!" Mary Putland exclaimed. "The pawnbroker!"

She had seen the boatloads of Corps officers going out to board each newly arrived convict transport and was no longer under any illusion as to the purpose for which they went. No comely convict girl was safe from them; under the guise of employing them as household servants, the officers demanded first choice, their noncommissioned officers followed them, and . . . Mary stifled a sigh. Her father disapproved most strongly of the practice and had made his disapproval known, but the Corps defied him, as they defied him in so many other matters, and for all he was governor and the King's representative in the colony, he had been powerless to put an end to the privilege they claimed.

Dr. Penhaligon was talking on, endeavoring to tell her of the happenings on board the *Mysore,* but she scarcely heard him, having no difficulty in visualizing the ugly scene. And of course Captain Kemp had been the instigator of the trouble; he was a man she particularly despised—a heavy drinker and a womanizer, and as she had let slip a few moments ago, it was said that he had been in business as a pawnbroker before buying himself a commission in the New South Wales Corps. Like the rest of the so-called "gentlemen by purchase," Captain Anthony Fenn Kemp had come to Sydney with the object of enriching himself, and this, according to her father, they had all contrived to do years before he himself had taken office as governor.

A faint cry from the sickroom banished all other thoughts from her head. Mary rose at once.

"My husband," she said, cutting Titus Penhaligon abruptly short. "I must go to him, I . . . poor soul, I wish that he could sleep." She held out her hand, and Titus bowed over it, murmuring his thanks for the manner in which she had received him.

"The laudanum I administered to him will help, Mrs. Putland," he assured her.

"And the nurse, too, perhaps," she suggested. "I will not forget your Mrs. Lamerton, Doctor." She looked up at him, a worried frown puckering her smooth dark brows, and asked in a whisper, "How long do you think my husband can endure?"

Titus stiffened, unprepared for the question yet sensing, once again, that she would not be put off by any evasions he might attempt.

"It is difficult to be exact, ma'am," he stammered, "but . . . perhaps a month, six weeks even. He has lost so much weight and he has little resistance—any sudden strain or shock could cause a serious setback, as I'm sure you will realize. I will do all I can for him, but—"

"But no more than Dr. Redfern," Mary put in. "I

understand. Thank you, Dr. Penhaligon. You have been very honest, and, believe me, I appreciate your candor and your advice, which I shall follow."

Nevertheless, it would be no easy task, she thought, as she hastened back to the sickroom. The now-disgraced Dr. Jamieson, who had first prescribed opiates and applied the leeches, had failed to halt the awful progress of poor Charles's illness, and Dr. Redfern's purging had, it seemed to her, only hastened his physical deterioration . . . and this in the space of little more than a year. Yet, when they had come out here with her father, their hopes had been high. Charles had suffered an occasional hemorrhage, but he had done his watch-keeping duties on board the *Porpoise* and served as squadron gunnery officer, and everyone—including her father—had said that the warmth and sunshine of New South Wales would restore him fully to health.

Instead, it was killing him. Mary felt tears come to ache in her throat. She paused in the doorway to compose herself, and then, pouring a glass of wine from the carafe Dr. Penhaligon had ordered for him, she carried it over to the bedside. Holding it up so that her husband could see it, she said with well-simulated optimism, "Charles, dearest, this will do you good. If I help you to sit up, do you think you could drink it?"

Charles Putland eyed her somberly but nodded.

"I'll drink the whole carafe, if you wish," he offered. The handkerchief he had been holding to his mouth was bloodstained, and he thrust it out of sight, letting her plump up his pillows before putting the wineglass into his hand. He sipped the contents appreciatively. "This is infinitely preferable to Willie Redfern's disgusting purgatives. You can tell him that, in future, I want to be treated by his assistant."

"Dr. Penhaligon is a most affable young man,"

Mary agreed, "and he has told me of a skilled nurse for you—a woman who came out with him in the *Mysore* and whom he recommends very highly. You would not mind if I engaged her to help me, would you?"

But he had not heard her. The glass slipped from his nerveless fingers and fell to the floor, and his eyes, she saw, were glazed and dull, the pupils widely distended.

"I'll sleep now, Mary," he whispered, "but stay with me, will you please?"

"Yes, dearest, of course I'll stay," she promised numbly, and had to fight back her tears as his hand moved blindly about the coverlet, searching for hers. She held it tightly and was rewarded by Charles's mumbled, "God bless you, my dearest love."

She would wait until he fell asleep, she decided, as she had waited so often in the past. The game of chess and dinner with her father would also have to be delayed, but Captain Hawley had returned from Coal River and would bear her father company until she herself could do so. He was a recent convert to the game of chess and played it hesitantly; he could not offer the challenge that she was usually able to mount, but . . . She smiled faintly. Her father had been very tense and irritable of late, his formidable temper all too easily provoked. Perhaps a victory over the chessboard would prove beneficial in more ways than one.

It was dark when Charles finally fell into a deep sleep, his hand relinquishing its limp grasp of hers, and Mary rose a trifle stiffly to her feet. She washed and changed in her own room and descended to the ground floor in search of her father, only to be informed by the young secretary, Edmund Griffin, that the governor was still in his office and had not yet ordered dinner.

"He has been talking with Captain Hawley for over an hour, Mrs. Putland," Griffin volunteered. "And I fear"—his tone was apprehensive—"that all is not well between them. His Excellency seemed more than a little put out. I do not know for what reason, but—"

"Order dinner, Edmund," Mary suggested. "Tell them to serve it at once, if you please . . . and to set a place for Captain Hawley. I'm sure that any differences which may have arisen can quite easily be settled over a meal, and I shall do my best to smoothe them over. In fact, I—"

"Captain Hawley has left, Mrs. Putland," the secretary put in apologetically. "About ten minutes ago."

"Has he? Well, it cannot be helped, I suppose." Mary sighed, conscious of an overwhelming weariness. A difficult evening was in prospect, she thought, with her father having to be placated and coaxed into forgetting whatever had been the cause of his difference with Andrew Hawley . . . and when she had been hoping to share the burden of her own anxiety with him.

Dr. Penhaligon's verdict had not, of course, been unexpected—she had known in her heart that poor Charles was nearing the end of his suffering. But that it should be so soon, a matter perhaps of weeks, not months, had come as a shock to her. They had been making plans for Christmas celebrations; a party for the children of Mrs. King's orphanage and a visit, if Charles felt up to traveling the short distance by boat, to Rose Hill House, in Parramatta, to give him a change of scene. But now . . . She drew herself up, lower lip trembling despite her determination to keep her emotions sternly in check. To Edmund Griffin she said tonelessly, "Be so good as to tell my father that I will wait for him in the dining room. And leave us alone, would you, Edmund? If anything is troubling him, I imagine he will tell me what it is. Perhaps Captain Hawley's report of conditions at Coal River have given him cause for annoyance."

But her father's arrival in the dining room, ten minutes later, warned her that the matter was more serious than she had anticipated. William Bligh's face was pale with anger, his mouth tightly compressed, and his language—although, as always, he tempered it in her presence—sufficiently vehement to arouse Mary's alarm.

"Disloyalty, damme!" he exclaimed bitterly. "That is rife throughout this whole infernal colony! It's what I expect from the blasted Rum Corps, and they seldom fail to display their animosity toward me. But when it comes from one of my most trusted officers, a member of my own staff—plague take it, Mary, is it any wonder that I despair?"

"But, surely, Papa, you do not mean that Captain Hawley is disloyal?" Mary protested.

"Yes, devil take him, I do!" Her father pushed his plate away from him impatiently and shook his head to her offer of wine. "No, no—order me tea."

"It is here, Papa, dear." She poured him a cup and set it in front of him and then, pausing beside his chair, let both hands rest gently on his broad, blue-uniformed shoulders. "Try to eat something, will you not? This is pork, and I instructed the cook to prepare it in what you always said was Otaheite fashion —with sweet potatoes and grapes, since there weren't any pineapples . . . and he has tried very hard. He is a good man, Papa, and most anxious to please you. Taste it, at least."

He humored her, digging an exploratory fork into the savory mess and, to Mary's relief, consented to eat a little of what she had piled on his plate. But whatever Andrew Hawley had done clearly still rankled, for he returned to the subject—though less wrathfully—when their second course had been served and the steward had withdrawn.

"The infernal fellow wants to throw in his commission and resign from the government service, Mary," he complained. "Now—at a time when he's one of the few I can depend on to do his duty and support me against the plaguey rum traffickers. Damme, daughter, Hawley's been my right hand . . . as he was when the blackguards of seamen mutinied at the Nore and refused to put to sea! I trusted him with my life, and he did not fail me."

"Then surely," Mary suggested mildly, "he must have a most pressing reason, Papa?"

"Dammit, of course he has! Or one he considers more important than the loyalty he owes me . . . he says he wants to marry and become a settler."

"Is that so unreasonable a wish?" Mary asked, with sad sincerity, thinking of her own marriage . . . now so tragically soon to be ended.

"Yes, by heaven it is, Mary—when the woman Hawley proposes to marry is in jail, awaiting trial on a capital charge!" her father assured her indignantly. "She's charged with harboring those miserable scum of Irish rebels who attempted to assassinate me, if you please!"

If his intention had been to shock her, he had succeeded. Mary stared at him, bereft of words, and he went on forcefully, "Furthermore, she is an emancipated convict, the widow of an escaper—one of that crew of villains Edwards of the *Pandora* brought back from Timor in ninety-two, with Heywood and the other mutineers from my ship. The gutter press in England made heroes of them, and they were all pardoned. Pardoned by the King!" William Bligh snorted his disgust. "This particular fellow's name was Broome, I understand, although he was using some other name

when he was serving his time here as a convicted
felon. Butcher, I think it was. I recall reading a gar-
bled account of his exploits in the *Chronicle,* in which
some damned know-all pen pusher had the effrontery
to claim that, as a feat of navigation, damme, Broome's
voyage from here to Timor excelled mine . . . because our boats were the same size and his course
was uncharted and because he had a woman and children on board! *That* woman, probably—the one Hawley's prepared to throw up his career for! Besides,
I—"

"But, Papa dear . . ." Mary cut him short, conscious of his increasing ire and anxious to avoid an
outburst. "Mr. Broome redeemed himself—Governor
King told Charles about him. It seems he served with
distinction in the navy after he was pardoned, and
that he became Captain Flinders's sailing master,
when he conducted his coastal survey in the *Investi-
gator.* Charles was only talking about it the other day."

She did not go on, although Charles had also told
her that the late John Broome had lost his life in the
Hawkesbury floods of the previous year whilst engaged
in a courageous rescue attempt. Her father remained
obstinately unimpressed.

"Well, it would seem that he, too, made an unfortunate choice of a wife," he observed dryly. "Hawley
tried to convince me that he has known this woman
since childhood and that she is quite incapable of villainy."

"Then perhaps she is," Mary felt impelled to reply.
She had always liked the quiet, reliable Andrew Hawley, and despite having no knowledge of his prospective bride, she found it hard to believe that he would
lie concerning her virtues or, come to that, endeavor
to conceal any lack of them. "The Irish rebels were
armed, were they not?" she reasoned. "If they forced
their way into Mrs. Broome's house and demanded

food and shelter, how could she resist them? She surely committed no crime that I, for instance, would not have committed in those circumstances, Papa."

He shrugged. "That is Hawley's contention, my dear child."

"Well, can you not believe it? Can you not take Captain Hawley's word for it?"

"It conflicts with the testimony of the arresting officer, Mary. In any event the woman will go on trial tomorrow—she will be given the opportunity to prove her innocence then."

"But you said she was facing a capital charge, did you not?" Mary persisted. "Does that mean that the poor soul will be on trial for her life?"

"Technically it does," her father conceded. "The Irishmen will hang, of course—their guilt is beyond dispute. And an example has to be made of them, in order to make it clear throughout this colony that attempts on the life of His Majesty's appointed governor cannot be made with impunity. But the woman will be shown mercy even if the court finds against her. I do not approve of hanging women, and I shall intervene on her behalf if necessary, so don't concern yourself on that score, my dear."

"What sentence will she receive, if she *is* found guilty, Papa?"

"Oh . . ." he frowned. "Banishment to Van Diemen's Land, probably. Hawley, damn his stubbornness, is determined to wed her, whatever the outcome of the trial! As determined as he is to quit the service and sweat his life away as a settler."

Mary sighed. "Could you not persuade him otherwise?"

"God's truth!" the governor exclaimed, exasperated. "Do you imagine I did not try? He has agreed to think the matter over, but he knows perfectly well that if the Broome woman is convicted, he'll have to resign his commission if he marries her. I could not retain him as a member of my staff in the circumstances, however badly I need him. And I *do* need him, devil take it!"

"But not so badly," Mary questioned, anxiously searching his face, "not so badly that you would use your powers as governor to order the charges against Mrs. Broome to be quashed?"

She was oddly relieved, although not entirely surprised, when her father shook his head emphatically.

"Even Hawley did not ask that of me, Mary," he reproached her.

"But you have the power, do you not?"

"Yes," he confirmed. "And the duty to review her case and the evidence against her, after the court has heard it. If I deem it justified, I can reduce or remit whatever sentence they have imposed, or even pardon her." His hand reached out to cover hers—"try to understand, Mary my dear. Men like Macarthur and Johnstone and the unspeakable Kemp have shown no compunction in twisting the laws of this colony to their personal advantage and for their own profit. But if I am to command respect as governor, and, indeed, if I am to govern, *I* cannot do so . . . and damme, daughter, I never will!"

Mary's eyes filled suddenly with tears.

"Dearest Papa," she whispered, in a choked voice. "I do understand and you are right, I know. I was sorry about Captain Hawley, that was why I spoke as I did. I . . . oh, let us hope that Mrs. Broome is innocent and that she is able to prove she is!"

"Amen to that, child," her father echoed. His expression relaxed into a smile of singular warmth and affection. "If your husband is sleeping, shall we indulge in a game of chess?"

Mary rose at once. "I will just look in to make sure that Charles is asleep, and then I should like a game very much, Papa." She hesitated for a moment, and then, crossing to his side, she kissed his smooth, freshly shaven cheek. "I truly think," she told him, "that I admire you more than anyone else in the world, Captain Bligh. And I am very proud to be your daughter!"

The six scarlet-uniformed officers composing the court of criminal jurisdiction filed into their seats, and in response to the usher's stentorian "All stand for His Majesty's justices of the peace!" the prisoners rose, with varying degrees of reluctance, to their feet. Joseph Fitzgerald, who was heavily chained, was the last to do so, aided none too gently by a constable, whose jerk on his leg irons was calculated to discourage any lack of respect he might be tempted to display.

Jenny, wearing only wrist fetters, rested her arms on the edge of the dock and looked uneasily across at the faces of her judges. She had no difficulty in recognizing them, and her gaze went first to Major Johnstone. Inclining now to corpulence, the acting commandant of the New South Wales Corps held himself with stiff military precision, as he unbuckled his sword belt and eased himself into the president's chair, after exchanging a coldly formal bow with Mr. Atkins, the judge advocate.

Captain Kemp was seated next to him; he made some demand of the clerk and swore audibly when it was not immediately answered, but then the usher supplied him with pen and ink, and he lapsed into smoldering silence, the quill grasped like a weapon in his right hand. The Corps quartermaster, Lieutenant Laycock, took the seat to the commandant's left, and to Jenny's surprise, he raised a hand in her direction and smiled . . . seemingly in reassurance.

She knew him better than she knew any of the others because in the past he had bought horses from her

and sought her advice when breaking them to the
saddle. Gratefully she acknowledged his smile before
subsiding onto the hard wooden bench which ran the
length of the dock. It was a relief to know that at
least one of her judges was well disposed toward her,
she reflected, since the adjutant, Lieutenant Minchin, and his friend, Lieutenant Moore—known to her
only by sight—both enjoyed a reputation for severity
on the bench.

The sixth officer was evidently a fairly recent arrival in the colony, for he was a stranger to her—a
coarse-featured, stockily built man of about twenty-
five or thirty, whose curiously light eyes contrasted
oddly with his darkly tanned skin and heavy black
mustache and side-whiskers. His name, she learned
when the clerk announced it, was Lieutenant Desmond
Aloysius O'Shea . . . an unmistakably Irish name,
and she saw Joseph Fitzgerald frown as he heard it.
But he held his peace, and, the initial formalities duly
completed, the prisoners were again ordered to stand
and the judge advocate shambled awkwardly to his
feet, a sheaf of papers clutched to his chest.

After consulting these, he read the charges. They were
addressed to all of them, including herself, Jenny realized, and couched in such a maze of longwinded legal
terms and phrases that she listened in unhappy bewilderment, unable to make out whether she, too, was
being charged with sedition and conspiracy, in addition to the expected charge of harboring and giving
comfort to those whom the judge advocate described
as "the King's enemies."

She caught the words "traitorous assembly" and
"rebellious opposition to the peace and tranquility of
the colony" and then, with a sinking heart, heard the
accusation that this had been "with the intent to overthrow His Majesty's Government and bring about the

death of His Majesty's governor and captain general, to wit Captain William Bligh, of the Royal Navy." In desperation she ventured to voice a protest against her inclusion, but Judge Advocate Atkins turned her interruption sternly aside.

"You will be permitted individually to make answer to the charges. Kindly remain silent until they are read to the court."

His rebuke frightened her, but Christie, who was standing beside her, put out a manacled hand to touch hers, and Jenny's heart went out to him in gratitude. The witnesses—who included Andrew and Tim Dawson and Tom Macrae—were not in court, but this, she knew, was British legal custom, which permitted their presence only when they were called to give their evidence. And Andrew, bless his kind heart, had been on hand to wish her well when, with their escort of constables, she and the Irish prisoners had halted outside the courthouse to have the connecting chains removed from their leg irons. Jenny drew in her breath sharply, as she heard the judge advocate say, "Joseph Michael Fitzgerald, you have heard the charges brought against you—how do you plead?"

The Irishmen's leader drew himself up to his full, impressive height. He replied courteously enough, but with a distinct edge to his voice, "I have to inform you, sir, that as Irish citizens none of us here present recognize the King of England or the authority of this court. We cannot therefore make any plea."

Mr. Atkins mopped his brow. He was, however, less disconcerted by Fitzgerald's reply than Jenny had expected . . . until she realized that he must have heard it many times before from others of a like persuasion and, indeed, had probably anticipated it, for he returned coldly, "You would be well advised to plead, Fitzgerald. If you do not, your trial will proceed and the assumption be drawn that you are guilty as charged. I say again—you have heard the charges. Do you plead guilty or not guilty to them?"

"And *I* say again, sir," Joseph Fitzgerald repeated defiantly, "this court has no jurisdiction over Irish citizens. I crave your indulgence, sir," he added, addressing Major Johnstone, "to enable me to explain why it is so."

The Corps commandant's reaction was slow; before he could utter the expected refusal, Fitzgerald had launched into a passionate denunciation of the suppression of freedom in his native Ireland.

"The King of England, sir, through his viceroy, seeks to hold Ireland in thrall by means of punitive laws, tyranically administered by alien soldiers and a Protestant militia. Those who, like myself, are of the Catholic faith, are mercilessly persecuted. They are deprived of their civil rights . . . no Catholic may sit in the Irish Parliament or hold a commission in the army or as a magistrate. Our peasants starve, sir, our patriots are massacred by the military garrison or hanged by the judiciary. If, as in my own case, they raise their voices in protest, they are accused of sedition and sent into exile here. And here, sir, as you must be aware, I and those who today stand charged with me have been flogged and banished to hard labor in the Coal River settlement or on Norfolk Island."

He talked on, his voice vibrant with the depth of his feelings, his arguments convincing, even to the most biased of his listeners and—seeming as if he did not hear them—he resisted all Major Johnstone's efforts to silence him.

"Ireland has been singular in suffering and in cowardice. . . . She could crush her tormentors and yet they embowel her. She could be free, yet she is enslaved! But now we are united in her cause, we no longer shrink from opposing an unlawful tyranny of a King we do not acknowledge or a governor who has no right to oppress or imprison freeborn Irishmen! We are pledged to fight by every means in our power until we have procured for Ireland her rights and her freedom. The lands which royal villainy wrested from us must be restored, and——"

Major Johnstone made himself heard at last.

"Be silent, man!" he thundered. "I will hear no more treasonable rantings from you, by God I will not! Make answer to the charges against you and sit down or I will have you gagged!"

Fitzgerald did not flinch; neither did he obey the commandant's angry order. "*You* are here, sir," he accused, with icy contempt, "to order our execution, whatever we may plead. So make a plea that suits you, so that our deaths may bear the appearance of legality—though I vow that will not erase them from your conscience."

"There are witnesses to your guilt," the judge advocate reminded him heatedly.

"I concede there are," Fitzgerald acknowledged, unabashed. "And the chief of them a creature whom you have suborned to turn King's evidence, that he may save his own skin!"

Beside her, Jenny felt big Christie O'Hagan start to tremble, but a glance at his set face and the bright anger in his blue eyes told her that he trembled from exultation rather than from fear. He flashed a smile at Joseph Fitzgerald, and she heard him say under his breath, "Bravely spoken, Joe! And 'tis the truth, so it is, every last word o' it."

Major Johnstone murmured something which was inaudible, save to those on either side of him, and then Captain Kemp said irritably, "Are we to be here all day, sir, whilst these insolent blackguards argue as to how and to whom they will plead? Gag this mendacious fellow and take his plea as guilty, for the Lord's sake!"

The judge advocate, who was perspiring profusely, opened his mouth to speak, but Major Johnstone roused himself and waved him imperiously to silence.

"Fitzgerald, do you deny that you and the men charged with you set an ambush for Captain Bligh, on the road between Toongabbie and the property known as Upwey Farm, where His Excellency was to attend morning service?"

The commandant's tone was placatory, even encouraging, and, clearly taken by surprise, Joseph Fitzgerald stared at him, frowning and, for the first time, unsure of himself.

"Come now, my good fellow," Johnstone urged. "After all the brave words you have addressed to this court, let us have the truth. Were you not seeking to strike a blow for the cause you espouse . . . a blow for Irish freedom?"

The Irishman's frown deepened. "I will admit we were, sir, yes, but we—"

"And what did you expect to achieve by your action?"

"Achieve, sir? I fear I do not follow you."

Major Johnstone heaved an audible sigh. "You spoke of tyranny and the oppression you claim to have suffered here. Was the purpose of your armed attack on the governor an attempt to end that tyranny?"

Once again Jenny was aware of Joseph Fitzgerald's hesitation. He glanced at Christie and, from him, to the three on the other side of him. Then, as if all four men had given him their mute consent, he inclined his head. Turning to face his questioner, he answered in ringing tones, "Our purpose was to rid this colony of the foremost of its tyrants!"

"You mean, do you not, that by taking the life of Governor Bligh you would be achieving your purpose?" Johnstone persisted. When Joseph Fitzgerald did not at once reply, he continued his probing interrogation. He was leading the Irishman, Jenny thought, in sudden alarm—deliberately inviting him to make the admission that it was personal animosity for Governor Bligh that had led him to plan the ambush. And Joseph Fitzgerald, for all his legal training and native intelligence, was falling into the trap which the New South Wales Corps commandant had set for him.

Twice the judge advocate endeavored to interrupt but was coldly ignored, and now the Irish lieutenant, O'Shea, at his commanding officer's instigation, joined in the questioning, citing examples of rebellious acts that had taken place in Ireland. In one of these Fitzgerald was compelled to admit having played a leading part, and—finally driven into a corner—he offered a plea of guilty to the charges on behalf of his associates as well as himself.

And this, clearly, was what Major Johnstone had been waiting for. The clerk of the court, who had been taking notes, signified that he had the prisoner's admissions written down in full, and the scarlet-uniformed president leaned back in his chair with a smile of satisfaction.

"You have the sworn and attested statements of the Crown witnesses, Mr. Judge Advocate, have you not?" he demanded. "In particular those given by the arresting officer, Lieutenant Brabyn, the sergeant in command of the governor's escort, and—ah—the rogue who has turned King's evidence . . . what's his name? Thomas McCann."

"Yes, sir, I have," Judge Advocate Atkins confirmed. "All are waiting to be called. And there are character witnesses who wish to make statements to the court, sir, on behalf of the prisoner Broome. They—"

To Jenny's dismay Major Johnstone cut him short. "There's no need to take up the court's time unnecessarily," he said, still smiling. "The prisoners have admitted their guilt, and it now only remains to sentence them. If you will be so good as to place the written statements before me, sir, we will consider them whilst we discuss what sentences are appropriate."

"This procedure is most irregular, Major Johnstone," Mr. Atkins warned. "I do not think that—"

Again he was interrupted. "I can see no irregularity in this procedure, sir. It's usual when those on trial enter a plea of guilty, is it not? However, if you are concerned by our failure to hear the character witnesses, then, by all means, let them offer written statements. We will consider them with the others. In any event, Mr. Atkins"—his smile widened—"the court is disposed to deal leniently in the case of the woman Broome, whose previous good character entitles her to the benefit of any doubt that may exist."

Jenny, straining her ears, heard his last words with heartfelt relief. Joseph Fitzgerald heard them, too; he started to speak but was silenced by the usher, calling loudly for the courtroom to be cleared. The constables prepared to separate the prisoners and lead them toward the cells, but Fitzgerald pleaded, "One moment, Constable, before you take us away." The constable shrugged good-naturedly, and the Irishman went on, his voice lowered, "Mrs. Broome, I did not intend to involve you in all this, believe me. Should it be necessary, I will inform the justices on oath that you are blameless. If"—his tone was wry—"if it is the last thing I do, and it may well be the last, I will see to it that you are cleared of all complicity."

Jenny thanked him without warmth. Had he inter-

vened when Lieutenant Brabyn had arrested her, she
might have been spared this ordeal and the humiliation
of her past week's imprisonment, she thought bitterly,
but he and the others were undoubtedly facing the death
sentence. Now was scarcely the moment to voice her
resentment. She laid her manacled hands lightly on his.

"I am sorry for you—for all of you—that it must end
like this, Mr. Fitzgerald," she told him sadly.

"We knew what we were doing and what consequences we should face," he answered. "Faith, all of us
escaped the gallows at home in Ireland, Mrs. Broome
. . . 'tis the fate of Irish patriots who battle to throw off
the English yoke. I've no regrets . . . save that we
failed. But rest assured, our countrymen here will not
forget us. They—"

"Enough o'that," the constable grunted, and grasping his chains, he dragged the Irishman away.

The court was reopened a scant twenty minutes later,
and there was, Jenny sensed as soon as she entered it,
a subtle change in the atmosphere. The officers on the
bench were, without exception, in high good humor;
Major Johnstone, in particular, was conversing in a low
voice, but with great affability, with the red-faced Captain Kemp, and he looked up with an oddly self-satis-
fied smile when the prisoners were once again lined up
in front of him.

The judge advocate and the provost marshal appeared, by contrast, glumly displeased and Jenny saw,
to her surprise, that Andrew Hawley had joined them,
his expression one of barely contained rage. But he
turned to smile in her direction as she took her place in
the dock; and, as he had done earlier, Lieutenant Laycock made her an almost imperceptible gesture of reassurance. Beside her, Christie O'Hagan whispered,
"Never fear, ma'am, I'll see you're not sent down wid'
us, so I will. I give you me sacred oath on it."

The usher called for silence; Major Johnstone rose, the clerk's notes in front of him, and an expectant hush fell over the shadowed courtroom as the sentences were read.

"On the charges of conspiracy and the attempted assassination of His Excellency Governor Bligh, to which you have all pleaded guilty, the sentences of this court are as follows. . . . Joseph Michael Fitzgerald—one year's banishment to Van Diemen's Land. Christian O'Hagan—six months' banishment to Van Diemen's Land. Liam Martin O'Rourke . . ."

Jenny listened in a daze, hardly able to take in what was being said. The sentences were so light as to be derisory, she realized, and . . . Her bewildered gaze went again to the faces of the six officers seated behind the long, paper-strewn table. Those of the younger of her judges were carefully blank, but Captain Kemp was grinning openly and Major Johnstone's round, well-shaven countenance expressed something akin to triumph which, it seemed to her, he was savoring to the full as he read from the clerk's written notes.

"For the theft of government property, to wit four horses seized under armed threat from His Excellency's bodyguard, the court sentences each and every one of you to a hundred lashes, which punishment shall be administered forthwith. For the illegal possession of firearms and rebellious assembly, an additional hundred lashes, to be administered at some future date, to be decided by a surgeon. . . ."

She had not heard her own name, Jenny thought, suddenly afraid. But surely, surely she had not been adjudged to be included in Joseph Fitzgerald's plea of guilty, which he had made for himself and those who had raided her farm? Beside her she heard Christie expel his breath in a long, pent-up sigh, as the sentence of fifty lashes for the theft of the horses was imposed on Thomas McCann and a hundred added for his theft of a pistol, the property of the assistant commissary, Mr. Robert Fitz.

"Jennifer Broome, widow of John Samuel Broome, deceased . . ." Major Johnstone paused to consult a fresh sheet of paper that the clerk had placed before him, and Jenny waited tensely for him to continue, the color draining from her cheeks and her mouth dry.

Judge Advocate Atkins leaned forward in his seat. "Sir," he began thickly, "I must point out . . ." But whatever he had intended to say was never said, for, ignoring his attempted interruption, the commandant announced with thinly veiled impatience, "Mrs. Broome, in view of the evidence of good character produced in writing before this court and pleas made on your behalf, it has been unanimously agreed that you shall be shown the utmost leniency. Accordingly I direct that you be released, with the proviso that, should you again commit an offense and be brought to trial, six months' deportation to Van Diemen's Land shall be added to any other sentence you may incur."

She had not been formally cleared of the charge against her, Jenny thought numbly, but that scarcely mattered now. She was to go free, which was leniency indeed. She could go back to Long Wrekin, to the children, to her land. Tim Dawson would have a hired boat and . . . She felt suddenly light-headed and giddy, the floor beneath her feet seemed to be rocking, the low ceiling of the courtroom closing about her ears.

Christie's fettered hands reached out to support her, but the constable thrust him away and, lifting her across his shoulder, carried her outside, to set her down on the steps leading to the street. From what seemed to be a great distance, she heard Andrew's voice raised in anger, demanding that her fetters be removed, and when, at last, her moment of weakness passed, she found herself held in his comforting arms, her wrists free of the irons that had imprisoned them.

"I'll have our banns called, Jenny love," Andrew told her gently. "And we'll be wed as soon as I can arrange for it. Because, by heaven, I'll not have owt like this happen to you again! Whatever Bligh expects of me, you come first. Although," he added grimly, "he's liable to expect plenty when he learns of this day's work."

"What do you mean?" Jenny asked weakly.

He helped her to her feet. "No need to concern yourself about that now, lass. I'm taking you to Mr. Spence's house—Tim Dawson says you're to stay there for as long as you want. Long enough, at all events, to greet Justin . . . the *Flinders* had been signaled off the Heads."

"Justin's back? Oh, thank God!" Jenny's joy and relief were in her voice, and Andrew smiled down at her indulgently.

"Aye, the lad's timed it well—he'll be here for our wedding. Come." He offered his arm. "Let's seek cleaner air, Jenny, my dear. The stench of what those misnamed officers and gentlemen have done—or endeavored to do—to Captain Bligh sickens me. And all because he's threatening to put a stop to their rum-trading profits!"

"Oh, Andrew, was that why they imposed such . . . such light sentences on the Irish Defenders? And"— Jenny caught her breath— "and on me?"

"Aye," Andrew confirmed gruffly. "Not that they had a whit of evidence against you, love, damn their eyes! But it'll be a brave man who bears the news to His Excellency. Atkins will drink himself into a stupor before *he* does, I can tell you. But there, enough of that, eh? You're free and we're going to be wed, which is reason to thank God, is it not, as well as for Justin's safe return?" He drew her closer to him. "When I've left you at the Spences' I will go and meet the lad and bring him to you. And we'll celebrate, Jenny, my own dear lass, and pledge our troth in a glass of wine."

Jenny walked beside him down the dusty street with her head held high. Andrew Hawley was a good man, she told herself—a good man and an honorable one, and she was fortunate that he should want her for his wife, fortunate indeed to be given the chance to love again, to love and be loved in return.

CHAPTER VIII

The next day was Sunday, and, as had become his custom, William Bligh reserved two hours between rising and breaking his fast to receive, in person, petitions and complaints from any, bond or free, who presented himself at Government House.

Most of the complaints were petty and concerned the buying and selling of farm produce and the repayment of debts, and the governor dealt with them swiftly but affably enough. His popularity with the free and emancipist settlers had increased during the past year, and a number of the petitioners thanked him, with genuine gratitude, for his efforts to improve their lot before—some almost apologetically—starting to air their grievances.

The vast majority of these pertained to promissory notes for sums borrowed following the Hawkesbury flood of the previous year and prior to his own arrival in the colony, and Bligh's temper rose, as settler after settler made the same complaint. The notes had been expressed in terms of bushels of wheat, at prices current before the flood, but now the claims for repayment were being made based on the present price of wheat—which had quadrupled, a punishing difference to the unfortunate settlers, few of whom had the means to meet such extortionate demands.

His own bailiff, Andrew Thompson, had been sued in the civil court by Captain John Macarthur, on precisely this basis, two or three months before, the governor recalled. Macarthur had purchased the note from its original holder in order, he could only suppose, to place Bligh in the embarrassing position of intervening on his bailiff's behalf at his peril. He had done so, nevertheless, and, as he had expected, had incurred accusations of bias and favoritism when he had ordered Thompson's debt to be reduced. Yet, in spite of this, the iniquitous practice was, it seemed, still going on, and most of the claims for repayment were being made in the names of Macarthur's fellow rum traffickers or their agents. He had seen no fewer than four this morning.

Bligh swore under his breath as a thin, gray-bearded emancipist from one of the more remote Hawkesbury settlements presented yet another note of hand, bearing a date in January 1806, and stated with stark bitterness that to meet it would spell his ruin.

"There's just the wife an' me, Yer Excellency," the old man added. "We lost everythin' in the flood, 'cepting the clothes we stood up in. Took us off'n the roof o' our cabin, Mr. Broome did, else we shouldn't neither o' us be 'ere now ter tell the tale. But it all went, sir, the cabin an' our wheat 'arvest an' we've only just rebuilt the cabin an' sown a new crop. I can't pay Mr. Underwood what 'e's askin'—I'd 'ave ter sell up if I did, sir, an' that's the gospel truth."

William Bligh reached for his pen. He wrote quickly and appended his signature with an angry flourish.

"Take this to the clerk of the civil court, my man," he commanded crisply. "And request him to stamp it.

I cannot revoke your debt, but I have restated the sum involved in cash, at the price your wheat would have fetched at the time you incurred the debt."

"God bless you, sir," the old settler managed. There were tears in his faded blue eyes as he thrust the governor's note into the pocket of his ragged breeches. "May you enjoy a long an' 'appy life. And my oath, sir, I'd thought ter see them scurvy Irish rebels strung up—'anged by the neck until they was dead, sir, fer what they tried ter do ter you! But the court let 'em off. Sent 'em ter Van Diemen's Land, they did, and—"

Bligh cut him short with a startled exclamation and then, controlling himself, dismissed him.

"That's enough, Edmund," he told his secretary. "I can see no more petitioners this morning. But by the living God, I'll see Atkins and see him at once! Did *you* know that Johnstone and his blasted crew had virtually pardoned the Irish scum who tried to assassinate me?"

Edmund Griffin shook his head in dismay. "No, sir, I did not. Surely it's not true—it can't be!"

"That old scarecrow seemed quite positive. And if it's common gossip, then why in hell was I not informed? Go and tell the infernal judge advocate to present himself here immediately. I shall have to see him and find out the truth of the matter before I attend church. Damme, I ordered a church parade for the plaguey Rum Corps, did I not?" The governor's face was white and taut with rage, and Griffin prudently retreated a pace.

"Yes, sir," he confirmed unhappily, "you did. But—"

"They shall damned well parade," Bligh said grimly. "And I shall inspect them. But I must see Atkins first . . . tell Jubb to set an extra place at table. And, yes, it might be as well to request Mrs. Putland not to join me until after I have dealt with Mr. Atkins."

His tone and the expression on his face boded ill for the judge advocate, Griffin thought, but . . . He himself held no brief for the drunken, incompetent Atkins, and he spared him no pity when, ten minutes later, he delivered the governor's summons and found the recipient of it still abed. Wakened by his convict servant, Atkins came stumbling into the untidy living room, twenty-four hours' growth of stubble on his cheeks and his speech so slurred as to be barely audible.

"I'll have to shave and dress," he complained. "What does he want, in such an almighty hurry, d'you know? Damme, it's Sunday, ain't it? Day of rest, or supposed to be."

"His Excellency will be attending morning prayer at the new church," Griffin retorted. "And the troops are parading at ten thirty. If you will take my advice, sir, you'll make all possible haste to wait on him."

He took his leave without disclosing the reason for the governor's unwelcome invitation, but it was evident that Atkins had contrived to work this out for himself when, as the young secretary closed the door behind him, he glimpsed the convict manservant leaving by the rear door and sprinting across to the rooms occupied by Lawyer Crossley, to summon Crossley so Atkins could seek his legal advice.

Both men presented themselves at the gates of Government House a commendable twenty minutes later, the emancipist, as always, neatly and soberly turned out, and Richard Atkins—to Griffin's secret amusement —wearing a freshly pressed suit but lacking hat and cravat. He escorted them to the door of the dining room where the governor, waited on by his steward, Jubb, was moodily consuming a belated breakfast. He greeted them with noticeable coldness, dismissed Jubb with a jerk of his bewigged head, and waved Atkins to the chair opposite his own. Ignored and uninvited, Crossley slid unobtrusively into a chair at the far end of the table, where he sat, studiously avoiding the governor's eye.

Griffin was about to leave them when a curt "No— stay and take notes, Edmund," from Bligh halted him in his tracks. With a reluctance he found it difficult to conceal, the secretary found pen and ink and seated himself at Crossley's side.

"And now, Mr. Atkins," William Bligh said, with heavy emphasis. "I'll thank you to give me a full report on the trial of the Irish seditionists who attempted— unsuccessfully, thank God—to assassinate me. You took their statements and, I presume, attended the trial in your official capacity?"

The expression on the judge advocate's long, sallow face was calculated to evoke pity rather than anger, and his hand was trembling visibly as he set down the cup of coffee that Griffin had poured for him, slopping most of its contents into the saucer as, all too frequently, was his practice.

"Yes, sir," he admitted wretchedly.

"Do you have a copy of the charges brought against the rogues?" Bligh demanded.

It was Crossley who supplied it, passing the documents across the table to his patron in silence. Atkins contrived to spill his coffee over one corner of the uppermost, and, muttering an apology, he dabbed at it ineffectively with his napkin before giving the sheaf of papers to the governor.

There was an ominous pause, whilst each sheet was minutely studied, and Edmund Griffin, wise in the ways of the man he served, waited with trepidation for the outburst. But it did not come; the governor had his temper under rigid control. Having read each of the charges, he bundled the papers together and pushed them in the judge advocate's direction.

"How did they plead to these charges?" he asked.

"They . . . they pleaded guilty, Your Excellency."

"And the woman—the woman charged with harboring them, Mrs. Broome—how did she plead?"

Richard Atkins shrugged helplessly. "In all honesty, Captain Bligh, I do not know," he confessed. "Conduct of the trial was taken out of my hands by Major Johnstone. It was he who summoned the prisoners to answer to the charges. I . . . that is, sir, I had the impression that Mrs. Broome entered no plea at all, but the clerk of the court entered hers as one of guilty and . . ." He launched into a rambling explanation, which left the governor still unenlightened, and Crossley diffidently intervened.

"Major Johnstone acted most high-handedly, Your Excellency. Mr. Atkins warned him repeatedly that his procedure was irregular, but he ignored the warnings. He read the written statements from witnesses but did not call any of them, sir. Having obtained pleas of guilty from all the Irish seditionists, he exercised his authority as president of the court and announced that it only remained for sentences to be decided, and he ordered the court to be cleared. And . . ." The lawyer hesitated, eyeing Bligh uncertainly.

"Pray continue, Mr. Crossley," Bligh urged, his tone still quiet and controlled.

"Mr. Atkins endeavored to advise him that witnesses should be heard, sir, and he—that is, Major Johnstone —stated firstly that the court would consider the witnesses' written statements. And then, sir, he announced that the court was disposed to deal leniently in the case of the woman Broome, because her previous good character entitled her to—ah—the benefit of any existing doubt."

The Broome woman again, William Bligh thought— the woman Hawley was so determined to marry. Well, perhaps in her case there had been room for leniency, but for the others . . . The fury he had kept in check rose like bile in his throat, threatening to break free of all restraint.

"Am I to take it," he managed thickly, "that Mrs. Broome *was* dealt with leniently?"

Atkins inclined his head wordlessly, and Crossley murmured details of the sentence imposed.

"And the Irishmen?" the governor pursued. "The foul, rebellious swine who did their damnedest to kill me, Mr. Crossley? I was informed, I trust incorrectly, by one of my petitioners this morning that they had been let off . . . is that true or is it not? Devil take you"—as Crossley remained mute—"answer me, man! Were these blackguards from the bogs of Ireland dealt with leniently, for all they pleaded guilty to the charges against them? Capital charges, damme!"

Crossley glanced anxiously in Atkins's direction and the judge advocate passed his tongue nervously about his lips. To his credit, however, he attempted to reply to the question. "Sir, they were sentenced to banishment to Van Diemen's Land. Their leader, Joseph Fitzgerald, for a year, the others for six months. And they were each ordered a hundred lashes."

"The floggings were for the theft of government property and the possession of firearms," Crossley put in, recovering his courage. He waited for the expected storm to break, and Edmund Griffin's hand shook as badly as the judge advocate's had done a short time before, so that he could scarcely retain his grip on the quill he was using. Atkins half rose and then subsided, shaking his balding head despairingly. All three were aware of the shortness of the governor's temper under provocation, and this was provocation indeed, which there was no avoiding.

But William Bligh had himself under a degree of restraint that astonished them all. He suppressed an oath and then, bracing himself, said with icy deliberation, "I recognize the malign influence of one man in this . . . a man who will stop at nothing to bring about my downfall, just as he brought about Hunter's and poor Philip King's. Johnstone is his tool, his puppet, damme! Macarthur tweaks the strings and his superior officer dances to his tune. But, by God, they shall not have their way with me! I'll see them in hell first."

"Amen to that, sir," Atkins ventured. He was sweating profusely, his face and brow beaded with moisture; he mopped vigorously with his handkerchief and gulped down the dregs of his coffee. Bligh had done no more than put his own suspicions into words, he reflected wryly. He had known from the outset that the manner in which George Johnstone had conducted the Irish seditionists' trial had been irregular and had guessed at whose instigation the Corps commandant had acted and, come to that, why. And yet . . . Atkins breathed an exasperated sigh. Johnstone had outmaneuvered him, driven him into a corner from which he had lacked both the ability and the legal competence to extricate himself—and thus, to his shame, despite years of experience of Macarthur's devious use of the courts to gain his own ends, his blatant flouting of the law.

The governor said, in a crisp, decisive tone that brooked no argument, "This parody of a trial cannot be allowed to stand, Atkins. The sentences must be revoked, the case heard again, with witnesses called on properly to give their testimony—and before a different bench."

"But Your Excellency—" Crossley began and then broke off, reddening under the governor's cold scrutiny.

"You are an expert in the law," Bligh told him. "And there has been, without any doubt, a miscarriage of justice. I shall expect you to look into the matter and advise the judge advocate as to his correct procedure. My God!" His composure vanished with alarming suddenness. "Convicts, infernal rogues of Irish rebels escape, with stolen firearms, and set an ambush for the governor of this colony—His Majesty's appointed captain general and viceroy, mark you, sir, not simply Captain Bligh of the Royal Navy. And they are virtually unpunished, thanks to the machinations of a set of unprincipled villains, masquerading as military officers, whose sole aim and object is *my* personal humiliation! Well, sir"—he rose wrathfully to his feet—"devil take them, I am not inclined to stomach such an insult, either as governor or as a post captain in His Majesty's navy! I don't care how you do it, Mr. Crossley, but see to it that a new trial is arranged and the miscreants justly dealt with . . . and by a bench of magistrates with respect for the law. Is that clearly understood?"

It was Richard Atkins who answered him. He rose, as Bligh had done, and faced him without flinching. "I will attend to it, Your Excellency," he promised. "Rest assured, sir, those assassins shall not go unpunished if it lies within my power to set matters to rights."

Bligh's anger faded. He bowed stiffly.

"I thank you, Mr. Atkins. And now I must give you good day—I am pledged to attend morning service at St. Philip's with my daughter." He added, almost as an afterthought, "It is, of course, Major Johnstone's privilege to nominate his officers to serve as justices on the criminal court bench, and he must be permitted to do so in this case. But I think it should be made plain to him that he would be ill advised to let his choice fall on any who served at the previous trial under his presidency. *You* will preside, sir, and I shall myself nominate three civilian officials to the bench. I'm within my rights, am I not?"

Atkins glanced at Crossley. The emancipist lawyer nodded. "As I understand the constitution, Your Excellency, you are completely within your rights," he answered readily.

"Good," the governor approved. He consulted his fob watch and moved toward the door, which Griffin hastened to open for him. "Good day, gentlemen. Edmund, be so obliging as to inform my daughter that I am ready to leave, if you please."

Mary Putland was awaiting him in the hall. She was in high good humor and the last vestige of her father's rage vanished at the sight of her. "My dear," he greeted her, "you look truly lovely! Is that a new gown you are wearing?"

Gratified that he had noticed her dress, Mary beamed with pleasure. "Yes, it is the one dear Mamma sent me by the *Mysore,* with the blue cloth and the silk stockings she sent for you, Papa." Mary executed a dignified little pirouette for his benefit. "It is of Chinese silk and in the latest London fashion—altogether different and superior to anything that has ever been seen in this country. Even poor Charles expressed admiration when I showed it to him."

"And doubtless it will provoke some envy in church this morning," the governor suggested indulgently. He offered her his arm. "Come, my dear—our carriage is waiting and I am, I fear, a trifle late."

The carriage, with its four horses and the mounted escort, covered the short distance between Government House and the recently built Church of St. Philip at a spanking pace. The parade ground, Bligh noticed, was deserted, and he clicked his tongue with annoyance. Evidently the Corps had not waited for his arrival as, out of deference, they should have done. He saw Andrew Hawley, riding at the head of his escort, glance across at the empty square and shrug, and his annoyance grew. Damn their impudence . . . this was another insult, another affront to his dignity as governor. Well, they should pay for it, by heaven they should . . . his inspection would be meticulous and long drawn out and the band ordered to play while he made it.

It was a hot day, the sun blazing down from a blue, cloudless sky, with the promise of more heat to come.

They would sweat in their damned scarlet tunics and leather stocks, these corrupt and drunken apologies for soldiers, but he would keep them there until he was satisfied they had understood that he was not to be slighted with impunity.

The carriage drew up outside the church portico, and as he prepared to alight, the governor saw another belated party ahead of him, hurrying in so as not to impede his entrance. He recognized Jasper Spence, with his good-looking young wife on his arm, and some children, whose faces were unfamiliar to him, and then, with a start of surprise, realized that the girl with them was Abigail Tempest. She was wearing a sprigged muslin dress, and looked as pretty as she had on the day she and her sister had taken lunch with the governor in Parramatta. At least now she was in better company, Bligh thought, than that of the Boskennas; and, of course, the Spences must have returned from Calcutta in the Indiaman that had been sighted off the Heads the previous evening.

Andrew Hawley, clearly with the intention of mitigating the Corps' insulting absence, dismounted his men and formed them up as a guard of honor on either side of the church door. Bligh alighted and turned to assist his daughter; he gave her his arm and together they walked slowly to the door, Mary patting the folds of her elegant skirt into place as a gust of wind caught it. The material was flimsy and the sunlight strong, and to his horror, her father realized that, as she halted in the open doorway, the effect was to make the beautiful garment all but transparent.

The church was crowded; the congregation came to their feet and with them the scarlet-clad rows of soldiers, their concerted gaze directed to the door. Bligh stepped hurriedly to his daughter's rear, but he was too late. . . . A man started to titter, others shook with laughter, and then ribald guffaws and chuckles rippled from pew to pew.

Bewildered and hurt, Mary turned beseeching eyes on her father, and the governor, white with rage, grasped her arm and led her up the aisle and into the pew reserved for them. As she dropped to her knees, he turned to glare furiously at the soldiers, and the sounds of merriment ceased abruptly. In the ensuing silence the chaplain's voice seemed strained and hesitant, his nasal north-of-Ireland accent unusually pronounced as he led the first psalm.

William Bligh, with his daughter's muffled sobs filling his ears, heard little of the service. Only once did the Reverend Henry Fulton's words penetrate his shocked consciousness, and this was when he called the banns of marriage between Andrew Hawley and Jennifer Broome. Bligh stiffened involuntarily, the blood rushing to suffuse his cheeks. This, he thought bitterly, was the ultimate betrayal . . . Hawley, damn his soul, had publicly joined the ranks of his enemies by announcing these banns.

He drew a swift, half-strangled breath, going back in memory to the time when he had first given his trust and his approval to the tall young sergeant of marines. As he had told his daughter only a short while ago, he had been given no cause until now to regret it. But now . . . plague take the fellow, he had found himself a woman and that was the end of his loyalty. And the woman was an emancipated convict, freed—presumably with Hawley's connivance—by Johnstone and his so-called justices of the charges of harboring the Irishmen who had tried to kill him.

Well . . . Calm returned and with it a solution. Hawley should join Colonel Collins in Van Diemen's Land, and he could marry the Broome woman there. In the meantime, as soon as this lengthy service came to an end, he could escort poor Mary back to Government House and look after her, while he himself put the infernal Corps through their paces on the parade ground.

The governor looked about him. The congregation was singing the final hymn, the soldiers joining in lustily, and not a soul looked up to meet his eye. Even Chaplain Fulton kept his gaze carefully averted as he intoned the blessing.

"The peace of God, which passeth all understanding, keep your minds and hearts in the knowledge and love of God. . . ."

But there could be no peace in the colony of New South Wales, Bligh thought bitterly. No peace between himself and the Rum Corps until . . . He turned to find Hawley at his elbow, his scarred face expressionless as he proffered a shawl, which Mary took from him with tearful gratitude.

And then the officer in command of the parade— Lieutenant O'Shea—claimed his attention, coming to a halt in front of him, ramrod stiff and unexpectedly correct.

"I have to beg Your Excellency's pardon for my men's behavior and to assure you, sir, that no disrespect was intended, either to Your Excellency or to Mrs. Putland."

"Is that so, Mr. O'Shea?" the governor challenged scornfully. "Then to what cause *do* you attribute it, pray?"

"Sir, it was coincidence. Your arrival coincided with an oafish jest on the part of a young soldier." O'Shea was very red of face and embarrassed, but he persisted. "The rogue stuck a long feather in his hair, sir, after he removed his headgear, and that was what caused the— the unseemly merriment. The man shall be flogged, sir, and the whole company shall—"

"I beg you, have some respect for my powers of

observation," William Bligh put in. He glimpsed Captain Kemp leaving the church among a group of civilian officials and their wives, and his thunderous summons brought the stout company commander hurrying to his side.

"Sir . . . Your Excellency requires my services?" Kemp was nervous but endeavoring not to show it. "This unfortunate affair . . . has Mr. O'Shea not explained the reason for it and offered an apology?"

"He has offered me a tissue of lies," the governor retorted. "Damn your eyes, sir, I am not half-witted!"

"No, sir," Kemp conceded. "But I—"

"My daughter was grossly insulted, Captain Kemp," Bligh accused, "by your ill-disciplined rabble regiment, by God! This is your company, is it not—the company of which you are supposedly in command?"

"It is, sir." Kemp drew himself up, abandoning all attempt at conciliation, his own anger matching that of the governor. "But if I may be permitted to say so, your daughter provoked the insult. Her dress, sir, was not— it was not decent, and my soldiers are men. They—"

Governor Bligh silenced him with a menacing look. "We will see what manner of men they are," he rasped. "March them onto the parade ground immediately, with their fifes and drums. And take command of them yourself, since Lieutenant O'Shea appears incapable of maintaining discipline. I shall inspect them, Captain Kemp, as you were surely aware I had intended to, before they entered the church. Had my orders been adhered to, this unhappy incident would never have happened. Your regiment is a disgrace to the colony and to the uniform they wear but, by the living God, sir, since I am given no other, I'll bring them to order!"

Kemp seemed, for a moment, as if he were about to resort to bluster, but O'Shea gripped his arm and instead he saluted woodenly, and, with the Irish officer at his heels, he strode across to the waiting ranks of scarlet-uniformed soldiers and, at the pitch of his lungs, gave the necessary orders.

The band struck up and the company wheeled down Church Street, their marching feet raising a cloud of dust from the worn sandstone.

His carriage had gone, Bligh saw. That, at least, was a mark in Hawley's favor . . . he had anticipated the need to hurry his poor Mary back to the sanctuary of Government House. But his escort had waited, men of the Sydney Loyal Association, volunteers upon whom he could rely . . . and their sergeant was holding a horse for him. Hawley again, he could only suppose, but all the same, if the damned fool insisted on marrying the Broome woman, he would have to go, for a time at least, because Sydney society, such as it was, would never accept her.

He stifled a regretful sigh and mounted the horse. With his escort jogging behind him, he rode on to the Corps parade ground with the dignity his office demanded, and, to his gratification, a group of settlers in homespuns cheered him as he passed.

Abigail was in a thoughtful mood when she returned from morning service to the Spences' commodious house overlooking Sydney Cove.

She had been as shocked as the rest of the congregation by the extraordinary appearance of the governor's daughter and by the soldiers' bawdy reaction to it and—like Frances Spence and Jenny Broome and most of the women present—had felt acutely sorry for poor Mrs. Putland.

But in general Sydney seemed to her a strangely unhappy place, with factional feuds and bitter resentment simmering beneath the surface, and the behavior of the New South Wales Corps—both officers and rank and file—the most alarming of all. She had seized eagerly on Tim Dawson's suggestion that she should assist him to bring his two elder daughters to Sydney, to enable them to attend school; but the reason for her eagerness was, she admitted to herself, the opportunity she had been afforded to escape from the Reverend Boskenna, if only for a week or two.

By rights, of course, she ought to have returned to Parramatta, to rejoin Mrs. Boskenna and her sister, Lucy, since this had been the original arrangement, but Mr. Dawson had contrived not only that she was to come to Sydney but also that Lucy should do so, as soon as a suitable escort for her could be arranged.

Abigail stifled a sigh and gave perfunctory attention to little Julia Dawson's plea for help with the sampler she was attempting, more than a little clumsily, to work, as a gift for Frances Spence.

"Take smaller stitches, Julia, dear," she advised, "and don't be in quite such a hurry to finish it. Your grandmother won't mind waiting, I feel sure."

"She's not my gran'mother," Julia objected. "She is only a step because she married gran'pa."

Another simmering resentment, Abigail thought, and none the less bitter because it was fostered by Henrietta Dawson whilst, seemingly, ignored by Frances. She filled in half a dozen neat stitches on the sampler, rethreaded the needle, and put it into Julia's impatient hand.

"There you are, dear—finish the last two letters in red, and I'll give you the blue thread for the next line."

Julia, tongue out in an effort to concentrate, went back to her seat and continued stitching, watched with a mixture of admiration and envy by her sister, Dorothea. They were both occupied, and Abigail crossed to the window, again busy with her own thoughts. Below her, close to the public wharf, the bluff-bowed Indiaman *Kelso* lay at anchor—the ship that had brought Frances Spence and her husband back from Calcutta.

Beyond her were two American trading barques and the graceful cutter owned by Jenny Broome's son Justin, lately returned from Van Diemen's Land.

Justin, tall and fair haired, but a trifle taciturn, had called the previous evening to take his mother away, in order to find accommodation elsewhere, in view of the Spences' imminent arrival. She had been disappointed, Abigail recalled, because, once again, she had had no opportunity to talk to Mrs. Broome—no opportunity, even, to express her pleasure and relief at the result of the trial. Poor soul, she had looked so wan and tired, so desperately strained . . . clearly it had been an ordeal for her, but now she had her handsome elder son to console her. And, of course, Captain Hawley, the publication of whose banns of marriage to her had caused almost as great a sensation in church this morning as Mrs. Putland's dress had done.

Suddenly Dorothea emitted an outraged wail. Before Abigail could stop her, she had seized the sampler and her small hands were tearing at the stitches, with Julia vainly attempting to preserve her handiwork.

"Children, children!" Abigail admonished them. "You mustn't quarrel!"

But, to her chagrin, both little girls ignored her. "You're a horrid, mean little *beast,* Dodie!" Julia cried. She struck her sister hard across the face, leaving the reddening imprint of her fingers on the plump cheek, and Dorothea retaliated with bunched fists and a well-aimed kick.

Had she and Lucy ever behaved like this to each other, Abigail asked herself, as she managed to separate them, and could recall no occasion when they had. Lucy was much younger than she was, it was true, and her health had never been robust, which was probably the reason, but she and Rick had never quarreled, either. Whereas these two spirited, self-willed little girls were always ready to quarrel, and their quarrels, all too frequently, ended in blows.

She dried Dorothea's tears with her handkerchief and was listening to Julia's indignant accusations against her sister when, to her relief, Frances Spence came into the room.

"What is this I hear?" she asked, flashing Abigail an amused smile. "Fighting? Shame on you both, and in Abigail's presence, too! I do declare you are exceedingly naughty, ill-mannered little girls. You will never grow up to be young ladies unless you mind your manners now."

The children were instantly on their best behavior. Whatever their mother might have impressed upon them regarding their true relationship to her, Mrs. Spence clearly had a way with both of them. The tears ceased, the quarrel was forgotten; Dorothea was taken onto her stepgrandmother's lap, while Julia proudly exhibited her sampler without offering any explanation for its crumpled state.

They made a charming picture, Abigail thought . . . Frances Spence, with her shining black hair and blue, intelligent eyes, was a beautiful woman and still far too youthful to be regarded as any kind of grandmother. Henrietta Dawson's barbed hints concerning her had made it plain that marriage to her wealthy father, Jasper Spence, had not removed the convict stigma Frances had endured, but . . . she was a lady, born and bred, and not the only woman of her class to be deported from Ireland for sedition. Even the acting chaplain, the Reverend Henry Fulton—who had conducted this morning's church service—had a similar background although he was of the Protestant faith. And there was Dr. D'Arcy Wentworth, in Parramatta, and the one-time naval surgeon, Dr. Redfern . . . so why, Abigail found herself wondering, should Henrietta continue to treat her father's beautiful wife as if—oh, as if she were an inferior?

And there was poor Mrs. Broome, too. She had been pardoned years ago—indeed, she had been a mere child when she had been transported to Sydney in Governor Phillip's first fleet, and Mrs. Pendeen with her. She had married a naval warrant officer, been granted land, and in spite of having been widowed, she had farmed her land in a manner that had evoked even Timothy Dawson's admiration. And yet, it seemed, because she had come out initially as a convict, she could be arrested and flung into jail, just on the word of a Corps officer whom everyone said was corrupt and drunken, just like the hateful Captain Kemp.

Abigail shivered. True, poor Jenny Broome had been released by the court, and Frances Spence had said indignantly that she had suffered an injustice; but that had not stopped the rulers of the colony from taking her forcibly away from her farm and her children. And there was Kate Lamerton, still, as far as she had been able to ascertain, languishing in the dreadful Factory for convict women in Parramatta. But . . . perhaps if she asked, perhaps if she told her about Kate, Mrs. Spence would give her employment, now that Julia and Dorothea were here for the start of the school term. She would need someone to look after them. . . .

"I fear," she began tentatively, "I shall never make a governess, Mrs. Spence. Julia and Dodie take no notice of what I tell them, and as for Alexander . . ." She spread her hands in a gesture of despair. "He won't even eat what I give him!"

"They are all horribly spoiled, the little monsters," Frances Spence asserted, with a meaning glance at the two small girls. "Indeed, I am not sure that they deserve the gifts their grandpa has brought back from India for them. Although perhaps," she added, forestalling a cry of disappointment from Julia, "if they were to present themselves to him in the withdrawing room, with very clean hands and faces and a pretty curtsy, Grandpapa might be disposed to relent. What do you think, Abigail?"

"I think he might," Abigail agreed, smiling.

The children needed no urging. "We'll go and wash now," Julia said. "And you need not help us, Abigail. We can manage by ourselves."

The door closed behind them and Abigail said ruefully, "You see? I inspire no confidence in them. But there's a very good woman I can recommend if you need help, Mrs. Spence. Her name is Kate Lamerton, and she came out with us in the *Mysore,* so I knew her well. But they sent the poor soul to the Factory at Parramatta, and I'm sure she is utterly unsuited to such work and quite miserable."

"It is a wretched place," Frances Spence admitted, "because the type of women who are sent there are . . . well, they are the least amenable to conditions here. But I will do what I can, Abigail. Kate Lamerton, you said. I'll remember her name. But surely, my dear"—she eyed Abigail thoughtfully—"you do not want to become a governess, do you? I had understood from Mr. Dawson that your father had left you well provided for, with stock and money to enable you to take a land grant. Is not your guardian, the reverend gentleman— I don't know his name—is he not making arrangements to that end?"

"The Reverend Caleb Boskenna," Abigail supplied. "And yes, he is." He had come briefly to Upwey Farm, she reminded herself, just before she and Timothy Dawson had set out for Sydney, to inform her that he had found a suitable farm some twenty miles higher up the Hawkesbury, whose owner was willing to sell, and where her father's grant could be taken up on virgin land adjacent to it. And he had been enthusiastic concerning its possibilities—an enthusiasm which, for some reason, Timothy Dawson had not shared, although all he had said was that the place was isolated.

She had wanted to see it for herself, but Caleb Boskenna had pooh-poohed the suggestion.

"It is ideally situated," he had told her emphatically, "and the existing buildings will enable your father's stock to be moved up there, as soon as I can hire a launch to carry them. But it is in too rough a state for you and Lucy at present, so you would be well advised to take advantage of Mr. Dawson's kind offer of hospitality in the meantime. Mrs. Boskenna will assist me to supervise the enlargement of the present dwelling place, which is a mere hovel, and we will send for you when it is put in order."

And because she was anxious to go to Sydney, Abigail had not insisted on seeing the farm right away—though perhaps she ought to have done. Abigail looked up to meet Frances Spence's searching blue eyes and managed an answering smile. "Mr. Boskenna is making all the arrangements. Papa's stock and the shepherd we brought out here with us, Jethro, are to go upriver by hired launch from the government farm at Parramatta. . . ." Under Frances's gentle probing, she told her what she could, but her underlying doubts and fears must have revealed themselves, for, when she had done, her hostess said quietly, "Abigail, my dear, I detect a note of uncertainty in your voice. Are you not happy concerning your guardian's arrangements for your future?"

How could she admit that she was not, Abigail asked herself—even to this kindly, charming woman who was, after all, a stranger? How could she explain her mistrust of the Boskennas when she had nothing tangible on which to base it? It was true that, in a moment of weakness, she had made frank admission of her feelings to Timothy Dawson, but he . . . what had he said? Something about the Reverend Boskenna being a man of

God and then, after that, he had changed the subject.

"No, I'm not," she evaded. "I should like to have seen the land Mr. Boskenna has selected for us—seen it for myself, I mean, since it's to be our home. And I had hoped that he would be willing to apply for Kate Lamerton to be assigned to us, as she herself wanted to be."

"And he was not willing?"

Abigail shook her head. "No. That was why I—that is, it was the reason I told you about her, Mrs. Spence. She is such a good woman and my sister, Lucy, who is very delicate, became deeply attached to her on the passage out. I really wanted her to come with us, but Mr. Boskenna would not hear of it."

Frances repeated her promise to inquire for Kate at the Factory and then, as Timothy had done, she went on to speak of other things.

"Mr. Dawson will make arrangements for your sister, Lucy, to come here next week," she said. "And if she is feeling up to it, she can attend the small private school Mr. Mann has set up, with Julia and Dorothea. You will probably be with us for five or six weeks—it takes time to erect farm buildings in the Hawkesbury Valley, you know, because all building materials have to go by boat."

"Five or six weeks!" Abigail exclaimed, unable to hide her delight at this prospect. "Oh, Mrs. Spence, how—how *lovely!*"

Once again she was conscious of Frances Spence's searching gaze and sensed her hostess's unvoiced sympathy, but despite this, could not bring herself to confide her fears concerning the Reverend Caleb Boskenna and his acid-tongued wife.

Mrs. Spence did not question Abigail's obvious relief. Instead she offered kindly, "We want you to enjoy your stay with us, Abigail dear. To meet people and visit friends and neighbors. My husband has a farm at Portland Place, which is not very far from Parramatta.

A manager looks after it, under Mr. Dawson's supervision, but we spend as much time as we can there, and I feel sure you would like to see it. You could gain a useful insight into how the land here is farmed and our stock is reared."

Abigail inclined her head eagerly and Frances smiled at her warmly. "But you are young, and, as I said, I want you to enjoy yourself here. Perhaps, whilst we are in Sydney, you have friends you would like to meet? I am making plans for a soirée to celebrate our return. . . . Is there anyone in particular you would care for me to invite? The *Mysore* has sailed, of course, but did you have friends among the settlers who came out here with you?"

There were the Trevempers, Abigail recalled, Chrissie and her master-carpenter husband, Robert, but . . . She looked at Mrs. Spence's elegant gown and hesitated. A soirée suggested high society; no doubt the governor and his daughter would be invited to such a gathering, the Corps officers and civil officials and their wives— even the hateful Captain Kemp—and they would look askance at honest tradesmen of Rob Trevemper's class. She was about to shake her head when she remembered Titus Penhaligon. A surgeon could hold his own in Sydney society, and Titus was of good family, possessed of impeccable manners. He had stayed in Sydney and was probably still here, for had not Governor Bligh promised that he would be given a post in the government hospital?

"There is the *Mysore*'s surgeon, Mrs. Spence," she ventured. "Dr. Penhaligon. I'm not sure where he is, but I—"

"Oh, my dear child!" Frances Spence was laughing. "Dr. Penhaligon will be taking luncheon with us today. He came out to the *Kelso* with the port health authorities, and my husband took a liking to him and invited him to call on us. Unless I'm much mistaken"—she gestured to the open window—"he has just arrived on our doorstep, and Dr. Redfern with him. Come . . . we will go and receive them, shall we?"

But it was not only Titus Penhaligon and his fellow surgeon whom they found in the handsomely furnished withdrawing room, talking to Mr. Spence and Timothy Dawson. The raised voices sounded angry, even alarmed, and Abigail halted in the open doorway at her hostess's heels, sudden fear setting her heart beating wildly.

Justin Broome stood in the center of the room, his blue eyes blazing and his face drained of color beneath its coating of tan.

"What is it?" Frances asked. She was at Justin's side, holding out both hands to him in swift, instinctive concern. "Justin, dear, what has happened? Surely Jenny, surely your mother—no harm has come to her, has it?"

"They have rearrested my mother," Justin told her thickly. "The constables, damn them, came to the Macraes' house half an hour ago and took her back to the jail! The governor has ordered a new trial—he's quashed the previous court's findings and Mam is to be charged again, with the Irishmen!" He drew a long, sighing breath, fighting down his anger, and went on, his voice flat and devoid of emotion. "Andrew Hawley has gone to intercede with the governor. He suggested that I should come here, sir"—he addressed Jasper Spence—"to request that, as a justice of the peace, you will grant her bail. I'll put up the *Flinders*, sir, as surety, and Andrew will offer recognizance of—"

Jasper Spence cut him short. "I'll see to it at once, Justin," he promised. "On my own recognizance." His eyes met those of his wife, and he smiled at her. "We'll bring Jenny back here for luncheon, Frances, my dear, if you can delay it for a while. Are you coming, Justin?"

Justin followed him without another word.

CHAPTER IX

The Reverend Caleb Boskenna, on his return to Parramatta, was summoned to the female Factory to perform what Superintendent Oakes described as "a ceremony to make honest women of half a dozen or so of our inmates."

In fact, when he presented himself at the straggling building, it was to find no fewer than seventeen prospective brides and bridegrooms, of whom several were still undecided as to their final pairings and were engaged in acrimonious argument which, before the service could begin, led to fisticuffs and hair pulling, and the intervention of Oakes's constables to restore order.

Caleb Boskenna watched the undignified riot with icy disapproval, thankful now that he had refused the superintendent's initial suggestion that the marriage services should be performed in the Church of St. John in Parramatta. The church—of which, in the Reverend Samuel Marsden's absence in England, Boskenna was the temporary incumbent—was for the weddings of respectable inhabitants, not for these foul-mouthed, quarrelsome Factory women. Mentally revising the scope and content of the sermon he intended to deliver, he caught sight of Kate Lamerton standing by herself in the doorway of the main weaving shed and beckoned her imperiously to his side.

She came reluctantly, mistrustful of him, but the chaplain's manner, if condescending, was pleasant enough, and, to her surprise, he greeted her by name.

"You are not taking a husband, then, Kate?" he questioned curiously.

Kate shook her head emphatically. Since being assigned to work in the Factory, she had witnessed the manner in which such marriages were arranged, and this had shocked her profoundly. Admittedly, few of the women with whom she was condemned to live and work were literate and most were of low moral character, former prostitutes and petty criminals, addicted to drink and unwilling to exert themselves more than was strictly required of them.

They were the dregs of Sydney's convict society, considered unfit to become officers' servants or soldiers' women and possessed of no domestic skills. In some cases they had fallen from grace since their arrival and been sentenced to toil in the weaving and carding sheds as punishment for habitual drunkenness or theft. In others they had been cast off by those who had initially taken them into concubinage, when the appearance in harbor of a newly arrived convict transport had afforded an opportunity for change and fresh conquest.

Marriage was their only prospect of escape from the Factory, but . . . Kate shivered, recalling the scenes which had led to this morning's jailyard ceremony. Superintendent Oakes—who was also Parramatta's chief constable and owner of the township's main bakery—had arranged to parade all the women desirous of securing a husband; and the prospective bridegrooms had been summoned to make their choice. The men in question were emancipists or convicts on ticket-of-leave, either gainfully employed or in receipt of a land grant, and each had to produce a government certificate of authorization before being admitted.

Kate glanced uneasily at the Reverend Boskenna's grimly set face, as a constable plied his lash with indiscriminate vigor among the quarreling women. Oakes, she recalled, had made a speech to them, as the blushing wife-seekers stood shuffling their feet at his back.

"These young fellers want wives. Any of you lasses wanting to make a respectable woman o' herself now has her chance. Step forward, all o' you, and let the boys take their pick!"

They had taken his invitation literally. Giggling and jesting obscenely among themselves, the women had formed a jostling line, and the men had moved slowly down its length. Some of the men were shy and awkward, with eyes on the ground, but most of them, long lost to shame, were frankly calculating and matching the women's outspoken comments and questions with equally explicit demands of their own. As each one made his selection, he took off his neckcloth and dropped it at the feet of the woman of his choice. If she picked it up, it was to signify that she had accepted him; but since there were fewer prospective bridegrooms than there were women anxious to gain respectability, quarrels were inevitable and fights commonplace.

Kate bit her lip, feeling tears start to her eyes. The work in the Factory was monotonous, but it was by no means overtaxing. She had acquired some dexterity at the loom and earned the respect of most of her fellow inmates, and having been promised an appointment as a supervisor from Superintendent Oakes, she saw no immediate need for escape. Least of all would she seek it by means of the Factory marriage mart, but . . . She blinked away her tears and made to return to the sanctuary of the doorway when, to her considerable astonishment, Mr. Boskenna put out a hand to detain her.

"Wait, if you please," he requested, his tone still un-expectedly pleasant, even friendly. "I have a favor to ask of you."

A favor . . . *from her?* Kate stared at him incredu-lously. Had it not been he and the red-faced Rum Corps captain who, between them, had been responsible for sending her here? They who had rendered it impos-sible for her to be assigned to Miss Abigail Tempest, as both of them had so much wanted? But she contrived to control her feelings of resentment and answered sub-missively, "If it's . . . that is, if it be in my power, sir, then o' course I'd do what I could." She added, with sudden hope, "If it maybe concerns Miss Abigail, sir, then right willingly—you know that."

The rioting women were under control now; the couples being urged into line, and the Reverend Bos-kenna's bearded lips relaxed into a smile. "It is indeed fortunate," he observed, "that I decided to hold these—ah—these wedding ceremonies here and not in church. They would have been most unseemly for the house of God."

Kate said nothing although, privately, she agreed with his conclusion, and he went on, again smiling at her, as if there had never been any differences between them. "Mr. Oakes tells me that your services as a nurse are being requisitioned by His Excellency, Governor Bligh. You are to assist in caring for his son-in-law, I under-stand."

Once again Kate stared at him uncomprehendingly. Superintendent Oakes had, it was true, hinted earlier that day that she might expect a change to her advan-tage, but she had supposed him to mean that her pro-motion to supervisor was imminent. Her heart leaped. "Oh, but sir, Mr. Boskenna, I—"

"You had not been told?" Boskenna suggested.

"No, sir, not a word."

"Well, it is the truth. You will be going to Sydney by

tomorrow's ferryboat. Now, as to the favor—Miss Abigail Tempest is in Sydney, residing as the guest of Magistrate Spence and his lady. Miss Lucy, as you may know, has been in Mrs. Boskenna's care, here in Parramatta."

"Yes, sir," Kate acknowledged, her hopes rising with each word the onetime missionary uttered. "Would you be wishing," she added eagerly, "—would you be wishing me to escort Miss Lucy to Sydney, sir, to join Miss Abigail?"

From someone, she could not recall from whom or even when, she had heard it said that the Reverend Boskenna's search for a suitable land grant had finally been successful. He had taken a grant on virgin land in the Hawkesbury area, and it stood to sense that he could not take either of his young wards there until a house had been built and buildings for the stock erected. His next words confirmed her supposition. He and Mrs. Boskenna would go to the grant, supervise the convict laborers and the moving of the stock and the house furnishings, and, in the meantime, Miss Abigail and Miss Lucy would be offered hospitality by Mr. and Mrs. Spence. And she, too, would be in Sydney, Kate thought joyfully, able to see them.

"Your responsibilities," Mr. Boskenna put in repressively, "will end, of course, when you hand over Miss Lucy to her kind hostess. In any event I imagine you will be kept busy at Government House. Lieutenant Putland, I'm informed, is very gravely ill." A constable approached, touching his hat politely.

"All in order now, yer reverence. The girls are goin' ter be'ave theirselves." He was breathing hard but grinning, the whip, with its long lash, dangling over his arm. "Put on quite a performance, the wicked besoms, but it were only their disappointment," he added with indulgence. "Not enough fellers to go around, see? But their turn'll come, that's what I tell 'em."

"Quite so, my man." Caleb Boskenna took his prayer book from the pocket of his ill-fitting tailcoat. "I did not find the spectacle edifying, and I intend to point out the errors of their ways to them, so make sure that you keep them in order." He nodded to Kate. "You will be so good as to call at my residence for Miss Lucy on your way to the wharf, Kate. You will save Mrs. Boskenna a tedious and unnecessary journey. It will mean that we shall both be able to leave in the oxcart first thing tomorrow, with Jethro and the stock." He did not wait for Kate's acknowledgment; walking with dignity to the improvised altar in the center of the yard, he faced the seventeen couples sternly and Superintendent Oakes, his this face beaded with perspiration, handed him a list of their names.

The ceremony which joined all seventeen in wedlock was swiftly concluded, but the sermon that followed kept newlyweds and congregation standing bareheaded in the hot sun for almost an hour. Kate, with past experience of the Reverend Caleb Boskenna's preaching, returned to her shaded doorway and, busy with her own unexpectedly happy thoughts, let his passionate denunciations pass unheeded over her head, catching only an occasional word here and there.

"Be not deceived," the chaplain thundered, as the women stirred restlessly and one or two muttered in blasphemous protest, "God is not mocked! Whatsoever a man soweth, that also shall he reap! I come not to call the righteous, but sinners to repentance. Forsake your evil ways . . . do not indulge in strong liquor, idleness, and promiscuity. Find salvation in hard work and Christian marriage, and abjure temptation. . . ."

He ranted on, but the women had had enough. Two or three started to sing, others caught the refrain and joined them in noisy chorus. The tune was that of a hymn, but the words were very different.

"We're Factory girls, refractory girls!" they taunted. "We're frail girls, pale girls, jail girls—keep nit and skip the bail girls! We're tried and true Old Bailey girls, the strip and rob you gaily girls, the true-blue gin and tatter girls—the assault and batter, Parramatta Factory girls!"

Caleb Boskenna's voice, powerful though it was, faded into inaudibility beneath the raucous laughter and the defiant chanting of the determined women. It was the first time Kate had ever seen him discomfited, and absurdly, she found herself wishing that Abigail could have been there to witness it. She herself remained silent, her expression carefully blank as, above the uproar, she heard Superintendent Oakes yelling for order. Francis Oakes was popular, on the whole, and the women obeyed him. In the sudden hush the Reverend Boskenna brought the service to a close, with an angry "You are dismissed!" and without the customary blessing. His departure from the jailyard was marked with a few ribald cheers, and then, it being Sunday and a day of rest, the yard emptied. The inmates who remained went in search of their hidden supplies of liquor with which—their former quarrels forgotten—to drink to the health of the newlyweds, prior to bidding them farewell.

The superintendent, glimpsing Kate, came over to join her, mopping his heated face.

"That was a rum do, right enough," he remarked ruefully, "but the reverend should'a had more sense than to start preachifying at a wedding. Or he should'a let 'em hold it in the church. They'd have behaved themselves in church, whatever he'd said about them bein' sinners and bound for hellfire."

"Aye," Kate agreed, aware that he was seeking no more than the truth.

"You come out with 'im, didn't you, in the same ship?" the superintendent pursued.

"Yes," Kate said. She smiled. "In the *Mysore,* and there weren't many ships as good as that one, Mr. Oakes. We was treated like 'uman beings . . . the master an' the surgeon, they was both kindly, decent gentlemen. An' the Reverend Boskenna, why he had us all converted almost afore we was out o' sight o' land. Model convicts we was, the lot o' us."

Oakes patted her plump arm. "Well, you're getting your reward, me lass—did the reverend tell you?"

"That I'm to go to Government House ter help nurse the governor's son-in-law . . . that what you mean?"

The superintendent nodded. "That's about the size o' it, Kate. I'll arrange for you to go to Sydney in the mornin'. You can call at the chaplain's residence on your way an' pick up the child he wants you to look after . . . an' you'll not need one o' my constables ter make sure you get there, eh?"

"No, I'll not need a constable," Kate assured him.

"You're a right good lass," Oakes told her, with sincerity. "Ought never to've bin sent here, but we'll miss you all the same. Like a plaguey lying-in hospital, this place is at times. What'll we do for a midwife when you go?"

"There's Sarah Burdo, Mr. Oakes."

"Aye. Gettin' a mite long i' the tooth an' in 'er cups most o' the time. But"—the superintendent shrugged—"she'll have to do, I suppose. Come back here, Kate, if you've a mind to. You could set up as a midwife here in Parramatta, no trouble. They say as your new patient's dyin', poor cove, so you may not be long down there at Government House. And I'd see to it that you got a house an' a few acres o' garden . . . there'd be no question o' you comin' back to the Factory, o' course."

Kate thanked him, and he left her with an invitation to call in at the government bakery before she picked up Lucy Tempest, promising a fresh-baked loaf and some sweetmeats to stave off hunger during the ferry's slow, twenty-mile journey from Parramatta to Sydney Cove.

Lucy was waiting for her when she knocked diffidently on the door of the chaplain's house early next morning. Two large oxcarts were standing outside, being loaded with household goods and sacks of provisions. Mrs. Boskenna, busy supervising a gang of convicts engaged in this task, hustled her young ward off with a very cursory farewell.

Lucy Tempest, Kate quickly realized, had changed—no doubt under Mrs. Boskenna's influence. On board the *Mysore* when, poor child, she had been so ill, it had been a pleasant and rewarding task to nurse her, for she had been both obedient and grateful, and a bond of affection had been forged between them, in spite of the difference in their stations. Now, however, it was evident that Lucy was aware of the difference. She addressed Kate by her surname, and with a convict pushing a handcart containing her trunk at their heels, Lucy loaded Kate with numerous items of hand baggage while she walked half a dozen paces ahead, free of all encumbrances, her manner one of conscious superiority.

Kate, who had been eager to learn of her charge's recent doings and to speak of her own unexpected change of fortune, finding her initial questions unheaded, lapsed into hurt silence, her plump cheeks pink with resentment. Behind her the convict with the handcart observed cynically, "She's a stuck-up little madam, that one, missus. Pay her no heed."

His words carried, for he had not troubled to lower his voice, and Lucy turned on him. "I could have you whipped for speaking so," she warned him shrilly, "and Lamerton for listening to you."

Martha Boskenna had threatened her in similar fashion, Kate recalled, but she said nothing, while Lucy tossed her head and affected not to see the male convict's derisive smirk. It was not until they prepared to board the ferry that Lucy deigned to speak to Kate again, and then it was only to order her in a peremptory tone to see to the bestowal of her baggage.

"You do not have to sit with me," the child added. "I prefer to be by myself."

"As you wish, Miss Lucy," Kate answered submissively, and found herself wondering, a trifle uneasily, whether her favorite, Miss Abigail, had also changed under the Dawsons' influence. It seemed unlikely—Abigail was made of sterner, less impressionable stuff than her younger sister. But if the treatment she herself might expect at Government House were of the kind thirteen-year-old Lucy was meting out to her, then—she smothered a sigh—she would have been better off at the women's Factory. At least there the position she had been promised was to have been one of authority, with her own room and an entire weaving shed under her control. And her skill as a midwife had not been wasted. . . . Kate smiled wryly. The Factory girls, even the single ones, gave birth with almost monotonous regularity, and as Superintendent Oakes had said, once she was granted ticket-of-leave, she would be free to set up as a midwife in the township and might even expect employment by the respectable inhabitants, as well as those under sentence in the Factory. Old Sarah Burdo, it was rumored, was a rich woman, despite a reputation for insobriety and lack of hygiene.

The ferry was starting to fill up. Government-owned and plying regularly between Sydney and Parramatta, it was intended to carry cargo rather than passengers, for whom the only accommodation was on the open deck. When a road gang, a ragged crew in leg-irons, came on board, and their overseer directed them to the after part of the deck, where Lucy had been sitting, the child took fright and, not entirely to Kate's surprise, came hurrying forward to join her.

The ferryman cast off from the wharf. The sweeps —each manned by two pullers—came out, and although there was only a faint breeze ruffling the smooth surface of the river, the lateen mainsail was hoisted, causing some confusion amongst those crowded on deck.

Caught up in the confusion, Lucy was breathless and considerably out of temper when she reached Kate's side. "Those rough, horrible creatures!" she exclaimed fretfully. "They were rude, Kate—they used blasphemous language, and they—they laughed at me when I bade them hold their tongues!"

"They know no better," Kate answered, careful not to betray the amusement she felt at her charge's discomfiture. "Just you sit down by me, Miss Lucy. They'll not trouble you when you're with me."

"Mrs. Boskenna should have hired a longboat for me," Lucy grumbled, "not sent me by the common ferryboat service. She is always saying that I must not mix with the convicts."

" 'Taint easy *not* to mix with them," Kate pointed out, "bein' as this is a penal colony." She folded her shawl and laid it on the deck for Lucy to sit on. "I'll warrant as Miss Abigail's learnt ter take the rough wi' the smooth by this time."

Lucy's thin, sallow little face expressed disbelief, and she countered resentfully, "Well, it will be different when we move to our own farm. Mrs. Boskenna says it is a long way from any other occupied property and miles and miles from any convict settlement."

"Where is it?" Kate asked curiously.

"On the Hawkesbury River," Lucy answered

vaguely. "You have to hire a boat from the wharf below Mr. Dawson's property. We shall have a house
there, built of brick and timber, and stockyards and
pens for the sheep and cattle my father bought at the
Cape. Convicts will have to build them, of course,
but when they are completed, we shall only employ
good Christian workers, Mr. Boskenna assured me.
He intends to select them with great care, and there'll
be Jethro—the shepherd who came out here with
us. . . ." She prattled on, but Kate only half-listened
to her boastful claims, beyond registering the fact that
the Boskennas' plans would take a considerable time
to put into effect, and in consequence, both Miss Lucy
and Miss Abigail would probably have to spend the
next month or two in Sydney. Her heart lifted, and
she looked forward with pleasurable anticipation to
the prospect of seeing Miss Abigail again—for she,
surely, would not have changed.

And there was the young surgeon, Dr. Titus Penhaligon, who, she had sensed, had taken a strong
fancy to her pretty Miss Abigail during the voyage
from Plymouth. Being a gentleman, however, and uncertain of his prospects in the colony, he had been
too scrupulous to declare himself. Perhaps he, too, was
in Sydney, and perhaps the government had given him
professional employment; so that now he could pay
his court to whomsoever he wished with a clear conscience.

Very little news from the outside world ever pene-
trated the fastness of the Factory, Kate reflected; it
was only because the Reverend Boskenna had told
her that she knew Abigail was in Sydney. There had
been no word, no visit, all the time she had been
confined to the weaving shed and exercise yard, but
someone—Dr. Penhaligon, probably, or even Miss
Abigail—must have recommended her to the governor's daughter, otherwise she would not have been

sent for. And there had been a rumor that had set tongues wagging—and which neither the superintendent nor his officials had denied—that an attempt had been made on the governor's life by some Irish escapers.

The attempt had been unsuccessful, Oakes had insisted, and the miscreants arrested and brought to trial, but it was possible that Governor Bligh had, after all, been wounded and that he, not his son-in-law, would be her patient. She hoped devoutly that he would not. There were rumors about Governor Bligh, too, about his uncertain and violent temper and, of course, about the mutiny on board his ship the *Bounty*. She had heard those before she had left England.

Kate shivered in the freshening breeze, feeling the ferry's deck cant beneath her, as the flapping sail filled. Lucy said reproachfully, "Kate, you haven't been listening! I asked you a question."

"I'm sorry, Miss Lucy—what did you want to know?"

"Whether you brought anything to eat," the girl repeated. She added plaintively, "I'm hungry. Mrs. Boskenna was too busy to prepare a meal before we left."

"Well, as it happens, I did," Kate told her, thankful to be able to gratify one, at least, of her wishes. She scrambled up and took the freshly baked loaf from Superintendent Oakes's bakery out of her basket. Lucy beamed and fell upon it ravenously, uttering no complaint at its lack of filling.

"Mr. Boskenna," she said, her mouth full, "intends to set up a mission on our grant—a mission for the aborigines. He says he will give them bread and endeavor to convert them to Christianity."

Kate stared at her. She had seen some of the native people in Parramatta and thought them savages; the women at the Factory, the older ones, who had had dealings with them in the past, had confirmed her view. The Indians, as they called them, were thieves and murderers, incapable of being civilized, and woe betide anyone with a white skin, male or female, who fell into their clutches.

"I'm learning to sing hymns," Lucy went on, "so that I can help him. He is a good man, Kate, a very good man."

"I don't doubt he means to be," Kate conceded warily, "but he'll be askin' for trouble, I reckon, if he tries preachin' to them blacks."

"Well, that is his firm intention," Lucy assured her. "Is there any more bread?"

Kate yielded up her second small loaf, and to her relief, when she had eaten it, Lucy lay down with her head propped on the basket and slept until Sydney Cove was sighted and the ferryman ran his unwieldy craft into its berth at the public wharf with the skill of long practice. There was a convict transport on the opposite side of the anchorage, with a water tender tied up alongside and men moving purposefully about her upper deck. Kate glimpsed the name *Edinburgh* painted across her stern and one of the ferry's crew, observing her interest, said flatly, "She's sailin' in a day or so for Hobart with a bunch o' folk from Norfolk Island and a score bein' deported from 'ere for their crimes. Poor devils, they don't know what they're goin' to!"

A shout from the ferryman sent the crewman scurrying off to attend a mooring rope, and Lucy wakened to stare about her in bewilderment.

"We're in Sydney," Kate told her. "And I think I see Dr. Penhaligon waiting for us."

"Not Abigail?" Lucy questioned, disappointed.

"I can't see her. Perhaps she'll come later."

Kate collected their hand baggage, and as soon as the mooring hawsers were secured and the wooden gangway in place, they went ashore, to meet Titus Penhaligon. With him was a slim, dark-haired lady in her early thirties, dressed elegantly but without ostentation, whom Kate guessed was Mrs. Spence, wife of the magistrate and shipowner, Mr. Jasper Spence, and Lucy's hostess. The doctor confirmed this in his introduction, and Mrs. Spence greeted both Lucy and herself with friendly warmth. She put out a hand to draw Lucy to her side and said, in a voice with a faint hint of an Irish brogue, "How very good of you to look after Lucy, Mrs. Lamerton. I had expected that Mrs. Boskenna would bring her, but . . ." Her smile expressed a certain lack of regret, and Kate found herself echoing it, as she explained the reason for Mrs. Boskenna's absence.

"I quite understand," Mrs. Spence answered. "And I have, on my part, to make Abigail's apologies. She kindly stayed behind to watch over the children, but she asked me most particularly to send her love to Kate . . . that is you, is it not, Mrs. Lamerton? She also asked me to say that she would see you at the first opportunity. Indeed, I would invite you to accompany us back to the house, but I understand from Dr. Penhaligon that you are needed urgently at Government House. He will take you there as soon as John has collected the baggage. John"—she gestured to a shirt-sleeved servant, with a handcart—"would you please see to it? Have you a trunk, Lucy?"

Lucy was staring at her in open-mouthed astonishment. Clearly, Kate thought, this was not the way Mrs. Boskenna had taught her to address convicts; Lucy's astonishment grew when Dr. Penhaligon relieved Kate herself of her burdens, tucking her basket

under his arm and transferring Lucy's hand luggage
to the cart. But the child roused herself sufficiently to
describe her trunk, and—her eyes downcast and studiously avoiding Kate's—she murmured subdued
thanks to no one in particular.

"You'll be pleased to be reunited with your sister,
after all this time," Mrs. Spence suggested.

"Oh, yes, yes indeed, ma'am," Lucy responded. "I
—I've missed her."

"And she has missed you, my dear," Mrs. Spence
said, "but I, for my part, could not have done without
her. She has been of the greatest help to me in what
has been an anxious and trying time." Her gaze went,
almost involuntarily, to the anchored transport, and
Kate was shocked by the pain in her blue, expressive
eyes. At a loss to understand the reason for it—for
surely the beautiful wife of a rich and respected magistrate could have no concern with exiled convicts, unless, perhaps, she had Irish friends among them—
Kate said nothing. Lucy, losing her initial shyness, was
prattling away eagerly now, asking about the children,
their names and ages, and Mrs. Spence replied with
charming courtesy, controlling whatever grief or anxiety she felt.

The trunk was unloaded and placed on the handcart, and Dr. Penhaligon hefted Kate's sacking bundle
onto his shoulder and bowed to Mrs. Spence.

"We had best be on our way, ma'am—Mrs. Putland is expecting us."

"And Abigail will be expecting *us*," Mrs. Spence
echoed, her smile returning with all its former warmth.
"The children can be a trial at times, little monsters!"
She shook Kate's hand and patted the young doctor's
thin shoulder with obvious affection. "You will, I
trust, find time to call on us again soon, Titus—you
are always welcome. And Mrs. Lamerton, too, when

she can be spared from her duties. Come, Lucy, my dear—our house is in the High Street, it's only a short distance from here. We'll walk, shall we?"

"And we will take a boat, Mrs. Lamerton," Titus Penhaligon said. "I have one waiting."

He talked of their patient as they were rowed across the cove, giving his professional opinion with regret. "He is sinking fast, I fear, and there is not very much that you will be able to do for him, poor fellow. But his wife—Mrs. Putland, His Excellency's daughter—is exhausted, nearing the end of her endurance. She is a brave and very conscientious lady, and she has hitherto refused to leave him or to entrust his care to anyone else. You will be doing her and the governor a great service if you can persuade her to take the rest she so badly needs." He outlined the treatment he had prescribed for the sick man, and Kate listened attentively.

"I will do my best, Doctor," she promised.

"Aye, I know you will." The surgeon smiled. "You're a fine nurse, Kate, and I've sung your praises to Mrs. Putland. All you have to do is win her trust. Dr. Redfern is officially in medical charge of the case, but I'm acting as his assistant until I am given a government post, and at his wish and Mrs. Putland's, I am visiting twice daily." As she nodded her satisfaction he added, his tone grave, "Quite apart from the effect the strain and lack of sleep are having on Mrs. Putland, the governor has his troubles, too, and he needs her support and her company. His wife is in England, more's the pity."

"Yes, sir," Kate acknowledged, with deliberate reticence. It was not her place to ask more on this subject, she decided; the young doctor had told her all she required to know. Instead, she inquired diffidently about Abigail Tempest and, to her dismay, saw him redden unhappily. But he answered readily enough,

"Oh, she is in her element with Mr. and Mrs. Spence and the Dawson children, who adore her. The Spences entertain a good deal, and Miss Abigail is immensely popular. Of course, that's only to be expected—she is so pretty and gay, and all the young officers pay court to her. But—" He broke off, his color deepening. "I see her when I can, and Mrs. Spence is exceptionally kind to me. But I've nothing to offer her, have I? Not even a government appointment, as yet."

The boat came alongside the government wharf. The bowman deftly wielded his boathook, and Titus Penhaligon leaped nimbly onto the jetty, holding out his hand to assist Kate to follow him.

"Just a step, now," he said, with a swift change of tone, indicating the white-painted, two-story building that Kate had previously only glimpsed from the *Mysore*'s deck. "That's Government House—your patient's rooms are on the upper floor, and I'll take you straight up. One of the men will bring your baggage."

Kate looked about her with interest. A flagpole stood at the rear of the jetty, with the Union flag flying proudly from its halyards. Behind it was a brick-built guardhouse, with a uniformed sentry pacing back and forth outside. A well-kept grass lawn, some flourishing vines, and a profusion of fruit trees lay behind the paling fence, and a graveled drive led up to the house itself, with a verandah shading its front door and lower windows. Four small brass cannon were ranged on either side of the door, one pair to the right, the other to the left, but they were unattended and Kate wondered whether they were merely for show.

The sentry slapped his musket butt in acknowledgment of Titus Penhaligon's approach, and another soldier came out from the guardhouse to open the gate, greeting him by name in familiar fashion. At the front door a manservant admitted them, and, having relieved

Titus of his hat, he accepted Kate's bundle and shabby
basket from the boatman with none of the disdain she
had anticipated. Instead, he gave her a friendly smile
and Kate warmed to him at once, liking his spruce
appearance and lined brown face, which suggested that
his real calling was the sea. He confirmed her supposition when he introduced himself.

"I'm George Jubb, ma'am, His Excellency's steward, previously in his service when he was Captain
Bligh of the Royal Navy. Quarters have been prepared for you in the next room to Mr. Putland, but
if there is anything you require which has not been
provided, you have only to inform me."

He led them across the entrance hall toward a narrow staircase, gesturing to a closed door on his right
as they passed. "His Excellency's office, ma'am. He
left instructions for you and the doctor to report to
him, but he's engaged at the present with a visitor,
so I think it's best for you to go straight upstairs. You
know the way, do you not, Dr. Penhaligon, sir? Mrs.
Putland is with the poor sick gentleman and—" He
was interrupted by a roar of anger, coming from behind the closed door of the governor's office.

Kate flinched as a string of oaths sounded in the
wake of the roar—oaths, she decided in shocked surprise, more suited to the quarterdeck than to the
austere and dignified surroundings of Government
House.

Jubb, however, seemed quite unperturbed. He exchanged a tolerant smile with Dr. Penhaligon and
observed shrewdly, "The trial of those plaguey Irish
rebels has caused His Excellency a deal of concern, and
Captain Hawley has not brought good news of it, I fear.
If you'll be good enough to excuse me, sir, I reckon I'd
best be on hand to see him out. You can find your own
way to the sickroom, can you not, sir?"

"Certainly I can," the young surgeon assured him.

"Don't let us keep you from your duties, Jubb, my dear fellow. We shall manage quite well."

He went bounding up the stairs, and Kate followed him, recovering her composure. What was a little bad language, uttered in wrath? Had she not heard much worse from the women at the Factory? The governor of a colony like this had plenty to enrage him, and had not the Irish rebels attempted to set an ambush for him and kill him? Small wonder if their trial had caused him concern.

Titus Penhaligon halted at the head of the stairs. He said in a confidential whisper, returning to the subject of their earlier conversation in the boat, "Talking of Irishmen, Kate . . . plague take the whole race, I say! There's one of them, a lieutenant in the Corps named O'Shea, who is setting his cap at Miss Abigail. And I very greatly fear that she favors the fellow. But keep that to yourself, will you? Only put in a good word for me if you can, next time you see her."

"Of course I will, sir," Kate promised readily. "You may rely on me."

"Bless you for a good-hearted woman!" He put his arm about her ample shoulders and hugged her, and then, still with his arm round her, moved forward to knock gently on one of the doors.

"Come in," a woman's voice invited wearily, and Titus pushed open the door.

"I've brought Kate Lamerton, Mrs. Putland," he began. "She's the nurse I recommended, and—"

"Thank God!" Mary Putland cried, and Kate, going to meet her, was instantly captivated by the beauty and sadness of her face. She dropped a dutiful curtsy as Mrs. Putland said, with deep sincerity, "No one was ever more welcome than you are, Mrs. Lamerton."

In the room below, which he used as an office, William Bligh exclaimed angrily, "Justice has been done, the devil take it, Hawley! A legally constituted criminal court has condemned my would-be assassins to hang. What possible objection can you have to that?"

"None, sir," Andrew Hawley conceded, keeping a stern hold on his temper. "It is in the case of Mrs. Broome that I believe most strongly that there has been a miscarriage of justice. Mrs. Broome had no part in the attempt on your life, sir, and she—"

"She harbored those who *had*—fed and hid 'em, damme! And provided them with weapons and a horse, did she not? Atkins said she did."

"The horse and the weapons were stolen from her, sir," Andrew protested. "And the Irishmen forced their way into her farmhouse under arms. She was convicted solely on Lieutenant Brabyn's evidence."

"And you don't regard Brabyn as a reliable witness?" the governor countered. "Well"—he shrugged—"come to that, no more do I. The fellow is a rogue and certainly he's no gentleman. But he gave sworn testimony to the court, did he not?"

"He did, sir. But so also did the witnesses to Mrs. Broome's character. Her record is exemplary since her arrival in this colony. The witnesses' written statements are before Your Excellency—" Andrew gestured to the piled papers on the governor's desk. "Mr. Spence is a magistrate, Mr. Dawson a substantial landowner, and—"

"Yes, yes, I've read them," Bligh said impatiently. "They speak highly of Mrs. Broome. But what sentence did the court impose on her, for God's sake? A mere six months' banishment to Van Diemen's Land—the same as the first trial judges imposed, when they virtually let the Irishmen off scot-free. If I remit her sentence, I'll have to remit theirs and make myself a damned laughingstock throughout the colony—and for no better reason than because *you* insist on marrying her!"

"I have offered to resign my commission in order to do so, sir," Andrew reminded him stiffly.

"No!" the governor thundered. "Devil take it, I need you! Can you not wait six months? They will be six critical months, Hawley—for this colony and for myself, as well you know. I need men I can depend on, men of proven loyalty . . . For the Lord's sweet sake, I am surrounded by traitors. The rum traders will move heaven and earth to get rid of me, so that they can preserve the source of their infernal profits! And," he added grimly, "I am heading for a showdown with Macarthur."

"Are you, sir?" Andrew's expression did not relax, but William Bligh was not looking at him. Searching amongst the scattered papers on his desk, he produced a letter.

"This, Hawley, is from the English missionaries in Otaheite, objecting to the presence of a notorious character by the name of John Hoare—a convict who escaped from this colony and, they inform me, landed from the schooner *Parramatta,* with the full knowledge and connivance of her master. And do you know who owns the *Parramatta?*"

Andrew, taken by surprise at the question, shook his head.

"Macarthur and his partner, Garnham Blaxcell," the governor supplied. "According to the regulations, they deposited a bond for eight hundred pounds as a guarantee that there were no stowaway convicts on board before the ship sailed for Otaheite. When she returns in a few weeks' time, I shall be compelled to make an official case of it and demand forfeiture of the bond. And Macarthur will fight—he'll fight me every inch of the way, you may be sure of that. It may well come to a trial of strength between us, Hawley, and the infernal fellow knows it. He's trying to get Atkins removed from the judge advocacy; he's persecuted poor Willie Gore; and he's engaged in vexatious legislation against both the Campbells. He's trying to clear his yardarm before the *Parramatta* case comes before the courts. And George Johnstone is backing every move he makes, with the support of that crew of blackguards he calls his officers!"

Andrew was genuinely shocked by the governor's revelations. On the other hand, Jenny had been sent on board the transport *Edinburgh,* on orders from the court, in felon's chains, to serve her sentence, and he was torn by his own conflicting loyalties. Bligh had threatened, following the calling of their banns of marriage, to transfer him to Colonel Collins's staff in Van Diemen's Land and then relented.

"I cannot remit Mrs. Broome's sentence," the older man said, in a much milder tone, "and then have you take her to wife. As a reasonable man, you must realize that, Hawley. To do so would destroy both your credibility and my own. . . ." He talked on, advancing reasons for his seemingly harsh decision, and Andrew listened with growing uneasiness. What he said was true, of course; an aide who was married to a convicted felon would become a liability. And a pardon granted solely to enable such a marriage to take place would scarcely redound to the governor's credit, which was already under attack. Yet Jenny was innocent—even Joseph Fitzgerald, facing the death sentence, had sworn to her innocence, but the court had ignored his plea on her behalf, just as they had seen fit to ignore the character witnesses.

Despite the fact that there had been three civilian magistrates on the bench, Brabyn's evidence had been accepted. Andrew's big hands clenched helplessly at his sides. Six months was a short enough sentence, even a merciful one if Jenny's guilt were beyond question, but it was not. And there were her children—young Justin, beside himself with anxiety, and capable of anything in his bitterness; William and little Rachel, safe enough in the care of the Jardines but deprived of their mother. Tim Dawson had promised to keep a watchful eye on them, and Frances Spence, who had been greatly distressed by the verdict, could be relied upon to take both children under her roof if need arose, yet all the same . . . Anger caught at his throat.

He said at last, reluctantly, when Governor Bligh fell silent, obviously expecting an answer, "I beg your forgiveness, sir. I have a duty to you whilst I wear the King's uniform, but I—"

"But you don't intend to do it?" Bligh accused, his temper again rising. "Well, damn your soul, Hawley, I'll not permit you to quit the service! You can get yourself on board the *Edinburgh* before she weighs and marry this infernal convict woman of yours in Hobart if that's what you want. When her sentence expires, you can come back to Sydney, and I'll give you some suitable military appointment. You can command the Coal River settlement or relieve poor Gore as provost marshal. But you'll not serve me as my aide. I need a man I can trust."

Andrew rose to his feet, to stand stiffly to attention. "Aye, aye, sir." The bitter rejection was deserved, he knew, but for all that it hurt him deeply after almost twenty-five years' loyal service to his Corps and the Crown. There was a chaplain on Colonel Collins's staff . . . they could be wed as soon as they landed. Collins was said to be an excellent administrator, with a reputation for just dealings, even with the worst of felons deported from New South Wales to his new settlement.

Andrew's flagging spirits rose. He made to take his leave, but the governor shook his head, frowning.

"On second thoughts, it would be inappropriate for you to take passage in the same ship as Mrs. Broome," he rasped. "You can follow her—I'll arrange for you to be given passage in a dispatch sloop when the next English mail arrives. In any event"—his frown deepened as he picked up a sheaf of papers from his desk—"these are the death warrants for the Irishmen, and I have signed them. There will be no reprieves—they'll all hang tomorrow morning."

"There may be trouble with the other damned rebels," he went on brusquely. "That fellow Fitzgerald will almost certainly make an inflammatory speech from the foot of the gallows. You will command my bodyguard, Hawley. I cannot trust the blasted Rum Corps. All right—that will be all. You may go."

Andrew bowed, his scarred face devoid of expression. It was an ill wind, he reflected wryly—at least he would have time to go to Long Wrekin Farm, see Jenny's two children, and ensure that the Jardines had money and were fully informed of what the next six months would require of them.

Justin would take him upriver in his cutter and would almost certainly be chosen to carry the dispatches to Van Diemen's Land, so that they could go together.

Reaching the door he turned, donned his headgear, and gave the governor an impeccable salute.

Bligh scowled at him and said regretfully, "Damn your eyes, Hawley—you were the best man I had!"

CHAPTER X

Frances Spence joined the noisy, catcalling crowd of convicts and emancipists gathered behind the ranks of the New South Wales Corps to witness the hanging of the five condemned Irish Defenders.

The soldiers, with muskets grounded, formed three sides of a hollow square, their scarlet-clad backs presented to the jostling throng and forcing them to keep their distance. William Gore, the provost marshal, attended by two constables, stepped out to read the sentences as the prisoners, their arms pinioned behind their backs, were marched to the foot of the gallows.

There was a priest with them, Frances saw, and she silently thanked God for that small concession to the preservation of their immortal souls. She had come alone, dreading the ghastly ordeal but feeling that she owed it to Joseph Fitzgerald to be present when he breathed his last. Her son-in-law, Tim Dawson, who might have accompanied her, had been compelled to return to his farm, and—she stifled a sigh—she could not, in all conscience, ask for her husband's escort. Jasper was a magistrate, and he did not share her faith

—indeed, he would almost certainly have forbidden her to go, had she told him of her intention. She drew her black shawl more closely about her, hiding the lower part of her face, as the thud of hooves and the jingle of bits heralded the arrival of the governor and his mounted escort, trotting across to take up a position some distance behind and to the right of the crowd.

There was, Frances was aware, a petition to be presented, pleading for clemency and signed by a number of Irish settlers—Protestants as well as Catholics, and including Sir Henry Brown Hayes and herself—but few cherished any real hope that it would achieve its purpose. Joseph Fitzgerald had not denied setting an ambush for the governor. At the second trial he had boasted of it, and it was now widely known that the original sentences had been a deliberate ploy on the part of Major Johnstone and his officers to anger and humiliate the colony's ruler. And poor Jenny had been, all unwittingly, caught up in the sorry affair. Frances's eyes filled with tears as she glanced behind her to where, in the cove, the transport *Edinburgh* lay at anchor.

If William Bligh had refused Jenny a reprieve, he was unlikely in the extreme to pardon the men who had tried to kill him. They would die, all five of them, and the *Edinburgh* would sail for Van Diemen's Land with Jenny on board . . . in the sick bay, if Captain Hawley had contrived to persuade the surgeon to move her there. She had clothes, money, and food—Frances and Jasper had seen to that—and Justin had been permitted to bid her farewell. Frances forced herself to return her gaze to the men standing at the foot of the gallows.

They looked calm, even proud, and despite the distance and the bobbing heads of the people between them, she could see that Joseph, his prayers finished, was smiling. Big, blue-eyed Christie O'Hagan was equally calm and at ease, although both were painfully thin, and Christie was limping. They had been flogged, she remembered, ordered a hundred lashes for possessing firearms at the initial hearing, and neither had fully recovered from the appalling treatment meted out to all those who were sent to Coal River. Perhaps—her teeth bit into her lower lip, seeking to still its trembling —perhaps death, even by the hangman's noose, was, to men like these, preferable to renewed exile and yet more brutal punishment.

Death would be martyrdom; their names would not be forgotten by Irish patriots, here or at home, for they had fought bravely in '98 and again out here, refusing to submit to tyranny, however insurmountable the odds. Joseph Fitzgerald had chosen his way, had known the risk he was taking . . . just as he knew now that Governor Bligh would reject the petition. An officer touched his pinioned arm, and, with something of a shock, Frances recognized him as Lieutenant O'Shea. He, too, was Irish and a frequent caller at her house since he had started to pay court to Abigail Tempest, but now . . . There was a bitter taste in her mouth as she watched the brief exchange between them, guessing its import. Joseph was to be forbidden the right to make the traditional address from the scaffold. That appeared to be the reason for O'Shea's intervention, his gesture to the hangman, waiting with a blindfold in his hand . . . oh, God, *no*! He should not be sent to his death like a dumb animal, robbed of the last chance he would ever have to declare his devotion to Ireland's cause!

The tears were streaming down Frances's cheeks, blinding her. She brushed them away with bunched knuckles, at once despairing and angry. When she looked again, Joseph had mounted the scaffold, still silent as the watchers stamped and shouted. The blindfold covered his face and the priest was at his side, murmuring a prayer he could barely have heard for the uproar.

A white-haired man in the rough clothes of a farmer, seeing Frances's tears, sidled close to her.

" 'Twas by agreement, mistress, ye understand," he confided. "Dey was fearin' trouble, if Joe got leave ter speak 'fore dey was after turnin' him off. So dey promised him a priest so long as he kept silent. But de rest o' us made no promises, so we did not." He raised his voice and shouted urgently, "Let's give de boys a send off! Up for de green!"

As if it had been a signal for which they had been waiting, people in the crowd started to sing. Some were in groups of half a dozen or so, some in pairs, a few, like Frances, were alone, and the singing faltered at first in untuneful disharmony. But then suddenly, as the hangman adjusted the rope about Joseph Fitzgerald's neck, the words came in heady, inspiring chorus.

"To live or die, to rise or fall—stand together, stand together! Oh, for the living—by the dead, stand together, true together!"

A moment later poor Joseph's thin, ragged body was dangling, swinging in a ghastly twitching momentum from the noose, and Frances closed her eyes, unable to bear the sight. But she went on singing as, growing bolder, more voices took up the refrain.

"We trust in God above us, and we dearly love the green. . . . Oh, to die for it is far better than be cursed as we have been! 'Tis the green, oh, the green is the color of the true! 'Tis the color of our martyred dead— our own immortal green! Up for the green, boys, and up for the green!"

Big Christie was standing beneath the gallows now, steadfast, unflinching, a smile on his lips, and the singing grew in volume, some of the English convicts joining in . . . probably, Frances thought wryly, without the least notion of the significance of the song but eager to give support to those whose lot was only a little worse than their own.

"And we've hearts—oh, we've hearts, boys, full true enough, I ween . . . to rescue and to raise again our own immortal green! Up for the green, boys, up for the green!"

Christie had gone; Frances crossed herself and breathed a prayer for his soul as his big, limp body was cut down. Liam O'Rourke endeavored to hold off the hangman; a high-pitched scream rose to his lips but was swiftly stifled. Seamus O'Mara, who had mounted the platform at his heels, offered his own neck and went before him. Luke Brady followed, and the wretched Liam, shamed into silence, was the last to be dispatched, as the singing went on. The troops—evidently under orders—stood steady in their ranks, making no attempt to quell the demonstration or to move the crowd on.

And the governor, Frances saw, when she ventured once more to look about her—the governor had ridden off with his escort, clearly in order to avoid trouble. She crossed herself again and made her way through the now rapidly dispersing throng into the High Street. It was, she realized—returning slowly to full consciousness of her surroundings—it was almost time for the children to go to school . . . and this morning Lucy would be going with them. Abigail would accompany them, of course, if she herself were not back in time; but she had promised to go with them and to introduce Lucy to the principal of the establishment, Mr. Mann. His house was to the rear of the official residences of the judge advocate, surveyor, and chaplain and almost opposite the Government House stables, a pleasant, brick-built house with a blue shingle roof and a large, somewhat untidy garden.

It was only a short distance from where she was, and if she crossed the Tank Stream beyond Mr. Garnham Blaxcell's house and turned to her right, she would almost certainly meet Abigail and her charges on their way. Abigail was a sensible, tactful girl; she would ask no questions as to the reason for her hostess's early-morning absence. Her mind made up, Frances crossed the road and quickened her pace as she made for the narrow wooden bridge over the stream, which had replaced the old stone bridge after its collapse a few months before. She had almost reached it when a horseman came cantering up behind her, and with scant ceremony, hardly slackening speed, went past her in a cloud of choking dust.

She recognized him instantly as Captain John Macarthur when he perforce drew rein at the bridge to clatter across it at a walk and then kick his horse back into a canter, as soon as the obstacle was behind him. He appeared to have come from Garnham Blaxcell's residence and to be going in the direction of Simeon Lord's and, to say the least, to be in a considerable hurry. At that moment Abigail and the children came in sight, having taken a shortcut past the lumberyard, and Frances threw back the concealing folds of her shawl, calling out to them to wait for her.

They did so, and she observed, with pleased surprise, that Titus Penhaligon was with them, Abigail's hand tucked demurely into the crook of his arm.

Her sad heart lifted, and although the singing of the crowd about the gallows still lingered in her memory, she was smiling as she went to meet them.

Simeon Lord witnessed John Macarthur's arrival through the small glazed window of the room he called his study. The hour and the speed of his coming augered ill, but Lord did not move from his chair. He employed a steward to receive guests, and it was early; he had not yet drunk the cup of hot chocolate he took habitually at this hour, and in any event, it would do the arrogant Macarthur no harm to be kept cooling his heels, whilst the steward came respectfully to ascertain whether his master was "at home."

That was the manner in which unexpected callers were treated in a gentleman's household. Simeon Lord smiled, a trifle smugly, to himself. He was not a gentleman, either by birth or upbringing. He had landed in Sydney from the transport *Atlantic*, in August 1791, having been sentenced to seven years' transportation for theft at the Lancashire Quarter Sessions the previous year. He had had the good fortune to be assigned to the then-adjutant of the Corps, Lieutenant Thomas Rowley, who was as deeply involved in the rum traffic as John Macarthur himself and, in his determination to make his fortune, no more scrupulous.

During the years of his enforced servitude, he had made handsome profits from the trade in liquor and other imported goods, both for his master and for himself. He already owned two houses and some extensive land grants by the time he was given emancipation and had entered into partnership with a first fleeter, James Underwood, and another emancipist, Henry Kable. Underwood had been a shipwright before his conviction, and their first venture had been building small ships with which, as their number increased, they had engaged in sealing and whaling, as well as importing trade goods from Otaheite and India. On his own account Simeon Lord kept a store and acted as auctioneer, retailer, and manufacturer, and for all that he had been an illiterate youth of twenty-one when he landed in the colony, he was now, at thirty-seven, one of Sydney's richest merchants, with no call to be subservient to any man . . . not even to the all-powerful Macarthur.

Nevertheless—he drained his chocolate, smacking his coarse lips appreciatively, and lumbered to his feet—Macarthur took offense all too easily, even when it was not intended. He never forgot a slight, and, as a succession of governors knew to their cost, he could be a vengeful and dangerous enemy. It would not do to keep him waiting.

"Jonas, you half-witted fool!" he shouted to his steward. "That's Captain Macarthur—show him in at once and serve him with fresh chocolate or tea or whatever he fancies. And see to it that his horse is attended to—bestir yourself, man!" He held open the door of his study, summoning a broad smile of welcome, both hands extended. "Come in, come in, my good sir! What brings you to my humble abode at such an early hour, pray?"

John Macarthur did not smile. His pendulous lower lip was drooping, his expression one of sullen resentment, but he sank into the chair Simeon Lord pulled out for him and accepted the chocolate the steward nervously offered him. From somewhere in the nether regions of the house a woman's voice rose in petulant complaint, and Lord said irritably, "Jonas, bid that fool woman hold her tongue. No, better still, pack her off back to the St. Patrick. Tell Tom Whittle he can find me a lass with more spunk to her. He—"

Macarthur put in, a distinct edge to his voice, "Oh, forget your infernal women, Simeon! There's trouble brewing and from at least three directions. You know they hanged the Irishmen this morning?"

"I heard they were going to," Lord affirmed. He reached for his tobacco caddy and thrust it across the ornately carved table in his visitor's direction. "Surely you expected it, did you not?"

"Yes, I suppose I did," John Macarthur admitted. He filled a pipe, moodily eyeing its bowl as his blunt fingers pressed the tobacco into it. "This is good stuff . . . where did you obtain it?"

"From Virginia," the emancipist claimed, with conscious pride. "Fill your pouch if you like it—I've plenty more." He hesitated and then added consolingly, "*Some* good has come of the Irish rebel affair. The Broome woman's on board the *Edinburgh,* and I heard, on good authority, that Hawley's being sent to Van Diemen's Land after her."

"Did you, by God!" Macarthur blew a cloud of smoke from between his pursed lips, the pipe in his hand describing an agitated circle. "Well, that's one less of 'em, praise be. But D'Arcy Wentworth is not to be reinstated in the hospital or on the bench, and Tom Jamieson's still on the black list and so's Harris. Now we're up against that infernal fellow Commissary Palmer and the two thrice-damned Campbells . . . and we are going to need a sympathetic bench, let me tell you, Simeon. We are going to need one very sorely!"

Evidently, Simeon Lord thought, he had come to the reason for his visit, and underlying it would be, without a doubt, a request—no, being Jack Macarthur, it would be a *demand* for his help. He reached for the tobacco jar and his own pipe, taking his time to fill and light it. "Why so, John?" he asked warily.

"Because," Macarthur returned, "that rogue John Glenn permitted a stowaway to land openly as soon as the *Parramatta* came to anchor in Matavai Bay. No waiting till dark, no attempt at concealment, and the wretched fellow managed not only to get himself intoxicated, but also to insult one of the miserable Biblethumpers who call themselves missionaries. And *he* has informed Bligh . . . your brig brought the letter from Otaheite!"

"But I see no reason why the matter should trouble you," Lord began, genuinely puzzled. "After all—"

"The stowaway, Hoare, was a lifer," Macarthur snapped. "He was posted as missing by public notice in June, and Glenn, instead of bringing him back, after all the fuss created by the missionary fellow, arranged for him to take passage on board an American-bound trader—which is the last we shall ever see of Mr. Hoare. Garnham and I executed the usual bond, but that unprincipled villain Gore insisted that we should each add fifty pounds to the normal eight hundred. He made some ridiculous claim that one of the mates impeded him in his search of the vessel before she sailed from here. Damme, Simeon, the *Parramatta* will be back in December, and there will be hell to pay!"

Simeon Lord continued to adopt an attitude of bewilderment, but his agile brain was racing, for it was evident that the expected demand for his aid was about to be made. Thinking to forestall it, he offered quickly, "I could send a fast cutter to intercept her and warn Captain Glenn off. The *Parramatta* shouldn't be too hard to find."

"And lose her cargo!" Macarthur retorted explosively. "Devil take it, Simeon, she's carrying pearl shell and sandalwood, as well as prime salt pork and New Zealand flax! It will be worth a mint here, and next to nothing at the Cape or Rio or even in Batavia. No, she must come back to Sydney—I cannot afford to stand that kind of loss, and why should I?"

"But are you sure you'll be called upon to forfeit your bond?" Lord argued. "It's almost six months since the *Parramatta* sailed. Hoare's escape will be forgotten by the time she returns. What's one escaped convict, among so many?"

"D'you imagine Gore will have forgotten? Or, damn his eyes, that the *Bounty* bastard will pass up an opportunity to make trouble for me? He most certainly will not!" The pipe stem cracked under the pressure of John Macarthur's agitated fingers, and he swore as he let it fall to the floor, crushing the clay bowl with his foot. "Oh, I'll fight any claim through the courts if I have to, and fight it all the way. But . . . there is an easier solution, if you're willing to help."

"If you and Blaxcell were thinking of asking me to buy the *Parramatta* from you—it would not work,

John," Simeon Lord said, anticipating the request. "If Gore remembers anything, he'll remember that *you* were the owners when Hoare stowed away in her, and the bond is in your names, yours and Blaxcell's, is it not?"

"Yes, of course it is."

"Then I would not be held responsible, even if I were the present owner."

"But Bligh might leave you alone—he has a personal vendetta against me. He—"

"He does not show *me* any favors, I do assure you," Lord said, with a rueful sigh. "No . . ." He affected to consider the problem, his dark brows thoughtfully puckered. "If they do make trouble for you, John, your best course would be to repudiate Glenn's action. He's known to be a rogue. Were you aware that he had taken a stowaway on board the *Parramatta*?"

"Good God, no! I'd have forbidden it if I'd had any notion of what he intended to do." John Macarthur's indignation seemed genuine enough, and Lord was quick to follow up his advantage.

"Then swear an affidavit to that effect," he advised. "Eat humble pie, for once, and petition the governor for your release from the obligation of the bond. If Captain Glenn is to blame, let *him* take the consequences. Hoare, I am sure, must have paid him well for his services. He was not without means, you know."

Macarthur pursed his lips and gave vent to a sigh of frustration. But he could not deny that Simeon Lord's suggestion had merit, and finally he nodded. "You are right, Simeon. If it should come to a showdown, then that is undoubtedly the best way to handle the matter. Glenn, as you say, is a dishonest rogue. Initially it will rest with Robert Campbell as port naval officer, and it's possible that I can square him. If he keeps his mouth shut and takes no action when the *Parramatta* enters the port, then there will be no harm done." He sounded considerably more optimistic, and Simeon Lord's brows rose.

"How," he asked, with sly interest, "do you propose to 'square' Robert Campbell? He's Bligh's most trusted ally, apart from our mutual friend Palmer."

"Every man has his price, Simeon," Macarthur retorted cynically, "even the righteous and God-fearing Campbells! And they've spent a small fortune building their wharf and warehouses on the west side of the cove, in the belief that—although they only hold the land on lease—they would be granted tenure in perpetuity. They—"

"Haven't we all?" Lord put in, suddenly anxious. "I'm in the same position in that respect, for God's sake!"

"Quite so, my friend," John Macarthur agreed, smiling. "One of *my* leaseholds, as it chances, borders the Campbells; and they would dearly like to have it." He rose, still smiling. "I must be on my way. Thank you for your hospitality, Simeon. Have you heard, by the bye, that Philip King is said to be dying? Major Foveaux mentioned the rumor in his last letter. He had it from Willie Kent, and he said, incidentally, that Hunter is pulling every string he possesses to have our Willie— who is now a post captain—appointed governor!"

"Kent?" Simeon Lord stared at him, open mouthed. "In succession to Bligh, d'you mean?"

John Macarthur moved toward the door. "In *place* of Bligh, God willing," he amended. "But keep that under your hat. There is also a faction endeavoring to advance General Grose's claims, and they are seeking royal influence on his behalf—that of the Duke of Clarence, no less. Interesting, is it not? I confess I should infinitely prefer either distinguished officer to the present incumbent, wouldn't you?" He did not wait for Lord's answer, but strode out of the house, calling impatiently for his horse. When a servant brought the animal, he mounted, offering a casually raised hand in farewell, and trotted off down the dusty street.

Macarthur was sitting very stiffly upright in his saddle, and his smile, Simeon Lord decided, lacked all vestige of amusement or, indeed, of humor.

Had he, the wealthy emancipist asked himself uneasily, made a very grave error in refusing to purchase the *Parramatta*? It would have done no good, but . . . He sighed as he saw his late caller turn into the gate of Thomas Reibie's neat, white-painted residence. Reibie's children were playing in the garden, and they called out in eager welcome. . . .

Apart from Simeon Lord's *Perseverance* and two trading brigs lying off the Campbells' wharf, the cove was deserted when Justin Broome ran his cutter *Flinders* into the anchorage.

The *Edinburgh* had sailed, he observed with a sudden sinking of the heart, and his mother with her. He glanced in mute question at Andrew Hawley, and the tall marine captain said flatly, "We can still go after her—aye, and make Hobart before she does. She's a slow sailer—she was sixty-four days on passage from the Cape."

"But there'll be no mail," Justin felt bound to point out.

"To the devil with mail!" Andrew returned irritably. "You are a free agent, are you not?"

"Aye, you know I am. But I had supposed that the governor would insist on keeping you here until he could send you with official dispatches."

"I don't intend to report to him, Justin," Andrew said. Justin eyed him doubtfully for a moment and then grinned.

"Then in that case, we'll sail first thing tomorrow if the wind doesn't change and I can get the provisions we'll need from Mr. Campbell. I'll have to take Rachel to Mrs. Spence's first, and then—"

"Leave the victualing to me," Andrew put in. "List what you want, and I'll see to it. You deliver your sister to Mrs. Spence."

"Aye, aye, sir," Justin acknowledged, with mock subservience; but his grin faded as he added, "*if* you are sure that the governor isn't likely to order your arrest for going absent without leave."

Andrew shrugged his broad shoulders indifferently. "I *am* on leave, damme, pending my transfer to Colonel Collins's staff in Van Diemen's Land. The worst he can do is demand my commission, and I've already offered him that."

"Yes, but I had supposed that you—"

"That my loyalty is to Captain Bligh, lad?"

"Yes, sir," Justin admitted, avoiding the older man's gaze.

"And so it has been, ever since the Nore mutiny, but he has flung it back in my face. *He* ordered me to Hobart."

"Because you want to marry my mother?"

Andrew inclined his head. "Aye—and because I asked him to pardon her after she had been unjustly sentenced. That . . . and other matters which have also strained my loyalty to its limit. He is a strange man, Captain Bligh. A man of many contradictions. He's a good governor, Justin, and he's done more than his predecessors to bring law and order to this colony and to ensure that the small settlers and emancipist landowners are given the chance to prosper. But he has a fiendish temper, and recently I've been the butt of it. He would not permit me to continue in his personal service, even if I desired to, and I do not."

"On Mam's account?" Justin suggested.

"That's only part of it, lad. I owe your mother my loyalty, too." Andrew clapped a hand on his shoulder, and his expression softened. "I gave her my word when she was a few years younger than you are now, and that's a long time, when you come to think on it. But speaking of time—it will be dark soon. Make out that list for me, will you please, and then go and waken the little lass?"

Justin moved to obey him. They had talked very little of Andrew's impending marriage to his mother, the boy thought as he descended to the small cabin in search of pen and paper. He had been half afraid to broach the subject, and during the two days they had spent at Long Wrekin, it had not been mentioned. For one thing, there had been so much to arrange with the Jardines and with Mr. Dawson, and for another, young William—little tartar that he was—had displayed his hostility to Andrew Hawley with embarrassing frequency. That, Justin felt sure, had been his stubborn young brother's real reason for refusing to quit the farm and accompany Rachel to Sydney—William did not want to take passage downriver in the *Flinders* when Andrew was on board.

Not that it mattered greatly; William's life was the farm and the sheep. He would be much happier working with Tom Jardine and the two native boys than cooped up in the Spences' house in Sydney, forced to attend school with the stuck-up Dawson girls.

Justin smiled to himself and concentrated on the list of provisions. Normally he carried a crew of two when he took the *Flinders* to sea, but he and Andrew could manage her—Andrew was a fair seaman, for all he was a marine—and that would mean a considerable saving in victuals and water. He had a coop of hens and a young ram, which Tom Jardine had provided unasked. They would have fresh meat and a few eggs, if the weather did not put the hens off their laying.

He finished his list, pleased by its modesty, and, rising from the chart table, parted the curtain which separated him from the cutter's sleeping quarters, to find Rachel already awake and struggling into her dress.

"Are we there, Justin?" she asked eagerly.

"We're there," he assured her, and bent to pick up the bundle containing most of her worldly possessions. "Come on deck when you're ready, lass. I'll haul the dinghy alongside and row us ashore."

It was dusk when he left Andrew at the Campbells' wharf, and darkness had fallen by the time he secured the dinghy on the opposite side of the cove. Relinquishing it to the care of the night watch on duty at the government wharf, Justin set off for Jasper Spence's house, with Rachel capering excitedly at his heels.

Abigail Tempest opened the door to them. Evidently the Spences were entertaining, for there were two carriages standing empty outside, and the sound of voices and laughter, mingled with the clink of glasses, caused Justin to step back in some confusion as Abigail peered out at him.

"Oh, it's you!" she exclaimed, recognizing him. "And your sister . . . Rachel, is it not?"

"Yes, Rachel. You . . . that is, Mrs. Spence is expecting her, isn't she?" For no reason that he could have explained, Justin reddened under her scrutiny. He had seen her before, of course, two or three times when he had come to the Spences' imposing residence; but on those occasions, he had been concerned only with his mother's arrest and trial, and had scarcely noticed how lovely she was.

He noticed now and was taken aback by the picture she made, framed in the lighted doorway, with her gleaming fair hair and smooth pink-and-white skin. She was wearing a gown that reflected the blue of her eyes, its shimmering folds emphasizing the graceful curves of her slim young body, and when she held out her hand to him, he could barely summon sufficient composure to take it in his own.

"We are all expecting Rachel," she said, smiling from one to the other of them. "Do come in, both of you. Mrs. Spence is in the dining room."

"But she has guests," Justin stammered, conscious of his shabby, seagoing clothing and his unkempt hair. "I'm just back from the Hawkesbury, and I—that is, I—"

"You will still be welcome," Abigail told him with sincerity. She took Rachel by the hand, but Justin, redder than before, shook his head.

"No . . . no, thank you, I cannot stay." He stepped into the hall in order to divest himself of Rachel's bundle and then swiftly stepped back. "Please convey my—my compliments to Mrs. Spence and tell her how grateful I am to her for having offered Rachel hospitality. My mother will be—" He was abruptly cut short.

"Why, Miss Abigail!" From the room beyond, a tall, scarlet-clad figure emerged, to stand protectively at Abigail's back. "What have we here—a sailor, by heaven! Is the fellow annoying you? Shall I send him on his way?" He saw Rachel then and stared at her in astonishment. "A sailor *and* a little girl who looks as if she's been plucked from the sea as well! Or am I, perhaps, out of order? Would they be acquaintances of yours by any chance?"

"Indeed they are, Mr. O'Shea," Abigail asserted. But she sounded amused, Justin thought angrily, as if she could see no intended offense in the young Corps officer's bantering words. "This is Justin Broome and his sister, Rachel, who is coming to stay with us . . . Lieutenant Desmond O'Shea."

"Ah, yes, that name is known to me," O'Shea said. His tone was still bantering, and he was smiling; but now, Justin decided, the implication was deliberately offensive. He drew himself up, controlling an impulse to smash his fists into O'Shea's smiling face. The Irish

officer had been a member of the court that had tried
and convicted his mother, he recalled, but in these circumstances—and in Abigail Tempest's presence—there
was nothing he could do, save swallow the insult and
withdraw with what dignity he could muster.

He made Abigail a stiff little bow, called out a stilted
farewell to Rachel, and excused himself. O'Shea's big
red hand pushed the door shut with finality, cutting off
the sound of Rachel's sudden wail of dismay at the
realization that he was leaving her. Justin hesitated,
sick with frustrated anger, but he had brought it upon
himself, he knew, invited the humiliation, standing
there, dressed as he was, staring at a girl he had failed
to be aware of previously. And she was beautiful . . .
dear God in heaven, she was beautiful!

He ran off his anger, pounding along the darkened
streets as if the devil were after him, but the vision of
Abigail Tempest, standing in the doorway in her blue
party dress, remained hauntingly in his memory as he
pulled the dinghy across the cove.

Andrew Hawley was waiting for him at the Campbells' wharf, the younger Robert Campbell with him, a
sack of provisions between them.

"I've supplied you with all you asked for, Justin, and
a water tender will top you up at first light." Robert
Campbell passed the sack down into Justin's waiting
arms. "I'll come out in the tender," he added amiably,
"to make an official inspection for stowaways, although
I can't imagine any escaper will want to exchange New
South Wales for Van Diemen's Land! Your bond's still
in force, is it not?"

Justin nodded. His mother had skimped and saved
to put up his bond and Andrew, it seemed, had paid
his dues in full to the Campbells. "Then I'll sail as soon
as I've taken on my water, sir."

"I'll inform my uncle," the younger Campbell promised. "You should make Hobart at least twenty-four

hours before the old *Edinburgh*—she only weighed
yesterday. But—you'll not be staying, will you, Justin?"

"Only long enough to see my mother wed, Mr. Campbell," Justin answered decisively. "My work is here."

"And we can give you plenty of it," Campbell assured him. "We've charters for the Hawkesbury and
Coal River piling up and not enough small vessels like
yours to take them. So drop into my office when you
get back." He turned to Andrew, holding out his hand.
"Godspeed, Captain Hawley, and may I be permitted
to wish you well in the future?"

Andrew thanked him and stepped down into the
waiting dinghy.

At six o'clock the following morning, the little
Flinders sailed out of Sydney Cove on a brisk south-
westerly wind. She was lying at anchor in the Derwent
River when the transport *Edinburgh*, a full ten days on
passage, tacked slowly up the estuary under her dingy
canvas, to bring to astern of a sealer which had piloted
her in.

Jenny came on deck from the sick bay to see a boat
put off from the straggling row of wattle-and-daub huts
and the tents which comprised the Hobart settlement
and, to her joy, recognized the uniformed figure in the
stern sheets as Andrew. A few minutes later, with a
swift lifting of her spirits, she saw that Justin was
seated beside him. It was wonderful, she thought, that
the two men who now meant everything in the world
to her—her son and husband-to-be—should be on their
way back to her.

CHAPTER XI

The Reverend Caleb Boskenna hammered the last nail into the row of roof shingles and, holding firmly to the upper rung of his makeshift ladder, brushed the sweat from his brow with the back of his hand.

It was hot work, the good Lord knew, but it was almost done. The primitive hut the previous owners had occupied was now converted to a sizable dwelling place, with brick foundations and solid timber walls. A brick chimney rose three feet above his head, already puffing out a thin column of smoke from the cooking fire below, at which a convict cook was turning a hindquarter of mutton on a spit under Mrs. Boskenna's supervision.

To the rear of the house, newly completed timber sheds and storehouses formed a neat half square, with huts for the workers they would employ and a fenced-in paddock, at present filled with Jethro Crowan's bleating Cape ewes. The ram—for which Edmund Tempest had paid a rapacious Dutchman fifteen pounds—was in an enclosure by itself. Jethro—that wretched excuse for a shepherd who was supposed to be caring for the Tempest flocks—said the miserable creature was about to die. If he let the ram die, he could expect—and would deserve—a flogging, the one-time missionary thought. Tempest should never have gone to the expense of bringing the fellow out here; he had lost eight lambs on the passage upriver in the launch, and two others had almost drowned, thanks to his carelessness during the unloading.

But the convict labor gang had worked hard and well, Caleb Boskenna had to concede. True, he had offered the superintendent a reward if the task he had set should be completed on time, and each man in the gang had earned himself the bonus of a promissory note—drawn on Tempest funds—which would buy him a gallon of rum at one of the taverns in the Rocks area of Sydney. It was the only way, Superintendent Oakes had assured him, to get the work-shy swine to put their backs into anything requiring effort, and *his* conscience was clear. *He* had not given them the liquor, neither had he permitted any to be consumed on his premises. If they wanted to sell their souls to the devil, they could do so in that sink of prostitution and iniquity whence he had recruited them.

But he had not been sorry, for all that, to see them go. They were a sullen, insolent bunch, only kept under control by the superintendent's lash and their enforced sobriety. Their blasphemous language and their foul-mouthed, bawdy quips had shocked him deeply, and to a man, they had been aware of it and indulged themselves in his hearing, whilst affecting to do so only when out of earshot. They had been particularly trying to his wife . . . so much so that she had refused to keep any of them on as assigned laborers, with the sole exception of the cook, who was an odd little Devon fisherman by the name of Larkin, under a life sentence for larceny and frightened of his own shadow.

For some reason Martha liked him, and he was, it had to be admitted, an excellent cook. Caleb Boskenna sighed. He would have to find two or three reliable men with agricultural experience when he went to Sydney to fetch his two young wards, he decided—convicts, of course, since emancipists and ticket-of-leave men were entitled to wages, in addition to their keep—but, it was to be hoped, men of sober and Christian habit.

He mopped his heated face again and, an arm firmly grasping the top rung of the ladder, took stock of his more distant surroundings.

The river, broad and swift-flowing, was half a mile away. The convict gang had built a small jetty from the plentiful supply of hardwood growing along its banks. That, of necessity, had been their first task, to enable their tools and the furniture and livestock to be unloaded from the two hired launches. The one Jethro had hired, from Parramatta, was old and worm-eaten, virtually in a sinking state, but it could be repaired; and he had bought it as it stood for little more than the value of its masts and sails, confident that he could make good use of it when it had been put to rights.

They were a long way from all other habitation here, the Reverend Boskenna reflected, the river their best means of communication. The half dozen or so small grants between this place and the main settlements on the lower Hawkesbury had been abandoned by their emancipist owners after the disastrous flood that, during the last year of Philip King's governorship, had spelled their ruin. Possibly some of them still held deeds to the land, but that scarcely mattered since they were not there to claim or work an acre of it, and if his sheep grazed there, who would be the wiser?

He found himself smiling as his gaze went over the shingled rooftop to the land he was legitimately entitled to fence and cultivate—in the Tempest girls' names, it was true, but as their guardian, with full authority. Almost as far as the eye could see, it stretched into the distance, up to the edge of the foothills of the Blue Mountain Range.

Part had been laboriously cleared by the original owners and an attempt made to take a crop from it after the trees were felled and the bush hacked down. But the rampaging river had wiped out their spindly wheat and swept away their maize, and in the silt the Hawkesbury had left in its wake, grass was growing . . . suitable pasturage for sheep, until hoe and plow should once again fit thirty or forty acres for autumn sowing.

It would be hard work, and he would need his convict laborers without delay, he told himself. In this strange country, with its topsy-turvy seasons, it was already summer; but the men he would employ would be convicts, and they could sweat through the hot, sun-bright days like any beasts of burden. That was why they had been sent here, to make reparation in honest toil for the crimes they had committed and the evil they had done. He need feel no pity for them, no concern . . . no more, certainly, than he had felt for the recently departed building gang, who had worked all the hours their God had given them for the promise of the liquor they would soon be pouring down their throats.

But when it came to permanently assigned convict laborers, it was essential that they should be sober, God-fearing, and . . . His wife's strident call broke into his thoughts.

"The meal is prepared, Mr. Boskenna! Where are you?"

She came to the door, peering shortsightedly about her, and then, seeing where he was, exclaimed reproachfully, "Oh, my dear, you should have kept the men back to do that! I had supposed them to have finished all the work."

"The shingles lacked a few nails, that was all. There was no sense in keeping those ruffians another day, when I could as easily hammer them in myself." Caleb Boskenna descended the ladder and, reaching its foot, took out a handkerchief to wipe his heavily bearded face yet again.

"It is hot," his wife said sympathetically. "But this is a pleasant place—indeed it is, now that those uncouth men have gone. And the garden will be useful and productive very soon."

"That it will," Boskenna agreed, glancing round approvingly. The garden of their new home had been well stocked, and the flood, fortunately, had done little serious damage. Fruit trees—apple, pear, and Cape citrus—were heavy with blossom, and although there were no flowers, such as an English garden might produce, there were root vegetables in plenty, some vines and tobacco plants, and a number of colorful native flowering shrubs growing just outside the newly erected wooden fence.

"We can be happy here," Martha Boskenna asserted, "but"—there was a hint of envy and regret in her voice—" 'tis a pity that we must share it."

"With my wards, you mean?" Her husband shrugged his bony shoulders. "There is no other way, and I shall have to go and fetch them very soon. We want no awkward questions asked concerning ownership."

"No," she conceded, "but the launch is not yet repaired, and you could not manage it alone."

"I shall go overland, on horseback, and hire a suitable sailing craft in Sydney." Caleb Boskenna outlined his plans, mentioning the convict farm workers he intended to bring back with him. "We are entitled to claim a year's supply of seed from the government store, as well as rations and tools."

"Are we?" Martha Boskenna frowned. There was an odd little smile playing about her husband's bearded lips, and her shrewd dark eyes searched his face as she waited for him to continue.

His smile widened. "We can be rich, as well as happy, if we play our cards right, wife. Do you suppose that I have toiled as I have solely for the benefit of others? Or chosen this land, solely because of its garden? We had nothing save Christian zeal when we embarked in the *Mysore,* trusting in the Lord to provide us with a means of livelihood. Well"——he waved a hand in an expansive gesture——"has He not done so?"

Martha Boskenna's eyes narrowed. It was seldom that her husband forsook the practiced rhetoric in which he normally spoke—even to her—but his tone, she realized, was curiously mocking, almost irreverent. She said in some alarm, "Mr. Boskenna, what of your wards? What of Abigail and Lucy? They were entrusted to our care, were they not? How can we——"

"Have faith, woman," her husband bade her.

"I have," she protested. "You know well that I have."

Caleb Boskenna rolled down his sleeves and, his arm about her waist, started to move toward the door of the farmhouse, compelling her to keep pace with him. He quoted sardonically, "If ye have faith as a grain of mustard seed, ye shall say unto this mountain, 'Remove hence to yonder place and it shall remove.' St. Matthew, my dear, seventeen, verse twenty."

"But, husband, surely you cannot mean——"

"With faith, my dear, all this"——he gestured toward the land—"shall be yours."

Martha was genuinely anxious now. "You have been too long exposed to the hot sun. How do you propose——"

His arm tightened around her. "Abigail will marry— she will attract suitors in plenty, for she is a comely girl. But *I* shall choose a husband for her, one who will not insist on a dowry. We are far from what they are pleased to call civilization here, and it will not be difficult to—shall we say, restrict the girl's callers."

"And Lucy?" Martha Boskenna asked.

"She will present no problem, my dear," her husband assured her. He paused at the door, sniffing. "I am hungry. Let us eat, shall we?"

During the first few days following her arrival in Van Diemen's Land, it seemed to Jenny as if time had stood still for almost twenty years, for the Hobart settlement was as primitive now as Sydney had been all those years before.

Colonel Collins, appointed lieutenant governor, had come here in January of 1804, after the failure of his attempt to establish a settlement on the mainland at Port Phillip. He had chosen a well-watered and breath-takingly beautiful situation for his new colony, over-looking Sullivan's Cove on the west side of the broad Derwent River. The settlement was some nine or ten miles above the mouth of the Derwent, which opened out into the inlet named Storm Bay by Captain Cook.

The harbor was vast, varying in breadth from two to eight miles, and the *Edinburgh*'s master had told Jenny that it was navigable for ships of the largest burden up to eleven miles above the settlement. But, save for the *Edinburgh* herself and a few small sealers and Justin's cutter, the anchorage was empty, the single wharf devoid of activity.

On one side of the stream dividing the settlement was a sprawling mixture of tents and ill-constructed wooden huts that housed Hobart's free and convict inhabitants. The lieutenant governor's dwelling—a mere cottage, woven of wattle rods and plastered with clay, with a grass-thatched roof and a turf chimney—was located on the opposite side of the stream, well away from the convicts' huts and the tents of his small force of Royal Marines. From its lofty elevation, Colonel Collins had an impressive view of the tree-grown mountains to the rear and across the Derwent River to the harbor's land-

locked eastern extremity, which had been named Double
Bay.

But . . . Jenny sighed, seeking vainly to ward off the
feeling of depression that her first impression of the
Hobart settlement had induced. She remembered Colonel Collins well as the young and incorruptible judge
advocate who had served Governor Phillip so efficiently
and with so much selfless devotion during Sydney's
early struggle for survival. Indeed, she reminded herself,
she had every reason to be grateful to him; he had
rescued her from Pinehgut. Later, he and his friend, the
late provost marshal, Henry Brewer, had recommended
her for her ticket-of-leave, and then for a pardon, and
they had seen to it that she had been granted her first
small-holding at Parramatta.

But with advancing years, David Collins had changed.
He now cohabitated with a slovenly convict woman,
and he seemed cynically content to permit the convicts under his charge to exist in squalor and idleness and the marines to relax their discipline. Andrew was as perplexed and disappointed as she was
herself, Jenny sensed, and although he had been careful
not to express his feelings openly, she was aware that
the lack of enterprise displayed by soldiers and convicts
alike had shocked him profoundly.

The evidence of it was everywhere. Save for a few
small vegetable plots in the immediate vicinity of the
settlement, little attempt at cultivation had been made.
The land was rich and fertile, yet a scant fifty or sixty
acres were under crop and little more cleared for sowing, with tree roots left in the ground. Such livestock
as the settlers had brought with them from the mainland roamed free, unfenced and generally uncared for,
gaunt creatures in poor condition.

Excellent timber for building abounded, but as yet,
apart from a government store on the wharf, and the

beginnings of a jail and a barracks, there were no public buildings under construction. Church services were held in the open air, and the hospital was still partially under canvas, its wretched inmates bedded, like animals, on dried grass and beneath a canopy of brushwood, which failed to keep out the mildest shower.

And, Andrew told her, after his first interview with the lieutenant governor, there had been no communication with Colonel Paterson's settlement at Port Dalrymple, at the mouth of the River Tamar, which—a hundred and thirty or forty miles to the north—had been established only eight months after Colonel Collin's party had landed at Hobart. An occasional whaler or a seal-hunting vessel called, in turn, at both ports and conveyed mail and messages, but no road into the interior appeared even to be contemplated.

Indeed, Jenny observed with bewilderment, the only road in the Hobart settlement was a dusty track, leading from the wharf to the oddly shaped house of Lieutenant Edward Lord, of the marines, which had been the first to be built in the colony—and the only one to utilize the native timber in its construction. The freshwater stream, on which Colonel Collins set great store, was choked with brushwood and fallen trees half a mile above the settlement, causing stagnant pools to form along its banks; but no one, seemingly, was willing to accept responsibility for its clearance.

There were over four hundred male convicts in Hobart, with two superintendents and fifty officers and men of the Royal Marines, but apathy and indifference appeared to have affected them all. A legacy, Jenny learned from the unhappy young wife of one of the assistant surgeons, of the failure of Colonel Collins's original attempt to establish a settlement at Port Phillip.

"Port Phillip was a beautiful place, and we loved it there," Mrs. Hopley said. "During the four months we spent there, I never felt one ache or pain, and I departed from it with more regret than I did from my native England. So, too, did my dear husband."

"Then why," Jenny asked, puzzled, "did you leave?"

"The whim and caprice of our lieutenant governor compelled us to abandon the homes we had built and the land we had cleared," the surgeon's wife answered bitterly. "We had worked so hard, all of us—the officers, as well as the marines and the convicts. We had achieved so much, we were well on the way to becoming a thriving community. But Colonel Collins insisted that the water supply would not suffice for our future needs and that the harbor and its approaches were dangerous. We came here most unwillingly, Mrs. Broome, and, I fear, we have lost heart. This place is a dreary desert which will never prosper, and I, for one, cannot feel secure. How can we be sure that the colonel will not decide to abandon this settlement as he did Port Phillip? He is a man of moods, missing his wife, I think, who refused to accompany him, and it is my belief that he would welcome any opportunity —any excuse, even—to order our departure."

Jenny refrained from comment. Mrs. Hopley, with great kindness, had offered her hospitality pending her marriage to Andrew, and it would be discourteous in the extreme to repay her kindness with criticism, whilst not fully understanding the reason for her attitude. Surgeon Hopley was one of the few officers who had brought his wife with him—as she had explained, Colonel Collins had not—and his house was large by Hobart standards. But it was uncomfortable, its furnishings primitive and convict-made, and the Hopley children were allowed, like the livestock, to run wild. True, they had servants—a marine orderly, a male cook, and a slovenly convict maid—yet Sarah Hopley took no pride in her home and seemed indifferent to the fact that its mud floors were unswept and her children uneducated and permitted to mix freely with the less desirable convicts' families.

As if she had guessed Jenny's thoughts, however, Sarah went on, "We took land when we first came here, Mrs. Broome—a grant of a hundred acres in the valley between here and Mount Table, about seven miles to the south. We built a farmhouse, pens and outbuildings for our livestock, and we started to clear the land, a little at a time. But"—her eyes, Jenny saw, were filled with tears—"the natives here, the aborigines, are more hostile than any in New South Wales. They stole our sheep and pigs, they murdered our shepherd; and then one day when Dr. Hopley was here, working at the hospital, a band of them raided our farm. I was there, with three of our children—little Bertha then just a babe in arms—and it was only by the greatest good fortune that we escaped with our lives. We hid, in a small storage shed which somehow escaped their notice. They set our house on fire, speared two of our convict laborers, and made off with the stock they did not slaughter." She shuddered at the memory, and her voice was a broken whisper as she added, "I walked back here with the children and the convict house servant who was with us, and that was the end of our farming. The attempts of others met with the same misfortune, Mrs. Broome. We stay here— we exist—in this settlement and long, with all our hearts, to go home. Thank God, it will not be long before we do!"

Jenny stared at her, appalled. "Can nothing be done to protect such farms as yours, Mrs. Hopley?"

The surgeon's wife shrugged her thin shoulders. "With fifty marines? I will concede that Colonel Collins does his best. He sends out punitive expeditions; they shoot as many Indians as they can, and the wretches retaliate by killing our people—they will not come to terms with us, as they have done in New South Wales. It is war between the aborigines and ourselves, and they are very numerous. We are only safe here in the settlement, and our farming is restricted to the riverside land, between Sullivan's Cove and Point Pierson." She gestured to the river, an enchanting sight in the bright morning sunshine, its near bank ablaze with golden wattle, its blue depths seemingly calm and peaceful.

It looked so lovely that Jenny caught her breath in wonder. "Perhaps the situation will improve," she ventured, "when the evacuation of Norfolk Island is complete. Many of the free settlers there were former seamen and marines who serve as militia. They are trained in arms, as well as being skilled farmers."

"It is possible, I suppose," Sarah Hopley conceded, without conviction. "But are we not also to have those convicts whose crimes, committed in New South Wales, earned them banishment from the mainland? Irish rebels and hardened felons, are they not?"

Like herself, Jenny thought wryly but, once again, did not give voice to her thoughts. As Andrew Hawley's future wife, she was acceptable, but as an emancipist, under additional sentence . . . She sighed, conscious of an all-too-familiar resentment.

The *Edinburgh* had brought a score of locally convicted felons from Sydney, as well as over a hundred from Norfolk Island, and a small guard of men of the New South Wales Corps, under a sergeant. None had come willingly, least of all the Norfolk Island free and emancipist settlers, who—although compensated for the loss of the livestock they had had to leave behind and promised substantial land grants in Van Diemen's Land—understandably felt aggrieved at being forcibly uprooted. They blamed Governor Bligh, Jenny knew from hearing them talk, but the orders the gov-

ernor was putting into effect came from the Colonial
Office.

"It is to be hoped," Mrs. Hopley said, with a hint
of asperity, "that none of our new arrivals will be
tempted to escape. Escapers from here do not live
very long unless they steal arms from the soldiers. One
or two have done so, and they now live by hiding in
the woods and preying on any who attempt to pass
them by. That is why there is no road, as yet, into
the interior, linking our settlement with Colonel Paterson's at Port Dalrymple . . . and one wonders if there
ever will be. Our deputy surveyor, Mr. Harris, talks
of the possibility, but that is all it is—a possibility. But
perhaps, as you say, Mrs. Broome, the situation will
be improved if our population is increased. Even the
most hardened felons can be put to work building
roads, can they not?"

"And houses," Jenny put in, thinking of the flimsy
wattle-and-daub quarters Andrew had been allocated
and which she would share with him, after their marriage. "And a church."

"A jail is our first priority, my dear," her hostess
told her, still with an edge to her voice. "Poor Mr.
Knopwood must wait for his church and we for our
houses—even His Honor the lieutenant governor does
not expect to have a residence worthy of his station
until the convicts are accommodated. But"—she smiled
suddenly and put an arm round Jenny's shoulders—
"when Mr. Knopwood returns from his voyage with the
sealers and can set a date for your wedding, I hope
that you will hold the ceremony here, in this poor
apology for a home. We will make it a celebration,
and I shall ask my husband to propose a toast to Abel
Tasman . . . and to Mr. Flinders, whose names I
have so often decried, because it is on their account
that I am here!"

Jenny studied her face uncertainly for a moment

and then stammered a grateful acceptance. Sarah Hopley was a strange, embittered woman but, at heart, a kindly one, she decided, and the offer was well intentioned and generous.

Colonel Collins—the only person to whom Andrew had confided an account of her trial and sentence— had given his official consent to their marriage, Jenny knew. He had given it readily but had advised discretion, for both her sake and Andrew's.

"What passes for society here," he had warned, "would not receive your wife were it known that she had been a convict. But I remember her as one of Governor Phillip's courageous Garden Women and one of those who set a fine example to us all, after our first landing, when she was only a slip of a girl. . . ." He had said more, and Jenny's heart had swelled with pride when Andrew had repeated it to her, but . . . She stiffened, meeting Sarah Hopley's dark eyes. It went against the grain to indulge in such deception and to accept kindness that would not have been offered had the truth been known, and she was tempted to reveal the truth, whatever the consequences. The absence, on a sealing expedition, of the chaplain, the Reverend Robert Knopwood, had delayed her wedding; had it not been for that, she would have been Andrew's wife now and . . . Jenny hesitated, seeking for words in which to make her confession.

Sarah forestalled her. "I know that you were deported here," she said gently. "The *Edinburgh* brought mail from Sydney, and I have a cousin there, a young man in the government surveyor's office, who writes to me regularly. He gave me a full report of your trial, Mrs. Broome, and I read it with indignation, for it was a gross miscarriage of justice. A ploy, my cousin told me, of the infamous Governor Bligh, whom he detests." Her arm tightened about Jenny's shoulders. "It was for that reason and *because* I knew that I extended my invitation to you. Believe me, my dear Mrs. Broome, I have not regretted it, for I have derived great pleasure from your company and conversation, and I shall, I trust, continue to do so after you are wed to Captain Hawley."

Jenny felt the color draining from her cheeks, and again she sought vainly for words. "Mrs. Hopley, I am . . . I am deeply grateful to you. I . . . that is, I—"

Sarah smilingly waved her to silence.

"I have been unhappy here and desperately lonely until you came and I was able to talk to you, as one woman to another. So I, too, am grateful." She added softly, "And rest assured, your—your secret is safe with me. I will confide it to no one, not even my husband, unless it is your wish that I should. And now let us make plans for your wedding . . . Mr. Knopwood will be back here before we are ready if we don't make a start. We must compile a list of guests to be invited—Colonel Collins, of course, and the other marine officers. And there is your son, is there not? The tall, handsome boy who, they tell me, is commander of his own seagoing cutter, although he looks too young for so great a responsibility. How old is he, Mrs. Broome?"

"Justin? Oh"—Jenny spoke with conscious pride— "he is almost sixteen, Mrs. Hopley. He gained his seagoing experience with Captain Flinders, who taught him navigation and mapmaking. He passed a naval examination for masters' mates two years ago, before a board of captains. He . . ." She glanced out, through the open, glassless window of the Hopleys' living room, to where Justin's small, graceful craft lay at anchor in the cove far below. The *Flinders* was too far away for her to make out whether Justin was on board, but he had slept there, she knew, preferring the cutter's cramped cabin to any of the dwelling places on shore. He was a creature of the sea, Justin—very much his father's son—and he was waiting only to see her married to Andrew. As soon as the ceremony was performed, he would hoist the *Flinder*'s well-worn sails and set course back to Sydney, where there was always work for such swift and handy craft to perform.

"You must have great satisfaction in him," Sarah began, and then broke off, pointing over Jenny's shoulder toward the entrance to the cove. "A ship!" she exclaimed excitedly. "One of the sealers, I do declare. Our chaplain will be returning to us before we know where we are! We must hasten with our plans, Mrs. Broome."

The Reverend Robert Knopwood came ashore that evening from the last of the sealing fleet to make port. Three days later he performed the marriage ceremony in the Hopleys' mud-floored parlor before what was, for the Hobart settlement, a distinguished company, headed by the lieutenant governor in full dress uniform.

With her tall bridegroom at her side and her son behind her, Jenny was proud and happy. Andrew made his vows in a firm, clear voice, her hand in his, and once again she had the illusion that time had stood still. Twenty years before, on the deck of the transport *Charlotte,* Andrew had declared his intention to take her as his wife, and they had made hopeful plans for the future they would spend together, in what had then been an unknown and alien land. He, who came of farming stock, had had no thought of a military career, but fate had taken a hand and kept them apart. Now, bearing the scars of sea battles in his country's service, he still wore the King's uniform and could look back on two decades of soldiering, whilst she . . . Jenny felt a lump rise in her throat.

She it was who had become the farmer and had

toiled all those years to wrench a living and the means of survival from that alien earth to which, as a convicted felon, she had been exiled. . . .

Memories came flooding back into her mind as she stood there. She remembered the terrible spectacle of Captain Wilkes's hanging, remembered his words moments before the executioner had placed the noose around his neck. *"I forgive all who ever did me any injury, save only one—the Judas who sold me for his own gain."*

And then Ned Munday had come running towards her, his pursuers hot on his heels, and he had thrust the purse he had stolen into her hands. They had accused her of being his accomplice; she had been arrested and sentenced to death. But Dr. Fry had paid a lawyer, and he had contrived to have her sentence commuted to one of transportation to New South Wales—or Botany Bay, as it had then been called. And she had been fifteen when that sentence was passed—fifteen. But . . . it was she who had aged, she thought ruefully; she, rather than Andrew, for all the actions he had fought and the wounds he had sustained . . . there was more gray in her hair now than in his. And yet, she had seen her dream come true . . . The lump vanished, and she found herself echoing Andrew's smile. On the banks of the Hawkesbury River, she had seen the fertile pastures, the flocks and herds and the rich fruits which Governor Phillip had prophesied would reward the labors of the husbandman. She had seen Johnny die and his children live, with Justin in his image; and, please God, when this, her second exile came to an end, she would return to her land, with Andrew as her husband—and no longer a soldier—to end their days as, twenty years before, they had purposed to begin them.

Andrew, in obedience to the chaplain's prompting,

slid the plain gold band that had been his mother's onto her finger, and she read his gladness in his eyes.

"I now declare thee man and wife," the Reverend Robert Knopwood intoned. "Those whom God hath joined together, let no man put asunder."

Colonel Collins was the first to step forward to offer his congratulations, Justin the second, a delighted grin spreading across his usually grave young face, as he hugged his mother and wrung Andrew's hand with touching warmth.

Sarah Hopley, with the aid of her convict servants, had performed miracles in her tiny, primitive kitchen, and the eating and drinking went on until well into the evening, toast following toast with ever-increasing enthusiasm.

It was dark when Jenny and Andrew finally took their leave to walk the hundred or so yards that separated Andrew's quarters from those of the Hopleys. But a whale-oil lamp had been left burning in an unshuttered window, and when they entered, Jenny saw by its flickering light that a bed had been added to its scanty furnishings. It was of rough-hewn local hardwood and draped with blankets she recognized as products of the Parramatta Factory, which she herself had given Justin for his cutter's bunk.

Andrew said, smiling, "Your son's wedding gift, Mrs. Hawley! The lad has worked on it like one possessed, scorning my help or anybody else's and determined that you should have a marriage bed that is worthy of you, even in this place. The mattress and the coverings reek of saltwater still, for all our efforts to launder them. But . . ." He stripped off his scarlet jacket, and, suddenly impatient, he closed his arms about her and drew her to him. "I've waited a long time to share bed and board with you, my dear lass, so for God's sweet sake, let's have no more delay! I

want you, Jenny, as I've wanted no other woman in
all my life . . . and I'll love you, I swear, until the
day I die."

Deeply moved by his avowal, Jenny raised her lips
to his, and his big hands cupping her breasts, he kissed
her with growing urgency before lifting her onto the
bed.

"Off with that dress, wife," he bade her, stepping
back, the belt at his waist already unbuckled. She
made to extinguish the lamp, but Andrew stopped her.
"No, leave it be. I'll not make love to you in darkness, when 'tis your face I've longed to see, all these
years past; your body I've wanted to take, instead of
some nameless whore's, chosen at random when my
ship made port. That's what my life has been, Jenny,
until now."

He was beside her, reaching for her, the breath
rasping in his throat as his mouth found hers once
again.

"There, my sweet lass, don't hold back! Give yourself to me and have no fear, for I love you truly.
Come to me, Jenny!"

His lovemaking was demanding and passionate, his
need of her not easily assuaged, but there were moments when tenderness outmatched desire, and Jenny
found herself responding with heady eagerness, holding back nothing, the last of her doubts concerning
the wisdom of their marriage vanishing as if they had
never been. She felt happy and secure and completely
at peace as, tiring at last, they lay together on the bed
her son had fashioned for them, her head on Andrew's
broad chest, his arm clasped lightly about her naked
shoulders.

"We could do worse than stay here, lass," Andrew
said softly. "I've been giving it some thought."

"Stay here, in Hobart?" Startled into wakefulness,
Jenny sat up, staring at him in disbelief.

"Aye, that's what I mean. Colonel Collins is a good and honest man. Oh, he's lost heart, as so many of his people have, but with the settlers from Norfolk Island soon to come here and plenty of convict labor, Hobart will grow. The land is good and the climate— better than in New South Wales, I believe. There aren't the droughts, Jenny."

Recalling all that Sarah Hopley had recounted of their early struggles against native predators, Jenny frowned. But with the population doubled or even trebled, the natives, however hostile to the new arrivals, would be compelled to keep their distance. And there would be no Rum Corps officers here, bent only on enriching themselves, no struggle for power between governor and military with Colonel Collins in command. As Andrew had said, he might have become disheartened after his failure at Port Phillip, but he was a good and honest man—an officer of Governor Phillip's stamp, with a record of integrity behind him and long experience of colonial administration.

"Tim Dawson would jump at the chance to buy your Long Wrekin land," Andrew went on, "and William and Rachel could come here to join us." He thought fondly of the two youngsters, now in the able care of the Jardines at Long Wrekin. Then he turned to Jenny and pulled her down beside him. "David Collins has said he will give me a government appointment if I stay, so I'd not have to resign my commission until conditions here improve. And I'd be free of any obligation to Captain Bligh . . . for 'twas he sent both of us here, was it not?" His lips brushed her cheek. "It's a prospect that bears thinking about. Let's sleep on it, shall we? We'll have a while yet before we need to decide."

As it happened, however, Andrew's decision was made for him only a week later, when one of Simeon

Lord's traders—the brig *Caroline,* on her way to the Cape—dropped anchor in Sullivan's Cove. Her master delivered mail from Sydney and orders from Governor Bligh for Andrew's recall by the first available ship.

"There's all hell to pay in Sydney," the *Caroline*'s master said grimly, "with the governor and Mr. Macarthur squaring up for a fight—in the courts, it's true, but a fight for all that. I'm damned glad to be out of it!"

The brig's master had brought no orders and no pardon for Jenny; when a ship to Sydney was available, Andrew would return alone. As it happened, Justin—who had departed two days before the *Caroline*'s arrival—came limping into Hobart on the afternoon of the brig's arrival, his mainmast sprung after he had encountered a severe storm off Cape Pillar. The stepping of a new mast of local pine took two days, so on the morning of the third day after he had received his orders, Andrew boarded the *Flinders* with Justin. Jenny stood and watched the departure of her husband and her elder son with tears in her eyes.

"Try not to grieve," Sarah Hopley offered consolingly. "Captain Hawley knows his duty. He would not be the man he is if he were to shrink from doing it, would he? And I feel sure that our governor's appeal to Governor Bligh on your behalf will be answered."

"Will it?" Jenny answered, with a bitterness she could not hide. "But when, Sarah . . . that is what I want to know? *When?*"

CHAPTER XII

To Abigail, enjoying to the full Frances Spence's indulgent and kindly hospitality, no signs of impending trouble between Governor Bligh and the military garrison were apparent. No one spoke of such matters in her presence, and the few hints and rumors that she overheard by chance held no significance for her.

Indeed, her only cause for anxiety was a letter from Mrs. Boskenna, informing her that the building work on their new land grant was almost completed and the house expected to be ready for occupation very soon. The convict superintendent of the labor gang delivered the letter some days after he and his men had returned to Sydney; but he had been able to tell her very little about the land or its prospects, save that it was isolated and would require extensive clearing before any planting could be done.

"But we built you a fine dwelling house, miss," he had assured her, with conscious pride. "And 'twas ready enough to move into when we left it, bar one or two finishin' touches the reverend was goin' to attend to hisself."

It had been this last statement that had worried Abi-

gail, since it could only mean that all too soon for her
liking, the Reverend Caleb Boskenna would arrive in
Sydney and announce his intention to take herself and
Lucy back with him. She had known, of course, that
they could not impose on the Spences' hospitality indefinitely, but she was happy here—happier than she
had been for years—and when the time came as, alas,
it must, she would be exceedingly sorry to leave.

Her duties were not arduous. She helped Mrs. Spence
to care for the Dawson girls and Lucy, but they spent
most of the day at Mr. Mann's school, and, in any
case, the Spences had a staff of willing and efficient
servants, and the house ran on well-oiled wheels. Jasper
Spence was wealthy, and there was no penny-pinching
in his household; his wife, it was true, made her own
clothes and those of the Dawson children, but she did
so from choice and because she was an exquisite needle-
woman. Abigail quickly learned some of her skills. The
dress she was wearing now was her own handiwork,
fashioned under Frances Spence's supervision and . . .
She smoothed its shimmering folds proudly. It was a
beautiful dress, and Titus Penhaligon, when he had
called earlier, had complimented her warmly on her
appearance.

She smiled to herself, recollecting and lingering over
the compliment. Titus had become bolder of late, and
she was glad of it, for he was not the only gentleman
to pay court to her, and although she had tried to indi-
cate that he was the one she most welcomed, he had
been slow to declare himself. He had been deterred—
on his own admission—by uncertainty as to his prospects in the colony, but now he was appointed an assistant surgeon at the government hospital, and it was he,
rather than any of his seniors, to whom the governor's
daughter, Mrs. Putland, confided the care of her poor
sick husband. Aided by Kate Lamerton, he had kept
the unfortunate Mr. Putland alive for longer than any-

one had dared to hope, and Kate was loud in her praise of his devotion and skill.

Abigail's smile faded as a loud knock on the front door was followed by the sound of a man's voice in the hall, asking for her by name. She recognized the voice as that of Lieutenant O'Shea and rose resignedly to her feet. The tall young Irish officer was the most persistent of her suitors; and, she reflected guiltily, she had given him encouragement in the hope that Titus might be roused by jealousy and for once forget his diffidence. That had not happened; instead of confronting his rival, Titus had held back, and even Frances Spence had begun to issue more invitations to O'Shea than she did to Titus, in the mistaken belief that it was he whom Abigail favored.

And Lieutenant O'Shea appeared to have more leisure than an overworked assistant surgeon could command; so that it was seldom, if ever, that he had to refuse the Spences' offers of hospitality. He came in now, smiling and confident of his welcome, to raise Abigail's hand to his lips with exaggerated courtliness.

"Ah, Miss Abigail, I'd hoped I would find you at home . . . and looking so pretty that, faith—you fair take my breath away! Stand there for a moment, will you please, and let me feast my eyes on you!" He held her at arm's length, clasping both her hands in his and subjecting her to a flattering scrutiny, his dark eyes bright and challenging.

He cut a dashing figure himself in his well-fitting uniform and polished top boots, Abigail was forced to concede, and there were times, such as this, when she was very conscious of his attraction and beguiled by his Irish charm. Yet she did not entirely trust him, although she could not have said why, for his behavior toward her had always been impeccable. There were rumors concerning him, gossip amongst the convict servants which suggested that, as an officer, he was far from popular with his men and actively hated by a section of the Irish convicts, of whom he had been in command on the voyage out from Cork.

But Frances Spence liked him, and she, surely, was in a better position to judge his merits than most, including herself. Abigail sighed, flushing under his prolonged and searching gaze.

"Mrs. Spence is out," she said, drawing back and freeing her hands from his grasp. "She has gone to fetch the children from school, and I—"

"Yes, I know," Desmond O'Shea returned, quite unabashed and even, it seemed, amused. "I met her on my way here, and she assured me that if you were in the house, you would invite me to take a cup of tea. Is that too much to ask? It's hot, and I've had a fatiguing ride from Parramatta."

"Of course it is not too much to ask, Mr. O'Shea. I'll order tea for you most gladly."

As he so often did, he had put her at a disadvantage, Abigail thought resentfully, making her appear ungracious and inhospitable, lacking in the courtesy Frances Spence always displayed to any visitor. She opened the door, intending to give the necessary order, but Mary Ryan, the younger of the two house servants, had anticipated it and came in, beaming, with a laden tray.

"I t'ought you'd be wantin' the tay, Miss Abigail . . . Mr. O'Shea, sorr." She set down her burden, dropped them a dutiful curtsy, and withdrew, leaving them alone together once more. Abigail poured from the silver Indian teapot, seating herself as far away from her guest as she could, but after accepting his cup, O'Shea, balancing it carefully, drew up his chair to face hers.

He said sourly, "Are you trying to avoid me, Miss Abigail?"

"No," Abigail denied. She lowered her gaze, acutely conscious of the heightened color flooding her cheeks, and murmured defensively, "Why should you suppose anything of the kind?"

"Your manner has been warmer in the past. Have I done something to cause you offense, perhaps?"

She shook her head, again recalling with shame the manner in which she had previously led him on. "Certainly not, Mr. O'Shea. It's just that I . . . that is—"

"I have a rival, have I not?" O'Shea suggested accusingly.

"A . . . rival?" Abigail's hand was trembling as she started to lift her cup, and hastily she replaced it in its saucer.

He captured her wrist, drawing her toward him and forcing her to look at him. "I'm not blind, my dear young lady. You have been seeing more than a little of that presumptuous young sawbones who came out with you in the *Mysore,* I'm given to understand. What's the fellow's name—Penhaligon, *Doctor* Penhaligon. That's so, *isn't it*?"

Abigail rounded on him with spirit, resenting his accusations. "I am free to see as much or as little of anyone I please, Mr. O'Shea, if it is any business of yours!"

"I intend to make it my business," O'Shea told her. His strong fingers bit into her wrist. "You must surely be aware of my sentiments concerning you, and I'll brook no rivalry from a miserable sawbones, Abigail!" She started to protest, but he cut her short and went on harshly, "Penhaligon's prize patient is dying, you know. And when he does die, our esteemed governor will have no further use for the fellow who's been pumping laudanum into his son-in-law and dancing attendance at Government House three times a day. Dr. Jamieson doesn't think very highly of him . . . he'll not keep him in Sydney for very much longer."

"What do you mean?" Abigail asked, in sudden alarm. "Titus—Dr. Penhaligon is appointed to the hospital here, is he not?"

"At the governor's insistence he was appointed temporarily. But he's attached to the Corps, and he'll have to go wherever the Corps commandant and the chief surgeon decide to send him." O'Shea permitted himself a thin smile. "I've heard it said that a surgeon is needed urgently at Coal River, Miss Abigail."

If he had been attempting to provoke her into a betrayal of her feelings, he had succeeded, Abigail realized wretchedly, for she had shown them all too plainly. Aware that her cheeks had drained of color, she took refuge behind her teacup but choked on the liquid and had again to set the cup down.

"I am paying honorable court to you," O'Shea reminded her, his tone no longer harsh but faintly reproachful. "And my prospects are considerably better than Penhaligon's, that's all I'm trying to make you understand."

Had his reference to Coal River and Dr. Jamieson been in the nature of a threat, Abigail wondered . . . was a posting to Coal River to be the price poor Titus must pay for his friendship with her? The friendship *she* had fostered and sought to encourage?

"I know," she began, "and I do understand, but I— that is, Lucy and I will not be here for much longer. We—"

Desmond O'Shea regarded her thoughtfully.

"That, too, I had heard."

"From Mrs. Spence? Did she tell you?"

He shrugged. "She mentioned it. But I chanced to encounter your guardian, the Reverend Boskenna, in Parramatta yesterday. He—"

"Mr. Boskenna! He was in Parramatta *yesterday*?" Abigail could not keep the dismay from her voice. If Mr. Boskenna was in Parramatta, then it meant that within a day or two he would make his appearance in Sydney. He would come here, to this house, to demand that she and Lucy accompany him to the new farm on the Hawkesbury River, for had not the superintendent of the convict building gang told her that the farmhouse was ready for occupation? She had hoped for a longer delay, but . . .

O'Shea inclined his dark head. "Yes, the reverend gentleman was negotiating with Captain Macarthur for the purchase of a ram from his herd. The one your father bought at the Cape had unfortunately died, I believe. He was also talking of chartering a boat, under sail, to convey you and your sister up the river, which, it seems, is the quickest means of access . . . and the least fatiguing. He himself had come overland, on horseback, and was exhausted from the heat."

The superintendent had said that the land Caleb Boskenna had chosen was isolated, Abigail remembered. She bit back a sigh and, regaining her composure, said quietly, "Then indeed Lucy and I will not be here for much longer, alas! Did Mr. Boskenna tell you when he expected to be in Sydney?"

"He was to conduct services in Parramatta this Sunday," O'Shea answered, with a faintly malicious smile, "in the church and at the Factory. I understand his sermons enjoy great popularity with the Factory girls, or so he informed me. May I trouble you"—he held out his cup—"for some more tea, Miss Abigail?"

Abigail reached for the teapot. Frances Spence, she thought, was being a very long time; usually she and the children were at home by now. But perhaps she had stayed to talk to Mr. Mann concerning their scholastic progress or had called for tea at the Reverend Fulton's, as she sometimes did. Though Mr. Fulton was a Protestant, he had given support to the cause of Catholic Ireland and been deported for it—so there was a bond of sympathy between him and Frances.

O'Shea's voice broke into her thoughts. He said, with well-simulated casualness, "I mentioned my attachment to you when I was talking to your guardian, Miss Abigail, and sought his consent to my courtship. He gave it readily, with his full approval, and invited me to pay a visit to your holding in the near future. I trust, therefore, that I may count on your willingness to receive me?"

What could she say, Abigail asked herself helplessly . . . how could she refuse, without antagonizing him and, perhaps, causing trouble for Titus? She answered flatly, "Of course, Mr. O'Shea, if you deem so long a journey worthwhile, I shall be happy to receive you. And—" Frances's lilting voice sounded in the street outside. Mary Ryan opened the door to her, and, to Abigail's relief, a moment later the children came running in, boisterous and laughing.

Desmond O'Shea rose at once to his feet. He paused only to greet Frances and exchange a few bantering words with Lucy and Julia Dawson, with whom he was a favorite, and then, bowing over Frances's hand, he took his leave, his parting words pointedly addressed to Abigail.

Fresh tea was brought, the children dismissed with Mary Ryan to tidy themselves, and Frances took her place behind the silver teapot. To Abigail's surprise she made no reference to her caller but said tensely, as the door closed behind the children, "Have you heard the news, Abigail?"

"You mean about Mr. Boskenna? That he is—"

"No, no." Frances shook her head. "The governor has ordered Captain Macarthur's ship, the *Parramatta,* to be placed under arrest and the forfeiture of his bond of eight hundred pounds. I can't fully understand for what reason, except that it is to do with a convict who escaped to Otaheite on board her, with the connivance of her master. Mr. Spence is very worried—he says that there may be serious consequences if Captain Macarthur contests the forfeiture, and everyone thinks he will do so."

Abigail, still too caught up in her own affairs to comprehend what her hostess was saying, stared at her in bewilderment. Sensing this, Frances patted her hand consolingly. "There, child, you can't know, can you? But I really think you *should* know—it affects the welfare and even the personal safety of us all. . . . My husband fears that this business of the *Parramatta* may lead to a trial of strength between Governor Bligh and the Corps if they champion Captain Macarthur's cause . . . and he is convinced they will. The situation could become very ugly. I . . . what did you say about Mr. Boskenna?"

"Only that he is in Parramatta, Mrs. Spence," Abigail stammered. "Mr. O'Shea met and talked to him there yesterday, and he will probably come to fetch Lucy and me in a day or so and . . . and take us back with him to the Hawkesbury."

Frances Spence eyed her pityingly. "And you don't want to go?"

"No, no, I don't, Mrs. Spence. Oh, I know you could not keep us here forever, but—"

"I should have been glad to, my dear child, believe me. But Mr. Boskenna is your legal guardian."

"Yes, he is. Only—" Abigail bit her lip in a brave effort to still its trembling. "The farm is miles from anywhere, and I shall hate leaving you. I—"

"And leaving your very ardent suitors," Frances suggested, misunderstanding her. "Dear little Abigail, nothing lasts forever, you know, and you may find that life on a Hawkesbury farm is pleasanter than you expect it to be." She drew Abigail into her embrace, letting the girl's fair head rest on her motherly shoulder. "But if my husband's fears prove to be justified, you may be better off well out of Sydney when the storm breaks, for things could become extremely unpleasant here for a time. I shall miss you, and you know, I hope, that you'll always be welcome here. There now, dry your eyes, my dear—I hear the children coming, and you'd not want Lucy to see you weeping at the prospect of your new home, would you?"

In the presence of the three girls nothing more was said concerning either Captain Macarthur's differences with the governor or the imminence of the Reverend Boskenna's arrival in Sydney. Frances Spence and her husband were engaged to dine with the Campbells, and they departed at seven in the new phaeton, which was Frances's pride and joy, behind the two well-matched chestnut geldings bred by Timothy Dawson.

The children waved them on their way, and the two younger girls, Julia and Dorothea, settled willingly to sleep after Abigail had heard their prayers and regaled them with fairy stories made up out of her head. Lucy, however, was fractious and reluctant to be packed off to bed, resorting to tears when her pleas to be allowed to stay up a little longer went unheeded.

"There's something *happening*," she insisted obstinately. "Something you were talking about to Mrs. Spence when we came in at teatime. But you stopped then and . . . you'd been crying, Abby. I could see you had! Why, tell me *why,* will you? I shan't go to bed till you do."

"I'll tell you," Abigail promised, yielding. "When you're in bed, Lucy, and not before. And *after* you've said your prayers."

Undressing, ablutions, and even prayers were swiftly and skimpily completed; then, with Lucy in bed at last, Abigail seated herself on the edge of the bed and, deftly plying a hairbrush, repeated what Desmond O'Shea told her of his meeting with their guardian in Parramatta.

"Then he'll be coming for us soon?" Lucy conjectured, seemingly not ill pleased by the prospect. "He'll take us back to our land by the Hawkesbury to settle?"

"Yes," Abigail confirmed glumly. "I fear so."

"Is that why you were crying and why you wanted to

pack me off to bed at the same time as Julia and Dodie, who are babies?" Lucy demanded. "Don't you want to go?"

"No, I don't want to go. I . . ." She could not speak of Titus to Lucy, Abigail knew; still less could she confide her dislike of the Boskennas or her suspicions concerning them. Lucy might not be a baby, but she was still a child of only fourteen, and in any case, since they must now look forward to living under the same roof as Caleb and Martha Boskenna, it would do more harm than good to turn her against them. She had got on well enough with Mrs. Boskenna in Parramatta, according to Kate Lamerton, and would probably continue to do so, left to herself.

"*I* don't mind going," Lucy said, as if she had read her sister's thoughts. "At least there'll be no school, and Mrs. Boskenna will teach me when she has time. And we shall have horses and miles and miles and miles where we can ride. I hate Sydney. The convicts are horrible, and even here one cannot avoid rubbing shoulders with them." She embarked on a story of one such encounter with a bunch of drunken convict women and then broke off, sensing that Abigail was not listening. "You," she stated deliberately, "do not have to leave Sydney if you don't want to, Abby."

"Yes, I do," Abigail countered. "It is our land, Lucy. The grant was made to Papa, not to Mr. Boskenna, even if he is our guardian. I've been thinking about it since I talked to Mrs. Spence. The money and the stock were Papa's, and you and I—and Rick, of course—are his heirs. I confess I do not want to go, but since Rick isn't here, I shall have to. It's my duty."

Lucy waved this aside. "You need not *stay*, Abby. You could marry Mr. O'Shea, could you not? He must have asked you, he's been coming here often enough . . . it's no secret that he's courting you. Mary Ryan says that he—"

"You should not listen to servants' gossip," Abigail reproved her sharply. "You know it's forbidden."

"If he had asked me," Lucy asserted slyly, "*I* would accept him. I wouldn't hesitate for a moment, truly I wouldn't! I think he's the handsomest gentleman I ever saw in my life. But I suppose," she added, with sisterly candor, "you are still mooning over Dr. Penhaligon, although he couldn't hold a candle to Lieutenant O'Shea! And he's not nearly so handsome, is he?"

"You are talking nonsense, Lucy," Abigail said, losing patience with her. "I'm sorry I told you anything now. I should have left you to find out for yourself." She rose, making to put out the lamp, deaf to Lucy's indignant protests. "Tomorrow I'll help you to pack because we shall have to be ready when Mr. Boskenna does come. Good night . . . and sleep well."

She was in the act of blowing out the lamp when Lucy said, sitting up, "Truly I would accept Mr. O'Shea if he proposes to you, Abby. Even if he does keep a convict girl in his quarters—Mary says they all do, all the officers. And he would soon send her packing if you were to marry him, would he not? He would have to because—"

"*What* did Mary say?" Abigail put in, shocked. "That Mr. O'Shea keeps a convict girl? Did she really say that?"

Wisely, Lucy did not remind her of her earlier strictures concerning servants' gossip. "Yes," she confirmed, and added, with a worldly wisdom far beyond her years, "but as I told you, she says they all do—I shouldn't be surprised if your saintly Dr. Penhaligon does, too. It's the custom because there are so few respectable young ladies here whom they can marry. Even Mrs. Boskenna, although she strongly disapproves, says it is inevitable when the women convicts are of so low a class as the ones they send out here. She was stunned by the behavior of the Factory women at Parramatta, Abby. You should have seen her face when some of them made advances to Mr. Boskenna in the street!"

"I'm glad I didn't," Abigail answered, still too shocked by Lucy's revelations and by her knowledge of such matters to reprove her a second time. She extinguished the lamp, burning her fingers in the process, and went out without repeating her good-night, her thoughts in confusion.

She was still far from clear in her mind as to her future course of action when, an hour later, Titus made an unexpected appearance. Mary Ryan showed him in and waited, unable to conceal her curiosity, for Abigail to order some refreshment to be served. But Titus shook his head to the offer. He looked weary and dispirited, his face even paler than its wont, and he started to pace nervously about the room until Mary finally, and with reluctance, accepted her dismissal and the door closed behind her.

"What is it, Dr. Penhaligon?" Abigail asked, anxiously searching his face. "Is there something wrong?"

The young surgeon met her gaze, his own troubled and oddly pleading. "Mr. Putland died this afternoon, Miss Abigail. Oh, I knew that there could be no hope for him, and he died peacefully, in his sleep, having made his peace with God. For his sake I could not wish it otherwise."

"Poor Mrs. Putland," Abigail ventured uncertainly. "She will be deeply distressed."

"Indeed she is, but she is bearing her loss bravely, and His Excellency is there to comfort her. This sad outcome is one we have all had to anticipate for some time past." Titus Penhaligon hesitated, and Abigail saw that there were beads of sweat on his brow and upper lip. Recalling Desmond O'Shea's hints as to the likelihood of his being posted away from Sydney should— how had he put it? *Should his prize patient die*—she drew her breath sharply.

"But surely," she began, "surely you——"

"There was some unpleasantness," Titus said flatly. "Dr. Jamieson, as surgeon general, had to be called in to certify the death, and there were words between him and the governor. I don't know what it was about. I didn't hear much apart from their raised voices. But then Dr. Jamieson came out like the——like the wrath of God and vented his spleen on me. I . . . I'm to be posted to Coal River, Miss Abigail!"

So Lieutenant O'Shea had made no idle boast, Abigail thought dully——he had known, it had all been decided before poor Mr. Putland's death. Indeed, the posting might well have been made at his instigation, for he was on terms of close friendship with the surgeon general, with whom Governor Bligh had previously had some differences. She asked, in a low, controlled voice, "When must you go, Dr. Penhaligon?"

"Tomorrow," Titus answered. "The supply ship is sailing tomorrow morning, and I'm ordered to go on board tonight. That is why I am here . . . there's so little time, and I . . . oh, Miss Abigail, I had to come. I had to ask you, I——" He broke off, suddenly bereft of words and gazing at her uncertainly, as if expecting her to chide him for his temerity.

Sick with misery at the thought of the imminence of his departure, Abigail prompted gently, "Ask me what, Titus? Tell me, will you not? I'm listening."

Her use of his Christian name gave him encouragement, as she had hoped it would. He reached out to take her hand, his own trembling. "Shall we go into the garden, where we won't be overheard?"

"Yes, I . . . if you wish, Titus." She led the way, unlocking the door at the back of the house which gave on to the Spences' spacious and well-kept garden. They walked, hand in hand, to the little grotto Frances Spence had fashioned, sweet with the scent of flowering shrubs.

Abigail seated herself on its wooden bench and turned to look at him, her heart in her eyes.

"Oh, Abigail!" Titus managed. "I had not intended to—to declare myself like this. I'd planned to take you driving, perhaps, or for a boating picnic. But there's no time, and I cannot leave Sydney without making my— my sentiments known to you. Although I expect you are aware of them, I—I must have made them so—so evident, for all I tried to conceal them. I . . . oh, Abigail!" He dropped to his knees, still clasping her hand in his, his whole body trembling now. "I love you. Dearest Abigail, I've loved you from the moment I first set eyes on you. But I could not speak, I could not beg you to— to do me the honor of becoming my wife, not until my position was secure, could I? It would have been irresponsible."

"Yes," Abigail agreed. "I suppose it would."

"But it *is* secure now," he asserted eagerly. "I am officially accepted into the government medical service. That means that I must go to Coal River, it's true, but I shall be able to support a wife and . . . I'll come back to Sydney or Parramatta the first moment I can if . . . if you'll marry me, Abigail. Please, my sweet darling, may I dare to hope that you will?"

"Oh, Titus, I will most gladly." Abigail was overwhelmed with tenderness for him. His had not been the romantic proposal of which she had dreamed, and he had made it with many hesitations, stammering in his anxiety and diffidence, but she loved him the more for that, and when he continued to kneel at her feet, her arms went around him, drawing him up beside her. "I love you, Titus," she whispered. "Truly I do. And I want to marry you more than I've ever wanted anything."

"You have made me the happiest man in all New Holland!" Titus exclaimed exultantly. "If only I had not to leave you, my darling."

He kissed her, gently at first and then with a passion that set Abigail's heart beating wildly, awakening desires of which she had never before been conscious. They clung together in a breathless embrace, Titus's lips on hers, on her eyes, on her neck, and in the hollow between her breasts, and she cried out in sudden fear, feeling as if her whole body was on fire, seeking fusion with his.

It was sinful, she thought—but no, how could it be sinful, they were to be wed, she had accepted him, and she wanted him so? Her attempts to hold him off, the result of her fear, grew more feeble as her desire mounted and her confidence and her love for Titus grew. What could be more right than this? One last time fear assailed her, and she spoke out: "Oh, Titus, I cannot . . . I have never been with a man before. No one has ever . . ."

"It is not wrong if we love each other and are to be wed," Titus insisted gently. "I want you to belong to me, darling, now and forever, so that no one can take you from me." His hands were gentle as they unfastened the buttons on her dress, and her heart stood still with anticipation and desire.

She hardly heard him now as her emotions surged, and she felt herself yielding to them. "Trust me, Abigail . . ." he was saying, and her heart gave assent. "Give yourself to me," he continued, "so that I may take the memory of your sweet loveliness with me when I go. I'll not fail you, dearest—I'll love you till the day I die. Believe me!"

"Oh, Titus, dearest, if this is truly what you want—"

With only the stars for witness, Titus took her with a tenderness that enthralled her the more for its awkwardness. For all that it caused her pain rather than pleasure, at first, she was enraptured, she was his.

He put her from him at last and said, a catch in his voice, "We must not do this again until we

are wed, beloved girl. But it need not be for long
. . . a few months, perhaps, until I can arrange for
my relief. But in the meantime, dearest, remember
that you are mine and are promised to me. And
please, my darling"—a hand beneath her chin, he
tilted her small, flushed face to his—"remember that
I shall be jealous of every smile you give to any other
man. Don't see so much of Mr. O'Shea. He will be
here in Sydney, of course, and you—"

"I shall not be here," Abigail pointed out, suddenly
glad of it. "Mr. Boskenna is completing his arrangements to take Lucy and me to the new farm on the
Hawkesbury. I think he will be here in a few days'
time, expecting us to return with him."

For a moment Titus looked relieved; then he
frowned, recalling his dislike of both the Boskennas.

"I shall come to you there, my love," he promised.
"And since Mr. Boskenna is your legal guardian, I
will make a formal request for your hand." He helped
her to her feet, carefully refastening the buttons on
her dress, and then drew her to him again, letting his
cheek rest lightly on hers. "I have to go, Abigail, although it breaks my heart to leave you. But I have
to pack up all my gear and go aboard the government
sloop tonight . . . Dr. Jamieson will be howling for
my blood if I do not! He wants me away from here
before the governor can stop it. But I shall write to
Captain Bligh . . . and to you, my dearest love. Although I may be there with you, in person, before any
letters can reach you. I know where the farm is, the
governor told me—it's nearer to Coal Harbor than
Sydney is. And"—there was a note of excitement in
his voice—"Mr. Boskenna is a minister of God, is he
not? He could wed us, Abigail!"

He left her with that hope and the reiterated promise that he would somehow find a way to join her in
her new home, and Abigail returned to the house and

her own bedroom, thankful to find that the servants had retired and there was no one to whom her absence must be explained. As she slipped into bed beside her younger sister, Lucy stirred and murmured something but did not waken. Abigail drew the covers round them both and composed herself for sleep, hugging her newfound happiness to her like a talisman.

She heard the phaeton draw up outside and the Spences' subdued voices as they reentered the house, but did not go to meet them. Time enough in the morning to acquaint Frances Spence with the glad news that she was affianced to Titus Penhaligon, she decided, and let her heavy lids fall.

Frances might not be pleased, since she had appeared to favor Mr. O'Shea, but she could not know—and must not be allowed to find out—on what terms Titus had parted with her. She was a woman, his wife in all but name . . . Abigail's lips curved into a smile as she drifted into sleep, no lingering twinges of conscience troubling her now. What they had done could not be wrong or sinful if, as Titus had said, they loved each other and were soon to be wed.

Her smile only faded when, in her dreams, she heard the splash of oars and watched Titus climb aboard the government sloop which, even as she watched, set sail and vanished into the darkness, bearing him swiftly away from her. . . .

Two days later the Reverend Caleb Boskenna presented himself at the house to announce, with a wealth of effusive detail, that he and his wife were now ready to relieve Mrs. Spence of responsibility for the care and well-being of his two orphaned wards.

He was profuse in his thanks and set himself out to win even Mr. Spence's approbation with the glowing account he gave of the new land grant and the work that had been done, in order to render it both habitable and productive.

"I have made arrangements to hire a suitable sailing vessel from Mr. Robert Campbell's yard," he said, beaming from one to the other. "The *Phoebe* will be ready in ten days' time, Mr. Campbell has assured me. She will accommodate us all, with our stores and provisions, and the three well-recommended convict laborers who have been assigned to me. If it is convenient to you, Mrs. Spence, ma'am, Abigail and Lucy may join me on board as soon as the *Phoebe*'s master informs me that she is ready to sail."

Abigail listened in resigned silence as Frances Spence gave her assent to this proposal, and it was of small consolation to learn that evening from her hostess that Lieutenant O'Shea had also been sent to Coal Harbor, in command of the troops there . . . and of Titus.

CHAPTER XIII

"The devil take it, George, I do *not* intend to forfeit my bond!" John Macarthur brought his clenched fist down onto the table with such force that the glass and chinaware with which it was set were sent flying. His wife, Elizabeth, eyed him reproachfully but said nothing, and Major Johnstone, visibly startled by his vehemence, grabbed his own half-spilled wineglass from the debris and swallowed what was left of its contents before committing himself to an opinion.

"You would be well advised to think what the consequences may be, John," he said cautiously. "They're within their rights, you know—all of 'em, Bligh included. You and Blaxcell don't have a case that would stand up in court, do you?"

"I can make one," Macarthur retorted sourly. "In fact I have . . . and in writing, too. Elizabeth, my dear, the copy of that letter I sent to Glenn is on my desk, under the paperweight. Would you be so good as to get it for me?"

Elizabeth Macarthur gathered up her skirts and rose, still without speaking, and her husband went on indignantly, "No sooner had the blasted *Parramatta*

dropped anchor in the cove than Robert Campbell—
on instructions from the plaguey governor, of course—
went on board, refused to pass her papers for entry,
and placed the ship and her company under arrest!
Then he hauled Glenn before the civil bench, and they
declared our bond to be forfeit."

"But there's no doubt of Glenn's guilt, is there?"
Johnstone questioned, frowning into his empty glass.
"Didn't he admit in court that he'd smuggled that
rogue Hoare out of the colony and arranged his passage to America?"

"Certainly he did," Macarthur conceded. "I don't
deny it. But damme, George, *I'm* not to be held responsible for Glenn's criminal actions! What he did
was without my knowledge and most definitely without my authority. I simply employed him to act as
master of the *Parramatta*." Elizabeth returned with the
letter he had asked for, and his expression changed as
he looked at her. "Thank you, my dear," he acknowledged, smiling his gratitude. God had blessed him in
his marriage, he thought; he possessed a wife who
was not only beautiful, but a woman of rare quality
and considerable accomplishment. And she was loyal,
supporting him staunchly in everything he did, and
giving him a family of whom any man would be proud.

For her sake, as much as for his own, he would
not submit to any official harassment that might destroy what they had built up, with such labor, over
the years—this farm at Parramatta—called Elizabeth
Farm, in her honor—and the fine grazing land at Cow
Pastures, which he had renamed Camden. *Bounty*
Bligh had threatened to deprive him of that land when
he had first taken office as governor, and by heaven,
he had done all in his power to implement the threat
ever since! He had not succeeded, but the memory
of that first acrimonious interview with him was still
fresh in John Macarthur's mind.

Automatically he refilled Johnstone's glass, the letter still folded in his free hand. He had gone in a conciliatory mood to request the allocation of the additional five thousand acres of grazing land promised him by Lord Camden and the Privy Council and had drawn the new governor's attention to the fact that he owned and had bred the only pure Merino flock in the colony. And Bligh, in an incredible display of ill-tempered prejudice, had rounded on him, damning the Privy Council and the secretary of state in the same breath.

"What have I to do with your sheep, sir?" the new governor had demanded. "What have I to do with your cattle? Are you to have such flocks of sheep and herds of cattle as no man ever heard of before? You have got five thousand acres of land in the finest situation in the whole country, but by God, sir, you shan't keep it!"

He *had* kept it, but he had never been given the balance of his entitlement and would not be so long as Bligh was governor. Macarthur could feel his own anger rising as he recalled the ugly scene which had marked the beginning of what some were pleased to call his feud with William Bligh. So far he had held his own, as he had done also with Bligh's immediate predecessors in the governor's office, but it had been a long and bitter struggle, with each of his victories dearly won.

Now, in this unfortunate business of the *Parramatta* and her ruffian of a master, John Glenn, he stood to lose . . . and not only financially. True, eight hundred pounds would be a heavy loss, but he could stand it and so could his partner, Garnham Blaxcell—they were both, thanks to their rum-trading ventures, wealthy men. No . . . Macarthur glanced again at his wife and, receiving her slight nod of assent, started to unfold the copy of his letter. It was a matter of principle and of prestige; the Corps against the governor, as it had always been, and he could not afford to give Bligh best. Johnstone, as commandant of the Corps, must be made to see that he could not.

Elizabeth excused herself, letting her hand rest lightly on his shoulder before leaving the room.

"Talk it over with George," she said quietly. "You know where I am if you need me, John, dear."

"Yes, of course," he agreed, and spread the flimsy sheet of paper out on the table in front of him. "This is addressed to Captain Glenn, under yesterday's date —December seventh, George. It reads: *'Owing to the action of the naval officer of the port, Mr. Robert Campbell, in placing the schooner* Parramatta *under arrest, I regard myself as having been virtually dispossessed of the vessel. I therefore give you, as master, formal notification that I have abandoned the said schooner and neither you, nor your crew, are henceforward to look to me for pay or provisions.'* "

He paused, looking expectantly across the table at his guest, and Major Johnstone, who had clearly anticipated the letter to be couched in more controversial terms, sighed his relief.

"I can see no objection to that, John. It's more or less a statement of fact, is it not?"

"Indeed it is," John Macarthur confirmed. "I sent Glenn a copy and instructed him to deliver it to the port naval officer, with the request that he take an inventory of all stores, provisions, and cargo on board the *Parramatta* before these are removed from her."

"Well?" The Corps commandant shrugged, the expression on his round red face frankly puzzled. "I can see no objection to that. You're within your rights, I'd have thought—you own her cargo."

"Quite so, my dear fellow." John Macarthur replenished both their glasses, but while Major Johnstone drank thirstily, he left his own untouched. He waited

302 William Stuart Long

and then said, with heavy emphasis, when he again had his guest's attention, "But I am *no longer the owner of the vessel!* Therefore I should not be obliged to forfeit my bond, don't you see? The *Parramatta* has been taken from me by the port naval officer, on instructions from the civil court which, needless to tell you, came from the governor. Rob Campbell is Bligh's man, George . . . and he's not to be persuaded otherwise."

"Is he not?" Johnstone sounded surprised.

"No!" Macarthur's tone was hard. "He's not. I tried weeks ago, before the infernal *Parramatta* came back here, and I failed to move him. He'll back Bligh, whatever the cost. But"—his pendulous lower lip was drawn back in an oddly humorless smile—"Mr. Campbell has played right into my hands without realizing it. He's put two constables on board the ship, to ensure that neither Glenn nor any of his people go ashore. *That* would be in breach of port regulations, according to Campbell."

"Yes, but I don't see how it affects the issue, John." The commandant picked up his glass and drained it. He had already drunk a good deal more than Macarthur. His voice was becoming slurred, his watery blue eyes bloodshot; but, ignoring these signs, his host quickly refilled his glass.

"Listen, George, my friend, and listen carefully, if you please," Macarthur begged.

"I'm listening, damme!" Johnstone protested. "Make your point, for God's sake!"

"Very well, then . . . it's this. By placing those two constables on board the *Parramatta,* Campbell has effectively removed her and her company from my control. Is that not so?"

Johnstone nodded slowly, "I suppose so, yes, but—"

"Plague take it, George!" Macarthur exclaimed, suddenly impatient. "I cannot be held responsible for a ship I no longer control, and I've now repudiated all responsibility for her in writing . . . putting the blame for this state of affairs where it belongs. On the port naval officer. The civil court cannot legally compel me to forfeit my bond."

"Well, your knowledge of legal procedures is much greater than mine," George Johnstone admitted. He again raised his glass to his lips, eyeing his one-time subordinate warily across its rim. Setting it down, he added uneasily, "But I fear you are treading on dangerous ground, John. You—"

"I'm making a stand, George—a stand against Bligh's intolerable tyranny!" For the second time John Macarthur brought his clenched fist crashing down on the disordered table. "As God's my witness, if some of us don't stand up to the bastard, he'll have us ruined! Look what he's done in the past eighteen months . . . consider the effect his damned orders and regulations have had on our trading enterprises. He's declared it illegal for us to import liquor and ordered that it can only be imported and sold under government license, at government-controlled prices. And who gets the licenses? Sniveling swine of emancipists, whose notes of hand aren't worth the paper they're written on. They are given land, stock, credit . . . anything they ask him for and be damned to the rest of us! Hell's teeth, George, must I spell these things out for you, when you know as well as I do what the arrogant bastard's intentions are? He wants to ruin us!"

"He is the governor," George Johnstone argued. "He has the authority and—"

"Has he? Are you sure he has?"

Alarmed, Johnstone shook his head, and Macarthur went on remorselessly, "Bligh's local regulations aren't even legal, George. I took counsel's opinion on that point and have it in writing . . . no order or regulation issued by a governor outside the United Kingdom can be binding or legal, *unless sanctioned by an act of His Majesty's Parliament*. I'm quoting from memory, but that's the gist of it, and it applies to all His Majesty's colonies and settlements overseas. It applies to *this* colony!"

Johnstone's alarm had visibly increased, and he passed a shaking hand across his mouth, as if to restrain himself from voicing an opinion on what he had just been told. Almost contemptuously Macarthur splashed liquor into his glass.

"Let's drink a toast, George," he invited, raising his own glass. "Down with the tyrant! Come on, man—you are the lieutenant governor, are you not? Don't you want to see an end to the *Bounty* bastard's tyranny?"

"You go too far, John. For pity's sake, you talk of treason, and I can't countenance that. I—" Johnstone choked in his agitation. "All this over a paltry forfeit of eight hundred pounds! It won't break you, and in any event, half of it is Blaxcell's, isn't it? You—"

John Macarthur cut him short. He said, controlling himself and speaking with quiet conviction, "You know it is not just that. I told you—I intend to make a stand, for all our sakes. But I cannot do it alone. I must be able to count on your support, George. The Corps are with me, Simeon Lord, the Blaxlands, Tom Jamieson, John Harris, of course, Wentworth, and Fitz, and Charlie Grimes. We've all of us had enough, and we're not going to see this colony taken over by the damned convicts and the so-called free settlers. We have too much to lose."

The hectic color drained from Johnstone's face. "The Corps?" he echoed. "*My officers* are with you?"

"To a man, George," Macarthur asserted.

"Then I . . ." The Corps commandant stared at him in shocked disbelief. "I cannot hold aloof, although, damme, I wish I could. But need it come to . . ." He shied from voicing his greatest fear and swallowed hard, as bile rose in his throat.

"It need not," Macarthur assured him, and laid a consoling arm on his threadbare scarlet sleeve. "Let us say that we are about to engage in a trial of strength, which has been threatening for a long time. Bligh is an arrogant tyrant, and he's using this business of the *Parramatta* as an excuse to pursue his vendetta against me . . . and through me, those of my associates he fully intends to begger, *if* he can. His object is to prevent us trading—you, too, George, as you well know, since you're in the syndicate with the rest of us. And he has a choice . . . damn his eyes, he can climb down or he can fight!"

"He will not climb down," Johnstone said unhappily.

"No, I do not think he will." John Macarthur's dark eyes held a bright gleam of anticipation. "In that case it will be a fight to the finish . . . and one I don't intend to lose!" He laughed softly. "I'd have avoided it if it had been possible—I even tried when I first heard of Hoare's escape, though you may find that hard to credit. I endeavored to work out a plan with Simeon Lord."

"Did you, John?" George Johnstone's echoing laugh was hollow, and Macarthur stiffened for a moment and then relaxed.

"Yes, I did. But the time had to come, now or later, and now I shall have most of the respectable inhabitants of this benighted place behind me, as well as the Corps. Bligh can count *his* supporters on the fingers of one hand—and he even got rid of one of the most devoted, our friend Hawley, without any prompting from any of us."

"There are the settlers," Johnstone reminded him. "Those on the Hawkesbury have just delivered a Loyal Address to him, with over a hundred and fifty signatures."

"But they are too far from Sydney to be able to intervene, my dear fellow," Macarthur said, smiling. He lifted his glass, which was still brimming over, and added pointedly, "Will you drink my toast now, George?"

"If you wish," George Johnstone agreed. He hiccoughed loudly and rose unsteadily to his feet, his own almost-empty glass in his hand. "What the devil was your toast? I've forgotten."

"It was 'Death to the tyrant!' " Macarthur supplied. He gulped down the contents of his glass and then flung it from him, to shatter in the stone-built fireplace at his back.

"I had thought it was 'Down with the tyrant,' " the Corps commandant objected. "And that's what I am drinking to, John. We want no violence here."

"Then pray that the tyrant provokes none," Macarthur retorted sourly.

John Glenn, master of the schooner *Parramatta,* watched anxiously as his mate and two of his seamen winched the longboat into the water. Beside him, one of the two constables posted to hold his ship under arrest repeated his earlier warning, but Glenn affected not to hear what he was saying.

The constable shrugged and crossed the deck to join his younger colleague at the taffrail.

"They've made up their minds," he observed unnecessarily, gesturing to the boat. "An' I can't honestly say as I blame 'em, Joe. No food, no water, an' no pay for a week, on top o' bein' kept cooped up on board this tub without leave to stretch their legs ashore! What else can the poor sods do but appeal to the gov'nor, seein' as their owner's abandoned 'em?"

"There's nowt we can do to stop 'em," the younger constable confirmed. He yawned loudly. "At least we c'n get some sleep once they're gone."

His senior shook his head. "That's where you're wrong, Joe, me lad. As soon as they have gone, you'll take our boat, quick an' lively, an' report 'em to Mr. Campbell. We got to keep our yardarms clear whatever happens. But you c'n bring back our reliefs when you come—we're over our time by a coupla hours."

"Very good," Joe agreed readily. "As soon as they've gone."

The longboat entered the water with a splash, and, standing upright in her bow, the mate hooked onto the *Parramatta*'s starboard chains and worked his charge alongside the rope ladder suspended from her entry port. Glenn jerked his balding head to the seamen waiting at his back and said crisply, "All right, my lads —over the side with you!"

He was a small, corpulent man, with a neatly trimmed beard and skin which—belying his calling—was the color of parchment. He thought, with restrained anger, as he watched his men clambering into the boat, that Captain John Macarthur had a good deal for which to answer concerning his treatment of them. While it was true that he had accepted a substantial payment from John Hoare to arrange his escape from the colony, he was by no means the only ship's master to succumb to similar temptation. If the price was high enough, they all took the chance, and usually, because the search on the eve of sailing was a formality and cursorily conducted, few were ever found out.

He had taken particular trouble with John, however, because the provost marshal in person had accompanied the men detailed to conduct the search, and it had been far from cursory—in spite of one of the ship's mate's attempts to keep it so. . . . Glenn scowled, remembering. For all their efforts, Gore and his fellows had drawn a blank and had let the *Parramatta* sail—although only just in time to save her illicit passenger from suffocation in the fore part of the hold, where he had lain buried beneath a hundred bales of stinking, unwashed wool. Then the passenger, Hoare, had gone and got drunk when they let him off in Otaheite, and that had been the start of all the present trouble. . . .

John Glenn grunted as he lowered himself into the longboat, and taking his grunt for an order, the mate cast off, and the men bent to their oars.

"We'll make for the government wharf," Glenn said. "And we'll keep together. I don't want anyone accusing us of riotous assembly or anything of that kind, understand?"

"But we're breakin' the sodding law anyway, ain't we?" the mate questioned uneasily. "By comin' ashore. And them constables won't waste no time informin' on us to the bleedin' port officer."

John Glenn gave him a withering glance. "We are seeking an audience with the governor, mister," he retorted repressively, "to petition him to right the wrongs our owner has seen fit to do to us. 'Tis Cap' Macarthur who's responsible, and I'm going to put the blame fairly and squarely where it belongs. And"—he tapped the hip pocket of his stained breeches—"just in case His Excellency won't give me an audience, I've written a full report for his consideration."

"S'pose 'e don't read it?" one of the men asked, his expression mirroring the mate's uneasiness. "S'pose the bastard governor claps us all in 'is bloody jail, Cap'n? Gawd, we could end up as convicts, the lot o' us!"

"We shan't, lad," Glenn assured him. "I had a little chat with Mr. Campbell, and I know what I'm doing. If the governor orders us back to the ship, then we go back, but the port officer's going to have to see we're fed."

"No run ashore?" the man demanded bleakly.

Glenn shook his head. "Without our pay, what's the sense in a run ashore? Get this into your heads, all of you—I'm aiming to force Macarthur to admit he owns the bloody *Parramatta*. Once he does that, we're in the clear, and he can argue the toss with the court or the governor as to whether or not he has to forfeit his bond. But he'll have to give us our pay and see we get our victuals, and that's all that concerns me."

"Yes, but Cap'n, surely we—"

"A plague on your infernal griping!" the *Parramatta*'s master exclaimed, his patience wearing thin. "Do what you're told, Eli Bates, or I'll have you clapped in Sydney Jail myself. All right—'way enough! Ship your oars!"

The longboat came alongside the wharf, and the mate wielded his boathook and jumped nimbly ashore, the painter in his hand. "One o' the constables is on his way to Campbell's Wharf, Cap'n Glenn," he warned as Glenn followed him on to the stone jetty. "D'you want me to come with you up there?" He jerked his head in the direction of Government House, marked by the pacing sentry at the gate, and the blue-tiled roof of the guardhouse to the right of it.

The master hesitated. The tall mate's support would have been welcome, but . . . He sighed, aware that he could not trust his men to remain in the boat without supervision. If he were too long at Government House, the chances were that—even without a penny to their names—one or two of them would make tracks for the drinking dens and whorehouses in the Rocks area, and if they did, he would be in serious trouble.

He shook his head. "No, bide here, mister. I want to see a full crew when I come back."

"Aye, aye, Cap'n," the mate acknowledged. He grinned sheepishly. "They'll all be here, don't worry— however long it takes you."

As it happened, Captain Glenn's call at Government House was brief. He returned to the wharf, his sallow face suffused with resentful color, and in reply to the mate's mute question and his men's muttered obsceni- ties, he said bitterly, "The bastard governor refused to

give me the time o' day. He sent his whippersnapper o'
a secretary to tell me that it's a matter for the judge
advocate, Mr. Richard Atkins, and we'd all be required
to sign affidavits before him if we wanted our complaints
heard." He spat his disgust into the still waters of the
cove and shrugged resignedly. "So that's where we're
going, lads, this very minute—to Mr. Atkins's residence,
the lot of us. It's only a step . . . up past the guardhouse
there and turn right. The sergeant of the guard will send
a soldier to watch the longboat if I ask him."

The men were silent, digesting this. Then Eli Bates
swore angrily. "An' after we done what they want,
Cap'n Glenn, does we get our victuals or will they send
us to jail?"

"We'll just have to find out," Glenn answered sourly,
"but I don't reckon they can let us starve. If we play our
cards right, maybe Mr. Atkins will stand us each two
penn'orth at Sarah Bird's. Come on, then, look lively!
And remember, lads—we all stick to the same story.
Don't any of you speak out o' turn. Just you back me
up, and we'll get even with *Mister* Macarthur for the
scurvy trick he's played on us."

He set off at a brisk pace in the direction from which
he had come, and his men fell in at his heels with varying degrees of reluctance, Eli Bates apprehensively
bringing up the rear.

"Mr. Atkins, Your Excellency," Edmund Griffin announced. Governor Bligh glanced up wearily from the
pile of papers which, as always, littered his desk, and
nodded his acquiescence.

"Very well, show him in, Edmund."

The judge advocate's appearance was not unexpected,
even if inopportune. After the call earlier that day of the
Parramatta's master, it was evident that some action
would have to be taken to deal with his complaint
against the schooner's owner. And since that owner was,

at least in part, John Macarthur, undoubtedly the action would have to be immediate and uncompromising.

Atkins entered, flushed and breathless, and William Bligh waved him to a seat.

"Well, Mr. Atkins?" he invited. "I take it you've interviewed Captain Glenn and his people?"

"I have, sir." Forsaking his usual wordiness, Atkins gave a brief summary of the affidavits he had taken, and then, a malicious smile curving his lips, he set the papers down on the desk and picked up a single sheet, already folded and addressed. "This is the letter I propose to have delivered to Macarthur, sir. I have a mounted messenger standing by, and, provided that it meets with your approval, it can be sent at once, so that he receives it this evening."

"So soon?" the governor commented.

"Yes, sir." There was no mistaking the malice in the judge advocate's voice. "He's gone too far this time, as I always knew he would one day. Sir, I should like to preface the letter 'In command from His Excellency the governor,' with your permission."

"Let me read it," Bligh said, holding out his hand. He frowned, seeing that the letter, in fact, was already prefaced as by his command, and, before reading further, he asked sharply, "Has Lawyer Crossley seen this?"

"Yes, indeed," Atkins assured him. "In Crossley's view, it could be more strongly worded than it is. But I deemed the tone sufficiently—ah—urgent to elicit an immediate response."

Bligh laid the letter down in front of him and read it carefully. It summoned John Macarthur to appear in Sydney the following morning by ten o'clock. His frown deepened as he considered the wording: ". . . *to show cause why the master, mariners, and crew of the schooner* Parramatta *have violated the Port Regulations by coming unauthorized on shore and to explain why you have deprived them of their usual allowance of provisions, which they allege to be the reason for this violation. . . ."*

"Macarthur repudiated all responsibility for the *Parramatta* in a letter he sent to Glenn, if you recall, sir," Atkins offered as the governor looked up, still frowning, to meet his gaze. "That was subsequent to the declaration by the civil court that his bond and Blaxcell's were to be forfeited."

"Yes, yes, I do recall that. But you cross-examined the fellow Glenn, did you not?" Bligh was impatient. "And he admitted his guilt?"

"Yes, he did, sir. To me and to the court. Macarthur hasn't a leg to stand on—he cannot repudiate responsibility for the ship and her company, any more than he can refuse to forfeit his bond."

"Does Crossley confirm it?"

"Most emphatically, yes. And about the letter . . ." As he spoke, Atkins was fumbling in the pockets of his shabby coat, finally bringing to light a crumpled sheet of paper. "This is a copy of Macarthur's letter which he instructed Glenn to deliver to Mr. Campbell in an attempt, I can only presume, to make his repudiation official."

"Or to drive the *Parramatta*'s people to flaunt our port regulations," the governor amended shrewdly. He glanced at the second letter, grunted, and returned it. "Mr. Atkins, there is more to all this than meets the eye. What is the sum involved in the bond—eight hundred pounds, with an extra fifty Gore made each of the owners put up? Nine hundred pounds in all. But the *Parramatta,* with her cargo, must be worth ten times that. Let us say, at a conservative estimate, ten thousand pounds. Admittedly John Macarthur is a rich man, but surely he must have a very good reason for repudiating his ownership of a vessel worth ten thousand pounds, in order to save paying a forfeit of nine hun-

dred? And"—Bligh's tone was suddenly excited—
"where does Garnham Blaxcell stand in the matter?
He's maintained a cautious silence, has he not?"

The judge advocate nodded. "Yes, indeed he has,
but—"

"In God's name, why?" William Bligh thundered.
"They're in partnership, aren't they? Blaxcell stands to
lose his share of the *Parramatta* and her cargo, thanks
to Macarthur's action, yet there hasn't been a peep out
of him! Hell's teeth, Mr. Atkins, suppose I tell Campbell to put the ship up for auction? I'm legally entitled
to give such instructions, am I not, if Macarthur and
Blaxcell continue to defy the court and refuse payment
of their bond?"

Richard Atkins looked startled. "Er—Mr. Crossley
considered that possibility, sir, but he was against it.
He—"

"In heaven's name, why?" The governor's temper was
rising. His judge advocate all too often had this effect
on him, he reflected resentfully, for Atkins was an incompetent fool, who now drank so heavily that his intel-
lect had deteriorated, and of necessity he depended on
the emancipist Crossley's guidance in virtually everything he did in his official capacity. Crossley was able
enough, but he was, after all, a convicted forger, disbarred by his benchers from legal practice in England,
so that his trustworthiness must always be a matter for
some doubt . . . although his shrewdness was not.

Bligh suppressed a sigh of frustration. "Damme!" he
exclaimed, making an effort to keep his annoyance within bounds. "Why the devil was Crossley against it, then?
It seemed the obvious action to take. If Macarthur has
abandoned the vessel, she can be put up for auction as
an abandoned vessel, surely?"

Atkins broke out in an attack of nervous perspiration,
and, a stained handkerchief between his shaking fingers,
he endeavored to mop his damp, heavily jowled face.

"In Crossley's view, sir," he managed at last, "Macarthur *wants* the schooner put up for auction, to enable him to sue Campbell in the civil court." Still sweating profusely, he outlined what the onetime King's Bencher had explained to him of the legal pitfalls. "The discrepancy in value between the bond and the *Parramatta* and her cargo would seem to justify legal action, sir," he ended. "If Macarthur did sue, he would in all probability win substantial damages, on the grounds that the naval officer had stationed guards on board, thereby depriving him of possession of the vessel and compelling him to abandon her."

William Bligh considered this reasoning in ominous silence. Then, still keeping a tight rein on his temper, he reread the letter Atkins had composed with even more care than he had given to it initially. He knew, of course, that there had been bad blood between John Macarthur and the judge advocate for years, and that this letter—worded as it was, with his own name as governor preceding the summons—amounted to an official command to Macarthur to explain his conduct.

It was a command that he would disobey at his peril, for all his wealth and arrogance. The governor glanced across the desk at Atkins, disliking what he saw, and found himself wishing that he might somehow contrive to avoid being drawn into the sordid affair. And yet he could not, devil take it! John Macarthur was a dangerous man who had actively and relentlessly opposed all his attempts to bring order and justice and prosperity to the colony he had been appointed to govern.

If he were to weaken now, when it seemed that, at last, as Atkins had claimed, Macarthur had gone too far, would he be given a second chance to put an end to the malign influence of the man from whom the rum traffickers of the Corps and the corrupt officials took their lead? It seemed improbable. To bring John Macarthur to heel—and to do so publicly—would achieve much more than Richard Atkins, pursuing his own personal vendetta, could envisage. But the end, surely, would justify the means?

William Bligh, shrugging his elegantly epauletted shoulders, said, without emotion, "Very well, Mr. Atkins—have this letter delivered at once. You say you have a mounted trooper waiting to take it to Parramatta?"

"Indeed I have, sir." Richard Atkins could not disguise his relief and satisfaction. He shambled awkwardly to his feet, reaching out to take the letter from the governor's hand, his own trembling visibly. "The *Parramatta*'s master and her crew are now on the public charge, sir. I took the liberty of informing Mr. Campbell, as port naval officer, that they were to be supplied from government stores, so long as they remain on board their ship."

The governor gave him a curt nod, which he accepted as his dismissal. The door had scarcely closed behind him than it was opened and Mary Putland peered inquiringly through the aperture.

"That unpleasant man has gone at last, has he? May I come in, Papa?"

Bligh rose and took her into his affectionate embrace, grateful for her presence. She was in widow's weeds, but they became her, setting off her slim figure and lovely oval face to perfection. Poor Charles's illness had taken a heavy toll of her. His death, for all it was expected, had grieved her sorely, but she had borne it all with courage and a dignified resignation. Even the funeral—conducted in the grounds of Government House with fitting solemnity and full military honors—had not weakened her resolve. Holding her in his arms, her father eyed her with conscious pride, and she smiled back at him bravely.

"I thought perhaps a game of chess," she suggested, indicating the board she was carrying. "You look as if you need a little relaxation before the guests start arriving for dinner."

"There is nothing I should like more, my dear," the governor assured her, "save for all the infernal guests to discover that they have previous engagements!"

"Well, we have over three hours before they fail to do so," Mary said. She laid her board on the low table on which they usually played, and began to set out the pieces. "Did Mr. Atkins worry you?"

"Not much more than he is in the habit of doing," her father evaded. He selected a pipe from the rack on the mantle shelf and raised it inquiringly. "You will not object if I smoke?"

"Of course not. Let me fill your pipe for you." Seating herself at the table, she took pipe and tobacco jar from him, her glance at his face more than a little anxious, as if his attempt at evasion had failed to convince her that all was as it should be. She waited, the pipe still unfilled, her smooth brow puckered, and, when Bligh offered no explanation, she prompted uneasily, "There *is* something wrong, is there not, Papa? Please tell me if there is."

Bligh's hand closed about hers. "There may be a storm brewing, Mary, my dear, but it need not concern you."

"What concerns you also concerns me, Papa," Mary reproached him. Under her gentle probing he recounted the details of his interview with Richard Atkins and what had led up to it. "Frankly, I'm not sure what the outcome will be. And Atkins isn't to be trusted—he is weak, motivated by personal spite, and his knowledge of the law is insignificant."

"And he drinks to excess!" Mary exclaimed distastefully. Her father did not contradict her; it was, he thought wryly, the truth, and he had said as much in a recent dispatch to the Colonial Office. But no move had been made to replace Richard Atkins in the office of judge advocate, and it was unlikely in the extreme that a more able man would be sent out in time to deal with the problems Macarthur was currently posing.

As if she had read his thoughts, Mary went on, "If Mr. Macarthur is involved, I fear you must anticipate the worst. Papa, dearest, I tremble for you, truly I do! Mr. Macarthur is a most devious and wicked person— and the Corps officers will stand by him against you, even if he is acting illegally." She sighed and again picked up the long-stemmed pipe, cramming tobacco into it with so heavy a hand that the governor took it from her with a rueful grimace.

"My dear, it will never draw if you overfill it. Leave it to me."

Mary clasped her two trembling hands in front of her. She said, in a strained voice, "I can never decide whether it is Mr. Macarthur or Major Johnstone I dislike more, for both are self-seeking and disloyal. And they are your bitter enemies, Papa! I . . . oh, goodness, when Major Johnstone appeared at poor Charles's funeral and offered his condolences, it was all I could do not to strike him!"

"He attended in his official capacity," her father reminded her.

"But it was such hypocrisy! And to intrude on my grief as he did was unforgivable. I wish you still had Captain Hawley here. Whatever you may think of his marriage, Papa, he has always been the soul of loyalty, and if Mr. Macarthur does intend to make trouble for you, you will need some trustworthy officers to back you up."

"I have sent for Captain Hawley to return," Bligh admitted, with unaccustomed humility. "It was a bad mistake on my part to banish him to Van Diemen's Land. He should be back in Sydney very soon."

"And his wife?" Mary persisted. "He married Mrs. Broome in Hobart, did he not?"

The governor was silent, busy with his pipe. When it was going to his satisfaction, he said flatly, "She may return when her sentence has expired. I have already been accused of tampering with court procedures, and I don't intend to lay myself open to such accusations needlessly—not even for you, my dear child. . . . Damme, Jamieson got on his high horse when I told him to cancel young Penhaligon's posting to Coal River! *He* tried to tell me I was usurping his authority as surgeon general, if you please, and I only gave the order because of your insistence, Mary."

"They had no right to send poor Titus away in the dead of night," Mary defended angrily, "and only a few hours after Charles had breathed his last. It was a deliberate affront to us both, Papa, and intended as such."

"I don't doubt it was," Bligh conceded, "but that is the way half the officers in this colony see fit to behave, plague take them! They constantly question *my* authority, and without loyal troops to back me up, I cannot assert it too rigorously. Unless and until"—he paused, recalling Richard Atkins's words—"unless and until one of them goes too far, and I can bring the weight of the law down on him with absolute justification. Perhaps the moment has arrived." He controlled himself and gestured to the chessboard with the stem of his pipe. "Let us have our game, shall we? I can do no more in this matter of Macarthur and his infernal ship until he answers the judge advocate's summons."

That answer, he thought, almost with relief, would determine his own, and if John Macarthur wanted a fight, then, before heaven, he should have one!

Mary eyed him for a moment in mute question, and then, well aware of the strain under which her father was laboring, she obediently turned her gaze to the chessmen. After a brief hesitation she made her first move. . . .

* * *

Macarthur's reply was delivered by the mounted trooper the following day, and Richard Atkins, to whom it was addressed, read it with mounting fury. Far from presenting himself in person to explain his conduct, the *Parramatta*'s owner merely offered the same excuses for it as he had before:

> You were many days ago informed that I had declined any further interference with the schooner —in consequence of the illegal conduct of the Naval Officer in refusing to enter the vessel and retaining the papers, notwithstanding I had made repeated applications that they might be restored.
>
> So circumstanced, I could no longer think of submitting to the expense of paying and victualling the officers and crew of a vessel over which I had no control. But previous to my declining to do so, my intentions were officially made known to the Naval Officer.
>
> What steps he has since taken respecting the schooner and her people I am yet to learn, but as he has two police officers on board in charge of her, it is reasonable to suppose they are directed to prevent irregularities, and therefore I beg leave to refer you to the Naval Officer for what further information you may require on the subject. . . .

Atkins, pausing only to seek the advice of Lawyer Crossley, went posthaste to Government House. The governor received him with noticeable coldness, but the judge advocate was too enraged for this to deter him. He waited, with barely concealed impatience, for Bligh to read the letter and, when he had done so, burst out explosively, "I am ready to take the necessary action, sir!"

"And what is that, pray?" the governor asked, his manner still cold and controlled.

"The issue of a warrant for the arrogant rogue's arrest," Atkins told him. His hands were shaking as he produced the warrant for inspection. "Crossley drew this up, sir, so it is perfectly legal. And Macarthur has declined to obey my previous summons."

William Bligh took several minutes to study the wording of the warrant and the charge it made, but, despite the appearance of calm he was at pains to present, he, too, was angry. John Macarthur had chosen to defy him and, once again, was calling into question his authority as governor. The moment had come; the challenge had been offered, and it could not be refused unless he— like his predecessors in office—were to allow Macarthur and his infamous Rum Corps supporters to get the best of him, at God knew what cost to the rest of the community.

And—come to that—to himself, since to admit defeat at Macarthur's hands would be to acknowledge his own inability to govern. Bligh's firm mouth tightened. For a fleeting moment he wondered whether the judge advocate's initial summons had been strictly legal and then dismissed the doubt. The summons had been prefaced in his name, as governor, and therefore amounted to a command from the official representative of the King . . . and John Macarthur had declined to obey it.

He had, as Atkins had claimed, gone too far and perhaps, God willing, laid himself open to an even more serious charge than that contained in the warrant, for which the sentence—if the court did its duty—might well be banishment from the colony of New South Wales.

The governor drew himself up. Sitting stiffly upright is his chair, he returned the warrant to Atkins's eager hands and said, with terse finality, "Very well, serve this on Mr. Macarthur without delay, sir. I take it that Mr. Gore will be trusted with its delivery?"

"No, sir." Atkins thrust the precious warrant into his breast pocket, his flushed, sweat-streaked face ugly in its malicious satisfaction. "Macarthur is at Parramatta, sir, so it will be the duty of Oakes, the chief constable of that township, to deliver it and, if it should be—ah—if it should be necessary, to place him under arrest."

He did not add that this had been Lawyer Crossley's ruling, but Governor Bligh, with a swift, frowning glance at his face, rightly concluded that it had and ordered crisply, "You had better set Crossley to work preparing an indictment, Mr. Atkins, and convene the civil court to hear the charges at ten o'clock tomorrow morning."

"The sixteenth of December, Your Excellency," the judge advocate echoed. "Very good, sir, I will attend to it."

He took his leave hastily and went out, a smile of pure pleasure curving his flaccid lips.

The governor expelled his breath in a deep sigh and returned to his papers, but the written words blurred before his eyes, and, superimposed upon them, it was John Macarthur's face he saw.

CHAPTER XIV

Justin tacked his cutter expertly into Sydney Cove, and, as her mainsail came down, Andrew, stationed in her bows for that purpose, let go her anchor and she came to within hailing distance of Robert Campbell's wharf.

The anchorage looked peaceful enough, with its usual complement of trading vessels, whalers, and river craft swinging to their moorings in the light offshore breeze. The colonial frigate, H.M.S. *Porpoise,* was absent, however, and remarking this as he came aft to assist Justin to stow canvas, Andrew said with relief, "The situation must have improved if the governor has let her go, don't you think?"

Justin, concentrating with the single-minded detachment he always gave to the securing of his small command, grunted indifferently and appeared not to have heard; but a little later, their chores completed, he dispelled his stepfather's brief illusion.

"She was due to go to the Cape for stores just after we sailed. I don't reckon the governor had much choice." He jerked his wind-ruffled fair head in the direction of the wharf. "But if you want to find out what's afoot, we could make our report to Mr. Campbell right away, before he comes to us. I see the *Parramatta*'s here."

"The *Parramatta*?"

"Aye—Mr. Macarthur's schooner." Justin grinned. "With two constables in uniform patrolling her deck and her hatches battened down."

The boy's sharp eyes had missed nothing, Andrew thought, but he asked, puzzled, "What does that signify, lad?"

"Trouble," Justin replied, still grinning. "She's under arrest. There was some story about her master having smuggled an escaper on board and given him passage to Otaheite. The provost marshal had her searched twice before she was allowed to sail from here. They found no one, but I suppose they've managed to pin it on her people now." He shrugged. "I'll get the dinghy."

Robert Campbell gravely confirmed this supposition when they joined him in his dockside office twenty minutes later.

"Sydney Town is agog, waiting for the storm to break, as I fear it's about to, and the wildest rumors are gaining credence—each wilder than the last. The most recent I have heard is that Mr. Atkins, as judge advocate, has issued a warrant for Mr. Macarthur's arrest, to be served on him today by Francis Oakes in Parramatta." The port naval officer spread his big, strong hands in a gesture of resignation. "Naturally, by reason of my office, I'm embroiled in the unhappy affair. I had to place the *Parramatta* under arrest, for a start. The civil court ordered her owners to forfeit their bond, and they both refused to do so—although the master made a full confession of guilt." He told of the crew's decision to come ashore in defiance of port regulations and then added, "Now the judge advocate has convened the magistrates' bench for tomorrow morning, and I am required to sit . . . presumably to hear the case against Macarthur. *If,* that is to say, he submits to Oakes's warrant and appears before us to answer the charges."

"Don't you think he will, sir?" Andrew asked, hearing the doubt in his tone. "Surely he cannot refuse to appear?"

"The good Lord in heaven alone knows what he'll do, Captain Hawley!" Robert Campbell returned. "He is as devious and unpredictable as they come. And who knows better than John Macarthur how to bend the law to his advantage? He's been doing it for years—harassing honest fellows like Will Gore and Lieutenant Marshall, and that poor devil Andrew Thompson, with his scurvy, trumped up lawsuits! This colony has suffered enough from him, and the governor has to make a stand against Macarthur *and* the Corps, who will, it goes without saying, support him whatever he elects to do. If we could rid New South Wales of the lot of them, it would be our salvation, in my view. My only fear—and it's one that haunts me—is what will be the consequence should we try and fail."

He spoke with deep feeling and Andrew, who had always respected his integrity and enterprise, nodded in sober agreement. "You can count on my support, Mr. Campbell, for what it is worth," he offered.

"Good—that's what I'd hoped. But it is a pity you are not a civil magistrate. You were never appointed to the bench, were you?"

"No, I was not. The governor—"

"The reasons scarcely matter now, do they?" Campbell put in. "But you *would* be eligible to serve on a military court, should it come to that, I presume?"

"I, too, presume so, sir. Unless His Excellency were to raise objections."

Robert Campbell smiled thinly. "Because of your marriage to this young man's mother, you mean?" His smile widened into warmth as he glanced across at

Justin. "He's a very fine young man, if I may say so, and a credit to both his parents. I have a proposition to put to you, Justin, when we conclude this discussion . . . so bear with us, will you?" He turned again to Andrew. "Did you bring your wife back with you from Van Diemen's Land, Captain Hawley?"

Andrew faced him squarely, his expression carefully blank. "No, sir. I did not receive official permission for her to accompany me."

"But you are returning to the governor's service?"

"I am, Mr. Campbell. In obedience to His Excellency's command."

Robert Campbell studied him for a moment or two in silence; finally, as if reaching a decision, he held out his hand. "Well, as far as I am concerned, you are very welcome. When you have reported your return to Governor Bligh, I should be more than pleased if you would dine with my family and myself. There may be fresh developments by this evening which would bear further discussion."

Andrew thanked him and rose to take his leave, but the big man waved him to wait.

"There is the proposition I want to put to Justin," he said, again smiling at the boy. "Tell me, have you a charter in prospect for the *Flinders,* or is she for hire?"

"I've nothing in mind, sir," Justin assured him, "save a visit, on my mother's account, to her farm at Long Wrekin."

"That is on the Hawkesbury, is it not—the holding beyond Dawson's property?" Receiving Justin's nod of confirmation, Campbell went on, evidently pleased, "Ah, then it will fit in admirably. I had accepted a hiring from that somewhat formidable parson, the Reverend Caleb Boskenna, to convey himself, the two young ladies who are his wards, and his assigned laborers to his newly claimed property on the Hawkesbury.

I've a map somewhere . . . yes, here it is." He spread the map out on his desk and, with a blunt forefinger, indicated the site of the new holding.

Justin studied it, his eyes, Andrew noticed, suddenly bright with interest.

"The vessel I had chartered to Mr. Boskenna—the *Phoebe*—ran aground three days ago and stove her bottom in off Manly beach," Robert Campbell explained. "Her damned skipper, I suspect, was drunk, though he won't admit it! But I haven't anything else of a suitable size to replace her, and Boskenna is giving me no peace. It would be of great assistance, Justin, if you would hire me the *Flinders* and take the holy man to his destination. You could call at your mother's farm on your way back. Boskenna's in a hurry. And I'd pay you a fair price for the hiring."

Justin's instant acceptance of the offer left Andrew faintly surprised, but he offered no comment, and the boy said eagerly, "I can have the *Flinders* ready to sail tomorrow morning, Mr. Campbell. She'll need swabbing down before the two young ladies come on board, and I'll require stores and water . . . and some blankets, too. And a good man to crew for me, if you can spare anyone."

"I can let you have Cookie Barnes."

"He'll suit me fine, sir. And if I give you a list of provisions, can I have them before dark?"

"You can have them in an hour—and Barnes as well, if you want him. I'll send word to the reverend gentleman that his waiting is over. Now, about the hiring charge . . ."

Andrew made his excuses and left the two of them to settle details of the hiring. One of Robert Campbell's oared boats took him across the cove to the government wharf. Pausing only to change into uniform at the house of William Gore, the provost marshal—who repeated the news Robert Campbell had already given him—he left his kit bag in the care of Gore's pretty young wife and went, with some foreboding, to report his return to the governor.

Bligh's reception was unexpectedly warm and affable. He said, after inviting Andrew to be seated, "You'll have heard what's going on, no doubt? You've come from Robert Campbell?"

"Yes, sir, I have, and I—"

The governor raised a hand to silence him. "I intend to deal with John Macarthur, once and for all, Hawley. But before I say any more, I should tell you that I have dispatched a full pardon to Hobart for your wife. She may return here by the first available vessel to touch there."

"Thank you, sir," Andrew managed. "Thank you."

Francis Oakes was in his bakery when the judge advocate's messenger dismounted from his lathered horse and thrust the warrant he had been ordered to deliver into his flour-caked hand.

The stout, perspiring Oakes read it with undisguised dismay, swearing under his breath.

"God in heaven!" he exclaimed, turning on the trooper, the warrant held at arm's length as if he feared that it would burn his fingers. "*I* can't serve this—*I* can't arrest Captain Macarthur! Here, take it back— serve the blasted thing yourself, plague take you! I'll have nowt to do with it. It's as much as my life's worth to cross that gentleman, an' Mr. Atkins knows it."

The trooper, who had ridden hard in the heat, visualizing the mighty draught of ale he would be entitled to demand at the end of his sixteen-mile journey, backed away in alarm.

" 'Tis addressed to you, Mr. Oakes, as chief constable o' bloody Parramatta. I've carried out my orders—I've delivered it to you, an' I ain't doin' no more, understand?" He clambered back into his saddle and, spurs dug deep into his mount's heaving sides, made off down the street at a shambling trot toward the Freemason's Arms.

Oakes stared after him, cursing helplessly. It was two thirty in the afternoon; the time when, as a rule— the last batch of freshly baked bread would be taken from the ovens—he sought his bed for a well-earned rest before his evening inspection of the Factory and the muster of his constables.

Not for the first time he found himself regretting the burden his various duties imposed on him. True, he was paid for his two official posts, as chief constable and Factory superintendent, and both enhanced his standing in the community; but the bakery was becoming increasingly profitable, with convict labor and girls from the Factory assigned to the work and demand for his wares growing almost daily. He could afford to resign from the constabulary, and indeed, he would probably be compelled to do so if he dared to enter Elizabeth Farm with the document he had just been given. Macarthur could surely see to that, through one or more of his many friends. . . . He read the warrant again, sweat breaking out all over his body and running in rivulets down his unshaven cheeks.

It was one thing to serve the plaguey warrant, but as for arresting John Macarthur and taking him to Sydney to face the magistrates' court . . . good Lord alive, Macarthur would probably shoot him in his tracks before they had covered half a mile! Francis Oakes drew in his breath sharply and glanced behind him to where the bakery workers were already starting to dampen down the fires.

Usually he made a point of inspecting and counting the loaves they had produced—being convicts, they were light fingered and prone to steal if he relaxed his vigilance. Today, however, he simply peered at the laden shelves without any attempt to check their contents and stumbled off to his own house, leaving the foreman to close up and dismiss his workers. The loaves of bread would be distributed in the morning.

Oakes's house—a substantial, brick-built bungalow in keeping with his position—was deserted, and Oakes recalled then that his wife and daughters had gone on a shopping expedition to Sydney. It was just as well, he thought glumly as, having refreshed himself with a long draught of beer, he lay down, fully clothed, on his bed. Clacking female tongues would be of no help to him when he sought to come to terms with his present problem.

He lay back, his head resting on his two linked hands, and tried to give the problem his full attention, but he was tired. He had started work at the bakery before dawn, and within a few minutes of lying down he fell into a heavy, dreamless sleep, his snores the only sound in the silent, empty house.

It was dark when he wakened and staggered dazedly to his feet. Memory returned and with it all his earlier doubts and fears. Plague take it, he thought wretchedly, struggling to light one of the whale-oil lamps, it must be almost five hours since the trooper from Sydney had thrust that damnable warrant into his reluctant hands and ridden off, caring little for the trouble he had caused.

The warrant would have to be served. That was his duty, and it was not one that he could foist upon one of his constables—he had to serve it himself, God help him! As the trooper had pointed out, it was addressed to him and bore the judge advocate's seal. He would invite official retribution were he to ignore it, and perhaps, if he were to explain the circumstances to John Macarthur and apologize for being the unwilling bearer of such an unwelcome summons, it would not be held against him.

Oakes picked up the lamp and went outside. He

drew water from the garden well, washed and shaved, and then dressed in his official uniform. There was no time for a meal; he would have to make do with a loaf of his own bread and the hunk of goat cheese which, it seemed, was all that his wife had left in the larder for his sustenance. He washed down his modest repast with several beakers of Cape brandy and then called at the police post for his horse. A considerably heartened Constable Oakes rode down Parramatta's dimly lit main street to pay his customary evening visit to the Factory.

This evening, as always, the women were bickering. There was a discrepancy in the weaving shed that smacked of pilfering; two of the inmates had to be consigned to the stocks for fighting, and there was a birth to record. Francis Oakes lingered over these routine tasks for as long as he reasonably could, refreshing himself with tots of rum in an effort to keep up his spirits, and taking his time over the handwritten entry in the birth register, which normally he left for the convict clerk to complete.

Finally, conscious that he could delay no longer, he remounted his horse and, with a sick sensation in the pit of his stomach, set off on the short ride to the Macarthur's imposing residence at Elizabeth Farm.

John Macarthur was enjoying a pipe of homegrown tobacco with his eldest son, Edward, before retiring for the night. Their talk was of wool prices on the steadily expanding home market and of increased yields from their fine Merino flock at Camden. The resulting profits were high enough to allow the purchase of Edward's commission in a good British regiment, and the boy, elated by his father's promise to set the money aside for this purpose, started eagerly to express his gratitude.

"Father, in truth I—" He was interrupted by an urgent pounding on the front door.

"What the devil!" his father exclaimed. "Who can it be at this ungodly hour? Damme"—he gestured to the clock above the fireplace—"it's gone eleven of the clock! Go and see who it is, Ned. If it is no one of consequence, bid him return in the morning. I don't know about you, but I'm done up . . . it's been a deuced long day."

Edward obediently tapped out his pipe and went to the door. There was a brief altercation, Macarthur heard his son's voice raised in protest, and then he came back into the candlelit parlor, red of face and clearly upset, with Francis Oakes at his heels.

"It's Mr. Oakes, sir," he explained, "and I had to let him in, he . . . he says he has a—a warrant for your arrest!"

"What's that?" John Macarthur was on his feet, his voice ominously low and controlled. "Come in, Oakes, for the Lord's sake! Is what my son says true? *Have* you a warrant for my arrest?"

"I regret to say I have, sir," Oakes admitted. "But 'tis no doing of mine, I give you my word, sir. I'd rather have cut off my right hand than serve it on you, but I ain't been given no choice, you understand. As head constable, I'm bound to obey the orders I'm given, and—"

"Yes, yes, I understand," John Macarthur interrupted harshly. "But what charges are brought against me? Tell me that, if you please."

"The charges are set out in the warrant, sir," Oakes stammered unhappily. "An' signed by Mr. Atkins, sir, as judge advocate. But I—"

"Let me read the infernal warrant, man," Macarthur demanded. "Here, give it to me. . . . Ned, a candle, boy, on the table beside me. I want to see what devilry that drunken swine Atkins is up to now!"

Both Oakes and his son obeyed him instantly.

The warrant spread out on the table in front of him, Macarthur read its contents with mounting indignation.

> Whereas complaint hath been made before me upon oath, that John Macarthur, Esq., the owner of the schooner *Parramatta,* now lying in this port, hath illegally stopped the provisions of the master, mates, and crew of the said schooner, whereby the said master, mates, and crew have violated the colonial regulations by coming unauthorized on shore, and whereas I did by my official letter, bearing the date the 14th day of this instant December, require the said John Macarthur to appear before me on the 15th day of this instant December, at 10 o'clock of the forenoon of the same day, and whereas the said John Macarthur hath not appeared at the time aforesaid or since:
>
> These are, therefore, in His Majesty's name, to command you to bring the said John Macarthur before me and other of His Majesty's justices on Wednesday next, the 16th instant December, at 10 o'clock of the same day, to answer in the premises, and thereof fail not.
>
> Given under my hand and seal at Sydney, this 15th day of December 1807.

The signature was Atkins's and the communication was addressed to Mr. Francis Oakes, Chief Constable of Parramatta.

John Macarthur swore softly and pushed the warrant across the table to his son. "You know, Oakes," he said, without raising his voice, "had the person who issued that pernicious document served it upon me himself—instead of charging you with the task—I would have spurned him from my presence, by God I would! As it stands, I shall treat it with the contempt it and its author deserve. In a word, Oakes, I shall ignore your damned warrant. Is that quite clear?"

"It's clear enough, Captain Macarthur sir," Oakes agreed ruefully. "An' if it was left to me, sir, I'd do no more. But, sir, it ain't left to me, is it?"

"What the devil are you getting at?"

"Why, sir," the chief constable muttered, avoiding Macarthur's cold gaze, "I'm ordered to bring you to Sydney to make your appearance afore the magistrates' bench tomorrow morning, sir."

"In felon's chains, Mr. Oakes?" John Macarthur challenged. "You're alone, are you not—and unarmed?"

"I thought it best to come alone, sir. I was hoping—well, that you'd appreciate my position and come with me of your own free will, like. Seeing as that warrant is official, sir."

"And if I refuse?" Macarthur's eyes were blazing, and Oakes backed away from him in alarm.

"They'd order me to seize you, sir," he answered, wretchedly conscious of his own powerlessness.

"And lodge me in your loathsome jail, I suppose," Macarthur flung at him. "Imagine that, Ned," he added, turning to his white-faced son. "Not only is that evil man Atkins determined to bring about my ruin—he and *Bounty* Bligh intend to treat me as a criminal! Well, Oakes, you can ride to Sydney and inform *Mister* Atkins and his bastard Excellency that I have committed no crime, and that—since my conscience is utterly clear—I decline to answer their summons."

"But, sir—" Oakes pleaded, his voice choked, "I'll be sent back. I'll—"

"Damn your eyes, fellow!" Macarthur was really angry now, his chilly control slipping. "If you come back, then you'd best come well armed, for I can tell you this—I'll never submit till blood is shed! Before God, I've been robbed of a ship worth ten thousand pounds by these—these unmitigated scoundrels, and now they seek to hound me into their courts on spurious charges!" He flung the warrant in Oakes's direction, grabbing it wrathfully from young Edward's nervous hands. "Take this infamous paper and return it to those who sent you here!"

"Father," Edward began, "I beg you to consider the consequences. Surely, sir, you—"

John Macarthur cut him short. "It's all right, Ned, don't worry," he said, with a swift change of tone. "If we let them alone, they'll soon make a rope to hang themselves."

"Sir," Oakes begged, in desperation. "If I'm to take this warrant back to Mr. Atkins, will you at least give me a letter, signed by yourself, sir, to make it clear that I'm doing so at your behest? If you don't, Captain Macarthur—if I go in without you, sir, they'll have me charged with dereliction o' duty, and—"

"Oh, very well," Macarthur agreed, with less irritation than he had hitherto displayed. "Ned—a pen, dear lad, and paper, if you please. I'll give this poor fellow his letter."

Edward, galvanized into action, fetched him a quill and an inkwell from his mother's bureau and, hunting in one of its drawers, found some sheets of writing paper. He set them down on the table, and his father started to write, the quill scratching across the paper in his haste. The letter consisted of six lines, and Macarthur said, not looking up, "I'll read this to you, Oakes. It's addressed to you and runs: '*You will inform the persons who sent you here with the warrant you have now shown me and of which I have made a copy that I will never submit to the horrid tyranny that is attempted until I am forced, and I consider it with scorn and contempt, as I do the persons who have directed it to be executed.*' There, my good man. . . ." He signed it with a flourish. Then he rose and waved Edward to take his place at the table. "The warrant, if you please."

"The warrant, sir?" Oakes echoed blankly.

"Yes—give it to my son. Now, Ned, be so good as to make a copy of this iniquitous document and of my reply. In a fair hand, boy . . . we may yet need copies to exhibit in court."

Edward, a worried frown creasing his smooth young brow, did as he had been bidden, and, meanwhile, John Macarthur reached for a handsome cut-glass decanter, standing on the sideboard. Pouring two glasses of brandy, he passed one to Oakes.

"I imagine this will be as welcome to you as it is to me, Mr. Oakes."

Francis Oakes thanked him obsequiously, relief at this ending to the unhappy affair evident in his voice and eyes as he raised his glass. "Your very good health, Captain Macarthur, sir!"

John Macarthur sipped his brandy in silence. When Edward had completed his copying, Macarthur took the warrant and his own note and offered them gravely to the head constable. "God speed you on your way, Mr. Oakes. But remember, will you not, that you will require to be armed if you come a second time seeking to tear me from the bosom of my family in order to confine me in your jail?"

"I trust it won't come to that, sir," Oakes assured him fervently. He set his empty glass down, bowed awkwardly, and made for the door.

When the sound of the muffled hoofbeats of Oakes's mount had faded into the distance, Elizabeth Macarthur came from her bedroom, white of face and wrapped in a hastily donned robe.

"I heard voices," she said, looking up anxiously into her husband's face. "John, my dearest, was it not Mr. Oakes who called on you? For mercy's sake, what did he want of you?"

Her husband told her in a few brief and bitter words,

pacing the narrow confines of the shadowed room, his voice harsh with remembered anger as, in the retelling, the full enormity of what had occurred was borne on them all.

"Bligh and that miserable drunken sot Atkins are determined on my ruin, Elizabeth," he said. "They have flung down the challenge, and I must accept it—I must fight them!"

"Did you not know that they would, John?" Elizabeth reproached him. "By taking the action you did over the *Parramatta*, did you not know what the result would be?"

John Macarthur caught his breath. There was a bright gleam in his eyes as he halted opposite her and took both her hands in his.

"Yes," he conceded. "I think, in my heart, I did. You heard my conversation with George Johnstone, of course, the other night. And you approved, did you not?"

"Let us say that I did not voice my *dis*approval," his wife amended. "For of what use would it have been to do so when you have made your mind up as to what course you intend to pursue?"

"But I shall have your support, my dear?"

"I am your wife, John. I will always support you."

"Right or wrong?" Macarthur suggested.

"I did not say that," Elizabeth countered. She glanced at their son, smiling although her eyes were suddenly filled with tears. "Ned, dear, what is your view?"

"I'm worried about the letter father gave Mr. Oakes," Edward confessed. "See for yourself, Mamma. It is dangerous—it is defying the authority of the magistrates, as well as that of Atkins, which would not matter so much. And I think it's implying an insult to Captain Bligh."

He gave her the copy, and Elizabeth Macarthur read it with furrowed brows. She said, with dismay, as she returned it to him, "I agree with Ned . . . it *is* dangerous. They could use it against you, John."

Macarthur read the letter again and shrugged.

"I was angry when I wrote it, but damme, you're both right! They could use it against me. Ned—" he turned to his son, but Edward forestalled him.

"I'll ride after Oakes and get it back, sir," he offered. "He's only been gone ten minutes. I'll have no trouble catching up with him."

He was off before either of his parents could reply, shouting for one of the drowsy servants to rouse himself and saddle a horse.

"You must keep a tight rein on your temper, my love," Elizabeth Macarthur advised gently when they were alone. "Bligh is notorious for *his* outbursts, as you well know, and you may well defeat him by provoking such an outburst. But not unless you consider every move you make and act calmly. Let *him* go too far."

"The swine already has," her husband retorted, but his anger had faded, and he eyed Elizabeth with deep affection as she refilled his glass and waved him back to his chair, seating herself on its arm beside him. "Ned will retrieve that infernal note of mine, and then all will be well."

But Edward returned, almost an hour later, and one glance at his face sufficed to tell both of them that he had failed in his mission.

"Oakes wouldn't give the letter back, Father," he said. "The wretched fellow insisted that he must keep it, in order to explain to the damned judge advocate why he had failed to bring you with him to Sydney. I offered him money—all I had on me—but he wouldn't listen. So I'm afraid—"

"But I am not," Macarthur assured him. He rose, elaborately stifling a yawn. "It cannot be helped, Ned, and it's my fault, not yours. Let us get some sleep, shall we? Tomorrow I shall go to Sydney and show myself openly round town. Let them try to prove their ludicrous charges, and I will cry 'Tyranny!' And"——he smiled from his son to his wife——"by heaven, I will sue Robert Campbell for depriving me of possession of the *Parramatta*! I'll swear a writ against him for ten thousand pounds!"

"Mr. Campbell is on the bench, John," Elizabeth reminded him.

He laughed and took her arm. "So much the better, my love. Johnstone and Abbott are also rostered this week. I shall not lack friends. Come—let us retire to bed. Tomorrow will be a busy day, I think."

Francis Oakes delivered the letter and an agitated account of his attempt to serve the warrant on Captain John Macarthur the following morning. He found Judge Advocate Atkins at breakfast, in the company of Lawyer Crossley, and observed without surprise that, despite the early hour at which he had presented himself, Atkins was far from sober.

Crossley, however, had all his wits about him, and, after a brief, whispered conversation with his legal superior, he thrust letter and warrant back into Oakes's hand and said crisply, "Take these to His Excellency the governor at once. When he's read them—unless he gives you any instructions to the contrary—return and make a sworn deposition before the bench as to your endeavor to serve Mr. Macarthur with the warrant. Is that clear? D'you understand what you're to do?"

"Aye," Oakes conceded reluctantly. "It's clear enough, but I done my duty, Mr. Crossley, to the best o' my ability. 'Tain't right to put no blame on me. An' if His Excellency's led to believe as I'm at fault, sir, I don't reckon as I've deserved it."

"Tut-tut, man, no one's blaming you!" Crossley retorted impatiently. "Just do as I tell you. The bench will be sitting at ten o'clock, and if Mr. Macarthur fails to present himself before them, then you'll be required to tell them why."

"Suppose he *don't* fail to present himself?" Oakes argued. "What then?"

Atkins belched loudly and waved him to silence. "Don't be a damned fool, Oakes!" he growled. "He's no intention of answering the charges. Off with you to Government House and hurry—we've no time to waste." He belched again and reached for the bottle in front of him, a gleam of triumph in his bloodshot eyes. To Crossley he added thickly, "We've got him by the short hairs this time, George, by God we have!"

Francis Oakes waited to hear no more. At Government House he was received by the secretary, who, to his unbounded relief, took his documents from him and left him to wait, sweating profusely, in the anteroom. The governor did not require to see him. Griffin returned a few minutes later to echo Lawyer Crossley's instructions to him to make his deposition to the magistrates when they assembled at ten o'clock.

"His Excellency desires Mr. Atkins to wait on him forthwith," the young secretary said, his tone a trifle uncertain. "Is he . . . ah . . . that is, Mr. Oakes, perhaps you would be so good as to inform him?"

"I will," the chief constable answered sourly, "but I reckon he'll need Mr. Crossley along to keep him on his feet!"

Edmund Griffin nodded in understanding.

"Then if you would please inform both gentlemen, and"—he returned the warrant and John Macarthur's letter—"take good care of these, Mr. Oakes. I think they will prove of great importance."

The magistrates, when they opened their sitting punctually at ten o'clock, clearly shared this opinion. Frances Oakes, under oath, gave his testimony after John Macarthur's name had been called and had elicited no response. The judge advocate, miraculously restored to a

semblance of sobriety, questioned him minutely as to
Macarthur's reaction to the serving of the warrant.

"You say that Mr. Macarthur told you that he intended to treat the warrant with the contempt which it
and its author deserved?"

"Yes, sir, them was his words. But . . ." Oakes
looked nervously about him, suddenly afraid that John
Macarthur might, after all, be somewhere in the shadowed courtroom. God in heaven, suppose he was? Suppose he was listening, suppose . . . but he was telling the
truth, no one could blame him for that, surely?

The judge advocate, prompted by Crossley, went on
relentlessly, "He said that he would ignore your damned
—and I quote—your *damned* warrant, Mr. Oakes?"

"Yes, sir," Oakes confirmed, mopping his heated
face. The bench consisted of Major Johnstone, the Corps
commandant; Robert Campbell, the port naval officer;
and John Palmer, the government commissary. He could
read no sympathy in their grimly set faces, although
Major Johnstone sought occasionally to interpose a
question that might be said to favor his onetime com-
rade in arms.

"Mr. Macarthur said," Oakes managed, "that he had
committed no crime, and that his conscience was clear.
Sir, he—"

"But he told you, did he not, that he declined to answer the summons to appear before His Majesty's justices of the peace this morning, in order to answer the
charges against him?"

"That is so, sir, yes."

"And—think carefully, Mr. Oakes," the judge advocate warned, "Mr. Macarthur told you that if you came
back for the purpose of enforcing the warrant, you had
best—and again I quote—'come well armed.' "

"Them was his words. That I was to come well
armed, for he'd not submit till blood was shed."

"They were words spoken in anger, surely?" Major Johnstone put in.

"Oh, yes, sir, they were indeed," Oakes agreed eagerly.

"Nevertheless those words show contempt for this court," Commissary Palmer pointed out.

"As also does Mr. Macarthur's letter," Atkins said, with heavy emphasis. He read it aloud slowly and, having done so, looked across at the unhappy Oakes. "This letter was written in your presence, was it not, Mr. Oakes? It was signed by Mr. Macarthur in your presence?"

"Aye, sir, I seen him pen it."

"He attempted to recover it from you, did he not, by sending his son after you to request its return?"

"Clearly because he regretted having written in such terms in the heat of the moment?" The intervention came from Major Johnstone, and again Oakes assented gratefully.

"But you refused to return the letter?" Mr. Campbell suggested, his tone curt.

"I couldn't give it back to Mr. Edward, sir," Oakes answered, reddening. "Your honors might not have believed that I'd served the warrant if I'd let him have it back. I had to keep it, sir." Campbell, he saw, was smiling; Palmer, too, appeared pleased on hearing his admission, and the judge advocate said approvingly, "You acted correctly, Mr. Oakes." He turned to face his fellow justices. "Gentlemen, I submit that John Macarthur is in contempt of this court and in clear defiance of the civil power of the colony of New South Wales. I ask you therefore to issue a second warrant authorizing Mr. Oakes, as chief constable of Parramatta, to take a party of armed constables to place him under arrest and lodge him safely in His Majesty's jail, pending his appearance before this court."

Oakes heard, with a sinking heart, their concerted assent. Even Major Johnstone, stony faced and unsmiling, raised no objection; the second warrant was signed and sealed and, drawing himself up, Oakes accepted it with what dignity he could muster.

"You know your duty, Mr. Oakes," the judge advocate bade him sternly. "Make diligent search for Mr. Macarthur at once."

The search was brief. John Macarthur made no attempt to conceal his presence in Sydney, and Oakes, with his armed party, found his quarry without difficulty at the house of the surveyor general, Charles Grimes. To his intense relief Macarthur submitted without resistance, even making a rueful joke of it, and, after a formal appearance in court, the bench of magistrates granted him bail, after committing him for trial at the next criminal court on January 25, 1808. Bail was set at one thousand pounds.

CHAPTER XV

Justin stood at the wheel of the *Flinders* cutter, completing his tack with the skill of long experience of the vagaries of the Hawkesbury River. His gaze, raised of necessity to the dingy canvas of his mainsail until he had brought the wind abeam, strayed—as of late it so often did—to the slim, beautiful girl standing a few paces from him.

Abigail Tempest had adjusted swiftly to conditions on board the cutter, taking an eager and intelligent interest in all that she saw and heard, and Justin, for his part, had been delighted to answer her questions concerning the farms and settlements they passed and the finer points of navigation, whenever an opportnuity to do so presented itself. Not, he reflected a trifle resentfully, that such opportunities were frequent . . . the Reverend Caleb Boskenna had seen to that.

The *Flinders* was crowded to the point of being overladen, with Boskenna and his two young wards occupying the cabin space, the cutter's holds crammed with government-issue tools and sacks of seed and provisions. Cookie Barnes and the three assigned convict laborers—as well as Justin himself—were compelled to bed down on deck when, during the hours of darkness, they came to anchor offshore. Boskenna's horse and the half-bred Merino ram he had purchased from Captain Macarthur also had to be accommodated—the horse was in the forward hold and the ram in a makeshift pen amidships, where the dinghy was normally secured.

He had made repairs to the dinghy before leaving Hobart, but . . . Justin glanced speculatively astern. He had not anticipated having to tow the patched-up craft all the way upriver to the Tempest holding, in order to load the bleating ram and its cage onto his spotless deck. But Caleb Boskenna had been arrogantly insistent, his concern for the apparently valuable animal equaled only by his determination to guard his two pretty little wards from all intercourse with their fellow passengers.

Boskenna, a somber, black-garbed figure, stood at Abigail's side, effectively cutting her off from Justin at the helm and frowning in disapproval whenever he observed the girl glance over her shoulder in his direction. Lucy, the younger sister, a pert, sly little creature, was permitted more freedom but—unlike Abigail—she scorned to take advantage of it, treating him, Justin thought sourly, as if his status were little higher than that of the assigned laborers or Barnes, the cook, who was a ticket-of-leave man, serving a life sentence.

He watched her, letting the wheel slip through his strong brown fingers, as she emerged from the cabin hatchway and, carefully avoiding contact with the three convict laborers who were huddled together on the weather side of the hatch coaming, went skipping across to the Reverend Boskenna, her small face anxiously puckered.

"Your horse, Mr. Boskenna!" Justin heard her exclaim shrilly. "It's fallen down and doesn't seem able to get to its feet, poor thing. I think you ought to look at it."

Boskenna clicked his tongue in exasperation and

glared angrily at Justin. "If that animal is injured, I shall hold you responsible, Master Broome!"

"I am not responsible for your livestock, sir," Justin reminded him. "The *Flinders* is not equipped to carry horses, as I told you before we sailed. It was only on your insistence that I agreed to make an exception and take your horse but, you must recall, sir, entirely at your risk."

He was on firm ground, and aware of this, Boskenna had to content himself with an irritable, "You are insolent, young man." Justin, unrepentant, suggested quietly, "I would advise you, sir, to see to the animal at once. A rope round its neck and hindquarters should suffice, with a couple of men to haul it up. If necessary, I can rig a winch, but that would take time and delay us."

Caleb Boskenna bit back an angry retort and, turning to his laborers, brusquely ordered them to follow him. The three—middle-aged men, with the hangdog air of those lost to hope and long since cowed by the ill treatment they had met with since receiving their sentences—got to their feet and shambled obediently after him. Lucy, pleased by the stir her announcement had caused, whispered something to Abigail and went cautiously in pursuit, anxious to miss nothing of the excitement.

Abigail stayed where she was for a moment and then, gathering up her skirts, she came to Justin's side. "Is it serious?" she asked. "I mean, could that poor horse be badly hurt?"

Justin shook his head. "It's unlikely—we had it pretty well secured. But there's not much space in the for'ard hold. The animal will be better on its feet."

"You could put it ashore if you had to, I suppose?"

"Yes," he agreed, "if we had to. As I told Mr. Boskenna, I could rig a winch and lower the horse into the water—let it swim ashore. But it would hold us up . . .

and I'm aiming to reach your property before dark if this breeze keeps up."

"Are you so eager to be rid of us?" Abigail questioned. She sounded hurt, and Justin reddened.

"I try to complete my charters on time, Miss Abigail. And we're overloaded. The *Phoebe*—the vessel your guardian originally hired—has more cargo and passenger space than my *Flinders*. I only accepted the hiring to oblige Mr. Campbell."

She eyed him in some bewilderment, and Justin's color deepened. She was so very pretty and charming, he thought, and fearing that he might unintentionally have offended her, he added quickly, "And because I realized that it would give me the chance to see *you* again."

"You did remember me, then?"

"Of course I did! How could I forget? I—that night I called at Mrs. Spence's house and you came to the door in your party gown, you made such a picture, standing there in the lamplight, I . . ." Justin broke off, stammering in his embarrassment. To cover it, he spun the wheel, bringing the cutter's head round and shouting to Cookie Barnes to haul on the weather jib-sheet. From below, a confused rumble and a stamping of hooves told him that the efforts of the Reverend Boskenna and his men had succeeded in restoring the horse to its safe upright position. This meant, of course, that the chaplain would be returning once more to the deck and that he would resume his all-too-strict chaperonage, thus precluding any chance of even the smallest conversational intimacy with Abigail Tempest.

It was one thing to reply to her questions in her guardian's hearing, but he wanted to forge a link between himself and Abigail, Justin decided. Indeed he wanted—more than he had wanted anything for a long time—to bid for her notice, her friendship, and perhaps even her feminine interest. He steadied the wheel, but

Abigail dashed his newfound hope before he could find the nerve to put it into words.

"Justin," she said, lowering her voice, "I am betrothed. That is, I have promised to marry Dr. Titus Penhaligon, but Mr. Boskenna does not know, and I . . . well, I don't want him to know . . . not yet. I . . . you will respect my confidence, will you not?"

Conscious of a swift pang of jealousy, Justin contrived to hide it behind a smile. "Of course I will, if that is your wish, Miss Abigail," he assured her.

"I've told you, because I . . . well, you see, I have a favor to ask of you," Abigail went on. She moved closer to him, and he caught a heady whiff of some faint, elusive fragrance that set his pulses racing. "You charter your *Flinders*, don't you—regularly, I mean?"

"Yes. That's how I make my living." He started to explain, but she cut him short, hearing the Reverend Boskenna's heavy footsteps on the hatchway ladder.

"Dr. Penhaligon—Titus—is at the Coal River settlement. They sent him there after poor Lieutenant Putland died, and I . . . I have a letter for him. You go there sometimes, do you not—you go to Coal River?"

"Yes," Justin confirmed. "I carry mail and prisoners there when the government gives me a charter. But I don't know when I'll next be given one."

"But you would know any vessel that was sent there?" Abigail persisted. When he nodded, she slipped a hand into the bosom of her dress, withdrew a folded paper from it, and held it out to him. "Please," she begged. "Will you try to see that this is delivered, Justin, even if you cannot deliver it yourself? I would be so grateful to you if you would."

It was, Justin told himself, at least something to earn her gratitude. The letter carried the fragrance of her person, and he took it from her, thrusting it into the pocket of his jacket as Caleb Boskenna stepped over the

hatchway coaming, his dark, bearded face flushed from
his exertions. He eyed Justin suspiciously for a moment,
but Abigail had moved away from him and was now
leaning over the lee rail, apparently absorbed in contem-
plation of a cluster of settlers' huts on the far bank of
the river. The chaplain contented himself with a curt
order to her to join her sister in the cabin.

He said irritably, in answer to Justin's inquiry concerning the horse, "We got the unfortunate animal up,
and it seems to have taken no harm. But the sooner we
put it ashore, the better. When do you expect to reach
our destination, can you tell me that?"

Justin grinned and gestured to a bend in the river a
little over a mile away.

"That's Pimilwi's *Yoolong*, Mr. Boskenna. Once we
round that, we'll have the wind full astern, and I reckon
we should be in sight of your place well before nightfall. If you are worried about your horse, I'll winch it
into the water as soon as we come to anchor, and it can
swim ashore." He was tempted to add that the animal's
owner might accompany it if he wished, but Caleb
Boskenna's expression was such as to discourage levity,
and instead he offered flatly, "If we make a start at first
light tomorrow, it will not take above two hours to
unload, with your men bearing a hand and so long as
your jetty's stout enough for me to tie up to."

In fact the unloading took even less time than he had
estimated; the three convict laborers and the Reverend
Boskenna himself, aided by the two men already there
—the cook and a Cornish shepherd named Jethro—
worked with a will. But Justin, anxious though he was
to head back to Long Wrekin during the hours of daylight, was hurt and disappointed when, the last cask set
ashore, Caleb Boskenna dismissed him with only a curt
word of thanks. There was no invitation to visit the new
farmhouse, no offer of a hot meal, and even more to his

chagrin, he was afforded no chance to take leave of Abigail Tempest.

Mrs. Boskenna, a thin-lipped, uncomely woman, took both girls with her to the house, and there they remained, hidden from Justin's sight behind its shuttered windows. He did not catch so much as a glimpse of them even when he cast off from the wooden jetty and dipped his tattered ensign in formal farewell.

But it was a different matter when, late that same evening, he brought-to off the familiar wharf which served his mother's and the neighboring settlers' farms and found Tom Jardine and William awaiting him, the former holding a lamp aloft to guide him in.

"I saw you, Justin. I knew it was the *Flinders* when you were more than a mile away, and I told Tom it was you!" William informed him excitedly, when he stepped ashore. "But Tom said it couldn't be you, even if it was the *Flinders*, because he'd seen her going upriver yesterday morning, and if you'd been on board, you'd have come in here. You wouldn't have gone sailing past Long Wrekin, Tom said. Why did you, Justin?"

"I had a hiring—folk and cargo to deliver," Justin returned shortly. "But I'm here now, am I not?" He hugged his young brother, and William, to his astonishment, clung to him in tears.

"The lad's missing his Mam," Tom put in, his tone defensive. "An' it give him a turn, you sailing past yesterday, Justin. Me, too, come to that. I didn't rightly know what to think. We've been a long time without news, you know. Last we heard was that your Mam had been sent to Van Diemen's Land in a transport from Norfolk Island."

"I've come to give you news," Justin said, "Willie lad, Mam's fit and well—and she's been pardoned! Captain Hawley had it straight from the governor the moment we landed in Sydney. And he and Mam are married—I saw the ceremony in Hobart. She—"

William's face, which had grown perceptibly lighter with the news of Jenny's pardon, had grown dark again as quickly, and now his cry of pain interrupted Justin.

"You left her there!" the boy accused bitterly. "You did not bring her back!" He jerked his hand from Justin's grasp and ran off into the darkness, sobbing as if his heart would break.

"What the devil!" Justin exclaimed, "How could I have brought her back if I didn't know of the pardon until we reached Sydney? For the Lord's sake, Tom, what has got into the lad? His Mam will be home soon enough, by the first available transport, the governor said."

Tom Jardine shrugged his broad shoulders resignedly. "Like I told you, the lad's been missing his Mam." He picked up Justin's canvas kit bag, hefted it onto his back, and jerked his head in the direction of the Long Wrekin farmstead. "My Nan's got a meal waiting, and she'll be better able than I am to tell you about Will . . . he talks to her. But the land's in good heart an' the stock flourishin', thanks to the help we've had from Mr. Dawson an' the other neighbors. . . . It's such good news you've brought; the boy will come round, soon enough, don't you worry. Your Mam will find everything in good order when she comes back, too." He hesitated, drawing in his breath sharply. "Could you say *when* she'd be comin', lad? It'd make such a difference to know—to the boy in particular, I mean."

Justin's mouth tightened. "No, I can't say when exactly, except that from what the governor told Captain Hawley, it will most likely be around the turn of the year. I myself had to come when I did—the governor had sent for Captain Hawley to come right away."

"That don't surprise me," Tom returned, a hint of anger in his deep, countryman's voice. "From all accounts Guv'nor Bligh's headin' for trouble, an' he's goin' to need all the support he can command." Again he hesitated, and then added, in a hoarsely confidential whisper, "The Hawkesbury settlers are formin' armed militia companies, Justin. I've joined, most of us have in this area."

Justin halted, to stare at his dimly seen face in bewilderment. "In the Lord's name, Tom—for what *purpose*?"

"For the governor's defense," Tom told him quietly. "Aye—and to take on the plaguey Rum Corps, if we have to! It could come to that, you can take my word for it." He laid a hand on Justin's shoulder, an odd little smile playing about his bearded lips. "No one's done more for the settlers than Guv'nor Bligh, an' most folks in these parts will bear that out. The Hawkesbury Loyalists, we call ourselves, lad, an' that's what we are . . . loyalists, you understand. If you're stoppin' here, you could do worse than join us."

"I'm not," Justin said, with finality. "I have the *Flinders* for charter, Tom. I can't stay here, you know that." The prospect of the settlers forming themselves into armed militia filled him with alarm. Mr. Campbell, it was true, had spoken of the possibility of confrontation between the governor and John Macarthur, and had said that the judge advocate had issued a warrant for Macarthur's arrest. But the matter was a trivial one, merely involving the forfeiture of the *Parramatta*'s bond. Surely even the arrogant Rum Corps would not dare carry their support for one of their erstwhile officers to the point of actively defying not only the governor, but also the colony's legally appointed courts of law?

He started to say as much, but Tom cut him short. "I know what I know, Justin," he stated, with conviction. "This colony's a powder keg, just needin' a spark to blow it sky, high. We're takin' precautions, that's all." He resumed his slow, measured stride along the rutted

track and went on thoughtfully, "When you go back to
Sydney, see if you can get Captain Hawley to come
here for a week or so. Truth is, we need a military officer
to train us. We can all use firearms, but we'll just be a
rabble unless we take a few lessons in military tactics
an' discipline."

Justin peered uncertainly at him but could read nothing in his face, save that he was in deadly earnest.

"Very well," he agreed. "I'll tell him, Tom. But I
reckon it'll all fizzle out. Mr. Macarthur will pay his fine,
and that will be the end of the matter, you'll see."

The lights of the farmhouse came in sight, and Justin
quickened his pace. To his relief William rejoined them
at the paddock gate, and they entered the house together
to a welcome from little Rachel and Nancy Jardine that
drove all other thoughts from his mind.

Only later when—their meal over and their news exchanged—he saw Tom pick up a musket and go quietly
out, did his uneasiness return. The Hawkesbury Loyalists evidently meant business and were taking a graver
view of the situation than he had supposed it merited—
for Tom, Nancy told him, had gone to drill with them,
as was now his nightly practice.

Answering the children's questions concerning Van
Diemen's Land and the Hobart settlement distractedly,
Justin decided not to delay his return to Sydney. Andrew must be informed of what was happening here and
through him, perhaps, the governor. And there was
Abigail's letter to be delivered.

Andrew Hawley was in attendance on the governor
when the secretary, Griffin, came with the unexpected
announcement that John Macarthur was urgently requesting a personal interview.

"Mr. Macarthur is most insistent, sir," Edmund Griffin added, sounding more than a little taken aback. "He
says he has some documents of considerable impor-

tance that he feels Your Excellency should be shown."

"Does he deem them of such importance that he must present them to me in person?" the governor demanded irately. "Damn his insolence! Tell him to give his documents to you, Edmund, and I'll read them when I have time."

"Sir, he is unwilling to entrust them to me," the young secretary answered apologetically. "He says they are originals which have urgent bearing on his impending trial before the criminal court."

William Bligh considered this statement, dark brows knit in momentary uncertainty; then, reaching a decision, he snapped, "Oh, confound it—I'll see him. But let the fellow cool his heels for ten minutes, Edmund. Tell him I'm engaged . . . and don't offer him refreshment."

"Very good, Your Excellency." Griffin withdrew, clearly not ill pleased by the instructions he had been given, and the governor turned to Andrew, still frowning.

"'What d'you suppose he wants, Hawley? You've been keeping your ear to the ground, have you not?"

"I have, sir, yes, but—" Andrew hesitated. Sydney was rife with rumor and speculation as to the probable outcome of John Macarthur's appearance before the criminal court. Indeed, in certain circles, the magistrates —and, in particular, Major Johnstone—had been harshly criticized for having referred the case from their own civil jurisdiction, when a fine could have been imposed and the matter concluded. But few expected the final verdict to go against the colony's wealthiest inhabitant since, in any event, the composition of the criminal court bench was exclusively military, and Macarthur's influence with the Corps officers was well known.

"Well?" Bligh prompted impatiently. "What's being said? And what's Macarthur been up to, eh? I'm told he's spent more time here than he has at Parramatta."

"Yes, sir, he has."

"Enlisting support from the scurvy rogues who call themselves King's officers, I take it?"

Andrew inclined his head. Anxious not to provoke the governor into a loss of temper, he continued to hesitate. Finally he said, choosing his words carefully, "He's succeeded in that endeavor, sir—the Corps are with him to a man. And most of the traders, too—Blaxcell, of course, Lord, Underwood, Kable, and Reibie, and the surgeons Jamieson and Harris, and probably D'Arcy Wentworth. The only officer who appears not to have given his support is Kemp . . . he and Macarthur have fallen out."

"Have they, now? That's interesting. Do you have any idea why?"

Andrew shrugged. "Nothing definite, sir. But I did hear that Major Johnstone has ordered Kemp to Parramatta and that Abbott is to replace him here."

"And serve as one of John Macarthur's judges, one presumes!" Bligh exclaimed. "His best friend and associate . . . well, I can put a stop to that if I have to. What else, Hawley? What's the general opinion?"

"That Macarthur will get off, sir—at worst with a fine and the forfeiture of his bond."

"Damn his eyes, I fear that is possible," the governor conceded, "though not if I can help it! God knows this colony will never prosper nor be at peace whilst that unprincipled villain remains here, flouting the law and lining his own pockets in any way he chooses. And I must depend on Atkins to trim his sails! A broken reed if ever there was one, Hawley . . . even when he's sober. What's the talk concerning Atkins, d'you know?"

There was a great deal of talk about Richard Atkins, Andrew was aware, and little of it in the judge advocate's favor. One persistent rumor had it that, from the outset, Atkins had been determined to avenge personal grievances suffered over the years at Macarthur's hands and that he had used his judicial office unlawfully to that end.

Conscious of the governor's eyes searching his face, he answered cautiously, "Sir, it's being said that Mr. Atkins has shown a strong personal bias against Macarthur, in that it was he who insisted on preferring criminal charges when Macarthur appeared before the civil court. And that, as judge advocate, he exceeded his authority by issuing a warrant for the arrest made by Constable Oakes."

Bligh gave vent to an angry imprecation. "God's blood, they're saying that, are they? No doubt the suggestion stems from Macarthur himself or from one of his cronies. Well, damme, Atkins may have personal reasons for wanting the mendacious rogue brought to justice . . . and so have I, on behalf of the settlers and in the interests of good government! But in this matter, I can assure you, Judge Advocate Atkins has *not* exceeded his authority. He has acted on my instructions and with my full knowledge and approval, every step of the way. My only fear has been that he would not act firmly enough, for his determination is weak, and his knowledge of the law leaves much to be desired. But for all that—" The governor's expression hardened, and Andrew saw that he was in the grip of a cold, controlled anger that was infinitely more alarming than any outburst of loudmouthed rage.

After remaining silent for a moment, he went on in a low voice, speaking more to himself than to Andrew, "If I must use Atkins's personal malice to enable me to rid New South Wales of that man and his like, then by God, I will do it . . . and with a clear conscience! Once Macarthur is broken and his malign influence removed, the rest will cease to trouble us or pose any threat to the colony's future. They'll toe the line, or they'll run. Damme, I'll bring charges against the scoundrel that he'll not be able to refute, even with Johnstone and Abbott as his judges. And if they fail in their duty, I'll see to it that—"

He was interrupted by the return of Edmund Griffin, red of face and apologetic. "Excuse me, sir," he began, "but Mr. Macarthur requested me to tell you that he—"

Bligh did not let him finish. "God in heaven!" he roared, losing his temper at last. "Is Mr. Macarthur out of patience? Does he not like to be kept waiting?"

"No, apparently he does not, sir," the secretary answered ruefully. "He's gone. But he said that if Your Excellency wished to speak with him, he would hold himself available. Er . . . he has pressing business and cannot waste time awaiting your pleasure, sir, that was what he said. He charged me to give you this note, sir, which he penned in my presence, and he also gave me a sight of the documents he had intended to bring to your notice, so that I might vouch for their authenticity."

"And can you?" the governor demanded, making an effort to keep his annoyance within bounds. "What are these documents, for heaven's sake?" He accepted the note with evident distaste, but did not open it, eyeing his secretary from beneath scowling brows. "Well, come on, come on . . . enlighten me, if you please!"

Edmund Griffin's color deepened and spread.

"Your Excellency," he stammered unhappily, "I am only acting as a messenger. I hold no brief for Mr. Macarthur, as you know, sir, and I did not read his note."

Bligh relented. "My dear boy, I realize that I had no right to vent my displeasure on you, but tell me about Macarthur's infernal documents."

"Yes, sir." Relieved, Griffin recovered his composure. "The first was a bill drawn by Mr. Atkins on Sir William Bowyer, for the sum of twenty-six pounds and six shillings, and dated fourteen years ago—July, seventeen ninety-three, sir. It was dishonored when first presented and is now held by Mr. Macarthur, who has claimed repayment, with interest, of the sum of eighty-two pounds nine shillings and sixpence, sir." The secretary referred to some notes he had taken. "Sir, there was a written reply attached to the bill, signed by Mr. Atkins, in which he agreed to repay the original sum, but disputed the claim for interest."

"Good God!" The governor was astounded. He met Andrew's gaze and spread his hands in a gesture of resignation. "Atkins must be mad! He could plead the statute of limitations . . . why the devil did he not do so?"

"Perhaps Macarthur's note will explain, sir," Andrew suggested. Macarthur, he recalled, had bought notes of hand before and sued for their recovery, but how, he wondered—how the devil had he managed to procure Atkins's fourteen-year-old bill?

Bligh grunted and, unfolding the single sheet of paper Griffin had given him, read from it in a loud and furiously angry voice. " *'I, the undersigned, do most earnestly entreat Your Excellency to appoint for my forthcoming trial a judge advocate who shall be disinterested. I am confident that, as governor, you would deplore the unhappy effect it might produce on the morals of this colony if it should appear that a judge has for two years resisted the payment of a just debt, without any reason to offer in his defense other than that he chose to take advantage of the merciful and indulgent spirit of his creditor . . .'* " He choked on the last few words, unable to restrain his rage. "God's blood, is there no limit to the fellow's effrontery! And what the deuce does he mean by saying that Atkins has resisted payment for two years?"

Edmund Griffin referred to his scribbled notes. "Mr. Atkins's reply is dated April, eighteen hundred and five, sir."

"What an unmitigated fool the man is!" the governor exclaimed despairingly. "You had better call on him at once, Edmund, and find out what he intends to do about this unfortunate matter."

"I do not think that there is much he can do, sir," the secretary said. "Mr. Macarthur has issued a summons against him, he told me."

"In the civil court?"

"Yes, sir. And I understand that he intends also to institute a claim against Mr. Campbell for the recovery of the *Parramatta,* setting a value of ten thousand pounds on the vessel."

In all the years he had served under him, Andrew could not recall having seen William Bligh so close to an apoplectic explosion of wrath. But somehow the governor managed to retain his self-control, though his hands were trembling violently as he picked up the sheet of paper which John Macarthur had addressed to him and read its final paragraph in an almost expressionless voice.

"He writes: *'If this withholding from me of my money be intended by the judge advocate as a sort of precursor of a more severe vengeance that he is meditating at my threatened trial, and if Your Excellency should continue to sustain his refusal to pay me, by not allowing me to prove my claim before a disinterested tribunal, I must submit with patience. Nor will I further trouble Your Excellency upon the subject until there may be an opportunity to send, with your dispatches, a memorial to His Majesty's Secretary of State for the Colonies. . . .'"*

He crumpled the paper and flung it from him across the desk, to stand for several minutes in an ominous silence, which neither Andrew nor Edmund Griffin— after exchanging anxious glances—dared to break.

Bligh himself broke it at last. "So the unprincipled rogue resorts to blackmail, does he? So he intends to refer the matter to the Colonial Secretary! Well, this explains why he waited two years to claim the debt . . . in the manner of all rogues, he anticipated that he might

one day require to discredit Atkins as judge advocate!
But I will not yield to such threats, by God, I will not!
Atkins's appointment to his office was made by His
Majesty's Government, and I cannot suspend him from
it even if I wished." He rose and started to pace the
room, striding from desk to window, his hands clasped
behind his back and his brows knit in concentration.
Griffin made to pour him a glass of brandy, but the
governor waved it contemptuously away. "Drink it
yourself, boy—I need no bottled courage to deal with
any rogue!"

"No, sir. I beg your pardon." Griffin retreated
abashed. "Do you wish me to reply to Mr. Macarthur's
demand?"

"To his earnest entreaty, you mean," Bligh cor-
rected, with heavy sarcasm. "Yes, by heaven, I do!" He
gestured to the desk, and the secretary obediently seated
himself at it, reaching for pen and paper. "Address it to
John Macarthur Esquire and acknowledge his communication. Inform him, in reply, that a Civil Court of
Jurisdiction is open to take cognizance of all civil actions and that he must seek redress there, if such be his
intention."

Griffin wrote swiftly. "I have that down, sir," he announced, looking up nervously. "Does Your Excellency
wish to add to it?"

The governor continued his restless pacing.

"Yes," he said, coming to a halt beside the desk.
"You may also inform Mr. Macarthur that, in view of
the fact that his own trial, on serious charges, is set for
January twenty-fifth, the matter which he has brought
to my notice cannot be considered as an object for discussion at this time by either the judge advocate or
myself."

Again the secretary's quill moved swiftly, and the
governor said, as he reached the last line, "Sign it on
my behalf, Edmund . . . and see that it is delivered im-

mediately. When you've done that, go to the judge advocate's residence and tell him to wait on me, accompanied by Mr. Crossley, at two o'clock this afternoon." He turned to Andrew and, addressing him for the first time by his Christian name, asked quietly, "Andrew, you are on good terms with Robert Campbell, are you not?"

"Yes, sir," Andrew confirmed.

"Good!" Bligh laid a hand on his arm, and he was smiling. "Then go and talk to him . . . tell him what is afoot, and say that he has my full support regarding the arrest of the *Parramatta*. Should Macarthur issue a writ against him for her recovery, he should seek the advice of Lawyer Crossley to enable him to make counter-charges. On no account is the ship to be released from arrest. Make certain that he understands that, will you?"

"I will, sir, certainly," Andrew assured him.

"Your loyalty is appreciated," the governor said. "And it shall not go unrewarded, I give you my word. Your wife has not yet returned from Hobart, has she?"

"No, sir, not as yet." For all his efforts to avoid showing his feelings, Andrew was aware that his tone of voice had betrayed him. He flushed under William Bligh's searching gaze. "There have been no ships, sir, since Your Excellency gave permission for her return. With your consent, I could charter my stepson's cutter *Flinders*, in which I returned, but—"

"There will be no need to expose her to the discomfort of a sea passage in so small a vessel," the governor put in. "The East Indiaman *Estramina* has been hired to transfer settlers and convicts from Norfolk Island to Hobart, and I am given to understand by her owners that she will call here after she has landed them, on passage to Bengal. Colonel Collins will see to it that Mrs. Hawley is given accommodation on board her, I feel sure. You'll only have two or three weeks to wait for your reunion with your wife, Andrew—perhaps less

—and in the meantime . . ." Bligh's pause was deliberate, his scrutiny intensified, and when Andrew remained silent, he went on, "I will have you sworn in as a magistrate—a role in which your loyalty to the Crown and to myself can be put to good use."

"I thank you, sir." If his acknowledgment sounded a trifle wooden, it could not be helped, Andrew thought. Appointing him to the magistrates' bench was a measure of the governor's renewed trust in him—even if the appointment was, or seemed to be, conditional on Jenny's continued absence from Sydney. In any event, so far as the forthcoming struggle for supremacy between Bligh and Macarthur was concerned, there could be no question of where his loyalties lay. Whatever he might feel personally about William Bligh as a man, he was the officially appointed governor and His Majesty's representative in the colony of New South Wales. If Macarthur and the Corps officers should attempt to challenge his authority, then—Andrew's mouth tightened—then they would be guilty of treason and it would be his inescapable duty to oppose them.

The governor said softly, as if he had read Andrew's thought, "With Crossley's aid, I intend to charge Macarthur with treason. But until the indictment is prepared, no word concerning my intention must reach his ears. Tell no one, you understand?"

"Very good, Your Excellency." Andrew drew himself to attention, bowed stiffly, and took his leave.

CHAPTER·XVI

John Macarthur was in high good humor as he thrust his way through the motley crowd thronging the tap-room of the St. Patrick Tavern in the Rocks area of Sydney Town.

It wanted only forty-eight hours to Christmas Day, and the tavern's customers were in a festive mood, not a few of them already inebriated, and the rest intent on following their example. Soldiers in the uniform of the Corps were the most numerous, and—Macarthur observed without surprise—all were drinking heavily, anticipating a brief leave from their duties and recklessly expending the pay they had just received on rum or beer for themselves and gin or ale for their female companions.

Seamen from the ships in harbor, emancipists and ticket-of-leave men, prostitutes and a few assigned convict servants, rubbed shoulders with the soldiers, exchanging banter and the occasional insult, but like himself, the majority were cheerful and in good heart if, perhaps, lacking in what the purists would have described as the Christian spirit. They would attend church services since these were compulsory, but the main interest in the celebration of Christmas in the colony lay in the issue of extra provisions by the commissariat and the officially sanctioned tot of rum each convict was allowed, for which no payment was demanded.

Macarthur smiled to himself, the smile ironic. Rum, he thought, could still buy men's labor, loyalty, and support, in spite of *Bounty* Bligh's efforts to suppress the traffic. He moved purposefully toward the bar, and two of the soldiers, recognizing him, called out to their comrades to raise a cheer.

" 'Tis Mr. Macarthur, boys—let him through now, will you? Your very good health, sir, an' the top o' the morning to ye! Hip, hip—"

The response was spasmodic, but flatteringly enthusiastic, and Macarthur called out to the barmaids, "See that their glasses are filled, girls, and you may present the reckoning to me."

The proprietor, the Corps sergeant major, Thomas Whittle, hearing his voice, came from the back premises to bow a welcome. He was not in uniform, but in his shirt-sleeves, a pen in his hand, and he offered obsequiously, "Come through to the parlor, Mr. Macarthur, sir, if you will, and I'll see that you're served there. What is your pleasure, sir? Cape brandy or a glass of Madeira?"

"I've not come to drink but to have a word with you in private, Mr. Whittle," Macarthur told him crisply. "And I'm somewhat pressed for time, so if you could give me your undivided attention for ten minutes, I'd be obliged."

"Certainly, sir. I'm at your service. Come this way, if you please."

There were two women in the parlor, one of whom was holding a pale, fair-haired girl of perhaps fifteen by the hand, over whose shoulders a shawl had been hastily draped. Beneath it she was naked, and Macarthur, meeting her frightened gaze, saw that she was weeping. Whittle murmured an apology and dismissed all three of them with an impatient wave of the hand. The girl's dress and her shift lay untidily on a chair, but one of her elders snatched up the crumpled garments, swept them into her basket, and beat a swift retreat, her companion and the weeping girl close on her heels.

Macarthur smiled. "Fresh talent, Mr. Whittle?" he suggested with amusement. "God's blood, you're a busy man!"

"I try to make a living, sir. And this is a busy tavern —I'm forever in need of girls to serve the bar." He pulled up a chair and invited his visitor to be seated, before crossing to close the door. "Now, sir . . ." He perched himself on the edge of the table, pushing aside the pile of papers on which he had been at work, and returning his quill to its holder. "What can I do for you?"

"First there's something I can do for you," John Macarthur said, ceasing to smile. "I've fifty gallons of American rum that I bought very keenly a little while ago. It's not the best quality, of course, but good enough. You can have it free of charge, provided you make it available to your men at half price on January the twenty-fifth. You know what that date signifies, do you not?"

Sergeant Major Whittle inclined his bullet head. "Yes, Mr. Macarthur, I do. Will you want your generosity known, sir?"

"You can mention it, yes."

"You'll be acquitted, sir, no doubt o' that, is there?"

"I hope not."

"It's a put-up job, sir," Whittle asserted stoutly. "That drunken swine Atkins has it in for you, and the governor's behind him. Two of a kind, they are. And as for Crossley—a bloody forger, yet he's permitted to ply his trade here as if he were an honest citizen!"

"Does Crossley ever drink here?" Macarthur questioned sharply.

"Here? No, sir, he don't." There was a wealth of scorn in the sergeant major's voice. "This place ain't good enough for him. He does his drinking on Church Hill, at The Settlers mostly, or at Sarah Bird's." He broke off, looking across at John Macarthur with narrowed eyes. "I can get to him there, if you should want me to, sir."

"I may want you to, Thomas," Macarthur confessed. "I've learned, from a reliable informant, that Crossley's being employed to draft the indictment against me. I don't need to tell you, I feel sure, that it will be of some assistance in my defense if I can obtain a sight of that indictment before the court sits."

"Nothing to it, Mr. Macarthur," Whittle assured him. "Leave it to me, sir. Is that all you want?"

Macarthur shook his head. "No. There are two other matters. First, I have received official notification that I must relinquish my fourteen-year lease on land I have held since Governor King's departure. Lot seventy-seven is said to be a church reserve." He shrugged his slim, elegantly jacketed shoulders. "I am forbidden to build on it and required to accept the leasehold of a similar size and value, of my choice, elsewhere in the township."

Thomas Whittle stared at him, his jaw dropping. "You did not agree to that, sir, surely?"

"Oh, I agreed, in order to keep the peace. Damme, Thomas, I do my best to accommodate Governor Bligh, you know."

"Yes, sir." Whittle's grin was skeptical.

"And what is the result?" Macarthur went on. "I chose a plot which His Excellency now insists is the *wharf* reserve, and, in a very high-handed manner, he tells me he has referred the matter to His Majesty's Government. Well, you know how long it will take for the Colonial Office to inform me of their decision, don't you? So—" He paused, looking unsmilingly into the

sergeant major's red, heavily jowled face. "I want a
fence erected round lot seventy-seven, Thomas. Can
you arrange for some of your soldiers to get to work on
it at once? They'll be paid for the work, of course."

"Soldiers, sir?" Whittle queried, clearly puzzled.

"That's right—soldiers. The damned provost marshal
and his constables will think twice before they intervene if the men are in uniform, will they not?"

Thomas Whittle reached absentmindedly for the bottle on the table behind him. Putting the neck to his lips,
he drank half its contents before replying. Then he said,
swallowing hard, "Right you are, sir. If that's your wish,
it shall be done. I reckon you know what you're doing."

"I do, Thomas," John Macarthur returned vehemently. "By God I do! I'm taking a stand against tyranny and injustice."

Whittle took another draught from his brandy bottle. "And not a moment too soon, Mr. Macarthur sir,"
he applauded. "You can count on me, sir, and on my
lads. What shall I tell 'em that you'll pay?"

"A gallon apiece," Macarthur said, without hesitation. "And good stuff—not the kind you concoct here,
my friend, with burned sugar and tobacco added to disguise the fact that it's diluted by fifty percent." He
laughed. "Come on, Thomas, you can't deny it."

"A man has to make a living," the innkeeper defended sheepishly. "And what was the other matter?
You said as there were two, I fancy."

"Oh, yes." Macarthur's eyes narrowed. "You know
Captain Hawley?"

"I'm not exactly on nodding terms with him, but I
know him, of course. Big gentleman, commissioned into
the marines . . . married an emancipist, they say, in
Hobart not long since. The woman that gave succor to
some Irish escapers . . . name o' Broome, wasn't it?"
Whittle again resorted to his bottle, looking suddenly
nervous and ill at ease. "He's not here at present, sir.

Gone up to the Hawkesbury, I heard, for his Christmas leave."

John Macarthur ignored the implication. "Captain Hawley," he said curtly, "has been sworn in as a magistrate at *Bounty* Bligh's behest, and I have reason to believe that there's a move afoot to have him nominated for the court at my trial."

Whittle nodded sagely. The drink was starting to take effect, dispelling his nervousness.

"I see, sir," he acknowledged. "And Captain Hawley's the governor's man, they reckon. You . . ." He hesitated. "What d'you want done about him, Mr. Macarthur?"

"I want him stopped, Thomas—prevented from sitting at my trial." The answer was crisp and John Macarthur rose to his feet. "I don't care how you do it, so long as it's done. Because if I'm *not* acquitted, there will be hell to pay, you can take my word for that." He moved slowly toward the door and, as if it were an afterthought, turned to face Whittle again. "They'll be after *your* leaseholding before long, you know. Lot fifty-four, isn't it, off Bridge Street?"

Sergeant Major Whittle expelled his breath in a long-drawn sigh. "I've started to build on the site, sir," he said, with apprehension. "Surely I'm entitled to build—they can't take it away, can they?"

"They can and by heaven they will, Thomas!" Macarthur told him. "That is, of course, unless—"

"Unless what, sir?" Whittle asked, now really alarmed.

"Well, unless the lease can be transferred to an emancipist or a reliable female—nominally, I mean, until the heat dies down. I can arrange it for you, if you wish—Mr. Grimes, the government surveyor, is a good friend of mine. It is Captain Bligh who is making all this fuss about the leases, not Grimes." Macarthur's tone was confident, his quick smile winning and devoid of guile. "Oh, come now, Thomas, trust me! Simply do what I have asked of you, and there will be no necessity to halt your building. And if you can have the fence on *my* site completed as early as possible in the new year, I'll double the quantity of American rum I promised you, damme if I won't!"

"Thank you very much, sir," Whittle managed. He slid from his perch on the table edge and hurried to open the door leading into the taproom. His enthusiasm had waned, but anxious not to betray any sign of faint-heartedness in the presence of the man he regarded as his greatest benefactor, he contrived a fulsome farewell for the benefit of his customers.

"The compliments of the season, Captain Macarthur, sir," he said, using the military title John Macarthur had once held. "Will you be spending Christmas here?"

"God forbid!" Macarthur denied. "I shall be spending next week with my family in Parramatta." Aware of the listeners hanging eagerly on his words, he added, raising his voice, "I am a churchwarden, and I shall be reading the lesson at the midnight service, as I always conceive it my Christian duty to do in this heathen place . . . whether or not I am the victim of malicious tyranny. I give you good day, Mr. Whittle. And rest assured that my nephew, Mr. Hannibal, will attend to the deliveries we discussed well before the due date."

The crowd parted to make way for him, and he was gone, leaving the proprietor of the St. Patrick Tavern to stare after his tall, immaculately tailored figure in scowling uncertainty.

Putting up the fence would be easy enough, he told himself, and if he arranged the matter through Sergeant Sutherland, he could plead ignorance should there be trouble as a result. Lawyer Crossley presented no problem, but how the devil was he to deal with Captain

Bloody Hawley, who was the governor's aide? Then he recalled the girl he had had to send away, on John Macarthur's unexpected arrival, and his scowl lifted.

"Jessie," he called to one of the barmaids. "Go and find those two women who were here with the lass. Name of Mattie Croaker, one of 'em was, and they called the lass Dorcas. Tell 'em I've a proposition to put to them and bring all three of 'em back here as soon as you can."

The barmaid obediently sped away, and Thomas Whittle returned to his accounts, a sly smile now curving his lips as he added the cost of the drinks Macarthur had ordered to his reckoning. According to the slate behind the bar, thirty-seven tots of rum had been served, but he rounded this figure up to forty. Adding a spoonful of vitriol with the sugar and tobacco he habitually put into each barrel certainly gave the stuff a kick . . . most of those Macarthur had treated were happily drunk, the rest in a fair way to becoming so.

Despite the fact that Sydney Town boasted close on a score of licensed taverns and three times that number of unlicensed grog shops and whorehouses scattered about the area between Sydney and the Hawkesbury settlements, the St. Patrick was making him a fortune. Time to sell out pretty soon, he thought, and join the ranks of the civilian merchants like Simeon Lord and Henry Kable, with his own trading schooners and a fine house on his plot at the back of Bridge Street.

So long as the *Bounty* bastard did not try to cancel his lease, with the house half-built . . . but Macarthur had promised to see to that. His smile widened.

The wisest move he had ever made, he reflected smugly, was to enlist in the Corps and . . . there were still other alternatives to becoming a civilian. He could purchase a commission with the money he took from the sale of the St. Patrick. Captain Thomas Whittle was a fine-sounding title, and as he totted up his profits, Sergeant Major Whittle savored the sound of it with intense satisfaction.

There were others who had risen from the ranks, he reminded himself—Minchin, the adjutant, Lieutenant Brabyn, Ensign Bell, Captain Kemp, and, of course, Captain Hawley, the governor's aide-de-camp, had once been a sergeant of marines. No doubt he owed his promotion to commissioned rank to *Bounty* Bligh's influence.

"They're here, Mr. Whittle." The voice of the barmaid, Jessie, broke into his thoughts. "Mrs. Croaker and Dorcas, like you said."

"Bring them in," Thomas Whittle ordered, "and then you can tell the other girls to close up until this evening. I want a bit o' peace."

The noisy clamor of protest from the taproom gradually faded into silence. Thomas Whittle put away his account books and was seated in his accustomed chair when Mattie Croaker reentered the parlor, dragging a weeping Dorcas unwillingly behind her.

Andrew Hawley returned to Sydney by road on December thirtieth. His time, he told himself, had not been wasted. Justin had taken him, with Timothy Dawson and his two young daughters, upriver in the *Flinders* on the twenty-second; he had stayed for a day or two after Christmas but had then departed, claiming vaguely that he had a charter to Coal River.

There had been no evidence, in the form of passengers or cargo, to bear out his claim, but Andrew had not disputed it. If the boy chose to lose money when he could have been coining it, that was his affair; the *Flinders* belonged to him—indeed, he had built her himself—and it was no part of a stepfather's duty, as he conceived it, to question Justin's decisions or his motives for arriving at them.

The information he had supplied concerning the formation of the Hawkesbury settlers' armed companies had, to Andrew's dismay, proved to be true. Tim Dawson had confirmed the fact, soon after they had weighed anchor, admitting, without apology, that he was in command of the first company to be formed.

"We cannot simply sit tamely by and allow the governor's authority to be flouted," Dawson had argued. "And it will be, I'm quite certain, if Macarthur has his way. He and his fellow rum traffickers—in the Corps and outside it—are not going to see their activities terminated and their profits curtailed without making a fight of it. And Bligh's made of sterner stuff than either Hunter or Philip King, Andrew. Besides, he has the home government firmly behind him, where they had not. Macarthur's influence with the Colonial Office counts for nothing now. He'll not contrive Bligh's recall, as he contrived poor King's. William Bligh can, and by God I believe he *will*, do what his predecessors failed to do—rid us of the infernal Rum Corps and their monopolies and make this colony the prosperous, productive land it should be. We must support him in return for what he has already done for us."

"But you are talking of armed support, Tim," Andrew had protested. "Your men are training with muskets, Justin says. Are you seriously suggesting that the Corps will rebel—that they'll take up arms against the governor?"

And Tim had answered vehemently, "I fear it may come to that, yes. Much, of course, will depend on the outcome of John Macarthur's trial . . . a trial he has deliberately brought upon himself. And what charges Bligh decides to bring against him."

He had been compelled to remain silent on that score, Andrew recalled, since Governor Bligh had forbidden him to disclose the indictment he was considering. But Tim Dawson was no fool; his silence had been

enough, and in the end he had agreed to meet and listen
to the loyalist settlers' views. He had found them convincing, the settlers themselves decent, honest men,
whose sole objective was to support the legitimate
colonial authority from whatever threat.

"We petitioned His Excellency, when he first took
office as governor, Captain Hawley," one of the older
men had told him. "We asked for reforms, an end to
the barter system that was reducing most of us to
penury, and over two hundred of us signed that petition.
And Governor Bligh acceded to our pleas." He had
produced a copy of the governor's order of February
fourteenth, and read it gravely. Andrew reined in his
horse as the flickering lights of Parramatta faded behind
him and repeated to himself the text of that fateful
order: "*'To remedy these grievous complaints and
to relieve the inhabitants who have suffered by the
monopolist traffic in rum, His Excellency feels it his
duty to put a stop to all barter in future, and to forbid
the exchange of spirits and other liquor in payment for
grain, animal food, labor, and wearing apparel or any
other commodity whatever, to all descriptions of persons in this colony and its dependencies. . . .'*"

"We couldn't ask fairer than that, sir, could we?"
the old settler had insisted. "And it's because Governor
Bligh has always treated us fairly and kept to his word
that we're ready to stand behind him now if he needs
us."

Well, it was to be hoped that he would not, Andrew
thought, and again kneed his tired horse into motion,
anxious to reach Sydney before the evening dusk turned
into darkness.

The rest of his visit had been, from his angle, concluded satisfactorily. He had spent Christmas and a
few days after at Long Wrekin, receiving a warm welcome from the Jardines and little Rachel, and a more

subdued and uncertain one from William. He had brought them presents from himself and Jenny and found the farm in good order, the Jardines coping adequately with the responsibility of running it, in Jenny's absence, and caring for the two children.

His final call had been on the Dawsons, when Tim had renewed his offer—made initially to Jenny—to purchase Long Wrekin lock, stock, and barrel.

"I'd pay her a fair price," he had said. "It's good land, and I can use it. And, as I promised Jenny when we first talked about the sale, I would keep on the Jardines for as long as she wanted me to. I'm presuming, you see, that when she does come back here you'll want to live in Sydney or within a short distance of Government House. Or—" He had hesitated, reading dissent in Andrew's face. "Don't you intend to continue in the governor's service?"

He had evaded the question, Andrew recalled, and found himself wondering why he had done so. Clearly he had to stay for as long as Governor Bligh needed him—he had made that decision after their last interview, a week ago—but after that? Would Jenny go back to Hobart with him, to start anew there, or would she want him to resign his commission and become a settler on the Hawkesbury, as they had originally planned? He would be guided by her wishes, but . . . His horse shied at a shadow on the road, and he swore, as he came close to being unseated.

So much in the future was unpredictable; so much hung on the result of John Macarthur's forthcoming trial and the Corps officers' reaction to it. And if, as Bligh wanted him to, he were to sit as one of Macarthur's judges, then . . . He shook his head helplessly. It would not be only his loyalty that was being put to the test but that of the whole of the New South Wales Corps, the colony's garrison, who wore the King's uniform and yet could not be relied on to bear allegiance to His Majesty's appointed representative, when he was in conflict with one of their own.

A light rain started to fall and Andrew hunched his shoulders and rode doggedly on. By the time he reached the outskirts of Sydney Town, the rain had become a deluge, and he began to regret not having halted at Parramatta for the night. As he trotted down High Street, a soldier called out to him, asking his name, but the man was obviously drunk, and, as wet as he was, Andrew ignored an unexpected offer from the soldier to stable his horse for him, surprised that it should have been made by one of the Corps. He left the horse—borrowed from Tim Dawson—in the care of a sleepy groom at the Spences' stables and, head down in the face of the driving rain, plodded grimly to the end of Mulgrave Street, its dusty surface now a sea of mud.

He was bone-weary and out of temper when he reached his own quarter, to find no lights burning there and his orderly presumably absent. As he struggled with rain-damp fingers to unlock the door, he heard a movement behind him, followed by the sound of loud sobbing, and the next moment a bedraggled figure precipitated itself at his feet, calling out to him for help.

Andrew's first impulse was to send the intruder on her way. He was worn out after his long ride and reluctant to become involved. Besides, there were all too many drunken women abroad in Sydney's streets during the hours of darkness, although the prostitutes in search of custom usually avoided—or were deterred from entering—the respectable residential quarter, which was spread out between Government House and the military barracks. But there was something pitiful about this woman's cries, and when she raised her face to his, he sensed, although he could not see, that she was young—a pathetic, ragged child, barely grown to womanhood.

He opened the door, searched for and found the oil lamp that was kept in the narrow hallway, and managed, after several abortive attempts, to light it. The sobbing creature followed him in, and when he raised the lamp in order to look at her, he saw that his initial impression had been correct. She *was* only a child, and he exclaimed in disgust when he observed that she had been the victim of a brutal attack which had left her face swollen and discolored, and livid weals, as from a whiplash, across her neck and arms.

Common humanity demanded that he yield to her distraught plea and give her temporary succor, at least. Only a man entirely devoid of compassion would send this poor waif back into the rain-soaked darkness, he told himself resignedly, and he could not bring himself to do so. Putting his arm round her and with the lamp in his free hand, he led her into his living room, where he lowered her gently into the only armchair the room possessed. From the sideboard he took brandy and glasses, poured out two stiff measures, and thrust one of them into the girl's limp hand.

"Drink this," he advised, "and you'll feel better."

She sipped gratefully, holding the glass in both hands against her chattering teeth, but she continued to weep until Andrew, fortified by his own draught, demanded sternly that she explain her arrival at his door.

"I . . . I was afraid. They beat me, and I . . . I ran away. I didn't know where I was going, but then I saw you, and I . . . I came to . . . ask you to help me. I thought they were still chasing after me, sir, and I . . . I wanted to hide from them."

"I see. Where did all this happen, child? Where have you come from?"

She waved a hand vaguely, as if uncertain even of her present whereabouts, and Andrew saw that she was shivering violently. He went into the bedroom, took a blanket from the bed, and wrapped it about her. His own clothing was wringing wet, and he divested himself of his jacket and shirt, and while the girl went on sipping her brandy, he donned his dressing gown before returning to her.

"Now," he urged. "Tell me your name, at least."

She shrank from him, her eyes filled with terror. "It . . . it's Dorcas, sir. Dorcas Croaker."

"There's no reason to be afraid, Dorcas—I shan't hurt you," he offered reassuringly. "But if I'm to help you, I must know something about you. For a start—how old are you? You can tell me that, surely?"

"I'm fifteen, sir."

"Convict or free?" Andrew persisted.

"I'm free. My ma's a convict, her and my auntie. I came out along with them, 'cos there was nobody to look after me."

"When, Dorcas? When did you arrive here?"

"A while ago. In a ship called the *Duke of Portland*."

She had been here for over five months, Andrew deduced, and was puzzled, wondering why she should so recently have been subjected to the beating which, judging by her appearance, had been inflicted with a whip. An attack by some lusting male might have accounted for the bruises had she offered resistance to his advances, but a whipping suggested that she might have incurred her mother's disapproval and been cruelly punished for it. But she had spoken of a chase and *they*. He put out a hand to take hers.

"Tell me what happened, Dorcas. Start from when you landed here from the *Duke of Portland*."

"Oh, they sent Ma and Auntie Alice to the Factory, at Parramatta," Dorcas answered readily enough, "and I was sent to Mrs. King's Orphan Home. I liked it there, sir. We was taught reading and ciphering, and the food was good. But then Ma and my auntie finished their time at the Factory, and they claimed me. They—"

she choked, hiding her tear-wet face from Andrew's searching gaze, "they wanted to . . . to sell me, sir. To some horrible old man in a tavern. And I . . . I didn't want him to buy me. My ma and the old man whipped me, and I ran away."

Her story was plausible, Andrew reflected uneasily. In London and other English cities, women sold girl children, of Dorcas's age and younger, into prostitution, sometimes for no more than the price of a few bottles of gin. Such women, deported here, would think nothing of continuing the practice and, he decided cynically, since many of the licensed tavern keepers in Sydney also ran whorehouses as a profitable sideline, there would be no lack of willing buyers.

He looked down at the girl, crouching like some small, frightened animal beneath her blanket, and realizing that she was watching him, he knew a momentary doubt.

Why had she come here, to him? There were other houses—many with lights still burning—that she must have passed on her way, houses with families, women and children in them, where she would not have been turned away. In the deluging rain, she must have run for some considerable distance, yet seemingly she had not halted, had not knocked on any other door to beg for sanctuary.

Her pursuers might, it was true, have been hard on her heels, but the watch patrolled this district and would certainly have intervened, had anything untoward attracted their notice . . . and the pursuit could hardly have been silent or, indeed, have gone unnoticed on a night like this. He hesitated, unwilling to put his sudden suspicions into words and anxious not to misjudge an apparently innocent fifteen-year-old child, whose fear was undoubtedly very real, and who could be telling the truth.

Andrew straightened up, frowning. Were his suspicions justified, he asked himself—could they be? It was possible that Dorcas had, as she had claimed, seen him as he approached his door and run to him on impulse, half paralyzed with terror. But then, mentally reviewing the route she must have followed, if she had come from the Rocks, he realized that she had passed the Orphan School, and suspicion hardened into certainty. If the chase she had described had been genuine, the Orphan School would surely have been her first objective.

"Dorcas," he questioned, a harsh edge to his voice, "do you know who I am? Do you know my name?"

"Why, yes, sir, of course I do." Taken by surprise, the girl sat up, meeting his gaze with a smile. "You are Captain Hawley, are you not? Captain Andrew Hawley of the—the marines, not the Corps. My ma said—"

A thunderous knocking on the door cut short her revelations, and Andrew swore in exasperation as a man's voice demanded admission.

"The watch, sir! Open the door!"

He did so, without hesitation, leaving the girl where she was, to find himself confronting two uniformed constables, in storm cloaks, and two bedraggled women who, at the sight of him, began an angry clamor.

"That's 'im, that's the officer! That's who abducted my child. If you go inside, you'll find 'er there, poor mite. Frightened 'arf to death she'll be."

"Go on—look for 'er, constable!" her companion screamed.

The leading constable tipped his sodden hat. "I'm sorry, Captain Hawley sir," he apologized, "but we've had a complaint against you."

"Made by these women?" Andrew returned coldly. "Convicts, I take it?"

"Yes, sir. Ticket-o'-leave convicts, both of 'em. But we have to clear the matter up, sir, with your permission." Embarrassed, the leading constable removed his hat. "Won't take more'n a few minutes, sir, if you'll let us in."

"Come in, by all means," Andrew invited, "and you'll find the girl here, but I did not abduct her. She accosted me when I was unlocking my door—I've just returned from the Hawkesbury—with some wild story that she had been beaten by her mother and was being chased. I took pity on her and let her in . . . but she's come to no harm at my hands, I can assure you. You'll find her in my living room."

"Right, sir." The two constables exchanged wary glances and followed Andrew into the living room. It was empty; the girl and the blanket with which he had covered her had vanished. With a shrill cry of triumph, one of the women made for the bedroom, urging the officers of the law to accompany her. Both responded with reluctance, their spokesman offering another murmured apology.

It was then that the full enormity of the trick that had been played on him dawned on Andrew. He did not need to go into his bedroom to guess what they would find . . . Dorcas, he knew, would be in his bed, with only the blanket to cover her nakedness, her bruised face and tear-filled eyes all the evidence they would require to substantiate the charge of abduction. Sickened and filled with impotent fury, he waited. The women's loud-voiced accusations and the constables' gruff rejoinders told him what he might expect when they returned to confront him.

And he had no defense; the girl would back up her mother's lies, tongues would wag, and his reputation would be left in shreds, even if no charges were leveled against him . . . and they almost certainly would be, since the constables would make impeccable witnesses. Clearly, the object of the sordid plot was to hold him up to ridicule, to make him a laughingstock throughout the colony, as a man who could have had any woman

of easy virtue he wanted but who, instead, had chosen
to abduct an innocent child.

Who, he asked himself bitterly—who had planned
this, and why? He knew the answer, almost as soon as
any questions occurred to him. The Corps were being
called upon to sit in judgment on one of their own, on
January twenty-fifth, and they wanted no officer of
another service to sit with them. Even Governor Bligh
—whilst he might insist on Richard Atkins continuing
to act as judge advocate, since the appointment was
made by the Crown—even Bligh would hesitate before
nominating his aide-de-camp, with such scandalous
gossip going the rounds concerning him.

And there was Jenny . . . Andrew drew in his breath
sharply. God in heaven, what would be her reaction,
when she came back here and listened to the clacking
tongues and heard the ribald laughter?

He dared not give his imagination rein, and when
the intruders came to stage their noisy confrontation,
he had himself under iron control, ordering the women
from his house in tones that brooked no argument, even
from them.

Left alone with the two constables, he said with icy
calm, "These accusations are utterly false and without
foundation. The women are lying and so is the girl. She
made her appearance exactly as I described to you.
Damn it, I have ridden from Long Wrekin farm, on the
Hawkesbury, and through this infernal storm into the
bargain! I had no desire for any woman, let alone the
time either to abduct that girl or to rape her. Until she
came to my door, with her plea for help, I had never
set eyes on her, I give you my word."

The constables were honest men, and as they again
exchanged worried glances, Andrew sensed that both
were inclined to believe him. The older, avoiding his
eye, said regretfully, "We have to report the matter, sir,
or be in neglect of our duty. I'm very sorry, sir." He

hesitated and added, still not looking at Andrew, "Maybe you could buy them women off, Captain Hawley. They're the kind that can be bought."

Undoubtedly they were, Andrew reflected, but they had already been bought, probably at a price beyond what he could afford. And in any event . . . He sighed, feeling suddenly unbearably weary.

"You must do your duty," he said, "and I commend you for the manner in which you have behaved in this unhappy affair. I shall make *my* report to Provost Marshal Gore in the morning. Good night to you!"

"Good night, sir," the men chorused.

They stumped out into the darkened street, leaving smears of mud from their boots as reminders of their presence, and both saluted before resuming their patrol. Of Dorcas Croaker and her unpleasant relatives there was now no sign. They had probably gone, Andrew decided, to claim the reward for their endeavors from whoever had hired them.

He shrugged helplessly and, stifling a yawn, crossed to the sideboard to pour himself a second glass of brandy, his hand less steady as he filled the glass to the brim.

CHAPTER XVII

Titus Penhaligon hated Coal River from the moment of landing from the government sloop, after the vessel had tacked her way past the odd, sugarloaf-shaped island known as Nobby's, which lay close to the shore at the river's entrance.

The island, Lieutenant O'Shea had told him with a sadistic smile, was used as a dumping ground for recalcitrant female felons whose conduct had failed to improve after the more usual punishments—having their heads shaved or being forced to wear iron collars —had been inflicted on them.

The settlement, also near the river's mouth, had been named Newcastle by Governor King, in an effort to dignify it. It was in fact a miserable collection of wooden huts and single-story houses for the Corps officers and superintendents, its largest buildings being the jail and the government stores. There was no courthouse, no church, and no hospital worthy of the name; the military commandant acted as both judge and jury, and religious services were held only when a chaplain from Sydney or a passing ship happened to call there.

There were sick and injured in plenty, but, Titus soon learned, most of them went untreated, since the superintendents were reluctant to report accidents, and the sufferers themselves—aware that their rations would be withheld if they did not work—preferred to endure their pain and keep their bellies filled. In any event the hospital was a patched-up wooden shelter, more suitable for the accommodation of cattle than human beings, open to the elements on one side and lacking blankets, mattresses, and any form of medical comfort, save an official issue of rum. Even this, his predecessor had told him before leaving, was intended solely for use when the amputation of a limb was deemed necessary.

"You'll receive a ration of bread," he had added cynically. "One loaf each week for each inmate—but you have to send an orderly to collect what's due from the bakehouse, and nine times out of ten the military and the overseers have claimed virtually all that's been baked, and you have to be satisfied with what is left. I did not encourage my patients to stay long, as you may imagine, and they weren't anxious to remain. A couple of the convict orderlies are good fishermen, and I used to go out after game whenever I could. There are kangaroos in abundance and plenty of duck a few miles up the river valley. So I kept them from starvation . . . but only just."

An inspection of the apothecary's store had revealed a similar dearth of provision for the sick, and when Titus had exclaimed in dismay at the sight of its empty cupboards and bare shelves, his predecessor's response had been a rueful shrug of the shoulders.

"Your duties, my dear fellow—your only *official* duties, that is to say—will consist of pronouncing convicts fit to receive whatever number of lashes the commandant has awarded them, and of declaring them dead, when the poor wretches expire. But if any of them die under the lash, you will be wise if you certify that death has occurred from natural causes."

That this had been no exaggeration, Titus soon learned from bitter experience. Coal River and Newcastle were designated places of exile for those felons whose crimes, committed since arrival in the colony, had merited sentence of death but who had been reprieved. A high proportion of them were Irish rebels, sentenced originally for sedition. The rest were thieves, murderers, and persistent escapers, some put ashore by the transports evacuating Norfolk Island—hardened criminals, considered too dangerous to be transferred to Van Diemen's Land.

They mined coal in crude tunnels driven into the sides of Nobby's Hill and Fiddlesticks Hill, working with pick and shovel in the ill-ventilated depths, and permitted out into the open air only on Sundays. Despite this and the constant danger of being entombed because of inadequate shoring-up of their dark burrows, most of them, given the opportunity, chose to work in the mines. The alternative, toiling with the lime-burning gangs in Fullerton Cove, was an even more dreaded punishment, and Titus understood why this was so when called upon to examine the bodies of two Irishmen who had committed suicide by drowning.

Both had suffered severe floggings before being put to work loading baskets of the unslaked lime into barges moored inshore. While they stood waist deep in the salt estuary water, the lime had entered their raw wounds, causing them such unendurable agony that they had preferred death to its continuation.

But, Titus recalled with bitterness, the commandant's reply to his indignantly voiced protest had been an indifferent shrug of the shoulders.

"Don't be a fool, Doctor," he had advised. "The scurvy swine have saved the government rope and spared the hangman a job! The rogues who are sent here have already forfeited their lives, and they're treated accordingly. We don't get many whose sentences are less than five years, you know, and two of those miserable Irish traitors were serving seven years for murder and rape. Forget about them if you've any wit. They're not worth troubling about."

But he could not forget, Titus had found. The brutality he was compelled to witness, the savage, inhuman treatment of the convicts and the incessant floggings tormented his conscience as a physician and demanded that he protest against their continuation, even though his pleas for mercy would be ignored.

He made no friends. The convicts saw him attending punishment and did not trust him; his patients in the hospital displayed the same suspicions concerning him, for all he made the most self-sacrificing efforts to feed and care for them. In their eyes he represented authority, and they rejected his overtures, giving him scant thanks for anything he did. The commandant held Titus in contempt as a fool and a weakling, and when he entertained in his spacious official residence, invitations were confined to his own junior officers. Titus reflected miserably that he had never passed the commandant's front door, and it seemed the lowest convict women were, in this respect, more privileged than the settlement's surgeon was ever likely to be.

All the officers—of whom there were four—had their female housekeepers; the convicts, confined ten to a hut, shared the services of women classified as hutkeepers; and the superintendents and the rank-and-file soldiers, as well as his hospital orderlies, were permitted to make whatever domestic arrangements they chose, with such females as were available.

Only he was alone, and as the weeks dragged past, he lapsed into a state verging on desperation, for which the sole remedy was to drink himself into oblivion. His hunting ventures upriver occupied many of his days, and these he enjoyed, finding interest in a study of the flora and fauna of the luxuriant valley and making contact with the gentle, friendly Awabakal tribe of aborigines, who also inhabited the valley and its surrounding woodlands.

At first, Titus recalled, he had spent his evening hours writing long letters to Abigail, pouring out his heart to her and telling her of his loneliness and despair, as well as of his love and longing. But although the pile of neatly penned epistles grew, there were so few opportunities of ensuring their safe delivery that, in the end, he ceased to put pen to paper. Ships called, at infrequent intervals, and their masters picked up mail, but this was either destined for England or addressed to Sydney; and when no answers came to the letters he had addressed to the Hawkesbury farm, he abandoned the futile endeavor to establish communication with his intended wife. Instead, such letters as he wrote were pleas to the governor and to the surgeon general for his relief . . . and these, too, went unanswered.

His greatest trial, however, was his relationship with Lieutenant O'Shea, which—never cordial—had now deteriorated into open hostility.

Seated in his small, wretchedly furnished living room, Titus poured himself an overgenerous tot of rum and gulped it down with scarcely a pause to draw breath. He had, of course, he now recognized, made a grave error when he had told the Irish lieutenant that Abigail Tempest had promised to wed him. He had blurted out the truth when O'Shea had taunted him, and since then . . . He sighed, looking back over recent events.

Ever since Titus had made that claim, O'Shea had spared no effort to make his life a misery, having him called out at night to treat some paltry injury to one or another of his soldiers, and demanding his presence at trials as well as punishments. Only two days previously a sergeant of the Corps—acting on O'Shea's instructions—had delivered the bodies of two would-be escapers to the hospital. Both were so long dead that putrefaction had set in, but the sergeant had insisted that a postmortem examination was required in order to ascertain the cause of death for the official records.

Titus shuddered, the ordeal of his hideous task still vivid in his memory, the ghastly stench still in his nostrils, for it had pervaded the whole hospital, and even his long-suffering patients had complained.

He reached for the rum bottle, feeling bile rise in his throat. Was there to be no end to his torment, he wondered desperately . . . no escape to Abigail's warm and loving arms, unless he arranged it for himself? But that would mean he would have to desert his post, give up the appointment to the colony's medical service and and the security this offered for his future—his future *and* Abigail's. He could not marry her if he had no means of making his livelihood. Although perhaps . . . He swallowed the contents of his glass, fighting down a wave of nausea.

Perhaps he did not have to depend on his medical training exclusively. . . . Abigail and her sister were the owners of the land grant the Reverend Caleb Boskenna had taken up on their behalf. He could work on the land, despite his lack of experience. Others did it, including town-bred convicts who had formerly lived by picking pockets and holding up coaches. He, surely, could do the same; and since he would be Abigail's husband, Boskenna could raise no objection.

Feeling suddenly as if a great weight had been lifted from his shoulders, Titus got to his feet, spilling the rum bottle in his haste. The devil take it, he told himself, he need not stay here . . . he was no convicted felon, serving a seven-year sentence! He was a free man, an officer, and there would be boats for hire in the estuary, a sealer, perhaps, calling in on the way to Sydney for her crew to spend New Year's Day there.

He made for the door, remembering, with a bitter jolt, that today was New Year's Eve. There would be some sort of celebration here. The commandant would no doubt invite O'Shea and the other officers to dine with him. The wretched denizens who subsisted in the tunnels beneath Nobby's and Fiddlesticks Hill would be permitted to crawl out of the darkness. The lime burning would cease for twenty-four hours. The barge crews would come ashore, and all of them—convicts, overseers, soldiers, and his patients in the hospital— would drown their sorrows in the officially conceded issue of rum which, by tradition, marked a public holiday in New South Wales.

Titus hiccoughed, turning to close and lock the door behind him with unsteady hands. He had taken only a dozen paces along the path which connected his quarters with the road to the wharf when, to his surprise, he heard a familiar voice call out to him by name.

"Dr. Penhaligon—I've a letter for you, sir!"

"Justin—Justin Broome? Oh, my God, but you're the answer to prayer!" Titus seized his unexpected visitor by the arm and, overcome by emotion, wrung his hand, his voice choked and his eyes suddenly filled with tears. "Have you come by sea? Have you come in your cutter?"

"The *Flinders*—yes, I have." Justin gestured in the direction of the anchorage. "She's there. And, as I said, I've brought you a letter. Miss Abigail Tempest asked me to deliver it to you." He fumbled in the pockets of his blue watchcoat and brought the letter to light, holding it out a trifle uncertainly.

Titus took it, choked again, and then, urgently grasping his arm, led him back to the house. "Please come in, Justin. I want to talk to you, I . . . I need your help desperately, my dear fellow. I . . . wait, please, I have to unlock the door."

Justin's blue eyes widened in shocked surprise as the two men entered the small living room, and he looked about him, taking in the unkempt state of the room, the scattered papers and the upended bottle on the dirty, rough-hewn wooden table. But he said nothing and waited, without impatience, whilst Titus Penhaligon unsealed and swiftly skimmed through his letter. The young surgeon was weeping openly now, obviously shaken by the receipt of the much-anticipated letter, Justin thought to himself, if not by the contents of it. As Penhaligon made no attempt to hide his emotion, Justin—unaccustomed to such displays of masculine weakness—hastily averted his eyes.

The poor devil had been drinking, he thought, trying to be charitable, although—judging by the number of empty leather-covered bottles and uncaulked rum kegs piled up against the wall—it seemed that he had fallen into the habit ever since his arrival in the settlement. And perhaps he had his reasons; it was commonly believed that conditions at Coal River were so bad that no member of the garrison stayed there for a day longer than he was compelled to. Governor King had sought to improve its image by renaming the river the Hunter and the settlement Newcastle, but the old names persisted and, with them, their evil reputation.

"You saw her, Justin? You saw Miss Abigail?" Titus said thickly, carefully folding the letter, his eyes still moist.

Justin nodded. "I took her, with her sister and Mr. and Mrs. Boskenna, to their grant, Doctor. It's an isolated place, which the natives call Yarramundie, five miles upriver from the Green Hills settlement. Mr. Boskenna chartered the *Flinders* to carry them, with their laborers and provisions and some of their stock, up the Hawkesbury from Sydney."

"And you talked to Miss Abigail—she asked you to bring this letter to me?"

"Yes," Justin confirmed.

"Did she—that is, did Miss Abigail tell you that she is betrothed to me? Did she say that she has promised to become my wife?"

Conscious of the resentment it would be unwise to reveal, Justin, looking down at his feet, reddened and agreed that she had. He replied as lucidly as he could to a spate of questions concerning Abigail Tempest's demeanor and her state of health, the size and condition of the buildings and the farm itself, and finally the means by which the holding could best be reached.

To this he answered unhesitatingly, "By boat, Dr. Penhaligon. But only a vessel of light draught can ascend that far up the river. There are shallows above the Green Hills where it's easy to run aground." He started to explain, but Titus Penhaligon cut him short.

"Your *Flinders* is built for such work, is she not . . . and you ply for hire?"

"Yes, I do, sir, but"—Justin faced him uneasily, anticipating his next question—"I have just accepted a charter from here."

It was as if the surgeon had not heard him. He asked impatiently, "What charge would you make to convey me to Miss Tempest's property? I—I'm not a rich man, Justin, but I'd pay you whatever you deem a fair price, and—" He frowned, subjecting Justin to a brief but thorough scrutiny. Then, evidently deciding to trust him, he lowered his voice. "I should have to—to leave here without drawing attention to my departure. Would it be possible to hide me on board your boat?"

"I suppose it would," Justin admitted reluctantly, "if I'd no other passengers. But as I told you, Dr. Penhaligon, I've agreed to take a charter to the Hawkesbury. One of the Corps officers was waiting for me when I came ashore, you see, sir, and we arranged the matter then and there. I'm to take him, with his orderly and his horse, and—"

"Who, for God's sake?" Titus demanded hoarsely. "*Which* of the officers, Justin?"

"Lieutenant O'Shea, sir. He told me that the commandant has given him leave. He—"

"Oh, God in heaven! I suppose I should have known what he would do—I should have been prepared for it! The swine will rob me of Abigail if he can. Damme, that's his intention! That's why he's going to the Hawkesbury, Justin, don't you see? But Abigail is promised to *me!*"

Titus Penhaligon's distress was so plainly to be seen that Justin—although unwittingly the cause of it—found himself apologizing. But when Lieutenant O'Shea had approached him earlier that day, with the offer of a charter, he had attributed no sinister motives to the offer. Indeed, he had welcomed it, since it would mean that he could turn his voyage to profit and, furthermore, could make another call at Long Wrekin on his way back to Sydney. He endeavored to explain, but Titus was too angry and resentful to listen.

"Can you not refuse O'Shea's charter?" he asked wrathfully. "Don't you realize what you are doing? Abigail Tempest is my affianced wife. He has no right to pay court to her, no right to visit her, the devil take him! You're taking him there, are you not—you're taking him to the Tempest farm?"

"Yes," Justin conceded. "That's to say I'm taking Mr. O'Shea to the Green Hills. He says he'll ride to Yarramundie from there. But I cannot refuse his charter, Dr. Penhaligon. I gave him my word, and he's paid me half the hiring charge in advance."

"I'd pay you double!" Titus offered recklessly. "Every penny I have, Justin!"

Justin shrugged helplessly. "I cannot go back on my word, sir, whatever you're willing to pay me. I'd take

you along as well, if you wish, and without charge."
He hesitated, recalling Titus Penhaligon's request that
he would wish to leave without attention being drawn
to his departure, and asked bluntly, "Are you deserting
your post, Doctor? Going absent without leave?"

"Yes, I'm afraid that is what it would amount to,"
the surgeon admitted. "I've repeatedly applied to be
relieved of this post, but without success, and I cannot
stand it any longer. This is a terrible place, Justin. To
be expected to practice medicine here is . . . oh, my
God, it is heartbreaking! You can have no idea." He
started to describe some of the scenes he had witnessed
and the treatment of the sick and injured and then
broke off, shuddering violently. "I cannot speak of these
matters without shame. And I am powerless to alleviate the suffering. As a mere assistant surgeon, I am
under the orders of officers like O'Shea, who have no
pity and do not even permit me to feed the patients
I have in the hospital. They return to the mines and
the limekilns when they can scarcely walk, rather than
starve on bread and water. And . . . Justin, there is
Abigail! I must go to her before O'Shea does. She is
promised to me, and she needs me!" Titus took out his
letter and waved it in Justin's face. "I beg you, Justin
. . . take me to Yarramundie when you go . . . hide
me on board if you must. You can do that, surely?"

It occurred to the boy then that his own feelings for
Abigail must pale into insignificance in the face of
Penhaligon's impassioned appeal. For all his natural
caution and a wary reluctance to commit himself to
any enterprise that might damage his reputation and
lead to the revoking of his trader's license, Justin was
moved by the young surgeon's plight. It would not be
difficult to smuggle him on board the *Flinders,* he told
himself, and once on board the cutter there was plenty
of space in the hold where he could lie hidden, in reasonable comfort, until their destination was reached.

"All right, Dr. Penhaligon," he agreed. "I can, and I will hide you . . . for Miss Abigail's sake. And I want no payment. Come to the main government wharf at midnight and wait by the shallow water beneath it. I'll pick you up in my dinghy. Lieutenant O'Shea and his servant should be tucked up in their bunks by then, and I'll post my lad, Cookie Barnes, as lookout, to make sure they stay there."

"Won't you be searched?" Titus questioned nervously. "They search for stowaways in every vessel that leaves here."

"They won't search the *Flinders* with an officer on board," Justin responded confidently. "The tide turns at five thirty tomorrow morning, and I aim to be off Nobby's Head by first light, ready to cross the bar with the ebb. There's a six-knot current to take us across. But if you're not at the wharf by midnight, I'll not wait for you, understand . . . I can't, for the tide won't."

"I'll be there," Titus promised fervently, and wrung his hand. "God bless you, Justin! I shall be forever in your debt."

His transfer, by moonlight, from under the tall timber piles of the wharf, went without a hitch, and when Justin edged his dinghy alongside the anchored *Flinders,* the seaman, Cookie Barnes, was on deck to assist him to climb aboard. The hiding place prepared for him was dark and airless, but by no means uncomfortable. Even when Barnes draped a tarpaulin over him, Titus found that he could breathe quite easily. Worn out by his exertions, he sank down amongst the pile of empty grain sacks and rustling straw that littered the hold bottom and fell asleep almost instantly.

Cookie Barnes, a wizened little man with a gap-toothed smile, wakened him some hours later with a beaker half-filled with rum and a plate of bread and cheese. The cutter was pitching heavily in what seemed to be a choppy sea, and as he drew back the tarpaulin to enable Titus to sit up, he observed cheerfully, "Blowin' a bit, sir, ain't it? We're off Barranjoey Head, but once we weather that we'll be in Broken Bay an' headin' for the estuary, with the wind in our favor. You all right, sir? Quite cozy, are you?"

"Very cozy, thank you," Titus assured him, conscious of a sense of intense elation as the mists of sleep dispersed and he remembered why he was here, in the *Flinder*'s tossing hold. To have left Newcastle and Coal River behind him was reason enough for elation, he thought, sipping gratefully at the rum. But when, in addition to that, there was the imminent prospect of holding Abigail Tempest in his arms once again, why then . . . He drained the beaker in silent toast to his beloved and smiled back at Cookie Barnes in the darkness. "I could not be better, believe me, Cookie!"

"Well, that's more'n can be said o' our other passengers, sir," Barnes told him, with grinning satisfaction. "Loo'tenant O'Shea's in 'is bunk, wi' the blankets over 'is head, and 'is poor sod o' an orderly's as sick as a dog in the for-ard 'old, tryin' ter keep the 'orse on its feet. Neither of 'em's likely to be troublin' you for a while, sir, so I'll leave the tarpaulin off so's you can breathe a bit o' fresh air. Don't worry—I'll be back ter batten you down again as soon as they show signs o' stirrin'."

He was as good as his word, and the day passed without incident, the *Flinders* moving smoothly up the broad reaches of the Hawkesbury; and the only evidence of O'Shea's presence on board was the faint sound of his voice, floating down occasionally from the deck.

The settlement at Green Hills was distant only thirty-five miles from Sydney, Titus knew, but the curves of the river, from its mouth, rendered the distance almost four times greater, and it came as no surprise to him when Cookie Barnes, delivering his evening meal, told him that they would shortly come to anchor.

"Mr. Justin's steppin' ashore for a couple of hours, Doctor. But you've no call ter feel no concern on that account, 'cause I'll be 'ere, an' I'll keep me eyes peeled. Best try an' sleep, sir, if you can."

Titus did his best to follow the little man's sage advice, but it was becoming unpleasantly hot beneath the tarpaulin cover and he could only doze intermittently, disturbed by the thud of O'Shea's booted feet on the deck above and the constant fear of discovery this engendered. The Irish lieutenant was restless and—from the sound of his voice, which was slurred and ill tempered—drinking fairly heavily and impatient of the delay as the night wore on.

Justin returned in the early hours from whatever mission had taken him ashore. Titus heard his dinghy come alongside and the greeting he exchanged with Cookie Barnes; then, from the cabin hatchway, a bellow from Lieutenant O'Shea set his heart beating in sudden fear. Justin descended the hatchway, and their voices carried quite clearly to Titus's hiding place, O'Shea's loud and accusing, Justin's quiet and seemingly calm.

"So this is what you get up to, is it—you trade in rum with the settlers? Oh, but you're a fine fellow, Master Broome, faith you are! And you make a good living, I'll be bound."

"I live by hiring my boat," Justin defended.

"And to whom do you hire her?" O'Shea's tone was scornful. "To that sanctimonious bastard Robert Campbell, who sets himself up as port naval officer and levies government dues on all incoming spirits with such diligence? He's your employer, is he not?"

"I charter the *Flinders* to him when he needs her, sir, but I also carry government dispatches and mail when they're put out to tender," Justin answered without rancor. "And now, Mr. O'Shea, if you'll excuse me, I want to get under way. The moon is up, and we can be off the Green Hills by midday if we take advantage of it."

Titus, hearing him start to move away, was conscious of relief. But his relief was short lived, for O'Shea was not so easily put off, and icy prickles of fear coursed down Titus's spine when the lieutenant roared, "Not so fast, Broome! You've not answered my questions, you young rogue, and I've a few more to put to you before I'm done."

"Ask away, sir," Justin invited levelly, "but we're losing time and a good breeze, I must remind you."

"To the devil with that!" O'Shea retorted. Hearing the menace in his tone, Titus Penhaligon licked at lips that had suddenly gone dry. He would have given anything in the world for a pull at the rum bottle from which, if his interpretation of the gulping sound was correct, O'Shea was refreshing himself as he talked. He must have drained it, for a dull thud suggested that he had thrown it from him, so that it bounced down the hatchway ladder and shattered at its foot. "Tell your rapscallion of a seaman to fetch me another bottle," the Irishman ordered.

"I have no more on board, sir," Justin told him.

"You mean you've sold all you had to the bloody settlers! What was in those sacks you took ashore in your rowboat, eh? Kegs of rum wrapped in sacking, in the hope that I wouldn't spot what you were at, I'll be bound! The truth, Broome—let's have the truth, boy!"

"They were sacks of animal corn, sir." Justin continued to address his interrogator with quiet courtesy, although now his voice was a trifle strained. "I took them from my mother's farm on speculation, intending to sell them to your commandant at Coal River, but he did not want them, so I sold them here. And now, Mr. O'Shea, as I said, I'd like to get under way. If you will be good enough to go to your bunk, sir, I'll get my anchor up."

For a moment the listening Titus thought that Justin had won the wordy battle. There was a brief silence, but then O'Shea exclaimed harshly, "The hold! Damme, you have a large hold for cargo, have you not?"

"I have," Justin admitted, "but it is empty. I'm carrying no cargo. See for yourself if you've a mind to."

Titus waited, tense with dismay. If O'Shea called the lad's bluff and came down to the hold, he was lost— the tarpaulin would offer scant protection from a determined searcher, and the damned lieutenant was clearly determined to prove that Justin was engaged in the smuggling of liquor.

"I'll avail myself of that invitation, Master Broome," the Irishman said. "Tomorrow, in daylight, before I go ashore." He hiccoughed loudly, tripped on the hatch ladder, and gave vent to a spate of obscenities.

"Let me help you, sir," Justin offered. "Your bunk's made up, and I'll have Cookie brew you a cup of chocolate if you'd care for one."

"Be damned to your chocolate!" O'Shea retorted ungraciously. "Let him call me with it when we're in sight of the Green Hills."

Their voices receded, and Titus, sweating profusely, lay back, the tension slowly draining out of him. He knew he would have to get away before Cookie Barnes served O'Shea his chocolate, and he could only hope that Justin would devise some way for him to make his escape. He heard the anchor come up and felt the water lapping against the hull as the sails filled, and the *Flinders* heeled before the brisk offshore breeze.

Justin came, moving softly on bare feet, to lift a corner of the tarpaulin and push a steaming mug through the aperture and into his hand.

"Chocolate, Dr. Penhaligon," he announced softly, "laced with the few drops of rum our passenger has left us . . . and I fear you are going to need it. You heard what passed between us, did you not? You heard what Lieutenant O'Shea said?"

"Yes, I heard." Titus sipped eagerly at the fragrant

brew. "Justin, do you suppose he *will* search this hold?"

"He'll search the whole damned ship from stem to stern if I let him," Justin returned, "*and* if he remembers—he was pretty drunk, so it's on the cards that he won't. But I don't feel inclined to take the risk of his finding you . . . unless, of course, you are prepared to face him. Why are you not?"

"No!" Titus's voice was shrill with alarm. "For God's sake, Justin, I dare not!"

"Keep your voice down," Justin warned. He added curiously, "Why—what could he do? You're not an escaped felon, to be shot on sight."

"No. But I have deserted my post and that is a court-martial offense." Ashamed of his earlier outburst, Titus gulped down the contents of his mug. "O'Shea is a Corps officer. He could arrest me and insist that you take me back to Coal River, and he could send his orderly with me, to make sure I did go back."

"But he's bound to see you if you are both going to the Tempest farm, is he not?" Justin reasoned. "He could still arrest you there, surely?"

Titus set down his empty mug, his hand trembling. He was suddenly appalled by the probable consequences of his impulsive decision to quit his post, and anxious to justify it, to himself as well as to Justin. "Abigail will hide me, for long enough for us to be wed. That's all I want, that's all I'm going for . . . to wed Abigail. I don't care what happens after that. And Mr. Boskenna is an ordained minister—he can wed us."

"But *will* he?" Justin was unconvinced, remembering the black-garbed, formidable figure of Caleb Boskenna, which had interposed itself between him and Abigail on the *Flinder*'s deck, forbidding all intimacy during their recent voyage upriver. "He guards her like a hawk!"

"Justin, I have been Abigail's lover," Titus confided. He felt Justin stiffen but went on obstinately, "I'm in honor bound to make her my wife. I have given her my

word, I . . . Boskenna cannot refuse to wed us in the
circumstances, can he? Not if that is what Abigail wants,
and it is. Her letter told me so! We love each other,
don't you understand?"

"I am trying to understand." Justin picked up the
empty mug, toying with it, his expression inscrutable in
the darkness of the hold. "I don't doubt the truth of
what you've told me, but—"

Sensing an underlying antagonism in Justin's voice,
Titus was puzzled, but to his relief, Justin went on, his
tone now crisp and decisive. "All right, Dr. Penhaligon
—I'll put you ashore just below the Green Hills settlement whilst Mr. O'Shea is still sleeping off the effects
of my rum, and I'll hold him and his orderly up for as
long as I can. Long enough to give you a head start, at
all events, although you'll be on foot, and he'll be
mounted. It won't be above nine or ten miles to Yarramundie overland. It's rough country, but I'll draw you a
map, so that you won't lose your way. You should get
there well before he does, if you keep going."

Titus started to thank him, but Justin abruptly cut
him short. "I don't much care for Lieutenant O'Shea,"
he said coldly, "so the choice isn't difficult, is it? And
since mine's the same as Miss Abigail's, there is no more
to be said. Get some sleep, Doctor. I'll waken you in
plenty of time."

Dawn was gray in the sky when Titus was assisted
into the dinghy by Cookie Barnes with the *Flinders* still
in motion and Justin at the wheel. There were no fare-
wells; with a whispered injunction to hide the dinghy in
the reeds, to be picked up on their return, Cookie un-
hitched the painter and Titus found himself swiftly
drifting into midstream in the cutter's wake. He un-
shipped the oars and, without difficulty, rowed ashore,
to discover plenty of concealment among the thick vege-
tation growing beneath the river's steeply sloping bank.
Satisfied that the dinghy was well hidden, he clambered

up the bank, paused to get his bearings and consult
Justin's map, and then set off on his journey at a brisk,
swinging pace.

The country was, as Justin had warned him, rough
and thickly wooded, but apart from a flock of brightly
hued parakeets disturbed by his passing he saw no other
sign of life. Able to remain safely invisible behind the
screening gum and ironbark trees, Titus's fear of pursuit
diminished, and he slackened his pace to a steady tramp.
He made good progress and had covered what he estimated to be about four miles by the time the sun rose;
so he halted, to eat the bread and cheese Cookie Barnes
had provided him, slaking his thirst at a small inland
lake, on whose mirror-smooth surface a pair of swans
floated majestically.

It was an idyllic spot, and Titus would gladly have
lingered there to dream of his coming reunion with
Abigail; but, aware that time was passing all too swiftly,
he got to his feet and regretfully continued on his way.
The sun, which had been only pleasantly warm until
now, rose higher, generating a suffocating heat, and
hordes of stinging insects came in clouds to torment
him, so that of necessity he had to slow down. He took
off his jacket and loosened the cravat at his neck and,
head down, stumbled wearily on, slapping ineffectually
at the winged tormentors which alighted on his sweat-
drenched face.

Some two hours later he glimpsed the river again,
shimmering in the distance, and with intense relief, he
emerged at last from the trees onto a patch of recently
cleared land. But it was littered with stumps and partially grubbed-up roots, and quickening his pace incau-
tiously, he tripped and wrenched his right ankle. Cursing, he stopped to ascertain the extent of the damage
and, a moment afterwards, heard the thudding of a
horse's hooves approaching him from behind. He spun

round, his heart pounding, to see out of the corner of his eye a flash of scarlet among the trees.

O'Shea, he thought bitterly, O'Shea, devil take him, must have seen through Justin's attempt to delay his landing! Or the horse was faster than either he or the *Flinder*'s young master had anticipated.

Cursing in futile anger, Titus stood motionless, watching as horse and rider cantered from beneath the flickering shadows of the tall gums. O'Shea had not seen him. He was not hurrying, and he was alone, his orderly evidently left behind to follow him on foot. It was possible that he was not engaged in pursuit, that he had been unaware of the presence of a stowaway in the *Flinder*'s hold, and if that were so, there was still a chance of escape, a chance that he might hide himself. But . . . Titus looked about him in despair, seeking concealment and finding none, for he was on open ground, without so much as a fallen log behind which to crouch.

Ahead of him, perhaps a hundred yards away, a clump of stunted bushes crowned a low, rocky knoll, and he hesitated, measuring the distance, his hopes rising. But then O'Shea saw him and put spurs to his horse, emitting a loud foxhunter's "*View Halloo!*"

Titus yielded to panic. His stomach churning, he ran, making for the knoll, and O'Shea came after him, shouting something he could not hear but which he took to be a threat. He pounded on, half blinded by sweat, letting his jacket fall from his grasp as he staggered unsteadily toward the objective he had chosen, his wrenched ankle slowing him down and causing him excruciating pain.

"Stop, you idiot!" O'Shea yelled. "Stop!"

Titus scarcely heard him. He reached the knoll, tripped over an exposed root, and fell heavily, striking his head on the sharp, jagged edge of one of the rocks of which the knoll was composed, and blackness closed about him.

O'Shea reached him and drew rein, flinging himself from his saddle, mouthing angry obscenities. His rein looped over his scarlet-clad arm, he bent down to turn the fugitive over, then lapsed into stunned silence when he saw who it was.

"Penhaligon!" he managed at last. "Why, you damned fool, I'd no idea it was you! My man told me young Broome was harboring an escaper, but . . . oh, get up, man, for the Lord's sake! I intend you no harm."

Titus Penhaligon's eyes, wide open and dark with fear, gazed sightlessly up at him, blood pouring from the ugly wound on his temple. O'Shea felt for his heart, then withdrew his hand hastily when he realized that there was no heartbeat. He sat back on his heels, frowning and undecided; then his horse nuzzled him and the momentary numbness passed.

"You've brought this on yourself, you thrice-damned idiot!" he said aloud. "But it'll be as much as my commission is worth if I let them find you here."

Bracing himself, he picked up the body of his erstwhile rival and laid it across his saddlebow; then, remounting with some difficulty, he kicked his horse into motion and rode slowly toward the river.

Justin was worried when, a little after noon, he cast off the hawser which had secured his cutter *Flinders* to the wharf at the Green Hills settlement and, under mainsail and jib, set his course downriver.

He had given Titus Penhaligon all the time he could, he reflected, but O'Shea's meddlesome orderly had reported his suspicions concerning the presence of an escaper in the main hold and . . . He swore softly, letting the spokes of the wheel slip through his hands as he completed his tack and brought the light, fitful wind onto the larboard quarter, to enable him to run close enough inshore to pick up the dinghy.

O'Shea had spotted the absence of the dinghy, and although his search of the hold had revealed nothing, the Irish lieutenant had issued a severe enough warning before going ashore.

"If I find the miserable felon you've let loose, I'll have you before the court, Broome—and that will be the end of your license," he had threatened. "And you might forfeit your master's ticket into the bargain! So have a care, my lad. Stick to your rum trafficking in future. There's less chance of your being found out if you do."

And he had departed, smiling, having refused to pay the balance of his hiring charge on the grounds that Justin would have received ample reward from the supposed escaper. Damn Titus Penhaligon, Justin thought —he should never have listened to the fellow's tale of woe. And he would not have done so, would not have lifted a finger to help him, had he admitted at the outset that he was Abigail Tempest's seducer. Although that claim might well be false. Miss Abigail was a lady, born and bred; not the kind, surely, to permit liberties to any man, least of all to a penniless surgeon.

"There she is, Mr. Justin!" Cookie Barnes, a hand shading his eyes from the sun's glare, had seen the dinghy. He gestured to it with his free hand. "Didn't hide her too cleverly, did he?"

"No," Justin returned shortly. He spun his wheel and brought-to within thirty yards of the missing craft, sails flapping as he spilled their wind. "I'll get her. Take the wheel, Cookie, and make another tack, just in case there's anybody watching . . . that miserable redcoat of O'Shea's, maybe. He wasn't in overmuch hurry to leave the Green Hills, was he?"

He divested himself of jacket and shirt and swam

across to the bank with the long, easy strokes he had learned as a child in the creek at his mother's first farm, outside Parramatta. By the time Cookie tacked back across the river to meet him, he had the dinghy in the water, careful not to put out from the shore until the *Flinder*'s slender hull and flapping mainsail hid his movements from anyone who might be watching from the cluster of settlement houses.

He clambered back on board, dripping, and flashed Cookie a boyish grin.

"All right, friend, let's be on our way to Long Wrekin and, it's to be hoped, a good, home-cooked meal for a change. Maybe they haven't quite finished their New Year's celebration. . . . I hope, anyway, that Nancy Jardine has kept some of that fatted calf they killed on the chance that we'd be back to eat it!"

But when they presented themselves at the door of the farmhouse just before dusk, it was to find a new and welcome cause for celebration, for Justin heard his mother's voice, coming from the kitchen. He thrust past William, who had opened the door to him, ignoring the boy's eager attempt to give him the news of their mother's return, and went to take her into his arms and hug her.

Andrew, he noticed, was not with her, and when greetings had been exchanged and the two new arrivals seated at the table, his mother said, "Andrew has involved himself in a scandal of some kind, Justin—a ploy, he is certain, aimed deliberately to prevent the governor nominating him to sit on the bench at Mr. Macarthur's trial. He thought it best and more prudent if I came up here for a while."

Justin studied her face anxiously, but seeing that it was serene and untroubled, he contented himself with asking mildly, "Not for any other reason, Mam?"

"Oh, no," Jenny assured him. "I was treated like a queen on board the *Estramina,* the transport that gave me passage back to Sydney . . . and equally well by Colonel Collins in Hobart. He wants us—Andrew and myself, and the children, of course—to transfer to Van Diemen's Land. To take land there and settle, with Andrew appointed to his staff."

Justin accepted a plate piled high with food, but for a moment he did not touch it, his appetite suddenly vanishing.

"Will you do that?" he asked, and waited tensely for her answer.

Jenny hesitated and then, to his surprise, inclined her head. "Yes, Justin, I think we will. There are wonderful prospects for settlers now that the people from Norfolk Island are being transferred in such numbers to Hobart. The land is being opened up all along the Derwent River, and there are enough troops at last to give protection from the blacks, even on distant holdings." She talked on, with infectious enthusiasm, and Justin listened, toying with his food, uncertain whether to be pleased or to regret the decision she seemed so eager to make.

But that she *had* made it, he realized when she said, "I am seeing Tim Dawson tomorrow, to arrange to sell him Long Wrekin. He has promised he will keep the Jardines on if they want to stay here, and they have told me they do. I shall join Andrew in Sydney, with the children, when the sale is completed, and the . . . the vexatious matter I told you of is settled. After Captain Macarthur's trial, perhaps. So much seems to hang on that, Justin, and people in Sydney are talking of little else. Some of them are even afraid that it may come to a trial of strength between the governor and the Corps, but I hope they are wrong. Andrew thinks they are."

Andrew was probably trying to protect her, Justin thought, recalling what Robert Campbell had said and the views Andrew had expressed to him concerning the possible outcome of Macarthur's appearance in the criminal court. If there was trouble with the Corps, his mother would be safer here than in Sydney, with Tom Jardine and his fellow Loyalist Volunteers to keep the peace. He glanced across the table at William, wondering whether he would be upset at the prospect of leaving Long Wrekin, but his young brother avoided his eye, seemingly intent on his meal.

As if she had read his thoughts, Jenny said gently, "Willie may remain here if he wishes, although I should like him to attend school in Sydney." She put out a hand to take Justin's, clasping it affectionately, and added, lowering her voice so that the two children could not hear, "All is well with us, Justin dear, I promise you. I am carrying Andrew's child, and I am glad of it. And in any case, we cannot leave for Hobart, even if we want to, until the governor tells Andrew that he no longer requires his services."

And that, too, would almost certainly depend on the outcome of Macarthur's trial, Justin thought, but he did not say so. Instead, he raised his mother's small, work-worn hand to his lips and, his throat suddenly tight, offered his congratulations to her on the coming child.

Later, however, when William and he were alone together, William confided hoarsely, "Mam's not as happy as she pretends, Justin. There was some girl in Sydney that Captain Hawley got himself mixed up with. . . . I heard her telling Nancy Jardine about it, and she was crying. *I* reckon that's why she's come here, 'stead of staying in Sydney Town with *him*."

Justin eyed him thoughtfully for a moment and then cuffed him soundly. "You're a damned little blabbermouth, William, like I've always said! I know you don't much like Captain Hawley, but he's a very fine man, and Mam loves him. So just you keep a still tongue in your head or I'll wallop the hide off you, understand? I'm going to stop here for a while, and I'll be watching you—aye, and listening, too. Now off you go to your bed."

Chastened, William did as he had been bidden, and quiet descended on the small farmhouse.

CHAPTER XVIII

It was Martha Boskenna who first became aware of the deterioration in Abigail's health, and she—rather than Abigail herself—who first suspected the cause of it.

The girl did not eat. She was pale and listless and obviously unhappy, and whenever possible, she avoided all other company—including that of her sister—preferring to wander about the new land grant by herself, sometimes on horseback but more usually on foot.

Leaving the management of the farm to Caleb Boskenna, she seemed to care little for what he did and to be indifferent to the plans he made for improvement in the breeding of stock and the clearing of additional land for planting.

Even his attempts to establish friendly relations with the native tribe in the area failed to arouse her enthusiasm. She watched him struggling to teach them to speak English, as a necessary prelude to their conversion to Christianity, but offered him neither help nor encouragement.

In striking contrast to her sister, Lucy, who had entered blithely into their new life, Abigail was uncommunicative and depressed, shut off from all of them in a solitary world of her own creation. She had gone downriver in the launch to attend the Christmas celebration service of worship, which Caleb Boskenna had conducted for the settlers at the Green Hills, but she had not contributed to its success in any way, Martha Boskenna recalled resentfully. Indeed, the wretched girl had barely opened her mouth . . . not even to join in the hymn singing that, to exiles in a heathen and inhospitable land, meant a great deal at such a time.

Unable initially to fathom the reason for her behavior, Martha decided to keep her under close observation, and it was as a result of rising one morning before dawn in order to follow her that a vague but unvoiced suspicion became certainty. Abigail had crept quietly from the room she shared with Lucy and, with a shawl over her nightclothes, had tiptoed in the semidarkness to the screened pit which served the three female occupants as a privy. And there, to Martha's shocked dismay, the girl had retched and coughed her heart out.

It was betrayal of her condition; the proverbial attack of nausea, in the early morning, that pregnancy induced, and there was nothing to do but tax her with it, in the hope of obtaining an admission before taking the disquieting news to the head of the household. But Martha hesitated, all too well aware of what her husband's reaction was likely to be and of the Christian fury she would provoke when she told him what she had learned. Certainly, the girl deserved to be punished, Martha thought, but as she stood, undecided, in the shadows beyond the wooden screen, Abigail emerged, a slim, white wraith in the dimness, still having to stifle her painful retching.

With her shawl tightly clutched about her, she set off at an awkward, stumbling run for the laborers' quarters on the far side of the fenced stockyard at the rear of the farmhouse. Shocked and incredulous, Martha Boskenna followed her at a discreet distance, saw her halt by the sheep pen, and, in response to her call, saw Jethro Crowan, the shepherd, come out to join her.

"Miss Abigail"—Jethro's voice was low but it carried clearly enough—"I weren't sure if you'd be comin'."

"I told you I would," Abigail answered. "Did you go to the Green Hills yesterday?"

"That I did, miss . . . promised you, didn't I? But there weren't no letter. I asked partic'lar, but the government storekeeper said nothin' had come."

"Oh . . . oh, I see." There was bitter disappointment in Abigail's voice and a hint of tears, but she controlled herself and thanked the shepherd gravely.

Jethro touched his forelock. "Storekeeper did say as one o' them aborigines told him there were a sailboat anchored a ways down the river, miss."

"A—a sailboat? Oh, Jethro, did you look for it?" Abigail seized on the hope his words had aroused, and Martha saw her clutch his arm in her eagerness. "Did you see whose it was?"

Jethro shook his head. "Nay, Miss Abigail, not I. You'm forgettin' it were dark when I did reach the Green Hills. Couldn't leave here afore I'd finished me work, now, could I, miss? The reverend would've had summat to say if I'd done that, sure enough."

"Yes. Yes, of course he would. I *was* forgetting, I—" Abigail repeated her thanks, waited for a moment, as if about to say more, but then, changing her mind, she gathered up her skirts and started back toward the house.

Martha Boskenna stepped swiftly into the shadow of an outbuilding. The girl passed her with only a few yards separating them, but—not having any idea that she had been followed—she did not look round or spare the outbuilding a second glance. Jethro, however, was more observant. He strode across to the outhouse door and, clearly suspecting the presence of an intruder, raised the heavy, crooked stick he was carrying in a threatening attitude, only to halt with a gasp of dismay when Martha addressed him authoritatively by name.

"Oh, 'tis you, Mrs. Boskenna ma'am," he managed uncertainly. "Is there summat I can be doin' for you, p'raps?"

"Indeed there is," Martha returned severely. "You can tell me, for a start, what Miss Abigail was doing here at this hour? Did she send you to the Green Hills to pick up a letter?"

"She did ask me to go along there, yes, ma'am," the shepherd admitted. "But 'twas in me own time, ma'am, not in workin' hours."

"And you brought her a letter?" Martha accused.

Indignantly, Jethro denied it. "Why, no, 'cause there weren't no letter to bring."

"But Miss Abigail was expecting one, was she not? That was why she sent you to the Green Hills?"

Jethro was loyal to his young mistress, but he was not overintelligent, and he fell easily into the trap. "Been expectin' that there letter a while now, Miss Abigail has," he explained regretfully. "But it ain't come, not yet, ma'am. Letters do take a time here, gettin' from one part to t'other. Even from Sydney."

"But this letter—the one Miss Abigail is expecting—isn't coming from Sydney, is it, Jethro?" Martha suggested shrewdly. "Do you know who would be writing her letters? Did she tell you?"

Belatedly realizing that he had said too much, Jethro shook his head sullenly and attempted to evade the question. "There be her brother, Master Richard—he'm in the navy, ma'am, a'servin' in one o' the King's ships. I do reckon as he'd write to Miss Abigail when he could."

"She would not send you all the way to the Green Hills after dark, just on the chance that there might be a letter from her brother, I'm quite sure," Martha said tartly. "Come now, Jethro—I want the truth, do you

understand? If you refuse to tell me the truth, I shall
have to report your conduct to Mr. Boskenna . . . and
you know what that will mean, do you not?"

It was evident that Jethro knew only too well. He
shrugged resignedly. "The letter was to come from Coal
River, ma'am, that was all Miss Abigail said."

It was enough. Lucy had talked of Abigail's romantic
yearning for Titus Penhaligon, Martha recalled, and of
how she had grieved when the young surgeon had been
sent to Coal River. Desmond O'Shea was also there, of
course, but if Lucy were to be believed, her sister's
choice had fallen on his rival. There had been nothing
between them during the voyage out in the *Mysore*—she
and Mr. Boskenna had seen to that—but under Frances
Spence's lax care, who knew what opportunities might
have been afforded them? Opportunities for intimacy,
for seduction. Martha Boskenna drew in her breath
sharply, hearing again Abigail's painful retching, and
left now in little doubt as to its cause.

Jethro muttered something about his sheep and
started to move away, but, with an edge to her voice,
Martha called him back. She said Titus Penhaligon's
name and the shepherd stared at her blankly; then,
when she repeated it, he gave his reluctant assent.

"Aye, from him. But there's been no letter, Mrs.
Boskenna. I'd take my oath on that."

"And the sailboat, the one you told Miss Abigail
about?"

"Like I said to her, I never seen it," Jethro retorted.
" 'Twas just some blackfellow's talk, but I thought
maybe it'd cheer her up."

Martha let him go and started slowly to retrace her
steps to the house, still undecided as to what action to
take. If she told her husband what she had found out,
then he would wring the truth from Abigail, at no matter what cost to her feelings. Perhaps, in common justice, she ought to speak to the girl first and warn her

that her guilty secret was discovered, her wicked, immoral conduct now known to one, at least, of her guardians.

But when she entered the house, Martha realized that she had been left with no discretion in the matter, for Abigail crouched weeping in the corner of the lamplit kitchen, and Caleb stood over her, his riding whip in his hand and his voice raised in thunderous condemnation.

That he had used the whip ferociously was at once apparent to his wife's alarmed eyes. Abigail's nightdress had been torn from her shoulders, and there were deep weals crisscrossing the naked skin of her back and arms and even one across her face, which had raised a livid bruise. But she wept soundlessly and did not cry out, and, seemingly unaware of Martha's presence—or indifferent to it—she did not look up when the door opened to admit her.

"So must sinners be punished for their sins against the Lord!" Caleb Boskenna proclaimed. "By chastisement must they be made to repent and, thereafter, humbly kneeling before Him, pray for His divine forgiveness!"

He raised the whip again, but Martha put out a shaking hand to restrain him. "Mr. Boskenna, that is enough! I beg you to leave her be!"

He let the whip fall and turned to look at her, his bearded face white as death, his eyes oddly glazed. For a moment he seemed scarcely to recognize her, but then he controlled himself.

"This girl," he said, in a strained but quieter tone, "despite her upbringing and the care we have lavished upon her, is a wanton! A wanton, Mrs. Boskenna, on her own confession! I was here, in this kitchen, when she endeavored to creep back to her bed without being seen, after consorting with one of the convict laborers— and in her nightclothes! And she admits that she is pregnant!"

"Yes, I believe she is," Martha answered, still retaining her grasp of his arm. "But the man responsible for her condition is not one of our laborers—there is that, at least, to be thankful for." Breathlessly, she recounted what she had learned from Jethro and, turning to Abigail, invited her to deny it if she could. "Surgeon Penhaligon has been your lover, your seducer, has he not? Answer me, Abigail!"

"We . . . we love each other," Abigail managed, in a subdued whisper. Holding her torn nightdress about her, she drew herself up into a half-sitting position and added, with a brave attempt to retain something of her lost dignity, "Dr. Penhaligon asked me to marry him, and I . . . I accepted his proposal. He will come here, so that we may be wed, as soon as he is granted leave of absence from Coal River. He *promised* he would come, Mrs. Boskenna. Truly he—does love me, and I—"

"But he has not kept his promise, has he?" Martha Boskenna countered scornfully. "He has not come, and he has not written to tell you that he is coming. You are a foolish, misguided girl, Abigail, and you have allowed yourself to be led astray by a feckless young adventurer who hasn't a penny to his name! You have disgraced yourself and betrayed the trust Mr. Boskenna and I resposed in you."

"She has behaved like the wanton she is," Caleb Boskenna put in. His tone was icy, but, to his wife's relief, his bitter anger had been brought under control. "We must pray for her, pray that she will see the error of her ways. She has disappointed me sorely—the more so, since I gave my consent to an honorable suitor, who asked in the proper manner if he might pay court to her, a young gentleman with excellent prospects." He turned to Abigail, his dark eyes curiously bright but wholly devoid of pity. "Lieutenant O'Shea, Abigail, was eager to wed you. He will not, I fear, wish to do so now."

Abigail hung her head, the tears falling again and running unstaunched down her bruised, unhappy face. But she said nothing, and Martha looked in mute question at her husband. He shrugged and offered harshly, "Lock her in her room, Mrs. Boskenna, on bread and water. You will have to let Lucy move in with you for the time being—she must not be told anything nor be allowed to speak to her sister, lest she too, become contaminated."

Martha nodded. "I expect the child is still asleep. I will carry her into my room before she wakens. Go and wash your face, Abigail, and then go to your bedroom."

Abigail obeyed without protest. Lucy had been moved by the time she returned to the bedroom, and Martha placed a Bible in her hands before closing the door on her, with a stern injunction to her to read it and pray for forgiveness.

"I cannot lock you in," she finished, "since there is no lock. But consider yourself banished from all other parts of the house and, in particular, from all contact with Lucy and that rogue Jethro Crowan."

Dusk was falling when Lieutenant O'Shea made his appearance. Martha saw him when he was still some way off, and recognizing him by his uniform, she hurried in search of her husband. Finding him in the feed store, she raised a cautionary finger to her lips and said, when he had dismissed the two convict laborers who were working there, "Mr. Boskenna, we have a visitor, and I think it is Lieutenant O'Shea. It is unfortunate, is it not? His arrival could scarcely have been more ill timed."

Caleb's heavy dark brows met in a frown. "It could not," he agreed. "And it goes without saying that he must not see Abigail in her present state. All will be lost if he does! But where, I wonder, can he have sprung from? We had no warning of his coming."

"Jethro spoke of a boat—a sailboat, he called it—

which was at anchor some miles downriver from the
Green Hills," Martha supplied, suddenly remembering
the conversation she had overheard between Abigail
and the shepherd. "He said that one of the aborigines
had reported it last night. But—" They looked at each
other in dismay, both struck by the same thought.
"Could it be," Martha asked, in a subdued voice, "could
it possibly be that Abigail was right, Mr. Boskenna? If
the boat has come from the Newcastle settlement, may
not her vile seducer have come here, as well as Lieutenant O'Shea?"

Her husband considered the suggestion, his frown
deepening, but finally he shook his head. "Not with
O'Shea's knowledge, wife—of that I feel sure. But if
he *has* come—with or without it—he will receive no
welcome from me."

"No, of course not." Martha moved toward the door
of the shed, straightening her apron. "But Mr. O'Shea
must be made welcome, must he not, for all his arrival
is so ill timed? Do you suppose that in these—these circumstances, he will keep to the bargain he made with
you?"

"Oh, yes, he will keep to it," Caleb asserted. "But we
shall have to tread warily, Mrs. Boskenna, for we have
much at stake. Far more than the paltry hundred and
fifty sovereigns of the late Mr. Edmund Tempest's estate
I promised the young gentleman . . . though he wants
that badly enough. And the girl, too." His expression
relaxed, suddenly, and Martha saw that he was smiling,
once more slipping into his accustomed role as the pur-
poseful, upright man of God. "It is a pity we did not
bring the midwife with us—what was her name? Lamerton, Kate Lamerton. But there is a woman of her kind
at the Green Hills, I believe, who will serve just as well.
Jethro can go and fetch her, since he is so eager to
spend his time there with the settlers."

Martha did not pretend to misunderstand him, and the color drained from her thin cheeks. "Suppose Abigail should refuse, Mr. Boskenna? After all, she—" Her eyes held fear, as she looked up at him. "And suppose Titus Penhaligon does come here, determined to wed her?"

"Penhaligon will be sent packing," he assured her. "By O'Shea as well as myself. And Abigail will be given no choice in the matter. She has sinned, and she must take the consequences. Come, wife"—he offered her his arm—"let us put a good face on it, for O'Shea's benefit. You can tell him that Abigail is indisposed . . . and this evening you can remove her, with her bedding, to this shed, for he must not be permitted to set eyes on her for a day or two."

"If you say so, Mr. Boskenna," Martha acknowledged submissively. She was leaning heavily on his arm as they went together to welcome the new arrival.

It was two days later when, in search of a missing ewe, Jethro Crowan stumbled on Titus Penhaligon's body, washed up among a clump of mangroves at the river's edge.

The body was bloated and already starting to decompose in the heat, but the shepherd recognized it; shocked and alarmed, he hurried back to give the Reverend Caleb Boskenna the tragic news. The chaplain, as shocked as he was, started to speculate as to the reason for the young surgeon's presence on their land, but Desmond O'Shea cut him short.

"So that was who young Broome had stowed away in his hold!" he exclaimed, in well-simulated surprise. "My fellow said he was hiding someone, but I searched and did not find a soul. Poor devil . . . I suppose he must have tried to swim ashore in darkness and drowned among the mangroves."

"But why should he try to swim ashore in darkness?" Boskenna questioned. "He would not have been welcome here, but for all that he may have decided to come uninvited, and—"

"He was probably trying to conceal his presence from me," O'Shea said. "I had chartered Broome's boat to bring me here, but Penhaligon did not apply for leave of absence. He must have quit his post without it and bribed Justin Broome to let him stow away, in case I tried to send him back to the Newcastle settlement. We were—ah—rivals, of course, for Miss Abigail's affections, but, devil take it, I'd not have attempted to stop the stupid young idiot from seeing her if that was what he wanted." He smiled and laid his hand on Caleb Boskenna's arm. "I've no reason to fear any rival, have I, sir? Least of all poor Penhaligon."

"No," Boskenna assured him warmly. "I do not think so, Mr. O'Shea."

John Macarthur was at the house of the government surveyor, Charles Grimes, when Sergeant Major Whittle presented himself at the door, in uniform, with the request that he might be received on urgent and confidential business.

A servant showed him in, and Macarthur greeted him with a pleasant smile. "Well, now, Mr. Whittle, what business is it that requires my urgent attention, pray? Do you bring me good news or bad?"

"It's bad, sir, I'm sorry to have to tell you," Whittle said. In uniform he looked flabby and overweight, but his manner—in marked contrast to that which he assumed when following his civilian occupation in the St. Patrick—was stiffly correct. "That fence, sir, the one you wanted my men to erect on your land off Church Street—" He hesitated, looking down at his well-polished boots and seeking to gauge the other's mood.

"Well?" Macarthur prompted, without impatience. "What happened to the fence?"

"My lads had to pull it down, sir, on orders from the governor," Whittle told him.

Macarthur sighed deeply. "I am indeed being victimized, am I not, Mr. Whittle? I own the leasehold, but am not permitted even to fence the land, still less to build on it! But *you* were permitted to continue your house building, I believe?"

"Aye, sir. Since you arranged the transfer of the lease, nothing's been said," the sergeant major confirmed. "The house is nearly finished, thanks to you."

"Yet *I* am singled out for unjust treatment," Macarthur observed wryly. "And, as you are doubtless aware—since you obtained the indictment from Crossley for me—I'm to be charged with virtually every crime that lying scoundrel and his crony the judge advocate can devise! Imagine it, Mr. Whittle. I am accused of raising dissatisfaction and discontent against the constitutional government, of endeavoring to bring His Excellency the governor into disrespect, hatred, and contempt, and, not least, of using false, libelous, and seditious words! In short, I am to be branded a traitor and a seditionist if *Bounty* Bligh and his supporters have their way."

He had spoken calmly and without heat, and Whittle, while protesting his ignorance of the charges and his disgust at the nature of them, eyed him with some misgiving. "Are you not angry, sir?"

"I am past anger," Macarthur confessed.

"But surely you're going to defend yourself, sir— you're going to refute the charges? I did not take time to read 'em after they . . . that is to say, after Lawyer Crossley let his papers fall out o' his pocket over at The Settlers, I sent 'em to you at once. Knowing how badly you wanted a sight of what he was cooking up. . . ." Whittle flashed him a conspiratorial grin, but finding this ignored, he added hastily, "You *must* defend yourself, Captain Macarthur, sir!"

"Oh, I shall, most certainly. Honor demands, however, that I must do so in the public court, so that the whole colony may know that these charges are entirely and utterly false. But you must understand, Mr. Whittle"—John Macarthur laid a hand on the older man's scarlet-clad arm—"the judge advocate has borne malice against me for years. In addition he is my debtor. He owes me a considerable sum of money, which he has unlawfully failed to repay. I have petitioned the governor repeatedly, in the interests of justice, to replace Mr. Richard Atkins by appointing in his stead a man— damme, *any* man—who can be relied upon to act impartially. But . . . he refuses. I cannot therefore expect a fair trial, can I?"

Whittle shook his bullet head in some bewilderment, and Macarthur went on, his voice now vibrant with feeling. "I once wore the uniform of the Corps, Sergeant Major, with pride, and, I swear to you, with honor and unswerving loyalty to His Majesty the King and his interests in this colony. But now, at Captain Bligh's instigation, my brother officers, my onetime comrades in arms, are to be compelled to sit in judgment upon me, presided over by an evil rogue, whose aim is to deprive me of my property, liberty, honor, and even of my life! Will you stand by and let one who has been a generous benefactor to you and to your soldiers go to that court hearing in fear of his life, Mr. Whittle?"

Whittle's expression was still one of bewilderment, but he shook his head again, this time with great vehemence. He had come simply to inform his benefactor of the enforced removal of his fence and had not anticipated an appeal to involve himself further. There was no doubt that Captain Macarthur had been his benefactor and that a reaffirmation of his loyalty was being called for and would not come amiss. He gave it and was rewarded by a warmly approving smile.

"You've served me well, Thomas, particularly in the —ah—the matter of Captain Hawley, who has not been nominated to sit as one of my judges."

"No, sir, so I understand. Although"—Whittle's tone was apologetic—"those grasping bitches I employed have retracted their evidence, bad cess to them! They—"

"It is of no consequence now." Macarthur waved the apology aside. "Now, before I let you go, there is one small service you can perform for me, if you will."

"You have only to ask, sir, but I—" Whittle was aware that this time his voice lacked conviction, and his gaze went, once again, to his polished boots. He was, he knew, already committed to John Macarthur's cause, for good or ill, and he could not back out now. "What can I do for you, sir?" he asked flatly.

"You can see to it that the court is well attended by your soldiers, Sergeant Major—in the public seats, of course—for as long as my trial lasts. And"—Macarthur led his visitor to the door, courteously holding it open for him—"you will not find me ungrateful and neither will they, I give you my word."

Sergeant Major Whittle drew himself up, gave him an impeccable salute, and marched off, a ramrod-stiff figure in his scarlet uniform.

Left alone, John Macarthur returned to the sitting room and seated himself at his host's desk. Drawing a sheet of writing paper toward him, he addressed a letter to the governor.

He began by employing the conventional courtesies:

> I must, with regret, protest most strongly against Your Excellency's decision to suffer Richard Atkins, Esq., to sit as a judge at my impending trial.

It is, I believe, my lawful right to request that an impartial judge be appointed.

He paused, frowning. Devil take it, the letter was not strong enough!

The reason on which I found my objection is that this gentleman is deeply interested in obtaining a verdict against me, insomuch that should he fail of so doing, he, in the ordinary course of things, must inevitably descend from the proud character of a prosecutor to the humble and degraded one of a prisoner, called upon to defend himself at the very bar to which he is about to drag me, for the false imprisonment I have suffered under the authority of his illegal warrant.

I would remind Your Excellency, furthermore, that Mr. Atkins has for years cherished a rancorous enmity against me, which he has displayed in the propagation of malignant falsehoods. . . .

That was better, he decided, after reading it through. Even if the letter failed to persuade Bligh to change his mind, it was at least calculated to annoy him.

He sealed it and summoned Grimes's servant.

"See that this is delivered to Government House, if you please," he told the man. "And should your master return during my absence, inform him that I have gone to the Corps officers' mess and that he is welcome to join me there."

"Very good, sir," the servant acknowledged. "Will you be requiring your horse, sir?"

Macarthur hesitated and then shook his head. "No, I shall walk. I have some thinking to do."

And indeed, he told himself, as he set off at a leisurely pace for the barracks, there was much to think about and plan, with his trial less than a week away.

With a modicum of luck, however, his judges—with the exception of Richard Atkins—would be in the mess, ready and willing to listen to whatever he had to say to them.

After that—this afternoon, perhaps—he would pay a brief visit to Parramatta to reassure Elizabeth, and young Edward and his nephew, Hannibal, could accompany him on his return to Sydney, in case they were needed.

He was smiling as he entered the Corps mess, his plan of action now clear in his mind.

Governor Bligh was at his desk when Andrew came to report to him on the evening of January twenty-fourth. He looked up to nod a greeting and gestured to a chair.

"Well?" he demanded brusquely. "What are the scoundrels up to? I presume they're making an occasion of it?"

Andrew seated himself in the chair the governor had indicated, eyeing him warily before committing himself to a reply. But Bligh appeared more resigned than out of temper; and he had, according to Edmund Griffin, made a conciliatory gift of a cask of wine to the Corps mess when Major Johnstone had sought his formal permission for the holding of a guest night, to celebrate the anniversary of the founding of the colony.

"Yes, sir, they are—quite an occasion."

"You've been to the barracks, I presume?"

Andrew inclined his head. "In common with half the inhabitants of Sydney, sir. They have the Corps colors flying outside the mess and the band playing on the parade ground." He described the scene in some detail and heard the governor give vent to a long, pent-up sigh.

"And the guests? Did you see who Johnstone had invited?"

"Some of them, sir, yes. The surgeons, Jamieson,

Townson, and Mileham—the Blaxlands, Jasper Spence, Grimes, of course, and Garnham Blaxcell. And Hannibal Macarthur was there; I saw him go in a trifle belatedly."

"Ha! What about his esteemed uncle?"

Andrew's mouth tightened. John Macarthur's performance had been, to say the least, theatrical. "He made a great point of being seen by the crowd, sir. I saw him walking up and down in front of the band. The bandmaster asked him his pleasure, and he requested the regimental march. Some of the people cheered him, and the soldiers on guard presented arms to him. He was still there when I left, sir."

"Was he, now?" Bligh swore disgustedly. "In all my years in the service, Andrew, I have never come across any man who could equal John Macarthur for sheer effrontery. In truth, I don't expect to! I presume his judges were all there?"

"I saw Brabyn and Laycock, sir, and the adjutant, Minchin. Brabyn had Dr. Harris as his guest, I think. At all events, Macarthur had quite a lengthy chat with both of them, before they went into the mess hall."

"It is all much as I anticipated," the governor said. "He's making damned sure they won't convict him, but what the devil can I do? Under the constitution of this colony, only commissioned officers may sit as justices in the criminal court, and it would take an act of Parliament to alter that. My only instrument of justice is the blasted judge advocate, and Macarthur has been bombarding me with demands that he be replaced because he's . . . damme, where did I put his latest humble petition?" Bligh sought among the papers on his desk and, finding John Macarthur's most recent letter, read from it indignantly. "Atkins, he claims, *'has for years cherished a rancorous enmity'* against him! Well, perhaps he has and small wonder, but it's still not within my power to supersede him. In God's name, I wish I could! It's a damned pity *you* got yourself mixed up with that young whore."

"Yes, sir," Andrew acknowledged. He had already suffered the rough side of William Bligh's tongue concerning the matter of Dorcas Croaker, and despite the fact that her mother had inexplicably withdrawn her charges against him, she had done so too late. Major Johnstone had refused, point blank, to nominate him as a member of the court, and even Jenny, when she had first disembarked from the *Estramina,* had been hurt and perplexed when the unpleasant story had reached her ears. But, wise in the governor's ways, Andrew made no attempt to excuse or defend himself, and Bligh, continuing to search among his papers, gave vent to an irritated exclamation as he brought a second letter to light.

"The devil take it! This is another humble petition, and it's one my daughter, Mrs. Putland, has urged me repeatedly to answer favorably! A plea from that young assistant surgeon, Penhaligon, to be relieved of his post at the Newcastle settlement. He was very good to my poor son-in-law, during his last illness—a most competent and reliable young man. I instructed Dr. Jamieson weeks ago to arrange for his relief, but a plague on the fellow, it seems he hasn't done so!" He picked up the small brass bell on his desk and rang it loudly.

Edmund Griffin, his secretary, responded at once, hurrying in from the adjoining room, which he used as an office. Bligh gave him the petition.

"For the Lord's sweet sake, answer this, Edmund! Tell Penhaligon that he's relieved and inform Dr. Jamieson that I want Assistant Surgeon Penhaligon sent back to Sydney with the utmost expedition. What vessels are due to call at Coal River in the near future?"

"None that I know of, sir," Griffin said, "but I'll make inquiries."

"Do so," the governor bade him, and then, as an

afterthought, he turned to Andrew. "What about that stepson of yours—what's the lad's name? Broome, is it not?"

"Yes, sir, Justin Broome."

"Does he not hire that cutter of his?"

"He does, sir, yes. But he's away on a charter at the present time, to the Hawkesbury," Andrew answered. "He should be back here fairly soon."

"Good, good!" Bligh approved. "Then, as soon as he comes to anchor in the cove, give him a charter from me—an official one. He can take Penhaligon's relief to the Newcastle settlement and bring Penhaligon himself back to Sydney. And I intend to have the commandant at Newcastle relieved as well, if I can prevail upon Major Johnstone to agree to it. If even half of what young Penhaligon has told me about conditions in the settlement is true, it's high time the sadistic swine entrusted with the command is replaced. I've another of Penhaligon's petitions here somewhere . . . ah, yes, here it is. Read it for yourself, Andrew."

Andrew obeyed and was appalled and sickened by what he read, set out carefully, with reference to names and dates, in Assistant Surgeon Titus Penhaligon's neat hand.

"Well," the governor said, when he returned the document, "we had better not keep my daughter waiting any longer for dinner, and there's really nothing more we can do here this evening. But I want you in court tomorrow, Andrew. Most of Sydney will be there, seeking places, I don't doubt, but I've instructed Willie Gore to reserve a seat for you."

CHAPTER XIX

The courtroom was packed to capacity, the rank and file of the Corps being much in evidence. A large body of them, led by Sergeant Major Whittle, had taken the seats reserved for the general public several hours before the court was due to convene, William Gore told Andrew in worried tones.

He added, lowering his voice, "I hope to heaven they don't intend trouble, for I have only half a dozen constables on duty here. Do you think it would be prudent to call up reinforcements, Captain Hawley?"

"Probably not," Andrew answered, after some thought. "It might be misunderstood. The troops aren't armed—they're here, presumably, on their own time, and are not intended to do much more than provide moral support."

"For whom?" The provost marshal challenged wryly. "The law or John Macarthur?"

Andrew shrugged and went to take the seat Gore had kept for him. He found himself next to Thomas Arndell, who had been assistant surgeon on board the transport *Friendship* of Governor Phillip's first fleet. Now aged and graying—as he himself was, Andrew thought ruefully—Arndell had retired from the government service, in order to farm at Parramatta.

Arndell eyed him for a moment without recognition and then smilingly held out his hand.

"Captain Hawley, is it not, of the Royal Marines and on the governor's staff? And married, I think I heard, to a most affectionately regarded friend of mine, who came out here as Jenny Taggart on board the same ship as myself?"

"That is so, sir," Andrew confirmed, accepting the surgeon's proffered hand.

"Thomas Arndell," the older man supplied. He asked about Jenny and then said, in a confidential whisper, "I have come to support the governor, for what that is worth, and also, I confess, out of a certain curiosity. I want to see how my near neighbor, Mr. John Macarthur, contrives to extricate himself from these charges, as undoubtedly he will endeavor to, although theoretically the odds are stacked against him. What, I have asked myself, will be his opening gambit? Attack or defense?"

It was not long before his question was answered. Punctually at ten o'clock the members of the court filed in—all of them in uniform and all officers of the Corps. They were followed by Richard Atkins, the judge advocate, who formally administered the oath to each in turn, as the law required, naming them in order of their seniority.

"Captain Anthony Fenn Kemp . . . Lieutenant John Brabyn . . . Lieutenant William Moore . . . Lieutenant Thomas Laycock . . . Lieutenant William Minchin . . . Lieutenant William Lawson."

Before Atkins himself could take the oath or read the indictment there was a dramatic interruption. John Macarthur, who had duly surrendered to his bail, rose to his feet. Standing arrogantly in the dock, he said in a loud and carrying voice, "Gentlemen, I wish to

protest against Mr. Richard Atkins's presence in this
court and to his presiding at my trial. He is an old
and inveterate enemy of mine, of whose vindictive
malice I have long been the victim and from whom I
clearly cannot expect the fair trial that is my right. . . ."

The rest of his protest was drowned in uproar, as
those in the body of the court gave him clamorous support, a number of them standing up and stamping their
feet, a few even shaking their fists in Atkins's direction
when he attempted to make reply.

Captain Kemp eventually restored order.

"Perhaps, sir," he said, addressing Macarthur, "you
would be good enough to inform this court in detail
of your objections against Mr. Atkins."

In the ensuing silence, a smile curving his lips, John
Macarthur delivered a lengthy diatribe, frequently referring to the pages of notes in his hand.

Most of his accusations were the same as those he
had previously made in his letters to the governor,
Andrew realized, recognizing a familiar turn of phrase
and the implied suggestions of bias and malicious
persecution on the judge advocate's part.

"Furthermore, gentlemen," Macarthur declared, "I
must tell you that Mr. Atkins has associated himself
with that well-known dismembered limb of the law,
George Crossley, to accomplish my destruction by
means of a conspiracy, entered into between them, to
deprive me of my property, honor, and life! Here gentlemen, is the indictment Crossley prepared. It was
dropped from his pocket in an alehouse and brought
to me. Read it for yourselves if you doubt my veracity!"

A gasp went round the crowded courtroom, as an
usher, in response to Macarthur's nod, took the paper
he was holding out and carried it across to the bench.
Richard Atkins, red faced and almost inarticulate with
rage, attempted once again to make himself heard.

"I declare that this is no court!" he bellowed. "The

trial cannot proceed until I am sworn in as president, and . . ." But, once again, he found himself shouted down. Leaving his papers on the table in front of the seated officers, he stalked across to the door of the courtroom and sat heavily down on a wooden form, normally occupied by a constable.

Captain Kemp waited until he had gone and then, quite good humoredly, asked for silence. His request was instantly complied with, and, turning to the dock, he asked courteously, "Have you anything else to tell us, pertaining to this matter of the present judge advocate, Mr. Macarthur?"

"Indeed, sir, I have," Macarthur responded. To Andrew's astonishment he quoted from a number of legal authorities affirming the right of accused persons to challenge their judges, and then, his voice rising to a throbbing, emotional pitch, he appealed to the bench of officers.

"You will now decide, gentlemen, whether law or justice shall finally prevail over the contrivances of George Crossley. You have the eyes of an anxious public on you, trembling—as I am—for the safety of their property, their liberties, and their lives!" He paused, but there was complete and expectant silence, and, as he continued, no attempt was made to interrupt him.

"To you, gentlemen, has fallen the lot of deciding a point which involves perhaps the happiness or misery of millions yet unborn, and I conjure you, in the name of Almighty God, in whose presence you stand, to consider the inestimable value of the precious decision with which you are entrusted!"

Again he paused, his gaze fixed unblinkingly on the faces of the men he was addressing, and all six gazed back at him, their expressions, Andrew saw with disgust, sympathetic, if not openly encouraging. Captain

Kemp, who had been noting his words on a sheet of paper in front of him, glanced up to nod approval.

Macarthur threw out both hands in a theatrical gesture of appeal and declaimed, "It is to the officers of the New South Wales Corps that the administration of justice in this colony is committed . . . and who that is just, gentlemen, has anything to dread?"

His harangue ended, and he sat down. Richard Atkins was instantly on his feet.

"I will order you to be committed to jail, Macarthur!" he shouted furiously. "For contempt of court and for uttering defamatory statements against me in the guise of a legal challenge that has no basis in law. You—"

Captain Kemp cut him short. "*You* commit! No, sir . . . but *I* will commit you to jail, by God I will!"

The soldiers started to cheer him, and Atkins, clearly aware that he stood no chance against their organized support for the man in the dock, waited until they paused to draw breath and then announced at the pitch of his lungs, "I declare this court adjourned! The courtroom will be cleared!"

He did not wait to witness the effect of his announcement but made for the door, slamming it shut behind him. Some of the civilians started to rise, Andrew and his companion with them, but Kemp attempted to call them back.

"Stay, stay!" he thundered. "Do not go out . . . we are a court, duly sworn. The trial will proceed!"

"There will be hell to pay about this," Dr. Arndell murmured. He grasped Andrew's arm. "We should go to the governor at once, Hawley."

"Yes," Andrew agreed, tight lipped and dismayed at the realization of his own powerlessness. The soldiers were there for a purpose, he knew, as two of them deliberately jostled him . . . and violence could well

ensue, should the provost marshal attempt to carry out
Atkins's instructions to convey Macarthur to jail. And
William Gore—brave man that he was—appeared to
be thrusting a way through the crowd, with two grim-
faced constables at his back.

It was Macarthur himself who intervened to stop
them. He was on his feet, shaking off the hand of one
of the constables posted, as the law decreed, to guard
him in the dock.

"Gentlemen!" His voice was firm and incisive and
the uproar faded. "Gentlemen, am I to be cast forth to
the mercy of a set of armed ruffians—the police?" He
pointed in Gore's direction and added contemptuously,
"I ask you to look at them. See, they have halted, but
they are preparing to lay hands on me as soon as I
go outside! I demand, sir—" His gaze went to Anthony
Kemp. "I demand a guard of soldiers, to protect my
life!"

Kemp's hesitation was momentary. "Your request is
granted sir," he returned, and a mob of cheering soldiers formed about the dock. From somewhere in the
rear of the courtroom half a dozen muskets were
brought and two sergeants distributed them.

In the confusion Andrew, with Dr. Arndell breathlessly at his heels, reached the door. The provost
marshal, white and tense, had gathered all his constables about him, and on his low-voiced order, they
marched out in a body. Andrew caught up with him
in the street outside, and Gore said bitterly, "They
intend to rescue him—damme, Hawley, I think they
always did! Well, the infernal fellow is out of my
custody, but he has not given bail, has he? I did not
hear Kemp ask for it."

"No, neither did I," Andrew admitted.

"Then I can obtain a warrant from the civilian magistrates for his arrest," Gore said. He glanced round

and, recognizing Dr. Arndell, asked quietly whether he would sign the warrant.

"Certainly," Arndell agreed, "but it will take at least three of us, Willie—if only to protect you. I think we should go to Government House at once and ask the governor for instructions as to how we should proceed."

Gore inclined his head. Some of the color returned to his thin cheeks, and he said forcefully, "The Corps have come pretty close to active insurrection here today, by heaven they have! And that damned court has no legal standing now. They have no judge advocate, and I have removed my constables from their posts in the courtroom. All they have is their own Rum Corps rabble!"

"Some of whom are now armed," Andrew reminded him grimly. "So it is an armed insurrection, and the governor *must* be informed. Let's get to our horses, gentlemen!"

Richard Atkins, attended by Lawyer Crossley and two clerks, caught up with them as they were about to mount. He had evidently refreshed himself from his hip flask, for his face wore its accustomed hectic flush. His eyes were bloodshot and red rimmed, but this was due more to anger and frustration than to the small quantity of alcohol he had imbibed.

"I am going to prepare a written report for His Excellency the governor," he said thickly. "Those blackguards who call themselves King's officers have refused to yield up the documents I had to leave on the table! The indictment, the statements of witnesses . . . everything pertaining to the trial! A pox on them!" His bloodshot eyes fastened on Andrew. "Inform the governor, Captain Hawley, if you please. Tell him I will wait on him as soon as I have drafted my report."

And, Andrew thought, as he assented to this request

—as soon as George Crossley had been consulted as
to the legal position, with all its complex implications.
Undoubtedly the sequence of events he had witnessed
in the courtroom a short time ago had been the result
of carefully coordinated planning, with John Macarthur
the one who had devised the plan. He had been the
schemer, and the officers appointed as his judges had
been fully conversant with each move he had made.
Kemp had known that he intended to make a lengthy
speech, calculated to defame the judge advocate—damn
it, as senior officer, Kemp had called for silence, to enable him to make it without contradiction or interruption! And the rank and file of the Corps, who had virtually filled the courtroom, could not have been there by
mere chance . . . they must have been ordered to attend.

Andrew swung himself into his saddle, and as they
rode together down Phillip Street, Dr. Arndell observed
in a shocked voice, "Macarthur *is* a seditionist. I was
not sure of it before, but I've no doubts now. He's
seeking a confrontation with Governor Bligh, and somehow he's contrived to suborn Johnstone and his officers
and men to aid and abet him!"

"He has implicated the members of the court up to
their necks," Gore put in. "Whether or not they realize
it, if Macarthur is guilty of sedition, so now are they.
They could all be arrested and charged with high treason, unless they dissolve the court."

Andrew kept his own counsel. William Bligh, he
told himself, was not the man to be coerced or intimidated by threats. If Macarthur's intention was, in fact,
to seek a confrontation with the King's appointed governor, he would find he was faced by a doughty and
courageous opponent. Short of inciting the Corps into
an armed rebellion, his ploy could not succeed, and
surely even John Macarthur would fight shy of rebellion?

Thomas Arndell's voice broke into his thoughts. "Did

either of you know that there are moves being initiated in London to have Captain Bligh replaced as governor? Strong representations have been made in high places, with a deal of influence behind them, to have Bligh recalled and replaced by General Grose or Governor Hunter's nephew, Captain Kent. I know because Willie Kent is a friend of mine, and he told me this in a recent letter. He would welcome the appointment, he said— but not, most decidedly not, if it meant bringing Captain Bligh home in disgrace."

Provost Marshal Gore snorted his disgust. "Grose was always hand in glove with Macarthur," he said. "He should content himself with his high command and go into battle against Bonaparte! But Kent is a decent fellow and a good officer—he would never let himself be made a party to Macarthur's dubious scheming. For God's sake, he knows what the' man is—an unprincipled adventurer, whose sole aim in life is to enrich himself! And to the devil with anyone who stands in his way, be he the governor or some poor fool of an emancipist settler!"

As they turned into the gates of Government House, the sentry on duty there snapped to attention, and a servant came to relieve them of their horses. When they filed onto the verandah which had been added to the front of the governor's residence, his secretary came agitatedly to meet them.

"His Excellency will be glad that you have come, gentlemen," Griffin said. "The wildest rumors have been reaching us as to what has happened in the criminal court. But surely—" He glanced anxiously from one to the other of them, his gaze finally coming to rest on Andrew's face. "Captain Hawley, is it true that they refused to swear Mr. Atkins in as judge advocate?"

"That was the start of it, Edmund," Andrew returned

flatly. "You'd better take us to His Excellency at once, and we'll give him a full report."

Governor Bligh received them in the room he used as his office. His daughter, Mary Putland, was with him, looking pale and worried, and in response to her plea to be allowed to remain, he waved her to a chair drawn up beside his own.

"You may hear what these gentlemen have to tell me about the court proceedings, my dear," he said, "but after that it would perhaps be best if you left us to talk things over."

William Gore gave him a brief but carefully worded account of the morning's happenings, and William Bligh's normally pale face became suffused with angry color. He listened for the most part in silence, only occasionally interposing a brusque question when the provost marshal's meaning eluded him or defied his credulity. Mary Putland wept silently, as the sorry tale unfolded, and when her father motioned her to leave the room, she kissed him fondly on the brow before obeying him.

Edmund Griffin returned from escorting her to the door with a letter in his hand.

"Jubb gave me this, sir. It's just been delivered by a sergeant of the Corps. He came from the court, he said."

Bligh accepted the letter and unfolded it. His eyes were ice cold when he looked up after a swift perusal of its contents. "This is signed by all six officers nominated to the court," he stated levelly. "In it they inform me that they have allowed Macarthur's objections to Atkins, and they jointly request that I appoint an acting judge advocate to preside at the trial. Edmund!"

"Sir?" the secretary was at his side.

"Is the sergeant waiting for my reply to this . . . this insolent demand?"

"Yes, sir, I understand he is."

"Then," Bligh instructed, "inform Captain Kemp that it is beyond my power to comply with his request. The appointment of judge advocate to this colony is a Crown appointment, and I cannot rescind it."

Griffin went to compose the governor's reply, and he had scarcely left the room when the steward, Jubb, announced that Mr. Atkins and some gentlemen were at the door, urgently requesting admission.

Bligh nodded his assent, and Richard Atkins came in, followed by Robert Campbell and John Palmer, the commissary general, with George Crossley bringing up the rear. Gore said, in a whisper behind his hand to Andrew, "Two magistrates . . . and Arndell's the third! They are all we'll need to issue a warrant if the governor gives his consent. And *then* we'll see what his armed ruffians can do!"

Atkins was in a state of considerable agitation. As he seated himself in the chair Mary Putland had vacated, Andrew caught a whiff of his breath and recoiled. But his manner was sober enough, despite his agitation, his plump hand quite steady as he laid his written report on the governor's desk.

"This has been hurriedly compiled, sir," he said, "but I have included my clerk's notes, taken down during this morning's proceedings. And Mr. Crossley has set out his opinion, in case any question as to the legality of those proceedings should arise."

"Don't you mean the illegality, Mr. Atkins?" Bligh countered sharply. He glanced through the clerk's handwritten notes, frowning as he did so, and Crossley supplied softly, "As Your Excellency rightly observed, the illegality is beyond doubt. The court, as it is at present constituted, has no standing in law. Under the letters patent of the second of April, seventeen eighty-seven, the duly appointed judge advocate is required to preside, and, in his absence, Your Excellency—"

"There is no court," the governor put in, with undisguised impatience. "Is that what you are saying, Mr. Crossley?"

"Precisely, sir. And in addition—"

It was Atkins who interrupted this time. He said angrily, "Furthermore, sir, when I sent a clerk to require that my documents pertaining to Mr. Macarthur's trial should be returned to me, this was refused. Captain Kemp and his officers have impounded them, sir."

"Including the indictment, Mr. Atkins?"

"Yes, sir. Although as you will see from the notes, Macarthur obtained a copy of the indictment prior to his trial. Crossley"—the judge advocate gave the emancipist lawyer a venomous glance—"permitted himself to be robbed of the indictment, and the thief—presumably confident that he would be rewarded—took it straight to Macarthur."

"I see. Well, we had best deal with the matter of your impounded documents at once," Bligh decided. "Edmund!" he raised his voice and the secretary came hurrying in. "Have you dispatched the sergeant with my note?"

Edmund Griffin shook his head. "No, sir. I have not quite finished writing it. I'm sorry, sir, I—"

The governor's hand waved him to silence. "Good!" he said. "We have another note to be dispatched to Captain Kemp and his associates. Address them severally by name and demand that they hand over to the provost marshal all documents pertaining to the trial of John Macarthur, which the judge advocate was compelled to abandon because of the unruly and disorderly behavior of those admitted to the courtroom. The sergeant can deliver both notes and you, Willie, had better take an escort of constables and go with him."

Griffin departed, and William Gore said diffidently, "Of course, sir, I will do as you wish, but my prisoner is seemingly still at large. No bail was imposed—that is, sir, he had yielded to his bail, but it was not renewed, and—"

"The court has no legal · standing, sir," Richard Atkins reminded him. He turned to the governor and added vindictively, "Kemp has no power to renew bail, sir, so strictly speaking, Macarthur is a prisoner at large and thus liable to arrest. We have three civil magistrates here, and the provost marshal. Should I not issue a warrant, with your consent, sir, for his immediate arrest?"

All eyes were on the governor's grimly set face, and he looked back at them, his own eyes bright with suppressed anger. But finally, after exchanging a few low-voiced words with Robert Campbell and the commissary, John Palmer, he said curtly, "No, not yet, Mr. Atkins. We will try to reason with them. In any event Macarthur is almost certainly in the courtroom with them, under the protection of the armed guard with which they've seen fit to provide him. An attempt to arrest him now could lead to bloodshed or even . . . God damn it, even to mutiny! At all costs we must avoid that."

For *Bounty* Bligh, Andrew reflected wryly, the very word held menace; even wielding the viceregal power and authority as he did, the *Bounty*'s onetime captain dared not take any action that might, however unintentionally, lead to mutiny. Although, heaven help him, a mutiny by the Corps could well be precisely what John Macarthur was seeking to provoke. He drew in his breath sharply and then expelled it in relief, as the governor silenced Atkin's indignant protests.

"We will await the answer to my notes," he said, "and take luncheon, whilst we are waiting. Gentlemen, I trust you will remain here and partake of such hospitality as I am able to offer you."

William Gore left to accompany the court messenger,

and, after a short delay, the others sat down to luncheon, joined once again by Mary Putland. It was a strained and somewhat silent meal, with Bligh talking to his daughter in light tones that, clearly, did not deceive her, and only Robert Campbell attempting to make the conversation general.

Gore's return, with a written refusal from the six Corps officers to hand over the judge advocate's documents, did little to reduce the strain under which the governor and his supporters were laboring.

"The damned scoundrels claim that they consider it necessary to hold the papers alluded to for their own justification!" William Bligh fumed. "They offer only to supply attested copies if I require them. But they have had the gall to send me a copy of Macarthur's objections to Atkins as judge advocate, to which, they say, they give unanimous support! The devil fly away with them for insubordinate rogues! Nothing, by God, *nothing* can justify their conduct!"

Both Atkins and Crossley attempted to speak, but Bligh ignored them, his temper, Andrew noticed uneasily, perilously close to erupting. Somehow the governor contrived to control it and, in a clipped voice, dictated a terse and peremptory reply.

"Inform them," he concluded, mopping at his face with his napkin, "that, without a judge advocate present, they do not constitute a legal court and have no right to continue sitting."

Edmund Griffin wrote swiftly. "Is there anything more, sir," he asked, looking up from the scribbled notes he had taken, "before I subscribe this in a legible hand?"

Gore cleared his throat nervously. "They might also be reminded, sir," he suggested, "that they have no legal right to retain custody of the prisoner."

"True," the governor conceded. "All right—add that, Edmund, if you please." He frowned, deep in thought, and then said harshly, "Have your warrant prepared, Mr. Atkins. These gentlemen"—he glanced from Campbell and Palmer to Surgeon Arndell, his brows lifting in question, —"these gentlemen will, I am sure, endorse it."

"Certainly, sir," Robert Campbell assented. He led the way into the secretary's office, and the other two unhesitatingly followed him.

Mary Putland stifled a sob and went to her father's side, putting her arm into his. "Dearest Papa," Andrew heard her say, very gently, "let me fill your pipe for you, and then let us take the air together, whilst we are waiting. You must not permit these wicked, unprincipled men to upset you too much. I will tell Jubb to serve tea for us on the verandah."

They went out together, leaving Andrew in the long, low-ceilinged dining room with Gore. The provost marshal said bitterly, "Mrs. Putland is right about their wickedness and lack of principle, by heaven! But they've thrown down the gauntlet, Hawley, my friend, and the governor has no option—he'll have to meet their challenge. The time for reasoning is past!"

And perhaps it was, Andrew thought, starting restlessly to pace from door to window of the shadowed room. "Under the Articles of War," he observed pensively, coming to a halt, "Kemp and his brother officers could be charged with mutinous assembly, I fancy, if they refuse to dissolve their court."

"With unlawful usurpation of the judicial power, at any rate," Gore returned. "And in John Macarthur's case with incitement to rebellion—for that, I am now convinced, is what he has intended from the start of this affair. Whether or not Major Johnstone knows it, the others do, I'd take my oath on it!"

"Where is Johnstone?" Andrew asked. "He's keeping his head well down, is he not?"

"He's at Annandale," Gore told him shortly, "nurs-

ing a few bruises he sustained after the mess dinner
when he fell out of his chaise. The hospitality," he
added dryly, "was generous, to say the least, and
George Johnstone partook of it . . . more freely than
most."

The others returned to the room, talking in low
voices, and, with the governor and his daughter on the
verandah outside, they waited with growing anxiety for
the reply from the criminal court.

It came at five o'clock, and, having read it in ominous
silence to himself, Bligh said, controlling himself with
a visible effort, "Captain Kemp informs me that they
have adjourned to await my pleasure, gentlemen. Before taking this step, however, they have admitted Mr.
Macarthur to his former bail and released him from
their custody. Futhermore"—his voice shook, for all
his attempts to control it—"this note contains an offer
to hand over attested copies of Mr. Atkins's documents
to anyone I may choose to appoint as judge advocate
in his place."

A concerted gasp from his listeners greeted this bald
announcement. Atkins was the first to speak.

"By God, sir!" he exclaimed. He had been drinking
steadily throughout the time of waiting and his voice
was slurred and overloud. "If Mr. Gore's prepared to
shwear—swear to it, we can issh . . . damme, issue an
escape warrant for Macarthur. He can be arrested and
lodged in the jail! In my absench no order to admit
the damned scoundrel to bail can be valid . . . ish that
not so, Crosshley?" Receiving Crossley's cautious assent,
he turned his gaze on the governor, and Andrew, watching him, became aware of how deep and personal was
his determination to bring about John Macarthur's ruin.

Atkins was an unpleasant man, he thought, unre-
liable, vacillating, and unworthy of the office he held,
but . . . what had Bligh said of him, in relation to Macarthur's impending trial and the confrontation he had

threatened? *"If I must use his personal malice to enable me to rid New South Wales of that man Macarthur and his like, then I will do it. . . ."*

Now, it seemed, Atkins's malice would have to be used and given free rein, since, for all his faults, he represented the law and the law could not be flouted, as Macarthur and the six Corps officers—appointed as his judges—were endeavoring to flout it.

Andrew stiffened as he heard the governor say flatly, "If Mr. Gore is willing, and the signatories in agreement, the warrant may be revised. But I think it is high time Major Johnstone was summoned to exercise active command of his regiment. Also, as I intend to order Captain Kemp and the others to present themselves here, tomorrow morning, it might be as well to have their commanding officer at my side when I address them."

There were murmurs of agreement, and Bligh looked at Andrew. "Johnstone is at his house in Annandale, I'm given to understand. I'll give you a letter, if you will be good enough to deliver it to him, Andrew."

"Of course, sir," Andrew acknowledged, pleased by the prospect of an hour or so in the saddle as a relief from tension.

Griffin, as before, took down the letter from the governor's dictation. It formally requested his immediate presence at Government House, on account, as Bligh expressed it, "of particular public circumstances which have occurred." He added, with a wry smile, when the secretary went to make a fair copy of the note, "You may inform him of what has been happening here in his absence, should he ask you. I imagine, however, that his officers will have kept him fully informed."

"I'm quite sure they will," Richard Atkins put in acidly. He tried, unsuccessfully, to suppress a hiccough. "Indeed," he finished, searching his pockets for a handkerchief, "I think it not improbable that you will find Macarthur there, Captain Hawley, as he is now at liberty." He took his leave of the governor and departed, leaning on Lawyer Crossley's arm, with the assurance that he would hold himself available at any hour of the day or night, should his services be required.

Bligh thanked him, with a noticeable lack of warmth, and when the door had closed on his retreating back, he turned affably to invite Robert Campbell and the commissary to remain as his guests for dinner.

"You, too, Dr. Arndell, if you have made no other plans, and Willie, my dear boy"—Bligh turned now to Gore—"there is no need, I think, for you to serve that warrant until tomorrow. Stay and eat with us."

Andrew drew himself up, bowed, and made his way to the secretary's office. Ten minutes later, with the governor's summons in his pocket, he set off on the four-mile ride to Annandale.

It was a little after five thirty, on January twenty-fifth . . . just twelve hours before the anniversary of the colony's foundation, which the New South Wales Corps had celebrated, prematurely, at their mess dinner.

John Macarthur left the criminal court in the company of his two bondsmen, Garnham Blaxcell and Lieutenant Nicholas Bayly, with his official guard, under Sergeant Sutherland, surrounding them. But when he saw his son Edward standing outside the building with two horses held by a groom, he smilingly dismissed his military escort.

"My thanks for your timely assistance, Sergeant Sutherland. Cut along now with your men to the Saint Patrick . . . Mr. Whittle has my instructions. He'll see to it that your devotion to duty is rewarded."

Sutherland did not question his decision. He saluted and marched his four men off, and only Blaxcell—

finding himself similarly dismissed—ventured a protest.

Macarthur clapped a friendly arm about his shoulders. "Have no fear, my friend—your bail money's in no danger. I shall be in court tomorrow without fail, so off you go with, it's to be hoped, a clear conscience. All is going most admirably according to plan."

Blaxcell shrugged his elegantly jacketed shoulders and went in search of his own horse. Macarthur strode on, whistling lightheartedly, with Bayly close on his heels. When they joined Edward, he led the two younger men aside, out of earshot of the waiting groom, and said in a much more urgent tone, "Garnham will lose his nerve if we're not careful. The greedy devil cares only for his cash . . . damn his eyes, he forgets I've saved him the forfeiture of his bond on the infernal *Parramatta*! You'd better keep an eye on him, Nick."

"I'll not say that will be a pleasure, sir," Nicholas Bayly returned, "but I'll do as you ask, naturally." He grinned, with sudden, youthful exuberance. "By heaven, John, you're a genius! Everything's going our way, damme if it's not."

Macarthur met his son's anxious gaze, shook his head in answer to it, and turned again to the grinning Bayly. "We've a ways to go yet, let me remind you . . . tomorrow will be crucial. And George Johnstone must be brought into it—we cannot afford to let him sit on the fence nursing his blasted bruises!" He hesitated, a thoughtful frown drawing his dark brows together. "On the other hand, he must not be brought in prematurely, and I feel it in my bones that the *Bounty* bastard may attempt to do just that. Whittle and his people are going to stir things up in town tonight. Bligh may decide to send for our friend George to order the troops out and restore tranquility by arresting a few drunks. And we do *not* want that, do we?"

Bayly's cheerful grin was wiped from his face.

"No. No, obviously not," he agreed hastily. "Is there

anything I can do? I could volunteer to command the riot squad or——"

"No, I think not," Macarthur decided. "Have you a horse here?"

"Yes, sir—at the barracks."

"Very well, then, Nick. Ride out to Annandale at once and warn your revered commanding officer not to accede to any request from the governor that he should come into town tonight. Tell him to plead illness . . . that's as good an excuse as any, and he can put his arm in a sling, in proof of it, if he hasn't already."

"Very good, sir," Bayly acknowledged obediently. "But should I not escort you to Dr. Harris's first?"

Macarthur shook his head. "Edward has a pistol. He can be my escort. Away with you, Nick . . . and thank you." Left alone with his son, he relaxed a little, putting his arm affectionately round the boy's slim waist. "Let's walk a ways, Ned. Just until I can get the stink of that courtroom out of my lungs."

"Is it prudent to stay here, sir?" Edward demurred. "Will they not try to arrest you?"

His father laughed. "Not whilst they suppose I've an armed guard of redcoats to protect me. Bligh will not want a pitched battle outside the court."

"Was it wise to dismiss the redcoats?" Edward questioned, still doubtful.

"Oh, yes . . . else I'd not have done so," Macarthur assured him. "I told you before, boy—I *want* them to arrest me. That will be the fuse to light the powder train, don't you understand? But I have one or two small matters to attend to first, and I shall require your help." He gestured to the waiting horses and added, as the groom led them toward him, "You can ride with me to John Harris's, and then I want you to go to the jail and tell Reilly that it is probable I shall be lodged in his custody tomorrow, at the latest . . . and just possibly tonight. Pay him well and warn him that he must be prepared to defend my person with his own life if need be—or, if he fears for that, he should at once inform Whittle and Sutherland."

Edward Macarthur nodded his understanding. They mounted their horses and, with the groom jogging behind them, set off in the direction of Dr. Harris's house in the High Street. When they halted outside the surgeon's gate, Macarthur asked sharply, "Where's Hannibal, Ned? Did he take news to your mother, as I instructed?"

"Yes, sir," Edward assured him. "He left as soon as your bail was granted, and he had a word with Mr. Simeon Lord in the courtroom."

"Good!" his father approved. "You've done well, Ned, my boy—you've done very well indeed! Come back here and join me, after you've spoken to Reilly." He swung down from his saddle, grimacing as a twinge of rheumatism passed through his right leg before he could put his foot to the ground. The panting groom hurried forward to his aid, and he relinquished his reins, swearing under his breath at the pain.

"Are you all right, Papa?" Edward called out apprehensively. He made to dismount, but his father waved to him to ride on.

"Too much standing," he complained. "But at least I've come to the right place . . . Dr. Harris can give me some laudanum if I need it." He smiled in dismissal and limped slowly to the surgeon's front door, to knock on it with his clenched fist.

John Harris, a thin, somewhat stooping figure answered the summons in his shirt-sleeves.

"I've heard!" he exclaimed, and wrung his visitor's hand, his blue, protuberant eyes alight with unholy glee. "The tyrant is brought to bay! Come in, come in, I beg you, John, and tell me how you accomplished it!"

"That, my dear sir, will be a pleasure," John Mac-

arthur assured him, "but I need a wider audience . . .
can you arrange it?"

"Certainly," Dr. Harris answered. "However," he
added complacently, "some of your friends and supporters are already here, awaiting you."

It was dark when Andrew returned to Government
House. Jubb, the governor's steward, ushered him in,
tapped on the door of the dining room, and stood aside.

"Go straight in, Captain Hawley, sir," he invited.
"His Excellency and the other gentlemen are still at
dinner."

They all turned at Andrew's entrance, the faces of
Robert Campbell, John Palmer, and Thomas Arndell
betraying an oddly similar anxiety, but Gore's and that
of Bligh himself devoid of expression, as if both were
anticipating the news he brought.

"Well?" the governor prompted, with only a hint of
impatience, gesturing him to sit down. "I take it Major
Johnstone has declined to accompany you? I am to be
deprived of his services at this crucial time?"

Andrew inclined his head regretfully. "I'm sorry,
sir . . . I did what I could to persuade him. He insisted
that he is too ill to leave his bed, having last evening
fallen from his carriage on his return from the public
dinner. His arm is heavily bandaged, sir—for which
reason he could not send you a written reply—and his
face is bruised. But I did not deem him seriously ill,
I must confess, sir—although when I endeavored to
impress the urgency of the situation upon him, he
claimed that to come to the city at this time might
well endanger his life."

The governor's color deepened and spread; fearing
an outburst, all those seated round the table eyed him
with varying degrees of apprehension. But, as he had
contrived to do throughout the long, nerve-sapping day,
he controlled himself and simply asked, with icy de-

tachment, "Was he, in your opinion, informed of what occurred in court today?"

"Yes, I am sure he was, sir," Andrew answered, without hesitation. "Lieutenant Bayly called on him before I did . . . I encountered him on my arrival, which was not, I think, what he intended, since he tried to avoid me."

"I see," Bligh said, his tone more resentful than angry, but his eyes dangerously bright. "So Johnstone's made up his mind to stand by his officers, which was precisely what I expected he would do. Well, I intend to order all six of them to appear before me tomorrow morning, and, if they fail to do so and instead attempt to reopen their court, I shall have no choice but to abolish it."

"Abolish the criminal court, sir?" Andrew echoed, startled.

"Set it aside," the governor amended wearily. "And place all judicial power in the hands of the civil magistrates, who will then be called upon to decide whether sufficient grounds exist for committing Macarthur's judges to trial themselves, charged with conspiracy and sedition. Judge Advocate Atkins—presumably after consultation with Crossley—has sent me a memorial, giving a review of the conduct of Kemp and his brother officers in court today." He picked up a bulky document from the table in front of him, and read from it: " *'The crimes these six named officers of the New South Wales Corps have committed amount to a usurpation of His Majesty's Government and tend to incite rebellion or other outrageous treason.'* "

Andrew could feel the color draining from his cheeks; he met Robert Campbell's gaze, and the tall shipbuilder inclined his head.

"It has come to that, Hawley. Believe me, we none of us like it any more than you do, but there is no alternative. In my considered view, John Macarthur fully intends to incite a rebellion, aided and supported by most of the Corps officers and certain civilian traders."

The others murmured their agreement, and Commissary Palmer said quietly, "Not to put too fine a point on it, Captain Hawley—the rum traffickers are fighting to preserve their monopoly, and you do not need me to tell you who they are."

"No," Andrew conceded. "No, sir, I do not."

It was an appalling situation, he thought, aghast, and yet . . . should they not have anticipated something of the kind? Had not the writing been on the wall, ever since William Bligh had taken office as governor and, in accordance with the instructions and wishes of the home government, issued his Order of Prohibition, which made the flourishing trade in rum illegal?

From somewhere in the depths of his memory he recalled the words of Bligh's speech, made when he had landed from the transport that had brought him here, and later reported in the Sydney *Gazette*: "*His Majesty's ministers have instructed me to exercise a rigid control over the trade in liquor, which is said to flourish here, to the detriment of morality and good order . . . and this I most certainly intend to do. . . .*"

And he had done it, Andrew reflected ruefully; Captain William Bligh had succeeded where his predecessors had failed. He had enabled the free and emancipist settlers to prosper from their toil on the land, had won their unqualified gratitude and support. Many of them, like Tom Jardine, had even armed themselves and formed their loyalist companies, ready if need be to fight in his defense, and—he felt his throat tighten— against the Corps, the colony's official military garrison, should Macarthur and his fellow rum traffickers succeed in inciting them to rebellion and mutiny.

Jubb placed a heaped-up plate of food in front of him, filled his glass, and then silently withdrew, to be followed a moment later by Mary Putland, who embraced her father and, her eyes brimming with tears, slipped from the room. Andrew drained his glass but pushed the plate away, his stomach churning.

The governor said bleakly, "Unless he gives himself up, Willie, you will execute the warrant for Macarthur's arrest tomorrow morning."

"Sir," Gore acknowledged. He hesitated and then asked quietly, "And lodge him in the jail, sir?"

"Devil take him, that's probably what he wants! But . . ." Bligh's temper, held for so long in check, suddenly flared. "Yes, dammit, where else should a traitor be lodged? He and his judges, too, for the scurvy blackguards they are! I am His Majesty's representative and governor, and, as God's my witness, I will see them all in hell before I'll permit them to defy my authority." He rose, dismissing them with a few crisp words of thanks. "I will expect you here, gentlemen, by nine of the clock tomorrow. Good night to you."

They dispersed without further talk, the three magistrates going out with Gore. Andrew lingered for a few minutes with Edmund Griffin, who, it was evident, was strained almost to breaking point, his face white and his hands clenching and unclenching at his sides.

"The governor should act tonight," he said with bitterness. "He should lodge them all in jail, Johnstone with them . . . now, at once! For God's sake, Captain Hawley—tomorrow will be too late!"

"It is his decision," Andrew reminded him. "Sleep on it, Edmund, as I am going to. When it comes to the point, I cannot believe that they will dare to act against the King's representative . . . not whilst they wear the King's uniform."

"God grant you are right," the young secretary said, forcing a smile. "I'll see you to the door."

Outside in the darkness all was quiet and seemingly peaceful. Andrew strode briskly towards the stables, only to be brought to a halt when a shadowy figure emerged from behind the building. Two others followed, and, as his eyes gradually adjusted to the dimness, he saw that all three were making for the nine-pounder guns which stood, in a symbolic line, on either side of the governor's residence.

That the men were intruders was evident from the stealthiness of their movements, but it was a moment or two before he realized that they were soldiers. Then one, kneeling beside the breech of the first gun, called out a low-voiced order to his companion, whom he addressed as corporal.

Andrew moved toward them, but before he could utter a word, something struck him a heavy blow from behind, and he crumpled up, lapsing into unconsciousness. . . .

He came to, with little idea of how long he had lain there, to find himself spread-eagled in the gutter and, stumbling unsteadily to his feet, saw that he was only fifty yards or so from his quarters. His head was aching unmercifully, but somehow he managed to stagger, like a drunken man, to his own door, pounding on it for admission with all the strength he could muster.

To his stunned relief it opened, and he saw Jenny standing in the lamplit hallway.

"Andrew!" she cried. "Oh, my dear, you're hurt! Your head is bleeding . . . lean on me."

His orderly came, and between them, they helped him into the living room.

"What are you doing here, Jenny, my love?" he asked her dazedly.

Jenny sent the orderly to fetch water and clean linen and, dropping to her knees beside him, took his hands in hers.

"I had the strangest feeling," she told him softly, "the feeling that you needed me, so I came with Justin in his *Flinders*. And my instinct was right, was it not . . . you did need me!"

"I was never so glad to see anyone in my life," Andrew admitted. "But for all that, my darling, I could wish you a thousand miles from Sydney at this moment."

He drew her to him, his head swimming, and she said softly, "Don't try to talk now, my dear. I've heard the rumors . . . Sydney is agog with them. Lie back now and let me attend to your poor head."

He tried to nod, to answer her, but no words came, and blackness closed once more about him.

When he wakened, he was in bed, the sun shining in through the narrow window, and Jenny lay sleeping beside him.

CHAPTER XX

Major George Johnstone was still in his bed the next day, January twenty-sixth, when his orderly announced the arrival of Dr. Harris.

"The doctor said to tell you, sir, that he must see you immediately. On a matter o' life an' death, sir, that's what he said."

Disgruntled, Johnstone bade the man assist him to dress, and, in uniform breeches and boots, with his gold-laced scarlet jacket draped about his shoulders, he joined his caller in his comfortably furnished drawing room.

"Well, Harris?" he demanded irritably. "What brings you here, for God's sake? I'm ill, damme! Is it *my* life you're concerned about—have you come to offer me the benefit of your medical skill?"

Harris shook his head. He was in a state of considerable excitement, and as he poured out his tale of the previous day's proceedings in the criminal court, the Corps commandant silenced him abruptly.

"Damme, I know all that—young Bayly was out here yesterday evening to tell me what was going on. *And* I've had another summons from the governor—it came

just before you did, hell and set fire to it! The infernal
fellow obviously imagines I'm using my injuries as an
excuse, for he writes that he supposes the same illness
will continue to deprive him of my services . . . and he
leaves it to me to judge whether Abbott should be directed to Sydney to command the troops in my absence!"

"Major, I fear you have not understood the extreme
gravity of the situation," Surgeon Harris reproached
him. "John Macarthur was seized this morning by Gore
and his ruffians—John is in the jail, sir, and in fear of
his life! It's said that the emancipist Crossley—who
seems to have gone mad—has gathered a gang of cutthroats with the intention of murdering him. If only for
John's sake, sir, you must come to Sydney without delay
and order his release."

"I can order it from here," Johnstone protested.

"No, sir, you cannot—believe me, the populace is in
a ferment, ready to rise in insurrection. Mr. Macarthur's
arrest has angered them greatly." Harris's voice rose.
"Bligh is in Government House, with a bunch of civil
magistrates, preparing to abolish the Court of Criminal
Judicature. They say he intends to set up a new court,
under his own presidency, and I know for a fact that he
has summoned the six officers nominated for John Macarthur's trial to appear before him and answer charges
of sedition. They've been summoned now, today, sir
. . . and they are *your* officers! You cannot stand by
and see *Bounty* Bligh have those officers and John himself tried and condemned out of hand for treason, when
their only crime is that they have opposed his despotic
tyranny. In heaven's name, Major Johnstone, do you
want their deaths on your conscience? They are all in
danger, and John in particular, if Crossley leads his
cutthroats to the jail!"

George Johnstone's thin, fair brows came together in
a pensive frown. He retained his calm, but he was wor-

ried, nonetheless. If even half of what Harris had told him was true, the situation was, indeed, extremely serious, he decided, and he would have no choice but to act . . . and act at once. The Corps would have to be called out to restore order in the streets and prevent bloodshed, and, if such a step were necessary, then he—he himself, and not Ned Abbott—must command them.

As if reading his unspoken thoughts, Surgeon Harris reminded him shrilly, "You, sir, are the commander of the Corps. You are the proper person, perhaps the only person with the power to put an end to what may well become a massacre. Suppose, sir, that the people take the law into their own hands? Suppose they try to free John and his judges by force? Do you imagine that the governor won't order the men of your regiment to open fire on them?"

That was, the commandant was compelled to admit, a possibility and a very unpleasant one. He sighed, already resigned to the task he must and was in duty bound to undertake. He had promised John Macarthur his support, but dear God in heaven, he told himself bitterly, he had never imagined what keeping that promise would entail.

"Harris, are you quite sure that there is a risk of an uprising by the populace?" he questioned sharply.

"I am in no doubt of it, sir," Harris asserted, with conviction. He added, with a swift change of tone, "I have a chaise waiting, in which I can drive you to the barracks. And, if you will permit me, sir, I can make your injured arm more comfortable before you don your jacket."

"Very well," Johnstone told him. He took out his fob watch. It was a little after four. By five o'clock he should reach the barracks. Time enough, God willing to prevent an insurrection.

At five, with his remaining officers clustered about him and all reinforcing Harris's arguments, he signed an order for the release of John Macarthur, and a squad of six men, under Sergeant Major Whittle, left the barracks to escort him to safety.

"Sound the drumbeat to quarters," the commandant instructed Lieutenant Minchin, his adjutant, "and muster the regiment under arms on the parade ground."

Minchin, beaming, hurried off to carry out these orders. At least, he told himself complacently, as the drums rolled and he waited for the men of the Corps to assemble, at least last night's work on the Government House guns had not been wasted. If *Bounty* Bligh managed to find a gunner to serve them, at the elevation to which he had set them, all four would fire harmlessly into the air.

"Sergeant Sutherland!" he bawled. "Open the bells of arms! Each man is to parade with musket and bayonet and with twenty-five rounds in his pouch."

Half an hour later the sound of spasmodic cheering heralded the impending arrival of John Macarthur, who was carried across the parade ground on the shoulders of his escort, to be followed a few minutes afterward by the six officers who had acted as his judges.

In the messroom, with its gleaming silver and long, highly polished dining table, George Johnstone awaited them. He said, when John Macarthur came up to him with hand extended, "God's curse, Macarthur, what am I to do? Here are these fellows"—he gestured to the officers on either side of him—"advising me to place the governor under arrest! But I confess I . . . damme, it's a most serious step!"

Macarthur smiled thinly, his lips tightly compressed. "If they are advising you, then, sir, the only thing left for you is to do it. To advise on such matters is legally as criminal as to do them. But if you will give me ten minutes, I will set down that advice as a petition to you, and we shall all of us append our signatures."

The petition, dated January 26, 1808, bore nine sig-

natures when it was offered to him. It read: *"Sir . . .
the present alarming state of this colony, in which every
man's property, liberty, and life is endangered, induces
us most earnestly to implore you instantly to place Governor Bligh under an arrest and assume command of
the colony. We pledge ourselves, at a moment of less
agitation, to come forward to support the measure with
our fortunes and our lives. . . ."*

It was addressed to Johnstone by name, as lieutenant
governor and commander of the New South Wales
Corps.

Still Johnstone hesitated. Macarthur linked arms with
him, and drawing him out of earshot of the others, said
in a low, controlled voice, "George, there will be hundreds of signatures on that petition when I have the
opportunity to collect them. All the respectable inhabitants will add their names, I promise you. You *must*
act upon it, for if you do not, there will be an insurrection and probably a massacre, and the blood of the inhabitants of Sydney will lie on you. You'll be held to
blame, for you have the power to prevent it."

George Johnstone bowed his bewigged head and responded with an oath. "So be it," he added, his tone
bleak as he divested himself of the sling Surgeon Harris
had fashioned for his injured arm. In silence he led the
way out to the parade ground, and Lieutenant Minchin
called the regiment to attention.

The sound of martial music, on fife and drum,
brought Sydney's inhabitants crowding into the dusty,
ill-kept streets.

At first few were aware of what was afoot; men
turned in bewilderment to their neighbors in the crowd,
asking in anxious voices for answers no one could supply. Then, as the dusk of evening fell, from the brothels
and taverns of the Rocks came a surging mob, egged on
by a handful of soldiers—the notorious Sergeant Major

Whittle at their head—and drunken cries of "Down with the tyrant!" and "Death to *Bounty* Bligh!" became ominously audible.

A band of Simeon Lord's seamen, holding flaming torches above their heads, came in a wild rush from the warehouses on the west side of the cove, and, well primed with rum, they added their voices to the din. The occupant of a house opposite the jail opened his door and, seeing the disorderly scene, hurriedly closed it again, only to be subjected to a storm of abuse from the seamen, who hammered with their fists on his door until he consented to join them. Others in adjacent houses soon followed his example, in response to the seamen's shouted threats, and there were demands to "Show a light in your window! All who are with us, show a light!"

Several bonfires—evidently prepared in advance—were lit at strategic points along the route from Barrack Row to the High Street.

The troops, some three hundred strong, swung smartly to the right to cross the Tank Stream Bridge. Major George Johnstone, mounted on a roan charger, rode at their head, showing no obvious sign now of the injuries resulting from his fall, which had earlier precluded his attendance on the governor.

At his back an ensign carried the colors of the Corps, his escort marching with measured tread and bayonets fixed, to be greeted with applause from the crowd, as the band struck up "The British Grenadiers," and the red-coated ranks advanced steadily toward their objective. Realizing that this was Government House, the crowd fell momentarily silent, but then a few bolder spirits took up the cry of "Down with the tyrant!" once more, and it was soon echoed by the mob.

Justin, who had come ashore only a short time before, found himself caught up by a second party of drunken, swearing seamen, and he was borne along with them, unable to extricate himself, as they staggered along, endeavoring to keep pace with the marching troops.

At the gate of Government House a single, small, intrepid figure barred their way, and Justin realized that it was the governor's daughter, Mary Putland. The shawl slipping from her shoulders, and her hair blown into disarray by the breeze, the slender woman faced the Corps and its commandant without flinching.

"You traitor!" she flung at Johnstone, as he reined in beside her. "You rebels! You have just walked over my husband's grave—have you now come to murder my father?"

The accusation, bravely delivered in a shrill, carrying voice, stung as it was meant to and gave even Johnstone pause. Then he recovered himself and motioned to the sentry on guard at the gate to take the governor's daughter in charge.

"Mr. Bligh will come to no harm," he stated coldly. "We intend only to place him under arrest."

Mary Putland broke away from the sentry's halfhearted grasp and ran, weeping, back to her father's official residence.

A mocking taunt followed her from somewhere in the close-packed crowd, the words drunkenly slurred but intelligible enough to the distraught girl as she stumbled up the low flight of steps to the verandah.

"Down with the tyrant!"

"Death to *Bounty* Bligh!"

Presently there was an outburst of cheering when John Macarthur appeared, borne shoulder high by half a dozen soldiers.

For all her fear of the crowd's temper, Mary Putland turned again to face the advancing line of redcoats.

"Stab me to the heart with your bayonets!" she challenged them. "Kill me, if you will, but respect the life of my father!"

The door behind her opened, and she heard Jubb's

voice, beseeching her to come inside. The steward and Kate Lamerton reached out to aid her faltering steps, but she seemed not to see them. "Papa! Oh, Papa, where are you?" she cried brokenly.

"His Excellency has gone upstairs to destroy confidential papers, ma'am," Jubb told her. He then left her with Kate and Mrs. Palmer, wife of the commissary, John Palmer; the two women had just emerged from the dining room.

Moving across to bar the front door, Jubb found he was too late . . . an officer of the Corps was pushing it open. "Inform Governor Bligh," the officer commanded arrogantly, "that we are here to place him in arrest."

Outside the troops had halted. Major Johnstone, on foot, drew them up into line facing Government House, and a small party, under Lieutenant Minchin, went to haul round the nine-pounder guns, so that all four were positioned with their muzzles aimed at the governor's residence, and charges rammed home.

The mob edged closer, held back by the line of soldiers, and they cheered wildly when they saw the commandant stride purposefully toward the open front door, attended by eight of his men and Sergeant Major Whittle, all with their muskets cocked and bayonets fixed.

Met by Jubb and the officer who had first entered Government House—Lieutenant Moore—with the information that the governor was not to be seen, the Corps commandant hesitated and then ordered a search. Whittle, with Sergeant Sutherland and Corporal Marlborough, led the rush upstairs, shouting hoarsely to his men, "Do your duty, soldiers! Spare no one!"

Johnstone, with Moore and Bayly at his heels, was conducted by Jubb to the dining room to find, as he had anticipated, that virtually all the governor's supporters were gathered there. He stood in the doorway, looking from one to the other of them, recognizing Griffin, the secretary; John Palmer, the commissary, with his deputy, John Williamson; Robert Campbell; the chaplain, Henry Fulton; and Dr. Arndell, Judge Advocate Atkins, and William Gore, the provost marshal. Only the governor's aide, the marine captain, Hawley, appeared to be missing and, of course, Crossley.

"I seek Mr. Bligh," Johnstone told them. "Where is he?"

A hostile silence greeted him. Then Robert Campbell stepped forward, a burly, dark-bearded figure, unabashed by the armed men at the commandant's back. He said coldly, "As you may observe, Major, His Excellency the governor is not here. For what reason and on what authority do you seek him?"

"To demand his resignation and to place him in arrest, sir," Johnstone snapped, "at the requisition of my officers and the respectable inhabitants of this town . . . and in order, God willing, to prevent an insurrection against him."

"You come with your regiment armed and in battle array?" Campbell questioned skeptically. "Come, Major Johnstone, is such force necessary?"

"In my considered opinion, it is, sir"—Johnstone eyed his questioner disparagingly—"for the preservation of Mr. Bligh's life, should popular fury against him and his agents erupt, as it seems like to do. To which end, gentlemen"—his gaze again went from Campbell's face to that of his brother-in-law, John Palmer, and thence to the judge advocate, who paled beneath it—"I have declared martial law, under extreme necessity. You will all be relieved of the offices you at present hold and will consider yourselves, for the time being, under house arrest. A guard will be placed on the door of this room, and you will kindly remain here until I can make other arrangements for you."

Voices rose in indignant protest, but the Corps commandant silenced them with a sudden outburst of anger.

"I am taking this action for your own protection, damme! The populace is inflamed against all of you for your support of the governor in his despotic tyranny. As for you, sir"—he turned to address William Gore—"charges of perjury have been brought against you. In addition, there are complaints that you conspired against the lives of the officers who composed the late criminal court. I shall have you removed, with the man Crossley, to the jail as soon as I have time to attend to the matter!"

He stormed out, giving the unfortunate provost marshal no opportunity to reply, and in response to his barked order, two of his men took up their positions, with muskets grounded, on either side of the closed door.

In the hall Lieutenant Minchin reported that a search had revealed no trace of the missing governor.

"Mrs. Putland is with Mrs. Palmer and the women servants in the room next to the secretary's office, sir," he stated. "We searched there, sir, and in the office we found clear evidence that drawers and cupboards had been ransacked and papers removed."

Bligh, Johnstone thought, the devil take him! He must have taken papers that were liable to incriminate him from the ransacked files; but if he had waited to do that, then he would have left himself with no time to escape from Government House. Therefore . . . he swore irritably.

"God's curse! Mr. Bligh must still be here, endeavoring to hide from us! Renew the search! Mr. Whittle—" Whittle was beside him, perspiring freely from his earlier exertions, his face a mottled red that came close to matching the color of his uniform jacket. Both he and Sergeant Sutherland had been drinking, their commandant realized, but he did not reprove them, simply ordered them to continue their hitherto abortive hunt for the missing governor.

Whittle, mouthing obscenities, gestured to the staircase. "Damn my eyes, sir, I will find him if he's to be found. Come on, my lads—up here with you! We'll go over the whole house, a room at a time."

Johnstone watched them go. There would be the very devil to pay if the *Bounty* bastard had fled—to the Hawkesbury, perhaps, where he could count on support from the majority of the settlers. A pox on the man . . . he would be out for revenge for this night's work, no doubt of that. And as commandant of the Corps, Bligh would hold *him* responsible. *He* would be arraigned for mutiny and sedition, *he* would be deemed the traitor, not John Macarthur. He turned to Nicholas Bayly and said sharply, "Send out a patrol to cover the Parramatta road and have a search made of the boats in the cove. Yes, and whilst you're about it, dispatch a galloper to summon Captain Abbott from Parramatta. I want him here first thing tomorrow morning."

"Very good, sir," Bayly acknowledged. He was smiling, unable to hide his satisfaction at the turn events had taken, and Johnstone swore at him.

"Wipe that smile from your face, you damned young puppy! None of us can afford to smile until we find Mr. Bligh. Where's Hawley, do you know?"

"No, sir, I'm sorry, I don't know. I haven't seen him all evening." No longer smiling, the young officer went about his errand. Ensign Bell, who had commanded the Government House guard, appeared from the verandah. "Sir—Major Johnstone sir, I—"

"Well, what the devil do you want?" his commanding officer demanded sourly. "Don't tell me you've permitted our quarry to escape?"

"Oh, no, sir," Archibald Bell assured him, "but there are a number of civilians, sir, asking that they be permitted to join you. The Blaxlands, sir, and Hannibal and Ned Macarthur, Mr. Grimes and Mr. Blaxcell, Dr. Jamieson and Dr. Harris, and—"

"But not," Johnstone interrupted, a harsh edge to his voice, "not John Macarthur?"

Bell shook his head. "I've seen him, sir, out there with the people. They're lighting bonfires and cheering him. But about the civilian gentlemen, sir . . . they are most anxious to offer you their support."

"Then admit them, boy," George Johnstone said wearily, "by all means admit them."

He would need their support, he thought grimly, their support and their proven complicity, the more so if John Macarthur chose to play the popular hero in front of the mob and to hell with him, and to hell with Fenn Kemp, too!

"Take a couple of men and search the stables," he growled at Lieutenant Moore, who came to report the failure of their second attempt to find the governor in any of the upstairs rooms. "He cannot have vanished into thin air, dammit! He's got to be skulking some-where in the—" A shout of triumph from the upper floor interrupted him, and Moore said excitedly, "By God, sir, I believe they've found him! Shall I go and see?"

"Yes," Johnstone snapped. Relief flooded over him, and he took from his breast pocket the letter he had prepared. It was addressed to *William Bligh, Esq., F.R.S.* No mention of His Excellency the governor general which, he told himself, was as it should be. Bligh's reign was over.

In the small, bare servant's room on the upper floor of his residence, Governor Bligh had found conceal-ment. Lieutenant Moore had put his head briefly into the room, but the governor had slipped behind the bed —which was the room's sole article of furniture—and Moore had withdrawn, calling out to the other searchers that the room was empty.

When the door had closed on his retreating back,

Bligh had returned to the task he had set himself, tearing into shreds the papers he, John Palmer, and Edmund Griffin had removed from the office files. They were papers that had to be destroyed—for the most part copies of letters he had written to the Colonial Office, including a report on the trial of John Macarthur that, alas, he had been unable to finish.

He could have made his escape, he reflected wryly— there had been plenty of time. Mary had urged him to go to the Hawkesbury, and Andrew Hawley had promised to find a seaworthy vessel in which to convey him there, and armed loyalists, ready and willing to give him whatever support he might require. But he had never yet turned his back on an enemy, and as His Majesty's governor general and official representative, it would ill become him were he now to take flight before an inglorious regiment which had rebelled in order to protect six of its officers—and one ex-officer—from trial and conviction for treason.

From the moment that Andrew Hawley had brought him the news of Macarthur's release from jail, he had known that the Rum Corps would rebel and endeavor to stage a coup. And when Richard Atkins had come, panic stricken, to report that their commandant, Johnstone, had called for the whole regiment to assemble, under arms, in Barrack Square, he had not doubted that an attempt would be made to depose him.

But he had not anticipated that they would dare attack his person, for all Atkins's panic and his assertion that they would . . . and yet they were here, in Government House, hundreds of them, armed and dangerous.

William Bligh swore under his breath, finding one of the documents too stoutly bound to be torn up, and, as booted feet sounded on the stairs, he thrust it impatiently under his waistcoat. Earlier in the evening he had donned full dress uniform, ready—as he had then supposed—to receive an orderly deputation of officers of the Corps and listen to their grievances. But instead —his fingers closed about the medal for Camperdown, which he had pinned to his uniform tailcoat—instead, the treacherous villains were, it seemed, intent on killing him, thus adding the crime of murder to that of mutiny.

The footsteps came nearer; there were raucous, drunken shouts and loud bursts of unseemly laughter, and the governor tensed, glancing up to the small window above his head. Hawley, he recalled, had insisted on going to the harbor to commandeer his stepson's cutter in case it should be needed, but . . . a pox on it, the window was too small! And even if his life were in danger from Johnstone's drunken and ill-disciplined soldiery, he would adhere to his initial decision—he would not be driven into undignified flight, perhaps to be caught in the act of forcing his large body through the miserable little aperture of the window. Hawley could go to the Hawkesbury and spread the alarm—the poor fellow had suffered an attack the previous evening, from an unknown assailant, and he was in no state for a fight with men of the Rum Corps now.

The door burst open, and, in the dim light from the window, William Bligh saw two soldiers enter the room, heard them cursing, and, glimpsing the flash of steel as the light struck them, realized that both had bayonets fixed to their muskets. He ducked down behind the valance of the bed—the subterfuge had served him earlier, when Lieutenant Moore had led the search—but, as he did so, the documents he had been attempting to conceal slipped from beneath his coat and fell to the floor with a faint thud.

"Wha's that, Sarn't Sutherland?" the first man exclaimed, startled.

"Whad'ya say, Mick? You hear somethin'?" The sergeant's voice sounded as if he, too, were tipsy, and Bligh silently retrieved his documents, edging further under the bed in order to do so. The next moment a bayonet tip made painful contact with his stockinged leg, and he heard the sergeant emit a yell of triumph.

"He's here—the soddin' guv'nor's here, under the bloody bed! I touched him wiv' me piece an' felt him move! Watch out for him, Mick!"

A hand grasped the collar of his coat, dragging him from his cramped and dusty hiding place, and the governor got to his feet, with what dignity he could muster, clutching at the sheaf of papers as they again slipped from beneath his coat.

The second man, wearing corporal's stripes on his arm, thrust a bayonet belligerently into his midriff and, as Bligh attempted to back away, shouted a warning.

"Damn your eyes, if you don't take your hand out o' there, I'll whip this into you, quick an' lively! Draw a pistol on me, would yer? Well, we'll see about that!"

William Bligh, recovering his composure, drew himself up. "Sergeant," he ordered sharply, "keep this man off—I am unarmed. Stand off, both of you!"

More soldiers came crowding into the room, cheering and jostling for a sight of him, and the sergeant, roused to a sense of the responsibility that went with his rank, shouted at them sternly to keep their distance.

"One of you cut along an' tell Lieutenant Minchin the guv'nor's been found," he ordered, and, turning to the governor himself, he added, courteously enough, "If you'll just stay here until the adjutant comes, sir, I'll see that you are treated as an officer and a gentleman."

Minchin entered a few minutes later, flushed and self-important, and Bligh said, before the lieutenant could speak, "I am not armed, Mr. Minchin, and I want your assurance that your men intend me no harm."

"Have a care, sir—he has a pistol," one of the men growled. "I seen 'im reach for it."

Minchin hesitated and then offered Bligh his arm.

"Keep the men off, Sergeant—the governor says he is not armed, and I will answer for it. Sir, if you will accompany me downstairs to Major Johnstone, I will pledge the safety of your life with my own. My men have been over two hours searching for you, and they're excited, but, I assure you, sir, they intend you no harm."

"Your men are out of hand and some of them are drunk," Bligh retorted coldly. "But I will accept your assurance. Where is Major Johnstone?"

"He awaits you in the government office, sir." The onetime artilleryman again offered his arm. Seeing no help for it, Bligh suffered himself to be led from the room, the soldiers standing back to permit him to pass . . . but now he read scorn in their faces.

The fact that he had endeavored to hide from them would be misunderstood, he thought bitterly—perhaps it might even be held to be cowardice. In the light of hindsight, it would have been better if he had waited with the others—with Campbell and Palmer and Gore and with his daughter—to receive them in the dignified trappings of his office. It might have been wiser still to have taken the chance of escape to the Hawkesbury when it was offered and to have called out the Loyalist Volunteers, for all it might have meant civil war and the inevitable bloodshed that would have followed. As he left the room he glanced at the torn shreds of paper which littered the dusty floor, and he stifled a sigh. Those papers had had to be destroyed, it was true, but Griffin and Palmer could have destroyed them. Perhaps, with their destruction, he had done more damage to his reputation than any of his letters to the Colonial Secretary or his reports on John Macarthur could have done.

Reaching the foot of the staircase, William Bligh braced himself, and, shaking off Minchin's arm, he strode with his head held high to where the Corps commandant awaited him—seated, to his outraged fury, at

his own desk, surrounded by the colony's principal rum
traffickers. The Blaxlands were there, Grimes and
Garnham Blaxcell, Dr. Jamieson, John Harris, and, in
the background, as if trying to escape his notice, Edward and Hannibal Macarthur, and four of the six
officers who had been nominated to the criminal court
—Brabyn, Moore, Laycock, and Lawson. Only John
Macarthur himself was absent.

Minchin related the circumstances in which his prisoner had been found, and, to his credit and Bligh's
intense relief, the adjutant did not dwell on the humiliating details.

George Johnstone picked up a letter from the desk,
the trembling of his hand, as he did so, betraying the
nervous strain he was under. But his voice was quite
steady as he read it aloud: " *'Sir, I am called upon to execute a most painful duty. You are charged, by the respectable inhabitants, of crimes that render you unfit to
exercise the supreme authority another moment in this
colony, and in that charge, all the officers under my
command have joined. I therefore require you, in His
Majesty's sacred name, to resign your authority and to
submit to being arrested, under which I hereby place
you.'* "

He looked up then, to meet Governor Bligh's angry
gaze, and hastily looked away. "Well, Mr. Bligh—what
answer do you give me? Will you resign your authority
and submit to being held in house arrest?"

His temper, Bligh knew, was perilously close to erupting. Somehow he contrived to keep it in check, the bile
rising in his throat and threatening to choke him. Dear
God, he thought, has it really come to this? Will they
put me up against a wall and shoot me to death if I
refuse their outrageous demands? Is that what they
want, Macarthur and these men he has suborned . . .
an excuse to put an end to lawful government in a fusillade of musket shots?

Looking about him he saw only hostile faces and armed soldiers lining the walls. Surgeon Harris's plump, unattractive face was a mottled pink, his eyes bright with malice; both the Blaxlands were regarding him with barely concealed triumph, Jamieson with contempt, as he whispered behind his hand to Macarthur's rogue of a partner, Garnham Blaxcell. Only Johnstone's eyes wavered, as if, even now, he felt some shame at the action he had taken, the orders he had given . . . or was he, perhaps, afraid of those he might have to announce, should his demands be rejected as unacceptable?

William Bligh hesitated for a long moment, undecided, but finally, smothering the rage that filled him, he inclined his head.

"You leave me no alternative, sir," he asserted with bleak resignation, "since you have come here at the head of three hundred men of your regiment against whom I am powerless. But what you and your officers have done this day is treason—high treason, Major Johnstone! And you will have to answer for it to His Majesty's Government in due course, as you well know."

"I can justify what I have done, sir," Johnstone retorted irritably. "I have acted to prevent a public uprising against you and have proclaimed martial law, to ensure that the peace is kept." He rose stiffly to his feet. "I shall have a guard posted here, sir, and shall require you to remain within doors, with your daughter and Mrs. Palmer, who has volunteered to keep her company."

"And the others?" Governor Bligh questioned hoarsely. "Mr. Palmer, Mr. Campbell, and the other civil magistrates?"

"The civil magistrates have been relieved of their offices, Mr. Bligh," Johnstone told him. "They are held in arrest at their homes, and I shall appoint their replacements tomorrow morning, from among my officers.

Mr. Atkins and Mr. Gore may face charges, together
with the felon, Crossley, whom you were unwise enough
to appoint as your legal adviser. He and Gore are lodged
in the jail, and your aide, Captain Hawley, will shortly
join them there. As possibly you expected, a search
party of my men arrested Hawley on board a seagoing
boat, in which he was preparing to escape to the
Hawkesbury—his purpose, one can only assume, to stir
up trouble there."

Bligh maintained a resentful silence, and Johnstone
bowed stiffly and led the way from the room, the rest
of its occupants trailing after him.

By nine o'clock, while the riotous celebrations in
the streets outside continued unabated, Government
House was silent, most of its rooms unlit and red-coated
sentries patrolling its shadowed garden, with their comrades posted in pairs at the gate and the front door.

The commandant of the New South Wales Corps and
his officers carried with them, on their departure the
seal of the colony, the governor's commission, and all
official papers that had not been destroyed. These
amounted to a considerable number, and, pushed hurriedly into boxes and mail sacks, they required a handcart to convey them to the Corps' barracks.

Upstairs, in the small room in which Governor Bligh
had been discovered, his valet, John Dunn—working by
the light of a single candle—swept up the piles of
shredded paper and consigned them to a bonfire at the
rear of the stables.

It was after ten when Jenny, a dark shawl about her
shoulders, closed the door of Andrew's quarters behind
her and, with trepidation, started to make her way on
foot to Government House.

Justin had come in search of her some hours earlier,
to warn her that the Corps had marched on Government
House and that it was rumored on all sides that Gov-

ernor Bligh had been arrested and was to be deposed.

"They say Major Johnstone is already styling himself lieutenant governor, Mam," he had told her, his blue eyes bright with anger, "at the request, it is claimed, of the *respectable* inhabitants. I don't know about that, but I saw quite a few folk being forced by the soldiers to sign their names to a petition . . . and at bayonet point. The less respectable are filling themselves with free liquor, which is being distributed by the Corps-owned taverns, and the soldiers in the streets are as drunk as lords."

He had urged her to remain indoors, Jenny recalled a trifle guiltily, as, indeed, Andrew had also advised, promising to come back for her when it was safe to do so. But neither of them had returned, and, aware that Andrew was still suffering from the effects of his head wound, she was worried. Before leaving her to go to Government House, quite early in the afternoon, he had talked of a plan he had conceived to persuade Governor Bligh to leave Sydney and take refuge with the Hawkesbury settlers, should the worst happen and the Corps rebel.

"As I am virtually certain they will," he had asserted, with grim conviction. "For it is the only way they can save six of their officers—and John Macarthur—from being charged with sedition. The officers, Macarthur's judges, have laid themselves open to such charges by their own actions, and Bligh's made up his mind to have them tried by the civil magistrates, with himself as president. And besides," he had added, "whoever knocked me out last night used a musket butt to do it, and I'd lay a pound to a penny that they were men of the Rum Corps, putting the Government House guns out of action."

Hearing drunken laughter and a man's voice shouting obscenities, Jenny quickened her pace. All about her, light glowed from within the houses; there were five or six bonfires in different parts of the town, and at one—a hundred yards from her, on the Barrack Square —a large crowd of revelers had gathered about what appeared to be an effigy, which they were carrying toward the flames. Most of the revelers were soldiers, and their voices carried to her clearly, leaving her in little doubt as to whom the effigy was intended to represent.

"Death to the   tyrant! Down with *Bounty* Bligh! Burn 'im alive, me lads, like 'e deserves!"

There were townsfolk among them, she saw, cheering with the soldiers, linking arms with them, lifting them shoulder high, but they—and the women with them—were far from being the kind that could be described as respectable.

By contrast, when she reached the gates, it was to find that quiet reigned in the immediate vicinity of Government House. A sentry challenged her, his musket leveled threateningly, but when Jenny gave him her name and requested that he permit her to pass, the soldier relented a little. He was young, and, if outward appearances were anything to go by, he was sober, yet the warning he gave her, in a hoarse whisper, filled her with alarm.

"I'd keep away from 'ere, ma'am, if you know what's good for you. Our commandin' officer's the guv'nor now, Major Johnstone, see, an' he's declared martial law. You could be arrested for wantin' to speak to Mr. Bligh, an' that's a fact."

"Arrested?" Jenny objected. "But I've committed no crime."

The young sentry bent closer. "Mr. Bligh's under house arrest, ma'am, an' his staff along wiv' 'im. I seen them take the provost marshal to the jail wiv' me own eyes, an' the gentlemen what was civil magistrates— Commissary Palmer an' Mr. Campbell an' the judge advocate—they've all bin marched out o' here under guard. Back to their own 'ouses, the sergeant said, not to the jail . . . though he reckoned as it won't be long afore they're sent there, too. I'd move along, ma'am, if I was you, honest I would. I don't want to call out the guard an' get you into trouble."

"I'm looking for my husband," Jenny told him. "Captain Hawley of the Royal Marines. Has he been put under arrest, do you know?"

The soldier shook his head. "I don't know nothin' about him, ma'am. Now, move along, will you, please? If the corporal o' the guard hears us, he'll be out, wantin' t' know what's goin' on."

He resumed his stiff march up and down outside the gate, and reluctantly Jenny did as he had bidden her and moved slowly on. But where, she wondered anxiously, was she to go? Where could she go and hope to obtain news of Andrew? Justin would be on board the *Flinders* at the anchorage, but she had no means of attracting his attention, and besides, since he had begged her to stay indoors, he would suppose her safely in Andrew's official quarters, with the door firmly locked against intruders. And perhaps it would be best if she were to return there. Andrew would come to her, if he could. If the Rum Corps had arrested him there was nothing she could do to free him at this late hour.

There was Frances Spence, of course. It would take her only ten minutes to walk from here to the Spences' house. She had stayed there overnight after disembarking from the *Estramina,* and although Frances had told her that she and her husband intended to make another voyage to Calcutta in the near future, no date had been settled, as far as she knew. In any event, Frances would welcome her, and it was possible that—since Jasper Spence was a justice of the peace—they might be able to tell her whether or not Andrew had been placed under arrest.

Jenny again quickened her pace, but as she reached the corner of Bridge Street, the noisy sound of raised

voices ahead caused her to hesitate. Outside the official
residence of the judge advocate a mob was gathering,
each passing minute adding to its number. Red coats
were prominent, and, indeed, soldiers in various stages
of inebriation seemed to make up the bulk of the crowd.
Once again there was a bonfire and—as they had done
a short while ago in Barrack Square—half a dozen
rank and file of the Corps were bearing a crude effigy
toward the leaping flames. The only difference was that
this time the effigy appeared to be of Judge Advocate
Atkins, with a rope about its neck, and there was wild
cheering when a man with pipe-clayed stripes on his
arm held it aloft, before hurling it into the fire.

Jenny decided that she had seen enough. She turned
back, intending to make her way by the shortcut the
children used when coming from school, passing outside the lumberyard, but she had walked only a few
hundred yards when she found her way blocked by
more soldiers. They were armed and under the command of a corporal, and she thought at first that they
were a foot patrol until she saw that a civilian was with
them—a man she did not recognize—who was calling
on passersby to sign a paper he was carrying. Most did
so without argument, but a few objected and received
a blow from a musket butt for their pains. Jenny guessed
that the paper was a petition of some kind, leveling accusations against the governor; the Rum Corps would be
seeking such documents, she knew, as a means of de-
fending their seizure of power. She endeavored to pass
unobtrusively by keeping to the shadows, but the corporal saw her and called out to her to stop.

She took to her heels and, having contrived to outrun
a halfhearted pursuit by one of the soldiers, found herself at last in front of the Spences' residence. Lights
shone from its windows, but, for all that, it was several
minutes before the door was opened in response to her
knock, and Henrietta Dawson stood framed in the aper-

ture. When she recognized Jenny, her expression hardened.

"What do you want?" she asked coldly, making no attempt to stand aside or invite her to enter the house.

"I was hoping that Frances—that is, that Mrs. Spence was at home," Jenny began, "and that she—"

Henrietta abruptly cut her short. "My father and his wife sailed for Bengal in the *Kelso* five days ago," she stated uncompromisingly, "and my husband is on our property at Upwey. I fear you have had a wasted journey, Mrs. . . . Hawley is your name now, is it not? You married Captain Hawley I believe."

"Yes," Jenny managed, feeling the resentful color rising to flood her cheeks at Henrietta's patronizing tone. "Yes, I did."

"Well, so far as I am concerned, Mrs. Hawley," Tim Dawson's wife informed her, "marriage, even to a King's officer, does not make any convicted felon socially acceptable and never will. So I must ask that you leave—there is no one here to receive you."

Her tone was one of icy disdain, and without waiting for Jenny's reply, she closed the door on her firmly, leaving her on the doorstep without apology.

Anger lent wings to Jenny's feet. By dint of using back streets and the path behind the lumberyard, she evaded the soldiers and the crowds they had gathered, and, to her heartfelt relief, she found Justin anxiously awaiting her return when she reached Andrew's quarters.

"They arrested Andrew," he told her, "on the suspicion that, because he was on board the *Flinders,* he was trying to escape. It was Governor Bligh's escape he was hoping to bring about, but the governor refused to leave. And now Major Johnstone has declared him deposed and he's being held under guard at Government House."

"I know," Jenny confessed. "I went there, but the

guard refused me admission. Have they taken Andrew
to the jail, Justin, do you know?"

Justin nodded, tight lipped. "He and Mr. Gore and
the lawyer, Crossley, I believe. But they cannot charge
Andrew with any crime—they will have to release him."

"Are you so sure?" Jenny countered bitterly. "It
seems to me that if they can arrest and depose the King's
appointed governor, there is little they cannot do. Once
they take the law into their own hands, no one can stop
them. They are burning effigies of the governor and
forcing people to sign some petition they've organized,
which I suppose is intended to justify their mutiny. Because that's what it is, Justin—the New South Wales
Corps has mutinied!"

Justin put his arm about her. "Aye," he agreed.
"That's about the size of it. Mam, pack a few things,
and let me take you back to the *Flinders*. You'll be
quite safe there. The soldiers won't bother anymore
about the vessels in the cove. They've searched them
once. Tomorrow I can make inquiries about Andrew,
and when they release him, I can take you both back to
Long Wrekin."

Jenny sighed but did as he had suggested, packing
the few garments she had brought with her into the
small wooden box that had served Justin as a sea chest
since the first time he had been to sea. She said, in a
choked voice, "Long Wrekin will not be ours for much
longer, Justin. I promised to sell to Tim Dawson."

"But you've not signed the deed yet," her son pointed
out. "You told me you had not."

"No," she conceded. "But I gave Tim my word."
She shut the chest and suddenly there were tears in her
eyes. "It will be a terrible wrench to leave Long Wrekin,
but Andrew wanted me here in Sydney, and . . . I cannot break my word to Tim, can I?"

Justin picked up the sea chest, hefted it onto his
shoulder, and, balancing it there with the ease of long

practice, held out his hand to her. "Come on," he urged.
"Let's get away from this place, Mam. The very air
stinks with the smoke of the redcoats' bonfires and the
smell of their rum. The air at the Hawkesbury will be
cleaner. And," he added, smiling down at her as she
followed him into the street, "Tim Dawson will understand, I reckon, if we stay on at Long Wrekin for a bit.
There'll be quite a few folk wanting to quit Sydney
Town now, because everything will be changed."

He was right, Jenny thought. After this night's happenings Sydney would change—the whole colony would
be ruled, once again, by the Rum Corps. The hard-won
progress made, over twenty years, by settlers and other
small landowners like herself would again be in jeopardy. All Governor Bligh's reforms and the orders he
had issued would be rescinded and the Corps left free,
as they had been in Colonel Grose's day, to return to
their profitable trading and to demand lavish land grants
and the monopoly of convict labor, as they had done
then. And there would be bloodshed if the settlers and
the Loyalist Volunteers attempted to oppose them.

She caught her breath on a sob, and Justin said, as
if he had read her thoughts, "There's Van Diemen's
Land, Mam. You said yourself that we could make a
fresh start there."

"Yes," Jenny agreed. "I did."

"It's liable to be a year, at least, before the government in London takes any action—if it takes action at
all." Justin's young voice held disillusion, "The Corps
will do all in their power to justify their rebellion, will
they not? And they might succeed."

"Yes, I suppose they might," Jenny had again to
agree.

"Well, Mam," Justin told her, "it would only take
me twenty-four hours to fit the *Flinders* for sea. And I
could come back for William and Rachel, if you and
Andrew wanted to remove to Hobart at once."

Jenny was silent, considering what he had said. Flight was a possibility, of course—indeed, it might become a necessity. "It will be for Andrew to decide, Justin," she said finally. "I think, myself, that he will stay and fight them in any way he can. He is not a man to run away from his duty, and his duty is to Governor Bligh."

Justin nodded and offered no argument.

John Macarthur found time, in the midst of the Corps' triumphant celebrations, to pen a brief note to his wife: *"My dearest Love, I have been deeply engaged all this day in contending for the liberties of this unhappy colony, and I am happy to say I have succeeded beyond what I expected. I am too much exhausted to attempt giving you the particulars, therefore I must refer you to Edward, who knows enough to give you a general idea of what has been done. The tyrant is now no doubt gnashing his teeth with vexation at his overthrow. May he often have cause to do the like!"*

He entrusted the note to his son Edward and, having seen the boy on his way, repaired to the officers' mess of the Corps for a nightcap. He found George Johnstone there, hunched glumly over a glass of brandy which, judging by his appearance, was by no means his first. Macarthur clapped him warmly on the shoulder.

"For God's sweet sake, what ails you, George, my dear fellow?" he asked, with well-simulated heartiness. "We succeeded, did we not? *Bounty* Bligh is deposed, and if what I learned from Sergeant Sutherland is true, the hero of Camperdown was proven a complete coward. Hiding under a bed, I gather, wearing his infernal gold medal and covered with feathers . . . what further proof is needed of his unsuitability to govern this colony? Lord alive, even London will believe it, if it's reported in the right way."

"Perhaps," Johnstone conceded. He took a sip of his

brandy, his blue eyes glazed and rimmed with red. "But it will be *my* head on the block if they don't."

Macarthur smiled. Ignoring the implication, he said smoothly, "You will have to bring me to trial on the same charges as that swine Atkins brought, to enable me to be formally acquitted of them. And I fancy you'll have to make an example of Gore and Crossley, George —and possibly Hawley, too."

"And Atkins?" Johnstone's tone was cynical. "Do you not want an example made of *him,* for God's sake?"

Macarthur's smile widened. "Where are your wits, George? You know the swine—he can be bought, and he must be, because he'll swear that black is white if he's handled the right way! Atkins won't stay loyal to Bligh for five minutes once he sees which way the wind is blowing. He'll have to be replaced as judge advocate, of course . . . and Charlie Grimes told me he fancies the post."

"I was going to appoint Ned Abbott," Johnstone objected.

"Yes, for my trial, perhaps," John Macarthur agreed, "with Nick Bayly as provost marshal, don't you think? He deserves to be rewarded."

Johnstone drained his glass and called to the mess waiter to refill it. "And what reward," he inquired thickly, avoiding Macarthur's eye, "do you expect, John?"

"I? Oh, nothing spectacular, my dear fellow," Macarthur assured him. "You could create an appointment —one that would occupy only my spare time. Secretary to the colony, perhaps . . . that would have quite a ring to it, don't you agree?" His gaze fell on a sheet of paper lying on the table, which Johnstone had attempted to cover with his hand. "What's this, George? Your first proclamation as lieutenant governor?"

"Yes," the self-styled lieutenant governor admitted, reddening. He uncovered the document and pushed it across. "I felt that something of this nature was called for, when I announce the lifting of martial law. Read it if you wish."

John Macarthur did so, his smile replaced by a pensive frown. The proclamation began: *"The public peace being happily and, I trust, permanently established, I hereby proclaim the cessation of martial law. I shall this day appoint magistrates and other public functionaries from amongst the most respectable officers and inhabitants. Justice shall be impartially administered, without regard to or respect of persons, and every man shall enjoy the fruits of his industry in security. . . ."*

Having read thus far, he shook his head. "Have I your permission to add to this, George? I think some praise to your soldiers should be offered publicly, and . . ." Picking up Johnstone's quill from the table, he wrote rapidly and then read aloud, " *'In future, no man shall have just cause to complain of violence, injustice, or oppression. No free man shall be taken, imprisoned, or deprived of his house, land, or liberty but by law.'* "
He paused and, receiving a faintly sullen nod of approval, read on: " *'Soldiers, your conduct has endeared you to every well-disposed inhabitant in this settlement. Persevere in the same honorable path, and you will establish the credit of the New South Wales Corps on a basis not to be shaken. God save the King.'* "

The Corps commandant gulped down the contents of his glass and rose, making a show of wincing at the pain in his bruised arm as he heaved himself to his feet.

"Well?" Macarthur challenged. "How does it sound?"

"It sounds familiar," Johnstone retorted, with heavy sarcasm, "and everyone will know who wrote it. But since you're to be secretary to the colony, my dear John, doubtless you'll feel the need to compose other such announcements, and this can be a start . . . and presumably you'll want me to sign it."

"Of course, sir. You are the lieutenant governor, are you not?" Macarthur was smiling again, pointedly refusing to be put out.

"So you tell me," Johnstone conceded. "But you will not, I trust, have too frequently to be reminded that mine is the head on the chopping block? I give you good night, John."

He walked out of the messroom a trifle unsteadily, not waiting for Macarthur's reply.

"Our next task," Macarthur called after him, "will be to make a report to Windham at the Colonial Office. But do not worry, George—I will see to it that you are not held to blame."

An almost imperceptible shrug of the commandant's epauletted shoulders was his only response.

CHAPTER XXI

News of the happenings in Sydney did not reach the Green Hills for close on two weeks, and then it was brought to the farm at Yarramundie by Desmond O'Shea's orderly, who had been sent there for mail.

A letter from Kate Lamerton, addressed to Abigail, was opened and read aloud by Caleb Boskenna to his wife, before Abigail was permitted to receive it. Having digested its contents, Boskenna sought out Desmond O'Shea.

"It would seem that your regiment has deposed the governor and is holding him in house arrest, Mr. O'Shea," he stated baldly, and then, as the young officer stared at him in openmouthed amazement, he repeated from memory the gist of what Kate Lamerton had written.

"God in heaven!" O'Shea exclaimed, scarcely able to believe what his host was saying. But he recovered his composure and added quickly, "I support what the commandant has done, of course—Governor Bligh was a damned tyrant. A despot who proved his incapacity to govern a ship's crew when he drove the *Bounty*'s people to mutiny. And his treatment of John

Macarthur was little short of persecution, from what
I've heard. To charge him with sedition was—damme,
Mr. Boskenna, it was quite outrageous! I don't wonder
that my brother officers felt compelled to take drastic
action, in order to save him."

"Mr. Macarthur has been acquitted," the Reverend
Boskenna informed him dryly, "by the same officers of
your Corps who were originally appointed to try him.
And if Kate Lamerton is to be believed, all the civil
magistrates have been deprived of their offices and several have been arrested. She says that Captain Macarthur has been appointed secretary to the colony and
that Mr. Gore and the emancipist lawyer, Crossley, are
expected to be deported to Coal River when they come
up for trial."

"They will deserve what they get," O'Shea asserted.
"But," he added grimly, "they will find Coal River hard
to endure. If I were in their place, I'd prefer the death
sentence. It is a cruel place."

"But you will return there, will you not"—Caleb
Boskenna's tone was still dry—"when you have succeeded in persuading my ward to accept your proposal
of marriage?"

Desmond O'Shea reddened. Since her recovery from
the indisposition from which she had been suffering at
the time of his arrival at Yarramundie, he had paid as-
siduous court to Abigail, but, he was unhappily aware,
without eliciting more than a lukewarm response. The
death of Titus Penhaligon had grieved her very deeply,
and the lovely, vivacious girl he remembered had become a brokenhearted stranger. She was not, of course,
suspicious; she clearly had no idea that he had had a
hand in the damned young idiot's unfortunate accident
and . . . devil take it, his conscience was clear! Penhaligon's death had been the purest accident, brought about
as much by his cowardly, panic-stricken flight as by
anything that he himself had said or done to cause it.

But for all that . . . O'Shea met Caleb Boskenna's searching gaze and his color deepened and spread.

"I am on furlough for a month," he said defensively. "And, in view of what has now happened, I think I'd be well advised to go to Sydney as soon as I can find transport. The vessel that brought the mail to the Green Hills will not sail until tomorrow morning, my man says —I could send him to book my passage in her."

"And what of Abigail?" Boskenna asked. "My promise of a dowry still stands, you know, on the—ah— the conditions I mentioned to you."

"That I renounce any claim she may have on this holding, sir?" O'Shea said. He shrugged. "I've no objection to that—I'm no soil grubber, and I've not the smallest desire to settle on the land."

"Well, then?"

Desmond O'Shea repeated his shrug. The dowry would, he told himself, come in very handy if he wanted to take a share in the Corps's liquor trading; he had no money, apart from his pay, and the profits to be made from the rum traffic were extremely handsome. With the governorship in Major Johnstone's hands there would be an end to Bligh's prohibition. Instead of being compelled to smuggle the stuff in, one could import it openly, with official cognizance and even approval, although, it was true, Johnstone himself had never held a share in the syndicate. But Macarthur had made his fortune from it, and . . . He hesitated. It was obviously important that he return to Sydney, for there would be rich pickings with the Corps in command, including appointments to offices which the civilian supporters of the late governor had been compelled to vacate. If he were not there to lay claim to one such, he would lose it by default.

Even so, the money was essential, if he was to have any hope of joining the trading syndicate, and Abigail

—if only she would consent to wed him—would be an additional bonus. A wife he could take into the colony's society and of whose charm and beauty he could be proud . . . to hell with it, he thought, he was in love with the girl! And he had long since tired of the wretched, uneducated convict women with whom, from time to time, he had shared his bed. They were slovenly creatures, devoid of interest to him, save in one respect, whereas Abigail . . . O'Shea's eyes lit with a speculative gleam.

Abigail was intelligent and well educated, a stimulating companion who would surely enhance his standing with both the Corps and the community and aid him in fulfilling his ambitions. It was a pity that, of late, she had not shown interest in him or sought his company as her sister Lucy had done, but Lucy was only a child, albeit a precocious one. He had bedded convict girls as young, but marriage was, of course, out of the question. It had amused him to let Lucy flirt with him on occasion; he had even responded to her coquettish overtures in Abigail's presence, in the hope of arousing the older girl's jealousy, but—he was forced to concede—with singularly little result. Abigail, so far as he was concerned, had remained apathetic and indifferent.

Conscious that Caleb Boskenna was eyeing him expectantly, O'Shea rose slowly to his feet. "I *have* to go to Sydney," he reiterated, frowning, "so I shall send my orderly to make sure that the mail boat will accommodate me. Whether I go alone or with Abigail as my wife rests, does it not, with her? Perhaps, Mr. Boskenna, you or your wife would put in a good word for me, before I again approach her? The time is short if this matter is to be settled before I leave your hospitable dwelling. And if it is not . . ." He paused significantly, aware that the Reverend Caleb Boskenna had his own reasons for wishing to see Abigail married and removed from the land grant that, by rights, she should have inherited from her father.

It was probably best, however, not to attempt to go into those reasons or even admit his awareness that they existed, however obvious they might be, since his own interests might be said to coincide with Boskenna's; but there would be no harm in stressing the urgency of the situation. In any case, with or without the bride he had sought, he intended to return to Sydney tomorrow; he had too much to lose if he stayed here in this isolated, godforsaken place, cut off from his regiment and from news of the changes that would no doubt be taking place following Bligh's downfall.

Besides, Abigail was unhappy here. She, too, felt cut off, and it was evident that she disliked her two guardians intensely. Probably she would welcome the chance to return to Sydney and civilization, and, since Penhaligon was lost to her, there need be no impediment to her marriage to Penhaligon's rival.

Desmond O'Shea moved toward the door. He said firmly, "It will not be likely that I shall come back here, Mr. Boskenna, and, in view of that, will you be so good as to arrange for me to see Miss Abigail alone? In about an hour, say, which will give me time to dispatch my orderly and my horse to the Green Hills, and" —again he paused to let his words sink in—"it will give you time to talk to the girl."

Boskenna nodded, his gaunt, bearded face wearing an expression O'Shea could not fathom, save that it boded ill for Abigail should she fail to comply with his wishes. But he thought no more about it and went out, whistling, to be followed by Lucy, who pursued him to the outbuilding where his horse was stabled. There she listened, with unconcealed distress, to the instructions he gave to his orderly.

The soldier saddled up and rode off obediently on his errand, and Lucy burst into hysterical tears.

"You're going—you're leaving us, Mr. O'Shea!" she accused him bitterly. "Oh, how can you be so cruel!"

Moved, in spite of himself, by her tears, Desmond O'Shea dropped to his knees beside her and drew her thin, childish little body into his arms. "There, there, child," he soothed. "It will not be forever, you know. And, God willing, I shall take your sister Abigail with me, as my wife. Things have been happening in Sydney which compel my return, and I—"

But Lucy was not concerned with happenings in Sydney. She whispered, gulping down her sobs. "Oh, I know—Abby told me. She had a letter from Kate Lamerton, who says the governor has been deposed. But that doesn't matter to us here, does it? You don't *have* to return."

"Yes," O'Shea answered, "I do."

"But"—her dark, tear-filled eyes held a pathetic entreaty as they met his—"why must you marry Abby? You—"

"Because I love her and because she will make me a wonderful wife."

"Has she said she will marry you?"

He could not evade the question. "I believe I can persuade her to accept me, Lucy."

His words caused a fresh outburst of sobs. "She doesn't love you," Lucy flung at him. "It was that oaf of a Titus Penhaligon she loved . . . you know it was!"

Desmond O'Shea put her from him. "Perhaps it was," he conceded, "but poor Penhaligon is dead, is he not? Abigail cannot mourn him forever."

"She *is* still mourning him," Lucy argued sullenly. "And she was in trouble with Mr. and Mrs. Boskenna about him before you came here. It was very bad trouble. Mr. Boskenna horsewhipped her, I think. And—"

"Don't be absurd, child," O'Shea admonished. "You are letting your imagination run away with you. Mr. Boskenna would do no such thing. Did you see him do it?"

Lucy shook her head. "No, but I heard him. And I'm not a child. I shall soon be fifteen, Mr. O'Shea. Oh, please"—she caught his hand, imprisoning it in both her own—"*I* love you, truly I do! Could you not wait for a little longer, until I am old enough to marry? Some girls marry at fifteen, and I . . ." She bore his hand to her lips, covering it with tear-wet kisses. Shocked by her intensity, O'Shea jerked himself free, his conscience plaguing him. The devil take it, he thought; had he encouraged her too much, thinking her only a child who was, as yet, incapable of adult emotions? She was an innocent, of course, unlike the convict girls he had been thinking about a little earlier, whose mothers were wantons and who were bred to prostitution. Lucy was of good family.

"I will put out of my mind everything you have just said to me, Lucy," he told her sternly. "You come of a respectable family—your father was a distinguished naval officer, and the Reverend and Mrs. Boskenna are, I am quite certain, doing all in their power to give you a good Christian upbringing. You must not behave as if you were . . . damme, child! I don't know how to put this, but—"

"Of easy virtue, Mr. O'Shea?" Lucy retorted defiantly. "That is how Mrs. Boskenna puts it."

"Then, yes," Desmond O'Shea conceded, suddenly at a loss and conscious of acute embarrassment. "All right? Then run along, if you please. I have pressing matters to attend to, which are no concern of yours."

Lucy reverted disconcertingly to childhood. Pausing at the door of the shed, she put out her tongue at him in urchin mockery, her big, dark eyes bright with malice. "*Mr.* Boskenna didn't say that Abigail was of easy

virtue," she cried shrilly. "He called her a wanton, so
there! I heard him with my own ears, Mr. O'Shea."

Then she was gone, sobbing with abandon, and Desmond O'Shea was left to puzzle over her parting words.
Deciding finally that they had merely been an expression of the child's jealousy, he went back to the farmhouse in search of Abigail, obstinately determined to
overcome whatever resistance to his proposal she might
offer.

To his relief, however, Abigail offered none. To his
formal request for her hand she inclined her head submissively, asking only whether or not Mr. Boskenna
had made clear under what conditions he would wed
her.

Surprised, he answered without hesitation, "Oh, yes,
Abigail, most certainly he did . . . and I have no objection. I want you for my wife, my dear. Damme, I have
wanted you ever since I first set eyes on you, on the
deck of the *Mysore,* when that drunken fool Fenn Kemp
mistakenly supposed you to be a convict wench!" He
smiled, holding out his hand to her. "You'd be ready to
leave for Sydney with me in the mail boat tomorrow
morning?"

"Yes," she agreed, and shivered. "I shall be thankful
to leave this place, Mr. O'Shea."

"Good!" he approved. "Then set to work on your
packing—one trunk and a valise should suffice for your
immediate requirements, and the rest can be sent on
later. I will make all the necessary arrangements with
Mr. Boskenna—we'll go on board tonight."

Still subdued and submissive, Abigail did as he had
bidden her.

Their brief wedding service, conducted by the Reverend Boskenna, with his wife and the convict cook
as witnesses, took place that afternoon. Lucy was present, as subdued and silent as her elder sister, and Boskenna curbed his usual verbosity, omitting to preach a

sermon and seeming, to Desmond O'Shea, as if his one desire were to conclude the necessary formalities as speedily as he could. He paid over the dowry, however, in gold guineas, and in return O'Shea signed a document, on his wife's behalf, relinquishing all claim on the Yarramundie land grant, together with its buildings and livestock.

Jethro Crowan and two of the convict laborers loaded Abigail's trunk and O'Shea's own light baggage into the decrepit launch that had been used to bring stock upriver, and Desmond O'Shea, although doubting its ability to remain for long afloat, escorted his new bride to the wharf an hour before sunset. They embarked, and with two Boskennas waving a no more than cursory farewell from the timber-built wharf, Jethro untied the painter and, using a long pole, pushed his unwieldy craft into midstream, steadying it with some skill. Aided by the current and the two convict laborers at the oars, the launch glided smoothly enough over the shallows and then, reaching deeper water, settled sluggishly, the rotting gunwales almost awash.

"She's right enough," Jethro assured his two passengers, deftly maneuvering his tiller, and grinning sheepishly from O'Shea to Abigail. "But if you'd be so good as to stand right here, behind me, Miss Abigail, and you, sir, would take the bow oar, she'll ride a mite better, I do reckon."

Cursing ill temperedly, O'Shea moved forward to seat himself on the bow thwart, and Jethro said, lowering his voice to a cautious whisper, "Miss Abigail, you'm married, ain't you, to Lieutenant O'Shea?"

"Yes," Abigail confirmed. She was not sure how much Jethro knew—or suspected—of her circumstances. Certainly the Boskennas would have told him nothing, but it had been he who had been sent to the Green Hills for the midwife, and . . . She shuddered in the warm dusk, remembering the agony she had endured at the dirty, probing hands of the foul-mouthed woman he had been instructed to bring back with him. She had tried to suffer the uncouth creature's ministrations bravely and in silence, but her anguish had been so unbearable that, in the end, she had cried out . . . and her shrieks of pain had carried until the midwife had stifled them with a thick cloth, pressed relentlessly against her twitching mouth.

Those in the farmhouse had not heard her cries; Mr. Boskenna had made sure of that, but the shed to which she had been taken was, she knew, within earshot of Jethro Crowan's hut. She had had no chance to speak to him alone since the night when Mrs. Boskenna had caught them together, but now . . . Abigail's gaze went to where her new husband sat, pulling unenthusiastically at his oar, and she found herself wondering whether it had been in order to talk with her in private that Jethro had made his request for assistance.

She looked up into his square-jawed, honest face and asked, in a whisper no louder than his own had been, "What is it, Jethro? Is there something you want to tell me?"

"Aye, Miss Abigail, there is," the shepherd admitted warily, "but seein' as you'm wedded to the gennelman, p'raps it'd be for the best if I keep a still tongue in me head. What's done can't be undone, can it? Still an' all, 'ee shouldn't never have wed him, Miss Abigail, an' that's a God's fact."

Abigail stared at him in puzzled and unhappy silence. "Why not?" she managed at last. "Why should I not have wed Mr. O'Shea?"

Words, she was aware, did not come fluently to Jethro's tongue. He was slow of thought, as he was to anger, but kindly and well intentioned, and, above all, he was unfailingly truthful. Whatever he had—or could be persuaded—to tell her concerning Desmond O'Shea would be the truth, but, as he continued to hesitate, her

own resolution faltered. She was Desmond O'Shea's
wife, for good or ill. Had she not promised only a few
hours ago to love, honor, and obey him, repeating the
words after Mr. Boskenna? Had she not vowed to
cleave only unto him, for better, for worse; for richer,
for poorer; in sickness and in health, until . . . Abigail
was conscious of an odd tightening of the throat.

Until death should part them—his death or hers.

With a sudden catch in her throat Abigail recalled
Mr. Boskenna's harsh, almost triumphant declaration
that Desmond O'Shea knew about the child—knew, too,
about the midwife's efforts to terminate her pregnancy,
efforts which had failed. She was still carrying poor
dead Titus's child and . . . She felt tears welling into
her eyes, at the thought of the painful interview with
the Boskennas, in which they had told her that Lieutenant O'Shea was willing to give the child his name and
wed her in spite of it, in return for a dowry, paid in
gold, from her late father's estate.

She had not inquired or even wondered why, Abigail reflected ruefully, although undoubtedly she should
have done. But with preparations already made for her
would-be bridegroom's return to Sydney, there had
been so little time. The proposition had been put to her
by Mr. Boskenna, with his wife urging her to accept it,
and, for the child's sake, she had agreed. Not only for
the child's sake but also, she was compelled to admit,
for her own. Marriage to Desmond O'Shea would mean
escape from Yarramundie and an end to the humiliating
accusations of wantonness and the endless prayers for
divine forgiveness to which, in their varying forms, she
had been forced to listen ever since her secret had been
discovered.

And Titus was dead. She could never wed him now,
would never see him again on this earth, never rebuild
the hopes they had cherished or find again the dreams

they had shared. All that was left of him was the unborn child he had fathered, now quickening to life in her slowly swelling belly.

The ungainly launch swung suddenly broadside onto the current, and Jethro's attention was distracted, as he struggled with the creaking rudder, endeavoring to right the boat. Desmond O'Shea cursed him savagely for a clumsy oaf, and, as if this had decided him, the shepherd gritted his teeth, and, having set his craft once more on course, he exclaimed with a wealth of bitterness, "Poor young Surgeon Penhaligon would be alive now, Miss Abigail, if it hadn't been for that rogue o' an officer there, that you'm just gone an' wed!"

"Jethro—" Abigail was shocked out of her self-imposed calm, but she kept her voice low. "What do you mean? What are you saying? Dr. Penhaligon was drowned—you found his body in the river, did you not?"

"Aye," Jethro conceded. "I found that poor soul in the river, all right. But he never did die o'drowning, Miss Abigail. There was a great bloody wound on his head, like he'd been hit wiv' some weapon—a club, maybe, or a sword."

"But you never told anyone that, did you?" Abigail questioned, in a small, shaken voice. "You did not tell Mr. Boskenna?"

Jethro shook his head. "Nay, he'd not have believed me—or claimed 'twas the blackfellers done it. But I asked 'em, I asked some o' the blackfellers. One of 'em said he seen what happened. He said he seen two *tulanis*—that's our people, in their lingo—one of 'em in a red coat, a-ridin' a big brown *yarraman*—that's what they'm callin' a horse, Miss Abigail. T'other was on foot an' limpin' like he'd hurted hisself. The blackfeller told me as there was a chase, an' the *tulani* on the horse was yellin' out, but the one on foot, he wouldn't stop, not till he was ridden down." Jethro paused, eyeing her expectantly. " 'Twas on that land we'm clearin' for maize—the *goorama,* them black folks call it."

It was a mile or more from the river, Abigail recalled. Tight lipped and numb with anguish, she whispered urgently, "Go on, Jethro."

"There's not rightly a deal more to tell," the shepherd answered. He shrugged his broad shoulders. "The blackfeller lost sight of 'em for a while, an' then he seen the redcoat leadin' his horse to the river, with the one he'd been chasing laid across the saddle. An' 'twas there, in the river as I found Surgeon Penhaligon, Miss Abigail."

Could what he had told her possibly be true, Abigail wondered wretchedly—was the word of an aborigine to be relied upon? That Jethro had contact with the tribe in the area she knew; and they were people who constantly moved around, seeing without being seen, never drawing attention to their presence. They left the white folk alone and were not aggressive, carful to avoid confrontation with the settlers and, in particular, with the Reverend Caleb Boskenna. So . . . they would have told *him* nothing. But Jethro was different; they were not afraid of him, and, on occasion, he had admitted giving them a sickly lamb, to ward off the hunger all of them suffered from when fish and game were scarce. A blackfellow *might* have talked to Jethro of what he had seen and . . . She drew in her breath sharply.

It was not, surely, a story that such a man could have made up?

She grasped Jethro's arm, her fingers trembling.

"Are you quite certain of this, Jethro? *Can* you be?"

He looked down at her, mute pity in his eyes.

" 'Twas I found that poor young gennelman's body," he reminded her. "An' 'tis certain sure he never died o' drownin', Miss Abigail. Like I told you—t'was a cruel blow to his poor head that killed him."

She had to believe him, Abigail thought, and had to fight against the tears that threatened to overwhelm her, as the realization that she was married to the man responsible for Titus's death slowly sank in. Titus's death . . . oh, God, Titus's *murder,* if what Jethro had told her was the truth. There was, perhaps, a possibility that it had been an accident. Visualizing the scene, as the shepherd had described it to her, she told herself that poor Titus might have fallen—fallen and struck his head. Desmond O'Shea was surely not capable of a deliberate attempt to kill him, although he might have ridden after him, enjoying the chase or, perhaps, even mistaking him for a runaway convict. But—if accident it had been—why had he not brought the body to Yarramundie, where Mr. Boskenna could have given it Christian burial? Why, instead of doing so, had he taken it, lying across his horse's back, to the river? Poor Titus had deserved better than that. . . .

She looked at Jethro, but his expression was inscrutable. Darkness was closing in now, the lamps flickering into life at the Green Hills settlement and rapidly coming closer, as the current carried the launch downstream toward the wharf and the sailing vessel tied up alongside. Only the boat's outline was visible, silhouetted against the lanterns on the wharf, by whose light men were loading cargo on board, and Abigail's hope that the mail carrier might prove to be Justin Broome swiftly faded. The boat was squat, lying low in the water and lacking the rakish lines and slender, graceful stem of Justin's *Flinders.*

" 'Tis the *Fanny,*" Jethro volunteered, as if she had spoken her thoughts aloud. "Mr. Lord's, she is, an' her master's Jed Burdock." He hauled on the launch's tiller and, having brought her head round, turned again to

Abigail and said, very softly, "I'm a-comin' with you to
Sydney, Miss Abigail, just to see you'm safe, understand?"

"Oh, Jethro!" Abigail exclaimed, torn between relief and fear for the possible consequences, if his decision to accompany them had been made without Caleb
Boskenna's consent. But he brushed aside her anxious
question, smiling in the darkness. "I be a free man, Miss
Abigail, not a convict. And my indentures was to Mr.
Tempest, not to no Boskenna, be he reverend or not,
understand? I can find work near Sydney Town—there's
many that'd be willing to employ a good shepherd,
never fear. An' maybe I'll find one as ain't so free with
the lash as Mr. Boskenna."

"Oh, Jethro," Abigail said again, finding herself suddenly choked with tears. "I . . . I . . . it's good of you.
I—"

Jethro took a hand from the tiller and gently touched
the small swelling on her belly. " 'Tis Dr. Penhaligon's
babby you'm carryin', ain't it, Miss Abigail? 'Twas him
you was plannin' to wed?"

"Yes," she admitted, making a brave effort to staunch
her tears. "I loved him, Jethro."

"You shouldn't never have wed Lieutenant O'Shea,"
he reproached her. "But don't 'ee worry—an' don't 'ee
say nothin' to him, Miss Abigail, 'bout what I told 'ee."

"Oh, but"—Abigail began—"I must, I—" Jethro's
hand came up, two fingers pressed lightly against her
lips. "Nothin'," he begged gravely. "Promise me that,
Miss Abigail . . . not tonight, anyways."

She gave her promise uncertainly and saw his smile
reappear. Then the settlement loomed up ahead of
them, and with a mumbled apology, Jethro grasped his
tiller, to bring the launch grinding against the stout tim-
bers of the wharf.

Desmond O'Shea abandoned his oar with a grunt of

relief. He assisted Abigail to disembark and, finding his orderly waiting, sent him to unload their baggage.

"Come on," he said curtly to Abigail. "You had better board at once. The moon will be up soon, and I'm going to tell the master of—what's the name of his tub? —ah, yes, the *Fanny*—that he's to cast off as soon as all our baggage is loaded. It will be cramped and damned uncomfortable, if I'm any judge, but presumably the master has some cabin accommodation. If he hasn't, then he'll have to give up his own."

His prediction proved, unhappily, to be accurate. The *Fanny* was a broad-beamed ketch, with most of the accommodation she possessed given over to cargo. There were hammocks slung in the forward hold for the use of passengers, but the only bunk was the master's, in a small cabin amidships, which was scarcely worthy of the name. Desmond O'Shea demanded and was duly given this, on payment of an additional charge, but Abigail was dismayed when she was conducted below.

The filthy blankets and unswept floor of rough deck planking allied to the stench of livestock and a blue cloud of tobacco smoke filled her with horror, but her new husband, it seemed, saw no reason why she should object to spending her wedding night in such surroundings.

"Undress yourself, my dear," he ordered, "and wait for me. I'll be no longer than I can help. But I want to make sure that fool of an orderly of mine has tied my horse up securely and that he has attended to the stowing of our baggage."

Abigail made to voice a protest, but he cut her short. "For God's sake, Abigail—you're my wife, are you not? And I've waited long enough for you!" He drew her into his arms, his kiss a lover's kiss, urgent and demanding, his tall body hard against hers.

She sought to back away, violently repelled, and hearing Jethro's whispered words drumming in her ears, recalling, with all its hideous implications, the accusation he had made. She needed time, she thought distractedly, time to consider the situation in which she now found herself, and, despite her promise to the faithful Jethro, she had to know the truth.

"Oh, please," she begged. "Not here, not now. I cannot, I—"

"A pox on it!" Desmond O'Shea exclaimed angrily, holding her closer, his tongue thrusting between her parted lips. When she made no response and again endeavored to free herself, he lifted his head and stood for a moment looking down at her, his eyes bright with resentment. Someone called to him from the deck above, and he answered irritably that he was on his way. Abigail felt his arms relax and, breathless and shaken, broke from his embrace.

"You'll need to learn wifely duty and obedience," he told her. "And, by heaven, I'll see to it that you do! Now"—he gestured again to the rumpled bunk—"undress and wait for me there."

"But it is filthy and foul smelling," Abigail objected, "and this cabin offers no privacy. I cannot do as you ask—I will not. I—"

"You'll do as I bid you," O'Shea retorted. He raised his hand and struck her a stinging blow across the mouth, from which she recoiled with a cry of pain.

"I'm sorry," he said, with a swift change of tone. Reaching for her hands, he held them imprisoned, but he was smiling, his earlier loss of temper seemingly overcome. "Your womanly modesty belies what your sweet little sister claimed concerning you! But . . . you've nothing to fear from me, my dear. I know how to bed a woman, and I'll deal gently with you, I promise . . . damme, Abby, I understand! You are an innocent, and you are afraid . . . that's natural enough. Now, do as you're told, like a good wife. I'll be as quick as I can."

He turned away, and, listening to his departing foot-steps as he mounted the short companion-ladder to the upper deck, Abigail was suddenly assailed by a host of tormenting doubts and fears, none of which sprang from the cause to which her new husband had ascribed them.

Was it possible, she asked herself anxiously *could* it be possible that Mr. Boskenna had not told him of her pregnancy? His assurance that he had done so had been part and parcel of the arguments he had used to per-suade her to accept Desmond O'Shea's proposal of mar-riage. She stiffened, recalling his words: *"Mr. O'Shea is willing to give your unborn babe his name, Abigail, and you would be foolish to refuse the chance he is offering you to regain your respectability. The Lord, in His in-finite wisdom, has moved him to give you this chance, and you will not be given another. . . ."*

Those words had weighed heavily with her, she thought, but . . . suppose they were not true? Desmond O'Shea had spoken of her as an innocent. He had . . . she choked on a sob. He had mentioned something Lucy had said, but . . . Above her head, feet thudded on the deck planking, and she heard raised voices and a shouted order to cast off.

The *Fanny* moved sluggishly from her berth and, with trembling fingers and a sinking heart, Abigail started to disrobe.

On deck Jethro Crowan waited, the shepherd's crook he always carried held firmly in his hand.

The moon had risen, but it was a cloudy night, with a strong if fitful breeze, and the *Fanny*'s master, Jed Burdock, after a few halfhearted objections, had finally agreed to sail without waiting for daylight.

Jethro glanced astern and, seeing the launch still tied up to the wharf, permitted himself a wry smile. The two old convicts had been dismayed when he had told them that they would have to row the decrepit old boat back to Yarramundie without his help, but he had remained deaf to their pleas and even to their threats.

"Go back without the poxy boat and see what his reverence has to say!" he had warned them, and both had lapsed into sullen silence, aware that his warning was no idle one. Even if they did contrive to return the waterlogged launch to its owner, they would probably earn a flogging for their pains, since his own absence would be hard to explain, he reflected; but he felt no qualms of conscience on that account. His duty was plain—and it was to look after Miss Abigail, not to work his guts out for the Reverend Caleb Boskenna.

He shifted his position as the *Fanny*'s grubby mainsail was hoisted, making sure that he was in shadow and unlikely to be noticed when Lieutenant O'Shea emerged from the stern hatchway. He had watched the redcoat officer take Miss Abigail below to Jed Burdock's cabin and had heard her cry out in pain a few minutes afterwards . . . and that cry had wakened an echo in his heart and strengthened his resolution.

Not that it needed strengthening, for he had known what he must do from the moment when Billy Larkin, the Boskennas' cook, had told him of the hurriedly conducted wedding. Miss Abigail had been in tears, Billy had said, at the conclusion of a lengthy interview with the reverend, which had preceded the brief religious ceremony.

For all that he was a simple man, slow of mind and of speech, Jethro's heart was quick to respond, and from the depths of his soul there arose a passion to right the wrongs done to his mistress—an urge to remove from the earth the one cause of her pain and travail.

He expelled a deep breath from between broken teeth. His father had broken those teeth when he had hit him in a drunken rage, and during the voyage out to Sydney, Surgeon Penhaligon had extracted two which had been giving him pain. He had been a good young man, Titus Penhaligon, and a fine surgeon, treating all the *Mysore*'s passengers with equal skill and compassion, whether they were convict or free. It was a thousand pities that the poor soul had met the end he had, for he and Miss Abigail would have married and raised a family and been a credit to the land of their adoption. But instead . . . Jethro glanced skyward, watching for the moon to go behind one of the scudding clouds.

He would have to choose his moment carefully, he told himself, uneasily aware that there would not be much time for him to do so. He could hear Lieutenant O'Shea blaspheming and shouting at his orderly, and the agitated stamping of horse's hooves in the afterhold. Fools, he thought scornfully—they should know better than to frighten that poor animal, which was already scared enough by the strange surroundings in which it had found itself, tied up with a bull calf and heifer from the Green Hills settlement, being sent to market in Sydney. You had to be gentle with animals, young ones especially, and . . . That thought brought him back to Miss Abigail. *She* was young, the good Lord knew, and she merited gentle handling, which she would not receive at Lieutenant O'Shea's hands, that was certain. Had he not already made her cry out, below, in Jed Burdock's cabin?

The stamping ceased, and he heard O'Shea's harsh voice, threatening the wretched soldier who was with him with a bloody back if the horse suffered any injury before reaching Sydney. That meant that the soldier would stay below, Jethro's mind registered, and O'Shea would be alone when he came on deck. It would have to be now—now or never—without giving him the chance to return to the cabin and Miss Abigail.

His fingers tightened their grip on the heavy shepherd's crook, and he glanced cautiously about him, to ascertain the whereabouts of the *Fanny*'s crew. Jed Burdock was at the wheel, his attention fully taken up with his steering; the two crewmen were forward, busy setting the jib and preparing to tack, their hands full, as the wind veered and the ketch heeled under its pressure.

Booted feet sounded on the ladder below him, and Jethro ducked swiftly down behind the hatch cover.

An eye for an eye, the Good Book said, and the Reverend Caleb Boskenna had taken those words as his text, more than once. *Thou shalt not kill* was, it was true, one of the Lord's commandments, but . . . had not Lieutenant O'Shea already broken it? Careel had sworn he had, Careel had been watching and had seen it all, crouched behind the trees at the edge of the *goorama,* and besides, there had been the ugly wound on poor young Surgeon Penhaligon's forehead. He had seen that with his own eyes, he . . . O'Shea's bare head appeared, level with the hatch coaming, and Jethro struck, aiming for the back of the neck.

The blow was one he had frequently had to use to stun a ewe required for the pot or to kill an injured lamb, and it was swift and skillful. O'Shea collapsed without a sound, and Jethro, leaning over and letting his crook fall, grasped him under the armpits. He paused, casting an apprehensive glance about him, and as if in answer to prayer, the moon vanished behind one of the racing clouds. Exerting all the strength of his sturdy body, he heaved O'Shea onto his back and carried him to the lee gunwale. Another heave and the red-coated figure fell into the river, making only a slight splash as the waters parted to receive it.

Jethro waited, breathing a silent plea to his Maker for forgiveness; then, seeing no movement, no attempt to swim or struggle to safety, he turned round and shouted at the pitch of his lungs, "Man overboard! Bring to, Mr. Burdock—there's a man overboard!"

Jed Burdock's reaction was predictably slow. In the cloud-dimmed darkness and with a gusting breeze, it was in any event no simple matter to lose way and bring the heavily laden ketch about, but he did his best, redoubling his efforts when he learned, from Jethro, the identity of his lost passenger.

"The Rum Corps lieutenant—Lieutenant O'Shea? God Almighty! Was he drunk or what? I never saw him go. O'Reilly, you goddammed idiot, let fall your sheet! I'm trying to back the mains'l."

Finally, he ordered the anchor dropped and his oared boat lowered. "We'll make a search, but God knows we're not likely to find him unless he can swim. Keep quiet a minute, the lot of you, and listen for him calling out."

But there was no sound, no swimmer breasting the darkened water, and, listening with the rest, Jethro breathed his relief. He saw Abigail come on deck, clasping her shawl about her slender shoulders, and he stood silent, leaving the *Fanny*'s master to break the news to her that her husband was missing. She took it quietly and waited, pale with shock, when the boat pulled away upriver to begin its search, O'Shea's orderly taking one of the oars.

After about an hour Jed Burdock fired off a rocket to summon his boat to return, and it was as he did so that the seaman O'Reilly emitted a triumphant yell.

"Somethin' red, so there is—agin' our hull on de lee side, Mr. Burdock! Looks like it's him an' de current's carried him down here."

The master peered over the lee bulwark, nodded his balding head, and then, recalling Abigail's presence, advised her, with gruff kindness, to go below.

"I'll come and tell you whatever there may be to tell, ma'am. But I fear you must prepare yourself for bad news. Your husband is not moving, as far as I can tell."

Abigail met Jethro's gaze across the half dozen feet of deck between them, and the shepherd could not fath-

om the look she gave him, save that it was at once
fearful and ashamed. But it was not accusing, and, as
Abigail walked slowly towards the midships hatch, he
heard Jed Burdock ask her if she wished him to put
back to the Green Hills.

Her answer, softly spoken and bravely composed,
sent a feeling of intense relief flooding through him.

"No, Mr. Burdock, thank you. I will go on to Sydney—I have friends there. And Jethro Crowan will look
after me if my—if my husband has met his end."

Then she was gone, and Jethro braced himself, sick
with apprehension, as the body of the man he had murdered was hauled onto the *Fanny*'s deck.

"Dead as a doornail," Jed Burdock pronounced,
after making a cursory examination. "Must have been
drunk, else why should he go over the side? And he
drowned, that's for sure. Didn't even struggle—still
wearing his boots an' his jacket, the poor sod." He
straightened up, with a resigned shrug of the shoulders.
"Have to be an inquiry when we get to Sydney, I suppose, but none of us saw what happened, did we?" No
one spoke, and he sighed. "All right, O'Reilly—get the
boat inboard, lad. I'll go below and break the news to
his widow, and then we'll get under way. I'll have a
word with his groom—the soldier—in case he knows
anything, but there's not much more I can do, is there?"
He hesitated and then addressed himself to Jethro,
" 'Twas you gave the alarm, was it not?"

"Aye," Jethro confirmed guardedly.

"But you didn't see him fall?"

"No, Mr. Burdock. I heard the splash as he went in,
an' I see who it was, that's all." He was twisting the
truth, he knew, but Burdock appeared to be satisfied,
for he nodded, covered O'Shea's body with some empty
sacks, and went below to break the news of his death
to Abigail.

Jethro waited, listening; then, as the boat came alongside, he roused himself and went to help O'Reilly with the winch.

A great deal—his liberty or perhaps even his life, he thought grimly—depended on what Lieutenant O'Shea's orderly had to say. But luck was with him to a greater extent than he had dared to hope it might be, for the soldier, questioned by Jed Burdock, agreed quite readily that his officer had been drinking.

"He had a hip flask, sir—allus carried one, Mr. O'Shea did. I seen him take a few pulls at it while I was movin' the horse. I dunno if he was drunk or not, sir, but he bawled me out something cruel when the horse started playin' me up." The man shrugged and added slyly, "He'd his new bride waitin' for him below . . . maybe felt he needed a mite o' bottled courage afore he went to her."

The *Fanny's* master reproved him sharply.

"She's a fine young lady and you've no call to make a remark like that. Any case, what I want you to tell me is whether you heard Mr. O'Shea cry out or saw him go over the side. Did you?"

"No, sir," the orderly answered, without hesitation. "I were busy with the soddin' horse. Didn't hear nuffink, an' that's the God's truth." He glanced across at the shrouded body and shrugged. "I'll not shed any tears for him, though, and I dare swear his fine young lady wife won't shed many neither. He were a swine o' an officer, Mr. Burdock, an' if you want my opinion, she's better off without him. Eh, Jethro?"

Jethro, taken by surprise at the soldier's unexpected question, felt the color drain from his cheeks. But Burdock seemingly did not notice his discomfiture, and his mute nod satisfied Lieutenant O'Shea's orderly.

It was easy to kill a man, Jethro reflected—as easy as O'Shea had found it. He moved toward the midships hatchway, intending to stand guard over it until his Miss Abigail left the cabin, and as he did so, he tripped over his crook, still lying where he had dropped it on the deck. Smothering an exclamation of alarm, he picked it up and, crossing to the lee bulwark, let it fall soundlessly into the river water.

That done, he regained his composure and went to squat down beside the hatch. From the cabin—contrary to the orderly's prediction—he heard the sound of subdued sobbing. When, at last, this ceased, Jethro let his head rest on the hatch coaming and, as he always did, fell into a deep and dreamless sleep.

CHAPTER XXII

On a gray morning in April 1808—some three months after Major George Johnstone had installed himself as lieutenant governor—John Macarthur strode into Johnstone's office, his face dark with anger. Close on his heels was Nicholas Bayly, the lieutenant governor's secretary.

"I tell you, John, he's not here," Bayly asserted, an anxious note in his voice. "If you could entrust whatever documents you want to show him to me, I'll see that he receives them as soon as he comes in."

Macarthur turned on him. "And when," he demanded coldly, "do you expect him to come in?"

Bayly shrugged. "I don't know. He's at Annandale. In an hour, perhaps. He—"

"Well then, damme, I shall just have to wait for him!" Macarthur frowned angrily, then reached into his pocket and took out a crumpled piece of paper which he thrust in Bayly's direction. "Here, look at this. I presume you've seen this—this so-called proclamation before?" Contemptuously, he read from it: *"His Honor the Lieutenant Governor, actuated by an anxious desire to preserve the rights and liberties of*

Englishmen inviolate, and to convince strangers resorting to this colony that they have nothing to apprehend from the oppression of power . . . hereby annuls and declares invalid the sentence of transportation pronounced against Oliver Russell and Robert Daniels, respectively master and mate of the vessel Brothers.' "
He replaced the printed sheet in his pocket. "Well, Nick, you know all about this, don't you?"

Bayly inclined his close-cropped head, his expression sheepish. "Yes, it was dictated to me. But for God's sake, John, as Johnstone's secretary I was simply obeying his orders! Didn't you *want* the sentences annulled? We both supposed you did."

"I wanted Russell given back his command, not merely exonerated, and George cannot say he wasn't aware of it. He knows I have a cargo of sealskins consigned to the *Brothers* and the London price won't hold as high as it is for very long. Besides," Macarthur added wrathfully, "he's bent over backwards in favor of the Blaxlands." He paused, as if gathering strength for the storm of fury that was sweeping over him. "Damn John Blaxland for the rogue that he is! I'm sorry, but I must say it—of all the turncoats who have come out against me, after supporting me during the trouble last January, he is the worst. And look at how lightly he was treated by the court, after his dreadful assault on poor Russell! What a scandal that was! The court found him guilty of assault and of trying to remove Russell forcibly from the *Brothers,* but all Blaxland got was a paltry fine of five pounds! Is that justice, Nick, by any standards? Why, even the *Bounty* bastard would not have countenanced it, I swear! It will be a happy day for the colony when we've seen the last of Blaxland, believe me!"

"Johnstone felt he had no choice but to acquiesce in the sentence. . . ." Bayly hesitated, conscious of what he owed to his angry visitor, yet compelled to defend the man he now served. "Er . . . he felt that to

do otherwise might give the appearance of influencing
the court in *your* favor."

"And Charlie Grimes made a confounded shambles
of the prosecution," Macarthur complained. "He is useless as judge advocate, Nick—my God, he's worse than
Atkins, and that's saying something, is it not?" He
swore softly. "Ned Abbott was better by a long chalk."

Nicholas Bayly sighed. "We all know that, John, but
he won't take it on again. He says he hasn't the time
or the necessary legal knowledge. And since we had
that infernal man Crossley deported to Van Diemen's
Land—devil take it, who has?" He gestured to the
desk, which was piled high with papers, and, after a
quick search, brought to light the one he was seeking.
Offering it for Macarthur's inspection, he said dryly,
"Mr. Grimes's resignation. It came in this morning—
His Honor hasn't seen it yet. Grimes brought it in himself and he told me, in confidence, that he's had enough
of New South Wales. *He* wants to be given passage
with John Blaxland in the *Brothers,* so that he can
deliver our official dispatches to Lord Castlereagh in
person."

"Harris wants to do precisely the same thing," Macarthur supplied, his pendulous lower lip drooping in
disapproval. *"John Harris,* would you credit it! Once
one of our most ardent supporters, Nick, as you know
well. But all those cowardly swine want is to save
their own skins, should the government in London, in
its wisdom, decide that we hadn't sufficient justification
for deposing the tyrant Bligh!"

"You should have gone to England yourself, John,"
Bayly said, his tone warily reproachful. "You have
a gift for oratory—*you* could have made out a case
that no one could refute. And they all voted for you
to be our official delegate at that meeting in February,
in St. Philip's Church, did they not?"

They had not only voted him in as delegate, John Macarthur reflected, with a certain bitterness, they had also volunteered to provide over a thousand pounds to cover his expenses . . . Lord Kable, Underwood, Blaxcell, and—damn their eyes—the Blaxland brothers had promised a hundred pounds each! Not that any of them had paid him a penny; they had promised but then they had gone back on their promises. Yet, at that meeting in the church, which had been very well attended, they had passed a resolution thanking George Johnstone for the wise and salutary measures he had adopted to suppress the tyranny of the deposed governor, and they had agreed to contribute toward the purchase of a sword, to be presented to Johnstone as a token of appreciation.

They had given an address of thanks to the Corps and one to himself, the wording of which might one day hang him, Macarthur recalled, his mouth twisting into a cynical smile. How had they expressed it? A pox on them—they were unprincipled turncoats! They had thanked him *"for having been chiefly instrumental in bringing about the happy change which took place on twenty-six January . . ."* But now . . . His smile faded, as he remembered the compliments he had received from men who had now turned against him, the way the populace and the soldiers had cheered him, after his final acquittal on Bligh's diabolical charges. Even Richard Atkins, drunken sot though he was, had given evidence that had assisted his acquittal, leaving the emancipist lawyer Crossley—and, of course, Governor Bligh—to shoulder the blame for the attempt to ruin him.

And Abbott, his friend of so many years, Ned Abbott had started to voice adverse criticism of Johnstone's administration in general and his own in particular. Ned was envious of course—most of them *were* envious, since his appointment as secretary for the colony, even though it was a post that involved a considerable amount of work and was unpaid. True, it gave him some degree of power and insured that George Johnstone looked to him for advice but . . . Ned Abbott had begun calling him "The Ruler" behind his back and Will Minchin had begun to complain that Macarthur had not, as yet, seen fit to use his power in order to reward those he had loosely termed his "friends."

Macarthur glanced at young Nicholas Bayly and some of the angry tension drained out of him. Nick was loyal, as loyal as Macarthur's own son Edward, and perhaps he was right; perhaps, in spite of the parsimoniously broken promises made at the meeting at St. Philip's Church, he *should* have gone to England. He had influence there, powerful influence still with Lord Camden, now president of the Trades Council, and could have gained the ear of the Prince of Wales through his physician.

"Why did you decide not to go back to England, John?" Bayly asked curiously, breaking the short silence that had fallen between them.

"My interests are here," Macarthur answered shortly. "My home, my family, and my fortune are all here, Nick. But—I might send Edward, if only in order to counteract such malice as Grimes and Harris may devise. Edward wants to take a commission in the army, in any event. . . . Yes, I think it might be wise to arrange a passage for him, as soon as possible. But not—" he made a wry grimace, "—not on board the infernal *Brothers,* even if Russell is reinstated! I'll be damned before I let my son set foot on any ship owned by the Blaxlands!"

"Edward would be an able representative," Bayly agreed. "And he'll do well in the army, if all the rumors of war are true and the Spanish do rise against Bonaparte." But Macarthur was not listening; he had started to rummage through the papers on Johnstone's untidy desk. "Where's that letter of resignation from Charlie Grimes?" he asked.

"It's there somewhere," Bayly began. "I put it there, ready for Major Johnstone's attention and—"

Macarthur's fingers closed about one of the reports and he read it, his brows knit in a thoughtful frown. "Good God, I'd forgotten about this! What was finally decided about it?"

"About what?" Bayly asked, somewhat at a loss.

"The report on two accidental drownings in the Hawkesbury." Referring to the paper he had picked up, he read out the names. "One was Desmond O'Shea of the Corps and the other that young assistant surgeon Mrs. Putland made such a fuss about . . . Penhaligon. He attended her late husband before he died and then Jamieson had him posted to Coal River."

Bayly took the report from him and, in turn, glanced through it. "A verdict of accidental death by drowning in both cases," he said. "Although there was a bit of a mystery about both of them. Penhaligon was absent without leave from Newcastle and had himself smuggled aboard one of the charter boats, from which, apparently, he drowned when he tried to swim ashore near the Green Hills. And O'Shea had just married—the elder Tempest girl—and was on his way with her to Sydney in a vessel called the *Fanny*. The report on him suggests that he fell overboard after he had been drinking."

"I don't recall him as a heavy drinker but"—Macarthur's frown deepened—"I imagine that a spell of duty at the Coal River settlement would drive most men to drink."

"Yes. There were no contesting depositions and seemingly nobody on board the *Fanny* saw what happened."

"And he was just married, you say?"

Bayly nodded. "The widow was recommended for a

small pension, but she's not in financial straits—my wife knows her and I've met her several times. She's in the temporary . . . employ, I suppose you could call it, of Mrs. Dawson, helping with her children and, my wife says, expecting one of her own. Rather a tragedy, when she lost her husband so soon after their wedding. She is a beautiful young woman. Er—Fenn Kemp was interested, until he learned that she was pregnant and—"

"Don't talk to me of Fenn Kemp," John Macarthur put in, a sharp edge to his voice.

"Is he one of those who have turned against you, John?"

Bayly shook his head before Macarthur could answer. "Well, no, not really," he admitted. "Or rather perhaps I should say that he's made it obvious, even to His Honor, that some recognition of his part in that tyrant Bligh's overthrow would be appreciated."

"That will come, Nick . . . and not only to Kemp, damn his eyes! I'll talk to George about it. If we have nothing else, we have plenty of land to grant to those who deserve it, have we not? And, I suppose, to a few who don't . . . let's call them the waverers. I—" Macarthur broke off, as the sound of horses' hooves on the newly graveled parade ground reached his ears.

Bayly went to the window. "His Honor the lieutenant governor has arrived, with escort," he said, without turning around. "Good! Now perhaps I can persuade him to sign some of these papers that keep piling up."

"Not until I've had a word with him, my boy," Macarthur warned. I must have this matter of command of the *Brothers* cleared up . . . damn it, my sealskins won't wait!"

But Major Johnstone, when he entered the office, clearly had other and more pressing matters on his mind. Seeing Macarthur, he slapped his thigh in what appeared to be relief. "John!" he exclaimed. "The very man I wanted to see! Sit down, my dear fellow, and cast your eye over this extraordinary document, because it's of vital concern to you."

Macarthur eyed him with some astonishment, but, seating himself in front of the desk, he accepted the proffered document. He read it through with rapidly mounting fury. Headed by Johnstone's name, as lieutenant governor, the document took the form of an address of complaint against himself, expressed in such strong terms as to be at once offensive and alarming. The signatories—of whom, he saw, there were almost twenty—described themselves as settlers, and they recorded their "surprise and alarm" at seeing John Macarthur, Esq., holding the post of secretary for the colony. The document went on to describe Macarthur as

> having violated the law and public faith, and having trampled on the most sacred and constitutional rights of British Subjects.
>
> Indeed, Sir, this gentleman has been the scourge of this Colony by fomenting quarrels between His Majesty's officers, servants and subjects, whilst his monopoly and extortion have been highly injurious to the inhabitants of every description.
>
> For these reasons, Sir, we the undersigned pray that the said John Macarthur should be removed from all Offices under the Government and prevented from participating in the administration of the Colony.

"God Almighty!" he gasped, coming to the end and staring incredulously at the signatures. "They wrote in these terms to you! They—"

"Not only to me, John," Johnstone put in sourly. "But also, I am assured on good authority, to William

Paterson at Port Dalrymple! They listed calamities which they claim have befallen the colony since *Bounty* Bligh's arrest and begged Paterson to return here at once and assume command of the Corps and the colony. They—"

"You permitted them to dispatch such a letter?" Macarthur's anger was in voice and eyes. "In God's name, George, are you out of your mind?"

"No, dammit, I'm not!" Johnstone, too, was angry. "The infernal letter had been smuggled out before I was informed of its existence."

"Do you suppose Paterson will act on it? Do you think he'll come back?"

George Johnstone recovered himself. "No," he declared cynically. "That is the very last thing he wants to do. Like Harris, he has had his fill of this colony— he wasn't ordered to Van Diemen's Land, you know. He went there at his own request."

Nicholas Bayly, who had stood in silence during the exchange between his two seniors, slipped quietly from the room, and neither sought to detain him; but, as he reached the door, Johnstone called out to him to bring in glasses and a bottle of brandy.

"There's more, John," he said, his tone oddly cold.

"What more can there be, for the Lord's sake?" Macarthur demanded.

"This," the lieutenant governor said. "It is a threat to your life, based on information presented by Gregory Blaxland and—"

Irately, John Macarthur cut him short. "If one of the damned Blaxland rogues is involved, then it's a ploy to try to alarm me. They *want* to drive me from the colony, for God's sake, by fair means or foul! Well, a pox on them, they will not succeed! They—"

"Fenn Kemp thought you would refuse to believe it," Johnstone put in, his smile faintly mocking. "For that reason he took Blaxland's statement and had made a sworn deposition, as a magistrate. I have it here, John, so perhaps you had better read it."

Macarthur flashed him a skeptical glance, but, as Nicholas Bayly returned with the brandy and glasses, he accepted a generous measure and started to read the short deposition, his eyes narrowing as he did so. Phrased in careful legal language and duly sworn and countersigned by Gregory Blaxland, it was a document calculated to shake even Macarthur's nerve and confidence. Referring to Magistrate Kemp as the "deponent," it ran:

> Deponent was informed by Mr. Blaxland that there was a plan laid at the Hawkesbury to assassinate Mr. Macarthur, and that there were people employed who would willingly sacrifice their lives to accomplish it.
>
> Deponent said he thought it was impossible but Mr. Blaxland replied that there were a number of Hawkesbury settlers in Sydney, and that there would be a great number there shortly. He told Deponent that although Mr. Macarthur had used him and his brother very ill in interfering with their Shipping concerns, he could not countenance the idea of murder being committed.

"Well?" Johnstone challenged. "Do you still imagine it's a ploy devised by the Blaxlands?"

Macarthur scowled at him and took temporary refuge in his glass. Finally, he questioned sharply, "Did he tell Kemp who was involved? Someone must be stirring up trouble amongst the settlers, organizing them—doubtless at Bligh's behest."

"The former governor is under strict guard," Johnstone reminded him reproachfully. "He is permitted to exercise in the grounds of Government House, but only under the escort of one of my men. He has no communication with anybody outside, and such requests or complaints as he makes to me are made in writing. No officer save the guard commander has access to him." He shrugged, sipped at his brandy, and added flatly. "Bligh can have organized nothing since his arrest, John. For the Lord's sake, he—"

"There are his servants," Macarthur argued. "And —why, damme, there's his aide, Hawley! *He* went to the Hawkesbury, did he not, after one of our courts released him?"

"True. His wife has a farm near Richmond Hill."

"Hawley should never have been released, George. Devil take it, we should have kept him in jail with Gore! Those two were the *Bounty* bastard's staunchest supporters." Macarthur's tone was edged with malice. "Why *was* he freed?"

"For the simple reason that no charges could be brought—or proven—against him," Johnstone returned with asperity.

"Well, they can now, damn his eyes! Look—" Macarthur pointed to one of the signatures at the foot of the settlers' address. "*A. Hawley,* d'you see, plain as day and one of the first names on the list! You can be sure that he's at the back of this infernal assassination plot . . . most of the settlers are emancipist peasants but Hawley's a marine officer, promoted from the ranks, and loyal to Bligh. He's our man, George, no doubt about it."

"And what do you propose I should do about it?" Johnstone's exasperation was unconcealed, but Macarthur ignored it.

"Order his arrest, of course," he retorted uncompromisingly. "Let Hawley stand trial."

"But you've no proof of his complicity. You—"

"Let him prove his innocence. He'll have his work cut out."

520 William Stuart Long

"That is hardly British justice, John. Why—"

John Macarthur gestured to the signature, a sneer on his face. "If you're too fainthearted to do what is your plain duty, George, then leave it to me. I'll order Hawley's arrest and make out the case against him."

"Charlie Grimes is acting judge advocate," Johnstone objected. "You'll have to consult him."

"Charlie Grimes's resignation is on your desk," Macarthur informed him, with icy contempt. "If you can find it amongst all that mess. He wants to be sent home, and Harris with him, to deliver our dispatches to His Majesty's Government. According to Nick Bayly he said he wants to be given passage in the *Brothers* and leave as soon as it's possible."

"Does he, now?" Johnstone was annoyed by what had all too obviously been a breach of confidence on the part of his secretary, but he contrived to hide his annoyance and, after a brief search among his papers, found Judge Advocate Grimes's letter of resignation. He was smiling as he read it. "Grimes and the much esteemed Dr. Harris?" he said pensively. "Why, my dear John, who better could we send as our advocates than two officers so well acquainted with the causes which occasioned the supersession of Governor Bligh? Harris in particular, since no person can be more competent to explain the situation than one of those who called upon me to assume command of the colony— and pledged their lives and fortunes to support the measure. As"—he added tellingly—"you did yourself, if my memory is not at fault?"

Unable to deny the implied reproof, John Macarthur reddened. "Do as you see fit in the matter," he returned irritably. "You are the lieutenant governor, are you not?"

"There are times when I have to ask myself which of us holds the reins of office," Johnstone admitted.

"Although, as I have mentioned before, John, it will be *my* head on the chopping block, if His Majesty's Government remains unconvinced of the necessity of the measures we took . . . don't forget that, will you?"

"Of course not," Macarthur assured him. He drained his glass and rose, feeling that the time for departure had come. With George Johnstone talking in this vein, no useful purpose could be served by prolonging the conversation.

"Are you going to let Grimes and Harris go?" he asked.

"I think so, yes. We'll be well rid of both of them . . . and Minchin, too."

Macarthur did not argue. "And what of the *Bounty* bastard's loyal marine, Hawley? Are you intending to order his arrest or shall I do so?"

George Johnstone shrugged his plump, gold-epauletted shoulders. "If you can make out a case against him—and I'm not sure that you can—then by all means order his arrest."

"Right." Macarthur gave his superior a mocking bow. "I will not only make out a case against Hawley," he asserted, with arrogant confidence. "I'll make him an example! I give you good day, Your Honor."

He was moving toward the door when he belatedly recalled the original reason for his visit. "George," he rasped. "Regarding Oliver Russell—you've pardoned him and the mate Daniels, I understand. But aren't you also going to reinstate them?"

To his annoyance George Johnstone shook his head. "I cannot," he answered, with unexpected firmness. "The most I can do is permit both men to take passage to England in the *Dart*, on Russell's written promise that he will report the matter to the authorities on arrival. After all," he added, in a more placatory tone, "the Blaxlands own a half share in the *Brothers,* which surely gives them the right to say who should command her, does it not?"

Macarthur opened his mouth to voice a sullen protest and then closed it again. So long as the infernal *Brothers* sailed, with his sealskins on board, what did it matter who was master? And John Blaxland had announced that he would also be taking passage in her. . . . Good riddance to him!

"George, my dear fellow," Macarthur said smoothly. "It won't do our cause any good for Paterson to return, will it? I'll send Walter Davidson to talk to him, just to make sure he does not suffer an attack of conscience. But I fancy the time has come to look into the question of some tangible—ah—recognition of the merits of those officers and civilian gentlemen who continue to give us their support, do you not agree? Shall we, perhaps, call a public meeting for the purpose?"

George Johnstone, with the uneasy conviction that he had been maneuvered into a position he did not greatly like, gave his reluctant consent to the suggestion.

"I'll announce it," Marcarthur promised. "After our ambassadors have departed these shores."

He was smiling as he went out, for it had occurred to him suddenly that Joseph Foveaux was due to return from leave in England within the next couple of months. Foveaux was senior to George Johnstone in the regiment and should therefore supersede him as lieutenant governor and . . . Macarthur's smile widened. He could handle Joe Foveaux with greater ease than he could handle George Johnstone, despite public opinion, and despite the dreadful song, or "pipe"—referring to himself by the hated nickname of Jack Boddice—that was making the rounds in Sydney:

That Turnip-head Fool,
Jack Boddice's tool
Stepped into Bligh's station—he dared not oppose.

*   *   *

Scurrilous things, these pipes, he thought, although he ought not to question their efficacy, since he had used them himself in the past with remarkable results. Perhaps this might be the moment to issue one aimed at the turncoat Grimes and his partner in disloyalty, Surgeon Harris.

First, however, there was the matter of the late governor's partisan, Captain Hawley, to be dealt with. . . . Still smiling, John Macarthur walked briskly into his own office. To the clerk on duty there he said, with curt decisiveness, "Give me pen and paper and then find Lieutenant Lawson and Lieutenant Draffin. Tell both gentlemen that I have need of their signatures to a warrant and ask them to oblige me by attending me here at once."

When the clerk had departed on his errand, Macarthur wrote out an order for Hawley's arrest and removal to the jail in Sydney to answer charges of . . . he hesitated for a moment and then penned the words: *conspiracy and inciting to violence.* That was comprehensive enough, he decided, and would suffice until he had had time to give more consideration to the precise nature of the charges.

Then, almost as an afterthought, he composed a second order, addressed to Sydney's chief constable, ordering the arrest of the Irish emancipist Sir Henry Brown Hayes. Hayes, a wealthy man, lived in a state of some luxury at Vaucluse but . . . due to Grimes's incompetence, his evidence at a preliminary hearing of the case against Provost Marshal Gore had been in Gore's favor. With Gore soon to be brought to trial, a second hearing of Sir Henry's testimony would be inadvisible. It was better by far, Macarthur thought, to have him arrested and, as soon as possible, deported to Van Diemen's Land.

Macarthur appended his own signature and seal to

both orders, and when the clerk returned with the two officers he had summoned, he spread both sheets of paper on the desktop in front of them, his explanation as to their import carefully worded.

"In the temporary absence of a holder for the office of judge advocate," he finished crisply, "your signatures, as magistrates and justices of the peace, will suffice, gentlemen, together with my own. Be so good as to add them, if you will."

Draffin scrawled his name without demure; Lawson, in the act of doing the same, asked cautiously, "I take it that the commandant is aware of what you are doing?"

"How could you imagine otherwise, my dear Will?" Macarthur demanded. "But ask him, if you've any doubts—he's in his office."

William Lawson shrugged and added his signature.

"Anything more, sir?" he asked, with formal politeness.

"No," Macarthur said. "That's all, thank you."

And it should be, he reflected. It should be all that was required to send both Gore and Hawley to Coal River for the next seven years. . . .

Justin learned of the warrant for his stepfather's arrest from Robert Campbell. The shipowner said gravely, "I obtained warning of this from Surgeon Harris who, as you've probably heard, Justin, is now working as assiduously to oppose our secretary for the colony as he once did in his support. He and the esteemed Mr. Grimes are both at loggerheads with the lieutenant governor and his chief adviser and are endeavoring to have themselves sent back to England . . . if possible, aboard the *Brothers*."

Justin stared at him incredulously. "Will they be sent home, sir?"

"It seems probable, from what I've heard. John

Blaxland wants to go, too." The big man smiled, eyeing Justin thoughtfully. "Blaxland, in despair since the *Brothers* affair, has asked me to give him passage in my barque *Rose* . . . and I've agreed."

Justin hesitated. "Can they really intend to arrest my stepfather, sir?" he asked at last, unable to take it in. "What crime can they accuse him of? He and my mother have done nothing, save farm the land at Long Wrekin."

"Captain Hawley had a hand in organizing the Hawkesbury Loyalist Volunteers, had he not?" Campbell questioned. "And would have called them out in Governor Bligh's support, surely?"

"He was prepared to," Justin admitted, with pride. "But the governor forbade it. He would not countenance civil war. Since then, since his return to the Hawkesbury, sir, as I said, my stepfather had done nothing to merit arrest."

"He signed his name to a petition for Macarthur's removal from the office of secretary."

"So did a score of others, Mr. Campbell!"

"True," Campbell conceded. "But since then there has apparently been a threat to assassinate Macarthur, and whether or not your stepfather had a hand in that, my boy, it would seem that he has been cast for the role of would-be assassin. He—" Justin attempted to voice a protest, but the older man waved him to silence. "No, lad, hear me out. I cannot be sure that all Dr. Harris's information is correct, but he is still nominally superintendent of police, here in Sydney, and, in that capacity, two warrants were delivered to him. One was for the arrest of Sir Henry Brown Hayes, the other for Captain Hawley's. The messenger supposedly made an error—the second warrant should have gone to that unspeakable rogue Reilly, promoted from head jailer here since Macarthur's sojourn as his guest, to chief constable in Parramatta. And it has just been sent on."

Justin's brain was racing now. "Do you mean, sir, that there has been some delay in serving the warrant?"

"That would seem likely. Time enough for you to warn him, Justin, granted a modicum of luck." Campbell held up a cautionary finger. "Reilly will almost certainly send one of his constables to request military aid in effecting the arrest, and that will take time, because the troops will have to go overland. My guess is that they will be sent from Toongabbie."

"Then I could be at Long Wrekin long before them!" Justin exclaimed. He got to his feet. "The *Flinders* is ready for sea and—"

"Not so fast, lad. Sit down and listen. You must not take the *Flinders*. You—"

"Not take her, sir? But I—" Justin reluctantly resumed his seat. "Why not, Mr. Campbell? She'd have the legs of anything they could send, if the troops don't go overland."

"But the *Flinders* is too well known," Campbell pointed out. "And you with her, Justin. Besides, Captain Hawley cannot elude arrest indefinitely if he stays in New South Wales—you'll not only have to warn him, lad, you'll have to take him back to Van Diemen's Land. But even if you managed to hide him on board the *Flinders*, don't forget, the *Porpoise* is back here now. If a chase were ordered, you would stand no chance against the guns of a King's ship."

Justin looked crestfallen. Campbell was right, he knew; even if he reached Long Wrekin before the soldiers, the *Flinders*'s arrival at the wharf could not be concealed, and he and his vessel would be put under arrest, his holds searched. . . . And if the *Porpoise* should be ordered to give chase, the *Flinders*'s speed would not save him from gunfire.

He looked up at Robert Campbell's bearded face and, to his surprise, saw that the big man was smiling.

"You can take my *Phoebe*, Justin. She's a fast sailer

and handy enough, and furthermore, she's fitted for
sea and expected in Hobart, in any event, on a mail
charter. So there should be no questions asked, if you
keep out of the soldiers' sight. You'll need a four-man
crew, but you and Hawley and Barnes can all handle
a sailing ship, and I can provide you with the fourth
man. What do you say, lad?"

Justin did not hesitate. Again he was on his feet,
eager to be gone. "I say yes, sir—and thank you."

"Good!" Robert Campbell approved. "But there's
one more matter we must deal with. I have a letter to
Colonel Paterson entrusted to me by those same settlers who, with your stepfather, signed the petition for
John Macarthur's removal from his infernal office. It is
confidential and dangerous, and, although I fear that
Major Johnstone may have got wind of its existence, I
don't think he's read the whole text and I don't think
he knows that it has not yet been delivered. Will you
deliver it before you go to Hobart?"

"Of course, sir," Justin promised, once again without
hesitation. He accepted the sealed letter.

"If you are caught with the letter on you," Campbell
warned, "you'll be sentenced to hard labor at Coal
River! So hide it well, Justin—and destroy it, rather
than permit it to fall into the wrong hands. Is that
understood?"

"Yes, sir."

"Very well, then I'll detain you no longer. Get
under way as soon as you can. I'll send a boat out to
the *Phoebe* to take off her crew—you pick up Cookie
Barnes and any gear you need from the *Flinders*."
Robert Campbell held out his hand. "May God go with
you, lad!"

Justin wrung his hand and left the shipping office at
a run. Barely an hour later he ordered the *Phoebe*'s
anchor weighed and her jib and topsail set. A party of
seamen on the *Porpoise*'s fo'c's'le paused in their task

of drying the frigate's sails and watched the colonial
vessel's departure with mild interest. From the *Porpoise*'s quarterdeck an officer courteously doffed his
hat, and Justin, hatless and unable to return the courtesy, raised a hand in token of farewell.

"Abigail!" Henrietta Dawson's tone was impatient.
"There is some person at the door asking to see you.
Go and deal with him, will you . . . and when you have,
it's time the children had their luncheon."

Abigail came slowly to her feet. She was in the
seventh month of her pregnancy, and the weight of
the child she was carrying made rapid movement difficult. Nevertheless, Henrietta did not spare her; she was
employed as the Dawson children's governess, and although there were plenty of servants, both at the
Spences' Sydney house and here, at Upwey Farm on
the Hawkesbury, she was held responsible for seeing to
all of the children's needs: their lessons—which had to
be kept up, when they were on holiday from school—
their meals, and of course their questions, which
seemed at times never to cease.

But, Abigail told herself, she was fortunate to be
given employment, a roof over her head, and three good
meals a day; the pension she had been granted, somewhat grudgingly, by the military authorities would not
have kept her in such comfort . . . and it would not
have paid Jethro Crowan's wages. As it was, Timothy
Dawson had taken him on as shepherd at Upwey, and,
with a large flock of purebred Merinos to care for,
Jethro was happier than he had been in the Reverend
Caleb Boskenna's service at Yarramundie—happier,
perhaps, than he had ever been. And she was glad of
that, for he was a good man to whom—Abigail caught
her breath, willing herself not to think of what she owed
to Jethro Crowan. To think of that was to admit . . . No,

no, she *would* not think of it. What was done was done and could not be undone. And she still had Lucy to worry about, still had to think of some way in which she could persuade Henrietta to allow her sister to join her.

When they went back to Sydney, perhaps she could suggest that Lucy's education was suffering and ask if she might resume at Mr. Mann's school. She reached the door onto the verandah and, in the strong midday sunlight, could not at first make out the identity of her unexpected caller.

"Mrs. O'Shea ma'am?" He came closer, hat in hand, a broad-shouldered, balding man of uncertain age, dressed in a shabby blue, brass-buttoned jacket. His voice was vaguely familiar but still Abigail was uncertain of who he was. Then she saw Jethro approaching and memory stirred. "Mr. . . . Burdock?" she managed, her voice not quite steady. "Mr. Jed Burdock?"

"Aye," he confirmed. "That's me—master o' the *Fanny,* dandy-rigged ketch."

Abigail's heart lurched. Now she knew who her caller was, and—it was evident from the look on his face—so did Jethro, as he mounted the two steps up to the verandah and ranged himself protectively beside her.

"You'm got no call to disturb Miss Abigail," he said aggressively.

Jed Burdock replaced his headgear and gestured to a small leather case, with brass-bound corners, which he had laid down in order to greet her. "But I do, Jethro, lad," he asserted. "That there case belonged to the late Mr. O'Shea, ma'am—and it's got his initials stamped on it, see? Only came across it a few weeks back, for 'twas under a pile o' junk in my cabin. And I've been aimin' to give it to you soon as I could, but I've been on a Norfolk Island charter, and then, when I asked for you in Sydney Town, I was told you'd left to come here. And," he added defensively, "this is the first chance I've had to come up the Hawkesbury."

"Oh," Abigail said flatly, avoiding Jethro's eye. "It's —it's very good of you, Mr. Burdock, to take so much trouble."

Jed Burdock picked up the case. " 'Tis locked, ma'am," he explained. "So I don't know what's inside it, but maybe it's money, and I thought—well, you being widowed like you were, you might be glad of it. Do you have the key, p'raps?"

There was a key, Abigail recalled, amongst what Quartermaster Laycock had described as her "late husband's effects." Most of those, Desmond O'Shea's uniforms, his horse and saddlery, his civilian clothing, had been auctioned in the Corps mess, according to custom, and the proceeds given to her. The key had been in the pocket of his scarlet jacket—the jacket in which he had drowned—and she had kept it, simply because she had not had the heart to throw it away.

She nodded. "Yes, I have a key, Mr. Burdock. But I—" She should reward him for his honesty, she knew, and she had a few notes of hand from the Corps auction. She excused herself and went to her room to fetch one. The largest was for five pounds and she returned with it. "Will you accept this, Mr. Burdock?" she asked. "As a—as a token of my gratitude for the trouble you've taken?"

He eyed the note uncertainly and then gave it back to her. "You'll need it more'n I will, ma'am, with your —ah—happy event to provide for. I'm pleased to be of service to you." He gave her the case, tipped his hat to her, nodded to Jethro, and made for the horse-drawn trap that had brought him from the wharf.

"That was good of Mr. Burdock," Abigail said to Jethro. "Very good."

"Aye," the shepherd agreed. "He'm a good man, Jed

Burdock. Let's hope there's summat in that little box as'll make it worth his trouble."

There was, however, no time to find that out now; the Dawson children were waiting for their luncheon, and, after they had finished, there would be lessons until five o'clock, then play—which she was required to supervise—the evening meal, and finally bedtime. Abigail sighed. Not until Julia—the eldest and last to retire—was tucked into bed would she have time to open the case.

She easily evaded Henrietta's indifferent questions concerning her caller and hurried into the big farmhouse kitchen, with little Alexander held firmly by the hand.

"See that they wash their hands and faces before you let them sit down at the table," Henrietta reminded her, as she always did. "Just because we live in an uncivilized society out here, there is no reason why the children should forget their manners."

"No, Mrs. Dawson," Abigail acknowledged. As the three children obediently attended to their ablutions, she slipped the leather case into her own room and forced herself not to think of it for the rest of the day.

Timothy Dawson came in at dusk. Abigail, busy supervising Alexander and Dorothea's preparations for supper, which they took in bed, heard him call out to his wife that he would have to go out again.

"I'll snatch a bite when the children have theirs," he added, "if Abigail will be kind enough to look after me."

"Of course she will," Henrietta declared, a note of irritation in her normally lilting voice. "But why have you to go out again, Timothy? I was hoping that we could have an evening together."

"Some urgent business to attend to, my dear," Timothy answered. To Abigail, when he joined her and his daughter Julia at the well-scrubbed kitchen table, and the cook had been dismissed, he said in a confidential undertone, "George Suttor had called a meeting of loyalist settlers, Abby—but don't breathe a word of this to Mrs. Dawson. You know that she holds strong views on the subject of our opposition to the illegal régime."

"Yes," Abigail acknowledged. "I do."

"I shall be riding over with Captain Hawley and some of the others and I may be late getting back. Could you see that there's a door left unlocked for me?" Timothy Dawson gestured to the door behind Abigail's back. "This one, preferably—and perhaps you could tell Jethro to take a watch on it, just in case any escapers happen to be about."

He left after a hurried meal; Abigail, at Henrietta's request, served her with a laden tray in her bedroom; and, having conveyed Timothy Dawson's instructions to Jethro and seen Julia into bed, she was free at last to retire to her own room and examine the case Jed Burdock had brought.

The key came to light, after some searching, and, to Abigail's relief, it fitted the heavy brass lock. She opened the lid, not knowing what she would find and conscious of an acute sensation of guilt as she did so. Desmond O'Shea was dead and . . . Her lower lip trembled and she bit fiercely into it. He was dead and the verdict of the court of inquiry into his death had been that it was accidental and caused by drowning— a verdict she had been virtually certain was incorrect but had not, by word or action, disputed. She had not disputed the verdict on Titus Penhaligon's death, either, and Jethro, called as a witness, had said nothing in his evidence of the wound on the poor young surgeon's head. They . . . Her searching fingers closed over a small leather bag—larger than a purse—lying in one corner of the case, half hidden among a miscellany of papers, old letters, and a pair of ivory-inlaid dueling pistols.

She opened the neck of the bag and spilled its contents onto the quilt covering her bed, having to suppress a cry of astonishment when she saw a small mountain of gold coins piling up as the bag emptied. By the light of her bedside candle the gold gleamed dully, the King's head catching the flickering beam of light. Abigail gasped—the coins were guineas. Breathlessly, she counted them, her fingers shaking.

There were a hundred and fifty of them—a hundred and fifty guineas, a fortune to her startled eyes and . . . close on three years' pay for an officer of Desmond O'Shea's rank, to the best of her knowledge. She started to pick up the coins in handfuls and thrust them back into the leather purse which had contained them. She could not keep them, she told herself, in all conscience she could not, for even though she was now his widow, she had never truly been Desmond O'Shea's wife. He must have relatives, a mother, brothers and sisters perhaps, with a better claim to this inheritance than she herself had.

It was possible that he had left a will; soldiers did, she had heard, since theirs was a precarious profession, and if he had, then it would almost certainly be among the papers in the case. Her conscience starting to torment her anew, Abigail continued with her search, placing the letters on one side, unread, and the pistols with them. There was a sheet of paper under where the pistols had lain. It was new, not faded as the flimsy papers of the letters had become, and it was folded in half and unsealed.

The will, she thought, this must be the will, and it would tell her to whom Desmond O'Shea had intended his money to go. She unfolded the paper and, moving nearer to the candle flame, could not suppress a cry of disbelief when she recognized the bold, sloping handwriting of—of all people—the Reverend Caleb Boskenna.

It was headed: *"Agreement between Desmond Aloysius O'Shea, Lieutenant, the New South Wales Corps, and the Reverend Caleb Boskenna of Yarramundie Farm, Hawkesbury River, New Holland, in respect of the hand in marriage of Abigail Mary Tempest, residing at the same address."*

There was a date at the foot of the page, beneath the two signatures, and Abigail deciphered it as the date of her wedding—February 11, 1808. She read on, having occasionally to go back, in order to interpret the exact meaning of the legal terminology employed.

But eventually the purpose of the agreement was clear enough even to her stunned and bewildered brain. Caleb Boskenna, her guardian—the guardian her father had appointed on his deathbed—had virtually sold her to Desmond O'Shea, in consideration of the payment of one hundred and fifty guineas, in gold, from her father's estate, as her dowry. And in return . . . A wave of shock and pain swept over her; blinding tears came and Abigail had to bite them back; the words on the page before her became blurred and indistinct, but she forced herself to read on.

In return for the dowry, Desmond O'Shea had relinquished, on his wife's part and his own, *"all claim, now and hereafter, to the land grant known as Yarramundie Farm, on the said Hawkesbury River, together with the livestock, growing crops, and buildings thereon in favor of the said Reverend Caleb Boskenna and his heirs, in perpetuity . . ."*

There was no mention of Lucy, nor of her brother Rick, and . . . Abigail's throat was tight. There was no mention of her pregnancy, and suddenly a bitter anger succeeded the shocked distress to which she had yielded, as the full enormity of what Caleb Boskenna had done—or attempted to do—began to sink in. Not only had he schemed to rob her of her inheritance, he had in addition condemned her to a marriage that could only have ended in misery, both for herself and her husband, when he learned that she was carrying another man's child. His rival's child, Titus Penhaligon's child . . . She stumbled to her feet, throwing the iniquitous agreement from her, and, as she did so, a violent spasm of pain coursed through her distended body.

Oh, God, she thought desperately, not now, surely not yet . . . the baby was only seven months, two months short of its full term. It could not, it must not come yet! She fought against the impulse to scream, and slowly, as if reluctant, the pain released its grip, the spasm passed, and Abigail managed to stand upright. She waited, the minutes ticking by, and then it came again, so severe that it almost wrung a cry from between her tightly clenched teeth. She must not waken the children, she told herself, or Henrietta, for what was probably only a false alarm, brought on by shock and . . . yes, anger. At this moment she experienced emotions she had never known before, all crystalizing in a deep and savage hatred of Caleb Boskenna.

When the pain passed, she returned everything to the leather case, including the gold and the hateful agreement that Desmond O'Shea had signed, and had just contrived to relock it when she was once again convulsed with pain. And this time instinct warned her that her hope that it was a false alarm was ill founded. The pains were too severe, following too swiftly one upon another, to be anything but genuine.

She considered rousing Henrietta and then decided against it. True, Henrietta was a woman, who had herself given birth to three children, but even so . . . Abigail managed somehow to stifle the moan that rose from her lips. Henrietta Dawson had undoubtedly had the services of a skilled midwife and one of the colony's best surgeons when she had brought her children into the world—her husband and her father were both wealthy men, well able to pay for such aid. But she would not know what to do, if unexpectedly called upon to assist another woman to give birth. It was a pity that her stepmother was still away—Frances Spence would have helped and could have been relied upon not to yield to panic. She . . . The pain ceased. Abigail dragged herself up, leaning on the bed and trying to think.

There was a midwife at Toongabbie and perhaps one at the Richmond settlement, too—she could send Jethro to fetch one of them. He would be awake; sitting in his hut, watching the unbarred kitchen door, as Timothy Dawson had bade him; and, if she could contrive to reach the kitchen, she could call him. Better, perhaps, to wait for the next pain and then go in search of Jethro.

The spasm came, so intense that she could not suppress her agonized cry, and when at last it was over, Abigail waited no longer. She staggered into the kitchen and flung open the door. Jethro came instantly, in response to her tremulous call, and one look was enough for him to shake his head to her stammered request that he go for a midwife.

"You'm too far gone for that, Miss Abigail," he told her gently. "The babby will come long before I could get halfway to Richmond." He smiled, putting an arm round her as another pain wracked her slight body. "Trust me . . . I'll take care of 'ee, never fear. Just you stay quiet, now, while I find a few things I'll need, an' then I'll carry 'ee across to my place." He did not suggest calling Henrietta; but, having assisted Abigail to a chair, he moved purposefully about the lamplit kitchen, setting a kettle of water to boil on the stoked-up fire, finding scissors and thread in Henrietta's sewing basket, and filling a jug with brandy from the store-room.

He made one hasty return to his hut; then, back in the kitchen once more, picked Abigail up in his arms and bore her across the yard, whispering to her reassuringly as if she were a child.

His hut, like Jethro himself, was clean and well ordered, and Abigail's fears left her when he set her down with infinite care on his own trestle bed, now draped with a sheet which he had taken from Henrietta's linen cupboard.

" 'Twill not be too long now, Miss Abigail," he asserted. "All 'ee has to do is bear down when I tell 'ee. Birthin' a babby's no harder nor birthin' a lamb, see, an' I birthed plenty o' lambs. Rest now, till the next pain comes."

She obeyed him without a second thought, and when —quite soon afterwards, it seemed to her—the baby came, her only concern was the fear that, because it was premature, it might not be alive.

But Jethro swiftly dispelled this fear.

" 'Tis a boy, Miss Abigail!" he told her excitedly. "Listen now and 'ee'll hear him cry!"

Abigail heard the crying, faintly at first but becoming stronger, and a few minutes later, Jethro held the tiny bundle up for her to see, pink faced, with a thin, downy suggestion of hair, peering out from the clean white shirt in which it had been wrapped.

"Just 'ee give me a minute or two to clean him up," the shepherd said. "An' then I'll give 'em you to hold. He'm little, 'tis true, but he'm strong an' he'm bleatin' louder 'n any lamb—hark to 'im!"

His cries were music to Abigail's anxious ears, and when Jethro carried him over and placed him in her waiting arms, she felt a surge of pride and happiness as he told her softly, "Here be your son, Miss Abigail. When both o' you's rested, I'll rouse up one of the men's wives an' take 'ee back to the house. Then no one needs to know who 'twas that delivered the babby."

"I'll know," Abigail answered. "I'll know and I'll always remember, Jethro . . . and I'll thank you from the bottom of my heart."

It was dawn when Jethro, with the sleepy-eyed convict woman in attendance, carried her back to her own room.

Neither Henrietta nor the children had awakened, and, Abigail realized, without attaching much significance to the fact, Timothy Dawson had not yet returned.

CHAPTER XXIII

William Broome whistled to his dog Frisky and the well-trained animal darted forward to head off one of the straying ewes. The wharf was in sight now, the stubby masts of the *Fanny* visible over the top of the shingle roof of the government storage shed.

There was another vessel, tied up astern of the *Fanny,* William saw, also a two-master, which he did not at once recognize. He kicked his mother's horse, Baneelon, into a trot, passing ahead of the small herd of ewes he was driving in order to obtain a better sight of the second vessel. It was then that he saw the soldiers, their scarlet jackets bright in the early morning sunlight, and with a sense of uneasiness, he realized that they were on guard over the wharf—two of them, with shouldered muskets, pacing as sentries at either end of the wooden jetty.

The presence of redcoats in this area always made for trouble, and with a cynicism beyond his years, William found himself wondering whose arrest they had come to effect. He had seen the *Fanny* on her way upriver the previous day; she was the regular mail and cargo carrier and her arrival was expected—

hence his own presence, with the dozen half-breed
Bengal ewes which his mother was sending to market
in Sydney.

He scowled, as he turned to look back at them. It
went against the grain, where he was concerned, to
sell any of the sheep they bred at Long Wrekin, but
his mother had assured him that there was no help
for it—these twelve were aging and at the end of their
breeding lives, fit only for sale as mutton. And the
cash they would bring in would pay at least part of
the wages of the extra laborers hired to assist Tom
Jardine with the now-completed maize harvest.

On the credit side, William told himself, the farm was
paying its way and nothing more had been said, by
either his mother or Captain Hawley, about the sale
to Mr. Dawson or their removal to Van Diemen's Land.
The possibility remained, he knew, in the back of
their minds, but—like the question of his own somewhat disrupted attendance at school—it was temporarily shelved, and he for one was not going to mention either subject in their hearing, lest they be con-
strained to take action.

Frisky started to yap, and he rode back to the dog's
aid, using his whip to muster his recalcitrant flock into
better order. Reaching the wharf, he herded them into a
small pen and, leaving Frisky to watch them, tied his
horse to a hitching post and approached the nearest
sentry.

"Well?" the soldier grinned at him in friendly fashion.
"What's your business, youngster? Sheep to market, is
it?"

"That's right," William confirmed. "Consigned to
the *Fanny*. And," he added self-importantly, "I have the
bills of sale made out for Mr. Burdock. Can I go on
board?"

"No reason why you shouldn't, lad," the sentry assured him. "We ain't here to stop commerce, only es-

capers." He lowered his musket, still grinning. "Pass, friend!"

Jed Burdock was on the *Fanny*'s deck. He greeted William with raised brows and an oddly conspiratorial air and, before the boy could present his bills of sale, asked him in a hoarse whisper if he had come on his stepfather's business.

Puzzled by the question, William shook his tousled fair head. "No," he returned. "On my Mam's, sir. *She* owns Long Wrekin, not Captain Hawley." He was still not reconciled to his mother's remarriage and was reluctant to acknowledge his new relationship to Andrew Hawley. To make this fact clear, he offered the bills of sale, gesturing behind him to where the ewes were penned. "You can see, Mr. Burdock—this is *her* signature on these bills, not his."

The *Fanny*'s master scarcely glanced at the bills before thrusting them into his pocket and bawling an order to one of his seamen to start loading the sheep from Long Wrekin.

"They're in the pen there, O'Reilly. Look lively, lad." William started to go after the man with the intention of helping him, but Jed Burdock's big hand came out to grasp him by the shoulder and hold him back. "Not so fast, you bleeding young whippersnapper! Mick O'Reilly can load your sodding sheep without you telling him how. Devil take you, boy, ain't you concerned about Captain Hawley?"

"No," William retorted, vainly trying to wriggle free. "Why should I be? He's my Mam's husband but he's not my father. My father was John Broome and he—"

Jed Burdock swore loudly and blasphemously. Then, lowering his voice, he said tersely, "I came back here last night, after transacting some private business ashore, and what did I find? Bleeding redcoats guarding the wharf because there's a warrant out for Captain Hawley's arrest and they're afraid he'll make a run for it! I'm held up and so's your brother, in the *Phoebe* and—"

"My brother?" William was startled, his jaw dropping. "Do you mean my brother Justin? Mr. Burdock, Justin owns the *Flinders* cutter—you know he does, sir. What's he doing with the *Phoebe*?"

"Trying to save Captain Hawley's neck, boy," Burdock answered uncompromisingly. "Like I would, if I could, damme! But the redcoats won't let any o' us off the wharf, so we can't even warn him. Here—" He released his hold and gave William a push in the direction of the *Fanny*'s gangplank. "Forget about your bloody sheep and go along to the *Phoebe*. Have a word with Justin—he's below, keeping out of sight. Maybe *you* could take the warning—them sodding sojers don't know who you are, do they?"

"No, sir, they didn't seem to." William swallowed hard, endeavoring to take in the situation. "You think they'd let me leave the wharf?"

"Why shouldn't they?" Burdock growled. "But talk to Justin. He'll know whether you're to be trusted—I don't."

William needed no second bidding. He boarded the *Phoebe* without attracting the attention of the sentries and found Justin waiting anxiously in the master's cabin. It was evident that he had been watching, for he said, without preamble, "Did Mr. Burdock tell you what's afoot? You know there's a warrant out for Andrew Hawley's arrest and that we're being held here, under guard?" William nodded.

"Yes, he told me, Justin. But why should they arrest Andrew? What's he done?"

"No more than most of the other Hawkesbury settlers who are loyal to Governor Bligh," Justin returned impatiently. "But he doesn't know and I cannot get to him to tell him he's in danger. Those soldiers came up here in an oared boat last night—they were here when I tied up and they refused to let me go ashore."

"*I* could go," William offered. "I could warn him." The resentment he had harbored for so long against the man his mother had married was still there, but, in spite of that, he told himself, he owed it to his mother to do what he could. She would not want Andrew Hawley arrested, and besides . . . He remembered suddenly the settlers' meeting to which Andrew had been summoned. He was always going to settlers' meetings, he and Tom Jardine and Timothy Dawson . . . they were organizing petitions, collecting signatures, which was perhaps why his arrest had been ordered, because the petitions were in favor of the deposed governor, Mr. Bligh. But . . . William drew in his breath sharply, remembering something else.

"Justin," he blurted out. "Captain Hawley went to a settlers' meeting last night. He hadn't come back when I left Long Wrekin with the ewes."

"Thank God for that!" Justin exclaimed. "Because it's the first place they'll look for him. D'you know where he's likely to be, Willie?"

Unhappily, William shook his head. "No. They were talking about it, he and Mam, but I didn't listen. I know he was going with Mr. Dawson, but that's all, Justin. I . . . I'm sorry."

Justin scowled at him and then relented. "You could not help it, I suppose. But Mam will know where he went, will she not?"

"Oh, yes, I'm sure she will."

"Right," Justin said, his tone crisp and decisive. "You came on horseback—then go back to Long Wrekin as fast as you know how and tell Mam. Then find Andrew, wherever he is. There's not much time, because the constable with the warrant has to come overland from Toongabbie, with the main party of soldiers. There are only four here."

"Only four?" William put in. "Surely you—"

Justin did not pretend to misunderstand him. "Yes—but they are armed and we are not. All the same, by your providential arrival, Willie, you probably saved my life. I was planning to tackle them if they were still here by nightfall and Jed Burdock hadn't succeeded in making them drunk." He shrugged. "That plan can be changed. When you find Andrew, tell him that I'm here and that I'll try to make it upriver and anchor off the Dawson's boatshed—he keeps a small oared boat in the shed. If the soldiers won't permit me to leave, tell Andrew to take the boat and drift downstream after dark. I'll be watching and I'll get him aboard—Jed will help me and it will not be his fault if those infernal sentries are sober." He paused, eyeing his younger brother searchingly, and then added gravely, "And, Willie, lad, you had best tell Mam that I shall aim to sail for Van Diemen's Land, once Andrew joins me. You understand, don't you, that he'd not be safe if he were to stay here?"

William, with equal gravity, assured him that he did. "Will Mam—" he began and broke off, reddening.

"Will Mam want to come with us?" Justin finished for him. "She'll want to, Willie, but I expect she will stay. Now off with you, lad, because the redcoats from Toongabbie will be here by nightfall if they bestir themselves."

William returned to the wharf as the last of his ewes was being driven unwillingly into the *Fanny*'s hold. The soldier who had admitted him was still on guard, but he had propped his musket against the storehouse wall and was downing the last dregs of a beaker with evident enjoyment, watched over by a benevolently smiling Jed Burdock. Neither the soldier nor the *Fanny*'s stout master appeared to notice him, and he slipped past in silence, to fling himself onto his horse's back. He whistled to Frisky and, with the dog running behind him, made for home, kicking Baneelon into a gallop as soon as he was out of sight of the wharf.

Jenny listened to the tale her younger son gasped out with an outward calm that was belied by the agitated beating of her heart and the fear his words engendered. She had no doubt that Andrew was in mortal danger; she knew John Macarthur all too well, and with even the bolder settlers now referring to him as "The Ruler," she knew his power.

To William she said only, "Andrew is at the Dawsons', Willie. They agreed to go back there after the meeting. Ask Tom to saddle two fresh horses, will you please?"

"But, Mam——" he was looking at her with dismay. "*You* can't go, not with the——the baby you're carrying. Leave it to me. Justin's told me what to do."

He was still so young, Jenny thought, meeting his anxious blue gaze. She could not—dared not—entrust so difficult and dangerous a mission to him alone. She would have to go with him, she—

"Tom could come with me," William suggested.

Jenny hesitated, wondering whether this might not be the wiser course. Tom Jardine was loyal and reliable; he would guard William's life with his own, and, if the soldiers came here—as come they undoubtedly would—before nightfall or early next morning, she might devise more subtle ways of delaying them than Tom could. Slowly, reluctantly, she inclined her head.

"All right, love. Ask Tom to go with you. You're sure you know what to do, what to tell Andrew?"

"I'm sure," the boy asserted stoutly.

"Tell him farewell from me, Willie." There was a catch in Jenny's voice as she faced once again the prospect of separation, of loneliness, of a husband at sea, cut off from her. She put her arms round William's thin young shoulders and hugged him. "Tell him I love

him," she added softly. "And take care, Willie—take
very good care of yourself."

" 'Course I will, Mam." William returned her hug
and then he was gone, shouting shrilly for Tom. A few
minutes later, when she had explained what was happening to Nancy Jardine in the kitchen, she heard the
thud of hooves and, hurrying to the door, watched the
two riders until they were out of sight.

Nancy said, when Jenny at last rejoined her in the
warm firelit kitchen, "I've made tea, Jenny. You sit
down and drink it and try not to upset yourself. I'll
take Rachel to my place as soon as I've finished up
here. It's best if she's not about when the soldiers come,
because they'll want to search this house, that's for
certain sure, but they may leave mine alone. Even if
they don't, it'll spare you the worry of her."

It would, Jenny thought—but that was the only
worry she could hope to be spared.

Left alone, she took up some of the pile of mending
that seemed always to accumulate; with her fingers
busy, she let her thoughts have free rein. Inevitably,
they were of Andrew and the months they had spent
happily together since her return from Hobart. He
was a good man, a loving and devoted husband, and,
sharing the work of the farm as they had, toiling side
by side with the stock and on the land, she had come to
care for him more deeply than—after the loss of
Johnny—she had believed it possible to care for any
man.

The rebel government—that was how she and the
majority of the Hawkesbury settlers referred to Major
Johnstone's administration still—had been unable to
bring any charge against Andrew after the governor's
arrest. He had been freed on the condition that he resign his official position and come here, as a settler
like herself. And he had done so, he had kept his word

. . . what charges could any of them, even Macarthur, bring against him now?

Her needle slipped, pricking her finger, and Jenny sighed at her own clumsiness, as tiny spots of blood stained the whiteness of the shirt she was patching. William had mumbled something about a conspiracy, she reminded herself, but surely there was no conspiracy —least of all on Andrew's part, unless the settlers' meetings and their petitions could be termed conspiracy? In that case they were all guilty—Tim Dawson, Tom Jardine, George Suttor, and the rest of them. True, there had been a move, a month or two earlier, to call out the armed Loyalist Volunteers in an attempt to free Governor Bligh, but it had come to nothing, at the governor's own behest. William Bligh wanted no deaths on his conscience, no risk of civil war, despite what the rebels of the Rum Corps had done . . . despite what they were still doing and the indignities to which they had compelled him to submit. . . .

The sound of a horse's hooves on the hard-baked earth of the fold yard brought Jenny to her feet. Surely William and Tom had not come back so soon? It was not yet dusk—they had been gone less than two hours. Moving awkwardly, she ran to the door, in time to see Nanbaree, the aborigine boy, leading a single horse into the stable on the far side of the yard—*Andrew's horse*, the young, newly broken chestnut he always rode. Then, to her shocked dismay, she saw Andrew himself emerge from the feed shed and come, without haste, toward her, calling out a casual greeting as he caught sight of her.

"Jenny, love, I'm home. I—dear God, lass, what's wrong? You're as white as a ghost."

For all the shock his unexpected arrival had caused her, she had the presence of mind to lead him into the house before she told him. He heard her out, his expression one of bewilderment as he took in what she was saying, and when she had done, he exclaimed incredulously, "A warrant for my arrest! Jenny, lass, that cannot be true!"

"Alas, it is, Andrew. Justin came here to warn you—Mr. Campbell told him, he sent him here to take you back to Hobart," Jenny managed, near to tears.

"In the *Flinders*?" Andrew was still incredulous.

"No—William says he has another vessel, one of Mr. Campbell's, but there are soldiers at the wharf, holding his ship and Mr. Burdock's *Fanny* in arrest, in—oh, Andrew, in case you tried to make your escape by river. Dearest, you must believe me. It is the truth and the soldiers will be here at any minute. They are coming from Toongabbie." Jenny's words were falling over each other, in her efforts to make him understand. "I—I sent William with Tom to Upwey, to the Dawsons', to tell you what Justin wants you to do. I thought you'd be there but—"

"I came straight here," Andrew said. He took her into his arms, holding her close, but now he was alert, alive to the totally unexpected peril in which he found himself and with no illusions as to the fate awaiting him, if he were arrested. Only the Corps officers sat in judgment in the criminal court now—Macarthur's tools, like their commandant, Johnstone—and they would show him no mercy, however outrageous the charges brought against him.

He thought fast, questioning Jenny meantime, and, when she told him that William had been allowed to drive his small flock of sheep onto the wharf and leave, after they were loaded, he gave vent to an exclamation. "Damme, love, that's it, of course! There's no time to round up any sheep, but there's a loaded feed cart in the shed. I'll harness two of the workhorses to it and drive it down to the wharf. The chances are that the soldiers on guard there won't know me by sight, and, in any event, Jed Burdock will see to it that they're well plied with liquor. When darkness falls, Justin will be able to slip away without them being any the wiser, given any luck at all. What do you say?"

Jenny met his gaze with resolution in her own.

"I say it's your best chance," she answered. "But it will be better still if *I* drive the cart and you hide yourself under the feed sacks."

"But in your condition—" Andrew began. "You cannot—"

"I can and I will," Jenny told him, her tone one that brooked no argument. "The child I'm carrying will want his father safe and well in Van Diemen's Land, not mining coal in Newcastle. Besides, the feed cart would arouse suspicion if it's left at the wharf unattended—and I can drive it back here." She gave him no opportunity for dissent, adding urgently, "Andrew, time is running out. Please, for God's sake, go and harness the horses whilst I get ready."

Her preparations, Andrew saw, when she came out into the yard, included a worn and ragged shawl for herself, a heavy blanket and a rolled bundle of scarlet cloth for him.

"Your uniform," Jenny said, when he pointed to the bundle. "You will wear it again when you are in Hobart or Port Dalrymple. And the blanket will cover you, if the sacks do not."

Andrew seized a minute of their swift-running time to kiss her tenderly. "You are a wonderful woman, my dear love," he told her. "And, God willing, our parting need not be for very long. After the child is born, Justin can bring you to me."

For answer Jenny, with brimming eyes, gestured him to the cart. He climbed in, clutching his bundle, and, having pulled the blanket over him, she mounted the driving seat and whipped the horses into motion.

They had covered almost a mile of the way when

the sound of a drumbeat reached them, and Jenny, with a whispered prayer, reined in the horses to a walk.

"The soldiers," she said, not turning round. "Keep well hidden!"

The soldiers came in sight, ten minutes later. A perspiring sergeant led them, with a mounted constable in his blue jacket and resplendent red waistcoat urging them on. But the men were exhausted and ill tempered after their long march, and they were deaf to his pleas and his obscenities. They shuffled along out of step with the drum, their muskets carried across their backs or slung from their shoulders, their stiff collars unhooked,

They scarcely glanced at the lumbering cart and its hunched, shawl-wrapped driver, as Jenny pulled onto the road verge to let them pass. The only question the sergeant asked was whether she had any water with her, and when she shook her head, he swore and went cursing back to the head of the column, reserving the most virulent of his imprecations for the constable.

Soon the dust raised by their marching feet settled back onto the rutted road and Jenny let her whip touch the flanks of the two sturdy workhorses and they broke into a trot once more.

They reached the wharf as the sun was setting, and the expected challenge did not come. Jenny drove straight onto the wharf, and Justin recognized her and came to her side, clattering down the gangplank at a run.

"The sentries?" Jenny said anxiously. "I thought they had set a guard on your ship."

Justin smiled broadly and pointed to the *Fanny.* "The offer of free liquor was too much for them," he answered. "They deserted their posts, every one of them. Is Andrew coming?"

"He is here," Jenny told him, conscious of a sense of heady triumph. "Please, Justin, get him aboard. We met the soldiers from Toongabbie on their way to Long Wrekin and I must go back at once."

It was the work of only a few minutes to free Andrew from his cramped confinement. Jenny would not let him prolong their farewell; a final kiss, without any tears from her to make the parting emotional, and as two seamen from the *Fanny* were summoned to unload the feed sacks, Justin cast off his borrowed vessel's moorings and hoisted sail.

The ketch, with mainsail and mizzen filling, headed out into midstream and came about. Justin, at her wheel, raised a hand in proud salute to his mother, before setting his new course. Jenny glimpsed a name painted across the ketch's stern—*Phoebe*.

"God bless you, *Phoebe*," she said, under her breath. "And God grant you may safely reach port!"

On the way back to Long Wrekin, Tim Dawson met her, with William and Tom Jardine at his side, and Jenny's spirits lifted, dispelling the weariness she had been feeling.

"I'll come with you," Timothy promised, when she had acquainted them with the good news of Andrew's escape. "The damned redcoats will be searching your house and buildings but I'll give them short shrift, don't you worry. Let Tom drive the cart and keep it out of sight until they've gone. I'll take you up with me—it will be less uncomfortable for you, Jenny, my dear."

Mounted on Timothy's horse and held firmly in his arms, Jenny let her head fall back on his strong, broad shoulder.

"We had a happy event at Upwey," Timothy told her. "Our little Abigail O'Shea gave birth to a son last night. He came a while before his time, but they say he's strong, and little Abby is in seventh heaven. Odd, because even though Abigail married O'Shea, Frances

always insisted that the girl was in love with that unfortunate young surgeon, Titus Penhaligon, and not
Lieutenant O'Shea. Now they're both lost to her and
all she's got is a tiny scrap of humanity I could hold
in one hand, but, as I said, she's ecstatic." He added
jokingly, "Don't you do anything like that, will you,
Jenny?"

"Give birth to Andrew's baby prematurely?" Jenny
responded. "No, Tim, that I will not."

"You must take care of yourself," Timothy warned.
He hesitated, pulling his horse into a walk. "In Andrew's absence, would you like to come to us at Upwey,
with William and Rachel?"

"Your wife would not welcome us," Jenny demurred,
her tone stiff. "You know she would not."

"She would have to, if I were to insist."

"Thank you, Tim. But I would not want you to."

"Well, there's Frances," Timothy said obstinately.
"She and my esteemed father-in-law will be back in
Sydney very soon. And I'm sure I don't need to tell
you that I am willing to buy Long Wrekin from you,
any time you want to sell, Jenny. You have only to say
the word."

"Yes, I know that, Tim." Jenny glanced at William
seated, like a tiny jockey, on his huge mount—a horse
that usually she rode—and caught her breath in a sigh.
"I'll manage. I want to stay. I—I have my roots here
now and so do Willie and Rachel. I should hate to
leave."

"Not even to join Andrew in Hobart?" Timothy
persisted.

Ahead of them Jenny could see the familiar buildings
of her home—the fold yard, the stables and outbuildings, the brood mares' paddock. Moving among them,
she glimpsed scarlet coats and knew that the soldiers
had begun their search, not waiting for her return. She
sighed again, in something approaching despair.

"I may have to join Andrew," she conceded unwillingly. "He will not be able to return here whilst the Rum Corps remain in power. But, pray God, the home government will act and rid us of them—and of John Macarthur most of all. This colony will never prosper for as long as they administer it solely in order to line their pockets, Tim. But perhaps Andrew will be able to persuade Major Paterson to come back. He was always the best of them, the most honest."

"Foveaux will come before him," Timothy retorted glumly. "He's expected, they say . . . and he's worse than Johnstone. His record at Norfolk Island was appalling. But—" He managed a smile. "I echo your prayer, Jenny. Let us hope that the home government *will* act and before it's too late for any of us."

He said no more until they entered the Long Wrekin yard. Then, after helping Jenny to dismount, he said crisply, "Away off to bed with you, my dear lass, and try to sleep. I'll deal with the soldiers and I'll send Nancy Jardine to look after you."

Jenny did as he had bidden her. But she could not sleep, and towards morning, watched over by an anxious Nancy, she gave birth to her fourth child. No life-giving cries heralded the poor little soul's arrival. Despite Nancy's skilled aid and her frantic slapping, Andrew's daughter lay limp and still on the coverlet of the bed, the still pulsating umbilical cord the only movement between mother and child. When even that was severed, Nancy sobbed out the bitter tidings and carried the tiny body away.

Jenny lay in silence, her face turned to the wall. Next day, white of face but grimly determined, she left her bed and went about her usual chores, deaf to Nancy's pleas and reproaches, ignoring the frightened glances her two other children gave her.

A life had been taken, she told herself, but life itself had to go on. That evening, sitting alone under a clump of gum trees at the river's edge, she repeated aloud the words Governor Phillip had said, when the colony was founded: "*'Here are fertile plains, needing only the labors of the husbandman to produce in abundance the fairest fruits. Here are interminable pastures, the future home of flocks and herds innumerable. . . .'*"

Those words, spoken so long ago, had been the mainspring of her life for twenty years, and, when she looked about her at her own fertile land and the sheep grazing nearby, she was conscious of a lifting of the heart.

Small though her contribution had been, those twenty years had not been wasted, and maybe, God willing, Governor Phillip's interminable pastures might yet be found, where the flocks and herds might expand, as he had believed they would. Found beyond the distant peaks of the Blue Mountains, towards which she was looking now, or in some other part of the vast island continent which poor young Matthew Flinders had mapped and surveyed, with Johnny's help and Justin's.

She had to hope, Jenny thought, not grieve. She had to go on and not look back with regret or self-reproach. And perhaps the prayer she had uttered and Tim Dawson had echoed would be heard, and the King and his government, in far-off England, would act before it was too late.

Quietly, as the faint breeze ruffled the surface of the river and set the leaves of the gum trees above her head gently rustling, she dropped to her knees and whispered her prayer again, adding another for Andrew's safe arrival, with Justin, at the end of their voyage.

CHAPTER XXIV

On July 28, 1808, the transport *Lady Madeleine Sinclair* came to anchor in Sydney Cove. From the window of her bedroom in Government House, Mary Putland—recognizing the ship as the one that had brought both Governor Bligh and herself out to the colony two years before—ran down to acquaint her father with the news.

She had hoped that it might cheer him, but, to her disappointment, it did not. William Bligh looked at her with lackluster blue eyes and asked flatly what comfort he expected him to derive from the arrival of yet another convict transport.

"A King's ship is what I want, daughter, and authority from His Majesty's Government to use her guns and her people against these miserable rogues who have usurped my official role! And against the *Porpoise* also, since her miserable curs of officers give me no support."

"But, Papa, dear," Mary pleaded "At least come to the window and see for yourself. There is quite a stir on the government wharf, with the Corps parading with their colors and their drums, and a boat has just taken Major Johnstone out to the ship. Surely some personage of importance must have come here—an emissary, perhaps, of the home government."

"It is more likely to be Foveaux," her father retorted irritably. "They're expecting his arrival from England, one of the rogues of sentries told me. And he's promoted to lieutenant colonel, the fellow said." But he brightened and, to Mary's relief, followed her to the vantage point she had chosen, taking up his naval telescope, the better to study the scene being enacted below them.

"Yes, my dear," he concluded, "it *is* Colonel Foveaux —see, that's him, on the lee side of the quarterdeck. And that infernal scoundrel Johnstone is bowing and scraping to him! He's senior, of course, and doubtless will take over command of the thrice damned Rum Corps. Mary, my dear, let us hope and pray"—he was suddenly excited—"let us hope that he will put an end to the mutiny in his regiment and order my immediate release and restoration to office!"

"Oh, Papa, I trust he has," Mary echoed. Without the advantage of the glass her father was using, she could not identify the figures on the transport's deck, but she was able to make out some blue naval uniforms amongst the military scarlet, and at least two small figures that appeared to be female. "Is Colonel Foveaux married?" she ventured.

Her father emitted a contemptuous grunt. "Yes, but to a very low class of woman—the widow of a sergeant of the Corps, who used to be his house servant. She made herself as unpopular as he did, when he governed Norfolk Island. I've heard it said that he hanged more convicts in a year than any previous lieutenant governor in the whole of his term of office! But . . .". He shrugged resignedly and lowered his glass. "I'll make you a promise, Mary, my dear. If Foveaux does as a loyal King's officer should and orders my illegal arrest to be terminated, damme, I'll receive both of 'em here!"

Mary smiled, without amusement, but answered dutifully, "Very well, Papa, I shall hold you to that."

On the government wharf the band of the Corps struck up a lively march and William Bligh turned his glass on them, swearing softly. "A pox on them! I suppose they'll have the effrontery to play 'God Save the King' when their new commandant comes ashore. But at least that scoundrel Porteous hasn't manned the *Porpoise*'s yards, so perhaps, after all, we may anticipate an order from Castlereagh." He snapped the telescope shut. "I cannot watch this—this cursed charade any longer, Mary. I'll write a note to Foveaux, so that he will receive it when he comes ashore."

Mary stifled a sigh. Her poor father occupied his endless, necessarily unproductive days writing letters to those he hoped might send him aid . . . there was one on his desk now, she knew, addressed to an admiral whose name eluded her, started but as yet unfinished. He wrote frequently and at great length to the Colonial Office and Lord Castlereagh but, fearful that his letters might be intercepted, was wont to hold them back until a reliable messenger or ship's master could be found to deliver them.

Recently he had told her that he intended to write to the Earl of Minto, the East India Company's governor, and in his epistles to her mother, Mary knew, he begged her to intercede in person with Sir Joseph Banks and to write, on his behalf, to other prominent persons—including those who had preceded him in office, Admiral Phillip and Captain Hunter. Governor King, she had heard, was dead—dead or dying, she was not sure which. News from the outside world was slow in reaching the poor prisoners in Government House. Perhaps, she thought, the rebel administration made sure that it was—perhaps they intercepted and read both incoming and outgoing mail, even her own private correspondence, as her father suspected. But

still he went on writing and, with Edmund Griffin's aid,
compiling a dossier on Major Johnstone, on Mr. Macarthur, and on the Corps officers—for disclosure, he
had told her, when these men were brought to trial.

Mary picked up the discarded telescope and, holding
it to her eye, studied the various people on the deck of
the *Lady Madeleine Sinclair*. Colonel Foveaux was a
tall, distinguished-looking man, in his middle or early
forties, as nearly as she could judge; his wife, though
perhaps inclined to plumpness, was by no means ill
favored. Major Johnstone, as her father had remarked,
was still dancing attendance on the pair of them and
. . . yes, there were Mr. Macarthur and his wife, and
Surgeon D'Arcy Wentworth—tried and convicted of
some crime and dismissed from his hospital post but
now, it seemed, back in favor with the rebel administration.

There was a diffident tap on the door and Kate
Lamerton came in. Dear Kate, Mary thought gratefully, as the woman bobbed her a curtsy. What a tower
of strength she had been, not only during poor Charles's
last, sad illness but also during the weary months of
what Major Johnstone was pleased to call house arrest
. . . and she herself called imprisonment.

"Yes," she said. "What is it, Kate?"

"I've had a note, ma'am, from my Miss Abigail."
Kate was beaming, and, contradictorily, her eyes were
filled with tears. "She's with Mrs. Dawson, at the farm
on the Hawkesbury, but they're expecting to come to
Sydney soon, when Mr. and Mrs. Spence return. And
oh, Mrs. Putland ma'am, Miss Abigail had borned a
little son, she says . . . premature but healthy."

"I'm glad," Mary said, having to make an effort to
recall who Abigail was. Then she remembered the two
young Tempest girls, who had come out here with Kate
in the *Mysore*, the orphaned daughters of one of her

father's onetime officers. They, too, had settled somewhere in the Hawkesbury area, with their guardian, a black-bearded, overpowering minister of a low-church denomination, whose interminable, ranting sermons her father had found particularly irritating, when he had been forced to listen to them.

She smiled, sharing Kate's pleasure in what for once appeared to be good news, and she added pleasantly, "I had not realized that Miss Abigail was married. My memory of the two girls suggests that they were of tender years, scarcely more than children."

"Miss Abigail's nigh on eighteen," Kate answered. "Married an' widowed, ma'am, all in a few days, poor young soul. But, there, she'll have the baby to console her now an' they'm both coming to Sydney, when Mr. and Mrs. Spence get back." She glanced wistfully out the window and bobbed another curtsy. "Have I your permission, ma'am, to go down to the wharf for a while?"

"Yes, of course you have," Mary agreed readily. "I suppose you want to watch the parade and the landing of the new commandant?"

But, to her surprise, Kate Lamerton shook her head.

"No, ma'am, not that. I don't hold with the Rum Corps, no more'n you do. A bunch o' money-grubbin' scallywags, the lot of 'em . . . and their commandants, whoever they are! But there be another ship signaled an' on the way in. I just want to see if it's the *Kelso,* Mr. Spence's ship, so's I can write to Miss Abigail an' tell her Mrs. Spence is back."

"Then go, by all means," Mary encouraged. "But," she added, in an anxious afterthought, "I hope you will not want to leave the governor's service when your Miss Abigail returns here, with her baby. I can't do without you, Kate."

Kate flushed with gratification. "Oh, no, Mrs. Putland," she asserted. "I'll stay for as long as ever you want me. Like Mr. Jubb, ma'am, I'd not dream o' leavin', not till His Excellency the governor is freed."

And how long, Mary wondered uneasily, would that be? But perhaps Colonel Foveaux's arrival did augur well; perhaps some of her father's reports and letters to the Colonial Office would elicit positive action and bring about his release and restoration to office.

But this hope was soon dashed. Governor Bligh's note, delivered to the new commandant at the barracks within an hour of his landing, brought an almost immediate and insolent response. Containing his fury with difficulty, the governor said, "The scoundrel has had the gall to inform me that he intends to carry on the government as before, with himself as lieutenant governor, if you please! If I desire my case to be heard, he suggests that I return to England for that purpose and offers to arrange passage for me, damn his eyes! Well, he may keep me prisoner as long as he likes but I will *not* be coerced into quitting my post at the behest of rebels and traitors, by God I will not!"

To Mary's distress her father spent virtually the whole of that day at his desk, rewriting his letter to Lord Minto, composing yet another long report for Lord Castlereagh at the Colonial Office, writing again to Colonel Paterson at Port Dalrymple and to Sir Joseph Banks and Admiral Pellew in England. His own mail, held up for two days, was belatedly delivered to him, and her mother's letter, Mary sensed—although couched in its usual concerned and affectionate terms—failed to dispel his bitter frustration or lessen the intense strain he was enduring.

Now even their games of chess, which he had previously enjoyed, ceased to give him pleasure or distraction; he paced the garden with short, angry steps, always with a soldier marching stolidly at his heels to preclude any attempt he might make to escape, and a guard at the gate to turn away would-be callers. She herself was permitted more freedom; she could drive out daily in her carriage but only with an escort of two mounted troopers, and an innocent complaint she made about the bad state of the road outside Government House—passed on in writing to the overseer by her father—brought an arrogant reproof from the new lieutenant governor.

Her father read it to her, choking with indignation, and later Mary reread it, unable to believe that even a Rum Corps officer could write in such a manner and with seemingly so little thought for the effect it would have on a man who had only his personal dignity left. Headed *Headquarters, 15 August 1808,* and addressed merely to *William Bligh, Esq.,* it ran: *"Sir: Some of the overseers having reported to me that you have thought it proper to give them orders respecting the execution of parts of their duty, I must acquaint you that should you do so again, I shall be under the necessity of taking some very effectual method of preventing any interference on your part in anything whatever relative to the affairs of this Colony."*

Mary wept, conscious that she had been the cause of his humiliation, but her father impatiently bade her dry her tears.

"They are unmitigated villains, all of them," he declared. "But by heaven, Mary, they'll not defeat me! That Indiaman the *Kelso* came into the cove yesterday evening, did she not? Well, she may have brought a reply from Lord Minto—God grant she has. I shall send a copy of Foveaux's insulting communication to Lord Castlereagh and tell his lordship that my sense of honor forbids me to quit my post as governor, unless His Majesty's Government orders me to do so. And . . . ask Edmund Griffin to attend me, will you, my dear? I shall write again to Colonel Paterson. He *must* return here and relieve Foveaux of command and I shall tell him so, in no uncertain terms!"

Mary left him to his letter writing, her eyes still filled with tears.

In the cramped, uncomfortable quarters allocated to him by Colonel Paterson at Port Dalrymple, Andrew, too, was engaged in writing letters.

The first, to Jenny, was deliberately optimistic. Justin, he knew, had informed her of their safe arrival, but he had not had the time since then to write to her at length, and now he endeavored to do so, describing his surroundings and the progress made by the settlement with as much enthusiasm as he could muster. It was not a great deal, and he did not attempt to persuade her to join him, for by comparison with Hobart, Port Dalrymple and the settlement known as Launceston—thirty miles from the river mouth—held little attraction for him.

True, the harbor was excellent and the Tamar River navigable for light draught vessels as far as Launceston, where the North and South Esk rivers joined, the former as a spectacular cataract, descending from the mountains. The majority of those who had taken land grants had chosen to do so on the banks of the North Esk; a few more adventurous spirits had established small farms further afield, in the district of Pittwater and inland from the North Bay, but, as the Hobart settlers before them had learned to their cost, attacks by hostile natives discouraged settlement too far afield.

And Colonel Paterson . . . Andrew gave vent to a frustrated sigh, pausing in midsentence, reluctant to put his feelings on paper, even to Jenny. Suffice it, perhaps, to tell her only that the lieutenant governor was a sick and aging man, more concerned for his health than for the future prosperity of the settlements he had been bidden to establish in this undeniably beautiful and fertile island.

Andrew conveyed this, choosing his words with care, and then went on:

> I miss you, my dearest wife, more than I can even begin to tell you. It is no exaggeration to say that I would give my right arm to be with you at this moment, in the happy warmth of the kitchen at Long Wrekin.
>
> I have been received very kindly by Colonel Paterson and his wife, but the colonel keeps me here; he will not permit me even to go on a brief visit to Hobart—why I do not know. Macarthur's partner, Mr. Walter Davidson, was here before me and has contrived to poison his mind where Governor Bligh is concerned. Truly, considering the colonel's feelings about Governor Bligh, I can foresee little hope of improvement, were the colonel to yield to the demands of the governor and our fellow settlers on the Hawkesbury and make his way back to Sydney, in order to relieve the present incumbent—who, we hear, is now Major Foveaux.
>
> I am writing at the same time as I write this to Tim Dawson, explaining the position to him. A transport, the *Maitland,* called here three days ago and her master has offered to take our mail to Sydney.
>
> There is a young naval officer on board, on his way to join the *Porpoise,* whom I was introduced to at the Colonel's residence. A fine young fellow —Midshipman Richard Tempest—who told me that he is brother to poor little Abigail O'Shea and the little girl who is still at Yarramundie, I suppose, and whose name is Lucy, if my memory serves me right.

I gave him what information I could concerning them both, and he was greatly worried about those his late father appointed as guardians to his sisters —the reverend and Mrs. Caleb Boskenna—for they are, he claims, frauds. The so-called reverend is not the possessor of Holy Orders but an embezzler fleeing from the authorities in Taunton, and he has proof of it. I trust, my dearest Jenny, that you will give him what aid you can to bring these people to justice. . . .

Andrew signed his name and began his letter to Tim Dawson.

In the privacy of his room which he called his sanctum, Caleb Boskenna unlocked his strongbox and took from it his copy of the agreement which the late lamented Desmond O'Shea had signed. Each of them had kept a copy, and Boskenna was anxious to recover the one that had been in O'Shea's possession on the night of his death. That and the gold, if possible—although the gold had in all likelihood been lost in the Hawkesbury, if O'Shea was carrying it on his person when he drowned. If not, then one of the *Fanny*'s crew almost certainly had stolen it from among his effects, after his body was recovered.

He had made exhaustive but carefully worded inquiries concerning the agreement, but he had learned nothing which would enlighten him as to the whereabouts of the document. All that the *Fanny*'s master, when questioned, had been able to tell him was that "the poor, sweet young widow"—as he had insisted on calling Abigail—had been given all her late husband's effects when he had landed her in Sydney.

Yet Abigail, in the two letters she had written to Lucy, had claimed that she was virtually penniless and, for this reason, had taken up employment as governess to the Dawson children. . . . Boskenna frowned, shaking his head in bewilderment. If the wretched girl had been given the agreement, if she had read and understood its import, then surely she would have taken some action by now—if not herself, then through Dawson or the lieutenant governor. But she had done nothing; she had not even tried to arrange for Lucy to join her. She had her duties, of course; Mrs. Dawson was reputed to be very demanding of all whom she employed, be they convict or free, but even so . . . it seemed odd that, as the months went by, Abigail had remained silent.

He reread the agreement and then replaced it in his strongbox, along with the rest of his personal papers and the deeds to the Yarramundie land. Perhaps his wife was right, he told himself, perhaps Abigail's conscience *was* troubling her, and she knew more than she was ever going to admit about the supposed accident that had cost her new husband his life.

"I cannot believe that he fell from the deck of that old tub, Mr. Boskenna," Martha had said after the news had reached them, "nor do I believe that he had imbibed an excessive quantity of drink. He wanted Abigail, did he not? He wanted her badly, and he had just wedded her. It's against nature to suppose that he would spend the night drinking with that orderly of his, leaving Her Ladyship alone in the cabin!"

O'Shea had not known that his pretty little bride was pregnant, of course—he would almost certainly never have wed her if he had. Shuffling through the papers in the box, Boskenna's fingers closed around a document which he had almost forgotten about. A wry smile curved his bearded lips as he recognized it for what it was. Couched in official language, it was a summons to appear before the circuit judge at the assize court in Taunton, England, to answer charges of fraud and misappropriation of church funds—charges brought against him as curate by the Reverend John Moorehead, rector of the Parish of Willerton, Somerset.

That summons had been the reason for his flight halfway across the world, he reflected. He had volunteered his services to the Missionary Society, assuming the role and title of clergyman—a role he had played often enough before. The Missionary Society—being at the time in need of preachers of the Word—had accepted him after only a token investigation of the credentials he presented.

The theft of funds from the Reverend Moorehead's church was but the last in a series of such crimes. Martha had been shocked initially when, some months after their marriage, she had found out the means by which her husband made his living. But she had finally accepted even this, for they had lived better than most others of a similar calling, and becoming his wife had been a step up in the world for her. Besides, she was loyal and had genuine love for him, as well as admiration . . . and she had simply shut her eyes to the fact that what he did was dishonest, only making it clear that she preferred his clerical role to any of the others he had played.

Boskenna sighed, wondering why he had kept the summons. It was no longer valid, of course, and could not possibly be enforced here, but perhaps it would be wiser to destroy it. In these isolated surroundings, with escaped convicts always a danger, the box might be stolen and broken open, and then heaven knew where its contents might end up. He tore the stiff paper into shreds and let his thoughts return again to the vexed question of Abigail and the strange, still unexplained death of Lieutenant Desmond O'Shea.

The rebel administration in Sydney had accepted the evidence of the *Fanny*'s crew and that of the girl herself, confirmed, presumably, by the orderly and the shepherd, Jethro Crowan. But, the case having followed so soon after the arrest of Governor Bligh, Major Johnstone and his officers had matters of more importance to cope with, and—like the Missionary Society in his own case—they probably had not troubled to go deeply into the whys and wherefores of the matter. They had seen no reason to suspect that O'Shea's death was anything but accidental. The death of the wretched young surgeon, Titus Penhaligon, had aroused even less interest and no suspicion at all—quite rightly so, since *his* death had clearly been accidental.

Boskenna locked the strongbox and rose to replace it on its accustomed shelf. Deaths, he reflected cynically, by accident, violence, or as the result of judicial punishment, were common enough in New South Wales. Convicts died in greater numbers and usually more violently than the honest inhabitants, but ill health and intemperance carried off quite a number of the respectable settlers, too. And in the more distant localities there were still attacks by the aboriginal tribes, aimed without distinction against settlers and escapers alike; many of these deaths were never reported.

He had considered—but then at once had rejected— some such contrived and violent solution to the problem posed by Abigail's sister, Lucy. The problem was not urgent: Lucy was firmly under his wife's influence, and indeed Martha had developed a fondness for the girl, as had he himself. This did not mean that he would permit her to stand in the way of the long-term plans he had made—too much depended on them for that. But, although she was still very young, he had detected signs of promiscuity in her and . . . Caleb Boskenna was smiling as he returned to his desk and reached, without much enthusiasm, for a fresh sheet of paper and his quill.

There was a sermon to prepare, for the inhabitants of the Green Hills settlement on Sunday, but that could wait for a little while, until the right text came to mind

and he could collect his thoughts sufficiently to concentrate on it. He scribbled a few words, then scratched
them out and let the quill fall.

He had, he decided, made a wise—even a subtle—
move, where Lucy's promiscuous tendencies were concerned, and as yet Martha had not observed or understood what he had done. And it was simple. On one
of his parochial visits to the Green Hills, he had met a
young ticket-of-leave convict by the name of Luke
Cahill—a handsome lad of seventeen or eighteen, who
had worked as a bank clerk and been deported for
stealing from his employers. The boy had been working
as an agricultural laborer and had been ready enough
to come to Yarramundie, to replace the absent Jethro;
and whilst it was soon evident that he was no shepherd,
he made himself useful in other ways, and Lucy had
not been slow to notice his good looks.

Up till now the two had done no more than eye each
other with mutual approval, but it would not be long,
Boskenna thought with satisfaction, before approval
turned to a deeper and more basic emotion on both
their parts. Lucy saw few young people of the opposite
sex; Luke Cahill was still recovering from the trau-
matic effects of his trial and conviction, as well as the
hardships which the long voyage out in a convict transport had inflicted on him. Marriage to Lucy when she
turned sixteen, and an agreement similar to the one
Desmond O'Shea had so willingly signed, would accomplish all that Boskenna had set out to accomplish,
without the need for anything more than gentle persuasion . . . and Cahill, being a convict, would scarcely
expect a dowry. He could be encouraged to apply for
a small grant of land, well away from Yarramundie,
and no suspicion could, in the circumstances, attach to
himself, as Lucy's guardian.

Unless, of course, O'Shea's copy of the agreement
were to fall into Abigail's hands. Abigail was highly in-

telligent, possessed of courage and a strong sense of justice; she would instantly realize the deception that had been practiced on her, and, God knew, she had little reason to wish to spare Boskenna, after the way he'd treated her. He shivered, remembering the brutal whipping he had given her, the taunts and the prayers that had been intended to humiliate her and break her spirit. Last but not by any means least, he recalled the efforts made by the slovenly midwife he had summoned, in the hope that the woman might be able to terminate her pregnancy. Even Martha had reproached him for that.

And Abigail's spirit had not been broken. All she conceivably lacked now was the means to bring charges against him. He dared do no more, where Lucy was concerned, unless and until he could be certain that the agreement with O'Shea really had vanished into the Hawkesbury's concealing depths. Abigail had her son now, and according to the revelations in her most recent letter to Lucy, Penhaligon's bastard love child was a source of great joy to her. Yet all the same . . . Caleb Boskenna reached once again for his pen, as a new idea occurred to him.

He would take as his text *Thou shalt not kill*, he decided and, without naming names, make it abundantly clear to the good folk of the Green Hills that Abigail O'Shea and the scoundrel of a shepherd, whom they knew well, were almost certainly guilty of scheming the death of Abigail's husband between them. . . .

His good humor thus restored, his pen moved swiftly over the paper. He was approaching the end of the second page when the door of his room was flung open and his wife appeared, white of face and clearly alarmed.

"What is it, my dear?" He rose at once, holding out his arms to her. "Is there anything wrong?"

"Oh, yes, Mr. Boskenna, indeed there is!" She clung

to him and he could feel her trembling. "That creature —that treacherous, murdering creature Jethro Crowan is back!"

Caleb Boskenna stared at her in disbelief. "Jethro—*here?* In God's name, wife, what does he want of us?"

"He says he wants to take Lucy away," Martha sobbed. "He says Abigail is in Sydney with Mrs. Spence and that she has told him to fetch Lucy. And he—he says he has a message for you. From Abigail that—oh, Mr. Boskenna, that concerns an agreement you made with her late husband! He—"

So his fears had been realized, Boskenna thought grimly. Abigail was threatening him. "Calm yourself, woman," he said, and thrust his wife from him abruptly. "I will deal with Jethro Crowan, by God's good grace I will! Where is he?"

"Outside in the yard," Martha managed, mopping her moist eyes with the corner of her apron. "And," she added fearfully, "Lucy is there too, with Luke Cahill."

"Go and bid Lucy return to her room. I'll be out in a moment," her husband promised. His musket was hanging on the wall behind his desk; he took it down and, tight lipped, carefully loaded and primed it. Then, the weapon held firmly at the ready in front of him, he followed Martha into the yard.

Jethro was there, calm and quite at his ease, smiling as he talked to Lucy and the Cahill boy, both of whom had ignored Martha's repeated bidding to return to the house. She stood a few yards off, helplessly wringing her hands, but when she saw her husband emerge with his musket, she set up a high pitched wail, unable to contain her anxiety. "Don't fire, Mr. Boskenna— please!"

It had been she who had first voiced the suspicion that Jethro was a murderer, Caleb Boskenna recalled, yet now the foolish, overwrought woman was begging that he be spared! He growled at her to come and stand behind him, but instead—seemingly deaf to his command—she ran to Lucy's side and sought to take the girl into her arms.

"Lucy, you cannot go with Jethro Crowan—you must not trust him! Mr. Boskenna will not hurt him, he will only send him away. And we want you to stay with us, child—we love you! Dear heaven, you know that is true!"

But Lucy evaded her embrace. "I don't know what is true or what isn't," she flung at her would-be protectress. "Jethro has told me a very different story and Luke heard him, did you not, Luke?" She did not wait for Luke's puzzled confirmation, but—looking oddly like her elder sister—she walked slowly and purposefully to take a stand at Jethro's side. "I'm ready to go with you, Jethro," she told him, her shrill young voice sounding like a knell in Caleb Boskenna's ears.

Angrily, he raised his musket to his shoulder, aiming it at Jethro's chest. "Stay where you are," he warned. "I'll blow you to damnation if you take one step from here with that girl!"

"You'm making a mistake, Mr. Boskenna sir," Jethro answered, without heat. "Did 'ee think I'd come back here alone?" He called, and from concealment in what had once been his hut, two dark, half-naked figures came padding softly towards him, each with a spear held menacingly above his head.

Aborigines, Boskenna thought, appalled—two of the wretched blackfellows with whom, when he had worked here, Jethro had consorted. Two of the elusive savages to whom he had attempted to preach the Word of God but who had repaid his overtures with contempt, choosing to rob him of livestock and maize, in preference to listening to his sermons and his readings from the Bible!

Losing control for a moment, he shouted at them to go away, but neither moved nor spoke, even when he turned his musket on them. They simply stood at Jethro's back, their spears still held high, their partisanship not to be doubted.

There was a tense silence, broken only by Martha Boskenna's frightened sobbing, and then Jethro said, his voice still calm and quiet, "There be a boat a-comin' upriver to meet us, Miss Lucy. If 'ee be ready, we could maybe go an' wait for 'un, on the wharf."

For answer Lucy—still looking, to Caleb Boskenna's angry eyes, like a mirror image of her sister—held out both hands to him. "I'm ready, Jethro," she said, with the same determination as before. "Let's not delay any longer."

The last remnants of Boskenna's control snapped. Was this to be the end of all his meticulous planning, he asked himself bitterly, the sole reward for all the months of toil he had expended on the land, in the conviction that it would one day be his? The musket wavered in his hands, but then he steadied it, peering along its barrel, to find not Jethro or one of the aborigines in his sights but . . . Lucy. She was going, she had made up her mind . . . going to Abigail, who had the evidence of his deception in her possession.

Not enough to convict him of any crime, perhaps, but enough, without any doubt at all, to deprive him of Yarramundie. His finger closed on the trigger; the musket fired but Martha screamed, putting him off his aim, and the next instant a spear came hurtling through the air, its aim, by contrast with his own, straight and true. Its barbed point struck with terrible force, to bury itself in his chest, in his heart, and he fell, to gasp his life away in a ghastly smother of coughed-up blood and an agony which was mercifully brief.

Jethro was the first to reach him and raise his head, with compassion, in an endeavor to ease his passing, but there was no breath in his body. When his weeping wife fell to her knees beside them, the shepherd could only reply to her despairing question with a whispered confirmation of her fears.

"He's gone, Mrs. Boskenna ma'am. There's naught you can do."

They carried the big, limp body into the house, and while they were doing so, an oared boat came alongside the landing stage below, manned by two settlers from the Green Hills.

"The *Flinders* is on her way up, Jethro," one of them said. "With Justin Broome and this young lady's brother." He gestured to Lucy. "We'll take her to meet 'em, shall we, and leave you to attend to matters here?"

Jethro considered the suggestion and then nodded. "Aye. 'Twill maybe be best if I stay. Young Luke'll help me, won't 'ee, lad? I daresay Mrs. Boskenna will need me for a while afore she leaves here." He laid his hands on Lucy's shoulders, turning her to face him. "You go on back to Sydney, Miss Lucy, an' try to forget what happened here this day. 'Tis best forgotten. But tell Miss Abigail not to worry her head about nothin', will 'ee please? I'll be watchin' out for when she comes along wi' that son o'hers, be it this year or next."

"Mr. Macarthur has fallen out with his onetime bosom friend, Colonel Foveaux," Jasper Spence announced with a certain undisguised satisfaction, as he seated himself at the luncheon table and picked up his napkin. "And Foveaux has relieved him of the post Johnstone created for him with such a furor. In future Lieutenant Finucane is to act as secretary for the colony, and, if you please, Simeon Lord has been appointed public auctioneer! Imagine it!"

He beamed from his wife to Abigail, helped himself from the dish the serving maid offered him, and added pointedly, "I'm aware, of course, that neither of you interests herself in the politics of this unhappy colony, but you will both, I feel sure, share my relief if, before long, Macarthur is driven to return to England."

Frances smiled back at him. "Yes, indeed," she agreed. "It will be the best thing than could happen, short of the governor's restoration."

"And you, Abigail?" Spence prompted.

"Abigail is anxious about her sister," Frances answered for her. "Are you not, my dear?"

"Yes," Abigail admitted apologetically. "I do beg your pardon, Mr. Spence, but I cannot seem to think of anything else just now."

"You've no occasion to worry, child," her host assured her. "Your brother and Justin Broome are two fine and most resourceful young gentlemen, and whatever the situation at—what's the name of the place? —at Yarramundie, I am confident that they will know how to deal with it, and with that unpleasant scoundrel Boskenna. So eat up—this is a most capital curry and you've hardly taken enough of it to feed the proverbial sparrow."

"I can't eat, Mr. Spence—truly I can't," Abigail evaded.

"Then drink, my dear—a glass of the brandy I brought back with me this voyage will restore your spirits." Jasper Spence made to fill her glass but Frances tactfully intervened to dissuade him.

"Leave the poor child be, Jasper. She will be all smiles once the two young gentlemen return, but now— quite understandably—she is distressed. Would you like to go to your room, Abigail, dear, and lie down for a while?"

Gratefully Abigail accepted her suggestion. Her brother's arrival, ten days ago, had been one of the happiest moments she could recall, and the more so because she had not anticipated it. Rick had grown almost out of recognition, in self-confidence as well as in stature. He was, as Mr. Spence had remarked, a fine young man, with the stamp of his naval training evident in manner and bearing. And he had instantly agreed to go to Yarramundie with Justin Broome, to whom he already, by coincidence, possessed an introduction from Captain Hawley, met at Port Dalrymple on his way to Sydney.

"The most alarming rumors are rife in England concerning this colony," Rick had told her gravely. "But it was when I found out the true nature of your guardians, the Boskenna's, that I decided I must come out here. I went to the old admiral, of course—Lord Ashton—and he worked the miracle. He not only had me appointed to the *Porpoise,* he arranged for me to take passage in the *Maitland* just three days before she sailed! And we made a record voyage—exactly four months and three days from Falmouth."

She had hugged him, Abigail remembered, and cried a little from the sheer joy and relief of seeing him again. And Rick had looked down at her with all his old affection and hugged her, too, exclaiming in mock wonder, "And when I find you again it is to learn that you are married and widowed and have a son! It takes some getting used to, Abby, I can tell you—especially when I learn I am an uncle and that my nephew is named after me. I'm glad of that, you know, and very proud—if just a mite fearful that, if I pick him up, my namesake will fall to bits in my arms."

"He will not," Abigail had assured him. "Dickon may look small but he's strong and resilient."

"Like his father?" Rick had questioned innocently, and she had smiled at him through her tears and nodded, deeming it best not to tell him more for the present.

Lucy was—she had to be—their first priority; in the light of the agreement Abigail had found in Desmond O'Shea's leather case and the information Rick had unearthed concerning Caleb Boskenna's criminal record,

Lucy might well be in danger. She had sent Jethro to
fetch her, it was true, as soon as she had come to her
senses after little Dickon's birth, but there had been
delays—partly caused by Henrietta Dawson's refusal
to let him leave Upwey in Timothy's absence and partly
by poor Jethro's insistence that he would go on foot,
rather than by river in the *Fanny* or one of the other
river vessels.

She had no means of knowing whether he had made
the overland journey safely or not; but Rick must have
caught up with him, in Justin Broome's fast cutter, and
between them they would surely contrive Lucy's release. As Mr. Spence had said, whatever the situation
at Yarramundie, Rick and Justin would know how to
deal with it. She was foolish to worry, but . . . Abigail
crossed to her baby's cot, her throat tight and aching.
Had it not been for the tiny scrap of humanity that was
her son, she might have gone with them and eased her
conscience on Lucy's account, instead of waiting here
so anxiously for news.

The baby stirred, sensing her presence. Suddenly
overwhelmed with pity and love for him, she bent and
scooped him up in her arms, holding him close, her lips
brushing his thin fuzz of dark hair. His eyes opened,
his small, perfectly formed mouth nuzzled her breast,
and carrying him over to her bed, she unfastened her
dress and gave him suck, finding at once release and a
new peace of mind in the age-old, primitive act of
giving him sustenance.

Later, when she had changed him, she restored him
to his cot and, as Frances Spence had so understand-
ingly advised, lay down on her bed and slept.

She was awakened by Lucy, who said simply, "Mr.
Boskenna is dead, Abby. A native killed him with a—
a spear. I saw it all. I . . . oh, *Abby*!" Suddenly she
was a little girl again, turning, as she always had, to her

elder sister for comfort, and Abigail's arms went round her.

"Don't cry, Lucy darling. Don't think about it, don't talk about it. You're here, safe and well, and that is all that matters."

"I *must* tell you," Lucy insisted, her voice choked with sobs. "Abby, I think Mr. Boskenna meant to shoot me. He pointed his gun at me, and there—there was a terrible look in his eyes. A—a look of hatred, as if he wanted me to be dead. But then Mrs. Boskenna screamed, and the aborigine threw his spear and it struck him in the—the heart. The musket ball went over my head—it missed me but it came quite close, Abby."

"There, there, darling," Abigail soothed, stroking her disheveled hair. "Now stop—you've told me all you need to. Don't say any more."

"I must say one more thing," Lucy whispered. She shivered in Abigail's arms but her sobs gradually subsided. "I don't ever want to go back there, to Yarramundie, not as long as I live. Rick says we can sell it, he's sure we can, if we recover the deeds. That's what you want, too, isn't it, Abby? *You* don't want to go back there, do you?"

Abigail's gaze went to her sleeping son and she was suddenly filled with a new resolution. "Yarramundie is our inheritance, Lucy," she answered softly. "And our lives are here now. Rick might go home, but we never shall. I think I shall go back to Yarramundie one day, for Dickon's sake. I believe I must."

"Well, I shan't," Lucy asserted, and broke into a fresh storm of weeping. Abigail's arms tightened about her small, trembling body, and she murmured endearments and offered consolation . . . but her own eyes were dry.

CHAPTER XXV

John Macarthur sat hunched in his armchair in the living room at Elizabeth Farm, staring with eyes that saw nothing into the crackling log fire. There was a glass by his side but he had not touched it, seeming to be unaware of it and of his wife's anxiously hovering presence in the room behind him.

It was she who finally ventured to break into his self-imposed silence. "John, my dearest," she began, her voice vibrant with emotion. "Please, I beg you, do not keep your troubles to yourself. I am your wife and I love you. I—"

"You must be the only living soul in this colony who does, Elizabeth!" he burst out bitterly. "Damn them, they are all deserting me, like rats from a sinking ship! Not one now even admits how much he owes me, and as for that unprincipled man, His Honor Colonel Foveaux, he is the cause of all the mischief. Truly, I regret having sent Ned home now . . . at least I could have counted on *his* continued loyalty."

"He will plead your cause in London, dearest," Elizabeth pointed out, "where you still have many good and influential friends."

"But it is here I need them," her husband retorted. "With the exception of Kemp, Lawson, and Draffin, there is not one of the Corps officers who affords me the least support. Abbott has turned against me, George Johnstone is only concerned to keep well in with Foveaux and that unspeakable wife of his. Tom Laycock is offended, because I would not recommend him for the provost marshal's office, and even Nick Bayly— for whom I did everything proper—has become a violent oppositionist! And all because he believed some lie Charlie Grimes told him about me."

"But at least Mr. Grimes has left the colony, John— you will not be troubled with him any longer." Elizabeth knelt beside him, to stir up the fire, and then sought to change the subject. "Our dear little Eliza seems to be showing quite a marked improvement this morning," she said. Their elder daughter was, she knew, the object of his deep and sincere affection, and her recent illness had caused him much concern. "She is asking to see you, dear."

"I'll pay her a visit," her husband promised, but he continued to brood, making no attempt to implement his promise. "They are a damned grasping, ungrateful set," he complained. "All of them—the civilians as well. I'm of the firm conviction, Elizabeth, that if I had yielded to them when I was secretary for the colony, the whole of the public property in the colony would not have satisfied them! They would still have demanded more—and for what? Reward for their part in bringing about Bligh's downfall, which was the outcome they all wanted? And look at that fat, greedy rogue Harris—my God, if ever there was a double-dealing rascal, it is he! Did he not agree—nay, damme, volunteer—to sail with Grimes and Minchin with our dispatches to the Colonial Office and then feign illness, in order to absolve himself of his agreement?"

"I think he really was most unwell, John," Eliza-

beth demurred. She rose, rubbing the dust off her
hands, and looked down in wordless pity at his hunched,
despondent figure. But he dismissed her suggestion in
regard to Dr. Harris.

"Not he, my dear. His illness was one of convenience,
diagnosed by himself because he thought it would pay
him better to remain in Sydney. Well, at least George
Johnstone saw through his miserable ploy and gave
him nothing. But," he added glumly, "Foveaux is making up for the omission—Harris has been given a grant
in the town, to keep him happy, Atkins likewise, to help
him change his coat, and Simeon Lord has been handed
the chance to make his fortune as public auctioneer!
God in heaven, Elizabeth, was it for the advancement
of men of their caliber that I risked my neck and my
honor, in calling for *Bounty* Bligh to be deposed?"

Elizabeth Macarthur, having no answer to this thorny
question, remained silent, and he went on, a harsh edge
to his voice. "Gore has got his just deserts, which is, I
suppose, something: seven years on the Coal River
should teach him a lesson. And I doubt that that dangerous criminal Crossley will be enjoying Van Diemen's
Land, any more than Hawley is—Walter Davidson
doesn't think very highly of Paterson's court at Port
Dalrymple."

"Will he come back to assume the government, do
you think, John, dear?" Elizabeth asked, seeking a
change of subject.

John Macarthur grunted contemptuously. "Paterson, d'you mean? Oh, he'll come back—he will have to,
if he is not to incur the Horse Guards' extreme displeasure. As the senior officer in the colony, he cannot
ride out the storm indefinitely in a settlement of only
a few hundred troops and convicts—not, at any rate,
without damaging his chances of promotion. But he
will make excuses and delay his return for as long as
he can. In the hope," he added cynically, "that Joe

THE TRAITORS

Foveaux and George Johnstone will contrive, between
them, to coerce the *Bounty* bastard to take passage to
England."

"Will they succeed in doing that?" Elizabeth's tone
was doubtful, and she was not surprised when her husband shook his head.

"They're trying, Lord knows. But Bligh's a damnably
obstinate devil. One day he writes that yes, he will take
passage in His Majesty's ship *Porpoise,* but then he
sends a long list of the witnesses he insists he must take
with him, and demands for alterations to be made to his
accommodation on board. His demands are refused, so
he mounts his high horse and writes that he'll stay
where he is. They don't meet in person, you know, he
and Foveaux—they communicate only by letter."

"Is that not rather—rather unsatisfactory, for both
parties?" Elizabeth suggested.

"Perhaps, but they appear to prefer it."

"Yet it achieves nothing?"

"No—just endless prevarication, on Bligh's part.
Everyone wants him to go, I need hardly tell you, but
he will not." John Macarthur permitted himself a wintry smile. "In one of the letters we intercepted, he was
writing to Lord Minto, in Calcutta, demanding troops
from the John Company to put down the mutiny on his
own! And in another he implored Admiral Pellew—Sir
Edward Pellew—to send him a ship of the line or even
a fifty-gun frigate, for the same purpose. Damn it, he
even revealed our defenses—or the lack of them—in
the hope of convincing the admiral that he need anticipate no serious opposition!"

"But were those letters sent on to England?" Elizabeth asked incredulously.

Her husband shrugged. "They had to be. He'd have
smuggled them out, if he thought they were not being
dispatched. He sent a long, complaining letter to Lord
Castlereagh in Campbell's schooner, the *Rose,* because

—as he explained to his lordship—he feared that if he consigned the letter to the *Dart* or the *Brothers,* his enemies would delay or destroy it. His enemies being the likes of poor young Ned, Minchin, and Grimes!"

"Suppose Admiral Pellew does send a ship of war here, what then, John? Would that not be disastrous?"

Macarthur's smile widened into a cruelly scornful smirk. "The good admiral has not replied; neither has Lord Minto . . . though doubtless both have forwarded the letter to His Majesty's Government for action, if deemed necessary. But, thankfully for us, His Majesty and his government are wholly preoccupied with the war with France. They have neither ships of war nor troops to spare for a penal colony half the world away, my dear Elizabeth."

"So Captain Bligh remains in arrest," Elizabeth said, and then added, with a hit of sarcasm in her voice, "and you, I suppose, remain unrewarded and unappreciated by those who have taken advantage of a situation you and only you had the courage and farsightedness to create?"

"That, my dear," Macarthur acknowledged grimly, "is one way of putting it. But it is, I suppose, the unpalatable truth. Yet I venture to forecast that in years to come, Elizabeth, *I* shall be recognized as having done more to bring prosperity to New South Wales than Bligh or Foveaux or Johnstone—aye, and more than Hunter or King! I shall have given this colony herds of fine, purebred sheep and a growing export commodity in wool. With your most valuable aid, my dear, I shall have achieved more than all of them put together . . . but they are fools, for they cannot see it!"

Moved by his words, Elizabeth went again to kneel at his feet. Her hands resting on his knees and her eyes bright with unshed tears, she said softly, "I know what you have achieved, John. And I am proud, so very proud, my dearest, to have played a small part in your achievement."

Her husband reddened. "I'm talking out of turn, Mrs. Macarthur. Damme, I'm even becoming maudlin, although I've not touched a drop of this brandy you insist on plying me with." He gulped down the contents of his glass and flung it from him, to shatter in the stone-built grate. "To the devil with the governor and Their collective Honors, the acting lieutenant governors! Let that drunken sot Paterson come back and do his worst. Let him bring Hawley with him, as a member of his staff . . . I will hold my peace. But now, my own dearest heart, give me your hand—we have a poor sick daughter to visit, have we not? In God's name, let us go to her!"

They went to the sickroom together, hand in hand.

On January 9, 1809—almost a year after Governor Bligh had been placed under arrest by his regiment—Lieutenant Colonel William Paterson returned to Sydney on board H.M.S. *Porpoise.*

Bligh watched the pomp and ceremony of the landing from the Government House window where, six months earlier, he had watched that of Joseph Foveaux. Still devotedly at his side, his daughter Mary sought by what means she could to raise his flagging spirits, and it was she who first saw the tall, scarlet-jacketed figure of Andrew Hawley standing on the wharf.

"Oh, Papa dearest, look!" she exclaimed. "I do declare that Captain Hawley has come back!"

The governor followed the direction she had indicated with his eye, not troubling to pick up his glass.

"Yes," he confirmed. "It is Hawley. Well, I am glad that he has survived, but I cannot see that his presence in William Paterson's entourage can in any way remedy my plight."

"But he has been a good and loyal officer," Mary reminded him. "Kate Lamerton told me that he was forced to escape to Van Diemen's Land in peril of his life. That villain Mr. Macarthur had sworn a warrant for his arrest, and the Corps would have served him as they served poor Mr. Gore, had he been brought to trial."

But her father merely nodded. "And the first thing he will do," he asserted coldly, "will be to make his way up the Hawkesbury to rejoin the emancipist woman he so unwisely married. *My* fate, devil take it, is in Paterson's hands!" He reached for his telescope, his mouth a hard, tight line, and focused the instrument on the man for whose return he had so often called in vain. "Damme, the fellow looks like death! He's aged out of all recognition, I dare swear he has—look at him, Mary, he's having to walk with a stick. And that scoundrel Foveaux is with him, talking his blasted head off! Filling his mind with infernal lies and accusations aimed against me, no doubt. I notice Johnstone's keeping well out of their way, and Macarthur's not even there."

"Is he not, Papa?" Mary's surprise was apparent.

"My dear child," her father retorted, snapping his telescope shut. "Macarthur, perdition take him, has had his day—he is out of favor with the rebel administration and, I am informed, spends most of his time with his ever-increasing flocks of bloody sheep at Camden, where he's built himself a palatial residence. He still has more money and owns more land and livestock than anyone else in the colony, and I don't doubt the scurvy rogue still imports twice as much liquor as the rest of them. You need spare him no pity."

"I did not intend to spare him any, Papa," Mary defended. "What I meant was—"

But her father was not listening. He said abruptly, "I shall issue the same order to Colonel Paterson as I did to his predecessor—my instructions, in writing, that he put down the mutiny in his regiment and release me from arrest forthwith. And I shall also order the *Porpoise* to remain here, pending my decision whether or not, on my release, to board her. I'll be in a position to judge what Paterson's attitude is likely to be, Mary, when he sends me his reply."

Colonel Paterson's reply—if less insolent than his predecessor's had been—left the governor under no illusions as to his attitude. It came promptly, addressed as always to *William Bligh, Esquire,* and, after stating that he intended scrupulously to adhere to the form of government presently in operation, Paterson demanded that, as a condition of his release from arrest, Mr. Bligh must agree to quit the colony and proceed at once to England.

He further stated that the transport *Admiral Gambier,* of five hundred tons, was standing by to receive Bligh, with his daughter, Mrs. Putland, and his staff and servants. His Majesty's ship *Porpoise,* however, could no longer be made available, since she was required to proceed to Norfolk Island to assist in the evacuation of its inhabitants.

"Papa, dear," Mary pleaded, when the contents of the new lieutenant governor's note were made known to her, "the *Admiral Gambier* is a new ship, and I am sure we should be comfortably accommodated. Could we not take passage in her? You have endured all that anyone could be expected to endure for nearly a year. You have suffered insult and indignity at the hands of these unprincipled rebels and the home government has sent you no help. Is it not time for you to leave?"

To her dismay her father shook his head, a gleam of anger in his tired eyes. "No, daughter," he returned firmly. "If I go, it will be in command of a King's ship or not at all. The *Porpoise* is under my orders, as commodore and senior naval officer, and I shall keep her

here, whatever demands that upstart Paterson may
make, and I shall tell him so."

His categorical refusal of the rebel administration's
terms was accompanied by an order to Lieutenant Kent
—in temporary command of the *Porpoise*—to place
Colonel Paterson under arrest. He did not expect this
order to be obeyed, Mary knew, but the outcome of
his having given it took him completely by surprise
and shocked him to the depths of his being.

Major Johnstone and Captain Abbott presented
themselves at Government House to deliver, on the
new lieutenant governor's behalf, a threat to remove
him forcibly to what they described as "less congenial
quarters" in the barracks, unless he issued an order to
permit the *Porpoise* to go to Norfolk Island at once and
himself board the *Admiral Gambier* without further pro-
crastination.

Mary trembled in terrified anticipation of her father's
reaction to his unprecedented demand, and poor young
Edmund Griffin was as alarmed as she was when he told
her of it.

"His Excellency had not set eyes on either of them
since the night Major Johnstone led the Corps here to
arrest him," the secretary said. "But they both marched
in, as bold as brass, Mrs. Putland, and confronted him
with that—that insulting threat to his person. Johnstone
was particularly arrogant and rude, but I do not think
that Abbott relished his role very much, for he said
little."

"And my father?" Mary asked steeling herself. "What
reply did he give them?"

"At first he was too stunned by their effrontery to
make reply. But then"—Griffin's voice held admiration
—"he pointed to the portraits of His Majesty, which
he had veiled following the rebellion, and reminded
them that they were addressing the King's appointed
representative and commander in chief. After warning

both gentlemen that they would have to answer for their mutinous treason against him when they were finally brought to trial, he refused their demands and observed—in a very dry tone of voice—that it was a fortunate circumstance which had caused him to cover His Majesty's face, so that he saw nothing of the scene. He—oh, truly, he was magnificent, Mrs. Putland! And he kept his temper . . . he simply ordered them to leave and they did."

Mary expelled her breath in relief. "Do you suppose they mean to implement their threat to remove him to the barracks, Edmund? Surely they will not dare?"

"I fear they do," Griffin confessed. "And that they *will* dare. It seems they are determined to force His Excellency to leave the colony." He hesitated. "I've heard a rumor that Major Johnstone and Mr. Macarthur will also leave for England, if your father does."

"*They* will leave?" Mary was taken aback. "For heaven's sake—why?"

"I can only presume in order to defend themselves against any charges His Excellency brings against them on his arrival in London. And also," Griffin added regretfully, "because Mr. Macarthur hopes to blacken His Excellency's good name and damage his reputation before there is any trial."

"According to my mother, that has been done already in their letters and reports. They have lied and lied, Edmund. They—" Mary broke off, hearing the sound of raised voices in the hall below. She hurried to the window, the secretary at her heels. "Edmund, in heaven's name—look! They are back, with a post chaise, both of them, and Major Johnstone is endeavoring to force his way in, past poor Jubb!"

"I must go to His Excellency's aid," Edmund Griffin exclaimed, on the verge of panic. "Stay here, Mrs. Putland, I beg you!"

But Mary ignored his well-intentioned advice. She

had inherited her father's temper and, descending the stairs at a run, was incensed at this flagrant attempt to humiliate him by laying hands on his person. She reached the hall in time to see Major Johnstone, his plump face aflame, struggling to propel her father out to the waiting chaise. He was backed up by two of the sentries, their muskets leveled on the startled menservants who had gathered in the hall. Jubb, nursing a bruised jaw, was leaning against the wall, while Captain Abbott held Edmund Griffin back, both hands grasping the secretary's collar.

Seeing Mary, he had the grace to offer a breathless apology. "I am sorry for this intrusion, Mrs. Putland, but it is necessary. Mr. Bligh is to be confined in the barracks—he will be driven there, under armed escort. But no harm whatsoever will come to you, ma'am. You may remain here until—"

Furiously, Mary cut him short. "I go where His Excellency my father goes, Captain Abbott."

"You will not be admitted, ma'am. You—"

"You are a coward, sir! Is there no limit to your treachery?" Mary flung at him, unable to restrain herself. She remembered that other occasion, when the Corps had come under arms to Government House and she had vainly attempted to bar their way. A terrible fear gripped her. "Is it now your intention to take my father's life? To—to order the execution of your lawful governor?"

The color drained from Abbott's cheeks. "Certainly not, ma'am," he denied. "I beg you to believe me and keep calm. Please, Mrs. Putland, I—" Releasing Griffin he held out both hands to her. "I'll take you to your room and—"

"Stand aside, sir," Mary bade him scornfully. "And do not dare to lay hands on me. I am going with my father."

She thrust past him, and, with fear and anger lending

wings to her feet, she gathered up her skirts and ran after the chaise. It was midday, the sun blazing down from Sydney's azure blue sky, and she was hatless, wearing only her thin house slippers. Neither heat nor discomfort could deter her, however, and when the chaise came to a halt outside the Corps' barracks, two hundred yards away, she had caught up with it. But her fear was in no way allayed when she glimpsed Colonel Foveaux standing by the door.

"My beloved child!" her father exclaimed, his voice harsh with concern. "What are you doing here? In the name of God, go back!"

Mary shook her head. Unable to speak from lack of breath, she took his arm when he descended from the chaise and, pausing only to cast a withering glance at the red-faced Johnstone, walked into the barracks at her father's side.

Foveaux did not speak or raise his hat as the two passed him, but his expression of dismay at the sight of her gave Mary satisfaction. Then his secretary, Lieutenant Finucane, was beside them, bareheaded and tactfully bowing.

"This way, if you please, sir—ma'am. You are to be accommodated in my quarters until your departure."

His quarters consisted of two small, sparsely furnished rooms, with a truckle bed in one and a sofa in the other. William Bligh, a suspicion of moisture in his eyes, led Mary gently to the sofa, but before he could settle her on it, Major Johnstone marched stiffly in.

"Sir," he announced brusquely, "I am directed by His Honor Lieutenant Governor Foveaux to inform you that you are to hold yourself in readiness to embark on board the schooner *Estramina* when she arrives in this port."

"And when will that be?" Governor Bligh challenged.

"I really cannot say, sir," Johnstone returned. "She

is expected in a week or so. I would draw your attention," he added, "to the presence of three armed sentries who have been posted outside this quarter to insure that you do not leave without Colonel Paterson's permission."

"Where is Colonel Paterson?" Bligh asked, keeping his temper with a visible effort. "Have you brought me here on his orders?"

"I have, sir," Johnstone answered woodenly. "His Honor is at Parramatta, but he will return for the purpose of arranging your passage to England. I give you good day, sir—Mrs. Putland."

Then he was gone, leaving father and daughter alone together. It was the final, bitter humiliation, and Mary, at last, took refuge in tears.

Justin brought word of Governor Bligh's new arrest to Andrew and his mother at Long Wrekin.

He had few details, save what he had gleaned from a few shore-going seamen who had witnessed the governor's short drive from Government House to the Barrack Square, but he said, when Andrew questioned him, "It appears that His Excellency was under restraint, with Major Johnstone and an armed escort accompanying him. And one of the sailors told me that there was a lady running after the carriage—Mrs. Putland, he supposed, since she seemed greatly distressed and hadn't waited to put on her hat, poor soul. But she's a brave woman—I remember seeing her stand at the gates of Government House last year, defying the troops to enter."

"You don't think," Jenny asked fearfully, "you don't think the rebel administration intends to execute the governor, do you, Justin?"

"There was no talk of that, Mam," Justin assured her. "Although with Colonel Paterson at Parramatta, there's no telling what Colonel Foveaux might do."

They both looked at Andrew and he shrugged despondently.

"After the manner in which Foveaux served poor George Suttor, merely because he refused to attend a muster, that particular scoundrel, it seems to me, is capable of anything! But—you say Paterson's at Parramatta, Justin, not in Sydney?"

Justin nodded contemptuously. "What you told us about him is proving right, Andrew. He's ensconced at Government House in Parramatta—drinking heavily, they say—and leaving the administration in the hands of Foveaux and Johnstone."

Andrew frowned. "Then he may not know about this latest move. Damn it, the man's almost senile! But I am quite certain he would never give his consent to the governor's execution, if he knew that there was any thought of it. I spent much longer than I wanted in Port Dalrymple with him, and for all his drinking, I know that he's no rebel. He disapproved very strongly of Johnstone's decision to depose Governor Bligh, and made his disapproval clear, both to Johnstone himself and to Lord Castlereagh, before he himself was persuaded to come back to Sydney." He turned to Jenny, a mute question in his eyes, and, reading his thoughts, she sighed deeply and laid her hand on his.

"Are you asking me to tell you that it is your duty to go to Colonel Paterson, Andrew?"

Andrew reddened. "Aye, lass, I suppose I am," he admitted, with reluctance. "But with the harvest not yet finished, I . . . damme, Jenny, love, I'll not leave without your consent!"

She smiled. "Will you not, my dear husband? Well, don't worry about the harvest—it is well enough advanced, and Tim Dawson will lend me one of his men, if I ask him. Go, dear heart, and with a clear conscience. I'd not try to keep you from your duty."

Andrew's relief was in his eyes. He raised her hand

to his lips. "Your mother is a wonderful woman," he observed to Justin, with sincerity.

"I know it," Justin said, and grinned across at her. "Shall I take you in the *Flinders,* Andrew?"

"No, I'll ride to Parramatta and go on from there to Sydney, if it's necessary," Andrew decided. "Stay on here, lad, until your Mam is ready to fill your holds with the Long Wrekin wheat, as we'd arranged."

"I'll do that," Justin promised. "And I daresay I shall be able to make myself useful, in your absence. William will see to that, if Mam does not!" He got to his feet. "I'll help you saddle your horse. Will you go in uniform?"

It was Jenny who answered. "Of course he will, Justin! He still holds the King's commission, and no rebel Rum Corps officer can take that from him." She, too, rose. "I'll put out your uniform and brush it, Andrew, while Justin attends to the horse."

Half an hour later Andrew set off. There was a road now, from the Richmond settlement to Toongabbie and thence to Parramatta, the last a carriage road, well constructed and in good repair. He pressed his horse hard, and, although he wasted little time, it was dusk when he reached Parramatta and trotted along the main street, passing Elizabeth Farm and the barracks on his way.

A carriage, drawn by two well-matched horses, and flanked by an ox-drawn dray, stood outside the Macarthurs' farmhouse, and, somewhat to his surprise, Andrew saw that both were being loaded with baggage, under Mrs. Macarthur's supervision. He saluted her and received a polite acknowledgment, but she offered no explanation and he rode on, thinking no more of it.

At Parramatta's Government House—a commodious, pleasantly situated single-story building, greatly enlarged from Governor Phillip's original Parramatta residence—a servant took his horse and the sentry posted at the door presented arms at the sight of his uniform. Colonel Paterson's charming white-haired wife, however, after greeting him warmly, expressed doubts concerning her husband's willingness to receive him.

"He is in bed, Andrew, and feeling a trifle off color, but perhaps, since it is you, he won't mind a short visit."

He had seen Colonel Paterson often enough when the colonel was what his wife had described as "off color," Andrew reflected with distaste; in Port Dalrymple there had been few nights when he had not drunk himself into a stupor. Admittedly the poor devil had never fully recovered from the severe wound inflicted on him when he had fought his duel with John Macarthur, and he complained that he was constantly in pain, but . . . it was small wonder that Foveaux and Johnstone were doing as they liked in Sidney.

And if Governor Bligh's life depended on his being able to persuade William Paterson to intervene, then it hung on a very slender thread indeed.

He smothered a sigh as he entered the lamplit bedroom, to find its occupant, as he had feared, stretched out, seemingly unconscious, on the rumpled bed. But he made an effort to rouse himself at the familiar sound of Andrew's voice.

"Andrew, my dear fellow!" he offered warmly. "Delighted to see you. Help yourself to a drink, if you feel like one." He pushed a bottle across his bedside table. "There's another glass somewhere, I think."

Andrew helped himself, feeling his mouth dry, but shook his head to the hospitable invitation to smoke a cigar. William Paterson lit one, propping himself up on one elbow, his bloodshot eyes apprehensively searching his visitor's face.

"What brings you here?" he demanded at last. "You haven't come for the pleasure of my company, have you?"

"No, sir, not this time," Andrew admitted.

"Then you bring news? Bad news, I suppose."

"I fear it may be, Colonel." As concisely as he could, Andrew repeated what Justin had told him of the circumstances of Governor Bligh's removal to the Corps' barracks, but before he had come to the end of his recital, Paterson interrupted him indignantly.

"George Johnstone was acting on my orders, damme!" he said irritably. "And on Foveaux's advice. They both agreed it was the only way to force Mr. Bligh to quit the colony—he'd have sat on his back-side in Government House till the last trump sounded, if we'd left him there. Devil take it, you've served with him—you know what a stubborn swine he can be!"

That, Andrew thought, was true. But he said, determined to make sure, "Then His Excellency is in no danger, sir?"

"Good God, of course not!" Colonel Paterson sat up, reaching for his glass. Finding it empty, he waved a hand at the bottle. "Fill that up for me, will you please?"

Andrew did so, and after draining its contents thirstily, the older man went on, his words—if not his slurred, resentful voice—carrying conviction.

"There has to be an inquiry, don't you see—probably a trial. But in England, not here; we cannot hold it here. His Majesty's Government must decide the matter, apportion blame, examine witnesses before a judge and jury. I had no hand in deposing Bligh, and I cannot take the responsibility of carrying on what, not to put too fine a point on it, Hawley, is an illegal government. Bligh *must* go back to London, and, if he won't go willingly, then we have to force him. I'm prepared to let him have the *Porpoise,* since he keeps insisting he'll only go in a King's ship, but when he's been told he can have her, he changes his mind."

The colonel, apparently quite sober now, sat bolt

upright, the glowing tip of his cigar waving in the air to emphasize the point he was making.

"Joe Foveaux is an unprincipled, cunning devil, and I hold no brief for him," he said vehemently. "And George Johnstone was nothing more than Macarthur's dupe, his tool. I know Macarthur, better perhaps than anyone else knows him, and damme, Hawley, I've suffered at his hands—the wound he gave me six years ago has never healed. The infernal ball is lodged in one of my lungs and it pains me, every time I draw breath."

"I know, sir," Andrew acknowledged, not unsympathetically. "But in the matter of Governor Bligh's confinement in your barracks, I—"

"A pox on it, Captain Hawley!" Paterson shouted explosively. "He is perfectly safe there—nobody's going to harm a hair of his head. It's Foveaux's idea to hold him in a subaltern's quarter, under guard, until he signs a written agreement to embark with his family and servants on board the *Porpoise* and proceed to England with the utmost dispatch. He's to be required further to give a solemn undertaking neither to touch nor return to any part of this territory, unless commanded by His Majesty to do so. And," he added feelingly, "I have ordered Johnstone and Macarthur to leave when Bligh does, on similar terms, with whatever witnesses they feel it necessary to take with them. The *Admiral Gambier* will take them, and she'll sail when the *Porpoise* does—the same day, dammit, the same hour! All I'm waiting for is Mr. Bligh's signature to the document we've prepared. When he's given me that and they've all gone, I shall endeavor to carry on the administration of this colony, until the Colonial Office sees fit to relieve me . . . and I hope to God that will be soon. I'm a sick man, Andrew."

He again thrust his glass in Andrew's direction.

"I came out with the Second Fleet, you know," he

said, a note of sadness in his voice, "as a young captain in the Corps, and, God help me, I've given nearly twenty years of my life to this colony. I don't like the present situation any more than you do, and it grieves me deeply to think that the Corps to which I transferred and which I now, for my sins, command, should have rebelled, mutinied—call it what you will. But the home government created the situation, by appointing *Bounty* Bligh in the first place, so the home government can sort it out."

He took the glass from Andrew's hand and raised it unsteadily, his eyes suddenly glazed.

"To the future prosperity of New South Wales!" he muttered. "Drink that toast with me and then go to hell, Captain Hawley! And if you want to satisfy yourself concerning Mr. Bligh—go to Sydney Town and talk to him. Tell Foveaux you have my permission to visit him. And if you do, then for the Lord's sake try to persuade him to take His Majesty's ship *Porpoise* and set course for England. That is all I want of him." He hiccoughed and then gave vent to a curiously shrill laugh. "You can count on a grant of a thousand acres of land at the Hawkesbury, my dear fellow, if your efforts are successful. Or you can go and govern Port Dalrymple, if you prefer it. But now just leave me in peace."

He let his glass fall on the coverlet, and when, after picking it up, Andrew looked at him, he was asleep, his mouth open, a thin stream of spittle coursing down his unshaven chin.

Andrew spent the night in Parramatta's leading hostelry, the Freemason's Arms, kept by a pleasant, elderly emancipist named James Larra. Over a substantial breakfast the owner regaled him with local news and gossip, and he was in a more optimistic mood when he set off for Sydney soon after eight o'clock the following morning.

His hopes of an interview with the governor were, however, speedily dashed.

"Mr. Bligh is permitted no visitors," Lieutenant Finucane told him, when he reached the barracks and made his request. "I'm sorry, Captain Hawley, but I am under the strictest instructions not to allow anyone to see him."

"Whose instructions?" Andrew countered.

"Why, His Honor's, sir—Colonel Foveaux's," the young officer asserted.

"And I have been given permission by His Honor Colonel Paterson, who is, I think, at present your acting lieutenant governor and commandant of the Corps. Does that not overrule Colonel Foveaux's ban on visitors to His Excellency the governor?" Andrew's tone was cold, and Finucane, clearly flustered, was compelled to concede that it did.

"Have you the—er—the order in writing, sir?" he asked unhappily.

Andrew shook his head. "No. You will have to take my word for it, Mr. Finucane."

"I—ah—I will report the matter to Colonel Foveaux," Finucane decided. "If he is here, I . . . Perhaps, sir, you will have the goodness to wait. I will have your horse taken care of. If you will step into our messroom, the mess waiter will give you some refreshment and—ah —I'll be as quick as I can, sir."

He was, in fact, gone for half an hour, and when he returned it was with Major Johnstone, who demanded, without the civility of a greeting, "Is there not still a warrant out for your arrest, Captain Hawley?"

Andrew controlled his indignation. "There is not, Major Johnstone. Your commanding officer, with whom I returned from Port Dalrymple, had it annulled. And now, sir, regarding my request to see Governor Bligh, made at the—"

But Johnstone did not let him finish. "No one is permitted to see the former governor. Unless and until Mr. Bligh gives us the pledges we require from him, he is to be kept here under strict seclusion. Those are my orders from Colonel Paterson, and without His Honor's written authority, I cannot give you permission to call on him. He will, I trust it is needless to tell you, be freed and allowed to return to his residence at Government House the instant he accepts our terms and conditions for his final departure."

"And when do you expect that to be, sir?"

"I have no idea," Johnstone snapped. But he relented a little and said, in a more placatory tone, "I hope you have been hospitably looked after? Let me offer you a drink. Corporal Marlborough—" The mess corporal was at his side, but Andrew refused the offer of conciliation.

"I beg you to excuse me, sir. Since my mission has proved fruitless, I will be on my way."

"As you wish, sir." Johnstone accorded him a stiff bow and strode out. Finucane waited until he was out of earshot, and then said quietly, "Mrs. Putland is under no restraint, sir. Would you like me to tell her that you are here?"

This time, Andrew accepted the proffered olive branch. Finucane conducted him to an empty office room, and, five minutes later, Mary Putland joined him there, her joy at seeing him ample reward for his long and hitherto frustrating journey.

"My father is well enough," she said, in answer to his inquiry. "Impatient and greatly frustrated, as you might expect, but we have in no way been ill treated. At first, poor soul, he was convinced that bringing him here was a—a subterfuge, that the rebels wanted to bring about his death without it being known that they had. He would not eat, fearing that they intended to poison him, but I asked that his food might be sent from Government House, and this was instantly agreed. The good Jubb brings and serves every morsel, and they have allowed Kate Lamerton to attend me. So . . ." Her smile was fragile, Andrew noticed, but Mary Putland had not lost her courage. "Tell me what is happening outside our prison."

He gave her what news he could, describing his interview with Colonel Paterson in Parramatta and adding that both Johnstone and Macarthur would probably sail for England if the governor did.

"Will His Excellency agree to the conditions they are demanding?" he asked. "Can he, in honor, do so?"

She spread her small hands in a gesture of helplessness. "Yes, I think he will have to, Andrew, for they leave him but little choice. He says that a promise, extracted under duress, by rebels and mutineers, cannot be binding, because he is still governor and His Majesty's Government has not released him from his office or its responsibilities. But . . ." She looked up at him with brimming eyes. "My poor father cannot stay here for much longer. If they give him the *Porpoise*, with Captain Porteous and not Lieutenant Kent in command, and if they agree to the release of poor Mr. Gore and other witnesses he wishes to have on hand in London, I believe he will accept their terms. I urge him to, I—"

"You?" Andrew questioned. "When have rebels ever defeated you?"

Mary Putland held out both hands to him, her smile returning. "My dear father is not defeated either! He is still the man who heroically brought the survivors of the *Bounty* to Timor in a cockleshell boat . . . still the captain whom the great Lord Nelson singled out for praise at Copenhagen! These unspeakable traitors have done all in their power to vilify him here and de-

stroy his good name in England, but have no doubt,
Andrew, he will fight back."

"I have no doubt of that," Andrew assured her, with
genuine conviction. Finucane's clerk came in, to request that their interview be concluded, and, still retaining his clasp of Mary Putland's hands, Andrew
added, "I am here to serve you and His Excellency
your father. How can I best do so?"

"By taking up residence in Government House,"
Mary answered without hesitation. "Until our return
there. Jubb will, I know, be grateful for your support—
he is seeing to our packing, although Colonel Foveaux
does not know that. I will tell my father of your visit.
Thank you for coming, Andrew. It has done my heart
good to see and talk with you again . . . and your continued loyalty to him will, I know, raise my father's
spirits." She let him kiss her hand and then turned to
the waiting clerk and said, with impeccable dignity,
"Very well, Mr. Gaudry, you may escort me back to
His Excellency's prison."

Three days later, Governor Bligh having agreed
to the conditions imposed for his release, he and his
daughter were back in Government House to make
their final preparations for leaving Sydney.

CHAPTER XXVI

The governor was leaving; he had gone on board the twelve-gun King's ship *Porpoise* three weeks after his return to Government House, and now all was activity on her deck as the crew prepared to weigh anchor.

A small crowd had gathered at vantage points about the cove to bid him a restrained farewell, the presence of the troops on the government wharf and on the road leading to it being sufficient to discourage any demonstration—whether of regret or ill feeling.

Her father had been unusually silent and withdrawn immediately prior to their leaving Government House, his expression grave and oddly inscrutable, and this worried Mary, for normally he talked freely to her, trusting in her discretion as much as in her loyalty.

The official leave-taking had been formal and, on the part of Colonel Foveaux, the reverse of pleasant. Indeed, Mary thought bitterly, Foveaux had gone out of his way to cause her poor father as much humiliation as, in the circumstances, he could. His officers had neither saluted nor ordered their men to present arms, and he himself had pointedly left the wharf as the boat from the *Porpoise* put off from it; while Colonel Paterson, although he had come from Parramatta the previous day, had not put in an appearance at all.

But, in spite of all their attempts to provoke him, her father had kept his temper. In full dress uniform, his sword at his side, he had cut a finer and more dignified figure than any of the military officers. He had turned a blind eye to their insulting omission of even the courtesies due to his naval rank, replying with icy calm to such remarks as they addressed to him, and he had, Mary told herself proudly, put them all to shame in consequence.

Nevertheless, knowing his temper, she was still worried; and because she had shared his ordeal, she was more aware than anyone of the frustration he had felt and the strain of the long months of enforced inactivity which he had endured.

On board the *Porpoise,* however, everything was being conducted with the traditional ceremony. A smartly turned out side-party piped him aboard, and Captain Porteous stood waiting, cocked hat in hand, at the head of his officers. He was, in fact, Mary knew, a lieutenant commander and did not hold post rank, but her father responded warmly to his greeting, addressing him as captain and returning his salute with punctilious politeness.

But he was unprepared for the shock of Porteous's next words.

"I regret, sir," the brig's commander announced, "that my health will not permit me to sail with you to England. I have been given a grant of land at Bringelly, sir, and it is my intention to retire from the service and settle there, to recoup my health. Lieutenant Kent is a most competent officer, and I have formally handed over command of this ship to him. So . . ." He saw the angry color rising to suffuse the former governor's cheeks and added hastily, "With your permission, sir, my gig is waiting. I'll go ashore at once."

"So you will join the traitors!" Mary heard her father accuse. "How much land did they give you, Mr. Porteous, to win from you the support you and your ship's company withheld from me?"

John Porteous remained obstinately silent.

"I shall not forget your conduct!" Bligh thundered. "And, you may be sure, Their Lordships will hear of it from me!" In a quieter tone he snapped, "Call away your boat. I shall not detain you."

Porteous saluted and descended to his boat, and, after a brief hesitation, Lieutenant Kent, hat correctly under his arm, stepped forward. "Your orders, sir?"

Still holding himself under stern control, Bligh answered curtly, "When the gig is recovered and secured, you may weigh anchor. I shall assume command of this ship in her commander's absence, and you will continue to act as her first lieutenant. Are all my witnesses on board?"

Kent braced himself. "Commissary Palmer is not, sir. Major Johnstone refused permission for him to leave, pending certain charges brought against him for —er—irregularities in his administration of Crown property, I understand, sir."

Mary, fearing the outburst that, she knew, must come, slipped unobtrusively to her father's side and took his arm. "Should we not ask to be shown our quarters, Papa, dearest? I—I am fatigued and the sun is hot."

He appeared, at first, not to have heard her, but then he said impatiently, "By all means go below, Mary. Mr. Kent, be good enough to detail one of your officers to conduct my daughter to her cabin."

It had been a mistake, Mary realized, but, thus dismissed, she had no choice save to accompany a tall, fair-haired midshipman below. He introduced himself very diffidently as Tempest and displayed great solicitude in his care of her, pointing out where her hand baggage had been placed in the small but comfortable cabin allocated for her use.

"Shall I pass the—that is, summon your maid, ma'am?" he offered. "Or have some refreshment served to you?"

Mary, rather than disappoint him, accepted both suggestions, but, when sounds from the deck above indicated that the gig had returned and was being winched inboard, she could contain her anxiety on her father's behalf no longer. She went back on deck as the anchor was catted, the seamen working the *Porpoise*'s creaking capstan with a will. Her attempt to keep out of sight was not entirely successful; her father, pacing the quarterdeck and calling out orders to Lieutenant Kent, did not see her, but Midshipman Tempest did.

"Mrs. Putland ma'am," he began. "How can I be of service to you? Perhaps—"

She silenced him with a finger held to her lips, and then, as the topmen of the watch pelted past, to swarm aloft in obedience to the order to set sail, she asked him nervously to conduct her to where she might take a last glimpse of Sydney. "I—that is, Mr. Tempest, His Excellency supposes me to be below and I don't want to be in the way."

He understood, smiled, and, a hand lightly on her arm, led her to the after part of the deck, where an open hatch gave her concealment.

"I'm on duty, ma'am," he apologized, "so I have to leave you. But if you need me, you have only to pass the word."

Left alone, Mary waited, her fears not yet allayed. The ship was under way, her topsails set and starting to fill, when a roar from the quarterdeck sent her heart plummeting.

Her father's orders, each following in swift succession, brought the *Porpoise* to, her larboard quarter broadside to the shore, with its clustered buildings and the slowly dispersing watchers on streets and wharves.

"Prepare to run out your larboard guns, Mr. Kent!" Mary heard her father's voice as clearly as if she were beside him. "Load with round shot and beat to quarters!"

"Load, sir?" Kent was aghast, his voice shaking. "With round-shot? I have a signal gun loaded, sir, if you wish me to fire a salute, I—"

"Salute—to rebels and traitors, by God!" Now, Mary realized, her father had lost control of his temper, and the fury in his voice shocked her. "Devil take you, Mr. Kent, I'm ordering you to perform now the duty you have failed to perform since the damned troops mutinied! Load and run out your larboard battery and open fire on the barracks!"

"But, sir—Commodore Bligh, with respect, sir—" Kent was frantic, his face drained of color.

"It will take only a few shots to bring those traitors to their senses. Lob half a dozen round-shot onto their blasted parade ground and they'll yield up the government. They are rum traders and merchants, not soldiers of the King. They've never been under fire. You're a King's officer, Mr. Kent—do you not know your duty?"

"Sir, I know my duty, I assure you." Kent had recovered from his initial shock and he came rigidly to attention. "I'll run out the guns, if you order me, but I'll not open fire. I do not conceive it my duty to take an action that must lead to the sacrifice of innocent lives. And you, sir, surely would not wish to cause loss of life? I cannot guarantee the accuracy of my gunners, sir, after so long without practice. If some of the shots were to fall short, innocent people would inevitably suffer."

"A pox on you, Mr. Kent," Mary heard her father growl. But, to her heartfelt relief, his voice had lost its earlier insensate fury; if not yet calm, it was resigned. "I will never rest until I have compelled those traitors to surrender to my lawful authority. You may secure your guns—as you have rightly pointed out, I would not wish to cause loss of life to any innocent people, however just my cause."

"Sir!" Kent acknowledged, expelling his breath in a ragged sigh. "Aye, aye, sir."

He started to move away, but William Bligh barked out a command to him to remain where he was.

"You will send a boat to the *Admiral Gambier* at her moorings, with instructions to her master that he is not to permit Major Johnstone to take passage in her. And then, if you please, you will inform your ship's company that it is not my intention that we should return to England."

"Not return to England, sir?" Kent echoed.

"That is what I said," the governor retorted. "We will set course for Van Diemen's Land. And when you have attended to these instructions, Mr. Kent, you will be relieved of your duties and are to consider yourself under arrest, pending a trial by court-martial. Is that understood?"

William Kent, tense and still pale, bowed his head in wordless submission.

"Then carry on, Mr. Kent."

Mary watched, in stricken silence, as her father turned on his heel and made for the midships hatchway. Then, choking back a sob, she followed him, the shocked expressions on the faces of the officers and men who had witnessed the ugly scene seeming to reproach her for her failure to prevent it.

When she reached the cabin, her father said, quite coolly, "We shall not be returning to England, my dear, until such time as His Majesty's Government instructs me to do so. It is my duty, as you well know, not to abandon this colony—regardless of any promises extracted from me against my will. I shall ask Colonel

Collins for aid to put down the rebellion, Mary. He is a good officer. He will not refuse me."

By nightfall the *Porpoise* had cleared the great harbor of Port Jackson and, under all sail and with a fair wind, had set course for the Derwent and the Hobart settlement in Van Diemen's Land.

The loyalist settlers in the Hawkesbury and Toongabbie area had composed a farewell address to the governor. Entrusted with its delivery, Andrew and Tim Dawson had arranged to take passage to Sydney in Justin's *Flinders,* and, with their harvest over, Andrew persuaded Jenny to accompany them.

She had demurred at first, making every excuse she could think of, but now, she decided, as she stood at her husband's side to watch the *Porpoise* leave the cove, she was glad that she had allowed herself to be persuaded.

It was a moving scene; a moment, perhaps, that would be recorded in the colony's history, even though it was a sad occasion, with a rebel regiment holding the ordinary people back from contact with their lawful governor and, with their bayonets, effectively ensuring that his departure invited no demonstration by those who regretted his going.

The settlers' address, however, had pleased him, Andrew had told her, as had the number of signatories to it. Jenny smiled to herself, remembering how it had begun. . . . *"We acknowledge the blessings we experienced under Your Excellency's firm, upright, and impartial administration."* And the tribute had truly expressed the feelings of those ordinary people, settlers and emancipists like herself, whom the soldiers were now holding back—Governor Bligh had indeed sought to protect their interests against the extortion of the rum traders of the Corps and those who, like Mr. Macarthur, had made fortunes from their illicit monopolies.

But at least Macarthur was going, and Major Johnstone with him. The *Admiral Gambier* was lying at
anchor, waiting for them to embark with, it was said,
Dr. Jamieson, Dr. Harris, and Macarthur's friend and
partner, Mr. Davidson. Jenny watched a heavily laden
oared boat go alongside the big transport, with her
sparkling new paint and her bustling crew; then Jenny's
gaze went to the little brig *Porpoise,* in which the governor was to take passage. By contrast the King's ship
was not only small—her dingy sails and the peeling
paintwork of her hull bore witness to her age and
arduous service. She . . . Andrew exclaimed suddenly,
distracting her thoughts.

"My God!" he said to Justin. "The *Porpoise* is running out her guns! What the devil does that mean?"

Justin raised the telescope recently presented to him
by Robert Campbell and focused it on the frigate. "The
governor is on deck," he said. "And Lieutenant Kent.
They seem to be arguing, and I can see Mrs. Putland
wringing her hands as if—here, you take the glass,
Andrew, and see what you make of it."

Andrew did so and Jenny asked uncertainly, "Is
she—is she going to open fire, do you suppose?"

"I hope to heaven she's not," Andrew answered.

They waited, Andrew and Justin both tense and apprehensive and Jenny frankly bewildered. Then Andrew
said thankfully, "The guns are being secured. Probably
the governor was simply providing them with some
practice drill—he always was a taut hand. Well—" He
grinned at Justin and held out his hand to Jenny. "It's
over and he's on his way. Let us pray that the home
government will take notice of the situation in this
colony before we're much older and send troops to replace the Rum Corps, with a commanding officer who
knows his business. But until that happens, we must put
up with His Honor Colonel Paterson and, alas, with
Foveaux. We—" Jenny tugged at his arm and he broke

off, to ask indulgently, "Whither away, love? There's no hurry, is there?"

"Frances Spence," Jenny said, pointing to a small, grassy knoll behind them, from which the small crowd of spectators was now moving. "And Abigail and Lucy, too! And, I do declare, Abigail has her baby and a nurse with her. Please, Andrew, bestir yourself—I've not set eyes on any of them for months past!"

It was, for them all, a joyous reunion. Frances embraced Jenny with all her old affection, and Abigail, flushing with pleasure, displayed her small son, taking him from the nurse's arms with touchingly maternal pride.

"His name is Richard, after my brother," she said. "But we all call him Dickon. And this is Kate Lamerton, Mrs. Hawley, who came out with us in the *Mysore*. Kate could have gone back to England with Mrs. Putland, but she's decided to stay. And when I return to Yarramundie, she will come with me."

"You're going back?" Jenny exclaimed, at once pleased and surprised that she should have made this decision. Justin, she knew, had not expected her to do so but . . . the girl had matured, she realized, covertly studying her lovely, glowing face and hearing the firmness in her voice. Abigail Tempest—Abigail O'Shea—had grown up and become a woman.

"She has made up her mind," Frances confirmed. "I shall keep Lucy here, with Julia and Dorothea, so that they may continue their schooling. And your William and Rachel may join them, Jenny dear, whenever you can persuade them to come. I shall be taking no more long voyages to India—Jasper says he is weary of travel and wants to settle down and do his trading from here."

They talked on, exchanging news and gossip, and then, above the subdued hum of their two voices, Jenny heard Abigail say, "May I charter your *Flinders* to take us to Yarramundie, Justin? Mrs. Boskenna has left—she is going home in the *Admiral Gambier*—so I can go when it suits you."

Justin's eager assent to her request startled even his mother. She turned to look at him, and what she read in his eyes told her that Justin, too, was fully adult.

Adult and, unless she was very much mistaken, in love.

Abigail went on innocently, "One of my brother's shipmates, David Fortescue, has asked me to marry him," and the light in Justin's blue eyes flickered and died.

Jenny slipped her arm into his. "Let us go back to Long Wrekin, Justin," she said gently.

EPILOGUE

The first news to reach England of the rebellion in New South Wales and the deposition of the governor was contained in the dispatches composed by Major Johnstone.

These were delivered to Lord Castlereagh, at the Colonial Office, in September 1808 by young Edward Macarthur, who had made the long voyage from Sydney in the schooner *Dart*. So anxious had he been to insure that they reached their destination with all possible speed that he had hired a fishing boat, off Start Point in Devon, to set him ashore there and enable him to proceed to London by post chaise.

His reception came as a severe disappointment to John Macarthur's devoted young son, and he wrote of it despairingly, a few days after his arrival: *"I was anxious to get to town lest the duplicates of my letters should be delivered before the originals of those from other persons, which might conflict with them. But our late affairs make little impression on the public mind and excite still less attention at the Government Offices, for Spain and Portugal attract all their attention and all their thoughts. . . ."*

In truth, Lord Castlereagh, who had also been appointed to the onerous office of Secretary for War, had little time to spare for the affairs of an obscure penal colony some fourteen thousand miles distant. News of Sir Arthur Wellesley's first great victories over the French in Portugal had stirred the whole country. The people talked of little else, the journals and newspapers published glowing descriptions and fulsome tributes to the heroism of the soldiers and their brilliant commander.

In the blaze of popularity resulting from the army's successes, the Duke of Portland's Tory government was content to shelve whatever problems might be posed by the mutiny of a single regiment in New South Wales.

It was only the following year—and after a succession of conflicting reports from Sydney and pressure from Sir Joseph Banks, on behalf of the deposed governor—that Castlereagh sought the British government's approval for effective action to be taken in regard to the colony's future. Given a free hand by the Prime Minister, Castlereagh decided that a military, rather than a naval officer, should be appointed governor. The post was offered to Brigadier General Nightingall, and on his accepting it, he was ordered to embark for New South Wales with his regiment, the 73rd Foot, which was to replace the New South Wales Corps.

In response to an appeal from Elizabeth Bligh, to whom word of Nightingall's appointment in her husband's place had caused great distress, Sir Joseph Banks again made strenuous efforts to see justice done to the deposed governor. Matters dragged on, and in December, Sir Joseph wrote regretfully that *"we must not flatter ourselves too much, dear Mrs. Bligh, with the hope that my friend and your husband will be permitted to retain his governorship of the colony."*

To Bligh himself, five months later, his distinguished patron wrote at greater length.

> I have made diligent enquiry by every means open to me into the charges of maladministration alleged against you by the persons who seized your person and your government and it gives me sincere pleasure to say that there is not any part of them in which, in my opinion, your conduct is not meritorious and such as I expect of you.
>
> The conduct of your enemies, on the other hand, bears evident marks of the revolutionary proceedings of the French, which I know not how to distinguish from treason of the deepest dye. They accuse you, indeed, of cowardice but, as that is with your disposition impossible, I entirely disbelieve.

He added the information that, because of illness, Brigadier General Nightingall had been compelled to withdraw his acceptance of the post in New South Wales and that, in his stead, his second-in-command, Colonel Lachlan Macquarie, had been appointed to the governorship.

The letter ended with Sir Joseph's assurance that the Colonial Office would see to it that justice would be done and his personal honor redeemed in the colony.

Thus it was that Colonel Lachlan Macquarie, commanding the 73rd Regiment of His Majesty's Foot, received his official instructions in writing, under the signature and seal of the colonial secretary himself.

Dated May 14, 1809, his orders were:

> That if Governor Bligh is still in the settlement, he is to be liberated from arrest and reinstated in his Office for twenty-four hours, fol-

lowing which he is to surrender the government
to his successor and return to England.

That Major Johnstone, of the New South Wales
Corps, shall forthwith be placed in arrest and
sent to England for trial. To enable Commodore
Bligh to understand the charges made against him,
a copy of Major Johnston's justificatory despatch
is to be placed in his hands, so that he may consider what evidence and what witnesses he will
require, in order to establish his charges against
Major Johnstone and certain officers of his Corps.

Since Mr. John Macarthur has been represented
by the late Governor as the leading promoter and
instigator of the mutiny against him, the said Mr.
Macarthur is to be arrested and brought to trial
in New South Wales.

All appointments to official office made since
the arrest of the late Governor shall be declared
invalid, and those officials who were removed from
their appointments by Major Johnstone are to be
restored to them.

Finally, the new governor was instructed to disband
the New South Wales Corps, which was to be then re-
designated the 102nd Foot and recalled to England.
All officers of the regiment, including Colonel Paterson
and Lieutenant Colonel Foveaux, were to proceed with
it, and all grants of land made by or to officers of the
regiment were to be canceled, without the right of re-
newal. Those made to other persons, if considered by
the new governor to have been honestly and impartially granted might, at his discretion, be renewed.

Like each of his predecessors before him, Lachlan
Macquarie studied the orders he had been given and
promised himself that they should be carried out. He
was a distinguished officer, who had seen active service
in America, India, and Egypt. A Highland Scot, he

had now succeeded to the command of a Scottish regiment, one of the best in the British army, and since it was to form his garrison when he reached New South Wales, his hopes and his confidence were high.

On May 10, 1809, he embarked with his new wife, Elizabeth Henrietta, the newly appointed judge advocate, Ellis Bent, and his lady, and four companies of his regiment in His Majesty's ship *Hindostan*. In company with a second King's ship, the *Dromedary*, carrying the rest of the troops and his second-in-command, Lieutenant Colonel Maurice O'Connell, New South Wales's governor-designate set sail for the rebellious and unknown land he had been appointed to rule.

The Explorers, *Volume Four in the magnificent six-book series,* The Australians, *follows the harrowing and inspiring adventures of Abigail O'Shea, Jenny and Andrew Hawley, and Jenny's first-born son, Justin Broome, as they try to put their lives together again after the trials and misfortunes of the Rum Rebellion.*

It is a time of healing, of new beginnings. Order must be brought to the colony, now nearly a quarter century old. The rebel New South Wales Corps must be replaced; roads and buildings—neglected during the rebellion—must be repaired; and the lives of all the inhabitants shored up and restored to hope for the future.

Before a new chapter in Australia's history can begin, the old must close—and it does so dramatically as William Bligh is restored to his full rank as governor—for one day. Here is the scene as you will relive it in the opening pages of The Explorers, *to be published by Dell, © 1981 by Book Creations, Inc.*

On January 17, 1810—two years after the commandant of the New South Wales Corps had arrested and deposed him by force of arms—Governor Bligh returned to Sydney.

On government wharf the troops paraded, with their colors flying and their bands playing, the new governor, Colonel Lachlan Macquarie, and his officers at the head of His Majesty's 73rd Foot brave in their tartan and scarlet, and, lining the road and the approach to Government House, the rebel Corps, now in the process of being disbanded and shipped back to England in disgrace.

The guard of honor formed up. The governor's barge, smartly manned by seamen from the *Hindostan*, put off with the second-in-command of the 73rd, Lieutenant Colonel Maurice O'Connell, in the stern sheets.

O'Connell had, in fact, gone out to meet the *Porpoise* the previous day, in order to inform Governor Bligh and his daughter, Mary Putland, of details of the reception being prepared for them. Today, standing at her father's side on deck, Mary was conscious of a fluttering of the heart as the tall, good-looking colonel once more saluted her father and bowed over her hand.

"All is in readiness, Your Excellency," he announced, with impeccable courtesy. "If you and Mrs. Putland would care to step ashore, His Excellency Colonel Macquarie and his lady are eager to bid you welcome."

"Where, sir," Bligh asked, when they were seated in the barge, "are we to be accommodated?"

He had become accustomed to slights from officialdom during the past few weary months, Mary Putland thought pityingly—Colonel Collins had treated him quite abominably, in accordance, she could only presume, with the orders sent to him by the rebel administration. They had held that he had broken his word when he had sailed the *Porpoise* to Van Diemen's Land, instead of returning in her to England, and, Mary reflected, he undoubtedly had gone back on the agreement he had made with Colonel Paterson of the Corps. But an agreement extracted under duress, by rebels and mutineers, could not be binding, her father had maintained . . . and, as the King's appointed governor and commander-in-chief, he could not abandon his post without orders from His Majesty's Government.

No such orders had ever reached him, and now, God willing, reparation was to be made and justice done to him at last. She looked proudly at her father and then waited, with a certain anxiety, for Colonel O'Connell's answer to the question he had asked. Clearly they could not expect to return to Government House. The new governor had arrived in the colony almost three weeks before; he and his wife and his staff would already be installed there and could scarcely be asked to move elsewhere for a mere twenty-four hours.

Maurice O'Connell met her apprehensive gaze and smiled at her warmly, admiration in his own.

"A house has been made ready in Bridge Street to accommodate Your Excellency," he said. "I hope and believe, sir, that you will find it both comfortable and adequate for Your Excellency's requirements. And, sir, His Excellency Colonel Macquarie would esteem it an honor if you and your daughter would take dinner with his wife and himself, this evening, at Government House."

Her father's acknowledgment was, Mary knew from long experience of him, cool and noncommittal; but Colonel O'Connell appeared to notice nothing amiss.

"We shall be near neighbors," O'Connell told her, with satisfaction. "And, my dear Mrs. Putland, if there is any way in which I can serve you, then you have only to ask, I assure you."

For no reason that she could have explained, Mary flushed under his scrutiny. For the past year she had lived on board the *Porpoise,* in an almost exclusively male environment, and she found herself wondering why, in Maurice O'Connell's company, she should suddenly start behaving—if not quite in the manner of a young girl—then scarcely in that expected of a widow in her twenty-seventh year. But . . . it was undeniably pleasant to be the object of so handsome an officer's interest and admiration, and she thanked him shyly for his offer to serve her.

The barge came alongside the government wharf, the crew tossed oars smartly, and the band of the new governor's regiment struck up the familiar music of "God Save the King," as the guard of honor came to attention and presented arms.

Governor Lachlan Macquarie stood at their head, tricorne in hand, his reddish hair ruffled by the breeze, his square, somewhat austere face wreathed in smiles. But then Bligh, in the act of advancing to accept Macquarie's extended hand, halted abruptly, as if taken aback; Mary, following behind him on Colonel O'Connell's arm, also came abruptly to a standstill, seeking the cause of her father's evident discomfiture.

She had not far to look. At Governor Macquarie's side stood the two rebel officers who had used him so ill—Colonel Paterson and Colonel Foveaux—both, it appeared, now ready to join in the expression of welcome.

Her father kept his hands at his side. He bowed stiffly to the man appointed to supersede him, and, pointedly ignoring Paterson and Foveaux, strode past them to greet, with great affability, the *Hindostan*'s commander, Captain Pacso, and his wife.

Colonel Macquarie's smile faded. "He has not changed one whit, sir," Mary heard Foveaux observe, his remark clearly intended to be audible, not only to Macquarie but also to those about him.

She tensed, but Maurice O'Connell's fingers closed gently about her arm, and her momentary anger cooled as she saw her father recover his composure and fall into step with young Captain Antill, the governor's aide, walking with head held high to inspect the guard of honor of kilted soldiers of the King's 73rd.

**The second volume in the
spectacular Heiress series**

The Cornish Heiress

by Roberta Gellis
bestselling author of
The English Heiress

Meg Devoran—by night the flame-haired smuggler, Red Meg.
Hunted and lusted after by many, she was loved by one man
alone...

Philip St. Eyre—his hunger for adventure led him on a
desperate mission into the heart of Napoleon's France.

From midnight trysts in secret smugglers' caves to wild
abandon in enemy lands, they pursued their entwined destinies
to the end—seizing ecstasy, unforgettable adventure—and
love.

A Dell Book   **$3.50**   **(11515-9)**
